THE FALLEN KING CHRONICLES

OTHER BOOKS

Dragon Riders of Osnen

The Price of Honor
Trial by Sorcery
A Bond of Flame
The Warrior's Call
The Coin of Souls
Wing of Terror
Eyes of Stone
Tooth and Claw
The Servant of Souls
Smoke and Shadow
The Dark Rider
The Song of Bones
Sword and Crown
Tides of Darkness
Wrath and Ruin

Marked by the Dragon

Scale of the Dragon
Egg of the Dragon
Call of the Dragon
Wrath of the Dragon

Dragons of Isentol

Throne of Deceit
Rune Marked
Empire of Serpents

Galactic Mercenaries

Steel for Hire
Steel for Free
Steel for All

THE FALLEN KING CHRONICLES

RICHARD FIERCE

Cover design by Kuro Ishi
Dragonsphere Interior Illustration by Nimesh Niyomal
The Fallen King Interior Illustration by JayGraphixx
The Valiant King Interior Illustration by JayGraphixx
The Restored King Interior Illustration by AegeanDesign

Dragonfire Press

e-Book ISBN: 978-1-947329-05-8

Print ISBN: 978-1-958354-31-5

First Edition: 2023

DRAGONSPHERE

INTRODUCTION

Year of the Divines 418

IT WAS DARK AND COLD.

The distant sound of dripping water echoed throughout the narrow tunnel, part of a large system of interconnected passageways and caves deep in the Viss Mountains.

A hooded figure navigated his way through them hesitantly, pausing every few paces to run his fingers along the stone walls. He desperately wanted to light a torch, but he knew it was a foolish thought. If he brought light into that chamber …

The figure halted as he felt the familiar sigils on the wall. He had traveled through this cave many times now, yet it seemed he could never memorize his way to the central chamber within the mountain.

"I sense you." It was a sound unlike anything in his most insidious nightmares. "Come forth."

An intense fear overtook him. His breath came short and quick and he could feel his heart throbbing inside his chest. His hands began quivering so he clenched them into fists, hiding them within his robes. Closing his eyes momentarily, he forced a deep breath before stepping into the chamber.

Every rational thought told him to flee. A horrible feeling wriggled its way into his heart, melting his resolve like wax in a fire.

"You have carried out my instructions?"

`1

The man crumpled to his knees. He could almost feel it hovering around him, able to see everything while he was as blind as a bat.

It was more of a demand than a question. The man could barely speak and meekly nodded his head. "I have arranged the bones in the cave as you said." Something colder than ice touched his shoulder, causing his entire arm to go numb. It could only be the touch of his unholy master.

"You have pleased me. I shall reward your obedience when all falls into place." It seemed to him that the words slithered across the cave like snakes, wrapping themselves around him.

"Yes … m-my … lord."

"They thought they destroyed me. But I cannot be destroyed … no, I am eternal. And now … I will unleash hell upon the land."

The man looked around futilely in the dark cave and could see nothing. But he could feel it. A shudder in the ground, a tremor in the walls. He could hear loose rocks clattering against each other as the rumbling grew stronger.

A wicked, cackling laughter erupted, making him flinch unexpectedly. Then silence. Suddenly there was a loud cracking sound as if something were splitting open. He heard a roar echo out across the mountains, but he also heard the distinct sound of flapping wings.

An ancient and mighty creature had been awakened. The man couldn't help but wonder: what have I done?

Death was coming. A dragon was coming.

"All of history bears false witness. Truth is only known by those who were present."

- from the Book of Faith

1

Year of the Divines 419

WHEN RUMORS OF A DRAGON attack reached Demetrius, he dismissed them almost immediately. Having lived in the port city of Radda his entire life, he had heard many wild stories from countless travelers. Everything ranging from giant squids in the open seas to horses with wings. Admittedly this was the first time he heard mention of a dragon, supposed giant mythical creatures that fed on the fear of people and could lay waste to entire cities.

"Rubbish," he said. "Children's tales told by parents to scare little ones into obedience."

"I believe it," the old sailor remarked enthusiastically. "Captain heard it 'imself. Says the whole city was burned to the ground and everyone killed."

"Then how did your captain hear of it?" Demetrius eyed his friend sternly. The man's face was covered in wrinkles and his hair bleached from constant sun. The man had been a sailor since he was not more than a boy and was prone to believe almost anything.

"What d'ya mean?" the sailor, Bannigan, asked.

"If everyone was killed, how did your captain hear this story? Who would have repeated it to him?"

The old man remained silent for a moment and scratched his prickly-haired chin. "It not be my place to question the Captain, silversmith."

Demetrius laughed heartily. "Nice cover up."

The sailor stomped his foot indignantly. "It ain't no cover up. I trust the captain's word. How's business?" Bannigan changed the subject.

"Profitable, as always. The war with Oakvalor hasn't put a pinch in anyone's pockets yet. I hear some of my fellow smiths have been requested to appear before the king, as to why is anyone's guess."

"Maybe the king needs more weapons."

Demetrius shrugged his large shoulders. He wasn't in the business of making weapons, so it mattered little to him. His craft was typically sought after by the well-to-do, custom pieces that didn't come cheap. Some people had so much money they apparently didn't know what to do with it. He could work with any metal he put his hands on, but he preferred silver. It was very easy to bend and could be cast or hammered which allowed him to form almost anything with it; from teapots to statues.

The clanging of the bell tower echoed loudly across the city, signaling noon. The bell tower was originally built to alert the populace of emergencies. Its main use now was to indicate the time. Bannigan clapped Demetrius on the shoulder and bid him farewell. "That's my call," he said, trying to be heard over the noise. Demetrius' shop was situated near the docks for convenience and the daily clanging of the bell had eventually become a normal sound to him.

"Be safe," he called out as the old man left. Bannigan waved to acknowledge he heard him. Not that anyone couldn't.

Demetrius was a large man with a thunderous voice. At six and a half feet tall, he was a beast of a man, with muscles so large that he had to be custom fitted for his clothing. His hair was light brown and cut short to keep it out of his eyes, and to keep it from being singed. His skin was a deep bronze color as he preferred to be in the sun most of his time.

He watched his friend until he could no longer see him among the crowd. He heard his name a few stalls down and glanced to see who said it. He could see a member of the king's guard talking to one of the vendors. The vendor pointed towards where he was standing. What in the Divines would a soldier of the crown want with him? He watched the soldier approach.

"Demetrius?"

The big man eyed the soldier warily. "Yes?"

"The silversmith?" he asked with an air of impatience.

"Yes."

The soldier withdrew a scroll from his belt and handed it to Demetrius. "What's this?" he questioned. The soldier shook his head. "Not my business, sir. I am just the messenger. I believe His Highness requests your presence at the palace."

"What for?" Demetrius probed.

"Not my business." The soldier's impatience was evident by his short, almost rude, answers. "I must be on my way, sir." The soldier turned and headed back from the way he came. Demetrius stared at the scroll, unsure if he even wanted to open it. Everyone knew he didn't make weapons. Why would the king summon him if he was seeking smiths to make his armies more weapons?

He snapped the seal in half and opened the scroll. It read:

To Demetrius the silversmith,

Greetings from the Esteemed Ruler of Talvaard, King Garun. Your presence is requested at the palace. Do not worry about your business. You will be well compensated. A carriage has been arranged to meet you outside the city of Radda at sundown. Do not be late.

King Garun

There was a fancy signature and the crest of the king, a phoenix bursting forth from a pile of ashes, at the bottom of the parchment. Demetrius sighed. He hated politics.

Dusk found him standing near the road at the outskirts of his hometown. He had closed his shop early much to his disappointment. There was a certain beautiful woman who walked by his stall everyday around the same time, usually carrying fresh bread. He had only noticed her because he caught her staring at him as she passed by one day.

Her look was one of admiration. At least, that's how he took it. She had smiled embarrassedly and blushed. And so, Demetrius made it a point in his day to watch her as she walked by and smile at her.

Closing early meant that he missed her. He was more than slightly frustrated by that, as he had finally worked up his nerve to actually speak to her. His hope was that she would let him get to know her and perhaps they would see where things went from there.

The carriage pulled up suddenly and Demetrius noticed that the sun was just sliding behind the mountains. "Well at least the king is punctual," he muttered beneath his breath. The door to the carriage swung open and a man dressed in plain clothes, probably a servant, stepped out. He motioned to the carriage and bowed low. "If you would, sir."

Demetrius dipped his head in thanks and climbed inside. A quiet whistle escaped his lips. The inside was adorned with all sorts of glittering shapes. He looked closely and recognized most of the precious stones. Diamonds and rubies comprised most of the decorations, but there were also a few sapphires and a couple stones he did not recognize. The fabric that made up the seats was comfortable and smooth to the touch. It was hard to tell whether the material was dark red or brown in the fading light.

Demetrius was impressed. He didn't expect to be brought to the palace in luxury. Granted he was known among the higher ups for his skills in crafting, but he was not of noble birth. And most, if not all of them, seemed to ignore the fact that he was much wealthier than most of them, anyway. The servant did not get back into the carriage, but instead shut the door and climbed into the seat with the driver.

He had a decent amount of time to think as the buggy headed toward Talvaarin, the city built around the palace. It was a thirty-minute trip to the palace by horse. After what seemed like hours to him, he felt a difference in the road. Instead of bouncing about on the dirt path, the ride smoothed out and he could tell they were now on the stone paved roads of the city.

The carriage came to an abrupt stop and the door swung open. The servant stood there and motioned for Demetrius to come out. He had gotten comfortable and it took him a minute to move. Why did the king want him to come so late in the evening hours, he wondered.

The servant led him through enormously tall double doors and into a massive circular room that was normally filled with nobles and commoners alike, usually bringing petitions and requests to the king or his advisors. The room was empty and their footsteps reverberated off the walls.

Demetrius looked admiringly up at the vaulted ceiling, rising sixty feet above him. Support pillars were spaced every ten feet, outlining the main walkway through the antechamber. "This is huge," he remarked to himself.

"Sir?" the servant looked back at him. Demetrius shook his head and the servant continued his hurried pace. A door in the middle of the far wall was flanked on either side by two giant alabaster statues of winged men standing at attention, their swords drawn and held up before them. Demetrius thought them an odd addition to the room. The walls were covered with portraits of regal looking men, whom he assumed were previous kings, and large brightly colored tapestries depicting scenes of long ago battles.

He began to wonder why he had never made a trip to the palace, if for no other reason than to say he had been there. The servant stopped before the door. "Wait here, sir," he said breathlessly before disappearing through the door. Demetrius looked down at the floor. Stone tiles, painted orange and yellow, ran the length of the entire room, forming a triangular pattern. The tiles outside the three-sided shape were bright red.

He assumed there was some sort of significance to the design, but it was lost on him. Demetrius looked back up and noticed the servant was staring at him. "His Highness will see you now." He held the door open and pointed down a long hallway. "It's the last door on the left at the end of the hall."

The big man nodded his head in thanks and walked to where he was directed. The hallway, large enough to comfortably hold two carriages side by side, was barely adorned at all. A guard stepped out from the shadows and startled him. "I didn't see you," he laughed nervously.

"That would be the point," the guard answered, his face hidden by the hood over his head. He patted Demetrius down for weapons and finding none, opened the door for him to enter. "Go to the center of the room and do not leave the circle."

"Circle? Why not?"

"Just don't."

Demetrius was starting to regret having made the trip. Then again, seeing how guarded the king was, he doubted he would have lived long had he refused to come. He walked to the middle of the room and noticed the circle design in the floor. He assumed that's where he was supposed to stand.

The guard shut the door and Demetrius was enveloped in darkness. He cleared his throat and the sound echoed eerily. Torches flared to life and revealed a large wooden chair with a man seated on it.

"Demetrius," the unknown man greeted. "I don't think we've had the pleasure of meeting before."

Demetrius wasn't sure if it was the king or not. And if it was, should he bow? He didn't answer. The man must have taken his lack of response as hesitance. "You can speak freely."

Demetrius felt a little better that he could speak his mind. He wasn't one to bite his tongue. "What is this about? Why am I here? I am a very busy man, and I have lost half a day's time—"

The man in the chair stood up swiftly and Demetrius fell silent. "I can assure you, master smith, that we are all busy. Some busy with tasks more important than others." The man tossed a leather pouch onto the floor in front of him. "Consider this payment for your time."

Demetrius didn't dare move from the circle to see what was inside, heeding the warning the guard had given him.

"Talvaard has a shadow cast over it, master smith. A shadow that threatens to consume us all."

Demetrius assumed the shadow was Oakvalor, the enemy kingdom that Talvaard had been at war with for as long as anyone could remember. "Then I must inform you, sir, that I am not a weapon smith. I make trinkets and items ordered for noble houses. I think you have erred in your selection of men to build your weapons of war."

"Do you think that I am ignorant of those in my kingdom?" the man asked, revealing that he was indeed the king. "I know what you are capable of, Demetrius, and I have not summoned you here to build weapons. At least, not in the sense that you are thinking."

"What do you mean?"

Several other torches lit up, as though by magic, and exposed King Garun in all his splendor. He was shorter than Demetrius by at least a foot. His hair was long and black, pulled back tight into a ponytail. His nose slanted down his face, reminding Demetrius of a bird's beak. His eyes were hazel and set deep in his head. The king was nothing special in terms of attractiveness. What he lacked in looks, however, was made up for in bearing.

His posture and demeanor exhibited a great deal of confidence and his general appearance was enhanced by his garments. His crown gleamed in the torchlight and gave the impression that it was made of silver. Demetrius knew it wasn't crafted of his favorite metal, but was instead made of something much more valuable: white gold.

It had three gems set in the front. A rare black diamond, twenty karats by Demetrius' estimate, in the middle, surrounded on either side by two green serendibite stones. It was a marvelous treasure. The king's shirt was turquoise and had a lustrous, dazzling sheen that only silk could give. His linen pants were a brilliant green color tucked into black leather boots. During the daylight hours, when dealing with matters of state, he would also wear a mantle that extended to the floor, joined at the neck and open down the front, that was emblazoned with the large phoenix crest on the back.

"I'm sure you have heard the rumors?"

"Of dragons, Your Highness?"

"Indeed. I can read the disbelief in your face. I know how you feel, as I too was of the same mind when word first reached me. I can assure you," the king's tone grew somber, "there is no myth to these tales."

Demetrius was dubious. "What in the name of the Divines are you talking about? Dragons? Winged creatures that fly and breath fire? You can't be serious, Your Highness."

The king's face remained solemn. "Had I not seen the creature for myself, I would be as doubtful as you, Demetrius. Unfortunately," he paused, gave a great sigh, and continued, "it is very real."

Demetrius was still in doubt, but he didn't further voice his suspicion. "What does all this have to do with me?"

"It is said that no one in Talvaard can work silver like you."

Demetrius had certainly earned a strong reputation for himself, but he was down to earth and didn't like to boast. "So I have heard," he replied, shrugging his large shoulders. "You still haven't answered the question."

The king closed the distance between him and Demetrius with a few quick steps. "I cannot reveal the details just yet, as I myself do not have them. All I know is that the skills of a silversmith are required, along with a few other details. Our ally," he used the word frostily, "does not have the privilege of metal smiths. And we lack what they have. So you see, master smith, you would be doing Talvaard a great duty."

"And if I refuse?" Demetrius asked, more out of curiosity than rebelliousness. A job for the king could prove to be very profitable.

Garun eyed him dangerously. "It would not be in your best interest … but you have a week to consider it."

Demetrius felt goose bumps run up his back under the king's baleful look. "I am loyal to my country, Your Highness. I would never refuse an opportunity to serve the crown."

Garun smiled, the first Demetrius had seen on his face, apparently pleased with the answer. "My servant will escort you out and deliver you back to your home."

"When will you require my services?"

"You will know," the king answered.

- Demetrius, silversmith

2

THE RIDE BACK TO RADDA seemed shorter than the trip to the palace. Demetrius pondered the king's veiled threat and his offer. He wasn't sure what Garun even wanted him to forge. And then there was the fact that the king believed there truly was a dragon rampaging across the land. He briefly toyed with the idea that the king had been drinking a bit too much wine. He didn't know the man personally, but from all accounts he was a man of intelligence, calculating, and courageous. The fact that he seemed troubled and had asserted to have seen the beast did add weight to his claim.

Perhaps Oakvalor had unleashed some sort of beast loose on Talvaard? Something frightening enough to make people think it was a dragon. Demetrius didn't know. He didn't care either. A job for the crown could make him rich enough to stop working. He could buy a house in Talvaarin and spend his days relaxing or sail the Ocean and see the world. He smiled at the thought briefly before pushing those notions aside. He had to do the job first. And he wasn't even sure that he could.

The carriage stopped and the door opened. The servant didn't bother to motion him out of the cab as he was already moving towards the door before it opened. The man stopped Demetrius and handed him the leather pouch the king had tossed him. He had completely forgotten about it back in the palace.

"The king said I will know when he needs me. How will I know?" he asked the servant who, in reply, shrugged his shoulders. So much for an answer, he thought.

He made his way down the worn dirt path that led through the center of the port city he called home. While his shop was located near the docks, his house was in the center of the town, where the "better" houses were. Radda was home to many merchants and traders, as well as some nefarious characters. Since the port's expansion some eighty years ago, the small town had grown to become somewhat of a city. While they didn't have the paved stone roads of Talvaarin, they did have some of the best inns.

One such inn was the Crab, owned by a wealthy sailor who had made his fortune in the crab fishing industry. Crabs were considered a delicacy, especially among the nobles. Having made more money than he needed, the sailor had retired and opened the inn. Demetrius would come here to unwind from his work.

He preferred it over the other places. It was newer than the others, and so had less sketchy individuals to worry about. He paused outside the doorway, considered calling it a night. He decided to have one drink and he would be on his way. He entered the building to find it mostly empty with the exception of two patrons. The barmaid, a young girl no older than twenty, was delivering a tray of food to one of the customers. The other customer appeared to be a woman, but he couldn't see her face and didn't recognize her as anyone he knew in the dim light.

He found a seat at an empty table and ordered some wine when the barmaid asked what he'd like. Demetrius laid the leather bag on the table and opened the flap to peer inside. His eyes widened when he was that along with gold coins, there was also some precious stones similar to the ones he had seen in the carriage. If this was just for his trouble of closing for one afternoon, he could barely imagine how much the king would pay for the actual job.

He slid the bag into his lap and kept one hand on it. The young girl brought him his wine and he sank down into the chair. The chairs were covered in soft cushions, another reason he preferred the Crab. Demetrius sipped his wine slowly, enjoying the taste and the solitude. While he did appreciate his customers, he needed time away from people in general to keep a cheery attitude.

Demetrius was still young, at least he considered himself so. He was almost thirty and had never married. Not yet, anyway. His mother had died giving birth to him and his father, a poor thatcher, had always been distant from him. Demetrius assumed his father's lack of attention was the result of the man's superstitious beliefs. He had viewed his wife's death as a bad omen for the character of the child. Whatever sinful things the child would do in the future resulted in the mother's death. A sordid payment of sorts.

Demetrius didn't hold a grudge against his father. Besides, he had an entire town full of people who helped raise him. The previous ruler, King Verin, had expanded the kingdom's trade routes with established nations across the Ocean and financed the expansion of all the ports in the kingdom. Since Radda was so close to the palace, it received preferential treatment. The city flourished and grew rapidly, bringing in people from all cultures of the world.

It was one of those people who had made the city his home that took Demetrius in as his own. Childless and widowed, the man took pity on him and made Demetrius his apprentice in the silversmith trade. And the big man had a knack for it. Under his adoptive father's guidance, he became one of the best in the kingdom. His goods were highly sought after, especially by the well-to-do.

His thoughts were scattered as the female customer stood up to leave. Her face was revealed by the lanterns that hung from the ceiling and he realized it was the woman from the market. His heart skipped a beat and he felt his stomach drop. What was wrong with him?

He stood up and their eyes met. He couldn't take his eyes off her which made her face flush pink. She smiled shyly and went to leave.

"Wait," he said gently. She looked back at him with a nervous look on her face. "At least tell me your name, woman."

She seemed to hesitate, as if she would not answer. Demetrius waited, thinking perhaps he was too forward. He wanted to know who she was.

"Tomorrow."

His confused look spoke volumes. "Tomorrow? That's ... different."

She shook her head and smiled. "I will tell you tomorrow."

"I won't be here. I must deliver some items to a customer. I will be gone for two days."

"Then when you return," she responded bashfully.

"That seems so long from now," he said, downcast.

"You have gone this long without knowing my name. What is a few more days?"

When he arrived at his house and slumped into bed, his thoughts were of the woman who seemed to have stolen his heart. He had finally heard her voice. And it was more beautiful than he imagined. As he drifted off to sleep, he was still smiling.

—

When the sun shining through the window woke him up, he groaned and rolled out of bed. His trip to Kish was at an end and he would be heading back home. He had not wanted to travel, but the customer had requested that Demetrius himself deliver the items. He tried to explain that he was a busy man, but his customer would not hear it.

Normally Demetrius would have merely declined the job, but the client offered triple the price for the trouble. He couldn't turn down the offer; it was a great deal of money. If there was one thing he loved more than his craft, it was money.

Besides that, the man was an ambassador to Treyfeth, a minor kingdom beginning to grow into a power to be reckoned with. Word was that he was cousin to the king, something that Demetrius considered more seriously now after having met the king two days ago. He certainly wouldn't want to offend a man who could have him thrown in the dungeon, or worse. All of the preparations were ready, the person he normally used had ensured all would be ready by dawn.

His client provided breakfast which he consumed quickly. He was impatient to see the beautiful woman again. Judging by their conversation at the inn, he sensed that what he was feeling for her was the same that she felt for him. He could hardly wait.

The journey took half a day, but it didn't seem to take that long as his thoughts were in the clouds. The city of Kish was located in the same direction as the Abbey of the Divines, the home of the monks. It was further east than the abbey, so he did not get the opportunity to glimpse their stone walls. There was one road that led out of Radda. It was a straight road north leading to Talvaarin, then it broke east and west from there. Far to the west was the nation of Oakvalor. He had never been that far west, as there was nothing but a lonely road that winded over the dormant volcano and the mountains that surrounded it.

He had no reason to go there anyway. Talvaard and Oakvalor had been at war with each other for the past thousand years, maybe more. When asked, no one could answer how it all started. Time had a way of erasing things. As Demetrius continued heading south, he thought he could smell smoke in the air. "Odd," he muttered to himself, attempting to block the sun from his eyes to get a better look ahead. He was still about a mile away and with the sun setting in the south, he couldn't see much. A foreboding feeling began to gnaw at him.

Demetrius urged the two horses pulling his wagon to speed up. As he got closer, the smell of smoke became distinct. The terrain was all flat grasslands except right outside the city, where small rolling hills slowed his wagon down. He could hear noises now, and he was gripped with fear. He leapt off the wagon before the horses had completely stopped and ran to the top of the last hill.

Fire raged across the city. Shrill, high pitched screams of women and children invaded the air, mingling with the shouts of men who were trying desperately to put out the spreading destruction. The smoke rising from the buildings was dark and thick, billowing into the air and blotting out the fading sun; a mere sliver of dimming yellow light on the horizon as it was.

The smell of burnt wood, and possibly flesh, reached him as a cool breeze blew in from the Ocean. The massive port city of Radda was now a charred wasteland. Demetrius dropped to his knees, overcome with emotion. This was his home from childbirth. The people he knew, the woman he had hoped to know, all burned up in the inferno. Tears stung his eyes as he thought of his father, too aged to have run for safely. He punched the ground, raising up dust and cutting his knuckles on rocks. He barely felt it. He punched again and again, wishing he would wake up from this horrible nightmare.

The soft nickering of a horse beside him seemed a strange and out of place sound. He looked up through tearful eyes to see a man dressed in soldier's clothes with the crest of the king displayed on the shoulder. His clothes were different from the soldier he had seen at the palace.

The man sat upon the horse, staring unfazed at the carnage. The man turned and looked down at him. Demetrius saw another emblem on the man's clothing, one he supposed was the symbol of a general.

"Where are the king's men?" Demetrius demanded, his voice breaking with grief.

The general turned his eyes back to the burning city. "Scattered throughout the kingdom dealing with similar situations." The man's voice was devoid of any genuine concern. Demetrius also looked back to the city. He wanted to rush down there and help, but he felt powerless and weak. He could only see a handful of people and they were trying to escape the flames, not put them out.

"It's time," the general said abruptly.

"Time for what?"

"To fulfill your obligation to the crown."

—

Demetrius rode in silence. He followed behind the general who didn't seem inclined to talk anyhow. He had fallen into a state of depressive calmness. He could feel tears sliding down his face but he didn't bother to wipe them away.

He wasn't aware that they had reached the castle until the general cleared his throat, breaking the silence. Demetrius looked up and saw the double doors that led into the palace. He looked over his shoulder, having some idea that maybe he would see his home, fine and undamaged as when he had left it. He saw only the ten-foot stone wall that separated the palace from the city of Talvaarin.

He slid off the horse and followed the general to the door, who entrusted him to the servant whom he had dealt with on his first visit.

The antechamber was filled with servants and soldiers alike, dashing here and there, at times almost running into one another. The entire palace was in chaos. Demetrius oddly found comfort in seeing many people eye him with frowning faces, the only way they knew how to express their condolences.

The servant led him through the doorway in the middle of the chamber with haste. "Where is the King?" the servant was demanding to those who passed them in the giant hall. Some shrugged, others didn't bother to answer at all.

Demetrius saw two women that appeared to be attendants, talking in hushed tones. As they passed by, he heard bits of their conversation and learned that Radda was only one of many cities across the kingdom that had burned to the ground. People were blaming Oakvalor and their king's wizard for the destruction.

While he still held reservations about Garun's story of a dragon, he didn't think there was any way Oakvalor's armies could burn so many cities without a single person seeing anything. The servant stopped at the end of the hall and glanced about. Demetrius wasn't sure what he was doing. A hooded guard stepped out of the shadows and the servant nodded back toward Demetrius. "His Highness has summoned the smith. Do not delay me!"

The soldier eyed Demetrius warily but did as the servant bade. He watched the soldier run his hand along the wall. Seeming to find what he was looking for, he removed a key from his belt and slid it into the wall. There was a soft click and the wall opened inward about two inches. Both the guard and the servant glanced around again.

"Come," the servant said, motioning Demetrius to follow him. He pushed the door and it opened silently. Once inside, the guard shut the door and Demetrius heard it lock. There were small lanterns every few feet, lighting what appeared to be another hallway. They walked straight ahead for about fifty feet before the servant turned to Demetrius. "I hope you aren't afraid of small spaces," he remarked as the floor in front of them slowly slid open, revealing stairs that wound downward.

"Where are we?" Demetrius asked. The servant stared at him intently before answering. "The palace that you see outside is only a small portion of the castle. The rest is hidden beneath the mountains.”

“Wait,” Demetrius grabbed hold of the servant’s arm. “We’re underground?” he asked incredulously.

“Not yet,” the servant smiled. He began to descend the stairs, then paused and looked sternly at Demetrius. “You didn’t see any of this.”

*"King Garun, needing an edge in the war with Oakvalor, had all
their smiths assassinated. This caused Oakvalor no end of trouble,
but the Oaks could boast of something Talvaard could not:
the power of wizards."*

- A History of Talvaard

3

DEMETRIUS FOUND HIMSELF FEELING A little claustrophobic. The
chamber he stood in was enormous in terms of open space, but the
knowledge that he was deep underground gave him chills. The idea
that more dirt and stone than he could imagine was being held up by
a few wooden beams was distressing. The air was cool, but he was
sweating so profusely his shirt was soaked. It clung to his skin and
made him even more uncomfortable. The servant had left him alone
in the room, and he was beginning to wonder what was taking so
long.

The door swung open and the same general who had met him
outside Radda strode in, followed by two guards leading a
blindfolded man in flowing grey robes. Demetrius looked
questioningly at the general. "This—" he waved towards the man,
"—is Vallen. He will be working with you."

Demetrius' brows rose. "Who is he? A prisoner?"

The grey robed man let out a chuckle. The general was not
impressed.

"He is King Manaem's wizard. We don't need the Oaks having
anymore advantages over us; hence the blindfold."

That put Demetrius on his heels. His initial shock, and then
anger, was apparent on his face. "I will not work with some fool from
Oakvalor," he cried angrily. "Especially not a servant of their king!
Is this some sort of joke? My home was destroyed and you come in
here …" his large body was shaking with rage.

"Be calm, silversmith. The Oaks," he used the insulting slang
term again, "are facing the same problems we are. King Garun has

issued an unofficial treaty of peace with Manaem. Do this task so we can be rid of the vermin from our land."

Demetrius almost refused, but the look on the general's face reminded him of the deadly stare of the king. He hated the Oaks as much as anyone else in Talvaard, but he valued his life and nodded in resignation.

"Follow me."

The general led them through a maze of passages and into a chamber similar to the one they left. There was a furnace and an anvil, as well as all sorts of tools hanging on one of the walls. "I still don't know what I am supposed to forge," he commented to the general, who in turn said nothing. He instructed the guards to take the blindfold off the wizard and left Demetrius in the room with him.

Demetrius looked at the wizard. He was young, perhaps younger than himself. His robes looked to be made of velvet. The man's hair was long and platinum colored, hanging down past his shoulders. His eyes were slate blue and brought the waters of the Ocean to mind. He carried an ordinary looking staff made of wood, but it was not to help the wizard walk.

The smith had never met a wizard. Before he was born, sorcerers were a common sight. A few bad seeds, however, caused a great persecution to break out against anyone who practiced the craft. The soldiers were able to quell the violence, but it was too late. Those who had not been killed went into hiding or gave up the craft altogether. It was whispered that the church had a hand in the revolt, but the Abbot condemned such accusations. It was also whispered that some wizards had the ability to control others with the power of their minds.

If the rumors were true … Demetrius suddenly wondered if this man had that power. He looked questioningly at the wizard, who frowned and muttered something about stupidity.

"Well?" Vallen said impatiently.

"Well what?" Demetrius answered.

"Are you ready to get to work or are you going to stand there until the beast destroys both our lands?"

"The king hasn't told me what to forge," he reiterated.

"I'm telling you what to forge, you fool."

—

Demetrius was the best at what he did because he worked alone. No one told him what to make or how to make it. His clients asked for certain pieces, true, but they did not dictate to him how to accomplish it. And that was precisely the reason he wanted to strangle Vallen. The wizard had drawn up a very specific blueprint and he insisted every detail be followed.

With each hammer blow, he would hear Vallen mutter something about "too much force" or "this is the best smith they could find?" Demetrius glared at him on one such occasion.

"Do you want to do this?" Vallen returned his glare but didn't say another word.

Demetrius prided himself on attention to detail, which was one of the reasons his work was so highly sought after. But this … this was just a round, hollow sphere of silver unadorned in any way. He had to shape it in two separate pieces, each one the wizard inspected meticulously. With both pieces complete, Vallen had him heat the metal pieces up so that he could engrave some sort of symbols onto the inside.

When Vallen was finished, Demetrius melded the two together, ensuring it was a perfect seal. For all the specifics, it looked like something he may have crafted when he was an apprentice.

"It looks unfinished," he lamented, turning his gaze to Vallen. For the first time since they had met, Vallen was smiling.

"It's perfect." Vallen reached over to pick up the sphere. "You are crazy, you blasted Oak!" Demetrius smacked the wizard's hand away. "The heat of the metal will burn the skin right off your fingers!"

The wizard's smile quickly vanished and turned into a scowl. "Watch what my craft can do." Vallen snatched the sphere off the anvil and held it close to Demetrius' face. "Do you feel any heat?"

To his surprise, Demetrius didn't. If anything, the metal seemed to be radiating a coldness. "What is it?" he questioned.

"This, silversmith, is a weapon beyond imagining. And it is going to save our kingdoms."

- a page in Vallen's journal

4

THE SPHERE HAVING BEEN FORGED and imbued with magic, Demetrius thought his task was done and expressed his desire to go back to Radda to help the survivors with the task of burying the dead and rebuilding.

"Out of the question," King Garun stated in a tone that allowed no room for debate.

"The task you required of me is complete," Demetrius returned irritably.

"On the contrary. The wizard requires your continued assistance. There is one last thing that the crown requires of you. You must escort Vallen to the dragon's dwelling and ensure the safety of the sphere when the wizard captures the beast."

"I am not a soldier, Your Highness. I couldn't possibly protect it better than your men of war."

They were in the same room he had first met the king in, which was just as dark and mysterious in the daylight hours. Garun dismissed the servants who were attending him and drew close to Demetrius. "Let me be blunt with you, since you are not wise in the ways of politics. I do not expect the wizard to survive the encounter with the beast." Garun's hazel eyes seemed to pierce his soul.

"Do whatever you must to secure the sphere for Talvaard's interests." Demetrius was catching on to the king's subtle words. "What interests would those be?"

Garun frowned. He was not accustomed to being questioned. "Let us merely imagine that it may be of use to us one day in the future. In the event that a certain kingdom begins to grow too powerful …" his words trailed off. He called his servants back into the room. "Take our guest to prepare for his journey," he instructed them.

"Where are we going?"

Garun smirked. "You are going to Kerosh Pass in the Viss Mountains. I will remind you of the importance of having that sphere brought back here."

"Why me?"

"Vallen trusts you now. Do not fail me," Garun warned.

The servants escorted Demetrius to a room located two doors down. He was given fresh clothes to change into, as well as a lightweight suite of chain mail. The wizard was also there, though he refused to take anything the servants offered to him. "I will not have it said I accepted anything without payment," was his excuse. Demetrius figured the real reason was because they were not made by Oakvalor hands.

"How does anyone know where this dragon lives?" Demetrius inquired, still having doubts that it even existed.

Vallen pointed to a large map that hung from the wall. "The border between our kingdoms crosses through the mountains of Ward and Viss. Within those mountains is a cave the creature calls home. We cannot hope to use the sphere within his domain, so we must draw him out into the open. One of the mountains is level at the top. That is where we will make our stand."

Demetrius was uneasy by the way Vallen seemed to be talking about their future encounter. Assuming the dragon was real, it was unlikely that he would be of any actual help to the wizard. Demetrius sighed heavily and half listened as the wizard babbled on. It was going to be a long journey.

—

Demetrius scrambled up the cliffside, almost slipping on the jagged rocks several times. The wizard had convinced him to enter the cave alone while the wizard stayed at the top of the mountain.

Demetrius initially didn't care as he still didn't believe there was a dragon. But seeing the massive creature inside the cave suddenly put a lot of things into perspective for the smith.

The beast had seen him and that immediately caused Demetrius to turn and run. No amount of money or threats from the king could make him stay and do anything. He reached the plateau, his only thoughts on escaping and running as fast as he could. Vallen stopped him in his tracks by letting fly a blast of lightning. "Stay focused. I cannot do this alone!"

He knew if he tried to flee that Vallen would kill him. The wizard might trust him, but that didn't make them enemies any less. The ground shook beneath his feet and he looked around frantically. A mighty roar of the dragon echoed off the mountain tops. Demetrius covered his ears, afraid he might go deaf from the sheer volume. The dragon shot up into the sky, a blur of red against the blue sky.

"How are we going to get the beast to land?" he yelled at Vallen.

Vallen withdrew the sphere from a leather bag strapped across his shoulders. "That is the good news. We don't need it to land. We just need it to fly overhead. It is a fire dragon, the deadliest of its kind. As in nature, fire can be extinguished by ice. The magic infused within the metal has a twofold purpose, the main being that it will keep the dragon's fire at bay. The other purpose is about to be tested."

Demetrius' face turned pale. "Tested? You don't know if your magic works? Divines save us!" Vallen ignored the smith's terror.

"This is not something that has been done before, but I know it will work. The magic will imprison the creature inside. I will distract the beast from there," he pointed to the edge of the plateau, "and you hold the sphere up in the air as the beast flies over." He handed the sphere to Demetrius.

"I thought this was going to kill the dragon?"

Vallen shook his head. "Dragon's cannot be killed. At least, not the way we can be killed." The sound of rushing wings filled the air, and Vallen sprinted to the edge of the mountain top.

"Where do I stand?" Demetrius shouted at the wizard.

Either Vallen didn't hear him or Demetrius didn't hear the answer. He threw himself to the ground as the massive dragon shot by. The dragon landed close to Vallen, dropping down onto an upraised platform of rock. Demetrius watched with panic as the beast spewed forth gouts of flame from its mouth.

He expected to see Vallen consumed in fire. A blue light flared to life and protected the wizard from the flames. The dragon went airborne again. The force of the wind from the dragon's wings seemed to be turned into a weapon and flung Vallen off the cliff.

Demetrius cried out and ran over to the edge, expecting the worst. He found Vallen holding onto the ledge. Using every last ounce of strength, he pulled the wizard back up.

Vallen's facial expression was all the thanks Demetrius needed. The dragon was circling high above them. "Get back over there, quickly." Demetrius held the sphere tightly and ran back to where he had been standing. Death seemed certain to him. The dragon shot downward, halting overhead and flying a complete circle.

There was a sudden eerie silence. Why couldn't he hear anything? He heard Vallen's voice inside his head.

If anything happens to me, keep the sphere safe! Do not let the safety of the world be jeopardized by the greed of men.

The dragon swooped over the plateau and Demetrius lifted the sphere high into the air as it passed above. The dragon jerked awkwardly in the air. All life seemed to leave the beast and it crashed with jarring force into the ground, rolling and tumbling toward Vallen.

The beast, and the wizard, disappeared over the cliff edge.

Do not fail!

Those three words echoed in his mind the rest of his life.

"The Eradication is a blight on our history, a disgraceful display of proselytizing by a man who did not interpret the Book of Faith properly. Though the church was strengthened in the long term of things, was it worth the incalculable lives of innocent souls? I think not."

- From the writings of Denrie'Aluth
Former Abbot

5

Year of the Divines 544

THE ABBEY OF THE DIVINES was an ancient structure, dating back almost a thousand years. The ruler of Talvaard at the time, King Beraiah, had converted to the worship of the Divines from the pagan religion that prevailed in the country. After his change of faith, he used the royal treasury to finance the construction of the monastery and issued a decree that all other religions were illegitimate.

The edict had angered the leaders of the major religions and instead of continuing their rituals in secret, they joined together and declared war on the king. What ensued came to be known as the Eradication. Beraiah hired mercenaries to track down and slaughter the rebels. It was a dark time in the kingdom of Talvaard as Beraiah enforced his new beliefs on everyone. Many of his top advisors resigned their positions, not wanting innocent blood on their hands.

Eventually the defiance from the rebellious people subsided and they converted to the new religion; or at the very least did not voice their opposition. As the years passed, and the Church of the Divines grew, the mercenary bands were replaced with loyalists, people devoted to the crown. Beraiah made them an official faction of the government and split them into two groups; his personal bodyguards and the Retribution.

The Retribution was a secretive sect that sought out those few who continued practicing the pagan religions and brought them to justice. They would be disbanded three hundred years later by the fourth great grandson of Beraiah, who believed them to be outdated and an unnecessary drain on the treasury.

Yet the Church of the Divines flourished in Talvaard despite its violent beginnings. The Abbey was the largest ever built, containing more than two hundred rooms. It was one story, made from the dark brown stone that could only be found on the Isle of Eio. Beraiah had spared no expense on the monastery, bringing in craftsmen and resources as far as the forested mountains of Eurista, half the world away.

No one was sure of the origin of the belief of the Divines, though it was rumored that Beraiah had indulged a missionary from some distant land and had been persuaded to abandon the traditional religion of his royal bloodline.

The monastery was massive in terms of square footage, larger even than the royal palace. It was situated outside the city of Talvaarin, the quarters of the palace and capitol of the kingdom for as long as anyone could remember. It was surrounded by an island of tall grassy plains with a single wagon-worn trail leading to it.

At one time, it had been open to anyone for prayer services and other ceremonies, but the Abbot in command closed its doors to the public when Demetrius brought the sphere to them. He claimed it was in the "best interests and safety" of everyone in Talvaard. It did spark some outrage from the king, who demanded that he be allowed to visit anytime he pleased, reminding the Abbot that it was, after all, the crown who paid for their building.

In a show of good will, the Abbot offered to send monks to Talvaarin each week to hold a prayer service and meet the needs of the people in the palace, to which the king agreed.

Inside the monastery, the monks continued their teachings by allowing only first born males into their ranks, referring to them as being 'consecrated to the Divines'. They took oaths of celibacy, forgoing their natural desires to serve the Divines.

Calderon was one such monk. He had entered the monastery at the young age of six, two years younger than what the Abbot normally allowed. His parents, devout followers of the Divines, had arranged for their son to be the exception to the rule. Many speculations followed as to how they managed it, but no one could decipher fact from fiction.

Nine long years had passed since the day his parents had dropped him off. Calderon had not seen them since. He could barely remember what they looked like anymore. The pictures he had conjured up in his mind when he first arrived quickly faded, leaving him with only a few distinct memories of events from his early childhood. He could not remember much outside the walls of the monastery. The monks were forbidden to leave without approval from the Abbot and Calderon was no exception.

It was past noon now, close to the first hour of the afternoon and the Abbot was winding down his exhortation. The Abbot, leader of the monastery and the priesthood in Talvaard, would preach his sermons each day at noon, and though he was typically long winded, todays seemed like it would be shorter than normal.

Calderon bowed his head as they closed the service in prayer. He quietly whispered his own invocation and rose from the pew. He searched the room but didn't see Velkyn in the audience. While attendance was not mandatory, his childhood friend hardly missed the daily service. He could always confide in Velkyn without fear of judgment. The two had become instant friends his first day in the monastery. Calderon had initially been shunned and bullied by the older boys because of his controversial admittance.

Velkyn, however, had taken justice in his own hands and pummeled a few of them. The masters had then punished Velkyn. His friend took it in stride and they became inseparable, doing all of their daily routines together. Calderon left the chapel and traversed his way through the winding hallways, occasionally glancing into private prayer rooms dedicated to the various Divines.

There was only one reason why his friend would miss the Abbot's sermon.

—

Velkyn finished his prayer and kissed the foot of the copper statue depicting Virtue and rose to his feet. Tomorrow would be the culmination of all his recent efforts. He would need all the favor Virtue would give him. The statue stood on a round dais made of curved red bricks that lifted the statue almost a foot off the floor.

The statue was probably decades old, but the lacquer that covered the statue gave the reddish-brown color a shiny complexion and made it appear new. Due to the fact that the metal turned green from oxidation, the monks had to import the protective lacquer from one of the islands on the coast and arrange periodical maintenance.

He pulled the hood of his robes over his head. "I always know where to find you," Calderon's familiar voice echoed in the chamber. Velkyn turned to face his friend. "That's because you know me." Calderon was almost the same height as himself, though slightly shorter. His head was shaved as was the custom for all of the monks in the monastery. Unlike himself, his friend had deep blue eyes whereas his were green. He was also the only one who knew about Calderon's disorder.

"Are you ready for the ceremony?" Velkyn smiled as he asked the question. He already knew the answer. Calderon was nervous. He knew his friend well, but he also could sense it in his spirit.

"My soul is ready, but my mind betrays me. I want this so badly," he raised his hand and clenched it into a fist with the last words. Calderon used his hands often when he talked. "I am afraid, though." Velkyn nodded in understanding. "I know. I have my own reservations about what lies ahead, but I trust that if I am not chosen, there is another path for me."

"My biggest concern is having my disorder discovered. Perhaps I am not meant to be the Musician. I do not feel right hiding the truth." Velkyn put his hand on Calderon's shoulder. "We all have secrets that we must bear. If you confess your weakness, you will never be the Musician. And they may even kick you out of the order. I believe you are making the right decision. Besides, you know my secret. I would surely be excommunicated for mine. I do not feel guilty. Neither should you."

Calderon's downcast expression brightened. "I suppose you are right."

"Have faith," Velkyn said empathetically. The two sat in silence for a moment before Calderon spoke. "I have never understood that phrase."

Velkyn's mind was wrapped up with his own thoughts. He looked at his friend confusedly. "What?"

"That phrase," Calderon repeated, waving his hands about as he talked. "Have faith. Faith is a Divine, so how do we 'have faith'? I've never understood it."

Velkyn contemplated the question. "That is the beauty and glory of her love. She gives of herself to us, filling us with her spirit so that we may not only believe she exists, but that we may be empowered to obey her commands. That is how we have faith." He smiled at Calderon's look of amazement.

"You are wise beyond your years, my friend. Perhaps one day you might be the Abbot."

Velkyn grimaced. "With all my heart I hope that not to be the case."

—

Velkyn was up long before he needed to be. He was too excited to sleep anyway, spending most of the night tossing and turning. Today was the ceremony that would decide his fate. He would be asked grueling theological questions about the sphere, as well as about its history. Then his strength would be tested in a battle with a master of hand to hand combat. Each candidate would be tested separately by different masters. Then the masters would convene and decide amongst themselves who would be the next Guardian.

The positions of Guardian and Musician were very similar with the exception that one played music to keep the enchantment on the sphere active. The Guardian's role was to guard the door to the sphere, literally, their entire life.

The Guardian would only get three hours of sleep each day when the Musician came to play their music. The Guardian's position was essentially useless, as the only enemy of Talvaard was Oakvalor. The two nations were at war, but the Oaks also served the Divines and the church kept itself separated from the political agendas of their royal counterparts.

The Musician was the more important of the two positions. It was the Musician who played the music that kept the freezing enchantment on the sphere. All magic expired over time without any influence. Demetrius himself had given them the musical notes needed to keep the sphere's magic from degrading.

Velkyn left his room and headed to the chamber where he had prayed the previous day. The sun had not yet risen, so he did not expect anyone to be using the room. Even though he walked softly down the stone hallways, the echo of his footsteps seemed loud in the silence.

He entered the chamber and stood before the statue of his favored Divine. He wondered if the statue was an accurate depiction of the deity. How the sculptor knew what the deity looked like was beyond him.

What if all he was praying to was a giant piece of elaborate metal?

One of the doubts that always seemed to dwell in the back of his mind had escaped his mental barrier. He drove the thought away and sighed in frustration. How could he be so wise and have so much knowledge, yet have so many doubts about his own faith? He knelt down before the dais and bowed his head in prayer.

Virtue ... I have sought your favor already, but I come before you again to pray for my friend. I know he is the best suited to be the Musician ... he has worked so hard to get to this point. If it is Your will, I pray that you would give him your favor as well.

Velkyn's mind began to wander. He thought of Nydel, his secret. Monks were forbidden to have relations, but he loved her. How could they justifiably ask him, or anyone else for that matter, to bury their desires and emotions? He refused to. She had been his closest friend before coming to the monastery on his eighth birthday.

He smiled at the thought of how she had snuck in to see him over the years, sometimes desecrating this very room with their romantic episodes. He didn't know how or when, but he would marry her one day. It may have been contradictory to be praying to the saint of Virtue considering his secret sin, but he didn't care.

His entire future rested on becoming the Guardian, and he would pray to whoever he needed to for success.

—

Velkyn had been drilled for the last hour on every deep subject based on the sphere. "Then Demetrius brought the sphere to the Brotherhood to keep it safe. Though our nations were at war then as they are now, they had banded together for the good of the world. The king of Oakvalor disagreed with King Garun's decision to keep the sphere here, but he ordered the bones of the beast to be brought to Oakvalor.

"Demetrius lived the rest of his life behind these very walls. The sphere is said to hold the soul of the fire dragon that brought massive destruction on both our kingdom, and Oakvalor's. Our order vowed to keep it protected and safe after the death of Demetrius."

"What if it doesn't contain anything at all?" the master inquired.

"That's a difficult but excellent question. The only way to know the answer is to stop playing the music that keeps the enchantment on the sphere. The better question would be, is it worth the risk to find the answer to that question? I do not believe it is."

"What if you spend your entire existence keeping it safe, only to find out that you wasted your life?"

"That is where faith comes in. I believe it though I have no proof. My faith drives my actions. If in the end there is nothing to what we do, did we really waste our lives doing what we thought to be just? I do not think so."

Velkyn was having trouble reading the master's faces. Was he answering the questions correctly? He could only hope.

"You showed a proficient level of training in your defensive skills. What if a member of the Brotherhood, meaning someone other than the Musician, sought to enter the chamber of the sphere—what would you do?"

"I would strike them down. Everyone in the Brotherhood knows the rules, and any fellow monk who breaks them deserves what comes to them."

"Please remove yourself from the chamber while we await the other masters." Velkyn turned and left the room, feeling unsure of how he did. Had he been too forceful in his answers? Was his hand-to-hand skill up to standard? Despite what he could glean from the masters, all of these and many more doubts assailed him as he waited outside the chamber. His thoughts turned to Calderon and he wondered how his friend was faring in his tests.

"Let your will be done," he whispered quietly, to no Divine in particular.

—

Calderon stood waiting outside the chamber he would be tested in. He could hear music playing through the wooden door, though it was muffled. His final and most challenging test would be to play his music for the current Musician. Calderon had only seen the man in passing a few times. Both the Guardian and the Musician led lives of solitude, kept away from the general population of the monastery.

A full hour of perfect notes without a single mistake was required to pass the test. He had been playing his flute more and more each day in preparation, but he had yet to make it more than thirty minutes without having to stop. All he could do was hope for the best. The music coming through the door stopped abruptly. Calderon leaned against the door and put his ear to the polished wood, hoping to hear what was happening. He could hear voices, but nothing audible.

He quickly backed away from the door when he realized someone was opening it. He turned his gaze up at the ceiling and pretended to be paying grave attention to the ceiling. One of the candidates walked out of the chamber, his face flushed red with embarrassment telling Calderon all he needed to know.

"Calderon," an elderly voice called out from the doorway, "it's time."

Calderon's heart began to race. His hands were sweaty, too. As he started walking towards the door, he dropped his flute. It clanged to the floor loudly, the sound echoing down the hallway. "F-forgive me," he stuttered, kneeling down to pick it up. He felt a weight on his shoulder and looked up. The Musician's hand was on him.

"Don't be nervous," the old man encouraged, "just breath."

Calderon nodded silently and stood up. If he was meant to be the Musician, everything would work out. All he could do was offer his best. As he entered the chamber, he noticed a single chair. The room was devoid of any other furniture. The only source of light was from a small window in the stone wall behind the chair.

The old man sat down in the chair and motioned Calderon to stand in front of him. "It is very important that you can endure physical strain. You will stand there while you play. Perhaps when you are my age, you will have the privilege of a chair."

Calderon wasn't sure in the dim light, but he thought he saw the old man smile. He breathed in deep, placed the flute to his lips, and began to play. He knew the song well, he had memorized it when he was young. He distinctly remembered when he knew he wanted to be the Musician. Everything now depended on this moment. He couldn't see anything with the light shining directly in his face. He closed his eyes to focus on the music.

The next thing he knew, the old man was standing in front of him. Had he fallen asleep? His felt his stomach lurch within him.

"You did well, Calderon." The old man smiled, then motioned to the door. Calderon followed the Musician's direction and left the chamber. His thoughts tumbled around in his mind as he made his way to his personal quarters. He was confused. What happened? He couldn't recollect anything.

—

Velkyn and Calderon had been summoned to the Abbot's chambers as the sun was setting. Both monks knew that because the smell of food was beginning to waft through the air. The monastery served two meals a day, always at sunrise and sunset. They both stood staring, entranced by the decorations that covered the walls. Tapestries, paintings, and other items practically hid every wall behind a multi-colored landscape of artistic beauty.

The desk, though made of wood, was plated in gold and silver. Red stones, possibly rubies, cast a reddish hue across the room in the candlelight. They were so awed by the wealth that surrounded them that they did not hear the Abbot ask them to sit down.

"You may be seated," the Abbot repeated after clearing his throat. Once they were seated, the Abbot stared intently at them from across his desk.

"These artifacts are beautiful," Calderon said quietly, feeling like he was in a holy place. The atmosphere of the room was hushed and serene. Speaking almost seemed sinful.

"Thank you. Most of these items the church has acquired through donations. The wealthy people of the city send them to us, not realizing we have no use for such things. Turning down their gifts would not be respectful, so we keep them here. I have called you both here for other business. The masters have made their decisions. While I do not completely agree with their ruling, it is not my place to challenge them. Tradition separates the duties of guarding the sphere from my duties as leader of the faith. With that being said, I must inform you both that only one of you have been chosen."

Velkyn shifted uncomfortably in his chair. Calderon didn't move.

"Velkyn, you have been chosen as the new Guardian. The previous Guardian, master Groves, passed away just this evening." Velkyn's face showed a mixture of joy and then confusion and finally, sorrow. "How …?"

"Age has taken its toll on his body. The Musician will not be far behind him. They do not live long after the choices are made, due in part to the fact that we do not choose candidates until we know the current protectors of the sphere are close to death. He died doing what he committed his life to; guarding the sphere. It was an honor to have known him." The Abbot paused before turning his gaze to Calderon.

"There was some debate about you," he said. "The Musician believes you are the right choice, but some of the masters who oversaw your other tests disagree. The majority voted to go with Sevrin. Were it in my control, I would honor the Musician's desire. But in this matter, the masters have majority power. I am sorry. You are dismissed."

The tranquility shattered like a mirror being tossed to the ground. Calderon sat in disbelief. Velkyn nudged him with his elbow and motioned with his head toward the door. Calderon stood up dazedly, and slowly made his way out into the hallway. Velkyn sighed softly. This was not part of the plan.

"I feel for him more than he knows," the Abbot said. "As for you, however, you must report immediately to your post. Under less saddening circumstances, you would work with the master until he left this world. I assume you know your duties?"

"Yes, I know them," Velkyn answered solemnly.

"You are also dismissed."

- from the Book of Faith

6

CALDERON PAUSED OUTSIDE THE DOOR to his room. How could they have chosen Sevrin over him? By all accounts, he had passed the other tests just fine. Maybe he had fallen asleep when he played his music? That wouldn't explain why the Musician wanted to choose him though. He could feel the tears welling up in his eyes. He didn't want to cry, but he couldn't help it.

He had worked for years to get here, but this was not the way he expected things to go. Perhaps he truly was not meant to be the Musician. He entered his room and hit his knees. He cried, and he prayed. And then he prayed some more. And cried some more. His tears were selfish, he knew. If the Divines had willed Sevrin to be the Musician, then he would have to accept that. But he didn't want to.

It was easier to be selfish. He should not allow himself to wallow in self-pity. He was stronger than that. He sat there on his knees, the hot tears streaming down his face. He was unaware of the passage of time. No light shone through his window. He didn't bother lighting a candle. He slumped down onto the cold stone floor and just laid there and stared into the darkness of his room.

When he woke up, small shafts of light were shining through his window. He was still lying on his stomach and his neck was a little sore from facing the same direction all night. A knock on his door startled him. "Yes?" he called out, not sure why anyone was knocking in the first place. It wasn't time for the morning prayers.

"Calderon," the Abbot's familiar voice rang, "I need to speak with you."

Calderon pushed himself off the floor with a grunt. He didn't bother trying to smooth his disheveled look. He opened the door and

`39

was greeted by the Abbot, who had a disturbing look on his face. "Due to unforeseen circumstances, you are now the new Musician. You will report to master Donovan this evening for instruction."

"Master who?" he questioned, only half awake.

"The former Musician. His name is master Donovan. And don't forget your flute." The Abbot turned and left, his departure as quick as his arrival.

"What just happened?" Calderon whispered to himself. Unforeseen circumstances? What did that mean? And why did he have a dreaded feeling about being the new Musician? He should have been overjoyed.

He wasn't.

—

Calderon made his way quickly to Velkyn's room. He knocked several times, but his friend did not answer. Could he be guarding the sphere already? He wasn't sure, but decided to go by the sphere chamber to see.

As he walked down the hallway that led to the room that housed the sphere, he saw Velkyn standing outside the door. "Velkyn!" he shouted. "I've got to tell you something!" As he approached his friend, Velkyn began to run toward him. "It's the strangest thing—" he began to say, but then Velkyn slammed into him, knocking him to the ground.

Velkyn's fists were a blur of raw fury, striking him in his jaw, neck, and chest. It was all he could do to try and block his face. The intensity with which Velkyn struck left no doubt in his mind that he was indeed the right choice for Guardian. "I'm the new Musician," he screeched.

As quickly as Velkyn attacked, he stopped. "Oh, thank Virtue," Velkyn gasped. "Why didn't you say so? I could have killed you!" Calderon could feel blood on his face, but he didn't know where it was from.

"How was I supposed to know you would attack a fellow monk within our own walls?"

Velkyn helped him to his feet. "Lesson learned. That is great news, my friend. What changed?" Calderon shrugged. "I'm not really sure. The Abbot came to my room and told me there were unforeseen circumstances."

"Like what?"

"I don't know. I'm going to ask master Donovan tonight."

"Who?"

"Master Donovan, he is … or was, the Musician."

"Somehow, I knew you would be chosen. I appreciate you coming to tell me, but you really shouldn't be here until you are supposed to play the music"

Calderon wiped his face with the sleeve of his robe. "I'm sorry. I didn't know."

"Don't worry about it. Go clean yourself up. Someone is bound to think you received a beating." Velkyn grinned at him.

—

The day didn't pass fast enough for Calderon. He went to the morning prayer ceremony, helped some of the newer monks with the cleaning tasks, and even spent some time in the library studying some old books about the sphere.

As the daylight began to fade and candles started to be lit, his anxiety about being the new Musician returned. He was uneasy about it, but he was also excited. Unfortunately for him, the uneasiness seemed to outweigh his joy. How could one live their entire life leading up to a single moment with anticipation, and then be so afraid of what would come next?

He met Donovan at the same chamber he played his music in. The old man was slightly shorter than him, about five feet tall. His head was shaved like all the other monks, but his wrinkles gave some hint to his age. He was one of those men who time had aged beyond years. His eyes were dark brown and seemed to pierce Calderon's very soul.

"Good evening," Donovan greeted.

Calderon returned the greeting and bowed his head to the old man. "The Abbot didn't mention the reason for the change. Do you know what happened?"

Donovan's face softened with what appeared to be sadness. "Sevrin, though not my first choice, did well. He played the music under my supervision and did everything the way he should have. Afterward, he fell ill. We assumed it was a minor thing, perhaps some bad meat. But he did not survive through the night. The poor boy died in his sleep."

Calderon frowned. "My heart breaks at this news. I have to confess something."

Donovan raised his eyebrows.

"I have worked and waited my whole life to be here, to be the Musician. But now that I am here and this is all happening, I am afraid. What if I mess up? What if I am not meant to be the Musician?"

Donovan did not answer immediately. "The Divines work their will out in ways that we do not understand. Their ways are not our ways. Their thoughts are not our thoughts. Yet everything works out in the end the way it was meant to. Sevrin's death is a part of their will, though how or why we will never know in this life. Fear is a natural response to the unknown. There is nothing wrong in being afraid. We all have fears; we are only men."

Donovan stared into Calderon's eyes with that piercing gaze. "The true test of a man is not whether he is afraid or not, it is how he responds. I will be here to teach you and guide you as long as the Divines see fit. And when death comes to me as it comes to us all, you will be ready."

Calderon had a puzzled look on his face. "Ready for what?"

"To be on your own, as the new Musician."

Calderon found being the Musician to be less overwhelming than he expected. There were two things that Donovan was very specific about. The time that he began the music, and how long he played.

"The enchantment that is bound within the metal of the sphere is old. It requires the music to be played daily to strengthen it. Every twenty four hours, to the minute, it must be played or else the enchantment will weaken."

"What happens if it weakens?" Calderon questioned.

"The soul of the dragon that is captured within is a fire dragon. The enchantment keeps the sphere cold, which ensures the beast is trapped inside. If the enchantment weakens, the temperature of the metal drops. And if that were to happen, the dragon would be able to escape. Were the dragon to roam this world again … it would be the end of things as we know it."

The old man knew more about the sphere than any of the books he had read in the library. He was older than any of the other monks, older even than the former Guardian. Calderon didn't like looking into the man's eyes. His piercing gaze made him uncomfortable.

"That is why you must never be late. The music must begin at the exact time, and it must be for a complete hour. If either of these guidelines are not kept, you endanger the entire world."

Calderon was silent in thought. "Why entrust something so important to the monastery? Why did the silversmith bring it to us? Why not destroy the dragon's soul instead of trapping it?"

Donovan shrugged his thin shoulders. "Why he chose to come here is a mystery. From what I have learned in all my years is that while a dragon's body can be destroyed, its soul cannot. They are from a time and world beyond ours. There are tales of wizards from ancient times that had dealings with the beasts, but dragons are sly creatures and often betrayed the wizards. No one knows where they came from or how they came to be in our world."

"What if I fail?" Calderon asked, hesitating to ask such a dramatic question.

Donovan didn't answer. Instead, he led Calderon to the chamber of the sphere. They relieved Velkyn and entered the room. This would be the fifth night that he played the music. Each night became less stressful. His sleeping disorder even seemed less active than he could ever remember.

He put the flute to his lips and began to play his music. Perhaps he had been wrong about his fears.

—

Velkyn had trained for years to make his mind more powerful than his body. Guarding a door that could be attacked for twenty-one hours a day, with only three hours to rest was no easy feat. The first couple days hadn't been too difficult, but it was beginning to catch up to him. He desperately needed sleep. It was hard for him to keep his eyes open. They were beginning to water and his eyelids were so heavy. He managed to make it to his room and slump into his bed. Sleep overcame him almost immediately.

His eyes shot open. How long had he been out? It felt like he had slept for hours. Panic gripped him as the thought that he might have overslept entered his mind. He heard a noise and sat up quickly.

"It's been a week since I've seen you," a female voice echoed in the darkness. Velkyn turned toward the doorway, where he heard the voice.

"Nydel … when did you get in here?" Velkyn whispered. He felt her soft hand touch the left side of his face.

"Just now. Why haven't you come to see me?" she whispered back, leaning in close.

"I was chosen as the Guardian. I get relieved late in the evening."

She hopped into the bed and straddled him. "I'm so proud of you!" she said excitedly as she wrapped her arms around him.

"Sshh! Not so loud, woman. Someone might hear you. I have to get back to my post soon. I only get three hours away."

"I saw you from down the hall, you just got in here. You must be exhausted," she pouted. "You are probably too tired …" she said sensually. She pulled her shirt off and tossed it to the side.

Velkyn shook his head and pulled her face close to his. "Mm … I missed you."

—

Velkyn arrived back at his post just in time to meet Calderon and Donovan as they were leaving the chamber. Donovan didn't say anything but continued on his way. Calderon stopped. "You look exhausted."

Velkyn waited until he didn't see the old man anymore. "Nydel came to see me."

"Here?" Calderon asked incredulously.

Velkyn smirked. "She's amazing. I *will* make her my wife one day." Calderon could only raise his eyebrows in response. He knew that wouldn't be very likely, but he didn't want to point that out.

"Are you going to attend the coronation?" Velkyn asked Calderon, abruptly changing the subject.

"The entire monastery is attending." Calderon responded. "Donovan just told me about it. How did you find out? And are you the only one guarding it?"

Velkyn shrugged. "I honestly don't know. I would imagine the other candidates will be under my supervision to keep it safe. I hear the king of Oakvalor will be present. Who knows what they might have planned. And anything that concerns the sphere comes to me first. After the Abbot, of course."

Calderon waited in silence a few moments to make sure Donovan was completely out of earshot. "I am playing the music by myself from now on. Donovan thinks his time is coming. I'm nervous about playing alone. What if—" Velkyn raised his hand to quiet his friend. "Trust in yourself, Calderon. You have too much fear about what might be, when you should live in what is. They were not wrong in choosing you. You'll be fine."

Calderon wasn't so sure of that.

—

It was hard for Calderon to believe it was time to play again. The days seemed to drown together. He had not seen Donovan at all since he played his music the night before. It was entirely possible he had passed during the night. Given the importance of the coronation, it was unlikely he would get the news of his mentor's death.

As he approached the sphere's chamber, a tingly feeling spread down his back. He reached down to rub the spot and the feeling went away, but he didn't feel right. He felt … off. Shaking his head, he continued on and relieved Velkyn from his duty. He pushed the door open and entered the dimly lit chamber, pausing to let his eyes adjust.

It was almost time.

Calderon placed the flute to his lips and breathed in deep.

He opened his eyes and was looking up at the ceiling. A horrible feeling of dread washed over him. He had fallen asleep! Calderon struggled up to his feet and tried frantically to determine how much time had passed. He pulled the chamber door open just enough to look out. Velkyn was not back yet. Perhaps he had only dozed off for a short moment.

He pushed the door shut and began to play his music like normal. As he played, he glanced around the room. The room was so dim, he wasn't sure how much time had passed, if any at all. Perhaps he had passed out and not fallen asleep? He wasn't sure. He eyed the sphere closely. It did not appear noticeably different, though he never really paid attention to what the sphere looked like. Calderon rested one hand on the sphere as he held a note on his flute.

It was cool to the touch, but he had only touched it once before. Was it always cool to the touch? He couldn't remember.

Calderon was so engrossed with the sphere he did not hear the door swing open. "Calderon," he heard Velkyn whisper. He spun around, startled by the sound. Velkyn stood in the doorway motioning him. "Your hour has passed, my friend. Come, your duty is complete for today. The sphere must be readied for the coronation tomorrow."

Calderon nodded, unsure of how long he had played his music anyway. He assumed he had played long enough to keep the enchantment strong. He left the chamber and stood in the hallway as Velkyn shut the door. "I will see you at the palace tomorrow. Do you suppose we will meet the new king?" Calderon asked as Velkyn took his post.

"If the Divines see fit to allow it," Velkyn responded. "You look pale. You should get some rest. Wait ..." Velkyn's voice lowered. "you didn't fall asleep, did you?"

"No, I didn't." Calderon lied. "I just feel a little weak now. I will see you tomorrow at the coronation. It will be exciting to see what lies outside these walls."

As troubled as Calderon was about his sleeping disorder having roused its ugly head, he had little difficulty sleeping through the night. As the light of dawn shown through the small window of his room, he was readying himself to see the palace for the first time in his life.

7

THE PALACE WAS BUZZING WITH rumors. Prince Ranaan sifted through the conversations of the servants as they dashed about, whispering in not-so-quiet tones. He feigned ignorance and continued making his way through the vast hallways that led above ground and to the throne room. The servants were always full of gossip and sharing the latest intrigue, but today was different.

Today, there was talk of death.

Barely reaching five feet, Ranaan was not an intimidating figure. His hair was black and of medium length, usually tied in a pony-tail. His bangs hung down in sharp points and he was always pushing them aside. His eyes were an icy blue and stood out vividly when he wore his formal white uniform. The youngest of his father's two sons, he would not take the throne but instead would be allowed to do with his life as he chose.

He reached the hidden doorway that led to the section of the castle that was above ground. At the end of the hallway was two massive wooden doors. As he approached he was greeted by two guards, one at each side of the entrance. They bowed low at his arrival. They grunted as they pushed the doors open, bowing once more as Ranaan swept past them without acknowledgement. The audience room was an enormous circular chamber. It was usually filled with nobles, but today it was empty.

His father was seated on the throne, a large oak chair plated in gold and silver. His brother, the heir to the throne, stood attentively at his side.

"You called for me father?" His voice echoed in the empty chamber.

Dagmar, his brother, had a grave look on his face. "He can't speak, Ranaan. His condition has worsened. The healers said—" his voice cracked and he paused. The emotional turmoil was obvious. "They said he won't make it through the night."

Ranaan stood in silence, unsure how to take the news. He loved his father dearly, but the man was nearing ninety and time had not been kind to him. A disease of the mind had consumed him and he was no longer the man Ranaan remembered. It was a confusing mix of emotions. Sadness at the imminent death of his father, but relief that his suffering would soon be at an end.

Byramm, the royal chamberlain, made his presence known by coughing softly. "Your Highness's," he greeted solemnly. "You know what this means."

Dagmar looked to Ranaan. "Do you object?"

"You know I don't," Ranaan replied, lowering himself to one knee. "I support your reign as king." He lowered his head in homage.

Their father, in a rare show of normalcy, reached up weakly and pulled his crown off. He looked at Dagmar and mouthed something unintelligible. Dagmar hesitantly took hold of the crown. Lifting it up, he stared at the large black diamond in its center. He looked to Ranaan, then to the chamberlain, and lastly, his father.

The old king nodded his head slowly. Dagmar placed the crown on his own head.

"Long live the king," Ranaan said.

There was complete silence. Byramm waited a few moments to speak, not wanting to ruin the moment. "My Lord's, I do not wish to rush your mourning, but there are things that need to be done. We must announce the coronation and summon the monks from the Abbey to bring the sphere." Byramm eyed Dagmar critically. "And we must summon the tailor."

—

"There is one more thing, brother." The tailor was busy taking Dagmar's measurements, her hands a flurry of fingers and measuring tape.

Ranaan looked questioningly at his brother.

"I am announcing a truce with Oakvalor."

Ranaan's face turned incredulous. "What! There hasn't been peace since … since anyone can remember. At least, not a real peace. How in the Divines are you going to manage a truce?"

"Marriage."

The tailor produced a plush violet robe and placed it over Dagmar's shoulders. Using needles and some sort of sticky parchment, she marked out where she would need to make cuts in the material. "I am going to marry the princess of Oakvalor. It is going to be announced at the coronation."

Ranaan was at a loss for words. "It is what is best for the people of our kingdom. And theirs. Enough blood has been shed in a war that neither side can win. No one can even remember how it started or why. It is time to leave our feuds in the past and work toward a better future."

Ranaan looked at his brother in a new light. He seemed wiser somehow. "It makes sense to me, brother. I'm not sure how the people will accept it. War is all we know. I stand behind any decision you make. And I will stand behind this one. My heart says peace would be a nice change, but my mind doesn't know what peace is."

"My prayer and my hope is that we can change that." Dagmar looked at himself in the mirror. "Do I look like a king?" he asked jokingly. Ranaan chuckled softly. He had to wonder if Dagmar meant 'we' as in he and his bride to be, or together as brothers. He supposed it didn't matter so long as the people of the kingdom were happy.

"You look noble to me, but what do I know?"

—

"No, no, no! You will stand here," the chamberlain screeched, pointing to a specific stone on the floor. Ranaan rolled his eyes at the old man. He reminded Ranaan of his grandmother, wrinkly and decrepit. Between the heat and the old man's irritating voice, it was all he could do not to snap. "Why does it matter where we stand, Byramm?"

Byramm's face turned a deep crimson color. "It is tradition! Which you apparently lack any knowledge of. You are fortunate you're not a child anymore."

Ranaan smirked at the chamberlain. "Careful, Byramm. I might break your hip."

"Please brother," Dagmar interjected, "we must get this right before evening. Two days from now is the coronation and we will have the entire kingdom watching. The less inexperienced we look, the better."

Ranaan conceded the point and stood where the chamberlain directed. That old man had been a pain, usually quite literally, when he was younger. Anytime he made a mistake, Byramm was always there to deliver discipline. Now that he was in charge of himself, he could pick at the chamberlain all he pleased with no painful retaliation.

The next few hours were full of boredom for Ranaan as the chamberlain laid out the course of events that would unfold leading up to the coronation. The monastery would bring the sphere out as a symbolic display of power, there would be a few speeches by the people who had helped raise the older prince, and once they were finished, he would be crowned the new king of Talvaard. The only thing that would be different from any other ceremony, at least according to Byramm, was the announcement of the marriage and treaty with Oakvalor.

"The general has tripled the guard in the event the people do not initially take to the idea. There will also be archers on the rooftops. We are not only protecting our new king, but also our new ally and his entourage."

"That should be plenty of protection," Dagmar said. "I've given King Elkanah permission to bring his bodyguard as well. We have made every preparation possible. Now we can only trust the Divines for the best."

—

The palace grounds were crowded with people who had come to see the crowning of the new king. Many of them had traveled hundreds of miles from all corners of the kingdom to glimpse the ceremony. The kings of Talvaard were known to live long and die of old age rather than of battle or disease, so the ceremony was a rare event.

Innumerable banners and flags of bright orange, yellow, and red lined the buildings and walkways leading up to the Palace Square. Why it was called a square, no one was certain. The stonework that laid out the area in front of the great wall which separated the actual palace and the Square was in the shape of a rectangle. Whoever had termed it a square, the description stuck.

Soldiers wearing ceremonial armor, emblazoned with the royal insignia of a phoenix bursting forth from a pile of ashes, stood guard along the streets to ensure order and keep the crowds from overwhelming the plaza where the sphere and the new king would be. Archers lined the rooftops with bows in hand, keeping careful watch. The entire population of the monastery, with the exception of the Guardian and those under his command, formed a large circle around a short pillar to the right of where the king would stand. Velkyn and the three former candidates for his position stood alert with their backs to the sphere, forming a protective square. An identical pillar to the left held the crown used only for coronations.

Prince Ranaan peered down at the scene below from the window of the throne room. Dagmar would pace the room, then turn, and pace back. "Are you nervous, brother?" Ranaan chided. "You act as though you have never stood before a crowd."

His brother ceased his march. "It is easy for you to be calm. You aren't the one who is accepting a crown that has many enemies. Not to mention the ire I may receive from the people of our kingdom with the announcement I make today. So yes, brother, I am nervous." Dagmar continued pacing back and forth.

Ranaan shrugged and turned his gaze back to the scene outside. He could see the glint of the sphere through the veil that covered it. Enormous groups of children waved miniature flags with the royal crest. It seemed that the people were happy. The Square was a much different place the night before when they held the funeral. The same people who were excitedly waving flags and banners were also the same people who had cried and openly mourned the loss of their previous king.

Ranaan thought about how his father looked inside the casket. He had always viewed his father as tall and strong, wise and venerable. Seeing him shriveled and pale just lying in a box made him conscious of the reality of death. It was no respecter of people or their status.

Trumpets signaling the approach of King Elkanah momentarily drowned out the sound of the people talking and cheering. Ranaan looked to see which direction the entourage was coming from and spotted them to the west. He could see about twenty men dressed in the colors of Oakvalor marching in front of a carriage.

"Brother," he said loudly, "our guests have arrived."

Dagmar seemed not to hear the news, so Ranaan motioned the guards to escort the visiting king to the plaza. "Have you seen her?" Ranaan asked aloud.

"Who?" Dagmar replied.

"Your future wife. Have you seen her?"

Dagmar still did not cease pacing the throne room. "No. Why do you ask?"

"What if she is ugly?" Ranaan laughed, though his brother did not.

"I do not see how the beauty of my queen has anything to do with bringing peace to our kingdoms."

"It doesn't." Ranaan answered. "Though it would be humorous for you to go into the history books as a king who married a repulsive woman." That did cause Dagmar to stop his pacing and glare at him. "Come now, brother," Ranaan left the window and embraced his sibling. "I only jest to lighten your heart."

"There will be plenty of time for you to jest after the ceremony," Dagmar said curtly. "Though … I do hope she isn't unsightly." He smiled at Ranaan and continued his pacing.

One of the generals appeared in the doorway. "Your Highness," his deep voice echoed in the giant marble chamber, "The king and his daughter await you in the plaza."

Ranaan removed the robe that lay on the throne and wrapped it around his brother's shoulders. "That's our queue."

—

Calderon could hear the Abbot arguing heatedly with someone in hushed tones. When he looked to see who, he was surprised to see Donovan. His spirits lifted when he saw his mentor, but when he realized his mentor was the one arguing with the Abbot, he got confused. He could only hear pieces of their conversation over the noise of the crowd.

"You must remove it," Donovan said.

"That will never happen. The coronation will begin any moment, and we will not insult our new king."

"Something is wrong … I feel … dangerous," Calderon strained to hear what Donovan was saying, but the crowd was getting louder. "It's not safe."

The sound of horns blaring overpowered every sound and shook the ground around them. "All hail Prince Dagmar and Prince Ranaan!" One of the heralds roared.

Calderon thought the crowd was loud before the princes arrived. The masses shoved forward and it was all the soldiers could do to hold them back. He could see a general barking out orders but couldn't make out the words. Then the two bothers entered the plaza, surrounded by a host of at least two dozen men armed to the teeth.

He had not seen much outside the monastery and was overwhelmed by everything.

He looked to where Donovan had been but the old man was gone. The Abbot seemed unfazed by whatever his mentor had said. Velkyn looked calm and composed compared to the soldiers fighting to keep the crowds at bay.

It took almost twenty minutes to restore order and get the people to be silent enough for the ceremony to begin. Despite the chaos of the crowds, everything seemed well orchestrated as each person who had written a speech about the new king came forward and spoke about their memories of Dagmar as a child and various other stories about his character.

As soon as the chamberlain finished talking, an odd hush fell over the crowd. Calderon wasn't sure why everyone suddenly went quiet. It was probably the only moment of silence he had experienced since leaving the monastery that morning.

Byramm approached the pillar that held the crown and gently picked it up. He turned to Dagmar and lifted the crown into the air. "It is my esteemed honor to name you, Prince Dagmar, as the new king, by royal lineage, over the kingdom of Talvaard and its people." Placing the crown upon Dagmar's head, Byramm turned to the assembly. "I give you King Dagmar!"

A great shout filled the air, though the people did not try to surge forward this time. Calderon noticed Prince Ranaan was staring at the sphere. The veil had been removed and it seemed so bright. Ranaan seemed to be entranced by the thing and oblivious to anything around him. The prince closed his eyes and opened his mouth in a scream that was lost in the sound of the thousands of people cheering.

Panic gripped Calderon as he wondered what was wrong with the prince. He was about to rush forward to help him but noticed that one of the soldiers came to his aid.

Ranaan kept shaking his head and seemed unsteady on his feet. It seemed to Calderon that nobody had noticed the prince's odd behavior. Suddenly Ranaan seemed fine. He stood straight and pushed the soldier away from him.

Calderon kept his eyes on the prince to see if anything else happened, but he seemed fine. Dagmar was trying to hush the crowd, and eventually Calderon turned his attention away from Ranaan.

"I have an announcement," Dagmar yelled loudly to be heard as the noise of the people died down. "We have long been at war with our neighbors, and I am sure you are all wondering why the king of Oakvalor is here for my coronation. Today the nation of Talvaard and Oakvalor put our feuding past behind us. Today, my people, we forge a peace that not even our forefathers imagined. Today, I will marry the daughter of King Elkanah and seal a treaty of peace between our kingdoms!"

There was complete silence. Calderon eyed the crowd. Everyone just stood there, staring at their new king with wide eyes and in some cases, wide mouths. Then someone in the back started clapping. Then another followed suit. And another. And another, until everyone was clapping in approval of the union.

King Elkanah brought forth his daughter and the people began cheering loudly again. To say the woman was beautiful was an understatement. Calderon was awed by her eyes. They were bright blue, and her white flowing dress made them seem all the brighter. Her hair was blonde and long, perhaps reaching the middle of her back.

The two kings embraced each other in a hug, and then Dagmar took the woman by her hand. "What's your name?" Dagmar asked embarrassedly.

"Nizana."

"It's as beautiful as you are," he complimented.

A great smile spread across her face, revealing her teeth which were just as white as her dress.

Despite the loudness and chaos of the crowd, Calderon was glad to have experienced this moment. "History in the making," he whispered to himself. He noticed Prince Ranaan was hovering toward the back of the plaza, his behavior seeming odd again. And then …

Calderon watched in sheer horror as a scene more nightmarish than anything he could ever dream played out before his very eyes.

Ranaan shoved his brother to the ground from behind. Unsheathing a sword from the soldier who helped him, he thrust the blade into Nizana's abdomen. Blood spurt forth onto Ranaan's hands and onto the floor. There was a wild look in the prince's eyes as he jerked the blade free.

Dagmar stared in horror and confusion, unsure of what to do. King Elkanah pointed at Ranaan and ordered his bodyguard to seize the murderer. The crazed look on his face made the guards hesitate. Then in a quick fluid motion, he swung the blade in a giant arc and decapitated his brother.

Time seemed to cease for Calderon, but for everyone else, all hell broke loose. The Talvaard soldiers, unsure of what they should do, grouped protectively around Prince Ranaan. King Elkanah's bodyguards did likewise and began systematically moving him away from the Square to the carriage, pushing their way through the distraught crowd.

People were screaming and trampling each other to get away from the horrific sight. Calderon's attention snapped back to the direction of the sphere when he heard the familiar voice of his friend Velkyn shouting for the monks to shield the sphere with their bodies. The thunderous sound of magic boomed and lit up the square in a bluish-green light and King Elkanah's carriage, and his entourage, disappeared from sight.

"So, there are wizards," Calderon whispered in disbelief. He felt a hand on his shoulder and looked up to see the Abbot. "Go with Velkyn and the others and take the sphere to safety." Calderon nodded and left the circle to join his friend. He noticed that the soldiers had moved Ranaan behind the stone wall of the palace.

"What in the name of the Divines just happened?" he yelled. Velkyn shook his head grimly. "I'm not sure, but it seems like a coupe just happened."

"A what?"

Velkyn pointed to the dead body of Dagmar. "An overthrow and seizure of the throne by a jealous brother. Come, we have to get the sphere back to the monastery."

The trip back was rushed and nothing like the trip earlier that morning. Calderon had been entranced by the beauty of the capital city and the surrounding countryside. Everything now seemed different. Velkyn personally carried the sphere and only allowed Calderon to walk near him.

"Why would the Prince kill King Elkanah's daughter, let alone his own brother?" one of the monks whispered to another.

"Why indeed?" Calderon looked questioningly to Velkyn.

"Your assumption is as good as mine," he replied, holding the sphere tightly to his chest. "Perhaps he wasn't happy with not being king."

Calderon's heart was heavy with grief. This was the only time he had left the monastery since he entered the sacred halls and it ended in bloodshed. A nagging thought in the back of his mind kept reminding him that the day wasn't over yet.

8

THE SUN WAS BARELY A sliver of dimming yellow light on the horizon. The few clouds in the sky shone red in the waning light of day above the low, forested hills of the Red Island. If one were watching from the hills overlooking the east or west parts of the valley at this time, he would have seen a shadow slowly stretch over to the south, creeping slowly down into the valley over the vast patchwork of fields, orchards, and pastures. All that could be seen of the Aiakh River was a dark ribbon, glittering like a long snakelike diamond in the last rays of the sunlight, winding its way north up the valley and out through a tunnel under the hills.

One could see the campfires of the ruby and iron miners being lit on the hillsides. The familiar sounds of cattle, sheep, and goats being herded into their caves just above the valley. The smell of dead fish that were daily brought upstream for trade with the farmers came up from the valley, rising with the heat of the day. Occasionally, a warm, gentle breeze would blow from the valley up into the hills, the richness and aroma reminding the entire island of the impending harvest.

A horn sounded, heralding the coming of night. In response, the sound of a flute playing an ancient melody rose from one of the campfires. It was a beautiful song, composed ages before the migration of the first twelve tribes of the Aihi into the Five Islands of Oakvalor. Such a song is very difficult to describe, as one would not hear the likes of it elsewhere. If one listened closely, you could hear voices coming up out of the earth, singing their ancient chant to the sound of the flute. The branches of trees rustled in the gentle breeze, humming along with the music. All of nature seemed to sing the song of the flute. If the song had words, one could be sure that all of the men, women, and children on the Island would have sung its chorus on that peaceful night.

All was peaceful on the Red Island as the sun set on that late summer evening. One felt like celebrating with every breath, such was the richness of the pre-harvest air. All the children were sleeping soundly in their beds, while the mothers prepared nighttime meals for their husbands coming back from a long day of work in the fields, pastures, and orchards.

As soon as the sun had set, the moon in its full brightness rose from the southern horizon. Proceeding, guarding, and following it were thousands of bright stars, lighting up the heavens. The sun had gone to bed along with the children of the valley, and then had come the moon, escorted by her children, to continue the great dance across the sky.

If any man by this time still had a trouble, discomfort, or sense of foreboding on his mind, it would have soon been forgotten. For once, all troubled thoughts and worries could be put aside until the morning. For just a few hours of time, man's mind could be at peace. All of the Red Island sang with that flute song, and the hearts of mankind sang with it. For just a short period of time, in the face of eternity, all was at peace.

The aged prophet made his way up the lonely mountain path after his journey to and from the busy streets of the capital city, Aicatan. He and his disciple, Lord Imen, had traveled much during the previous week. After four days of treading the valley roads, a week of sleeping in the cramped rooms of the city inns and taverns, and many rigorous ceremonies and rites of passage, both master and—especially—pupil were glad to be returning to their peaceful homes on the mountain, and looking forward to a comfortable rest in their own beds.

The prophet, called Lord Aio, would have had little trouble hiding behind any medium sized tree trunk or small boulder without having to crouch low or stand sideways. His pupil, who was of average height and build, dwarfed him considerably. His scarred, withered arms told of many long death matches. What little muscle that could be found on his diminutive frame would have been hard enough to force any Cannibal to leave the morsel in frustration, claiming it in the primitive Cannibal tongue to be a peculiar type of stone. His brown, oven-baked face—but one of the many perils endured—was decorated by a long, unkempt and unwashed scarlet beard, framed on top by hair of similar color, length, fashion, and state. The dark eyes sinking deep into his face had not lost the fire of youth, but had been stoked with over a century of war and wisdom. His thin, cracked, dry lips almost matched his face in color.

His earthen-colored traveling cloak was covered with dust of a slightly lighter hue. His feet and ankles were so caked with dust, sticking to his skin from the sweat caused by wearing sandals for an extended period of time. The aroma of pipe-smoke mixed with the odors of sweat and old age emanated from his body.

They halted for a moment. The prophet inhaled deeply, feeling the warmth and richness of the air surge throughout his entire body, restoring some of his long-lost youth.

"A fine evening, Lord Imen," he said.

"It is, Lord Aio," said Imen, attempting to catch his breath before the tireless prophet continued the seemingly endless march.

The Lord Aio nodded. "The Ai has shown us favor in giving us such an evening. One hundred and forty-three years ago this hour, the personified Ai, the Great Aio, appeared on this Island."

The young High Priest wiped the sweat off his forehead as he gazed out over the Island, looking over every twist in the river, every small campfire, every stone and tree, the moon and every small star, and every lighted window that was visible in the valley; hearing every miner's flute and every grazing beast that was raised in the valley; absorbing every breath of wind, the odor of fish and manure. All of this, the good and the evil, the agreeable and disagreeable, the pleasant and the unpleasant, had been made by the Ai. All living and non-living things were of the Ai.

In the past—he had been told—the Ai had spoken to mankind through visions, or through the clouds, and sometimes in a great, blinding white light. However, the Ai, for a short period of forty-eight years, came to the Five Islands in the form of a man. It was at that very hour, and on that Island, one hundred and forty-three years before, the Ai has chosen a place for his unannounced arrival. For a moment, Imen forgot all of his troubles, discomforts, fears, and even his exhaustion in that thought.

Following that brief pause, they continued their arduous climb up the narrow, steep, winding trail for what seemed to the pupil to be an hour (though it was probably a good deal less than half). It had always amazed Imen how the decrepit old mentor always managed to be a good three paces ahead of the young warrior, never tiring or seeming to need a rest, while the youthful student felt as if his legs would fall out from under him.

They came to a place where the ground leveled off, surrounded on all but one side by high rock formations. In the center of this area lay five large, flat stones arranged in a circle, all of them large enough for one to sit upon with space left over for a staff, cloak, or a sword. If one were to look over the side not surrounding the mountain, he would have seen a patchwork of fields and orchards spread from beneath him, allowing him to view almost the entire valley.

The Lord Aio suddenly stopped, staring into a space that had opened up in the side of the mountain during his absence. For what seemed like an eternity to Imen, he stared in amazement and terror at the opening, never once blinking or letting his gaze shift from the tunnel before him. If he had not been paralyzed by the sight, his body would have shuddered violently. The look of death shone in his eyes.

Imen, at the sight, felt a mountain of fear fall upon him. He had heard of this omen, its meaning, and its history, yet he had never seen it until now. He wished he could have run and hidden, or better yet, jumped off the cliff wall that fell below him into the valley. The Tunnel had again been opened.

"This cannot be happening," stated Imen, the shock evident in the shaking of his voice.

The words of Imen breaking him from his stupor, the Lord Aio shook the dust of the ground off his traveling cloak, muttering to himself in the ancient tongue of the Ai.

"The Tunnel has again been opened to us," he said to Imen, "and troubled—nay, far worse than troubled—times are to come. The East Wind grows bolder than ever; life eludes the West Wind; the fire grows cold. Sit upon this sacred stone, Lord Imen, and guard the Tunnel with your life. Let no one pass in or out unchallenged. I feel that an evil has come upon the Island. An evil I have not known for almost ..."

Wincing as if feeling pain from some terrible memory, the Lord Aio turned quickly and walked up the path to his hut. After his master was out of sight, Imen sat down with his sword drawn, his eyes searching, and his ears ever attentive.

He could feel the cold winds of danger and fear cut through him like a sword. The ancient melodies played by the miners, and the warm, peaceful atmosphere that had just a few minutes earlier dominated the entire Island was suddenly gone. He shivered a bit, even though the night was warm and the weather fair and despite wearing a traveling cloak.

Just a few minutes before, he thought only of a long, peaceful sleep. Now, he felt as if he had awakened to find himself living in one of his worst nightmares. Every rock looked as if to conceal a ghoul, a Cannibal, or an Orc behind it. Likewise, every tree was the dwelling place of evil spirits. Imen felt as though the Tunnel itself would swallow him. The smallest sound was an army of demons. Every few minutes, Imen would check behind the rock he sat on to assure himself that no danger lay hidden in its shadow.

What reason had he to fear? He had been hungry. He had been without necessities. He had suffered pain. He had been betrayed. He had seen war. He had seen defeat. He had seen death, and had even faced it a couple of times. He, more than the population of the Five Islands, would know what it meant to have troubles. But the Tunnel? Nay. Although the High Priest knew of troubles, the opening of the Tunnel meant troubles of the worst kind. Atrocities that had caused even the greatest warriors to cower and flee as children escaping some punishment for some seemingly great offense, tortures that had caused even the most devout Priests to publicly denounce the Ai and claim allegiance to the forces of evil. A living death within a living death, as the Lord Aio had described some of the wars he had fought in during the time of the opened Tunnel.

High Priest over the Red Island was he, and a proven warrior. High Priest and warrior. On this night, however, he felt more like the small child that has strayed from his mother in a place he does not know. Although the Lord Aio and the other four pupils were just a few minutes' walk up the mountain trail, well within earshot, he felt as though even his closest of friends had betrayed and deserted him in the thick of a battle.

The Tunnel had again been opened, and although he knew not what would happen, impending doom lurked behind the mask of that once peaceful evening.

- Father Ean

9

AT FIRST GLANCE, TO SAY that he was an elderly person would have been the grossest of understatements. So numerous and deep were the wrinkles that creased his aged face, he was almost beyond recognition as a man. The darkened, earthen color of his face, the large forehead, the small, black deep-set probing eyes, the slightly pointed ears, a long, crooked hawk-like nose that looked as if someone had pulled on it too long, and a thin, slightly darkened pair of dehydrated lines he called lips did not help. The unmistakably human salt-white beard that hung from his protruding chin was the only thing that identified his human ancestry at this point in his life.

Beginning at the top of his head, coming down to the side in both directions forming an arc, his head was adorned with thin, dirty white hair of moderate length resting upon his shoulders. For the most part, this was unkempt and in it, one could find the remains of dead insects, traces of spider's webs, leaves, twigs, and almost any other type of small objects that can rest in one's hair. On very special occasions, he would wash it, comb through it with his eleven gnarled fingers (their appearance more like claws), and thread an intricate pattern of vines, leaves, and wildflowers into it. He had not had such as occasion of celebration in over ninety years. The greasy quality of his hair, as well as the dirt and filth that had claimed his head as a permanent habitat were quite conspicuous.

His tall, bony frame was clothed (if at all) in the leaves of the oak tree, woven together in a complex pattern by a myriad of pine needles. He would have two sheets of this covering, one in front, the other in back, connected on the sides and top by long, thick blades of grass or even the vines from his extensive vineyard.

Regardless of what ages he had seen come and go, he had towered above even the tallest of men from each race. Although not

`65

carrying a single drop of giant's blood in his veins, he appeared as one with a tall wisp of a body, strong arms of immense length that one would think they could stretch to the ends of the world, claw-like fingers, and the thin, stick-like legs and feet that could have been mistaken for roots taking into account the leaves and twigs in his hair and the leaves that covered his body.

On this particular morning, he sat at the edge of the lush, green forest on the Island of Cerel, his eyes peering down into the bustling commerce and life that was characteristic of any bay in the dominion of the Five Islands. Well hidden from view, a sighting of him by one of the people in the town below would have upset the whole of the Five Islands. It had been centuries since any man had ever seen him, much less spoken to him. Even to the Council of High Priests, he was merely a legend, a story told among the more youthful circles sitting around the campfires. There had not been need for an appearance for a very long time, and he felt no desire to appear.

He had begun to feel the pangs of old age settle in about one hundred years before. From shortly after the founding of Oakvalor as a nation, he had forsaken the path of the rest of men and chose to serve the Ai, to look after and tend Oakvalor. On choosing this, his body and functions had changed dramatically. He had become one with the earth, his body aging ever so slowly. However, as all men did at some point in their lives, he would have to die. He did not expect to admire the bay from his camouflaged position again.

Looking down upon the bay at the brightly colored ships, the acreage of canvas used for sails, the fathoms of rope and netting, the crates, the sailors and vendors, the merchants, and the many people there to see what goods were to be had after market day, he could not help thinking about how much things had changed, yet how little the Aihi themselves had changed. The race had been much the same when he had been a part of it, caring only for its immediate pleasures, at most, thinking of how to build a strong financial foundation for the next generation. The Aihi had not changed.

He had changed, however. He had at one time been as those he viewed from afar, seeking pleasures that he knew would satisfy him only a short while. Perhaps it was the long centuries of his work that had caused the change, or the knowledge he had accumulated during that time. Perhaps it was from having seen the history of Oakvalor.

Maybe his longevity. It could have been all four reasons, or even others unsurmised. "The answer will be known but to the Ai," he thought. "Perhaps I shall be informed after my death."

Having seen millions of people, empires, races, and even ages come to life, bloom, and then whither one would expect him to be an authority on death. This was the farthest thing from the truth. Although he had seen death in all different manners (even having caused it on occasion), his extensive knowledge ceased its long reach when it came to this concept. He had spent his entire life helping things to live and grow, giving life to the plants and animals of Oakvalor and the Five Islands. What lay beyond the moment of the body's death, not even he could foresee.

For the first few centuries of his work, he had feared death more than pain, hunger, or fire. Having seen the ages rise and fall, having witnessed most of Oakvalor's history— the extremes of evil and good—he no longer feared death. And despite his lack of knowledge on the subject he would have welcomed it at any time.

He sighed. To be even as blissful in the ignorance of these people once again! He had seen too much, had lived too long. He longed to purge himself of his body, to finally join with the Ai.

A hand came to rest upon his shoulder. "A fine bit of handiwork, brother."

Without turning, the old man nodded. "The work of my master, the Ai."

"It would have been destroyed by these creatures we let populate it without your help."

"Perhaps," he pondered. "Perhaps. It will not be long now, however, before I must select for myself one who will carry on my work. I have not much longer as the gardener of Oakvalor. I wish to live no longer. I beckon death. It draws nearer, as we speak."

"Nearer, brother. It has been many a century since I said those exact words. How correct was the wise man that said, 'The parting of oneself from one's body brings momentary pain, but ever after, blissful rest.'"

The old man closed his eyes and nodded. "Blissful rest. When I undertook the task of tending Oakvalor, I was young and restless. Perhaps a touch of foolhardy."

"Foolhardy!" interrupted the other speaker. "It becomes you less to speak of it as such. Curious, maybe, as is the nature of all men, but foolhardy? Nay."

"Curiosity then!" continued the old man. "And overflowing of it was my cup. I had seen nothing of the world's horizons surrounding the Five Islands. I was young, even to the standard of the time. Did I care for the life of the farmer, the herdsman, or the miner? Nay, I was the explorer. Before I had reached the age of thirty-three, I knew everything there was to know about the Five Islands. The mountains, the valleys, the mines. It was I who first discovered the Tunnel."

"No small feat," commented the speaker.

"At the time, no," said the old man. "But of what purpose did it serve my lust for wandering? Did it satisfy? Nay. It only increased my appetite for more."

"That I remember," said the speaker. "Our father would not allow us to take one of the boats any farther than a mile past the outer coasts."

"They would not have lasted half that distance," said the old man, laughing. "That much knowledge I have gained from my work."

"That you have. You have tended not only father's nets, our uncle's fields, but you have gardened a nation. You have seen everything that was worth seeing, as well as everything that was not worth seeing. If a new field was ploughed, you knew of it before the man's neighbor heard a sound of the plough animal. If a new pocket of rubies was struck, you knew of its worth in countless ways before the miner recognized the stone. If furnaces beneath Oakvalor have displayed their glories through the tops of the mountains, you welcomed the spectacle while most creatures in fear would run for cover. Many great empires have risen, their numbers far beyond even my reckoning, only to become no more than the soil in which a child's garden in planted. You have even seen the Great Lord Aio face to face, a thing that even I cannot boast. It was destiny that called you from our mother's womb."

"Yes, it would seem that I would be the most fitted to the task. However, it is because I have seen the good, the evil, the land, the mines, the mountains, the empires, and a great deal of the history of Oakvalor that I wish to die. There are no more mountains to climb, forests to probe, valleys in which to run. My lust has been sated and has become distasteful to me. I am tired, brother. I wish no more to explore the new. I can but revel in the memory of the old."

"Perhaps it is not that you are tired of the new, but that you tire of that which you know. An eternity would scarce suffice the time necessary to explore completely even one room in the House of the Ai. Think on it. You have lived long in Oakvalor, long so that even the marvels of this place are common and wearisome. Your desire to explore and discover has not yet been sated, but has merely soured in the absence of novelty. The House of the Ai? You need not worry about running out of worlds to explore. It is more than even your mind can comprehend. Even I, the long-dead mortal fisherman who wished for nothing more than his boat and nets, have developed a taste for exploring."

"You make me feel as the youth I once was, many ages past. The energy, vigor, strength, and unfettered curiosity that our father would whip me for! To have that again! To explore and to discover again! You tempt me, brother, to follow you back this very moment!"

"And as much as you deserve," said his brother, "I would relish in the company of my now much older brother again. You have served well. You have, however, but one more task before your time."

The old man turned and smiled. "A word from the Ai. Such as I have not heard since the beginning of my changed life, and from you, who have not walked Oakvalor for many a thousand years. I live only to serve. Speak on, brother."

"This task will require all of your abilities, and perhaps cause you to discover a few others. You have heard of the advance of Orlek."

The old man spit on the ground in response. "He was a good pupil. He could have served alongside me, maybe even succeeded me. A much earlier death for myself. His is the dominion where even I will not dare to tend. The reek of such evil I cannot bear."

"That he could have succeeded you," said the messenger. "I have only this for you: You are to do whatever you can to assist the new Lord Aio and his followers. However, you are not to make an appearance unless it is completely necessary."

The old man sighed. "I do not have any love for man. Only the Ai. Neither do I love death or peddling it. The only appearance I wish to make is before the Ai himself in His own House. However, I will do what my master has asked. Now, for the sign of your master."

"You were never able to give up the traditions considered old even in our time," said the messenger, laughing from the memory that had been unearthed after millennia of burial.

"I trust you," said the old man. "You are my brother, you are my blood. However, the law is the law, and the law is still in effect. I will not be caught neglecting it. If it was practiced for the message of a mere tribal leader in our day, should we not use the same if not greater precaution for the Ai?"

"You are a true servant of the Ai, brother. Your sign. Look behind you."

The old man slowly turned, a grin mixed of shock and joy forming on his face at what he saw, and their numbers. That which he had not seen in Oakvalor for many centuries. He turned to the messenger. The man had left as he had come, silently and unnoticed.

"Farewell, my brother," he said. "Our day of reunion shall not await me much longer. I shall meet you once more, this time in the House of the Ai." The old man turned to his new—or old—friends. "Greetings, cousins," he said, embracing each of their scaled necks. "It has been a long time."

One of them shot a wisp of smoke out of his nostril in affection. "Much time indeed, Father Ean."

"Too much time," said another. "The Serpentauri have been long in waiting for the day we should return to Oakvalor and avenge ourselves."

"Your time has come, my cousin. It has come," said Father Ean. "A pity you did not come to me these hundred years. I am old, and my powers are not what they used to be."

The first of the Serpentauri to speak reared on his hind legs, bellowing in a long column of fire and smoke. "You have not to fear of such, lord, nor to dwell on an imagined weakness. I am Kelros, Chieftain of the Serpentauri that live, descended from our ancestors of Orlek's golden age. You have as many of us as live to stand behind you."

Father Ean nodded. "Although I would have you stomach your fire until your time to fight has come, I accept your pledge. The battle we fight will not be anything as simple as the one which was fought those generations past. Our enemy has grown strong and all the more bitter in ninety-five years. He has remained alive all this time, an advantage over yourselves."

"We remember. Although the Aihi might let such things slip their memories, the Serpentauri never forget. We have had just as long as Orlek to remember, perhaps longer. Should we die in battle, better that we die a thousand deaths than back down against an enemy of more advantage, though our race should live to rule Oakvalor."

The old man nodded. "You might think it stupid of me when I ask, but where has been the dwelling place of the Serpentauri these centuries past? I had noticed a drain on the magic that gives life to Oakvalor, but had always thought it to be the festering hole in which Orlek lies."

Kelros laughed. "You were probably correct in the assumption that the dominion of our old friend Orlek is responsible for the drain on magic, although I suppose that we just might have been responsible for a small portion of the loss. The race of the Serpentauri somewhat … died out … after the fall of the age of Orlek, at least, that is, disappeared from the Five Islands."

Father Ean nodded in remembrance, allowing the chief to continue. "There is a land to the East, far beyond the limits of the maps and charts used even today. You have been there, I presume?"

"That I have, and know it well," said Father Ean. "Continue."

"A large number of our people set off to the east in whatever boats we could find that had not been destroyed in the battles in an effort to escape the wrath of Orlek should the outcome of the war have been favorable to the orcs. We sailed east with the hope of finding some haven of safety for our race. The boats, built by men for men, did not accommodate us well and had not been built to withstand such a voyage, the length of which our ancestors could not surmise. Many boats fell apart, the occupants drowning. Those vessels that survived the journey were seriously leaking and had become dangerously waterlogged by the time land had been sighted. We were unable to travel further, and the land was to our liking, so we settled there."

The Serpentaur's tongue flicked out across his nose. "Why you had not discovered our presence is a mystery. Perhaps we were guarded by some strange magic."

"Perhaps we were," said the second Serpentaur.

"A fantastic story of perseverance, cousins," said Father Ean. "I still do not see how even one of those boats could have lasted such a journey. I am surprised that our harbors held anything seaworthy after that battle."

"Unbelievable it is, even to us," stated Kelros, smoke slowly trickling up from out of his large mouth. "Even more a mystery, however, is the tale of our return."

Father Ean rested his chin on the top of his staff. "Please tell me this as well."

The Serpentauri began to mumble among themselves, until one said, "We do not remember, Father Ean. We fell asleep this past night. When we awoke, we were sitting here, in this forest. A man approached us, telling us to remain here in silence until you should come to us. You were sitting on that rock when the same man came and spoke to you."

A fourth Serpentaur stepped forward. "Now that we have told you our history, what are our plans? When, Father Ean, do we begin?"

Father Ean laughed. "You must be patient, and not show yourselves until the proper time. The old Great High Priest has been killed, and no doubt his body has been discovered and is being buried this day. The new Great High Priest has yet to be given the Red Sword, the new Council of High Priests to be ordained. We must wait until the battle has begun. I swear to you by all that I was, am, and will become and all that we labor towards that you shall have your revenge."

"Then may the Ai hasten the start of the battle," said Kelros, "and may I live to see the victory, or die amidst the lifeless bodies of my enemies. Victory or my death, for I shall not back down, even if I am the last of the Aihi forces standing. Life for myself on the victory of the Ai and his people. My blood is fairly wagered."

A fifth spoke up. "What are we to do for now, Father Ean?"

The rest of the Serpentauri mumbled in agreement with the question. "He is right," stated Kelros, "for we cannot hide ourselves in this place much longer."

Again, a general agreement from the group. Father Ean sat down again, looking out over the bay. "We have before us a few choices. I could disguise you all as common animals …"

"And be captured and hunted by men. Or eaten by the animals of the forest?" interrupted the second one.

Father Ean continued, ignoring the remark. "The Tunnel entrance has been opened. I suppose that just this arm of the Tunnel would be sufficient to conceal you. A bit dark, though."

"The Priests of this island, at least while our race walked Oakvalor, have guarded the entrance to an opened Tunnel most heavily, letting no man, woman, orc or any other thinking creature enter. Even disguised, we would be destroyed. I say we stay to the places on the Island that are traveled little, such as the Deep Woods," said Kelros.

Father Ean pondered the option a moment. "True. However, there are some, mostly youthful adventure seekers, that still enter the Deep Woods. What would you do if one of these were to discover you? Roast him alive? Nay. The Five Islands will need that hand of the sword before our time is through."

One of the younger of the Serpentauri walked over to Father Ean, nudging him on the shoulder with his snake-like nose. "The choice is difficult. I, for one, would not lead my people to their deaths, nor wish to cause a friendly hand the same affliction. On this Island, there are not many choices available. We do not know of the habits of these people so changed from the stories handed down through the generations. We can only make a decision and hope it to be the best. You, Father Ean, know this land and its people. You have seen the changes of this race even before our people made alliance with them. You were born as one of these people. We let you decide for us, Father Ean."

Father Ean paused for a few seconds, then grinned. "The Ai's pardon on the poor pupil in green armor that watches the entrance of the Tunnel this night."

Ideas of what was to happen already forming in their minds, the rest of the Serpentauri began to laugh, almost losing control of their fire all at once. After a bit they calmed down, waiting for the sun to bid Oakvalor goodnight. Clouds lined the horizon. The stars would dance behind the billowy curtains that night, almost no light being left for the Tunnel guard to see by. A small amount of magic would be sure to get them past the guard unnoticed in the dark of night. They had but to wait.

10

PRINCE RANAAN'S ATTENDANTS WOULD NOT come near him. No one would except for the chamberlain. Byramm stood in the royal audience chamber, trying desperately to sort through the actions of the young prince. Why would he kill his own brother? And worse, why would he give more reason for Oakvalor to continue the war with them? Prince Ranaan strode into the chamber and sat upon the throne that had long been his father's.

"My Prince," Byramm began. Ranaan looked to him and held his hand up, silencing the chamberlain. "Am I not king?" he asked. "Yes, my lord, but there is the ceremony to make it official. Plans must be made to—"

"I am king," Ranaan interrupted, his tone ending the argument. "I do not need a ceremony to make it so. Call for my generals." Byramm shifted uncomfortably. "My lord?" Ranaan motioned for Byamm to come near. "My brother thought to unite our kingdoms in peace through marriage. There can never be peace. Elkanah sought only to subvert our kingdom through his daughter. My brother was weak to think there could ever be peace."

Byramm shook his head. "You do not believe that." Ranaan glared at the chamberlain. "Do not presume to tell me what I believe. I will not suffer fools. Now call for my generals."

Byramm left the chamber to do as he was bid. Something was amiss. He had raised both Ranaan and his brother from birth and knew that this was not Ranaan's character. Something wasn't right, and he was going to find out what.

Soon after, the men who had faithfully served Ranaan's father as the leaders of the kingdom's military had gathered before the throne.

"I demand your loyalty as my father did," Ranaan said, standing tall and straight before the group of generals. Some of them began whispering. One of the men, Lord Sius, stepped forward. "Your father did not demand our loyalty, he earned it by fighting beside us. You haven't even wielded a sword."

Ranaan smirked at the brash general. "I thought you might say that. Hear me out before you make your decision." Sius conferred with the others, then nodded to Ranaan. "We will listen."

The dragon's spirit that had possessed the prince could feel the man's own spirit battling against its will. The dragon easily pushed the man's spirit aside, but could feel him still, trying to fight. This man was persistent. The creature only needed the body long enough to get his own back. "We have long been at war with Oakvalor. My brother thought wrongly to join us with our enemies. That would never do. No, we must drive our enemies out."

"Out?" asked Sius.

"We must drive them out of their own land. We must recall all of the troops and march against Oakvalor. We will drive them out before the might of our armies. My armies."

The look on Sius's face revealed his incredulity. "We cannot simply call them back. Especially not the men who protect our western borders. And even if we could, it would take weeks just to get them here. It would take months to mobilize them all. Add to that the setup of provision lines, ensuring we have enough water for the troops and the animals … it is not as easily done as you would think, young Ranaan."

"King Ranaan, and do not forget my title again, Sius. Either you will carry out my orders or I will appoint someone who will. Someone more loyal to the crown." Ranaan smirked at the general. Lord Sius knew to who Ranaan was referring. A talented young upstart who had earned his way into the dungeon through some disreputable acts. "When do you want to march?" Sius questioned.

"Immediately," Ranaan answered tersely. "My lord," Sius began. Ranaan interrupted him. "You will take the troops still stationed here at the castle immediately, and those recalled will follow. Consider them reinforcements."

"I refuse," Sius said defiantly. He crossed his arms over his chest to accentuate his point. A few of the other generals followed his example. Ranaan's smile left his face quickly and he stared at Sius for long moments. "It wasn't a request." Sius didn't answer, but kept his posture of insolence. Ranaan nodded his head and several heavily armed men stepped out from either side of the throne. "Take them to the dungeon," Ranaan said. "And release Maverick and bring him to me." The guards grabbed Sius and the few men who stood with him and led them out with their weapons drawn.

"As for the rest of you, I am honored by your loyalty," Ranaan smiled again, but it was not out of joy. "Ready the men and march first thing in the morning. I will have Byramm send out the recall orders without delay. I want a report every two days. As soon as you cross into Oakvalor and reach Palindrom, inform me at once. I will ride to meet you. I would watch the city burn to the ground."

The generals nodded their accord and left the audience chamber. "The dungeon, my king?" Byramm asked hesitantly. "We cannot afford men who will not obey the crown to be running about Talvaard. It is for the safety of the kingdom. Now go and issue a recall of all soldiers. They are to report to the castle. If I have already left for Palindrom, they are to march straightaway to meet the armies there. Oakvalor will fall within the week."

Byramm wasn't so sure about that last statement. Talvaard had long been at a disadvantage due to the fact that Oakvalor had wizards among their cities. Oakvalor might fall, but at what price? Byramm determined that he would follow the king's command. Perhaps he would expound on the orders. Yes, he decided. He would add a few things to ensure there was no miscommunication. He walked with a surety to his step that he had not had since the days of Ranaan's father.

Ranaan finished the remaining affairs of state and retired to his personal chambers. He gazed out one of the windows. It had been too long since he flew above the clouds. The dragon, Cordathvellonth, yearned for his body. He had been promised mountains of gold if he would terrorize Talvaard. Yet that blasted orc Orlek had deceived him. Orlek promised that no wizard had the power to come against him, and yet one had crafted a spell strong enough to wrench his spirit from his body. Blast that wizard! He had killed the wizard in the end, true, but he had spent the last hundred something years trapped in a cold ball of silver.

And so, he would raze Palindrom to ensure that would not happen again. He had hoped the king of Oakvalor would have used his bones to decorate the royal carriage. Then he could have resurrected his body and assumed his true form.

Instead, Cordath had learned that some fool had the idea to use his bones as decoration for one of Oakvalor's war machines. Now he had to live inside this wretched human until he could find a way to get near his bones. Perhaps when his newly acquired armies marched into Oakvalor, they would bring forth their war machine. Cordath smiled at that.

Yes, he could feign retreat and goad Oakvalor into pursuit. And at the right moment, he would fuse his spirit with his body once more. Then he would slaughter every man, woman, and child as retribution for his imprisonment. Cordath felt Ranaan's spirit shudder under his thoughts. Cordath flashed some of his memories at Ranaan, visions of entire cities burned to the ground, mutilated bodies by the hundreds that littered desolate landscapes.

Cordath took pleasure in Ranaan's torment. Orlek had summoned him to this world, but when Cordath was finished with his fiery rage, this world would be nothing. And after he had destroyed everything, he would go back to his own realm. The following morning, when the armies of Talvaard began their march, Cordath knew he was one step closer to annihilating this pathetic world.

11

IMEN MOURNED THE TRAGIC CIRCUMSTANCES that found him the temporary leader of the four other pupils. First, the reopening of the Tunnel, and then the death of their beloved master, murdered within the walls of his own hut; a symbol drawn on his back in blood.

The Lord Aio had been murdered the night of their return from Aicatan, the night they had discovered the opened Tunnel. A quick glance at the inside of the hut, the burn marks and gashes made in the walls and on the furniture, the scattered papers, the books, writing materials and weapons tossed carelessly around the room, and the shredded clothing told of a great struggle. The body of the Lord Aio was found in the center of the hut, facedown, a symbol carved into his bare back. Only one thing could have caused the incident to go unnoticed to the group of five pupils, considering all the noise that must have been made by such a struggle: magic. A strong, evil magic.

Certainly, with the unexplained murder of the Lord Aio, the young High Priest would rise to yet a new level of leadership and seniority, having pupils of his own, each one listening intently to every sound that would come out of his mouth as if it had come from the Ai himself. He would continue in his priesthood, most likely as the High Priest on one of the four other islands. Although his power would not be of a political nature, his influence would stretch even into the Great Cabinet. He would have power over the beliefs of hundreds, perhaps thousands, of gullible people. If he said that milk came from horses, all the milkmaids on the Island he presided over would attempt to milk their horses. He would have the ability—which he would never exercise—to corrupt his position and deceive the people for his own gain. All however, without the Lord Aio to guide him.

Imen doubted himself. He was being thrust into a position of leadership that he did not feel himself capable of holding, in a time when one would need such self-confidence more than any other. Imen wished that he could have died with the Lord Aio, or perhaps even in his stead. He had always wished to be the great leader, the great warrior, the Great High Priest. At this time he did not wish for any political influence or moral power. As his dream became more of a reality, losing its sheen, as the burdens gained weight, he felt an increasing desire to give it all to anyone. Even to Erasan, the pupil maladroit. Having raised himself on the streets of the city, the fourth-year pupil was afraid of very little. At least he would have accepted any type of challenge such as this with the enthusiasm and determination to conquer an army of orcs.

Even more than his desire to delegate his responsibility elsewhere, he wished that he could have had the Lord Aio to guide him in his new role. He had expected him to be there with him when he had been appointed High Priest over the Red Island, just a few days earlier. Now, to be placed even higher in the hierarchy of High Priests, he had no one familiar to guide him as the storm approached.

The body of the Lord Aio had been taken care and disposed of according to the ancient customs of the Aihi. So as not to discourage the people of the Five Islands in letting them know that one of the greatest warriors and priests in their history had not merely died, but had been murdered, the occasion went unannounced outside of the small group of Priests, Priestesses, and pupils. Nonetheless, there was much weeping as the earthen mound covered the lifeless form.

The aged prophet had been the beloved master to many for over a century, and of the five pupils, to Lord Imen the longest. As a child, Imen had seen much of the High Priest, usually from a distance, and had thought him to be a small, harmless yet frightening old man. As he departed his youth for a life in the service of the Ai, the harmless old man gradually grew larger in the pupil's eyes, the essence of wisdom and strength. The two had fought together during Imen's early days as a pupil and as a warrior-priest, each saving the other's life many times during battle. Over the years following the wars, the Lord Aio had become somewhat of a father to Imen. As Imen prepared the body, performed the rites of burial, and led the group in songs of mourning, he found his grief of a greatness that would not allow the tears to form. The whole of the ceremony had found new meaning for him, the High Priest finally understanding the importance of the ceremonies of burial and the honoring of the dead. The Lord Aio had died, the part of Imen that lived life seemingly dying with him, disappearing with the full shovel of earth on the burial mound.

The dawn of the eighth day after his death marked the end of the week of mourning. A messenger, the pupil Erasan, was sent to summon the Lady Melar, High Priestess of the Island of Ban, in order that she should take her place as the Great High Priestess.

Although the others did not recognize—much less understand—the symbol cut into the Lord Aio's back, Imen understood it altogether too well. Immediately after Erasen's departure for the Island of Ban, Imen had sent the Lady Moren to Aicatan to warn the Great Cabinet to mobilize all available military units from the various armies of the Five Islands. It was for the same reason that Imen had sent the Lord Forgotten Man to warn all who remained faithful to the Ai on the Island to either take up arms and prepare for battle, or to take up their things and flee to the mountain.

It had been three days since the three messengers had gone out from the mountain. Only Imen and Las remained. Imen spent most of his time looking over the valley from the Clearing of the Five Stones, near the Tunnel entrance. Las worked at preparing the huts for the new Great High Priestess and whoever else might be moving in or out, busying herself with every task imaginable, accomplishing very little for the amount of effort invested.

At dusk on the third day, Las had run out of tasks to complete, while Imen continued to look out over the valley. It was on that evening the young Priestess chose to interrupt the thoughts of her senior.

She sat on the stone nearest the right of the High Priest.

"Sitting all day, looking over the valley will not bring him back or cause our three messengers to return more quickly, you know."

Imen's gaze ahead did not falter. "As busying oneself with futile tasks does not cause time to alter its course for the faster?"

She laughed, probably for the first time in the eleven days that had passed since the return of Imen and the late Lord Aio. "You are starting to sound more and more like the Lord Aio."

Imen turned his head toward her, raising an eyebrow. "Am I?" he asked.

Las nodded. "You are also starting to act like he used to. Why do you sit and stare at the valley all the time as he did?"

Imen returned his gaze to the valley as he pondered the question. "I used to ask myself the same question of the Lord Aio for the six years in which I studied and trained for the priesthood, and in my ten years as a priest. I believe now that I understand somewhat. For one, when sitting here, I am not taxing an ever-limited supply of energy on pointless errands and labors."

They both laughed at this.

After a few moments, Imen went on explaining. "Having put mourning for the loss of the Lord Aio behind me, I have been thinking these past three days. Thinking about the recent twist in what will be the history of our people that has put me in this temporary position of authority. Thinking about what will happen to us all. Thinking about the death of the Lord Aio, his murder, the hut, the body, and the …"

He stopped himself short, his composure normal, and his eyes telling of unfathomable torture. He shook it off, yet not before Las noticed something.

"The symbol in the Lord Aio's back?" she asked of him. "It was the one thing that you could not take your eyes off while investigating the hut."

Imen quickly turned to her, the pain in his eyes returning with a deeper ferocity. It took him a full minute to quell the inner disturbance. As it subsided again, the fire died within his eyes. He cleared his throat and spoke.

"You are quite observant. I tried my best to hide my reaction to the symbol. I see that you have been wondering as to its meaning."

"When he died, you became our leader, for the time being. I would imagine the others observing you just as closely, as well as wondering about that symbol."

Imen smiled. "For reasons that have not been forgotten with the death of Lord Aio, this is something that has been kept within the confines of the High Priest Council ever since Lord Aio became the Great High Priest. It is probably better if you do know. You are to be a High Priestess someday, and judging by recent events, you will not have to wait long. These things have already begun to pass. I see no reason why you should not be informed."

He stood, taking his staff, drawing the symbol in the dirt.

"Many years ago, the Great High Priest Dazu called Aio, while on his deathbed, made a prophecy which is recorded in song. He spoke of the returning of evil into the Five Islands. An evil so great it annihilated the Serpentauri, and all but destroyed our people."

"Orlek!" Las gasped in a fearful recognition.

"That is correct," said Imen as he continued. "Our deceased master, Daio called Aio, was present as the successor took the position of Great High Priest. Since his death, the song has been taught to all who are to become High Priest and High Priestesses. I myself have known this song for scarcely a month. However, considering all the events foretold are taking place as we speak, I believe that now is the proper time to be teaching you."

Las positioned herself into an upright posture, listening attentively, as Imen destroyed the symbol with his foot and, singing, began to draw another one with his staff. A line to draw the horizon; a small circle depicts a moon. A banner abreast the bright sun to hail the impending doom.

There was a moment of silence as both High Priest and Priestess took in the full meaning of what had just been sung. It seemed as if all life had frozen for a short moment after he finished. Nothing stirred, not bird, not beast, not fish, not man, not woman, not child. The wind seemed to stop blowing. The river seemed to stop its steady flow toward the sea. The sun seemed to hold its position, giving off the waning light of day for just a few moments longer.

Imen broke the silence. "Tell me, Las: what do you know of our history concerning Orlek?"

Las looked up at the darkening sky, searching her memory. "I admit my knowledge concerning this is limited," she said, somewhat sheepishly. "Just what I learned in the school as a child."

Imen frowned. "Very well, then. Much of this you will have heard before, but at least some should be new to you. To properly tell this story, it must be started from the beginning. Over two thousand years ago, before the Great Ai, before the twelve tribes of the Aihi had united to form the Republic, there lived on the Five Islands the cave-dwelling orcs, the legendary fire-breathing Serpentauri, and the Cannibals, as well as the Aihi.

"The four groups battled amongst themselves, no race seeming to gain any sort of advantage, each struggling futilely for mere survival. This went on for five hundred years. The twelve tribes had been reduced to no more than twelve small families. the Orcs, a small band of paranoid, dangerous cave dwellers. The Serpentauri had taken to isolation in the area on the coast of the Red Island where we have built Aicatan, and the Cannibals eating leaves, insects, animals—and, occasionally, themselves—in the hills.

"Out of desperation, the Twelve Tribes of the Aihi united and chose from among themselves a leader who would travel to the caves, the coast, and the hills to speak to the other three races about peace. This representative's name was Daio, now called Daio the Uniter. After many man-to-man struggles and death matches with members of each race, he finally united the Aihi, Serpentauri, and the Orcs under one central government, controlled by a council consisting of a representative from each race. The Cannibals continued to live in their primitive state in the hills, not willing—and perhaps too primitive—to join with others.

"For the next thousand years, the three races prospered working together. The Orcs mined the hills, the Aihi farmed the valley and raised cattle and sheep, along with helping to mine the hills and fish the rivers and the sea. The Serpentauri took part in every activity, using their breath of fire and their great strength to help till the fields, herd livestock, and carry loads of product. Commerce developed between the Five Islands and the mainland of Oakvalor, which resulted in the king of Oakvalor buying the Five Islands. Each race became more adept in magic and science. Every once in a while, a band of Cannibals would enter the valley or raid a mine, killing a few Orcs or men.

"Toward the end of that thousand years, an Orc by the name of Orlek was elected to the Council as representative of the Orcs. Of the races, Aihi included, he surpassed all in knowledge and power.

"For many years, he led his race and the whole of the Five Islands in becoming the strongest and wealthiest civilization. Through his discoveries, magic had peaked to a point that has not since been bested. No other nation would have challenged the Five Islands in any move it made. Even the king paid tribute to the Islands. A citizen was considered poor if he did not have at least ten slaves and double his weight in gold and rubies. Orlek became a symbol of pride for the Five Islands."

At this point, Las spoke up. "If I remember something about this period of history, Orlek began to delve very deep into the magical arts. From my understanding, he was on the verge of discovering the secret to all magic and power."

Imen spat on the ground. "Yes, I suppose you could say that. Could one also say that he was about to benefit the three races and, eventually, the entire world with this last secret? That because of overwork and exhaustion he went mad, all but destroying the Five Islands?"

Las looked down. "That is what they said, what I was taught at …"

Imen spat on the ground again. "*School?*" he finished for her, the contempt in his voice unconcealed. "You would be best not to accept as fact anything you have learned about our history in school. I call them not teachers. Agents of Orlek would be more appropriate."

Las gave him a nod partly indicating agreement, partly indicating her impatience for an explanation. Imen continued with the story.

"It is true, that Lord Orlek came close to the discovery of this great and terrible secret. It might even have been that his original intentions were to use it for the good of the Five Islands. However good his intentions, he was not able to control his knowledge. In the end, the knowledge and magic controlled him.

"For many years, he remained mostly in the solitude of his tower, allowing only a few select orcs to see him, and not too often at that. When he did come out, it was only for a mandatory session of the Council. Even in those sessions, he was not of much help to the Council or the Five Islands, usually deferring any important decisions or economic matters to the other two members, taking on only small responsibilities concerning magic, none of which he ever fulfilled.

"All the while, he had been using his chief advisors, all Orcs, to spread sentiment against the Aihi and the Serpentauri among the Orcs, teaching them certain depths of the magical arts as favors for those who were successful, usually torturing to death those who were not.

"The Five Islands were losing their power in the world. Those nations who had once paid us tribute ceased to do so, using that money instead to build their armies and wage war against one another. The stronger nations even maneuvered their armies to positions in which they could easily attack the Five Islands, resulting in the endless war with Talvaard. With an Orc population unwilling to do anything with or for the other races, our armies began to dwindle. Ruby production all but stopped and our treasury was steadily growing smaller.

"It came time for the Council members of the other two races to confront him. He was either to find some way to prevent the Five Islands from an almost inevitable fall, bring them back to their former glory, or to abdicate his position, letting another Orc be elected in his place."

"I don't imagine he was all that pleased," said Las.

"You are correct in your understatement of his emotions. He was infuriated. The moment he was given that ultimatum, he drew his sword and beheaded the Aihi Councilman. He managed to kill the Serpentauri member as well, but not without his left arm being burned so badly that it completely fell off his body.

"Within the hour, the entire Orc army he had been building on the Red Island had been mobilized and had begun marching to occupy Aicatan, led by the magically empowered Orcs. The mass of bodies was so great, it completely covered the valley floor. It was evident that much innocent blood would be spilled before the end.

"The other inhabitants of the Five Islands were not without advantage, however. Aicatan, although it lacked natural defenses, employed every able body male citizen into its army, as well as keeping large reserves from the other Islands. The Orcs within the city were easily done away with at no loss to the city guard."

Las interrupted his telling of the story again. "Having heard that, what little I know is starting to make sense to me. I believe—correct me if I am wrong at any point—that after the death of the two council members, a civil war broke out. The Orcs and their vast numbers against the Aihi and Serpentauri, A good deal of the Serpentauri and men in the hills and the valley were killed within minutes of Orlek taking control of the Council building, outnumbered and caught off guard. A few managed to escape to the cities, giving warning to the people, allowing them to make what preparations that could be made."

Imen nodded. "So far, you are correct. Please continue."

"The combined efforts of the Aihi and what remained of the Serpentauri were able to repel the Orc attacks on Aicatan for some time," she continued. "They had the Council building surrounded, but because Orlek gave them little trouble, they were content to keep him prisoner, concentrating most of their strength on the city walls.

"When it started to seem that the Aihi-Serpentaur forces would prove victorious, Orlek began his attack from within. Buildings went up in flame for no apparent reason. The group of men surrounding and guarding the Council building suddenly found themselves naked, armed with flowers. It was then that the city began to concentrate its efforts on the Council building, allowing most of their outer defenses to disappear altogether.

"At this point, Orlek put up a magic field around the building to shield himself from his attackers. Then the Orc militia began its invasion of the city. What few handfuls of men that had been left to the walls had already been eliminated with the next attack, and those that fought to get to Orlek were being cut down from behind. Despite all their desperate efforts, the main body of the army turned to fight the Orcs. The Orc lined advanced, destroying everything in its path, drawing nearer to the Council building and their dark Lord Orlek.

"The use of magic was not limited to Orlek and his minions, however. A few men still practiced it at a powerful level, though none as powerful as Orlek. It was through their combined efforts that they were able to break down the magic defenses of the Orc King. Although they died from their overuse of magic, the inner forces stormed into the Council building and threw Orlek out of a high window onto the ground, where everyone near was able to hear the snap of bones and see his lifeblood drain from his body.

"Having seen their leader supposedly dead, and feeling the absence of his magic, the Orcs took to a madness, most of them killing whatever they could find, including themselves. The rest fleeing the Five Islands to the mainland of Oakvalor."

Imen laughed. "Very good. I give you far too little credit for the time spent studying history in school."

Las shrugged. "Knowledge of the past has its advantages. For the most part I knew all of that history, save the corruption of Orlek. The schools and libraries never fail in failing to teach in a precise, consistent, and accurate manner concerning that. They claim not to know the cause, yet believe that it could be excused as a madness from overwork."

"Interesting how that information never falters in its absence from the minds of the people. Very well. In continuing, our people had another four hundred years of peace and prosperity. All the Orcs had fled to the Viss mountains in Oakvalor and the Serpentauri died off after Orlek's death. What remained of men on the Five Islands began their attempt at rebuilding into what they were in the 'Golden Age'. The sciences and magics, however, were ignored in the stead of more primitive ways of life and development. It was science and magic that had brought them to the depth at which they were, and the Aihi did not wish to experience such again.

"For a time, the people followed the Ai with every twitch of their muscles. Quickly, however, through corrupt priests, they forgot about the Ai, reducing him to a legend that their parents would tell them in front of the hearth, or the name that the teachers and priests used in frightening followers into obedience.

"A little over a hundred and forty-three years ago, there appeared a young child, who was called Aio. Although very few people would believe it at the time, he was the Ai, put in human flesh. At first, only twelve men believed. Among these were the Great High Priest Dazu, called Aio, and his successor Daio, called Aio, who was the last living man to have spoken with the Great Lord Aio. Over ten years, they united the priests of the Five Islands, commenced reform among the priests and schools, and brought a large portion of the people back to a following of the Ai.

"Aio had many enemies, however, among some of the middle and lower levels of the priesthood as well as in the Cabinet. His actions had cost many of them their political power, as well as their control over the people. Many corrupt priests had had their cloaks shredded because of this man who claimed to be the Ai. To rid themselves of him, there was only one solution: invoke the old magics."

"Wasn't the use of magic in times of peace forbidden by the Aihi law at that time?" asked Las.

"It was punishable by death," said Imen. "This did not cause the enemies of the Great High Priest to hesitate in their actions. They were afraid of Aio nonetheless, and made sure that nothing of their deeds became known.

"Many attempts were made to kill him through various magical and scientific methods, all quite unsuccessful. In desperation, the renegade priests made the decision that almost destroyed the Five Islands: through a meticulous search, they were able to locate and summon the reincarnated spirit of Orlek."

At this, Las looked a bit puzzled. "This is one part that I have not yet fully grasped. In one section of the histories, it says that he was thrown out of the Council building window, that the cracking of his bones was heard. At the point in history where you have arrived in your retelling, he is alive and reincarnated?"

Imen nodded. "No one to this day has delved as deep into the magic as had Orlek. All that we have been able to decide is that during his experiments with magic, he found a way to detach his spirit from his body at the last possible moment, and then find another body in which he could abide. How he was able to do it, no one can say.

"The rest of the history you know in detail. I shall recite it briefly. Orlek had come into power, eventually becoming ruler of a land far to the north, populated chiefly by Orcs and sorcerer men. When he was summoned, one could expect that he was more than delighted at an invitation to destroy not only the Great High Priest, but also the incarnation of his greatest foe, Lord Aio, the personification of the Ai. He stretched out his spirit into the Five Islands, telling the conspirators that he would come immediately. He neglected to tell them of the great force of Orcs that he would send to precede him, or of his plans to take control over the Five Islands from them. At the beginning of the fortieth year of the Lord Aio, the first of his forces landed on this Island.

"The war that ensued continued for almost four years. Everyone on the Islands that had conspired against the Lord Aio either changed his mind or had been killed in battle after joining the Orc army. At the end of those four years, it seemed that neither side would gain any advantage. Both Orlek and the Five Islands had poured the blood of their armies like water. The valley floor became black with the bodies of Orcs, our rivers ran red with our own blood. It was then that Orlek decided to show his strength in full."

Las nodded. "It took all the magic of the High Priests just to repel this last attack. A dragon was released into Oakvalor and Talvaard, and even the body of the Great Lord Aio was destroyed in this battle."

"Along with Orlek's. It has been said that the two departed to battle in the spiritual realm. As Orlek's physical body was robbed of life, so was he lost to the Five Islands. He is but a distant memory, if that, in the minds of the people.

"He has, however, remained quite alive in the minds of the High Priests. In the mind of the Great High Priest Dazu, especially. As you know well, he was one of the greatest prophets our history has ever known. It was said that he was, when prophecy came to him, able to leave his body and go to the places and times where the prophecies would take place. He knew that whatever battle fought by Aio and Orlek in the spiritual realm would not finish itself out there. It would have to end here, on the Five Islands, where it started almost six centuries ago. On his deathbed, he asked for a pen and parchment. He began to sing the song which I sang to you as he drew the symbol from which I have drawn. He prophesied of the coming of Orlek to retake the Five Islands, an admonition to the Aihi."

For a moment, neither of them spoke. Imen was content to sit watching the valley beneath him, not waiting for a response. Las sat doing the same thing, wishing she could say something. Anything.

She sighed. "One can never fully appreciate what one has until one has it no more. Everything about the Lord Aio and his early years as a priest was known to me. I realize now, especially with what is supposed to happen, that I have taken all of my advantages for granted."

Imen looked at her, smiling in response. "It might not be that your labors here were quite as useless as I had thought. One of the messengers, along with another, approaches as we speak."

A few seconds later Erasan and another figure cloaked in brown turned the corner. One could see the glint of white armor, the color of the Island of Ban, in the last rays of sunlight. Yet it was not Lady Melar that came with Erasan but the eldest of her pupils, Lord Arum, who had also been considered for the High Priesthood over the Red Island. It was not the coming of Lord Arum that set the Priest and Priestess sitting on the stones ill at ease, but the absence of the Lady Melar. The ceremonies were to be performed the next day. Although it was most likely that Arum would be chosen as High Priest of the Red Island, Lady Melar would also have been present.

None of this, however, was enough to prepare Imen for what was to come. Lord Arum came and knelt at the High Priest's feet, saying, "Hail Lord Imen called Aio, Great High Priest of the Aihi!"

Imen stood, facing the bowing Priest. "Greetings to you, Lord Arum. You seem to be a bit mistaken. I am merely the lowest of the High Priests. Where is the Lady Melar?"

Arum got up, his long, bony frame a few inches taller than Imen's. "There is no mistake, my lord. As for the Lady Melar, her end was much the same as that of the Lord Aio and the other three."

"The others?" asked Imen, choking on the words.

"The entire Council, save for yourself, murdered in their own huts, the symbol cut into their backs."

12

SHORTLY AFTER ARRIVING BACK AT the abbey, Velkyn and Calderon were both summoned to the Abbot's chamber. They walked together through the stone halls quietly, each absorbed in their own thoughts. Calderon kept replaying the terrifying events of that morning in his mind, desperately trying to figure out why Prince Ranaan would have murdered his own brother.

Perhaps what Velkyn said earlier about a coup was the truth. Maybe the younger prince was not happy with being second in line for the throne and murdered his brother out of anger and jealousy? Yet from all that he had heard, both princes were respected and mature, never having any real dispute with one another. It didn't add up.

"The world feels ... darker somehow," Velkyn whispered to Calderon. "I feel it in my spirit. It is as though some unseen force blankets the land." Calderon didn't respond. He considered his friend's words. While he didn't feel what Velkyn spoke of, it did make sense to him. Perhaps the darkness that Velkyn felt was behind the actions of the young prince.

They reached the door to the abbot's chamber and paused, glancing at each other. "What do you think he wants?" Calderon asked softly. Velkyn shrugged in response. "Only one way to find out."

Velkyn knocked on the door, but there was no answer from within. He waited a moment and then knocked again, louder this time. The door swung open silently and they were greeted by Donovan. The former Musician said nothing as he walked out in what Calderon thought was quite a hurry. The Abbot sat behind his desk writing. Without looking up he told them to shut the door and have a seat.

They sat down and waited for the Abbot to speak. The old leader of the monastery finished writing and folded the parchment in three creases. Lifting the burning candle that rested on his desk, he poured the hot wax onto the paper. He removed one of the rings that adorned his fingers and pressed it into the quickly cooling wax, leaving an imprint of a flag with a water drop in the center, the official seal of the church. He set the letter to the side and looked at the young monks.

It seemed to Calderon that their leader had grown older since that morning. The lines of age creased his face and his eyes seemed dimmer. "We are in danger." Calderon and Velkyn exchanged looks. Velkyn turned his gaze back to the Abbot. "The sphere is safe," he managed to say before he was silenced by the Abbot's upraised hand.

"That may not true," the Abbot said. He ran his hands through his thinning white hair and sighed aloud. "We fear that the dragon may have escaped the sphere somehow."

"How?" Both monks echoed in unison.

The Abbot shook his head hopelessly. "Donovan thinks the enchantment has failed, perhaps the magic was too old to be strengthened by the music. We can only speculate. He has gone to see if our fears prove to be true." Velkyn realized then why he had been summoned with no one left to protect the sphere. His protection may no longer be required.

"How can he know if the creature is no longer bound within the sphere?" Calderon spoke up.

"Donovan has been the Musician longer than any other before him. He has been in the position since he was barely eighteen and he is now ninety. He has studied the sphere longer than anyone of our brotherhood. If anyone could know, it would be him."

Calderon felt fear welling up in his stomach, threatening to overwhelm him. He cracked open his mouth to speak, but nothing came out. His life was over. He had messed up and there was nothing anyone could do to help him. He decided then to confess hiding his condition and express his fear that he had fallen asleep when he was supposed to play the music.

Velkyn sat forward in his chair, staring intently at the abbot. "What if it is true? What if the dragon has escaped … what does that mean?"

"Absolute destruction," Donovan's voice answered. Neither Calderon nor Velkyn heard him enter. "That is what is upon us," his tone was grave and ominous. Donovan walked up to them slowly. "The sphere's magic has failed."

All three men turned to look at Donovan, alarm evident on their faces. The Abbot rose from his chair. "And so it begins."

"What begins?" Calderon looked questioningly from Donovan to the Abbot. He had the feeling that they knew something he didn't.

"It is written that the dragon, before it was captured in the sphere, wreaked havoc across the land. It burned entire cities to the ground with its very breath. The only reason it was stopped was because of Oakvalor. The people there do not fear wizards as the people of Talvaard do. What begins, Calderon, is the quest to save our world. In order to recapture the dragon's spirit, we must first know where it is. The wizards of Oakvalor are our only option."

Velkyn sputtered in disbelief. "Our kingdoms have no love for each other, everyone knows that." The Abbot smiled at him. "True, but the church's loyalty lies to the Divines, not to the crown. We have allies there that will aid us. And the wizards, though they have helped their king in the past, do not concern themselves with politics. They will know the importance of this task."

"We have lost enough time already." Donovan added. He and the Abbot shared a knowing look. "Make the preparations." Donovan nodded and left the room. Velkyn and Calderon stared at their leader, waiting for further explanation. "Neither of you are ready for this, but you will not be alone. Donovan is going with you."

"Going with us? Where are we going?" Velkyn wasn't sure he fully understood the Abbot's meaning.

The Abbot stared at him, the old man's eyes drilling straight into his soul. He slumped into his chair dejectedly. "To Oakvalor, my son. You are both going to Oakvalor."

—

Calderon sat upon the edge of his bed, trying to prepare himself mentally for the journey he was about to take. He should have been getting some rest, but his mind was racing. Truth be told, he was a little curious and a lot afraid. Curious about the world outside the abbey, yet afraid of the unknown all at the same time. He had to travel light and only bring the things he absolutely needed. They would travel by horseback until they reached the mountains, but then they would have to pass through on foot.

The Abbot had shown them to a room full of miscellaneous items that the monks did not have any need for. He had taken a thick brown traveling cloak trimmed in black silk and some leather boots. They would be leaving under the cover of night so as not to draw any unwanted attention and there was only a few hours of daylight left. He was glad that Donovan was going with them, despite the fact that he was so aged. He trusted him and found comfort in the fact that he was so knowledgeable.

He extinguished the candle on his desk then laid down and tried unsuccessfully to fall asleep. Not far from Calderon's room, Velkyn too sat pondering what lay ahead. Unlike his friend, however, he was not afraid. He was pleased to be leaving the abbey. Adventure was calling his name. He had written a note to Nydel and would leave it for her in the event she didn't visit him tonight. He couldn't leave her behind. He was confident that she would find some way to come with him. Velkyn smiled as he thought about her.

She usually wore her hair down and the long black strands reminded him of the ravens that often flew into the fields around the abbey, always trying to eat the crops. Her eyes were bright green and shined like her free-spirited soul. Every detail of her face was etched into his memory, every moment spent with her locked into his remembrance. He loved her with every fiber of his being. Velkyn stretched out across his bed and stared at the smooth stone ceiling, running their last encounter back through his mind.

He drifted off to sleep peacefully.

Calderon was awakened in the middle of a pleasant dream. Velkyn stood over him, shaking his shoulder. "Time to leave," he said softly, as if fearing his voice might be heard throughout the abbey. Calderon pushed himself into a seated position, hanging his feet off the edge of his small bed. Donovan appeared in the doorway. "Grab your things and meet me in the courtyard by the main gate. And make haste," he added, almost as an afterthought. Then he was gone.

"I'm not sure about this," Calderon said quietly. Velkyn's excitement showed in his demeanor. "What do you mean? We will finally get to see what lies beyond these walls, probably farther than any brother before us has traveled. What are you unsure of?"

Calderon couldn't quite put his finger on it, but there was something at the edge of his mind that gave him the uneasy feeling that life would not be the same after this journey. "There isn't anything specific," he said, "but I have the feeling we will soon learn things that will change our lives. It's as if there is a veil, and something—whether good or ill—is waiting behind it to be revealed. And I am not sure that I am ready for it."

Velkyn stood in silence listening, taking in the words of his friend. "If what you feel does come about, do you think that though you are not ready now, you will be when it happens? The Divines will work everything out as it should be. Now come on, we need to leave."

Calderon wasn't sure why, but he didn't think Velkyn's last statement was true. He decided there was nothing that could be done about it and got up off his bed. He had slept in his new leather boots and grabbed his cloak off the chair by his desk before following his friend out of the room. He looked back one more time, staring into his room. He wondered how long it would be before he saw it again. They made their way down the halls and to the courtyard. They found Donovan waiting for them at the main entrance. "Don't we need a couple more of our brothers in order to open this gate?" asked Velkyn as they approached Donovan.

"We would if we were leaving through it," Donovan replied. He smiled at their look of confusion and motioned them to follow him. The old man led them along the east wall. Stopping abruptly, Donovan felt along the stone until he found one that felt loose. He grunted as he pulled on it and was rewarded when a grinding sound revealed a hidden doorway. "We are going this way," he told them, "to avoid being seen leaving. We don't need to draw any unwanted attention to our departure."

They pulled the stone door open enough to fit through. On the other side of the door was a steel handle attached to the door. They used it to pull the hidden door closed behind them. Calderon heard the soft nickering of horses before he saw them. Three horses were tied to one of the many wooden posts along the side of the abbey that were used for the delivery carriages. Calderon eyed them warily, having never ridden one before. "Are they safe?" he asked.

Donovan untied the reigns of each horse and handed one of the reigns to each of the monks, keeping hold of one for himself. "They are safe. Don't be afraid, Musician. They will speed our journey considerably." Donovan placed his foot into the stirrups and climbed atop his mount with a practiced ease. Calderon and Velkyn, having never ridden before, looked from their mounts to Donovan, and then back to their horses. Shrugging, they mimicked the old man and attempted unsuccessfully several times to climb onto their own horses before finally finding success.

Calderon gripped the horse with his knees tightly, afraid of falling off. Velkyn seemed to have better balance and merely held onto the reigns for stability. "You seem to be comfortable riding for someone who's lived in the abbey their entire life," Calderon remarked to Donovan, still trying to find a comfortable way to ride his mount.

"There are many things about me that may surprise you. With such a long journey ahead of us, I am sure you will learn a lot more about me before the end." With that, he pulled the reigns of his horse and turned eastward. It took both young monks a few minutes to get their mounts to follow their commands as Donovan did not give them any help. "You said the end …" murmured Calderon, "… the end of what?" Donovan looked over his shoulder at his pupil but offered no explanation. He urged his horse forward and turned his eyes back to the east.

The young monks were finding it much easier to get their horses to follow commands as they rode. "While time is something we don't have enough of, we must conserve the energy of our horses for now. We will stop to rest at an inn when the sun begins to set if the horses can make it that long." The horses trotted along at a leisurely pace. "What about food and water?" Velkyn asked.

Donovan reached behind him and patted a large sack tied to his saddle. "We each have enough to last us a couple days. We can buy whatever we need when we stop each night." Velkyn seemed pleased with the answer and merely nodded to himself. Calderon wondered how his mentor knew where they were headed and voiced as much. "I have been this way before, many years ago," answered the old man. Calderon looked to Velkyn. "Do you think he's hiding something?" he whispered.

Velkyn nodded his head. "We all are hiding something. The better question would be what is he hiding. Only time will tell."

—

The day was long and uneventful. They had traveled without seeing much of anything or anyone except the occasional merchant caravan. Earlier in the day Donovan had pointed to their left as the road they traveled on forked that direction and continued straight, telling them that the castle they had visited the day before was that way. They had continued straight, the scenery nothing but tall grassland as far as they could see.

They didn't talk much as each of them were occupied with their owns thoughts. Velkyn thought about Nydel and wondered if she had snuck into the monastery and found his note yet. He looked behind him several times, hoping to see some sign of her trailing them, waiting for the opportune moment to meet with him. He was greeted by nothing except the empty road and the tall grass which swayed in the gentle breeze.

Calderon's thoughts were far different from his friend's. He missed the stone walls of the abbey the moment they were out of sight. As hard as he tried, he couldn't push the sense of foreboding from his spirit. There really wasn't anything to justify his fears other than the fact that everything outside of the abbey was unknown to him. There was also the new emotion of distrust he felt towards his mentor. He thought the man was no different than himself or Velkyn, that he had entered the brotherhood at a young age and had never ventured out. His assumptions didn't seem to line up with who the old man actually was. He also found himself wondering about the people of Oakvalor. The only thing most people knew was they were the enemy and nobody could remember why. Was the brotherhood there as devout in their faith as the men of his abbey? Was their king a believer in the Divines as well? He found that notion hard to fathom considering the ageless war both kingdoms were waging against one another. If they shared the same beliefs, whatever petty grievance they had with one another would be overlooked because if you shared the same values, you would be on the same page and fight for what mattered, not one another. All this and more swirled within the young man's mind.

Donovan was as unreadable as a blank page. He had learned many things during his long life, and if there was one thing that he knew was a mighty advantage, it was being able to conceal your emotions and intent. He hadn't survived this long by luck. The young monks traveling with him were clueless to the world outside the abbey, and though he mostly pitied them for it, he also envied them. To be oblivious to the things he knew and was burdened with, the things his hands had committed … he pushed the past out of his mind and thought about the journey that laid ahead. He wondered how much Oakvalor had changed since the last time he had seen it. He knew they would find help there, but he didn't know if they would find answers. The wizards there were not loyal to anyone but their craft, but he didn't know if the monks there held true to their faith over the king as those in Talvaard did. He had never seen the abbey in Oakvalor, but he had heard of its existence.

The sun had begun its descent behind the mountains and the sky slowly changed colors on the horizon. Deep oranges and reds lined the clouds and both young monks were awestruck by the beauty. "It's amazing," Calderon remarked in a hushed tone. "Indeed," Donovan said, "It is a sight that never gets old. Look there," he pointed. "The first stop of our journey." They could see a small building in the distance, perhaps another half hour of riding left to reach it.

"We won't make it before dark," Velkyn stated. Donovan turned and looked at him. "Not at this pace," he agreed, grinning. He nudged his horse and the animal picked up speed, going from their slow pace to a fast run. Calderon and Velkyn followed the old man's lead, urging their horses in the same manner. They were thundering down the road, the gentle breeze seeming to gain strength and began to blow their hair around wildly. They made it to the inn with their quickened pace in half the time it would have taken. The horses were breathing heavily when they stopped.

Calderon had trouble getting off the horse and ended up slipping and falling face first into the ground. He pulled himself up, the embarrassment evident on his face as he spit dirt. Velkyn stifled his laughter. A young boy, possibly no older than twelve, came to collect their horses after they had pulled their belongings off and the boy led the horses into the stable that was located behind the inn.

Donovan turned to the young monks when he was sure no one would hear their conversation. "If anyone makes conversation with you, do not tell them where we are going or what we are doing. If knowledge of what has happened with the sphere were to become known, it could cause fear among the people that would result in chaos. As best as we can tell, there is almost no travel from Talvaard to Oakvalor. If people get the wrong idea, they might see us as traitors and we would be in no end of trouble." Calderon and Velkyn exchanged glances. "Is there food here?" Velkyn asked. They all laughed at the remark and Donovan nodded.

The interior of the inn was old and worn. Rough boards attached to the walls gave the place the appearance of a rustic wood cabin. From behind the badly scratched bar a woman took orders. Ten tables were arranged in a haphazard manner, each surrounded by three stools. Around those tables was a minimal crowd, although busy for this inn. The three monks made their way to an empty table and sat down. Calderon was relieved to be off the horse, but his backside was numb and his lower back was a bit sore. He couldn't wait to lay down. After a few minutes, the woman from behind the bar made her way to them.

"Evenin' gents. Welcom' ta the Sly Mare. What'll ye be havin'?" she asked. The monks found her lack of proper speech annoying. Donovan didn't give them the chance to speak and answered for them all. "We will take three orders of whatever the special is, and three mugs of water." The barmaid grinned at him and he noticed most of her teeth were missing. "Water? We ain't servin' no water 'ere 'cept ta 'orses. Ale er cider?" she asked him, still smiling. "Cider." She offered a mock curtsey and sauntered off behind the bar to place their order.

"Who doesn't have water?" Calderon asked, baffled. Donovan looked at his pupil and again found himself envious of his ignorance. "We probably will not find water at any of these types of establishments. They specialize in tasty alcoholic drinks."

Calderon's eyebrow raised. "Why would people pay to lose their common sense?"

Donovan shrugged. "Only the Divines know."

The barmaid returned several minutes later with the mugs of cider and made a second trip to bring their food. On each plate was a mound of chopped, skinless potatoes covered in butter and salt. She casually tossed three forks onto the table as she walked away. Velkyn, who had yet to speak, commented on her behavior. "She seems rude." Donovan merely nodded his head in assertion before closing his eyes. The two young monks lowered their heads and Donovan said a prayer over their meal. "Not everyone in our kingdom follows the precepts of the gods. Especially so as we get to the fringes of Talvaard. Our order has a rough history." None of them had eaten since midday and found themselves a lot hungrier than normal.

They ate in silence. Calderon mentioned the odd taste the cider had and Donovan knew it was not virgin. He didn't think one mug would hinder his companions and he let them drink it. Velkyn was busy watching the people in the inn. There was a man at the bar who appeared to be taking an interest in the conversation at a table near him. Velkyn shifted his attention to the table as well and took note of three men. He listened to their conversation and shook his head. All three of them were drunk.

—

Julian Brathenworth had misplaced eyes. He knew this fact for whenever he stared directly ahead at the beer in his glass, one eye thought it mostly empty; the other mostly full. What other explanation was there for this differentiation of opinionated eyesight than misplaced eyes? He held one unsteady hand before his face and closed his left eye. He concentrated upon the glass behind his hand as he opened his left eye and closed his right. His hand moved. He repeated. Yes, he was sure of it; his right eye made his hand appear higher than his left. Therefore, his eyes were all wrong. "Crap!" he slurred.

"What's that gov?" A pale faced man with a lengthy mustache directed at him. Julian blinked several times and then turned his gaze upon his verbal aggressor. His puffy red lips pursed as he drew breath. He took an absent swipe at his straight shoulder length hair but missed. "I think I said crap," Julian replied, making three attempts at his glass before his hand grasped it. While continuing to stare at the man, he raised the glass to his moist lips and swigged.

"Argh, that it is, but we drink the piss, eh?" The man chuckled, took a gulp of his own brew and then turned his attention back to his own table and his two companions. Julian sniffed hard as he again turned his back to the group. With nothing better to do, he began to eavesdrop.

"So, Theo, what do you say?" One gruff voice asked. "What do I say governor what do I say?" replied the man who had addressed Julian. "Yes, what do you say?" asked a third.

"I say … do you like beer nuts?" the familiar voice of Theo. That was followed by a series of humming and crunching, then some general noises of affirmation. "Now … where was I?" said the gruff voice.

"You was talking about adventuring."

"Oh yes, I was. So, what about it?"

"I don't know, you were the one discussing the topic. I was just listening politely," said Theo. "Of course, I was doing the discussing. You would hardly talk about adventuring. You are not an adventurer. But you could be."

"Could I?"

"That is what this conversation is about."

"And what about beer nuts?" munched the third.

"Beer nuts … what's the fascination with beer nuts?" said the gruff voice. "I guess they're delicious." Again, more grunts and crunches. All was quiet for a short time. All except breathing and crunching.

"I'll do it!" Theo yelled, rising to his feet with one hand over his heart. "Good for you son, good for you," acknowledged the gruff voice, having finally received his answer. "Do what?" asked the third, spraying broken beer nuts from his mouth as he talked.

"Right. Now what's the plan?" asked Theo.

"The plan … argh, the plan. The plan is simple. As adventurers, we need adventure."

"Oh, that is true, very true," mumbled the third through a mouth full of beer nuts. "And the best source of adventure is Dillenger."

"Oh yes," burped the third, "Dillenger is full of adventure."

"So, let's go get Dillenger!" Theo yelled. "We would, but …" At that moment, Julian decided to pitch a sale. He spun his stool gracefully on one leg so as to face the mob of adventurers. After rotating too far and too vertically, be picked himself up off the floor and presented himself to the crew.

"Gentlemen, I believe I can help you … for a price." The three stared at Julian for a moment, munching beer nuts. Julian averted his gaze, sought some inspiration and began afresh. "I am Julian Brathenworth, magician for hire."

"For hire … for hire," the gruff voiced man said with increasing zeal. "And what would we want to hire a magician for?"

"I believe you are adventurers," Julian said, proudly giving a knowing leer. "That we are gov, that we are," said Theo, stroking his mustache with a soggy finger. Silence.

"Well then, mayhap you could use a man of magic?"

Silence. Julian waited patiently.

"Why?" asked the third, whom Julian deduced looked a little like a weasel, with beady black eyes, greasy black hair, and a pointy nose. "To aid with your adventuring," Julian offered. All three stared at Julian, confusion on their faces. "I … do magic," Julian said tentatively.

"Oh," said the weaselish man, "magic. But I don't have any kids."

"What the hell are you talking about?" Julian warbled.

"You do party tricks, right? I don't have kids, but thanks anyway."

"No, no, no. I do proper magic. You hire me and I provide you with magical services so as to aid you in your adventuring."

"What adventuring?" inquired the third.

"You are adventurers, are you not?!" Julian screamed. "That we are gov, that we are," Theo smiled, stroking his mustache again. "Then you must need help on adventures?"

"So, you can help us with magic on our adventures?" questioned the gruff voiced man, who had remained silent until now. "Yes," sighed Julian, relieved to be getting his pitch acknowledged. "How much?"

"Right. I demand an equal share of profits, nothing more."

"No, how much help?"

"What?"

"How much help can you give?"

"Oh. I … can give …"

"Do you like beer nuts?" asked the weasel man. "Yes … I guess …"

"Excellent. You're hired," winked the gruff voiced man. Julian looked from one man to the next, took a large swig of beer and then collapsed onto the floor. Either the alcohol had knocked him out, or the conversation had.

Velkyn snorted derisively and turned his attention back to his own table. He somehow felt less intelligent having heard that conversation. The barmaid came to collect the plates as soon as the three monks had finished eating. "Will ye be havin' anythin' else?" she asked Donovan. "We would like a room for the night," he answered, finishing his cider and handing her the empty mug.

"With yer meal an' room, it'll be thirty silver." Donovan withdrew a small leather pouch from his robes and counted out the appropriate amount and handed it to the woman. She double counted it, smiling at him the entire time. Nodding in satisfaction, she left the table and came back a moment later with a key. "It be the door with a three on it," she said. Lowering her voice and leaning in close to the old man, she added, "Might want to keep an eye on your belongings. Things be comin' up missin' a lot lately." Donovan understood her meaning and smiled in thanks for the warning. He looked to the young monks after she had left.

"We should take turns watching our door," he said lowly. The two nodded and rose from their chairs the same time Donovan did. They followed him across the room to the left where a small flight of stair led them to the area of the inn that housed the rooms.

The beady eyes of the weaselish looking man followed them until they were out of sight. Looking to the man with the gruff voice, he smirked and nodded.

13

"IF I AM FORCED TO eat another one of these particularly disgusting cave creatures again, I shall …"

"Peace, Kelron," interrupted Kelros. "At least in the Tunnel's darkness, we do not have to look upon them too much. Besides, by looking at you with the light of one's fire, one could hardly say that your appetite has decreased significantly from this most undesirable fare."

Kelron looked down into the darkness in the direction of the large lump of flesh, blood, and scales, the like of which having been the sustenance for the two hundred Serpentauri during their residence in the Tunnel. He belched, a ball of flame erupting from between his fangs, his forked tongue flailing wildly about his open mouth. For a moment, the small segment of the Tunnel lit up by the almost blinding flash and then returned to its usual darkness. "Your skin does not draw so tightly over your bones either, Kelros. How can you stand to eat these things anyway?"

"What else is there to eat?" replied Kelros, somewhat irritated at his friend's constant complaining. "It's a lot better than having to eat ourselves like the Cannibals of this Island. Did you know that if enough of these creatures band together, they could kill an unsuspecting Serpentaur and reduce him to pile of whitened bones within an hour? They even eat the scales and the coat. Quite a gruesome spectacle, from what Father Ean has told me. It is most important that we eat them before they eat us."

Kelron turned his head to the invisible stench in front of him. "Even so, I still do not understand why you do not leave the Tunnel—or at least allow the rest of us to do so—and eat an animal that makes its habitat above ground and lives off something other than feces and rotting carcasses of its fellow cave creatures."

"Because," said Kelros, leaning his head down into the creature's body, ripping a limb off with his massive jaws, swallowing it whole. "Father Ean has ordered that we stay in the Tunnel, where we will be unseen by men who would destroy us or attempt to use us for ill purposes. I might also have you remember that both you and I fare much better than our brothers in the center point of the Tunnel where the five branches meet. Father Ean has let us come this close to the entrance on the Red Island. At least there is some small chance of getting some animal strayed from its home on the mountain."

"I would question the thinking behind his decision to keep us hidden. I feel no need for protection from men. As for stray creatures from the over-world, I have not yet seen one since we entered the Tunnel," said Kelron, reluctantly biting out a large piece of flesh from the mess in front of him, hardly taking the time to chew it as he forced the seemingly resistant food down his throat, trying his best—unsuccessfully—not to taste it.

"I haven't seen much of anything since we entered the Tunnel," stated Kelros.

"Indeed Kelros," said the young Serpentaur. "It has been a long time since we have entered the Tunnel."

The elder Serpentaur took another bite from their meal, swallowing the rancid morsel. "It has been some eight or nine days we have lived here in hiding, I would imagine."

"Thank you so much, Kelros, for letting me know information that will make the rest of my eternal stay here much more bearable, being able to count the endless days we waste in here, while the Ai knows what is going on up there that might require our assistance," said Kelron sarcastically, stamping a hoof impatiently. "I am sure it will be of such great joy to the rest when we tell them that."

"I am sure it will," snapped the elder of the Serpentauri. "It certainly amazes me how much patience I never knew I had, having been stranded in this Tunnel for over a week with you as a test of it. Now, if you will shut your ever-opened jaw and stop complaining, Father Ean is coming. I would prefer to listen to some new news from above ground for a change."

Except for a smoke-filled snort in reply from Kelron, the two Serpentauri remained in silence as they heard the footsteps of Father Ean grow steadily in volume as he drew closer. "Greetings, cousins," said Father Ean, invisible in the absence of light. "How fare you in the darkness of this Tunnel?"

"If you could call it fare, we have plenty of these stomach-wrenching little …" said Kelron, stopping himself so as not to offend Father Ean. "We do not seem to be dying of starvation, Father Ean," he finished.

Ignoring his friend's comments, Kelros lowered his head to what was left of their meal and set it ablaze. The smell of burning scales and flesh almost caused the Serpentauri to vomit.

"A light by which to see, and no great loss of good food to Kelron, although our stomachs do seem to agree on the matter of food. Tell us, Father Ean: what news today, or tonight for all it really matters, do you bring from the Red Island?"

Father Ean cupped his hand over the top of his staff, putting the weight of his body on it, resting his chin on his hands. A large sack lay by his feet.

"Just about sunset when I entered the Tunnel," he said. "As for news? Mostly ill news, yet maybe some might seem good to the two of you."

"I was afraid of that," muttered Kelron under his breath.

"Become familiar with it, my cousin," replied the old prophet. "You will hear much more such news, and most likely far worse in the near future. Both the Lady Moren and the Lord … the Lord … the Lord … I cannot seem to remember his name. The Priest and Priestess I told you earlier about have both returned from their journeys into the Island."

"How did they fare?" asked Kelros.

"The Lady Moren was somewhat successful in her task, and was able to push whatever body now governs the Five Islands into mobilizing the Priesthood's allotted five hundred men and any who wish to join, one hundred for each Island."

Kelron snorted into the fire, his flames disappearing into the burning carcass. "They mock the Lord Aio. Only five hundred?"

"Only five hundred," confirmed the aged man.

Kelros flicked his forked tongue about. "And of the Lord … the Lord … the other one. The Priest. What of him?" Father Ean looked about him, finding a large enough stone near the fire to his liking and sat on it.

"Much the same, only worse. Of all the Priests and Priestesses on this Island, one has promised his full and unconditional loyalty and aid. The rest have—in a more courteous manner—refused to even acknowledge the Lord Imen his new position."

Kelros lowered his head. "Pity for the Aihi. It was not as hard for our race those five hundred years past. What precious few surviving priests lived on the Five Islands at the time of our ancestor's departure fought alongside us. This group of priests sounds to be the type that would fight against us."

"Yet by the Ai," said Kelron, "how are we expected to fight a host of Orcs in the thrall of Orlek—may he eternally rot in the Endless Depths—with five hundred fighting men, maybe two hundred Serpentauri, an ancient, though powerful, gardener, a handful of warrior priests newly ordained, and a tenth of the farmers and laborers on the Red Island?"

Father Ean sighed. "With only what we have, it cannot be done. It is impossible. I have faced many great difficulties in my all-too-long life. The empires have risen and fallen under my watchful eye. The world has undergone changes in such a manner and to such lengths that your language would not have words for it, and I was present. I have fought alongside the greatest of warriors, and have helped to defeat the greatest of foes. Even with my assistance, however, this trial that faces the Lord Imen has only been surpassed by one other, some ninety-five years ago. As with this battle, Orlek was the enemy."

"Yes," said Kelros, his serpent head nodding. "And this time, the Council of the High Priests is not aided by the Great Lord Aio being present among its members. If I recall your stories correctly, Father Ean."

"In the physical sense, no," said Father Ean. "However, this half-millennium old battle is between Orlek and the Ai, not between Orlek and the Aihi, though the Orc king would wish to destroy all men, Serpentauri, and his own people as well. We can rest assured that the Ai will enter the battle," he paused, "in his own time and manner."

The old prophet pulled the large sack in front of him, opening it up. "I have something for the two of you. It is not much, but even I make difficult of stomaching the provisions of the caves and tunnels, and I can sympathize with your plight. My innards turn at the thought of eating a creature of this Tunnel, or any tunnel, for that matter."

He proceeded to take out two objects, both somewhat round and covered with feathers with two thin, scaly legs limply hanging from one end of each. Both were a dark brown in color, covered in blood, sticking to both the sack and Father Ean's hands. "These used to be chickens, although the struggle which ensued obtaining them has changed that somewhat. I didn't want to use too much magic. The Priests would notice any excessive use of magic, and I wouldn't want to betray our presence for the wholeness of two dead birds."

Kelron stared at the two chickens. "After our rather distasteful diet these past days, it looks delicious. Not that I am saying it wouldn't be delicious otherwise. You will be partaking with us, Father Ean?"

Father Ean shook his head. "With your appetite, Kelron, I doubt there would be any left for Kelros, let alone myself. Besides that, I do not make it a practice to eat flesh, though I have had it in lieu of starvation at times. Before my return to the Tunnel, I overstuffed myself with the fruits of the laborers that tend the orchards. The Ai has blessed them with an excellent harvest this season. Most likely the last one for some time."

"That is too bad," said Kelron. "Fruits are usually too small for a Serpentauri to taste, unless eaten in large quantities. I am particularly fond of a good wheat … harvest, as I believe men call it. Where we come from, it grew wild in a small valley. Every autumn day when the harvest was good, I would venture to the edge of that field and help myself to some. Wheat is quite good when it is fresh."

"Some!" cried Kelros, half choking on his small meal, blackened and smoking feathers flying out of his mouth. "As if there would be any left for the rest of us."

Kelron appeared to glare at Kelros out of his serpent eyes, hissing. "At least you were given your fair portion when we would feast together.

Kelros reared his head. "If one could call it a portion compared to yours, yes. Although I do agree with you on one point: your daily trips to the wheat fields would definitely redefine the word 'feast'. Your eating habits are about as disgusting as our meal. You even eat the chaff."

"You should have tried it. It isn't that bad," said Kelron.

Kelros sighed in frustration, smoke and tiny flames coming out from between his jaws. The old man sitting on the rocks, almost forgotten in the exchange between the two Serpentauri, began laughing. "I shall certainly remember to bring some wheat to you, Kelron, the next time I leave, if that is even necessary."

The Serpentauri looked across the fire at Father Ean. "What is your meaning?" asked Kelros, cocking his head to one side. "You mean to turn these cave creatures into a field of wheat? At least it would put an end to my friend's incessant complaint."

Father Ean shook his head. "Not at all. Although I have never considered that idea in my thousands of years as the gardener of Oakvalor. It would make them more lovely to look upon. I meant that I intend for the two of you to come with me to watch the Ceremony of Ordination of the High Priest Council …" he said, noticing the pleasantly surprised looks on the faces of the two Serpentauri, "… from a distance, but were a man to come near us, I am afraid that even my magic would not suffice were I hiding someone other than myself."

Kelron shrugged. "Magic, science, prophets, priests … all the same to me. I possess no magic, and do not mind it, as long as it does not harm me. I say that one's fire is as good a defense as any, at least for a Serpentaur."

Father Ean looked upon Kelron for a few seconds. "You do not believe in the importance of magic, do you good Serpentaur?"

The hungry one shook his head. "Not really. Don't worry yourself. I can see how it would have its function in certain lives. Otherwise I would be feasting upon wheat instead of being holed up in a tunnel, even if that tunnel happens to be the Tunnel."

Father Ean turned his eyes down, staring at his feet for a second. "You have much to learn, Kelron. The influence which magic has upon us as living beings is far greater than even I can imagine. How does the sun continue its daily trek, age upon age unending, giving light by which to see and a magic by which even the growth of wheat is aided? Or how does the moon and her children, the stars, do homage to their master and bestow the beauty of their light upon the people? What makes earth suitable for crops, or wheat to grow wild on a deserted, unknown land?

"There is a magic running deeply through everything that lives and does not live. The fact that the body of a man, Orc, or Serpentaur can live, that we think beyond the level of the two birds that have been devoured us a result of the magic. Even you have magic, Kelron, however limited it may be."

Father Ean stood up, stretched, and looked once more upon the two creatures in front of him. "Think on that, both of you, while I am gone. I must see to the other Serpentauri."

Kelros and Kelron both nodded as he stepped around the fire, heading for the deeper parts of the Tunnel. "Ai'au c," they said in unison, using the ancient tongue of the Aihi. "May the favor of the Ai be upon you."

The aged man looked back at them, their massive figures but shadows framed by the firelight behind them. "Ai'au cn," was his reply.

"Most men can survive hardship, but if you want to test his character, give him power."

- Lord Aio

14

"ALL FIVE, MURDERED?" ASKED IMEN, his face quickly losing its color. He shook his head. "Surely you jest, Lord Arum."

"As well as I might wish that I could, you of all people would know me better than to make light of such heavy matters, Lord Imen," said Arum. "Erasan and I arrived on the centermost Island at roughly the same time. We found the other three messengers waiting for us. It is they who have given us this tragic news."

"The other three messengers were sent back to summon those who are to succeed the deceased High Priests and Priestesses," Erasan added, "while we traveled here before them. The Ceremony of Ordination will take place the dawn following their arrival."

Imen sat back down on the stone, feeling the burden he was to bear settling upon his shoulders, slowly beginning to crush him. "Why must such a thing happen to me?" he prayed silently. "I am not ready. I cannot. Yet I must."

He looked upon the three people standing around him. Two of them were good friends, two of them fellow pupils of their deceased master. The death of the Lord Aio having repeated itself with the other High Priests and Priestesses on the other Islands, all three of them would look up to him almost as to the Ai Himself. They would follow his every word. In turn, it would be his word that would guide each follower to victory and safety, or to death and defeat. The correct command could save the lives of many, while the wrong command could be that which would lead all of his close friends to their deaths. Would he be forced to sacrifice these three and many others with them in loyalty to the Ai?

Every muscle in his body strained, all but forcing him to fling his body over the cliff face to certain death at the foot of the mountain. His mind battled with equal force to overcome his instincts. He sat upon that stone, his body tense, his mind fighting against his body and for control.

One more blade of grass. One more blade was all that was needed. All that was needed to break him. The troubles that were to come upon him by omen of the open Tunnel had already begun.

Las laid her hand upon his shoulder.

"It is difficult for us all, Lord Imen, when those who mentored us and guided us have departed, more so in the manner of this particular departure. Even more difficult it becomes when we must don their cloaks, seemingly too small to fill them."

At the voice of the soon-to-be High Priestess, Imen nodded, his muscles relaxing, his mind having temporarily won the battle. "It is difficult, however, for each of you. Lord Arum, you are to become a High Priest, and to sit at my right hand. You will have me to guide you. Fortunate is the Lady Las, who in becoming High Priestess of the Red Island will have not only myself, but also the rest of the Council to look to. To be envied are you, Erasan. You are yet a pupil, and will have all of us to hold your hand the entire way. Yours is but the responsibility to follow those who lead. As for me? Am I to be the one that stands in front, blindly leading everyone across the unknown parts of the future? The way is dark to my eyes. Who have I?"

"You have the Council of High Priests," said Arum, "as well as every Priest and pupil on each of the Five Islands."

"Perchance a mighty band of the Followers, or the military forces of the Five Islands," said Las, trying her best to sound hopeful.

Erasan cut in. "If I may be so bold as to speak to the Lord Aio, as you are soon to be called, Lord Imen. As well as to the soon-to-be High Priest and Priestess Arum and Las," he paused, "he has the Ai."

All conversations immediately came to a halt, everyone looking to Erasan in silence, allowing the weight of his words to beat down upon them. Imen turned and smiled at Erasan. "You have learned well, pupil, under the Lord Daio, called Aio, to remind Lord Imen of the most basic of the basics. I must now accept what I am to become. The way is still dark, but no longer does a blind man lead his sightless followers."

In saying this, he looked upward. The moon lived still, and the stars danced about her, beautifully decorating the blackness that dominated the sky. He still had one to follow. One unlike the Lord Daio called Aio that would never be found murdered in his hut. Not even one like himself, unconfident and afraid of leading everyone into the mouth of the giant Demon of Aihi legend. One far different.

He shifted his attention to the Lord Arum. "I mourn with you your loss, and grieve with you for your advancement in the hierarchy of the priesthood, yet still envy you your position as lower than mine. Of the two, yours is the smoother path, for the time being. Very well then. Hail, Lord Arum, High Priest of the Island of Ban."

Arum grinned. "Hail, my lord."

The white-clad High Priest turned to the Lady Las. "And hail the Lady Las, High Priestess of the Red Island."

Las giggled softly. "Hail, Lord Arum, Lord Aio. If we are done now with our greetings, might we best be in shelter? Darkness has already overtaken us, and the night's weather to the east bodes ill with me."

"A wise decision and great observance on your part. I am sure the Lord Arum is exhausted from the undoubtedly strenuous climb up the mountain. You will have him in your hut, Erasan?"

"As you wish, Lord Imen, called Aio."

Imen let loose a small laugh as he led the way farther up the mountain trail to the huts.

The next three days were spent working, preparing for the ceremony, moving the belongings of Imen and Las into their new huts, and each reviewing the business of the person whose position they were to take. During the afternoon of the first day, both the Lady Moren and the Lord Forgotten Man returned, bringing news of their journeys to Aicatan and to spreading the tragic news and warning to the Followers.

"Hail, Lord Imen!" panted the Lady Moren, nearly collapsing on one of the stones. "Hail!" came the unnoticed reply from the Lord Forgotten Man as he stood, half asleep, next to the Lady Moren. Immediately Las came to their sides, two pitchers of water in her hands.

"Hail, Lady Moren, Lord Forgotten Man," said Imen, slowly turning toward them, breaking his gaze from the valley. "What news do you bring from Aicatan, Lady?"

Drinking half the pitcher in one gulp, unceremoniously pouring the rest over her head, she caught her breath. "To call it either good or bad would be to look at it in the broadest sense," she said. "The Cabinet was, of course, skeptical. However, the opening of the Tunnel did give way to a general concern among them."

The Forgotten Man slowly gulped his water down, yawning. "What did they do, or have they yet to decide?" asked Las.

Moren laughed. "With a little help, I might be able to bring them to a quicker, more favorable decision. They do not know what to do about the main body of our armies, they being occupied with other matters, but according to ancient laws, one hundred men from each of the main Islands, along with any who of free will choose to aid us, are to be mobilized on demand and put in the command of the Great High Priest. The company from the Red Island should arrive at the foot of the mountain within a few days.

Imen shrugged. "That can be expected, although we shall need much more than five hundred if we expect to ward off the invasion."

"Invasion?" asked Moren. "That is why I was sent to Aicatan? Knowing that, I could have convinced the Cabinet to mobilize quite a few more from among the armies. Any idea on who is attacking?"

Imen shook his head, his face grim. "The worst has happened. Orlek is alive, and will most likely wish to return."

Moren's face turned white, her studies of history as a child coming back to her memory. "Orlek?" she asked, her voice shuddering. "Was he not killed, many years ago?"

Imen nodded. "That he was." He paused. "Twice." He then, with the help of Las and Arum, recounted what he had told Las the day before, as well as what happened on the other Islands. When they had finished, Moren pushed herself up off the stone. "It seems as though great tragedies have struck all of us, Lord Arum. However, I envy not your new position."

Arum solemnly nodded. "Indeed, tragedies strike all of us. Every Priest on the Five Islands by now grieves with you, feeling your loss as their own."

Moren pushed her long, dark brown hair back with her hands, squeezing the water out of it. "Such is my story," she said, "with one small hope. More discouraging is the account of the Lord Forgotten Man, if you wish to hear it."

All looked toward the Forgotten Man, who by this time was beginning to doze off. At the sound of his name, he groggily opened his eyes, yawning. He stared blankly at the rest of the group.

"My story," he droned in a low, monotone voice typical of a creature that has not slept well, "might be similar to that of the Lady Moren, yet much more disturbing. The Priests of this Island might be the youngest our history has seen, but must they be the weakest, the most skeptical and power hungry? Rejection. That is all I received for warning the Priests. Of course, they were courteous, as is customary to a priest of higher seniority, but their unbelief was tangible, even through the front of respect. Of the ten, only one I could discern actually believed my story and agreed to give us any help. He said he would warn the Followers under his care and have them make standard preparations."

"The others?" asked Imen, taking in what had been said, evaluating his next action.

The Forgotten Man yawned, sipping water once more. "They tried to sound as helpful as they could. Empty words. They agreed to talk to the Followers under them. The next time I come to them, a general consensus of the Followers' opinions on the matter will be given to me. They would promise me nothing more."

Imen solemnly nodded at the report of the Forgotten Man. Erasan gritted his teeth, suppressing his anger at the backslidden priests, a few of whom had been his best friends during his earlier years of studying for the Priesthood.

"'Tis grievous news you bring us, Lord Forgotten Man," said Imen. "It will make our task much harder. It might be too late for some people. I believe I shall meet with some of our 'Priests' soon."

"Who, pray tell, was that one good Priest?" inquired Las. "He might be of some help to us."

The Forgotten Man pinched himself, trying to keep awake. "Interesting that you of all people would ask, my Lady. He inquired into your well-being. He was the youngest of the Priests. His name was Eroz."

Both Las and Imen nodded, smiling in spite of the ill news. "Eroz?" said Imen. "How could one forget a pupil such as Lord Eroz?"

"A pupil," explained Las, "studying for the Priesthood two years ago. As good a man and Priest as one could ever meet. After being ordained, he was sent to do work away from the mountain. I must have caught his eye. Never could stand looking at him, however. A likeable person, but he had such a horrid face." All six laughed, the Forgotten Man in his fatigue managing to chuckle somewhat.

"Although I have seen naught of him in my last year here as a pupil," said the Forgotten Man, "then after my work on the Island, as a Priest, I still saw nothing of him."

Las, having finally regained her breath, leaned against the rock wall. "You may tell him, then, when you return that I still think his face to be quite ugly."

More laughter ensued. When the laughter died down, all present fell silent for a few minutes, each deep in their own thoughts. It was Moren who decided to break the silence.

"The dawn after the ceremonies have been completed, I will leave to prod the Cabinet to make a quicker decision." Imen shook his head. "No. I shall go. I am to be the Lord Aio. Not only is it my right and duty, my presence in my new position might just offer them more incentive to act."

"Nay, lord," said Arum. "If anyone is to go, it is I. It is not customary for the Great High Priest to serve the function of his own messenger, except in time when the positional influence or use of magic is completely necessary."

"Neither is it customary for a messenger, regardless of his level in the Priesthood, to serve such a function on the Island of another High Priest. To report of happenings on the Red Island would not only be highly improper, but would no doubt push us farther back then where we started. If I am not to go, a messenger from this Island will be sent."

Las cut in with her opinion. "If we are to follow the customs of the Priesthood to the letter, I would be the one to go. As the new High Priestess of this Island, my word is to be honored as having come from the Great High Priest and the Ai Himself, and might be enough to sway the opinions of more than a few members of the Cabinet. Your place, Lord Imen called Aio, is where you are, sitting on that stone. My work is to this Island. Your responsibility is to the entire Five Islands, and mine to just this one."

"She is right, Lord Aio," said Erasan somewhat timidly. "If I may be so bold as to speak, my Lord, you will be needed for the managing of the affairs of the Five Islands combined. The affairs of this Island might need close attention as well, but that would be the duty of the High Priestess and Priests of this Island."

"Very well then," said Imen, a bit cross at having been corrected by his soon-to-be pupils. "It shall be the Lady Las." He got up from his seat on the stone. "I have yet more moving of materials from my hut to my new hut to finish before the day is out." He looked over at the Forgotten Man. "If I were that poor Priest," he said, loud enough to wake the sleeping priest, "I would wake up for a time long enough so that I could be accompanied by the new Great High Priest to my hut where sleep would be slightly more comfortable than on such a cold, hard stone."

Imen achieved more than the desired effect. The Forgotten Man, having been shocked awake at the loud voice of the new Great High Priest, immediately jumped, his cloak falling out of place. He quickly bowed to Imen, causing his cloak to fall completely over his head. While struggling to get it off, he tripped, falling face first on the ground, entangled even more in the folds of his cloak.

The others laughed, helping him to his feet and removing the cloak from him. The exhausted—and embarrassed—priest quickly grabbed his cloak from them, folded it over his arm, and red-faced walked up the trail to the huts with Imen.

15

CALDERON WOKE WITH A START. Sunlight was beginning to filter through the patched material over the window that was considered a curtain. He sat up quickly and looked to see if Velkyn or Donovan were up. He could tell by their rhythmic breathing they were still sleeping. It had been his turn to watch the door. It seemed that his disorder had reared its ugly head again.

Calderon went to stand up and almost screamed out. A horrible burning pain shot through his legs and lower back. He gave up trying to move and realized this was most likely caused by gripping the horse with his legs the day before. He grit his teeth and tried hard not to move at all, hoping vainly that if his legs were still he wouldn't feel the pain.

"Mother of Faith!" Velkyn swore loudly. Calderon realized his friend must be experiencing the same feeling of pain. "I can't move!" He didn't bother to respond. He noticed Donovan was awake now as well. "What's going on?" the old man asked as he rolled out of bed, seeming unbothered by any pain himself.

"My legs are on fire!" Calderon yelped. Donovan chuckled knowingly. "I forgot you two have never ridden before. Unless the inn has any salve, we may lose a day to let you two recuperate. I'll ask when we …" he paused mid-sentence as he looked around the room. "Where are our bags?" he asked suddenly. Calderon and Velkyn forced themselves out of bed against their bodies' protest. Their bags, which they had set on the floor next to the single chair in the room were missing.

Velkyn met Calderon's eyes and knew immediately what happened. "I … I must have fallen asleep," Calderon muttered sheepishly. Donovan sighed. Calderon waited for the verbal lashing, but it never came. "We can buy more supplies," Velkyn said, attempting to be of some help and come to his friend's aid. "All the money we had was in my leather pouch. And it was in my bag,"

Donovan replied. "Don't worry about it," he added, sensing Calderon was beating himself up over it.

"Perhaps there is someone who saw something, saw who took our things and where they went." Donovan tried to make his tone sound hopeful, but he knew better. Things were likely to get more difficult than they already were. They were going to have to track them down. "Get dressed and meet me downstairs," the old man instructed. He looked into the mirror that hung on the wall next to the chair, patted his hair down, and walked out of the door.

Calderon looked to Velkyn. "I think my disorder is going to get us in a lot of trouble. Maybe I should just go back to the abbey." Velkyn slowly walked over to him. "Calderon, I don't think you understand. This isn't about you. This isn't even about me, or Donovan. It's about something bigger than that, something bigger than us." He forced himself to walk over to the window, ignoring the pain in his legs. Velkyn pulled the curtain aside and stared out at the mountains in the distance. "This is about the kingdom. Maybe even the world. The task set before us is going to require much. It may even demand our lives …" he trailed off, pausing as if thinking about something. He turned from the window and looked at his friend. "Are you ready to make that sacrifice, if it comes? To give your life for others?"

Calderon didn't answer. He didn't have to. If his friend didn't know the answer, he obviously didn't know him that well. He didn't want to die. Especially not for people he would probably never know. It was selfish, but he didn't care. He wasn't like Velkyn, willing to do whatever it takes for the good of the kingdom. They left the room in silence and limped down the stairs to where they had eaten the previous night. They found Donovan at one of the tables with two plates of food waiting. The only other patron in the room was the man Velkyn had seen the night before, the one who had passed out on the floor. He was holding something against his head, apparently nursing some sort of bump.

The two young monks sat at the table and looked questioningly at Donovan. "I thought we didn't have any money?" Calderon asked quietly, looking around warily even though they were essentially the only ones in the room. Donovan smiled and nodded toward the barmaid behind the counter. It was the same woman from the night before. "It's already been paid for. No one saw anything. She said that this has been a problem only recently. Guests stay and then their things go missing. No one ever sees anything or anyone. It is not going to be easy, but we have to find them. We won't make it through the mountains without supplies. We have to retrieve our things."

"We could turn back," Calderon said. "We only traveled one day." Donovan was shaking his head as the young monk spoke. "We can't afford to lose any more time. The creature," he lowered his voice, "if it finds a way to restore its body, will be almost impossible to stop."

Calderon looked at his plate which had scrambled eggs and some hard biscuits on it. It didn't look very appealing, but he decided to eat it anyway. He chewed a mouthful of eggs and thought about what Donovan said. Velkyn was devouring his food with a vengeance. Calderon looked back at Donovan. "The dragon was stopped before. Why would it be impossible to stop it now if it was stopped before?"

Donovan bit his lip. "The kind of magic that was used then … doesn't exist now." Calderon looked confused. "What do you mean?" Donovan tried to explain. "Each wizard specializes in a specific type of magic. They can cast any kind of magic, but the type they are most adept at is much more powerful. Each wizard explores their powers on their own to learn their capabilities and limits. Wizards create their own spells once they progress in their knowledge. The spell that was used to capture the dragon was made specifically by the wizard who cast it. That is why I said that kind of magic doesn't exist. If the wizards in Oakvalor can find the dragon's spirit, they can reactivate the magic in the sphere. Spells like that can be reactivated, but never recreated. At least, not the way it worked originally."

"You know a lot about magic," Calderon said. Donovan shrugged. "I have studied many books. With knowledge comes strength." They finished their meal and were talking with the barmaid about possible places where they might find who stole their things. Velkyn noticed the man from last night was looking their way and listening to their conversation. "He's a wizard," Velkyn said to Donovan. "I think his name is Julian. He was trying to find work last night." The old man looked at Julian. He stared at him for a moment before looking back to Velkyn. "No, he's not."

"How do you know?" Velkyn questioned. Donovan sighed. "We're still in Talvaard. If he were a real wizard, he certainly wouldn't be parading that knowledge about. The Massacre might be a thing of the past, but people still don't trust those who practice magic." As they rose from their chairs, so did Julian. They thanked the barmaid for the food and the information and left the inn, making their way around the back to collect their horses.

"Gentlemen," a voice rang out. Donovan turned to see Julian stumbling toward them. "I believe I can help you," he said, brushing off his pants and straightening his shirt. "I am Julian Brathenworth, magician for hire."

Donovan snorted in response. "You are not a wizard." Julian's face scrunched up in a look of indignation. "I most certainly am," he shot back. "I can do magic." This last sentence was laced with smugness. "Even if you were a wizard," Donovan said, "we don't need one. We've got enough to deal with right now. And if I were you, I wouldn't be telling people I was a wizard, even if I was. The people here aren't so accommodating to wizards." Turning back toward the stables, the three monks collected their horses and thanked the young boy who had made sure they were taken care of. As they came out, they found Julian waiting for them.

"Let me demonstrate," he offered. He put his two index fingers to his head and began mumbling something under his breath. Seeming to discover something, he looked back at them and smiled. "You're looking for something!" Donovan urged his horse forward and rode past the man without a second glance. Velkyn followed suit, but Calderon held back.

"What are we looking for?" he asked Julian, wondering if the man really did have some magical powers. Julian glanced about as if he were going to reveal some sort of secret. "You're looking for … something that belongs to you." Calderon frowned at Julian. "Some magic," he said. He urged his horse to move, feeling the burning pain in his legs starting to feel like a thousand tiny ants biting him. The man wasn't as useful as Calderon thought.

"I know where they went," Julian added, almost as an afterthought. This stopped all three of the monks. Donovan looked at Julian from over his shoulder. "You know where who went?"

Julian realized that he might have found his in. "The people you are looking for. I know where they went. But you will have to take me with you." Donovan looked at the two young monks, then back to Julian. His conscience told him it was a bad idea. The man was obviously a schemer, but if he did know something about their missing belongings …

"Do you have a horse?" Donovan questioned. Julian shook his head. "No. I have something better." He disappeared into the stable and returned a moment later with an odd-looking creature. It was much shorter than their mounts and covered in grey fur. A dark brown stripe ran the length of its body, beginning at its nose and continuing to its tail. A similar stripe ran from one shoulder to the other, forming what looked like a cross shape.

It was an odd sight to the three of them, and Julian riding the creature made it look even more ridiculous. "Where are we headed?" Donovan asked, eyeing Julian dubiously. "South," Julian answered, "to Dillenger."

"Dillenger? Why Dillenger? I hear it's full of nothing but cut-throats and thieves." Julian nodded. "That it is. It's also a place full of adventure. We will certainly find them there."

"How do you know we will find who we are looking for there?" Velkyn chimed in. "How do we know you didn't take our things and you are leading us off to be killed?" Julian looked shocked that someone would accuse him of such things. He forced his animal to stop and looked at Velkyn. "Because I can do magic," he said with a wink.

—

Dillenger was a dilapidated town. The entire place was once protected by an enormous stone wall that rose at least twelve feet high. Here and there, entire sections of the wall lay crumbled upon itself or entirely missing. The three monks and Julian entered the town through a large archway that used to be a guard house. The massive iron gate was useless now and lay rusted on the ground.

Calderon looked warily at the various buildings that were abandoned, or at least appeared to be. Where many of the doors and windows should have been, boards and soiled sheets covered the openings. He half expected an army of thieves to jump out from the shadows of each alleyway. He looked to Velkyn, whose face was as stoic as if it were made of the same stone as the walls around the city. Donovan was keeping his gaze straight ahead, and Julian was babbling on about the history of the place. None of them were listening to him though. They didn't see anyone—not even in the shadows—as they made their way deeper into the city.

As they headed toward the center of the city, the buildings became more maintained, some of them even painted and operational by their outside appearance. As they rounded a corner they could hear the faint sound of music. It got louder as they approached a two-story brick building. A sign hung over the front entrance that was weather worn and unreadable. "Maybe we can find some answers in there?" Velkyn said, pointing. They all exchanged glances and decided it was a good place to start. A long wooden rail ran the length of the front of the building and they used it to tie their horses up.

Julian pushed the doors open and noted the well-oiled hinges that allowed it to open silently. That was evidence that the place was used often and seeing it as a good tiding, he led the monks inside the building. The walls were adorned with all sorts of paintings and the floors were polished to a clear shine. The elegance of the interior belied the room full of customers, all of whom appeared to be criminals. There were several people working behind the bar.

All but one of the tables were taken, and as Julian looked about at all the patrons, he recognized three men, the same three men from the previous night. "There," he muttered to Donovan, nodding his head in their general direction. "I am about sure they are the men you are looking for."

Donovan led them to the empty table and they all took a seat. Donovan leaned into the middle of the table, motioning for the two younger monks to do the same. "This is a dangerous place. I suspect if we accuse those men of taking our things, the whole inn might attack us. We need to figure out if these men really do have our things before we accuse them. Any ideas?"

"We could find out where they are staying and search their room," Calderon suggested. Velkyn smiled and looked at Julian. "We could send him over there. Let them take him in on their 'adventuring' and find out for us." Donovan considered both options and honestly didn't have any ideas himself. The quicker they retrieved their stuff, the quicker they could get back on the road to Oakvalor. Donovan glanced at Julian, and though he still didn't trust the man, he knew their options were limited and they were short on time. "Go work your 'magic'," he said sardonically.

Julian pushed his chair out and stood up, pausing a moment to smooth out his clothes, and then walked over to the table where the three men were sitting. "'Ello," he greeted them. "I am Julian Brathenworth, magician for hire."

—

"Stay close and keep quiet," Donovan bade the younger monks. After a considerable amount of time, and ale, Julian had convinced the three men (again) that he was a magician who could help them. The men had left the inn with Julian in tow, and the three monks followed them from a safe distance.

They made their way down several streets, seeming to travel deeper into the city. The buildings all looked similar in design to those near the nameless inn they had just left. "I still don't trust this Julian," muttered Velkyn, casting wary glances every few steps. "That makes two of us," Donovan replied. "But he is the only lead we have." They watched as Julian and the other men stopped at one of the buildings. One of the men produced a key and unlocked the door. They entered the building and the sound of the door closing echoed off the neighboring buildings throughout the street.

"Let's get a closer look," Donovan suggested. They moved quickly but quietly down the cobblestone street and bent low under the windowsill. Donovan pressed his ear against the wood. He could hear voices, but nothing distinguishable. He was startled suddenly when a loud thump sounded, followed by what sounded like laughter.

"What do you hear?" Velkyn asked, continually scrutinizing their surroundings. "Not much," Donovan admitted. "Let us go in and demand our belongings," Velkyn said, pointing at the door. "Our time grows shorter the longer we spend here."

Donovan considered the young man's words. It was true that time was slipping away, but he didn't feel comfortable barging into the Divines knew what-and possibly getting them all killed. Their mission was bigger than some highway thieves. "You are the only one skilled in the art of fighting," Donovan finally said, looking to Velkyn and Calderon. "Then I'll lead the way," Velkyn answered simply. Donovan sat silent for long moments, unsure what to do. Finally, he shrugged and pressed his ear back to the wall. He didn't hear anything now. "I leave the decision to you two," Donovan said.

Velkyn and Calderon looked to each other and nodded in silent agreement. "We can't leave him here," Calderon finally spoke. "Not in good conscience." Velkyn took that as his sign and nimbly leapt over to the door. He centered his concentration and focus. In a blur of movement, he spun in a complete circle, lifting his leg as he came full turn and slammed his foot into the door. Whether it was locked or not, Velkyn couldn't tell. It probably wouldn't have mattered either way, as the old wood splintered under the force of his kick. The door flung open and he charged in immediately, Calderon and Donovan running in behind him. Pain flooded the left side of Velkyn's head and he crumbled to the ground. He could hear shouting and assumed it was his companions, but didn't have time to sort out the sounds as darkness overtook him.

Calderon saw the man hit Velkyn with a wooden pole and watched as his friend hit the floor. It happened too fast for him to yell a warning or intervene, but he quickly ducked as he ran through the doorway, narrowly missing a similar strike from his right. He dropped down beside Velkyn and could see a large welt across his face. He looked behind him as he heard a grunt and saw two men wrestling with Donovan. Julian lay crumpled in a heap in the corner of the room. He saw the third man, possibly the same man who knocked Velkyn out, calmly walking toward the struggling men. He lifted the wooden pole up as if to strike the old monk, and Calderon jumped up and threw himself bodily at the man.

The unexpected force dropped the man to the ground and Calderon desperately tried to wrest the makeshift weapon from him. The man was much stronger than Calderon expected and he was quickly overwhelmed. The man punched Calderon in the mouth several times, causing the monk to lose his grip on the pole. The man untangled himself and kicked Calderon hard in the ribs. Calderon gasped audibly as the air in his lungs rushed out painfully and watched helplessly as the man dropped Donovan with a bash to the head.

It was all he could do to try and force air into his body. The three men drug Velkyn and Donovan beside Calderon and tied them all together with their backs facing each other. Apparently thinking them immobile, they went into another room. Calderon was able to find his breath after much effort and heard a groan. He looked over in Julian's direction and saw him stirring. "Julian!" he whispered as loud as he dared. "Julian! Are you all right?" Another groan was all he received.

Velkyn and Donovan began moving and he struggled to face them. The ropes didn't have much slack and so he wasn't able to see their faces. "What happened?" he heard Velkyn's familiar voice say. "Shh," Calderon replied. "Keep your voice down. We were ambushed. They must have seen us following them."

"What'ev we got 'ere?" a voice interrupted. Calderon didn't even notice the three men had reentered the room. One of them, the one who had spoken, reminded Calderon of a weasel. The one holding the wooden pole, judging from his demeanor, seemed to be the leader. He was tall and broad shouldered with a bald head and a black beard that was thick and bushy. The third man was taller than the weaselish man, but shorter than the leader. His face was pale and he sported a lengthy mustache that used to be popular among the men of Talvaard.

Julian groaned again and the pale faced man walked over and helped him to his feet. "Seems we have some thieves looking to steal from us," the big man with the beard said. His voice was deep and gravelly. "What should we do with them, Theo?" the big man asked, looking to the man who had helped Julian. The pale faced man, Theo, stroked his mustache as if in thought. "I never seen a man killed by magic," he said with a smirk.

The leader looked at Julian. "Well magician, it seems your services are needed. Give us a show." Julian's face paled and he looked feebly to the three monks. Theo pushed Julian forward. "We are not thieves," Donovan said.

"No?" the big man questioned. "Then why were you sneaking around outside my house?" Donovan was moving his hands behind him, trying to loosen the rope that bound Velkyn's hands. "Someone stole from us. Took everything we owned. We came here hoping to find our stuff." The leader frowned. "Are you calling us thieves?" The man that resembled a weasel snickered.

"I don't believe I made that accusation," Donovan replied. "We are just looking for information." He was having a hard time loosening the rope. The big man didn't seemed convinced. "Continue," he bade Julian.

"Wait," Donovan pleaded. He could feel the binding giving way and worked his hands furiously. "Let me fully explain." Julian began weaving his hands in the air, forming odd looking shapes and whispering something unintelligible. Donovan slid the rope off Velkyn's wrist and shouted "Now!"

Velkyn quickly sprang into action. He pushed himself onto his feet and turned to his assailants. He somersaulted over his companions and landed in front of the leader, knifing his hands into the throats of weasel and Theo. Without pausing, he slammed his head into the big man's face and was rewarded with the crunch of cartilage. Julian quickly fled into the other room. Donovan and Calderon helped each other to their feet and worked together to untie the rest of the rope. Theo and weasel were making choking noises and grasping at their throats. The big man's nose was bleeding, but he wouldn't be as easy to take out. He grabbed Velkyn by his robes and pulled him in close and returned the monk's head butt.

Velkyn's head snapped backward and he felt his own nose running with blood. He brought his arms up, palms together, between the big man's arms and pushed them outward, breaking the leader's hold on his robes. He struck out with his fist, attempting to punch the man in the throat. The big man merely slapped his hand away and tried to grab the monk again. Velkyn ducked under his reach and snapped his foot up and forward, connecting with the man's kneecap.

The big man fell back with a pained roar and crashed to the floor. Julian came running back into the room with three bags that Donovan recognized. "I told you they had your stuff!" Julian shouted as he continued across the room and out the door. Donovan and Calderon followed quickly behind him, and Velkyn brought up the rear ensuring they wouldn't be followed. The day was nearing an end and the three monks were lost. Julian was waiting for them at the end of the street waving his arms excitedly. "Come gentlemen! Hurry!"

They reached him and each grabbed their own bags. "Thank you," Calderon said sincerely. "You didn't have to help us." Julian waved his hand. "I doubted you," Donovan chimed in, "and I apologize for judging you unjustly. We are indebted to you." Velkyn kept his eyes on the house they escaped for any sign the men would come running after them. "You hired me, remember?" Julian winked at them. "And maybe you can pay that debt … some other time. I'm afraid I must take my leave of you gentlemen now. Safety and such," he smiled. "Follow this street and turn left, go to the end of that street, and turn left again. That will put you on the street with the inn. Can you find your way out of the city from there?"

Donovan nodded. "I'm certain we can. Thank you again, Julian." Velkyn clasped Julian's hand. "Until next time," he said. Julian smiled and off he went, disappearing down another street and out of their view. "Make haste," Donovan said as he glanced down the way they had come. "I want to be long gone from here."

The two young monks nodded their ascent and followed Donovan's quick pace. They were leaving the city's crumbled walls almost an hour later, headed back toward the mountains.

16

THE SUN PEERED OVER THE southern hills of the Red Island with a seeming reluctance, hesitating slightly before continuing its journey upward into the sky, greeting that portion of Oakvalor in its full brightness. The moon had already deserted the expanse, leaving it full of the trailing stars until the time when the sun should blot out their trek over the horizon with its glorious presence.

Not a cloud, gray, black or otherwise was to be seen on that day. On all areas of the Island not shaded by some larger body, such as the mountains or trees, the morning dew glittered with the beauty of diamonds, countless as the grains of earth of which Oakvalor was composed.

The side of the mountain facing the valley was by no means covered in shadow, allowing the three watchers at the peak to see what transpired below them with perfect clarity. For any ceremony, this was a more than perfect morning. One almost would have felt that such a ceremony could not be done with a greeting less worthy than the one given it by the sun. "Fortunate, for the moment, is this young Council," thought Father Ean. "Even the appearance of the Great Lord Aio was not hailed with such splendor."

Father Ean had been watching as the pupils from the other four Islands began their trek up the mountain's trail the evening before, and he had run into the Tunnel to wake up the two sleeping Serpentauri. After having passed by the Tunnel's guard unnoticed, they found a perch at the top of the mountain, just close enough to see, yet just far enough not to be seen.

They had spent the remainder of the night on the top of the mountain, waiting for the ceremony to begin. Except for a few words about the absence of any morning meal from Kelron, the hours of waiting were spent in complete silence. For the first in almost two weeks, the Serpentauri were able to hear the sounds of life outside the Tunnel. Even to Kelron, whose mind was preoccupied with food, it felt like a dream to be able to see the stars, hear the chirping of the crickets, and to experience being under the sky again.

Father Ean motioned the two Serpentauri to watch closely as the Lady Moren and the pupil Erasan quickly walked down the trail in the brisk dawn air, readying the Ceremony of the Clearing of the Five Stones for the ceremony. Cloaks of all colors were spread out at the foot of each stone, a sword thrust into the ground next to each cloak. A ring was placed upon each stone.

Once this task had been completed, the Lady Moren and Erasan walked to the edge of the cliff overlooking the valley below, preparing to call all Priests on the mountain to arise and to take their part in the ceremony that was about to be started.

Erasan pulled a small, hallowed out wooden rod from the folds of his pupil's cloak, examining closely the holes that had been put into it. "What is the reason for hesitation?" asked Moren, impatient for the ceremony to begin.

Erasan looked up from the instrument. "I am sorry, Lady Moren," he said. "I just hope that Lord Imen will not mind us using his flute for waking everyone up." Moren slowly shook her head. "Have you not been studying the histories, specifically where they speak of such events?"

"From my recollection, there is really only one example to look upon. When the Great Lord ..."

"I know, I know," said Moren impatiently. "It cannot be helped. You now hold the only musical instrument on the mountain at this time, and are the only person on this mountain other than Lord Imen who can intelligently breathe through that thing and make sounds to become music. The ceremony requires music for the waking of the new Council or Council members, and would it be proper for Lord Imen to wake himself up with the music when he is to be given the Red Sword?"

"I would suppose not," said the young pupil. "Very well, Lady Moren. The sun has risen, and so must the rest of the mountain." He lifted the flute to his lips, playing the same melody that had been played the night the Lord Aio was murdered. At first—to the disapproval and impatience of the Lady Moren—the sound was weak, his breath barely making any music come out at all. Gradually, however, Erasan gained more confidence in his playing, the sound becoming stronger, sweeter. Life seemed to surge anew through everything that could be seen at the music played by the pupil. The sun, its lower part finally escaping the bonds of the horizon, seemed to shout for joy in all its splendor in thankfulness for its very existence.

Erasan turned around after finishing the song, finding most of the group already standing behind him, listening to the music. The Lord Arum, the Lady Elaran, the Lady An, and the Lord Irn stood in their places beside the stones respective to their Islands, a sword in front and a cloak to the left of each of the soon-to-be Council members. Lady Las had positioned herself in the middle-front of the stones, kneeling. A suit of armor lay in front of her. The Lord Forgotten Man stood guard at the part of the trail leading to the valley, while the Lady Moren had moved to the part of the trail leading toward the huts. Imen was not present.

Erasan bowed to the group of his superiors. The Lord Arum nodded in reply. The Lady Las smiled. All attention was quickly turned to the sound of the footsteps on the trail, coming down to the Clearing of the Five Stones.

All the Priests and pupils present knelt down on their right knees as Imen appeared from the bend in the trail. He bowed quickly, acknowledged Erasan, and slowly walked to the center of the Five Stones, facing the valley.

"Fellow Priests and pupils," he said, addressing the entire group. "We gather here now to ordain a new Council of High Priests, an event such as has not been seen in the past century. The histories concerning this ceremony are quite vague, and not much applicable to the situation we find ourselves in. We have, by studying deeply of the histories, found what we need to know in the carrying out of this ceremony but for one thing: Who is to ordain the Great High Priest? There has been only one in the history of this Council worthy of self-ordination. In other cases, there were other High Priests who could very well perform the task. We have neither this morning, aside from myself. Who shall ordain the Great High Priest? The question ran through my mind a thousand times as I slept and as I walked to this Clearing, and I have only one method in mind that I would think proper for such an occasion in the situation we find ourselves."

The Priests held their breath, waiting for him to finish. Erasan trembled slightly, mostly out of nervousness at the importance of what he was witnessing and participating in.

"The Ai shall ordain, and the Ai shall revoke ordination. Erasan," he said, looking directly at the young man facing him. "My lord," said Erasan, standing up from the kneeling position. Imen smiled. "Take the red cloak off of the ground, and help me put it on. If I be not the man ordained by the Ai, than may this cloak be drenched with water, and may I be soaked through my armor and my undergarments."

Erasan slowly dropped his flute on the ground. He solemnly walked over to the centermost of the Stones, picked up the cloak in front of it, and spread it open behind Lord Imen, allowing the High Priest to put his arms through the armholes. When the cloak rested on Imen's shoulders, the pupil stepped back a few paces, waiting in silence for whatever would happen next. All the Priests watched in silence for something, anything, to happen. After what seemed an eternity, Imen cleared his throat.

"Erasan, feel the cloak. How wet is it?"

Erasan stepped back up to Imen, taking a part of the cloak in his hands, feeling it for any bit of moisture. "It is completely dry, my lord," he said. Imen smiled, nodding at the pupil. "Remove the Red Sword from the ground," he ordered, pointing at the Sword. Erasan promptly obeyed.

The High Priest continued. "Should I be unworthy of this holy position which I bestow upon myself, then may this sword turn to lead as my hands close over the hilt, and may I not be able to hold it above the ground."

Erasan handed the sword to Lord Imen, waiting for the worst to happen. Imen held the Red Sword for a few seconds, then in one quick motion causing Erasan to lose balance and fall on his back, he swung the sword high into the air. The early morning sunlight penetrated and reflected off the rubies that studded its hilt, casting a wondrous red aura over the Circle. The sword itself seemed to shimmer without the aid of the sun. The Priests, Priestesses, and Erasan looked up in awe at the wonder they were witnessing.

As quickly as the miracle had started, it ended, the sword losing its magical light. Imen lowered it to the ground, holding it out to his side. His breath was quick and heavy, as if he had climbed the mountain trail again. The rest of the Priests and Priestesses looked at him worriedly, yet said nothing as he continued.

"Lord Arum, a Priest of the Island of Ban, come forward."

The tall, thin young man arose, a breeze blowing his back-length black hair behind his shoulders, leaving a few loose strands near his face. When the Lord Arum was not a pace's distance from the Great High Priest, Imen raised the Red Sword between them, broadside out.

"Do you, Lord Arum, warrior and Priest of the Island of Ban, pledge your life and blood in service to the Great High Priest, the Red Sword, and the Ai?"

"I so pledge," said the Lord Arum, his face stern and solemn. "Raise your right hand," said Imen, turning the blade of the Red Sword out.

Arum obediently raised his right hand, bringing it close to the blade of the sword. Imen immediately touched the blade to the Priest's hand, pulling it back quickly. A dark, red ribbon of blood was left where the Red Sword had touched. A corresponding red liquid dripped from the blade.

Imen smiled, motioning for Arum to turn around, facing the rest of the clearing, and below that, the valley. Erasan, without having to be told, picked up the white cloak, handing it to the new Great High Priest.

"Of this cloak cometh knowledge and the wisdom to use it. Should you be unworthy of the blood oath which you have taken, and of the cloak which shall be placed upon you, may you babble like the foolish child when this cloak rests upon your shoulders."

Imen then proceeded to open the cloak, placing it upon the Priest. Arum immediately smiled, looking up to the sky, saying nothing.

As Imen looked to the Stone to his right, Erasan, on one knee, held the White Sword out to him. Imen nodded at the pupil, taking the sword. Arum turned around, again facing Imen. "As it has been said in the prophecy of the Lord Dazu called Aio, 'From the White Sword cometh wisdom, and many great tasks for you to do.'" Imen paused a moment. "The test of worthiness by wisdom has been passed. Should you be unworthy of this sword, may you be unable to perform the next task I give you, no matter how its simplicity."

He handed Arum the sword, saying, "Raise the sword above your head, Lord Arum, Priest of the Island of Ban." As if by itself, the sword was lifted high above Arum's head, the diamonds glittering in the sunlight. Again, it seemed for a brief moment that the sword itself produced light.

As the Lord Arum lowered the White Sword, Imen nodded at Erasan yet another time, and this time, the pupil bringing to him a large ring, cut from a single diamond, the ancient Aihi symbol for the Island of Ban cut into its intricate design at the top. "Although this object has no known value where magic and science are concerned, it is the symbol of the High Priest's position. Honor this symbol with a service equal to the honor that this ring gives you."

He then took the ring from Erasan and placed it on Arum's finger. "By the ceremonial powers vested in me of the Ai, and according to the customs of the ancient Aihi, I hereby ordain you, Lord Arum, now High Priest of the Island of Ban, next in the line to bear the Red Sword."

Arum knelt again, before returning to the stone closest to Imen's right, only to bend the knee again. The Lady Elaran, kneeling, stood up next, her tall, strong heavyset frame solemnly lumbering toward Imen, coming to a halt in front of him. Although she did not look so tall from a distance, anyone could tell that she was at least a head taller than Imen.

"Do you, Lady Elaran, warrior and Priestess of the Island of Carn, pledge your life and blood in service to the Great High Priest, the Red Sword, and to the Ai?" said Imen again, holding his sword in between the two in the same manner as with Arum. "I so pledge," said the young Priestess, raising her right hand without waiting for instruction to do so.

The blood pledge was repeated, the stain more visible on the Red Sword. Imen took the black cloak from Erasan, who had been holding it, waiting for the chance to give it to Imen. He motioned Elaran to turn around, facing the growing Council.

"This cloak shall be more a protection to you then will the shield you carry with your armor, for while wearing it, you can neither be wounded nor become ill. Should you be unworthy of this cloak, may your face break out in boils, and may you die of painful sickness at my feet in the presence of those gathered here."

The group gasped at hearing the consequences of unworthiness. Elaran became tense, knowing the type of death she faced if she were not meant to wear the cloak. "Into the will of the Ai I place my life and my body," she murmured.

Imen spread the cloak open, standing on his toes and stretching his arms in order to rest it on Elaran's shoulders. The Priests and Priestesses held their breath, waiting to see what would happen to the giantess of a Priestess. Elaran closed her eyes, expecting the worst. Elaran waited for a few seconds after the cloak had come to rest on her shoulders, Imen having drawn back. Eyes still closed, she reached her hand to her face, feeling around for any deformities that had not been there earlier. Breathing a sigh of relief, she turned around, facing the new Lord Aio again.

Imen took the Black Sword from the waiting Erasan, holding the hilt toward the large Priestess. "From the Black Sword cometh healing for those wounded and without rest," he said. "Should you be worthy to wield the healing power of this sword, may its hilt heal your hand from the wound inflicted by the blood pledge."

She grasped the sword in her right hand, immediately dropping it to the ground. Not only had the sword cut on her hand disappeared, so had all the other scars and scratches that hand had obtained through the various activities of a Priestess.

Imen next took a ring from Erasan, cut from a single piece of onyx. As with the White Ring, the symbol of the Island of Carn carved into the plain smoothness of the stone. "This ring which I now give you, although it has no magical or scientific powers, is a symbol of healing, to be worn only by the greatest healer of the Five Islands." Imen placed the ring on her finger, surprised at how smooth the ring slid onto Elaran's thick, strong finger. "By the ceremonial powers vested in me by the Ai, and according to the customs of the ancient Aihi, I hereby ordain you, Lady Elaran, now High Priestess of the Island of Carn." The High Priestess bowed on one knee to Imen, returning to her place at the stone to the left of Imen, then bowed again, facing Imen.

The Lady An hesitated a few seconds before standing up. Although very small and quite thin even while wearing her blue armor, she was not the frail Priestess that the sight of her figure led many to believe. A very young Priestess, yet already a veteran of war, her small size and peculiar skills with the sword had kept her from death many times, and had been the downfall of many seasoned warriors.

She stood before Imen, repeating the blood oath as had Arum and Elaran. The Great High Priest had to bend down a bit to complete this task, the part of the Red Sword that had performed the blood pledge covered and dripping with blood. Imen then spread the cloak, preparing to place it on the young warrior-priestess. "You, Lady An, who have fought well with the sword and have lived because of it and by it, may your body fall backward onto the Red Sword should you be unworthy of this cloak, that by the sword you may die."

Imen placed the cloak on An's shoulders, making sure the size would not cause it to slip off. He then quickly knelt, holding the Red Sword that she should fall on it if not one of the chosen by the Ai. The Lady An suddenly doubled over, away from the Red Sword, as if having been struck in the stomach. She immediately came back to an upright standing position, not having fallen onto the Red Sword.

By the time she had turned around to face Imen, the new Great High Priest was holding out the hilt of the Blue Sword to her. "From the Blue Sword many wonders that only the Ai can best," he said. "Should you be worthy to wield this great sword, may you with it perform a wonder for us."

The Lady An grabbed the Blue Sword, immediately thrusting it into the ground. The ground began to shake slightly, the quake growing in intensity the longer the sword was in the ground. A shocked look came over An as she tried to pull the sword out. The shaking of the ground, however, had become so violent by that time that she could barely hold onto it. She was shaken off her balance, landing on the ground, her body swinging with the shaking of the mountain as her hands kept a hold on the Blue Sword. Imen attempted to stumble over to help her, but fell hard on his back, feeling a sharp pain, his breath becoming short.

In an effort to push herself off the ground and to try to yank the Blue Sword free while standing, An took her hands off the Blue Sword. The shaking immediately stopped. Imen raised his eyebrows, immediately closing his eyes tightly in a wince as he got up, his back unable to completely straighten, having been injured by his fall during the short, violent tremor. "I suppose that we have our wonder, although I would have preferred a thunderstorm or a fire show in the sky to that," he said.

The rest of the Council, ordained or no, began returning to their kneeling positions, each grimacing at the pain from some hurt caused by the 'wonder' of the Blue Sword.

The Great High Priest took a blue ring, cut from a single piece of sapphire. Its design was simple, being no more than a couple straight lines crossing each other at certain irregular places on the ring. The symbol of the Island of Sares—the Island from which she came— was carved onto a flat part of the ring. It too, like the ring's design, was quite simple.

"This ring, Lady An," said Imen, "is the symbol of your High Priestess-hood, stained through the centuries by blood, sweat, flesh, goodness, and honor, not by disgrace, cowardice, or evil. Let not so much as a speck of dust mar its future." The ring was then placed on her finger. "By the ceremonial powers vested in me of the Ai, and according to the customs of the ancient Aihi, I hereby ordain you, Lady An, now High Priestess of the Island of Sares."

The High Priestess bowed to Imen, returning to the outermost stone to the right of Imen. A tall young man, his skin drawn tightly over his face as if nothing but skin and bone composed his body, rose from a kneeling position, approaching the Lord Imen. He had no hair on his head, but instead proudly wore the scars of many wounds and injuries to his head in place of the hair.

Imen looked up, the Lord Irn seeming even taller now that his back was bent. They went through the blood oath quickly, the blood dripping down the hilt of the Red Sword. As the blood oath was finished, Imen motioned the tall man to stand up. "Lord Irn, of all the members of this Council gathered here, you alone have shown no deceit, even as a child so young to not know the better. Within you is honesty and integrity without flaw or blemish. Should your blood oath have had the smallest part of any deceit, may the weight of this cloak bear you to the ground."

He took the green cloak from Erasan, putting it over the tall, thin body of the new High Priest.

"Put me down! Put me down!" shouted Irn angrily in a high pitched nasal voice. "If it won't stop I'll have it burned when I get to the ground," trying to remove the too large, yet too short cloak as he began floating up into the air. The cloak immediately set him down, as if to say that it did not wish to be burned. Those of the new High Council not in too much pain to laugh did so. Irn frowned, walking up to Imen, brushing off the cloak.

Imen took the Green Sword from Erasan and held it out, hilt forward, to Irn. "The Green Sword shall bring back the past in the form of the Great Serpentaur. This, Lord Irn, is the prophecy which all High Priests of the Island of Cerel dream every night to come within their time, yet dread it with the passing of every day. With this sword comes not a test of worthiness, but a blessing: that you might be the worthy bearer of this sword in the fulfilling of this prophecy." He handed the Green Sword to Irn, who solemnly bowing, accepted it.

A green ring was then handed to Imen, cut from a single piece of emerald, the symbol of the Island of Cerel carved into it. "This ring, Lord Irn," he said, "is the symbol of your high Priesthood. No finger that has worn this ring has ever belonged to one of the false tongue. Do not let your finger be the first." Irn held out his hand allowing Imen to put it on his finger. "By the ceremonial powers vested in me of the Ai, and according to the customs of the ancient Aihi, I hereby ordain you, Lord Irn, now High Priest of the Island of Cerel."

Cerel's new High Priest walked back to his stone, the outermost to Imen's left. Las timidly walked forward, her red armor shining in the rising sun. She bowed to Imen as she neared him, standing up again and repeating the blood oath as those who had gone before her. "Lady Las, Priestess of the Red Island," Imen addressed her. "The high Priestesshood of the Red Island offers no magic cloak to the one who claims this title. No powerful sword is given. No perilous test of worthiness is taken. There is only this …" he said, motioning to Erasan, who promptly placed the ring, cut from a single ruby, into his hand.

"This ring is the symbol of your high Priestesshood. It has but one power: while you remain worthy and the rightful bearer of it, it will never slip off your hand. Should you ever commit an act that would prove you less than worthy to bear this ring, it would burn your finger as fire, until you would cast it away from you. Bear this ring well, and do not give yourself reason to remove it." He then placed the ring on her finger. "By the ceremonial powers vested in me of the Ai, and according to the customs of the ancient Aihi, I hereby ordain you, Lady Las, now High Priestess of the Red Island."

Las bowed, returning to her place directly across from Imen.

Imen, still bent over from his injury, motioned for the new Council to rise. "May the Ai grant this Council the wisdom with which to lead our people in these ever perilous times, and may we be granted the power with which to carry out wise decisions. I hereby, as spokesperson for the Ai, ordain this High Priest Council, to lead and serve the Five Islands of the Aihi in the name of the Ai."

He walked past the other five members of the Council, motioning to Erasan to follow him. He motioned for the other two priests to come near to him as well. "Have preparations made for a meal in my hut. Prepare also a resting place for the Lords Arum and Irn, and Ladies Elaran and An. When you are done, do as thorough a search as you can of this mountain. Magic is in use here on this mountain, apart from the wonders of the ceremony. Faint traces, but there is definitely some magic. I can feel it. Erasan, I have a task for you when these are finished."

—

Father Ean got up, stretching. "Took them long enough," he said, watching the sun near its zenith. "I suppose the two of you are hungry?" The two Serpentauri nodded. "I can smell the ripe wheat from here," said Kelron, stamping a hoof.

"We had best wait a bit longer," said Father Ean. "The Priests and Priestesses must travel to their huts, rest, eat, feast and whatever else civilized men do. We must wait until such a time as they are all inside their huts, engrossed in whatever activity they happen to partake in."

Kelron raised his head. "You speak of civilized men, Father Ean. Do you not consider yourself to be civilized?"

Father Ean laughed. "I once considered myself civilized, although I cannot speak for the other men of my time who knew me. Now, that is the last word that be used to describe the gardener of Oakvalor."

Kelros nodded. "How long shall we wait, Father Ean?"

Father Ean looked down upon the deserted Council Circle. "A short time. Your feasting shall be worth whatever longer wait you must suffer."

17

THEY LOST ALMOST TWO FULL days, but they had finally passed the Sly Mare. They didn't stop at the inn again, choosing instead to put more distance between themselves and the three men who might have killed them. At the base of the Viss Mountains rested the last sign of life until one crossed over the mountains. The monstrous line of rugged terrain stretched from the Ocean hundreds of miles north straight to the Deadland. The mountains were the official boundary between Talvaard and Oakvalor. Once they traveled into Oakvalor, they would have to rely on help from their enemies to find their way to the monastery of their brothers.

They set up a makeshift camp in a small clearing of trees close to the stables of the small town that named itself after the mountain range. The population of the town had steadily declined over the years as most of the youth had gone off to join the king's army. Viss's only inn was more a shack than any actual accommodations, and none of the few rooms it had were available. The monks made the best of it, tying the flimsy limbs of the small trees to each other, which helped to make a sort of roof covering. The sky showed no signs of rain, but one could never be too prepared.

"The trail through the mountains is not well worn. People do not cross the borders enough, for obvious reasons," Donovan said later that evening, as the sky turned black except for a few visible stars. Calderon stretched out on the ground and used his sack as a pillow. "I suppose the people there will not be so inclined to help us," Calderon remarked aloud. Donovan and Velkyn made themselves as comfortable as possible on the hard ground as well. "Don't be quick to assume," Donovan replied. "There is not much difference between the people of our respective kingdoms. They will not know we are from Talvaard unless we share that information."

They remained in silence for long moments before Velkyn broke the peaceful hush. "Do you think we will succeed?" That simple question, asked with such honesty, seemed to weigh them all down heavily. "We must have faith in the Divines that we will," answered the old monk. "Without faith, we are nothing."

Calderon wondered, not for the first time, if their faith might be misplaced. "Have you ever …" he started to say but instead fell silent. "Speak honestly," Donovan bade quietly. "Have you ever wondered if, maybe, our belief in the Divines is … wrong?" Neither monk responded and so he continued. "Not that our faith in the higher powers is wrong, but that the ones we place our trust in is? I have lived in the monastery walls most of my life, and yet I have never once heard my prayers answered. Am I alone in this?"

In the far distance, they could hear the howling of wolves. Calderon noticed then that the moon was full this night. "I suppose we have all questioned ourselves, and our faith, at some point in our lives. But the Divines do not just speak to us through prayer. They speak to us through other people, and through the holy Scriptures." Silence fell over the three, and yet again it was Velkyn who broke it. "I have never heard my prayers answered either."

No one spoke after that, and eventually they all fell asleep. As Calderon's eyes got heavy and he began to slip away into sleep, he vaguely heard "Neither have I."

—

Daylight brought the chirping of birds and the sounds of the small town coming to life. Calderon opened his eyes and sat up to find Velkyn and Donovan missing. Their packs were still there, but he didn't see either of them. His neck was stiff and he rubbed it for a moment before getting to his feet. He assumed they must have went into the inn to get some breakfast and started that way when he saw them coming back towards their camp. "Sleep long enough?" Velkyn asked, smiling to show he was jesting with his friend.

"Perhaps too much," he smiled back, rubbing his neck again. "Where did you two go?" In answer, Velkyn produced an apple and a small chunk of bread. "For you. Eat quickly though. Donovan says it will take us most of the day to reach the other side of the mountains. He wants to be in Oakvalor before dark."

Calderon nodded and ate, consuming the food as hurriedly as he could while still enjoying it. They strapped their packs on and untied the tree branches that had given them shelter. Donovan was right that the path was not worn, they almost missed it entirely. Once they got going, they found the trail was straight and the climb easy enough. It seemed they would make good time, until the trail began winding in wide circles and became steeper. An hour into their journey, Calderon and Donovan began to feel burning in their legs. Velkyn, being much more physically fit, was having less trouble.

The sun crested the top of the mountain peaks and the air warmed considerably, making the three monks uncomfortable in their thick brown robes. They began to sweat profusely and eventually had to stop to rest and to eat. They didn't talk much but focused their energy on simply making the climb. When they finally reached the peak of the trail hours later, they stopped to admire the scenery.

They found the air was thin this high, and the clouds seemed to rest upon the surrounding peaks. It was quiet. Too quiet. It unsettled Calderon, who expected to hear the many sounds of wild animals. Calderon looked down into an enormous valley that swept from the base of the mountain and out as far as he could see. Off in the distance he could see small tendrils of smoke rising lazily into the air. "Palindrom," Donovan said, seeing the direction where Calderon was looking. "I have heard it is a city of unrivaled beauty, where one can find the answers to almost any question."

"How?" Calderon asked, not taking his eyes off the distant city. "The Hall of Mirrors," Donovan answered. "It is said that the wizards created it in the early days of discovery, when no forms of magic were prohibited. It is a hallway that contains magical mirrors that show the future. It is for that reason we go to Oakvalor. If we can get the wizards to allow us use of the Hall, it is likely we will find the dragon's spirit."

"How do we get them to even hear our request?" Velkyn asked, coming to stand beside the old monk. "That is why we seek out our brothers. They will be the ones to help us."

The rest of the journey was much easier as they now traveled downhill. They saw the occasional signs of what appeared to be animal crossings. At one point, Calderon thought he saw someone in his peripheral view. He stopped and searched his surroundings, but saw nothing. Shrugging, he continued down the trail. It was well past midday when they were a few hundred feet away from the valley. They still had a few hours' worth of daylight left. As they came around a bend in the trail, they could hear voices.

Donovan held his hand up, motioning for the two younger monks to stop. He crouched down behind a large boulder and peered down the trail. He saw a number of soldiers wearing the customary bronze armor of Oakvalor's military. The old man looked around and knew this was the only way down. Heaving a sigh of resignation, he stood and beckoned the two young monks to follow him. They stepped into the open and continued down the trail.

If the soldiers noticed the three monks, they didn't act like it. When they were a stone's throw away, one of the soldiers stepped forward. His hands were wrapped around the shaft of a spear and he placed the butt end into the dirt and leaned against it. "What is your business here?" he questioned.

"We are on a pilgrimage," Donovan answered, meeting the soldier's gaze. "We have been traveling to the holy sites of the Divines." The soldier's eyebrows raised in curiosity, or was it confusion? "Divines?"

The soldier drew closer to the old monk. "What is your name? And where do you hail from?"

"My name is Donovan and I hail from a distant land," the monk answered cryptically. "As I said, we are traveling to the holy sites of our faith, the Divines. Is that not allowed?"

The soldier didn't answer for long moments. "I'm afraid I don't know what you are talking about. Who are the Divines?" That question set Donovan back on his heels. How did this soldier not know about the Divines? Even the most remote villages knew of the Divines. "We are seeking our brethren in the chapel of Hermiston."

"The ruins?" the soldier still seemed confused. "I am not sure what faith you follow, but here in Oakvalor we follow the Lord Aio of the Five Islands."

This was a surprising turn of events to Donovan. What did the soldier mean by 'ruins'? And who was Lord Aio? "I have been gone from my home a long while," Donovan said, lowering his voice so that Calderon and Velkyn could not hear him. "What do you mean the ruins? Has the chapel at Hermiston been destroyed?"

The soldier shook his head. "No, not destroyed. Abandoned." Donovan's face turned incredulous. "What did you say your name was again?" the soldier asked.

"Donovan."

The soldier scratched his beard. "Donovan … Donovan …" his face lit up with recognition. "… the Donovan?" The old monk hushed the soldier and glanced over his shoulder at his two young counterparts. "The same. I am on a mission of the utmost importance and I need to get to Hermiston." The soldier bowed low and stepped aside, allowing the three monks to pass. Donovan shook his head in confusion. Why would the chapel be abandoned? That thought haunted him the rest of the way.

—

The Chapel of Hermiston was a tall structure of salt-and-pepper colored granite. The walls soared up roughly twenty feet high, with a taller tower at each of the four corners of the chapel. In the center of the front wall was an archway that served as the entrance. As with most of the chapels, they were constructed without gates to allow anyone entrance. The three monks made their way into the courtyard and found it eerily empty.

"Where is everyone?" Calderon questioned aloud. Donovan didn't have an answer. How could he know what happened? "Look around … see if you can find anyone or any sign of what might have happened," the old monk instructed. They separated and went through the various rooms within the structure, searching everywhere. An hour later they met back in the courtyard. Velkyn shrugged his shoulders. "No signs of any kind of battle," he said. "It doesn't appear they left in a hurry either," Calderon added. "Everything is intact and nothing appears to be missing."

Donovan considered their words but did not say anything. "This is going to hinder us getting an audience with the wizards," Donovan finally said. "The question is, where are all the people? They couldn't have just left."

"Or could they have?" Calderon responded. "There is nothing to support an attack or the threat of one. What if they all simply left? When was the last time the Abbot heard from this chapel?"

Donovan cleared his throat. "He hasn't."

Velkyn and Calderon's eyes widened in surprise. "What do you mean he hasn't?" Velkyn demanded. Donovan held his hands up to calm them. "The Abbot has not heard anything from this chapel since he was ordained," the old man paused, "and neither had his predecessor." The two young monks stood silently. "We never thought anything ill had happened, we merely assumed they were not in need of anything from our central abbey. But this," he swept his hand out, motioning toward the chapel, "this is disturbing to say the least."

"What do we do now?" Velkyn asked. Donovan gave a cursory glance about the courtyard. "We don't have time to investigate these new revelations. We must find a way to meet with the wizards on our own." His tone did not inspire confidence in the young monks.

A loud clatter sounded then, and all three monks spun about quickly. A man, wearing robes and a cloak that looked similar to their own, stood staring at them. "Who are you?" Donovan questioned. "Are you a brother of this chapel?" The man shook his head but offered no explanation. "Are you following us?" Calderon asked, thinking back to the mountain path and how he thought he saw someone. Again, the man shook his head. They watched him warily, for he carried a sword across his back and they were unarmed.

Finally, the man spoke. "I am Erasan, servant to the Lord Aio." Donovan immediately recognized the name Aio, the same name the guard had mentioned. Who was this Aio, he wondered. "I am Donovan, and these—" he waved to the young monks "—are Calderon and Velkyn. We are brothers from the Abbey of the Divines in Talvaard."

"What brings you here?" Erasan asked. "Do you not know this place is forbidden?" The monks looked at each other uncertainly. "We did not know that," Donovan answered honestly. "We have not heard from this chapel in a very long time. Why is it forbidden? Do you know what happened here?"

Erasan laughed at them. "Truly you do not know," he said, more of a statement than a question. "This place is forbidden for it is a place of idol worship. The Great Lord Aio taught that there is only one, and that it is he." Seeing confusion, and possibly alarm, on the faces of the three men, Erasan grew distrustful. "Why are you here?" he asked again.

"We could ask the same of you," Velkyn answered. "If this place is forbidden, why do you stand in its midst?"

That put Erasan back a step. "I am here at the behest of the Lord Aio." Donovan raised his hand to silence what Velkyn was about to say. "We are here because this place is under the jurisdiction of the Church of the Divines," he said. "It is not forbidden to us, it is a holy place. Your clothes are like ours, with little major differences. Do you know what happened here? We have no time to spare and we are on an important task."

Erasan walked over to them, his steps slow and measured at first, then bold and quick. "I do know what happened here," he answered. "And I will tell you, but you must tell me some things as well."

"Very well," said Donovan, seeing no other way to get any answers. Erasan pointed to the south. "I am from the Five Islands, where the Great Lord Aio was born one hundred and forty-three years ago. This forbidden place at one time had many people living in its walls. But they left."

"Left?" Donovan asked, confused. "Why would they leave? Did they build a new chapel elsewhere?" Erasan shook his head. "They left this place and the beliefs it held them to. This place represents what some see as truth, but what we know as false," he said. "There is only one, and that is the Great Lord Aio."

"Where did they go?"

"They left to follow the Ai. Word of him and his deeds spread even to this place," Erasan said. Donovan couldn't believe it. How could anyone abandon their faith for another? Something didn't add up. Something sinister was going on here, something far more dangerous than a dragon loose upon the land. They had already run into delays, but perhaps this Erasan would have some answers that might give them direction on their next step.

"Let me tell you why we are here," Donovan said. "This may take some time."

—

She swung her sword, a deadly looking weapon, with such ease that anyone who had seen her wield it knew without doubt she was well versed with it. Her body was lithe and agile, stepping this way and that, her sword like an extension of her physical body, striking this way and that. She fought no foes this day, but instead was practicing, ensuring her body was in peak condition. She had too many enemies to count, which left her overly cautious. She dipped low, sliding her foot across the ground in a sweeping motion that would have taken the feet out from under any opponent. Without any hesitation or pause, she leapt up and spun about, kicking the same foot outward and landing back down on her feet with perfect balance.

"Jovanna!" she heard him shout her name.

Jovanna turned to face him, twirling a strand of her black hair with her finger and pulling it behind her ear and away from her face. "I trust you come with good news," she said as he approached her. "M'lady," Julian said, kneeling down before her. "Rise," she said, motioning him to stand.

Julian rose to his feet and brushed the dirt off his pant legs. "Well?" she demanded impatiently. He smiled at her and produced a large silver ball. There was nothing remarkable about it. "You are sure?"

Julian nodded. "Yes. Three monks stayed at the inn I was at when I was trying to infiltrate a group of thugs from Dillenger. The closest chapel is the Abbey of the Divines, so they must be from there."

Jovanna took the sphere from him and turned it over in her hands, studying its surface. "It seems to match his description," she said finally. It was smaller than she expected, fitting in the palm of her hand and being slightly larger than an egg. She opened a small pouch on her belt and slid it inside, pulling the drawstrings tight. "You did well. Where are they now?"

Julian shrugged. "I know only that they left quickly after our run in with the thugs. They headed back towards the east as far as I can tell." Jovanna pondered her options. "Perhaps they will realize it is missing and come looking for Julian?" she hinted, turning her blue eyes to meet his gaze. "It's possible," he conceded. "Though I think they will have much trouble indeed if they try to find me."

"Did you use the guise I told you to?"

Again, Julian nodded. "I told everyone I spoke with I was a magician, as you instructed." Jovanna grinned, she liked his obedience. "And?" she asked.

"No one seemed to care, or believe, that I was a wizard," he answered. "Though I was also at the edge of the kingdom, where many probably turn a blind eye."

"Go farther," Jovanna instructed. "Go to the city of Talvaarin itself and do the same. We shall see how long the memory of its people are. Return to me in two weeks' time." She turned and began to walk towards the small shack she currently used as home.

"M'lady," Julian called after her. She stopped but did not turn around. "My payment?" he asked. Jovanna turned her head to look at him. "Your life is payment enough, don't you think?" The threatening look on her face was more than enough for him to know that no threat lurked behind that mask, but only promises of utter pain.

"Right," he said, hesitating only a moment before quickly leaving. She was beyond dangerous, he knew.

18

THE THREE MONKS AND ERASAN made camp outside the ruined chapel of Hermiston, mostly due to the fact that Erasan refused to stay in the place, using the words 'accursed' and 'forbidden'. Erasan informed them that the area was safe and there was no need to set a watch. They each made their own makeshift beds and settled in.

Long after everyone else had fallen asleep, Velkyn lay awake staring at the night sky. He considered the last week and all that had transpired. He had traveled so far and seen so much, and yet he had barely entered the kingdom of Oakvalor. What other amazing sights would he see? What other knowledge would he gain? A sound nearby interrupted his thoughts. He sat up slowly, casting his gaze about and trying vainly to see what might have made the noise. Velkyn rose to his feet and made his way cautiously in the direction he heard the sound.

He paused, the shock evident on his face as he saw his beloved Nydel reveal herself from behind a small copse of trees. "Velkyn!" she whispered, a bit louder than she had intended. Velkyn took her into his arms and hugged her close. "I missed you," he said softly, giving her a gentle kiss. "And I missed you," she replied, returning his kiss. They held each other in silence for long moments before Velkyn pushed her back at arm's length. "Why did you come here? And how did you get past the guards at the mountain? You know it isn't safe."

Nydel smiled reassuringly at him, trying to distill his fears. "I got here two days ago. I thought you'd be here, but this place was empty. I looked around some and decided to wait for you. Your letter said you were headed here for answers. I was afraid you had already come and gone." She leaned into his embrace, brushing her fingers along his jaw line and up through his hair. "Come," she said, leading him by the hand. "I found a place for us." He glanced back at his friends. Velkyn knew they shouldn't separate from the others, but he knew too what she wanted. His own body wanted it as well. He allowed her to lead him into the abandoned chapel. They went through the courtyard and into one of the rooms that once was used for prayer. Nydel pushed the wooden door closed.

Velkyn pulled his robes off and laid them on the cold stone floor. They began kissing and caressing each other, slowly moving to lay down atop his robes. She made sweet noises and he knew she was ready for him … had missed him as he had missed her. "I want to spend my life with you," he whispered to her. That seemed to make her even more wild with passion.

A loud bang echoed in the room and Velkyn quickly looked up. The door had been kicked open and three figures stood in the doorway. "I can explain—" Velkyn began.

"What'ev we got 'ere?" a familiar voice chimed. Velkyn felt his heart jump in his chest when he recognized the gruff voice of one of the thugs. He pushed himself to his feet and stood defensively in front of Nydel, who covered herself with his robes. "Leave," Velkyn warned, "or I will cause you much more pain than the last time we met."

The three thugs laughed. The weaselish man rushed into the room then, eagerly swinging a metal rod. Velkyn brought his hands up to block the rod while simultaneously angling his foot up to kick Theo, who followed behind the weasel. Theo grunted as Velkyn's foot slammed into his stomach. He staggered back, obviously struggling to breath. The weaselish man kicked out at Velkyn and swung his rod back and forth in an attempt to strike the monk. Velkyn was too quick though, and he dove into a roll, coming up behind the weasel and delivering a solid punch to the man's lower back, followed by another punch to the back of his neck. The weasel didn't fall, and so Velkyn kicked the back of the man's leg, which resulted in the weasel dropping to his knees.

An explosion of pain ripped through Velkyn's head and he fell forward, crashing hard into the wall. He looked up and through his blurred vision he saw the gruff voiced man, wielding a similar metal rod as the weasel. "Ye caused us a 'ho'lotta pain, monk. Now we're gonna cause ye some pain." Theo and the weasel had recovered and stood over him. "Get 'im on 'is feet," gruff said. The two thugs jerked the monk up roughly to his feet.

"See'in as how ye took somethin' from us, we're gonna take somethin' from ye." Gruff switched places with weasel. Velkyn's vision was beginning to clear and he saw the weaselish man unbuckle his pants. "She'll even the score, me thinks." Velkyn struggled against their grasp but he couldn't break free. "Get away from her!" he screamed. Gruff punched the monk in the mouth, causing blood to drip from his lips. "Ye shut yet mouth if ye know what's good for ye," gruff said. Nydel tried to fight the man as he ripped the robes off of her, so weasel punched her in the face, knocking her flat onto the floor. He invaded her body with his hand and turned to his fellow ruffians, but more specifically Velkyn.

"Oh, she is ready, she is." He grinned wickedly and began to rape her. She screamed and struggled, but he was much stronger than her and kept her pinned down as he did his business. Velkyn fought with all his strength to get free, but the two men just punched him into submission. "Ye're gonna watch it," gruff said heavily. "Be quick about it," gruff yelled at weasel. "It's my turn next."

Velkyn watched helplessly as each of the thugs took turns raping his beloved Nydel. He could taste blood in his mouth and feel his left eye swelling up. When Theo had finished with her, she merely lay there feebly, her head twitching every so often, as if in some silent plea to stop. "I will kill you," Velkyn threatened weakly. Gruff held up his metal rod and looked Velkyn in the eyes. "Ye just try it." He lifted the rod up and swung it hard, bashing the monk in the left side of the face. Velkyn crumpled unconsciously to the floor. "What of 'is friends?" Weasel questioned.

"Who cares," gruff answered. "Leave 'em to die." Gruff looked down at Nydel and spat on her. "Tell yer monk we're even." The thugs left then, leaving Velkyn a bloody mess and Nydel laying naked and bruised.

—

Velkyn grunted as he opened his eyes. Or perhaps it was only one eye that was open, as his left seemed not to comply. He reached up and gingerly touched the skin around his eye; it was fat and puffy. And it hurt worse than his legs did when he rode the horse. Everything flooded back to him then, and he sat up quickly. Too quickly, for the room spun and he vomited. He spat the nastiness from his mouth and crawled over to Nydel. She lay very still but he could see that she was breathing.

"Nydel," he whispered softly. "Are you … are you okay?" He put her hand in his and she whimpered and pulled away. "It's okay, my love. It's just me." He tried to comfort her again, but this time she screamed and thrashed at him. Velkyn could feel the tears well up in his eyes. How could they have done this to her? How could people be so vicious to one another? He needed help. Calderon, he needed Calderon. Nydel was still lying on his robes. He stood up unsteadily, using the wall for support until he felt as though he might be able to walk. He moved over to the doorway and looked out, not sure if the thugs were gone.

It was still dark. There didn't seem to be any sign of the men, so he stepped out and made his way out of the courtyard and towards their camp. The air was warm but it felt cool to him with nothing but his loincloth on. He made his way slowly to where his companions were sleeping. Finding Calderon, he shook his friend gently. It didn't do anything, so he shook him harder. Calderon's eyes opened lazily. Seeing Velkyn's battered face, he immediately was wide awake. "What happened?" he asked, and Velkyn covered his friend's mouth. "Not here," Velkyn whispered and motioned toward the chapel.

Calderon got up and helped Velkyn walk. When they were a safe distance away, Velkyn told Calderon what happened. "How did they find us?" Calderon asked. Velkyn merely shook his head. "They must have followed us here," Calderon mused. Velkyn led his friend into the room they were assailed in to find Nydel in the same spot. "She won't let me touch her," Velkyn said brokenly. Calderon knelt beside Nydel and reached out to put his hand on her forehead. She jerked and moved her head away from him. Calderon bit his lip and looked to Velkyn. He had his back against the wall and was staring forlornly at Nydel. Tears flowed freely.

Calderon didn't know what to do. His knowledge of healing was almost nonexistent and he had never seen anyone who had gone through something so horrific. "We could take her to Donovan," he said, but immediately Velkyn was shaking his head. "If anyone finds out, I will be kicked out of the brotherhood. And what does the old man know about healing?" Calderon nodded in concession, but they couldn't just do nothing. "Maybe we can take her to a town somewhere and get her some help?" Velkyn considered the option. "We will have to wait until morning. We can't move her in the darkness. We don't even know where we are," Velkyn said.

"I agree," Calderon replied. "Do you want me to stay with you?" Velkyn shook his head. "No, I will be fine here with her." Calderon stood up and stared down at Nydel. He ignored the fact that she was completely nude, instead focusing on her bruised face and soul. He tried not to cry as he headed back to their camp, wondering how it was that such evil could exist in mankind. It was one of the many mysteries he could not unravel. He lay down but could not sleep. His mind was heavy and his soul was troubled. When the sun began to light up the sky, Calderon was still awake.

—

Velkyn opened his right eye. His left was still swollen shut. He looked to where Nydel was … only she wasn't there. Velkyn scrambled over to make sure he wasn't seeing things. She was indeed gone. He grabbed his robe and put it on, rushing out into the courtyard and calling her name. He didn't see her anywhere. He noticed Calderon making his way into the courtyard. "Nydel is gone! I can't find her!" Calderon started to respond but stopped mid-stride, his mouth dropping open in horror. Velkyn could feel a deep fear rise in his throat. He turned around to see what had so horrified his friend.

Nydel's body was hanging from the wall. Velkyn dropped to his knees and cried out. Calderon could only stand in horror. Her body was hanging from a rope that had been secured to a metal hook in the wall. Her lifeless form dangled from the other end of the rope. Erasan had called the place accursed. Cursed indeed.

19

"I'M LEAVING," VELKYN SAID QUIETLY. He and Calderon walked several feet behind Donovan and Erasan. The old monk and the priest of Aio were talking about the differences between their faiths. "What do you mean?" Calderon looked to his friend. "What do you mean you are leaving? Leaving where?"

Velkyn met his gaze and Calderon could see the tears, barely being held back. He couldn't blame his friend for being so sorrowful. He had lost the woman he loved, and his secret was now known to Donovan. While Donovan had no authority to cast the young man out of the brotherhood, he didn't deny that the Abbot would do so. "I will not be welcomed back into the abbey. You know that."

Calderon shook his head. "I do not know that. And neither do you. Where would you go? You do not even know where you are." Velkyn stopped walking and turned to Calderon. "You know where I must go. There must be justice for this crime." Calderon's face turned to a horrified look. "Velkyn … there are proper ways to handle this … you can't just …" he trailed off as he looked at his defeated friend. He realized that nothing he said would dissuade him from this course. "How will you know where to find them?"

"I will go to the Sly Mare. If I do not find them there, I will go to Dillenger. I will not stop until I find them. I will travel as far as it takes. I will destroy anyone and everything in my way." Calderon noticed Velkyn had clenched his fists. The sheer rage, hatred, and sadness that his dear friend harbored was so intense, Calderon feared he might snap then and there. He tried his best to console Velkyn, but he knew that ultimately his friend would leave. "I don't know what to do without you," Calderon said sadly. "You have been my friend, my only friend, since we were young. I will not stop you, neither will I tell Donovan when you leave. Just do it when I am unaware. It will be easier that way."

Velkyn considered his friend's words and offered a smile. "I can do that." The two traveled in silence for hours afterward. Calderon took in the beautiful scenery. It was much different than what he was used to. The tall grassy plains around the abbey instilled a peacefulness that he had grown to love, but Oakvalor was like another world entirely. He could still see the mountains they had crossed over clearly in the distance. They walked along a well-built cobblestone road which carved its way through the valley that stretched from the mountains to their west all the way to a massive forest to the east.

Velkyn kept his gaze at the ground, only occasionally looking up. He was lost in the swirling chaos that was his thoughts. He wanted to fulfill his obligation to recapture the dragon's spirit, but his love for Nydel compelled him to exact revenge on those thugs. He wasn't sure he could really abandon Calderon and Donovan after coming this far. He would sleep on it and decide the following morning.

Calderon learned from Erasan that one of the kings of Oakvalor had worked to pave all the main roads to every major city. It made it easier for merchants to travel farther and faster, boosting the economy. It also made it easier to move armies faster, though which reason was really behind the upgrade of the roads was anyone's guess.

Erasan was an odd one, Calderon thought. The man called himself a priest of Aio. From what he had gathered, some divine figure named Aio came from the heavens and took on flesh, living among the people of the Five Islands. It was Orlek, a powerful Orc wizard turned evil who did battle with Aio and supposedly had resurrected himself more than once. It sounded more like folklore to Calderon, but the more he pondered it all, he had to wonder if there was at least some ounce of truth to what Erasan claimed. In all his years, Calderon had not once been given an answer to his prayers, or been shown a sign of the Divines' will for his life.

They had traveled nearly the entire day, stopping only a few times to eat and rest their feet, before finally they saw the tall gray walls of Palindrom. "The city of wizards," Donovan remarked. "Built long before the kingdom of Oakvalor was a united nation." Erasan looked at the old monk. "You know much about this land for one not from it."

Donovan didn't reply, but instead continued talking about the city. "Palindrom is the center of the world as far as the wizards are concerned. When men first began to realize their gifts in the magical arts, they banded together and traveled in small groups, living in tents. Not unlike the tribes of the Five Islands," this comment he directed to Erasan. "But one of the leaders, the man who would become the first head of the arts, Palin decided it would be easier for them to study magic in a central location that was open to all. The knowledge gained from the wizards would be shared with anyone who wanted to know the secrets. Thus, Palindrom was conceived and then built. The city around the main structure built up over the years that followed. Many people do not know this, but Palindrom isn't really a part of Oakvalor. It is considered an autonomous state within the kingdom's boundaries."

As they neared the city, Calderon noticed several forms, probably guards, patrolling along the wall. As they neared the entrance to the city, they saw many people lined up waiting to enter the city. "This is different," Donovan muttered. Calderon looked to the old man with a raised eyebrow, but Donovan didn't notice.

At the gate were guards who were questioning the people seeking admittance. They didn't turn anyone away, but seemed to be asking a few questions and then motioning people in. "What's going on?" Calderon asked, but if Donovan or Erasan knew, they didn't answer. After nearly twenty minutes, the monks had reached the main gate. As Calderon looked at the guards, he noticed they were not dressed like the guards he had seen in Talvaard when they attended the coronation.

The men wore swords at their hips, but they did not wear any armor. They wore some sort of shiny clothing that looked like silver, yet it was obviously made of cloth. They also wore red capes that stretched from their shoulders down to within a few inches of the ground. One man, whom Calderon assumed was a captain of some sort, wore a blue cape. "Reason for entry?" one of the guards asked without looking at them. He was holding up what appeared to be a crystal. "We are looking for a place to stay the night," Donovan said, looking intently at the man wearing the blue cape. The crystal began to glow a light red. The guard holding it looked up at them. "He's lying," the man said.

The man wearing the blue cape stepped forward and surprised them all. "Donovan?" he questioned, tilting his head slightly. "I would recognize that face no matter how long I had not seen it. It's been too long, old friend!" Calderon and Erasan were greatly confused, and Velkyn seemed to be off in his own world. Donovan, however, knew that he would not be able to hide things much longer.

"Indeed it has, Anton. I come bearing some ill news, I fear." Anton held his hand up. "Not here. Come, we will set you up at the keep. Who are your friends?" Donovan pointed to Velkyn and Calderon. "These are my fellows from the abbey, and this man—" he pointed at Erasan, "—is Erasan, a priest from the Five Islands." His tone made the last part sound like a question more than a statement. Anton nodded and motioned them to follow him. "When the last of the people are in, close the gates," Anton ordered the two guards.

They followed Anton inside the walled city. "What is all this?" Donovan asked, nodding to indicate the guards. "These are dark days," Anton said ominously. "Many things have changed, most of them recently." Anton would say no more, even though Donovan prodded him the entire way. The city was massive in terms of size. It had grown to capacity within the protection of the walls, and so to continue building, they began adding second, and in some places, third stories to the existing buildings. As it was the end of the day, people had begun cooking and they could smell many different scents in the air, all of them mouth-watering.

Anton led them through the city until they finally reached an imposing structure. It was different than any of the other buildings they had passed, and it was definitely the largest in the city. There were no guards posted at the gates of this building. Anton led them inside. There was a small girl waiting in the antechamber that served as a waiting room. "Take our guests to the dining area. I will be there shortly." The girl bowed to Anton and began walking towards one of the doors. "Don't let her appearance fool you," Anton warned them. "She is not what she seems."

The girl turned back and smiled wickedly. Calderon could feel the hairs on his neck raise. "What is she?" he whispered aloud. Anton looked at the young monk and smiled. "A succubus." Calderon didn't recognize the term but it didn't sound good. They all reluctantly followed her anyway. Donovan hung back until they were gone and turned his attention back to Anton. "What is going on?" he demanded.

Anton's face took on a more somber look. "There are rumors of war," he said. Donovan shook his head. "Oakvalor and Talvaard have been at war for years." Anton looked around and lowered his voice, as if someone might hear him although no one was in the room. "I am not talking about that war. Although, we do have reports that the young prince of Talvaard killed his brother and the daughter of Elkanah, Oakvalor's king." Donovan nodded to confirm the story. "I was there. I saw the entire thing myself."

Anton shook his head. "The newest word is that Talvaard's armies march toward Oakvalor as we speak." Donovan seemed confused. "We traveled the main road to get here," Donovan said. "I saw no signs of any army." Anton nodded. "I hear they are slow moving. There is also rumor that they don't want to march, but the new king demands it. There is worse news still," he said, lowering his voice even lower. "Orlek has taken a new body." Donovan laughed at his old friend. "Don't tell me you believe that crazy priest's stories?" he said. Anton didn't laugh. "You have been to the Chapel of Hermiston?" he asked. Donovan nodded. "Then I trust you see the truth of the word of Lord Aio. You have been gone a long time, Donovan. You left when we were young and adventurous, but many things have happened here since you left."

Donovan stared at Anton. The two of them had grown up together, studying the art of magic right here in Palindrom. Donovan saw his friend had aged better than he had. While Donovan had spent his years behind the walls of a monastery, Anton had spent his days training as a warrior-mage. Adept at wielding a sword just as much as magic, a warrior-mage trained for many years to attain the perfect balance between the two skills. Donovan had been sent by the leader of Palindrom to ensure the safety of the sphere. They had made many attempts to have the sphere brought into the care of the wizards, but the monks of the abbey had declined every time. Anton's hair was once brown but had been lightened considerably from his many days in the sun. His skin was a deep tan color, and his body was thin and muscular. Though they had studied together, Anton was ten years younger than Donovan.

"Erasan told me about this supposed Aio. Is there really truth to this?" Anton nodded his head. "There were whispers of this new faith when we were young, but that's all it was; whispers. Turns out there was much truth to the whispers."

The door of the front entrance flung open and a young man rushed inside. Both Anton and Donovan turned to see who was barging in. The man quickly bowed to Anton and held up a letter. "Jovanna?" Anton asked hopefully. The man shook his head. "No, Captain. Worse!" Anton held up his hand to silence the messenger. He turned to Donovan and smiled. "I'll meet you in the dining room shortly. I have some things to attend to. I won't be long." Donovan hesitated. "Who is Jovanna?" he asked. Anton shook his head. "No one to concern yourself with," he answered curtly. They stood in silence for a moment before Donovan finally left. Anton took the letter from the messenger and read it. He lowered the missive and stared off, then reread it. "Has this been verified?" he asked.

"Yes, Captain. I came as soon as I could. Everything you read is true … all those people … what do we do?" Anton knew this was beyond anything he had experienced, beyond anything anyone here had experienced. Except for him. "Take this to Cygnus at once. He will know what to do."

The messenger took the letter back and rushed off. Anton had seen many things, and had heard many stranger things. This was not strange. It was pure evil, and he knew that Orlek's hand was behind it. When he felt he had composed himself, he joined the others in the dining room. They were all seated and eating quietly. All three monks and the priest regarded him with interest as he took his seat. The young girl set a plate of steaming food before him and moved off into the shadows. Several torches lined each wall every four feet, except for the corners of the room where darkness remained. Anton ate his food absently.

Donovan had had enough. "Anton, I know I have been gone for a very long time, but that does not excuse you from keeping me involved in the dealings of our order. What in the Abyss is going on?" he ended his shout by slamming his fist onto the table. Everyone looked at the old man, startled. Even Velkyn, who had been in some sort of trance looked up. Anton stared at him from across the table, but not in anger. "A storm has wiped out the Five Islands."

Erasan gasped, or would have had his mouth not been full of food, and he choked and began coughing. Calderon and Velkyn didn't understand the implications of it, and Donovan fell back speechless in his chair. "The report tells of a strange storm that battered the Islands and destroyed everything. They don't think anyone could have survived. The ocean is littered with debris, but most of it is floating bodies …" Anton's words died as he imagined the horrific scene. "Something isn't right," Donovan said shakily. "Storms hit the Islands often. What do you mean a strange storm?"

Anton shrugged his shoulders. "I do not know. Witnesses on the coast said it was not like any storm they had ever seen. I suspect there was magic involved in this. Though whether it is Orlek or Jovanna, it is yet to be seen."

Donovan leaned forward. "Who is Jovanna?" he questioned Anton for the second time. Anton rubbed his hands over his face and he suddenly seemed much older. Heaving a great sigh, he answered the question. "Jovanna was an orphan that displayed obvious talent with magic. The people who took care of her brought her here to Palindrom to see if we could 'help' her." Donovan made an exasperated noise. "I know," said Anton, "I know. They didn't understand that this was not something that could, or needed to be, fixed. We offered to take her into our care and they did not protest much. She was only six and she had taught herself to cast a fireball."

Donovan raised his eyebrows, obviously impressed. "Six? That's incredible." Anton nodded. "Cygnus said that with training she would rival even the famed skills of Palin himself."

"Cygnus is still alive?" Donovan asked, surprised. Anton nodded. "And hasn't aged a day, it seems. Jovanna was an eager student, but she also had a dark side. There was an accident in the halls one night and several students were found dead, apparently burned alive. She was blamed and there were enough witnesses for

Cygnus to pronounce punishment on her. She was given forty lashes minus one with the whip. That only seemed to fuel her anger."

"Burned alive with what?"

"Magical flames."

Donovan looked skeptical. "The halls of housing are protected by anti-magic. How could she have cast magic so powerful that the anti-magic would not stop it?"

"Exactly," Anton said. "Cygnus tried to figure that out as well, but he could find nothing conclusive."

"She sounds dangerous."

"Exactly," Anton said again. "We knew she was a liability waiting to happen. By the time we had enough evidence of her breaking the wizards code, she could not be found. She abandoned Palindrom and we have yet to find her. She is very powerful. Powerful enough to hide from scrying stones," he added, referring to the stones they used to see over vast distances.

"Perhaps it is a good thing she is gone?" Donovan suggested. Anton shook his head. "There is nothing good about that one. She craves power, and will do anything to have it. We fear she seeks the sphere."

Donovan looked down. "That is the ill news I bring. The creature has escaped." Anton sputtered. "What do you mean it escaped? How? You were ordered to protect it with life and limb!"

"I did!" Donovan shot back. "For most of my life I have kept it safe. But something happened. The magic must have weakened and failed. I believe it escaped during the coronation in Talvaarin."

Anton digested the words. "Where is the creature now? And where is the sphere?" Donovan pointed toward Calderon. "The sphere is safe in his bag. But as to the location of the creature, I do not know. That is why we are here. We need to use the Hall of Mirrors."

"Out of the question," Anton replied. "The danger is too great."

"I know it is dangerous, but that does not negate the fact that we must use it to find the creature. You must know this."

"You misunderstand me," Anton said. "Jovanna tampered with the magic of the mirrors. If she were to find out that the creature is not bound in the sphere, she would surely use that knowledge against us. She is a formidable foe, and we are already pressed with Talvaard threatening invasion at our door and Orlek with his orcish hordes preparing in the mountains. Oakvalor is surrounded by enemies and now the priests of Aio lie dead in the ocean. We cannot risk it."

Donovan knew Anton's words were not merely spoken in frustration. The embers of a war unlike any other were heating up, and soon a raging inferno would spread across the land. "We cannot afford the risk of the dragon gaining his body back. Where are his bones?"

"They decorate the king's war machines."

Donovan remained silent in thought. "Perhaps they are safe there. I need to use the mirrors," he said with a tone of finality.

"That is unlikely to happen," Anton responded. "Cygnus has forbidden any use of them." Donovan felt helpless. He had to find a way to use the Hall of Mirrors. "Then what do we do?"

"That, gentlemen, is the question." Everyone at the table turned to see Cygnus standing in the doorway.

20

JOVANNA HAD LEARNED LONG AGO to trust no one. Her own parents had abandoned her when she was four, scared of what their daughter might be. She had scrounged in the trash heaps of the town, fighting with rats and other vermin to simply stay alive. When the local orphanage took her in, they soon began treating her like her parents did. Jovanna knew now that it was fear that caused people to act the way they did toward her. Fear of the unknown often caused people to treat others differently.

She knew she was different. Even when she was four, she knew she was not like other children. Not like anyone, regardless of age. But when she had been brought to Palindrom, she felt like she finally belonged. The people there were more like her than anyone she had encountered before. They could summon fire like she could, they could do things other people could not. And yet, as time went by, Jovanna realized even the wizards of Palindrom were not the same as her. She was different. She could 'see' the magic. No one, not even the half-blood Cygnus, could do that. And so, some of them treated her differently, just like everyone else in her life. She grit her teeth in anger at the memories.

They had given her knowledge to control the gift, true, but they could not wield the magic as she could. She had been laying in her bed trying to sleep one night when she realized something. There was nothing wrong with her. There was something wrong with everyone else. She was above them, had been given a gift that no one could fathom. She had learned when she was young that in order to get what you needed, you had to take it. No one was going to help you and certainly no one cared.

And with that thinking, she also decided that since she was above everyone, she needed to rule over them. Why have the power and not use it? But she was only one person. She could not defeat everyone single handedly, even she knew that. But if she had someone or something to help her achieve her rise to power … and that thinking had led her to the decision to steal the sphere. No, not steal it. To take it. She was not a thief, she was a taker. A doer. She had left Palindrom because she knew they were going to try to stop her. She knew they were searching for her too. She could feel the emanations of the crystal magic, could feel the eyes searching, ever searching.

If there was one thing she could do well, it was hide. She had to when she was younger. But soon, very soon, she would no longer have to hide. Jovanna smiled at that. Now that she had the sphere, she would release the dragon and use it as a tool to her ascension. The sun was rising and the sky was bathed in reds and oranges. She held the metal sphere up in the increasing sunlight and knew her time was at hand. She placed the sphere on the ground, using a few rocks to keep it from rolling around. Once she had bent both king and peasant to her will, she would seek out Orlek and destroy him as well. He was the only one that could stand against her, she was confident of that. The wizards had grown soft in their teachings. They had ceased to study the old books, to learn the old magic. She was different.

She unsheathed her weapon, a light-weight, short-bladed sword. It was plain in decoration except for the hilt which was shaped like a dragon's body. The pommel was the dragon's head, its mouth stretched wide in a silent roar. The blade looked ordinary, yet it was anything but. She tilted her head to each side until it popped. Raising the sword, she brought it down hard onto the sphere's surface. The sound of clanging metal rang out, and then a heavy thud. Her blade had cleaved right down the middle of the sphere and into the ground.

She smirked. That was easier than she expected. She bent down to inspect the sphere and the smile left her face. The magic had all but faded from the sphere. And the dragon's spirit was not inside. She swore silently, sheathing her sword angrily. She had been so close—and now this!

She forced herself to calm down. Anger would get her nowhere, despite how good it felt to be angry. She picked up the two halves of the sphere and stalked back to the building she was currently staying at. The door banged shut behind her and she slung the pieces into a leather bag. "Never send a man to do a job right," she muttered.

Julian had his uses though, she had to give him that. He was one of the first she had recruited into her cause. She had several spies in various places now, all of them reporting to her weekly.

She knew that Talvaard's armies were marching toward Oakvalor, but what she didn't know was why. The kingdoms had been at war for hundreds of years, but no actual fighting had happened in quite a long time. She pondered that, along with all the other information delivered to her of late. A knock at her door drew her from her contemplation. "What is it?" she demanded, expecting it to be the young man who had been following her around lately. He was infatuated with her but the feelings were one sided. She needed a man as much as she needed a dog; the upside being that a dog licked itself.

She was surprised to hear Julian's voice on the other side of the door. "Come in," she instructed. The door swung open and Julian sauntered in. "All goes well, my lady." He halted suddenly, her gaze cutting through him like a pair of daggers. "Where did you get the sphere?" she questioned.

"From the monks I told you about. They—" In one swift movement she pinned him against the wall, drew her sword, and had the sharp blade pressed against his throat. "I know who you got it from, I said where?"

Julian swallowed and a thin cut appeared on his neck. "The … uh, I found it in one of their b-bags in Dillenger. They seemed to be headed east before a couple of thugs robbed them. I don't know where they were going, they seemed to be very private men."

Jovanna glared at him, but she knew he was telling the truth. He was smart enough to know better than to lie to her. She released him and straightened his shirt. "I find it interesting that the sphere is supposed to be guarded within the Abbey of the Divines, and yet these monks were strolling along the countryside with it in their bags. Why do you think that would be, Julian?"

Julian wasn't sure where she was going with this. "I can't say I have a guess, my lady."

"Of course you don't. You are a man, and men don't seem to think much. The sphere is empty. The dragon is not bound within it anymore. Which means that it is roaming about somewhere. I need to find it." She paced the length of the room, turned on her heel, then paced back the other way. She did this several times before she looked up and saw Julian still standing there, apparently not sure what he should be doing. She was about to yell at him but remembered one of the tasks she had given him. "What was the reaction of the people when you told them you were a wizard?"

Julian smiled meekly. "They arrested me."

She raised an eyebrow. "Yet you stand here?" Julian nodded. "How?" she asked. "They realized that I was not really a wizard," he answered. She snorted derisively. "If they will not welcome their new ruler willingly, then they will bow to their new ruler at the end of my blade. Get out of my sight," she said scathingly. He bowed low and opened the door to leave. "Any new orders?" he asked hurriedly.

"Stay alive," she warned. Julian shut the door and scurried off. Jovanna continued her pacing. "Something happened," she reasoned aloud. "Perhaps the monks released the dragon ... no, that's not right. They had it with them and they were traveling east." She stopped her pacing. "East," she repeated. Her face lit up with realization as she began to put the pieces together. "They are headed to Palindrom!" She whirled about and grabbed the bag containing the halves of the sphere.

She would need to renew the magic and seal it back together, but it would work. "That's why he ordered the invasion," she breathed. "The creature wants its body back!" She would have to get close enough to the prince for the sphere to work its spell, but she was confident there would be many diversions to keep the beast occupied. She slung the bag over her shoulder and knelt down. She withdrew a small piece of chalk and traced a circle along the floorboards. She unsheathed her sword and ran her finger over the blade, cutting herself. Pressing her finger onto the top of the circle, she mixed her blood with the chalk, tracing over the chalk circle with her bleeding finger.

When she finished, she scrutinized her work, ensuring there was no gaps in the circle. She stood up and prepared herself for the magical journey. She would have to locate the prince quickly. If the wizards knew she was near, she would be just as much a target as the possessed prince. She gritted her teeth. This part always sucked. The floor opened up and swallowed her.

21

DONOVAN STARED AT THE LEADER of Palindrom. Anton was not lying when he said the man had not aged. Donovan remembered the man clearly from his early days here. Cygnus was tall, yet not overwhelmingly so. Standing nearly six feet, his body was lithe and his movements graceful. His hair reached midway down his back and remained a golden blonde color. There was no sign of wrinkles on his face and his eyes were as bright green as they had been the first time Donovan saw them.

"It is good to see you again, Donovan. I did not think I would see you so soon, though. It has been, what, sixty years?" Donovan smiled. "At least," he replied. "You haven't changed a bit in all that time."

Cygnus returned the old monk's smile. "I have changed, just not on the outside." Calderon looked with incredulity from Cygnus, to Velkyn, then to Donovan, and finally to Anton and Erasan. Erasan seemed like Velkyn now, as he was in a deep silence and tears ran down his cheeks. Calderon had nearly forgotten that Erasan was from the Five Islands, the same Islands wiped out by the storm. The priest didn't make eye contact and just stared blankly at the wall.

Anton looked to the young monk. "Who is that?" he asked Anton. "That is Cygnus, the head of the order of wizards and has been for nearly two hundred years."

"Two hundred years? The man looks barely into his twenties." Anton smiled at the ignorant monk. "Cygnus is a half blood. His mother was human, but his father was an elf from the Deadlands." Calderon still looked confused. "The Deadlands is the land north of us. It is a dangerous place. Elves and many other races call the place their home. Cygnus's mother was raped by an elf when her village was attacked by a raiding party. Cygnus is the product of that unfortunate union. It seems he favors more of the elf side, I think.

Elves are long lived creatures, but they are evil. Cygnus is a credit to his race."

Calderon felt as though he had learned more about the world he lived in within the last couple of weeks than he had his entire life. Foreign lands, different races, the absolute evil that resided in mankind. It all seemed too much.

Cygnus took a seat at the table. "The devastation to the Islands is surely the work of magic. We have yet to locate Jovanna, but the signs of Orlek's impending invasion are obvious. The thing that baffles me is why Talvaard marches full force to our land." Cygnus drummed his fingers on the table. "The loss of the tribes of the Aihi surely puts us at a disadvantage." He looked to Erasan. The priest met his gaze. "I am truly sorry for your loss. If there is anything I can do, please do not hesitate. Our city is your home as long as you will it. From everything gathered, we suspect you are the only priest alive." Cygnus paused to let his words soak into the young priest.

"According to your customs, this would make you the new Lord Aio." Erasen's eyes widened. "I am not worthy," he whispered. "That is understandable, and I would not blame you, nor would anyone I suppose, if you chose not to take the calling. Think about it." Cygnus looked to Donovan. "Your mission was to keep the sphere safe. Is it with you?" The old monk nodded. "Yes, we have the sphere with us … but the creature is no longer bound within it."

If Cygnus was surprised, angry, or feeling any other emotion, it did not show. He merely nodded, his fingers continuously drumming on the table. "So then the beast roams the land in spirit …" his words trailed off and he rose slowly to his feet. "What is it?" Anton asked, noticing the difference in his superior's demeanor.

"It makes sense now. How I did not see it before …" he was shaking his head. Everyone at the table watched Cygnus, waiting for him to explain. When he didn't, Anton pushed him for one. "A dragon is a mighty beast, but it is limited to a physical form, just like any other creature. There is limited knowledge on them, as they are not originally from our world. What I do know is that, like Orlek, they have the ability to resurrect themselves. They only need their bones to do so. This is why Vallen decided to imprison it within the sphere. If they would have killed the dragon, it would simply have raised its own body from death. A dragon's soul is eternal, at least from what we know, and so it had to be confined inside something that could keep it there."

Everyone continued staring at him, still not understanding. "The dragon has to have a body to do anything … it must have possessed the prince of Talvaard!" Gasps filled the dining room. "That would explain why he murdered his brother," Donovan conceded. "By all accounts, he didn't want the throne. His body must be the pawn of the dragon."

"Then we must draw him out of Talvaard," Cygnus said. "Why would we do that?" Calderon asked. "Could the dragon not just as easily kill us in the body of a man?"

"Yes," Cygnus answered. "But since we have the sphere, we can still use it. The magic cannot be replicated, but it can be strengthened. With the enchantments reinforced, it can be used to recapture the beast."

"They have it here right now," Anton mentioned.

Cygnus seemed pleased with that. "Very good. Take the sphere to Antimodus. He will strengthen the enchantments. You four go and get some rest. I fear we may need all of you before the night is over."

They all stood up and Anton instructed the young girl to escort the monks to empty rooms for the night. Donovan waited until they had all left with the exception of Anton and Cygnus.

"I have a request," Donovan said to Cygnus. "I need to use the Hall of Mirrors." Anton was shaking his head. "You don't need to. We know where the dragon's spirit is now." Cygnus didn't answer, but listened to them both. Donovan sighed. "We are assuming that the dragon has taken the prince's body, but we do not know that for certain. We must be sure."

They both looked to Cygnus to settle the issue. "Your request is not an easy one to grant. A former student named Jovanna has messed with the magic that is in the mirrors. We are not sure what she has done to it. We do not know if it will kill the user, or if it will show them false images. As you are aware, the mirrors were crafted by Palin himself. Jovanna is a nuisance to be sure, but she is capable of anything dealing with magic. I fear what may happen if I let you use the Hall.”

“I accept the risk,” Donovan said. “I am an old man and I have lived my life. Let me use it and know that I accept willingly anything ill that may come of it. Your conscience can be clear.”

Cygnus hesitated. The man knew the risks, to be sure. Yet Cygnus was keeper of the Hall, and if something happened, he could be blamed. Was it worth the risk? He couldn’t know the answer to that question. “I approve your request. But use it now and quickly. You will need to be rested.” Donovan bowed in thanks and made his way toward the Hall.

“Are you sure about this?” Anton questioned. Cygnus shrugged. “I am sure of nothing these days.” And then he departed also, leaving Anton with his thoughts.

22

MORNING CAME ALL TOO QUICKLY for Calderon. He felt as though he had barely fallen asleep when the sun began peeking through the small window of his room. A storm had arrived during the night and the incessant tapping of rain drops pelting the glass pane had kept him awake most of the night. Or at least he blamed the rain. If he was honest with himself, he would have to blame himself for his lack of sleep.

The news of a dangerous woman seeking the sphere and the armies of Talvaard marching on the city they were in troubled him deeply. He couldn't fight well and had never been trained with a blade. What good could he do in a battle that had nothing to do with him? That was a lie too. The truth of it was that he was responsible for the dragon. If he would never have fallen asleep, the beast would still be bound by the magic. He sighed as all of the thoughts and doubts from the night before reared their ugly heads in his mind again.

He had begun to wonder about this Aio and his priests. Calderon had somewhat decided to visit the Five Islands if they survived the chaos to seek out his own answers. But now that hope lay in the bottom of the Ocean. He forced himself out of bed and stretched before making his way to the window. The rain had stopped early in the morning and the clouds were beginning to break. Shafts of sunlight slanted at an angle from the sky, coming to rest on the ground and bringing their warmth with them. His room was towards the back of the structure, and so he did not see the sprawling city. He saw the stretch of valley that met the forest in the east.

He wondered what lay within the woods. Considering everything he had seen recently, he assumed the forest could be home to any number of things. Calderon turned from the window and retrieved his brown robes. He had laid them across the desk, which happened to be the only thing in the room besides the bed. He sniffed them and scrunched up his nose. They were starting to smell like sweat. He was accustomed to washing his robes daily at the abbey. Numerous days on the road had caused the bottom of them to fray and stain with dirt. He made a note to find somewhere he could wash them.

He put the robes on and stepped out into the hallway. Velkyn had gotten the room across from his. His friend was an early riser, so he expected Velkyn to be up and ready for breakfast by now. He knocked on the door. After waiting a long moment, he knocked again.

Nothing. Calderon tried the handle and found it unlocked. He pushed the door open and walked in to find the room empty. As realization struck him, his heart sank. He would not find his friend; would probably not see him again. He shook his head at the futility of Velkyn's self-made mission and went back to his room to collect the sphere. He was supposed to take it to someone named Antimodus. He rummaged through his bag but he couldn't find it.

He knew it was in there. He had packed it in his bag himself, and no one had touched it … he began to panic when he remembered the thugs who had stolen their bags back at the Sly Mare. Turning the bag over, he dumped all the contents onto the bed. It wasn't there. Terror gripped him. Without the sphere, they couldn't stop the dragon. A knock on his door startled him. He opened the door to find Donovan standing there.

"Where is Velkyn?" the old monk asked. "I'm not sure," Calderon answered. It wasn't really a lie. "We have a bigger problem." Donovan stepped inside the room. "What's the problem?" He looked over at the mess on the bed. "Where is the sphere?"

"That's the problem," Calderon said softly. "It must have fallen out or it was taken when we were robbed back in Oakvalor." Donovan's gaze narrowed on the young monk. "Velkyn and the sphere disappear at the same time, and you don't see anything odd about that?"

"Why would Velkyn take the sphere? He isn't a wizard and he has no use for it." Donovan considered the argument. Still, something wasn't right. Why would Velkyn suddenly disappear unless he was doing something he shouldn't. "Come with me, we need to inform Cygnus—"

The deep, long blare of a horn overpowered Donovan's words. A few seconds of silence, and then another identical blare sounded. "What is that noise?" Calderon asked.

"It's the city guard warning of danger."

Calderon ran to the window and looked out. "I don't see anything," he said over his shoulder. Donovan nodded. "You wouldn't from here. It's coming from the front of the city."

The sound of footsteps echoed in the hallway. The two monks saw more than a few wizards hurriedly pass by. "Follow me. And stay close. We don't need anyone else to go missing," the old man remarked. Calderon respectfully adhered. They followed the wizards through the confusing maze of hallways until they reached the antechamber that led outside. The place had become organized chaos as groups of men and women dressed similar to the guards from the city gates the night before came and went.

"They are battle mages," Donovan explained. "They are trained in the art of magic and with weapons."

"Who are you?"

Donovan looked curiously at Calderon. "Who are you really?" the young monk asked again. "You know things about this place and you know some of the people here. You are hiding something, and I want to know what it is."

"That's not important right now," Donovan said, trying to avoid the conversation. "It is to me," Calderon replied testily. "I will not follow your lead anymore until you tell me what is going on. Who are you?" he reiterated. The old monk stared at Calderon, struggling with something internally. "I am not a monk," he finally said. "Before I tell you anything else, if we even have the time, you must promise not to tell anyone back at the abbey."

Calderon nodded silently. "I am not from Talvaard either. I was born here in Oakvalor, in this very city. I trained as a wizard within these halls."

"Why do you claim to be a brother of the Divines?"

"The leaders of Palindrom have long sought to bring the sphere out of the abbey and secure it here. Each time the request was issued, the abbot—regardless of who led it—refused. The monks have turned it into some sort of holy item of their faith. They do not understand that there is nothing sacred about it. It is merely a round piece of silver inscribed with magic. When the dragon was loosed by the hands of Orlek, no one could stop it. Talvaard and Oakvalor had been warring over dominion of the Five Islands for years, but both kings realized that unless they put their feud aside, everything would be destroyed by the beast.

"So the two kings united toward the common goal of stopping the dragon. Talvaard did not have wizards, but Oakvalor did. And Oakvalor did not have metal smiths because assassins from Talvaard had killed them all. Had either side have had both, there would surely have been no alliance. As the dragon was trapped in the sphere, the creature's body crushed the wizard who imbued the magic, leaving only the metal smith to protect it. Despite the protests of both kings, the smith took the sphere to the monks of the abbey. The king of Talvaard respected the monks enough not to try to take it by force. The wizards of Palindrom, in reward for their help in defeating the dragon, were given autonomy from the kingdom of Oakvalor and could not be convinced by the king to help take it. Nobody could forcefully take the sphere without causing either a civil war, or an all out blood bath between the two kingdoms. Since we could not bring it back here, we had to find other ways to safeguard it."

"By infiltrating the brotherhood?!" Calderon shouted in anger. "How could you make the vows with no intention of keeping them? They are sacred!"

Donovan tried to calm the young monk. "I kept an open mind to the teachings of the Divines. I even dared to believe they truly existed and guided the lives of men." Donovan shook his head. "But I am convinced now more than ever before that the Divines do not exist. I do, however, believe that there is some divine being who created our world and sustains it all. But I do not think we can really know that being."

The old man's honesty not only checked Calderon's anger, but it also left him without words. It was as if Donovan had looked into Calderon's own soul and put into words how he felt. Yes, he was angry that Donovan could take the vows of their brotherhood with no faith in them, but was he mad at Donovan specifically or at the possibility that all he claimed to believe could possibly be wrong? He didn't have time to delve any further into the conversation as Cygnus strode into the room, preceded by ten wizards. Two men followed behind that Calderon assumed were either bodyguards or more wizards.

"Donovan, I need you on the walls with me. Your companion should stay here and seek shelter in his room." Cygnus made a motion with his hand and five of the people with him rushed out of the door and into the city.

"What's happening?" Donovan asked. Cygnus paused as the horn sounded again. "The armies of Talvaard are before us. There is something … ominous … in the air," the half-blood said. "Did you find the truth of our assumption last night?" he asked. Donovan didn't know how to answer the question. The mirrors had showed him many things, but he did not know what was real, and what was a possibility. "I am led to believe that the dragon has indeed possessed the prince of Talvaard."

Cygnus drummed his fingers in the air, something he did when he was thinking. "Did you have Antimodus strengthen the magic of the sphere?"

"We don't have it. It seems to be missing, possibly stolen by thieves while we were on the road traveling here."

Cygnus, despite the disappointing news, did not show any emotion or frustration. He continued drumming his fingers in the air. "This will make things difficult. If the dragon comes here in his borrowed body, we will not be able to capture him. You know as well as I do that we cannot replicate the magic of the sphere."

"Could you not expel the creature from the man's body?" Calderon chimed in. "Force the dragon out? Then the prince could call off his army. Is that possible?"

Donovan looked to Cygnus. The half-blood stopped drumming his fingers. "It is possible, but I do not know that the cost is worth whatever the gain might be. And there is no guarantee that the creature will not simply take another body. It can possess anyone."

"Anyone except you," Donovan said.

"We don't know that for certain."

"What do you mean he can't be possessed? Why not?" Calderon asked.

Cygnus pulled the sleeve of his robes up, revealing countless symbols tattooed into his skin. Calderon looked them over but could not read any of them. "The elves of the Deadlands have very unique practices," Cygnus explained. "They tattoo spells into their skin with special ink. The flesh must heal before the spell can be used, and the spell is limited to only a few uses before the tattoo fades from the skin. The longer the tattoo stays in the skin without being used, the more powerful the spell. It is believed that there are spells that can keep one from being possessed as there are many dark creatures that walk the Deadlands with the elves who have that ability." Cygnus paused. "But dragons are not from our world, thus there is no guarantee it will work."

The horns sounded again, but instead of the two notes, it sounded three. "Our enemy nears," Cygnus said. "We must decide on a course and act quickly."

"I think we should take whatever measure necessary to expel the dragon from its host. It is a risk, true, but with the prince free to think on his own, he should cease the actions of his army," Donovan decided. Cygnus looked to Calderon. "You are not a wizard, but I find that there is much wisdom in the counsel of many. What say you?"

"I agree with Donovan's logic," the young monk replied. "Remove the leader."

"I will do what I can," Cygnus said. "Let us survey this army." Cygnus led the way out of the antechamber and out into the city. Calderon headed back to his room, hoping he could navigate the unfamiliar halls himself. There was no panic or discord in the streets. There really weren't many people out, and the ones that were seemed to be heading to safety. "We have seen many battles, and our walls have never been breached," Donovan heard someone say.

"We have never fought a dragon," Cygnus said in rebuke. "Do not let your pride affect your decisions." The man took the reproof in stride. They made their way through the empty streets and to the front of the city, then climbed the steps that led to the parapets.

"War machines," one of the guards reported as they looked over the wall. Tall structures jutted up from among the ranks of soldiers. The number of troops was incalculable, their line slowly stretching out around the walled city. As they marched closer, the defenders of the city could begin to make out formations. Most of them were ten men across and ten deep, with a captain leading each group.

"Steel your hearts," Cygnus bade them. "We slaughter innocent people driven by a fiend. If you have any hesitations, remember that you defend our own innocent people against the cruelty of a foul beast."

When the first rocks began to crash against the walls of Palindrom, all doubts of whether or not what they did was right quickly fled.

23

THE ABYSS SWIRLED PAST HER. The clawed hands of demons reached out for her, wanting to tear her flesh off. She could feel the heat of the hellfire and hear the screams of the tortured. The faces of her attackers glared at her. Thankfully the magic kept them at bay. It was the fastest way to travel, but it was also the hardest. Jovanna feared very little, but every time she traveled this way, she felt like a small child scared by the unseen monsters under her bed. Only for Jovanna, they weren't unseen. They were very real, and if she were to make even the slightest mistake in the magic, there would be nothing separating her from the demons that desperately wanted to feast on her.

She felt a shudder as the magic ripped a hole in the ground above her and thrust her up ten feet into the air. Her arms and legs flapped about wildly as she attempted to right herself. She twisted her body and managed to land on her feet with a jarring thud. Several soldiers stood nearby, staring dumbly at her. She drew her sword and rushed forward. The sight of the ground spitting out a woman had momentarily distracted them, but they were trained men of war and quickly gained focus and drew their own weapons.

There were six men, all fitted with heavy armor and ready for battle. Jovanna knew she wouldn't be able to fight them all at the same time. She could use her magic, but that would alert the wizards in Palindrom and she couldn't risk it. That left fight or flee. She growled in frustration as she dodged past the soldiers. She sprinted as fast as her legs would carry her, trying to put some distance between them and herself. Luckily the magical tunnel had put her out toward the outer edge of the army and gave her a chance to hide. The wide valley would have left her out in the open, but since she was nearer to the forest, it offered her a chance to hide. She turned a corner and dove headfirst into a thicket.

The soldiers rushed by a few moments later. She waited to make sure they weren't coming back before she climbed out of the bushes. "Easy enough," she boasted, still breathless. She walked deeper into the forest, looking for a suitable spot for what she would need to do. Seeing a small clearing among the trees, she made her way toward it. As she neared it, she could hear what sounded like voices. Using the trees as cover, she stepped lightly, avoiding stepping on anything that would alert whoever was ahead. She stopped when she saw two men. They were talking, but she couldn't make out what was being said.

Jovanna reached into her leather bag and produced a small stone. It was a dull grey and polished to a smooth shine. On one side was a symbol that had been painted with some sort of ink. It was one of the trinkets she had taken from Cygnus before she left. She pressed her forehead to the stone until she felt it warm up. She looked to make sure the men were still there before she hurled the stone into the air. Her aim was true and it flew through the branches of the trees without hitting anything. It hovered in the air high above the men, but the magic was linked to Jovanna and she could now hear them talking.

"The creature has possessed Ranaan, the prince of Talvaard. And he walks among the troops now, commanding the assault against the city. The dragon is a mighty foe. The wizards will be hard pressed to win this battle," this from the taller of the two men. She couldn't make out their details as they were both wearing hooded robes. The shorter figure had a raspy voice that reminded Jovanna of an old man she once knew when she was young. "What of the sphere?"

"It has been taken from the monks that guarded it. They do not seem to know where it may be. Should we intervene?" The raspy voiced man didn't respond immediately. "Let us see how it plays out. If all seems lost, we will step in. But we mustn't be seen. We only keep the balance, nothing more."

"He didn't keep the balance," the tall man said. Jovanna wanted to try to see their faces, and she began slowly moving closer. She pressed her hand against a tree. Its bark was old and rotted and chunks of it fell off and noisily hit the forest floor. The two men whirled about and Jovanna almost gasped audibly. The taller man wasn't a man at all. He was an elf. The other man seemed more like a man, but his face was wrinkled beyond anything Jovanna had seen before. The elf drew up his sleeves revealing tattoos that covered the lengths of his arms and began to trace his finger along them. The smaller man slapped the elf's hand. He shook his head and in a burst of light, the men were gone.

She wasn't sure if they had actually seen her or not. She thought she was well hidden. Who were those people? And what were they talking about? The shorter man mentioned something about a balance. A balance of what? She stayed put for what seemed like an eternity before she was sure that she was alone.

Jovanna stepped out from the trees and retrieved the stone before moving to the clearing and pulling the halves of the sphere out of her bag. She laid them on the ground beside each other and produced a small pouch. She opened the flap and reached inside, dipping her finger into a thick, liquidy substance and coating the edge of each piece. She used a leaf to wipe her finger clean, then tossed it aside. She sat down cross-legged and closed her eyes. She concentrated on the symbols drawn on the inside of the piece to the left. She could see the symbols were dim, hardly glowing at all. The magic was very weak. Using her mind's eye, she could see the fragments of magic that floated about the world, and lifting her hands, began to sweep them toward the sphere.

When she had gathered numerous pieces of the fragments, she began to hum softly. The humming helped her to keep her concentration and had nothing to do with the magic. She began to touch the fragments, gently pressing them into the symbols. It was a time-consuming process, as it was difficult to grab hold of the fragments. After roughly twenty minutes, the magical symbols began to glow brighter. Slowly at first, but as she added more fragments, it began to glow all the brighter. Once she was satisfied that the spell was strengthened sufficiently, she began work on the other piece. This was the skill that the other wizards didn't understand. They didn't believe that she could see the magic. When she was young, she believed the fragments of magic were fairies that wanted to speak to her.

Jovanna finished the task and placed the two halves together. She grabbed a few more fragments and used them to ignite the substance on the edges. The sphere flashed brightly and then went dark. She opened her eyes and lifted the sphere up. It was almost impossible to see the line where her sword had cut. She smiled, pleased with herself.

She would need a way to get close to the prince. That was her objective, but she couldn't help thinking about the elf and the man. Why were they here in the woods? She put everything back into her leather bag and stood up. She forced the thoughts of the men out of her mind. It was time.

—

"She has the sphere," the elf remarked. They were surrounded by an invisible barrier that kept them from sight and muted their words. The shorter man nodded, watching her with interest. "They say she can reconstruct spells created by other wizards," the man rasped. "What do you think she plans to do with it, Jerik?" the elf asked.

The shorter man, Jerik, shook his head. "That remains to be seen." He turned his gaze to Cahenrair the elf. "Be prepared," Jerik warned.

"For what?" Cahenrair asked.

"To set the balance, whatever must be done."

—

Jovanna stood at the edge of the forest. She could see stones flying through the air, flung from giant war machines. Thousands of soldiers were spread out before the city walls. "Fools," she said to herself. If they thought throwing rocks against the walls would knock them down, they would surely be disappointed. No army had breached those walls in the history of the city.

It would take much more than catapults to bring them down. She knew Cygnus would not offer a counter attack. He was too weak to use force. She was extremely surprised when, a moment later, a bolt of lightning blasted forth and struck one of the catapults, sending splintered wood everywhere. She fell back a step as the air reverberated with a resounding boom. It would be difficult enough to reach the prince with all the soldiers protecting him, and now the wizards were launching magic from their walls!

She growled in frustration. She didn't have any other choice. She would have to use magic to reach the prince. She pulled the sphere out and held it in one hand, and with the other she drew her sword. She was done hiding. She was done running. She was different.

She cast her magic quickly and furiously, weaving layer upon layer around herself, fashioning a thick shield of magic. She closed her eyes and waved her sword about, gathering fragments into her spell, causing it to fluctuate and tighten. Jovanna opened her eyes. She rushed across the valley, heading straight toward the army. The first few groups of soldiers had no idea what hit them. She hurled bolts of lightning from the tip of her blade, sent blasts of scorching fire from the other hand holding the sphere.

When they struck at her with their swords, they were flung back by her shield. She was unstoppable, a raging force of burning hatred. And she was headed straight for the prince.

24

"WHAT IN THE ABYSS IS that?"

Cygnus looked to where one of the guards was pointing to see a form running through the soldiers on the field below, waving a sword and surrounded by blue pulsating light.

"Anton," Cygnus said, "She is here." Donovan and Anton looked down to see Jovanna dealing out death and destruction to everything in her path. "She looks angry," Donovan observed. "She's always angry," Cygnus replied. "We must stop her from whatever she is plotting. Send the guards." Anton looked at Cygnus warily. "Send them into that?" he said, motioning toward the army at their gates. "We will create a diversion," the half-blood said. "She must be stopped. Send them now."

Anton bowed and rushed off to obey. Moments later, a handful of men were seen running from the gates out into the valley. Donovan moved over to where Cygnus stood. "What makes her so dangerous?" he asked.

"Many things, but specifically her lack of concern for anyone or anything other than herself. She has passion, but it is not tempered with responsibility." The old monk nodded and looked back toward the building where Calderon was. He hoped the young man was okay.

—

Jovanna was laying low everyone that came against her. She was vaguely aware of her surroundings. Her sole focus was reaching that blasted creature. Her blade bit into the flesh of a soldier who got too close to her. Her shield was holding strong, but her strength was beginning to fail her. It was only adrenaline and anger driving her actions, causing her to move one foot in front of the other in a determined pace. She did take notice of the four guards of Palindrom moving to intercept her. She cursed silently, knowing she couldn't keep up her rampage.

She could see the prince, see him waving his men toward her. They didn't seem to want to obey, but their fear of him had them moving hesitantly toward her. The guards were also closing the distance. She was running out of options. She was tired of running. This was supposed to be her moment. She mustered her last bit of strength and hurled herself magically into the air, narrowly missing a rock launched from one of the few remaining catapults. Jovanna flew through the air, siphoning off some of the magic from her shield to give her the distance she needed. She landed a few feet away from the prince. His eyes widened when he saw what she held.

"Now I have you!" she shouted triumphantly. The possessed prince rushed her. She tossed the sphere onto the ground and watched as it began to glow. An unearthly growl issued from the man's mouth. Jovanna ducked as a spear was thrown at her from one of the nearby soldiers. The glowing sphere seemed to falter and change colors. "No!" she shouted, knowing the magic was not working properly. She came at the prince with her sword, slashing this way and that. Ranaan moved fast and dodged her attacks, sending his foot out to try and take out her knee. She managed to twist out of the way and avoid impaling herself on the sword of another soldier.

Lightning arced from the walls of the city, destroying the remaining war machines and blasting groups of soldiers aside. Blackened scorch marks littered the valley. Jovanna was trying to keep out of Ranaan's reach and get to the sphere to correct the magic.

Too late, she realized, as the sphere went dim. She rushed toward it only to be blown backward as the sphere erupted in a massive explosion. The blast leveled everything within a few hundred feet, blowing soldiers apart and scattering body parts. Ranaan barely seemed affected. Jovanna crashed to the ground and didn't move. All of time seemed to stand still as everyone slowly realized what happened. Cygnus was shouting orders, the generals of the army were dashing about madly, trying to organize the chaos that was their forces.

Cahenrair appeared on the battlefield not far from Jovanna's lifeless body. "Get back to the hellspawn you came here from," he said to Ranaan. The prince's face turned into a scowl and he glared at the elf. "Come, let me feast on your body," Ranaan said.

The elf pulled his sleeves up and began running his finger along the tattoos that covered his skin. Ranaan threw himself bodily into Cahenrair and the two crashed to the ground, punching each other and thrashing about. Cahenrair got to his feet, his robe twisted and caught from the struggle. He shrugged the robe off, revealing his tall slender body covered in nothing but a loincloth and many, many tattoos. The elf quickly traced his finger over several of the tattoos, enacting the magic.

A concussive blast of invisible force struck Ranaan as he was trying to get up. It knocked him backwards. As he closed the distance, the elf summoned more of his spells, one after another. Wicked looking green flames singed Ranaan's hair and face. Ranaan clawed at his skin, struggling to control the body of his host and keep the man's spirit at bay. "I can't do anything in this body!" he shouted.

Cahenrair quickly touched a couple of his tattoos, causing them all to come alive with a pale light. His body became wrapped in the same light and he wrapped his arms around Ranaan. "Let us see how you fare through this!"

His body exploded.

—

Jerik knelt beside Jovanna's body and felt for a pulse. Nothing. Everyone was distracted with the battle between Cahenrair and Ranaan. He placed his hand on her forehead and whispered a few words. He would take her body back with him. They both disappeared, just in time to miss the elf destroy himself and Ranaan.

The explosion sent blood and bone flying in all directions. The beast that had possessed Ranaan could feel his spirit fading. No, fading wasn't right. His soul was … breaking. He silently cursed the elf and his magic until his last moment of his conscious existence. The creature's soul dissipated into the wind.

- Calderon

25

CALDERON SAT ON THE EDGE of the bed, feeling a slight tremor here and there as the rocks from the war machines slammed into the walls. He felt out of place. He was not a wizard, and certainly no soldier, yet here he was, in the middle of an important battle. And somehow, he had managed to lose the sphere.

"At least things can't get much worse," he muttered to himself. He stood to stretch his legs and walked over to the window. He couldn't see the battle from his view, but he could hear it. He had never seen battle, but he had read books written by people who had. He could imagine the screams, visualize the bloody and wounded. It was enough to make him gag. He could never bring himself to kill another man. He heard something then, a slight rustling perhaps, that drew him from his contemplation. He turned to find a man in his room.

The man was of average height, pretty close to Calderon's. He wore robes like a monk, but they were black instead of brown. A hood was drawn over his face and he stood silently. "Yes?" Calderon asked. There came no reply. "Can I help you?"

The man reached up with thin, pale hands and pulled his hood back. Calderon almost gasped aloud. The man was bald, with a thin line of gray hair along his chin. His eyes were green and seemed slightly clouded. Calderon almost thought the man might be blind. Or at least not far from it. The thing that made him almost gasp was the jagged scar that covered the man's neck.

"Can you speak?" Calderon asked, his hands instinctively covering his own neck. The man nodded. "I can speak," he said, his voice a whisper. "Though not very well. I have come to bring you information that you may find valuable." Calderon was confused. Information? For what? "Would you like to sit down? The room is more for sleeping though." The man shook his head. "I do not have time," he replied. "You have heard of Orlek?"

Calderon nodded. "I have heard the name, and a little about him. To be honest, I don't know that I believe the stories. They seem like folklore to me." The man stared at him, his gaze like burning coals. Calderon shifted uncomfortably. "Stories? They are not mere stories," the man replied, stepping closer toward the monk. "They are realities. There is nothing that has been uttered about Orlek that is not true. And he lives still, even now, and plots the end of mankind."

Calderon backed up a step at the man drew near. "Who are you?" Calderon asked. Fear was beginning to make it hard to talk. The man waved a hand dismissively. "My name means nothing to you. Let me tell you my story, and then you can decide what you believe. This," he pointed at the scar on his neck, "is from a crossbow accident when I was a child. A hunter in our village accidentally shot me. I lived, but I had lost my voice. I studied magic in hopes of finding a way to heal myself. Unfortunately, magic does not heal as I found out later. Only Aio can heal, and I did not turn to him. I suppose I was talented, as the mysterious Guardians approached me with an offer to join them."

"The Guardians? Who are they?" Calderon asked. The man grunted. "Have you lived in a monastery your whole life? Everyone knows about the Guardians."

"I have lived in a monastery most of my life."

The man laughed then. It sounded more like wheezing to Calderon. "The Guardians are men, and some who are not men, who work to keep the balance of the world in order. They are few, but they are powerful, chosen by the leader of the Guardians for their talents, whether magical or otherwise. They cease to exist to the world, but are always behind the scenes, ensuring the balance. I was chosen to replace one who had died. I thought that if anyone could heal me, it would surely be the Guardians. Yet not even they could fix my voice," he seemed saddened suddenly, as if remembering it clearly. "I was upset and began to despair that I would never speak again."

"You speak now," Calderon said, pointing out the obvious. The man nodded. "One day, when I was in the mountains, I was approached by Orlek. I knew who he was and knew that he would bring nothing but trouble. I almost summoned the other Guardians so that we could defeat him, but he made me an offer that has become my biggest regret. He offered to give me my voice back."

"I thought magic cannot heal?"

"It can't. What Orlek did was beyond magic. It was …" his voice trailed off and his eyes shifted back and forth, as if seeing something. "It was something entirely different. I had only to gather some bones for him and he would give me my voice. It seemed simple enough, but I did not realize whose bones I was gathering."

"Bones?"

"Dragon bones," the man said. Realization struck Calderon suddenly. "You gathered the bones of the dragon for this Orlek?" The man nodded. "I did not know then what I was doing. I simply wanted to speak again. Once I saw what the bones were for, and saw the terrible destruction the creature caused, I regretted my actions every day. Orlek did give me my voice back, but it was not what I expected. I am here in front of you, and you can barely hear me."

It was true. Calderon found himself leaning toward the man to hear what he said. "Why are you telling me this?" The man suddenly seemed very old. "I seek to make amends for what I helped unleash. I have lived longer than any man, but my time grows near. I want to give you the knowledge that I have, that Orlek might be stopped. Forever this time."

"Why tell me? What can I do? I am no wizard." Calderon didn't like where this was going. "That is exactly why I have come to you. You do not crave power as wizards do. And when you traveled through the mountains, Orlek did not sense you."

"How did you know—" Calderon paused. He remembered the trip down the mountain, when he thought he saw someone from the corner of his eye only to find no one there. "You were there, on the mountain?" Calderon asked.

The man nodded. "I was there. I could feel the power of the old man that traveled with you, as well as the spirit of the other monk.

But I could not sense you, and neither could Orlek. I bring you this because I believe you can reach Orlek without him knowing you are there. And you can do what no one else has been able to do.”

“What is that?”

“You will kill Orlek.”

That put Calderon on his heels. “I have not killed anyone. I cannot kill anyone. I do not believe in murder.”

The man laughed again. “Do you believe in justice? Do you believe in doing what is right? Orlek seeks the destruction of mankind. Ever since his first defeat he has sought to annihilate man. If the death of one could save many, why would you not kill the one?”

Calderon couldn’t argue with the man’s logic. He did believe in justice. But he did not believe he was strong enough to carry it out. He could not be trusted with such an important task, especially not with his sleeping disorder. And then it dawned on him. His disorder had not reared its head since his watch at the Sly Mare. Was it possible that his disorder was gone? He was at a loss. He had struggled his entire life with falling asleep at the most inappropriate times, yet he hadn’t had any issues since the inn.

“I am not a soldier,” Calderon said. “I have no skills, no talents. This is not something you should entrust to me.” The man nodded. “That is why I know you will succeed. Orlek will never see you coming.”

Calderon sat in silence. He had no more argument in him. He could not deny that if Orlek could not sense him, he might really be able to get close enough to strike him down. But what if Orlek did sense him? What if Orlek killed him? Velkyn’s words echoed in his mind: Are you ready to make that sacrifice, if it comes? To give your life for others?

He sighed resignedly. “What must I do?”

26

THE FORCE OF THE BLAST that destroyed the body of the prince shook the earth. Most of the men of the Talvaard army were flung to the ground. Donovan and the men on the wall grabbed onto whatever they could to keep from falling.

"What just happened?" Donovan yelled, his ears ringing from the blast. Cygnus didn't answer. The half-blood wasn't sure himself. The army would have gone into complete chaos if not for the generals. Cygnus motioned Donovan to come near. "We must parlay," he said. "With the prince gone, the army is in the hands of the generals. We must convince them we are no threat."

Donovan agreed. "Take my bodyguards," Cygnus said, pointing at the two tattooed elves that stood close to him. I'll raise the flag." Donovan took the stairs down to the courtyard and waited at the gates. Cygnus had the flag raised and waited for the sign to be returned. It was.

The gates opened and Donovan headed out, escorted by the elves. By the time he reached the tent that had the flag flying, several of the generals had already gathered. He bowed when he reached them, giving the proper respect as protocol demanded. The generals bowed back. "It is our desire to see you leave in peace," Donovan said. "Palindrom is a city of peace, not of war. We take no issue with you, and ask that you hold the same toward us."

One of the generals, an old veteran, took the lead. "We didn't want to march in the first place," he said. Donovan sighed in relief. "Our men just want to go home. We agree that there is no qualms between yours and ours. We honestly don't know what happened to the king. It seems he lost his mind in the end." The general seemed bitter. A horn sounded out from the army, startling everyone in the tent. A messenger came stumbling in, sweaty and breathing hard.

"Calm yourself," the general said. "Get him some water." Someone handed the messenger a water skin. He drank deeply and paused to catch his breath. "We have enemies approaching," he gasped. "Orcs! Thousands of them! They cut off our supply lines in the mountains and are marching this way now!" His legs gave out and he collapsed. Several men lifted him up and carried him out of the tent. The general looked to Donovan, troubled.

"Orcs?" he asked aloud, looking to his fellows, then back to Donovan. "I haven't heard of Orcs in the mountains." Donovan shook his head. "I have heard a lot of things lately. It wouldn't hurt to be prepared. I'll report to Cygnus and get word back to you. We can use our magic to confirm the report." The general seemed pleased with that and dismissed the monk.

He ran back to the gate, the elves following him without question. Donovan could hear the generals roaring out orders behind him. It seemed one battle had ended, only for another to begin. Cygnus was waiting for him in the courtyard. "They are leaving?" he asked Donovan.

"Not quite. We need someone to use the crystals. A man reported an army of Orcs marching from the mountains." Elves rarely ever showed emotion, and Cygnus, though he was a half blood, was no exception. So it surprised Donovan to see the color drain from his face. "Orlek makes his move," Cygnus said ominously. "So it is here, before the walls of Palindrom, that the fate of our world will be decided. Come, we must prepare." Cygnus turned and left. Donovan looked to some of the guards standing nearby. "Get someone to use the crystals, will you?" One of them nodded and left.

Donovan followed Cygnus back onto the walls. "The Talvaard army is between us and whatever is coming. What is there to prepare for?" Donovan asked, looking to Cygnus. The half-blood stared out at the valley. "They cannot stop what is coming. The Orcs will overrun them and hit our walls with ease. Orlek is leading them, and he cannot be stopped. We can fight and hope to dwindle their numbers, or we can run. But I see no victory in either option."

Donovan started to respond but stopped short when he noticed Calderon making his way through the courtyard. The young monk made his way up the stairs to stand beside Donovan. "It isn't safe out here. You should go back inside."

Calderon shook his head. "There is something I must do. But I will need help."

—

Calderon stood at the entrance to the cave. They had flown him on the winds of magic to the mountains. It was the only way to get there quickly and safely. He only hoped the magic didn't give him away. The man had told him there were symbols etched into the walls that would help him find his way into the main chamber of the cave. He stared into the darkness. Taking a deep breath, he plunged into the darkness. The air was cooler inside the cave, an immediate difference from the outside. The robed man had warned him not to light a torch.

That was severely going to hinder him, but there was no way around it. Calderon put his hands on the walls and felt along the cool stone for the symbols. After traveling a few feet, he found the first symbol. The first step toward the chamber, the last step to his destiny.

—

Cygnus and Donovan watched the battle unfold in the valley below. The Orcs had come storming into the valley, hacking and slashing at the Talvaard army. The soldiers were holding their own, but they were steadily being pressed back. "Their line isn't going to hold," Cygnus remarked. "We may have to open the gates and let them into the city. What do you think?" he turned to Donovan.

"Do we have enough room? There are many men."

Cygnus nodded. "There are many, but a lot have fallen, and countless more will fall before it is over, I fear. We can only hope Calderon knows what he is doing." The Talvaard line of defense began to crumble. Chaos erupted and a retreat had been signaled. "Open the gates!" Cygnus yelled.

The guards obeyed and opened the massive gates. The soldiers began to run into the city. "What do we do now?" Donovan asked.

"We wait."

"I am left with the feeling that war solves nothing, that to win a war is as disastrous and costly as losing one."

- Donovan

27

THE AIR SMELLED OF MOLD. A few times, his hand had touched something wet and he would quickly jerk his hand away. Calderon was beginning to think he was lost within the tunnels of the cave. He didn't know which way went where, and he hadn't felt a symbol in any of the walls recently. He was about to turn around when he turned a corner and felt a horrible sensation in his stomach that made the hairs on his arm raise.

He could see nothing. He didn't hear anything either. Yet the feeling was there, as if something lurked around him, waiting to devour him. He breathed as quietly as he could and listened. Still nothing.

He slowly took a step. And another. His hand felt the wall curve away from him, out of his reach. He hoped he wasn't about to step off into a deep hole. He took a few more steps. And then he heard it. At first, he thought it was the echo from his breathing. But Calderon wasn't rasping. The sound could be coming from anywhere in the chamber, he realized. And he was blind in the darkness. How would he see what it was, and if it was Orlek, how would he see him to attack him?

A voice froze him in his tracks. "I hear you scurrying, rat. Come to me and let me feast on your flesh." The voice was weak. Calderon thought the voice was speaking to him, but discovered that thankfully it was not. The voice was talking to what it thought was a rat moving about the cave.

Could the weak voice be Orlek, the magic-wielding Orc? Judging by the voice, Calderon figured him to be weak and near death. How could something so weak pose such a threat to the people? He shrugged his doubts away. He had seen the army of Orcs marching into the valley. He steeled his nerves and forced himself in the direction he thought the voice came from.

He nearly tripped. He yelled at himself in his mind, listening. He could hear something shuffling around, coming nearer. His hands began to shake. Calderon didn't know what to do. He didn't want to risk injuring himself, but what if Orlek realized he wasn't a rat? He forced himself to calm down. Pulling the dagger that the robed man had given him out from his belt, he clenched the hilt tightly in his hand.

He heard the voice muttering something unintelligible. There was no other way around it. Calderon pulled out a flat stone that Cygnus had given him. The man told him not to use any light, but he couldn't see a blasted thing. He tossed the stone into the air and it lit up, momentarily blinding him. He heard a screech and gained his vision back enough in time to see something flying toward him. They crashed to the ground in a heap, and something was clawing at Calderon. The blade fell from his hand and he lashed out with his fists, pummeling with all his might.

He managed to push the thing away and scrambled to his feet. He saw the glint of metal in the dim light and quickly retrieved the blade. Whatever had attacked him was hiding in the corner, where the light didn't reach. Calderon cautiously made his way toward the shadows. The creature came hobbling out toward him. If this was Orlek, the creature was far from intimidating. It was thin and skinny. Its skin was reddish-brown and hung loosely from its frame. Scraggly long black hair covered its head. Two large teeth jutted up from its bottom jaw, protruding from its lips.

The creature was certainly ugly, but nothing frightening. Calderon held the blade out in front of him in an attempt to keep the thing at bay. It seemed to work as the creature paused, looking at the blade intently. "Where did you get that?" the creature rasped.

"From one you drew into your dark scheme," Calderon answered, using the phrase the robed man had told him. The creature laughed, a guttural, raucous noise. "I used him as I have used so many others," Orlek said. "I told that fool the magic was unpredictable at best. It was never meant for humans. Why have you come here?"

Calderon fought the feeling of despair. It was thick, palpable. "I have come to kill you," he said. Orlek laughed again. "I have died many times. You may kill me, and you may not. Though if you do, what good will it do? I will merely rise from the grave once again."

Calderon shook his head. "Not this time." He lunged forward, attempting to stab Orlek in the chest. Orlek was weak and his body was deteriorating, but he was not slow. The orc leaped out of the way, turned around, and slugged the monk in the shoulder. Calderon tumbled to the ground under the forceful blow, scraping his hands and knees on the rocky floor of the cave.

Orlek needed a new body. What kind of havoc could he create if he took the body of a man? The thought repulsed him. Maybe he would just kill the human and eat him. He shambled over to the man. Calderon slashed Orlek across his foot. The orc cried out in pain but did not flee. Calderon got to his knees and rammed his shoulder into the creature, forcing Orlek to trip and fall backwards. Calderon was on him quickly, straddling the orc. Orlek moved his arms frantically, trying to push the man off of him. His strength was failing him.

Calderon forced his left arm under Orlek's arms and pushed them up, leaning forward and using his weight to hold them up. His brought his right hand in, still holding the dagger, and plunged the blade into the orc's chest. Orlek howled in anguish, and Calderon withdrew the blade and stabbed again and again. A rush of anger and emotions swirled within the young monk. Anger at this creature for causing so much evil, anger that he had lost his friend Velkyn to madness, anger at the men who raped Velkyn's woman and stole their belongings.

He stabbed Orlek again and again, losing himself in his anger. Orlek had long since stopped moving, his blood a massive pool around his body. By the time Calderon came to his senses, he had stabbed the orc more than a dozen times. He sat atop the dead orc, his breath coming in heaving gasps. When he had caught his breath, he pulled himself off Orlek's body and grabbed the dagger. There was one thing the man had told him was of extreme importance, otherwise Orlek could bring himself back to life. Calderon grabbed hold of the orc's hand and pressed the blade into the armpit, severing the arm. He began removing Orlek's limbs, one by one.

He had almost finished when the light of the magical stone began to sputter and crackle. Calderon looked at the stone, still hovering in the air. The light would start to dim and then flare up briefly dimming once again.

Calderon realized too late. That was no ordinary light. Calderon flung the limbs in different directions, grabbed Orlek's head by the hair, and ran toward the tunnel that brought him into the chamber. The light dimmed, then faded altogether. And then it exploded. Calderon crashed to the ground, smashing his head onto the rocks of the cave floor. Darkness, silent and comforting, took him.

—

Donovan watched the soldiers of Talvaard. They had snuck out of the back gate of the city and split into two groups, each group heading around the city and toward the front. They were going to try and route the orc army that had gathered at the front of the city. "They are outnumbered," Donovan remarked to Cygnus. "It was not my decision," the half-blood said. "The generals decided it amongst themselves."

Donovan knew that. He just felt obligated to say something to try and stop them. It was a suicide mission. "Do you think Calderon will succeed?" he said aloud, not really asking anyone.

Cygnus didn't say anything. He hadn't taken his gaze off the mountains for the last twenty minutes. "They seem to be waiting," Donovan said. Cygnus nodded. "They await the right opportunity. Probably nightfall," the half-blood answered. A rumbling sound like that of thunder filled the air. All eyes, including the orcs', went to the sky. The Viss mountain, it appeared, had exploded. Dust and debris filled the air and tremors shook the ground.

"Orlek is dead," Cygnus said incredulously. "He did it. Calderon slew Orlek!" Donovan was just as surprised. He noticed the Talvaard soldiers had taken the advantage of the disturbance to launch their attack against the orcs.

The creatures might have outnumbered them, but they didn't stand a chance. The route was working and the orcs began to scatter. "The four winds take them," Donovan cursed. He looked back to the mountain. "What of Calderon? Why did the mountain explode? Where is he?" his tone was frantic.

Cygnus laid his hand on Donovan's shoulder. "It is unlikely we will see him again. Take comfort in his sacrifice, my friend. Because of him, many will live." Donovan burst into tears. His eyes blurred. He could barely see the orcs fleeing the field in all directions. "It's over," he vaguely heard Cygnus say. "It's finally over."

Donovan was going to miss the young monk. He had really grown fond of him. He slumped down with his back against the wall. "What now?" he asked, his tone pleading. Cygnus knelt beside him. "Now?" The half-blood paused and looked across the city. "Now, we work toward peace."

EPILOGUE

JOVANNA OPENED HER EYES. HER body was throbbing with pain and she couldn't see from her left eye. She attempted to sit up but the pain was too much. She slumped back down. She lifted her left hand, excruciating pain lancing through the limb. Her skin was splotched black and red. It was slimy looking and appeared to be covered in some kind of salve. She reached over to feel it with her right hand.

"Don't touch it."

The voice startled her. She looked the other way and saw an old man standing there. "It's my arm. I'll touch it if I want." The old man smiled and shrugged. "I'm only trying to help."

He seemed familiar to her for some reason. "Where am I?" Jovanna asked. The old man drew near to her. "You are safe. Do you remember what happened?" She stared at him with her good eye. She tried to remember, but all she got was a swirling mass of fog in her brain. "I rescued you from a battlefield," he said.

A battlefield … she tried to remember. "There was an army," she said softly, trying to piece the fragments of memory together. "A city." It all came back to her. Her eyes widened. "The dragon in the prince! I had the sphere …" she went quiet, looking at the man distrustfully.

He nodded knowingly. "I know. I was there. Like I said, I rescued you from the battle. My name is Jerik. And I know you are Jovanna. I have heard many things about you and your unique gift. Perhaps when you feel better we can talk more about why you are here."

Jovanna rolled onto her side to better see the man. "Jerik," she whispered. She had seen him before. In the forest, talking with another man. "I saw you," she said. "In the woods with another ..." she glanced about the room. Jerik smiled. "Yes. You are coming back better than I expected."

"Back? From where? Was I dead?" she asked, confused.

"Nearly," he answered. "Your soul was on the fringes of your body. I managed to coax your soul to come back."

"Why would you help me? No one has ever helped me," she said pitifully, a single tear sliding down her cheek.

"We will talk more about this when you are feeling better," he bade gently. "Get some rest, Jovanna. And welcome," he added. He turned to leave the room.

"Welcome to what?" she called out.

"To the Guardians," he answered. Then he turned and left.

THE END OF BOOK 1

THE FALLEN KING

"Darkness gathers in the West. It is approaching ... and there is no escape."

—A beggar on the streets

1

"YOU LOOK RIDICULOUS," ARAMIS SCOFFED.

Melchiades gasped in offense. "I will have you know that this is the current style in the court of your father." Aramis's attendant, and best friend, was constantly changing his wardrobe to mimic the nobles. "You look like a bird, Mel. Take that thing off."

Melchiades wore a medium-sized black hat with massive green plumed feathers that rose up from the back of the hat like some sort of sprouting plant. Mel shook his head indignantly and sputtered, which made him look even more like a giant peacock. Aramis burst into laughter and pointed to the door that led out of his personal quarters.

"I can't take you seriously. Now go and do something about your hat. I will meet you in the courtyard when I am ready." Mel sighed but did as he was ordered. When Mel had shut the door behind him, Aramis stripped his clothes off and tossed them onto the floor. The maidservants would gather them in the morning. They were muddy and smelled of sweat, the byproduct of his earlier escapades.

He stepped in front of the ornately decorated mirror that hung upon the wall next to his closet door and examined his reflection. His brown hair had lightened considerably in the last few weeks. His time outside with the soldiers must have had something to do with that. Stray hairs were beginning to grow along his jawline and chin. *I need to shave,* he thought.

He flexed his left arm, and then his right. They certainly looked larger. His abs didn't show, but he knew they would take longer to appear. A light yellow and green splotch the size of a fist mottled the skin below his right shoulder, just above his nipple. He gingerly touched it and winced at the pain. He had fallen from a horse and landed chest-first onto a rock.

It was a minor injury, but it was still sore. He hadn't bothered the court physicians with it, though his mother would be furious if she found out. He was the only son of the king, and she doted on him. He stepped into the closet and frowned. Mel had chosen something equally hideous for him to wear. "I don't think so," he muttered. Aramis grabbed a plain blue tunic and a pair of black pants. He liked simplicity, something that couldn't be said of Mel.

Melchiades was the son of a noble whose estate was on the edge of Oakvalor's eastern border. Some small house of nobility that he wasn't familiar with. He had arrived two years previous with instruction to serve the king in any way deemed appropriate. His father had plenty of servants, and so ordered Mel to attend his son.

Aramis had hated him at first. His ridiculous clothing, his odd accent, and his ardent faith in a god Aramis had never heard of. Over time, however, he began to respect the man. He was just as skilled, perhaps more so, than his father's finest soldiers and had a keen intelligence for matters of state. He didn't care for Mel's faith, but he admired his loyalty. Mel never skipped his private prayer time.

He slipped his freshly polished boots on and checked the mirror again. Nodding in satisfaction, he walked over to the window. His room was at the top of the keep and afforded him a magnificent view. Dusk was quickly approaching, and the lights of the city were beginning to burst forth into life. There was a ball tonight to celebrate his father's thirtieth year of reign, as well as Aramis's eighteenth year since birth.

Sadness welled up inside him as he thought about the day that should be joyous. His beautiful sister would not be present. The traitorous younger prince of Talvaard had murdered her, along with his own brother, before the two kingdoms could be sealed with peace by her marriage to the new king of Talvaard. His eyes filled with tears. He reached up and quickly wiped them away.

The sounds of the city below faintly reached his ears, pulling his mind away from the dark thoughts. He could barely make out the men returning from the mines. The smell of cooking fires and the meals they boasted made his mouth water. It reminded him of the roasted deer that was waiting at the ball.

He turned from the window and quickly left his room. Aramis

didn't care much for the political nonsense that usually overshadowed his father's parties. The nobles were like a bunch of spoiled toddlers, whining and sniveling when they didn't get their way. And if there was one thing Aramis couldn't stomach, it was whining.

The hallway was a long corridor that stretched from the Royal Wing—where his father's chambers were—to the massive winding staircase known as the Circle that led down to the throne room. Aramis made his way toward the Circle. The walls of the hall were lavishly decorated, with giant richly colored tapestries and murals by famed artists throughout the land.

He passed a few guards who were stationed in the hall to keep curious guests from exploring the restricted areas of the castle. They stiffened at his approach and saluted as he passed. "Prince Aramis," they greeted formally.

Aramis nodded absently, thinking about the food that awaited him. He descended the Circle with measured steps, careful not to trip on the bright red runners that carpeted each stair. Despite the many servants who had toppled down the Circle, his father refused to have them removed.

He reached the bottom of the Circle and was greeted by Mel. "What are you wearing?" he demanded. "I picked out the best design for you to wear, and you come out wearing *that!*" Mel shook his head, which caused the feathers to sway back and forth.

Aramis smiled. "You know I don't like your taste in clothing if that's what you call it."

Mel feigned a look of anger and turned around as Aramis passed, escorting him out of the keep and into the courtyard. The sky had darkened considerably. A line of fire bowls glowed brightly, leading the way across the stone courtyard to the auxiliary building where his father always held his parties.

"It's going to be a smashing evening," Mel remarked enthusiastically. Aramis grunted in response. Mel gave him a sideways glance. "Did you invite Hanna to accompany you tonight?"

"Of course not," Aramis replied.

"Why not? I thought she rather enjoyed the royal parties?"

"Exactly. I don't want her to *expect* my invitations. I'm not sure where things between us are going, anyway."

"Your father likes her," Mel said with a grin.

"My father likes any pretty girl with money who shows an interest in his son. He has a legacy to think about."

"So, you wouldn't be terribly upset if she just happened to come of her own accord?" Mel asked, turning his gaze away from Aramis suspiciously.

"You didn't!"

"I would *never*," Mel breathed, aghast.

"Blast you, Mel. She won't leave me alone for weeks after tonight. Sometimes I don't know why I put up with you."

Mel laughed. "Please announce the prince," he instructed a servant who stood beside one of the fire bowls. The young man bowed and ran ahead of them. "Did you have to do that as well?"

"It's protocol," Mel answered.

"Now everyone will know I've arrived."

"That's the general idea."

Aramis sighed. "I hate the nobles."

"Hate is a strong word, don't you think?"

"Fine. I *dislike* the nobles. I won't put up with their petty complaints when I am king."

Mel didn't bother responding. Two large wooden doors were pushed open by several guards as they approached. Mel took the lead and entered first. A loud cheer rang out as Aramis entered. A wave of heat immediately hit him. With so many bodies in one place and no windows for ventilation, the heat was stifling.

Aramis spent the next hour talking to the many aristocrats who served in his father's court. It was completely un-enjoyable, but he suffered through it for the sake of his father's reputation. He couldn't care less what they thought about himself.

When he had finished exchanging pleasantries with the nobles, he made his way to the bar and began to partake of the various wines and liquors, mixing them with abandon. Aramis was vaguely aware of his father retiring from the party, not unusual for him. He might be healthy for his age, but he was no longer a young man.

Mel was participating in some new popular dance with several people, all wearing similar ridiculous looking hats. He would never understand 'fashion'.

"There you are," Hanna's familiar voice sounded beside him. He downed another cup of whatever he was drinking and turned to face her.

She was beautiful. Her long hair was a light blonde color and reached past the middle of her back. Her eyes were a brilliant blue, the bluest he had ever seen. That was one of the things that initially attracted him to her.

"Hannah," he said, smiling dumbly. Something in the back of his mind told him to keep his mouth shut, but he didn't listen. "I was hoping you'd be here."

No, I wasn't.

She gave him an enormous smile. His heart began to beat quickly. Inhibitions were all but gone, it seemed. She leaned in close to him and whispered, "I have a gift for you in honor of your life celebration."

"If it includes you, I can't wait to have it."

Why did I say that?

She blushed and shook her head. She held up a small wooden box. He hadn't even noticed she had anything in her hand. He accepted it from her and fumbled clumsily with it before opening the thing. Inside was a silver pendant inscribed with his family's crest: an oak tree with three branches. They represented the ideals his family strived for. Courage, honor, and justice.

"Thank you," he breathed. "It's beautiful. Like you." He allowed her to clasp it around his neck, then he ran the fingers of his right hand through her hair. Her smell was more intoxicating than any alcohol he'd ever tasted.

"My Prince," Mel interrupted. "It's time to retire for the evening."

Aramis sighed. Mel was a blessing to him, as well as a curse. "You're interrupting Hanna," Aramis informed him. He turned his attention to his friend and winked. "You should retire without me," he whispered. Or at least he thought he whispered. Everyone nearby could hear him.

"It's quite all right," Hanna interjected. "I'll see you later." Aramis wasn't sure if she was stating a fact or asking a question. She curtsied and took her leave. "You're a killjoy sometimes, you know that?"

Mel grinned in reply. "I'm protecting you from yourself. Someone has to when you fill yourself with this stuff. Did you eat anything?"

Aramis shook his head. He had forgotten about food with all the nobles buzzing around him. Mel disappeared through the crowd of people and returned a few minutes later with a plate full of venison. "Eat this and then you can retire from the festivities."

Aramis grabbed a piece of the meat and stuffed it into his mouth. "The night has hardly begun. Why would I retire now?" he asked.

"I knew you would forget," Mel said. "You told your father you would go on the hunt with him tomorrow. And the night is later than you realize. It's after midnight."

Aramis cursed under his breath. "I did forget. Blast it, Mel! I hate going on those boring hunts. Sitting around for hours, listening to old men recount exaggerated tales of their 'glory days'. I prefer a *real* opponent. One who thinks and reacts. Not an animal that walks into a trap."

"I can imagine," Mel replied. Aramis cleared the plate and drank another cup of wine. "I think I will retire now."

Mel escorted him through the throng of people and to the doors they entered through earlier. Just as before, several guards pushed the doors open and saluted the prince. Mel thanked them for their service and led Aramis along the lighted path back to the keep.

"Should I assist you to your chambers?" he asked. Aramis waved his hand dismissively. "I'm not needy like my father," he answered. "I'll see you in the morning. And for mercy's sake, wear something practical tomorrow."

Mel bowed low in response.

Aramis left him behind as he entered the keep and ascended the Circle. The guards he'd passed earlier were no longer present. His father had probably released them earlier. He meandered along the hallway, humming an old song his mother used to sing to him.

Reaching his room, he paused and briefly considered going back down to the party. Perhaps Hanna would still be there …

He decided not to. It would be hard enough to get up already. Aramis entered his room. He kicked off his boots, neither landing near the other. He pulled his tunic over his head and tossed it to the floor.

Something glinted in the mirror as he passed it. He stopped to look and realized it was the pendant around his neck. He had already forgotten Hanna had given it to him. He admired it in the mirror. She was a clever one. Now he had to give her a gift, which would be seen as a move of official courting.

"I have no idea what I should get her," he muttered. He walked over to his window and opened it, letting the cool breeze in. Maybe it was the alcohol, but he was burning up.

He spied his father's window. Light shone from the room and he could see his father's servants fawning over him and preparing him for bed. If he could hardly stand Mel doing it for him now, what would it be like when he became king?

Aramis pushed the thoughts from his mind. His father was healthy and strong, unlikely to pass the crown down anytime soon. And that didn't bother Aramis one bit.

He was about to turn and climb into bed when he noticed something unusual from the corner of his eye. Leaning forward, he squinted and tried to see better. It looked like a shadow. It hovered in one spot for a moment, then shifted upward. It was almost like a pattern. Hover, shift.

"What is that?" he whispered to himself. As though fate had timed it perfectly, the moon illuminated the shadow for just a moment. It was a man. Yet why would a man be scaling the side of the …

Assassin!

Aramis turned and dashed across his room. As fear swept through him, he began to sober up. He threw the door open and dashed past a few startled servants. He sprinted through the hallway, his heavy footsteps muffled by the thick rugs that lined the floor. He glanced down every side passage, looking for guards. He didn't see any.

"Guards!" he shouted, "Guards! To the King's chambers!" He had no idea if anyone heard him. He ran faster, his legs burning from the effort. Two massive wooden doors separated the Royal Wing from the rest of the keep. Normally there were two guards positioned here, but he saw no one. What was going on? The doors were heavy, but he threw himself bodily into one, sending lances of pain through his bruised chest.

The door swung open slowly, just enough for him to squeeze through. And then he was running through the Royal Wing, his breath coming in ragged gasps. Was it possible the assassin had made it into his father's room yet? He didn't know. A lone soldier stood guard beside his father's door. Aramis almost slammed into him before stopping his momentum.

"Where … are the … others?" Aramis demanded, sucking precious air into his lungs.

"My lord?"

"Get … reinforcements! Hurry!"

The guard seemed confused. Aramis grabbed the soldier's sword and shoved him out of the way. "Do as I command! Get reinforcements!"

The guard bowed hastily and ran off down the corridor. Aramis kicked the door twice before it opened, splintering the wood and breaking the latch mechanism. He strode into the room to find his father—and the servants—staring at him in surprise.

"What is the meaning of this, Aramis?" the king demanded.

"Father! Step away from the window!"

"Have you gone mad, boy? What are you doing?"

Aramis rushed to the window and looked down. He didn't see anything or anyone. He pulled the window closed and locked it. "Father, I saw a man climbing the wall. He was clothed in black. It was an assassin, I'm sure of it. Did anyone come in through the window?" he asked the servants. They were looking at him as if he were crazy, but they all shook their heads.

Perhaps he had made it in time.

"A man climbing the … impossible! Aramis, what's going on? Are you drunk? Where are your cloth—?" Aramis cut him off mid-sentence. "I'm telling you, I saw someone from my window climbing the keep. Where are your guards?"

"What are you talking about? They are outside."

"There was only one soldier out there." Aramis's mind was racing. "I think you are in danger. We should go."

"In danger of who? We are not at war."

Aramis went to the door and peered down the hallway. *Where are they?*

"I beg to differ," an unfamiliar voice said. Aramis spun about and saw a strange man among the servants. His father kept only female attendants. The man brandished a dagger. "Kings always have enemies."

"Drop it," Aramis warned. He held the sword up before him and slowly advanced toward the man. The servants squealed in terror and scrambled to get out of the way.

"Why would I do that?" the man replied. "That just wouldn't be fair." The assassin rushed the king. Aramis threw himself into a roll and came up onto his feet in front of his father, deflecting the man's dagger with his sword. He launched a series of furious thrusts at the man, all of which the assassin managed to avoid. He could hear a commotion in the hallway and was relieved to know the guards were coming.

"You've failed," Aramis said triumphantly. "The guards will be here in a moment and you will be hanged at once."

The assassin flashed a smile at him. "That may be." Then the man rushed him. Aramis swung the sword as fast as he could, but he couldn't match the assassin's speed. He received several nicks along his left arm. The servants fled out into the hall, screaming as they ran.

Just a few more moments.

The assassin attempted to slide past his left, but Aramis stopped the man with an awkward swing of his sword. Seeming to anticipate the move, the assassin halted his momentum and pivoted, using Aramis's body as leverage to propel himself past the prince's right.

Aramis turned too late to catch the man, and the man lunged at the king with the dagger, trying to land a killing blow. His father was no novice to battle, however. He ducked down and grabbed the assassin's wrist, twisting it and jabbing the man's elbow with his palm. The dagger clanged harmlessly to the floor.

"Who sent you?" the king inquired angrily.

The assassin smiled again. "Wouldn't you like to know, *Your Majesty?*" The man used the title sarcastically. Aramis could hear the rattle of the soldiers' armor.

Any moment.

He held the sword out and pressed the tip of the blade against the man's side. "If you move, I'll gut you," he promised. "Answer my father's question. Who sent you?"

"It should be obvious," the man responded, "You know him."

The assassin deftly slipped his hand out of the king's grasp and slapped the flat of the sword blade hard, jerking the hilt out of Aramis's hand. In a fluid movement more graceful than anything Aramis had ever seen, the assassin grabbed the sword and drove it into the king's chest. Blood spurt forth and the king cried out in agony.

Aramis's eyes widened in horror and he lunged for the assassin. The man stepped out of his reach and landed a solid blow to his jaw. Aramis staggered back from the force and tried to maintain his balance. The assassin retrieved the dagger from the floor.

"Now your hell begins," the man said. The assassin pointed to Aramis's left arm and muttered something in a strange language. An intense burning flared through his arm. And then the assassin's cape fell to the floor and the man was gone.

Aramis didn't believe his eyes. Did the man *disappear*? He rushed to his father's side and grabbed the hilt of the blade. "Don't die, father. We'll get you to the healers. I promise!"

A contingent of guards entered the room. "He's killed the king," one of them shouted, "Seize him!" Confusion swept over Aramis like a cold ocean wave.

I didn't kill him! His mouth wouldn't work.

The soldier who he'd ordered to get help walked up to him and shook his head. "You killed him with my sword?" The soldier kicked him in the face. He collapsed onto the floor and there was only darkness.

"One decision does not define a man. Though it certainly changes him."

—Prince Aramis

2

Aramis opened his eyes.

His head was throbbing. His mouth was dry, as well as his throat. The revelry from the night before, most likely. He tried to sit up but found his wrists bound at his sides by manacles.

"What the …?" the words were barely more than a whimper. His head rolled to the left. It was dark. Mostly. As his eyes adjusted to the gloom, he noticed a dim light flittering at the edge of his vision. His right eye felt swollen and he couldn't see clearly out of it. He surveyed his surroundings. Stone walls and a metal gate.

Where am I?

Aramis tried to jerk his arm free, resulting in pain shooting through his wrist. His hand was wet and sticky with something, but he wasn't sure what. He forced himself to calm down and breath. That was probably the only thing that didn't cause him pain.

His thoughts were groggy. He remembered the ball. The nobles, Mel's outlandish dancing. He also remembered drinking. How could he forget that? Going back to his room, though, that was merely fuzziness. The cool air of the strange room brought his attention to the fact that he wasn't wearing a shirt.

I remember talking it off … I looked out the window … the window!

The memory washed over him, overwhelming him with the horrifying knowledge that his father was dead. The tears stung his swollen eye, but he couldn't hold them back. He sobbed for long moments before regaining control of his emotions.

The man who had killed his father would pay. He would send the armies out to hunt the assassin down. Aramis vowed to himself that he would personally kill the man responsible.

With his father dead, that meant that he was now the king. A terrible weight settled over him. He knew one day the throne would be his responsibility, but not now. Not like this. He thought he could hear voices. They spoke quietly, and he couldn't make out their words.

Aramis continued staring in the direction of the light, trying to determine where he was. He had no idea whether it was morning or night. He didn't recognize anything. The sound of jingling keys startled him. The metal gate swung open and an indistinct form stepped inside.

"You're awake," an unfamiliar voice said. The tone was gruff and reminded him of the soldiers he spent his days with. "It's about time. He must have roughed you up good."

"Who?" Aramis tried to say, but his throat was too dry and constricted to manage more than a mumble. A fit of coughing overwhelmed him. "Save your energy," the man bade him. "You'll need it. You can believe that."

There was something about the way the man said those words that unsettled him. What did he mean? The man came close and knelt down beside him. Aramis couldn't make out the man's features in the darkness. The man was fidgeting with something.

"The blasted thing is stuck," he muttered to himself. An earsplitting screech caused Aramis to flinch. The bed he was manacled to begun to rise.

After a minute or so, he was completely vertical. Were it not for his bindings, he felt as though he would have fallen onto the floor. At the bottom of the bed, where his feet were, was a thin metal lip that rose off the bed. His feet rested on it, which kept them from dragging on the floor.

Then he was rolling toward the gate. The bed had wheels. That was interesting. The man rolled him out of the room and into a short narrow hallway. He could see now the light that had caught his eye before was only a torch on the wall, one of a few that were spaced irregularly along the hall. He was wheeled down the hall and to the left, into a similar room. This one had an open doorway; no gate.

A brazier filled with burning coals gave the room a reddish hue. The man left him facing the glow of the brazier. Aramis didn't mind at all. It felt good. He hadn't realized before, but he was shivering. The warmth was a welcome indeed.

"Sit tight," the man said. "He'll be along shortly."

Aramis considered responding but decided not to waste his breath. The man probably wouldn't answer anyway. He gazed at the glittering coals for what felt like hours, though how much time had truly passed he couldn't guess. Time ceased to have meaning in the darkness. The sound of heavy footsteps echoing through the hall broke his reverie.

"Lord Aramis."

The use of his name gave him pause. Wherever he was, this man recognized him. The new person came around and stood in front of Aramis. The angles of his face were sharp and defined. His hair was black; his eyes light gray. He stood as tall as Aramis, though the prince was at least a foot off the ground in his wheeled bed.

The man offered a slight bow. He seemed to analyze Aramis with a critical eye for a moment, then turned to one of two tables that stood to each side of the brazier. A silver carafe and a wooden cup were the only adornments. The other table was covered with a white cloth. The man lifted the carafe and poured a liquid into the cup.

He exchanged the carafe for the cup, then turned back to Aramis. He lifted the cup to Aramis's lips, but Aramis refused to open his mouth. It was probably poison. "It's water," the man said as if reading his mind. "Drink."

Aramis hesitated, then allowed his lips to part far enough for the man to pour the liquid into his mouth. The water was cool and refreshing, soothing his dry throat. He could feel the water run down his esophagus and into his stomach. It was an odd feeling. He drank the entire cup. "More?" the man asked.

Aramis shook his head. "Where am I?" he asked softly.

"You are in the keep. The dungeon, specifically."

The dungeon? "Why?"

The man seemed surprised at the question. "For murdering your father—the King—of course."

"I didn't …" Aramis sighed. "I didn't kill my father. Why would I?"

"I was hoping you would tell *me* that," the man answered. "There are several witnesses who say they came upon the scene. You had your hand on the weapon. A sword you took from one of your father's guards, I believe. Do you deny it?"

"I deny killing my father, yes. If I had my hand on the sword, I don't remember. There was a man who scaled the wall of the keep. *He* killed my father."

The man folded his arms across his chest. "You expect me to believe a man climbed the walls of the castle? That's a task I would say is impossible. And your father's wizards have warded the entire castle against magic."

"I thought the same. But it happened. I saw it with my own eyes. I ran to my father's room to warn him, but the assassin had already entered through the window when I arrived." His throat was constricting. "May I have some more water?"

The man nodded and refilled the cup. Aramis downed it all. The water intensified his feeling of hunger. "Suppose someone was able to do as you say. Where then did he go?"

"After he stabbed my father, I tried to attack him. He eluded me and then … then he disappeared. I don't understand it myself," he said, seeing the doubt evident on the man's face.

"There are two types of people in this world," the man said. "Those who hide the truth, and those who reveal it. I am of the latter of the two. My name is Jarn, and I have a long list of truths I have revealed. The tale you have crafted is a clever one, I will grant you that. But I will get the truth out of you, one way or another."

"That is the truth," Aramis protested. "Why would I lie about it?"

"Men lie for various reasons. I believe you wanted the throne. Your father was healthy, and you were impatient. Hence, you murdered him."

"I did not kill my father." Tears welled up in his eyes. The man spoke so nonchalantly about the death of his father, as though he couldn't see how torn up Aramis was about it. He loved his father more than anything.

Jarn pulled a ring of keys from his belt. He fingered through them until he found the one he was searching for, then unlocked the shackle that held Aramis's left arm. Aramis groaned in relief.

Jarn walked over to the table that was covered with the cloth, grabbed the edge, and pulled it over beside Aramis's bed. He placed Aramis's hand onto the table and cuffed it into place with a metal shackle attached to the table.

"I almost believe you," Jarn said. Turning to the brazier, he retrieved a pair of tongs from a hook set in the wall. Using the utensil, he dug through the coals and withdrew one.

"Almost," he said. And then he promptly placed the coal on the back of Aramis's hand.

Aramis sucked in his breath, then let out a shriek of pain. The coal burned his flesh, a searing intense sting. It was all he could do to say, "Stop!"

Jarn waited a few seconds more before removing the coal and placing it back in the brazier. "That was quick. I have found that pain usually helps one to remember the truth--."

Aramis grit his teeth against the pain. "I, I … didn't …"

Jarn frowned. "A pity. I thought you would come clean quickly. No matter. I have several ways to get what I want." He placed the tongs back onto the wall hook, then removed the cloth from the table. An array of various wicked looking tools and a few vials greeted him.

He picked up a small hammer and an odd-looking tool that resembled the tongs, but smaller. "Water eases the pain of burns as I'm sure you are aware. Would you like me to pour some onto your hand?"

Aramis remained silent. Jarn nodded as if expecting as much. "These are forceps. You may not be familiar with them, but you will be well acquainted shortly." Jarn angled the forceps so that the prongs were horizontal. He placed the nail of Aramis's index finger between the edges of the forceps.

"Some like to heat the prongs up until they are red hot," Jarn said. "I prefer not to. Brace yourself. This is really going to hurt." In one fluid motion, Jarn clamped the prongs down and yanked his arm backward.

Aramis screamed again as his nail was ripped off. Blood welled up from his nail bed. The pain was agonizing. He got lightheaded and thought he might lose consciousness. "That is only half of the procedure," he vaguely heard Jarn say. "This is the second half."

He watched his torturer raise the hammer. Everything appeared to be moving in slow motion. The hammer descended, smacking directly in the middle of his finger. Aramis both heard and felt the bone crack beneath the blow. The pain was too much for him to bear. He could feel the darkness closing in. He invited it to take him.

In the distance, he heard Jarn's voice, "Not so fast." A sharp smell in his nostrils brought his senses reeling back. Jarn was waving one of the vials from the table under his nose. "I cannot do my duty if you aren't feeling the effects of my methods. We have only just begun. And you will not pass out. I will not allow it."

The next twenty minutes were the longest and most brutal Aramis had ever experienced. Jarn proceeded to tear the nails from the remaining four fingers, breaking the bones afterward with the hammer. And each time Aramis thought he might find relief from the pain in the darkness that threatened his vision, Jarn would wave the vial under his nose.

Finally, when Jarn broke the last finger of his left hand, he questioned Aramis further. When Aramis held to the fact that he had not killed his father, Jarn got frustrated and left the room.

Aramis was weak. His muscles shuddered involuntarily. His battered fingers were numb and useless. His eyes had ceased to produce tears. His mind was deadened by grief and pain.

I'm going to die.

The realization didn't scare him. It was more of a psychological surrender to the fact that his life was at an end. Jarn seemed passionate enough that he would end up killing him trying to get a confession. And Aramis refused to lie about doing it for the sake of respite. To do so would dishonor his father's memory.

His eyes took in the carnage of his mutilated hand. He noticed something else. A faint black mark on his forearm. Perhaps it was a trick of the light, or merely a bruise, but there was a shadowy symbol in his flesh.

Strange.

Then his vision blurred and he closed his eyes to keep from being sick.

—

"Aramis! Lord Aramis!"

Aramis cracked his eyes open slowly. He awoke to find his attendant Melchiades staring at him. "Mel?" he croaked. His hand was still numb, and his entire body was aching.

"Praise Edria! I thought you were dead. Don't move," Mel warned. He struggled with the shackles that kept Aramis bound to the bed. He growled in frustration. Aramis watched through blurred eyes as Mel searched the table covered with torture instruments.

Grabbing something thin, he slid it into the keyhole and jerked it back and forth viciously. He issued a laugh of triumph as the manacle made a click and popped open. He did the same to the other one. As soon as his bonds were released, Aramis fell forward weakly.

Mel quickly grabbed him to keep him from crashing onto the floor. "I fear I must ask you a foolish question, my Prince. Are you able to walk?"

Aramis shrugged weakly. "Water," he whispered, nodding toward the table with the carafe. Mel hesitated, then grabbed it and helped Aramis drink.

"I don't mean to be inconsiderate to your pains, but we must make haste. The guards will be back at any moment."

Aramis lay in silence, forcing his body to obey his will. He could sense an urgency in Mel's voice and trusted his friend enough to know there was a good reason behind it. He drank some more water. "Help me up."

Mel complied, pulling Aramis by his arms and onto his feet. He was able to stand up without help, but he didn't know if he would be able to walk on his own. He tried to take a step and almost collapsed.

"Here," Mel said and wrapped Aramis's arm around the back of his neck. "Lean on me. It will slow us down, but we don't have any other options." Aramis didn't say anything, choosing instead to conserve his energy. They walked out of the room and into the hallway. "I don't know where we are," Aramis admitted.

"No worries, my Lord. I know this place well." Mel motioned to the right. "That leads to a stairwell that takes you up into the main keep. This way," he pointed to the left, "is the way we are going. There is a hidden tunnel that will take us out by the river."

Aramis didn't know what was happening, other than the fact that Jarn assumed he was guilty of murdering his father. "What is going on, Mel? I'm so confused."

"Come, I'll explain as we walk. We must hurry." Leaning most of his weight onto his friend, Aramis followed Mel's lead. The corridor seemed to be fairly straight, other than a few passages that broke off to the sides.

"The king has been killed," Mel said tentatively. Aramis nodded silently. "Rumor among the court is that you are responsible for the act. Some believe it, others do not. Fortunately, none of the nobles are squabbling for power."

That surprised Aramis immensely. He figured without his presence to hold the kingdom together, there would be much infighting.

"The people know you are being detained, but I highly doubt they know you are being tortured down here. There would be rioting in the streets. Jarn is a seriously disturbed individual." Mel paused and cocked his head. "They're coming." He quickened his pace and Aramis struggled to keep up.

"Forgive me, my Prince." Mel shook his head despondently. "I should have escorted you to your chambers that night. I failed in my duty."

"It's not your fault," Aramis replied weakly. "You didn't know what would happen. No one could have known what last night held."

"Last night? You've been gone three days."

Aramis's surprise was broken by the sound of guards shouting. "They know," Mel said. "Quickly!" They tried to pick up their pace, but Aramis was too exhausted.

They continued down the hall until it ended in a cul-de-sac. The walls were smooth, marred only by several torches. For a dead end, the area was well lit. "Are we going the wrong way?" Aramis asked tiredly. Mel shook his head. "The entrance to the tunnel is hidden. There should be a stone or something out of place. That is the trigger to open the door."

Aramis leaned against the wall as Mel searched for it. He could hear the voices of their pursuers closing in. Five armed and heavily armored guards came around the corner.

"Halt!" One of the guards stepped forward from the others and drew his sword. The other four also unsheathed theirs. "By order of the King, you are hereby detained for the unlawful release of a prisoner."

Mel turned to face the soldiers. "The King has been murdered, you inconsiderate fools! This man is Prince Aramis, now King Aramis. Show some respect."

"I know who he is," the leader of the group said, staring at Aramis. "We've been ordered to execute him." The soldier turned his attention to Mel. "As well as anyone aiding him."

"I wouldn't do anything hasty if I were you," Mel said. Aramis looked at him. There was something about his friend that seemed different.

"Surrender willingly and your death will be painless," the soldier promised. A large smirk spread across Mel's face.

"Take him," the leader ordered, pointing his sword in Aramis's direction. Aramis tried to move away from them, but his legs gave out and he collapsed face first. The two guards moved in to grab him.

Mel leaped forward suddenly, landing in front of the prince and shielding him with his body. Aramis rolled onto his back. What he watched unfold was like something out of a dream.

The air around Mel shimmered with mist. The torches darkened momentarily, flaring erratically. The mist began to coalesce around Mel's body, shifting and transforming into armor.

Silver and flawless, the armor was similar to plate mail Aramis had seen before but unique in a way he could not explain. The soldiers hesitated, unsure of what to do. Mel held his hand out and a sword formed, the same color and style as his armor.

One of the guards turned and fled, obviously wanting no part in the fight. The leader looked from Mel to Aramis, then back to Mel. He rushed forward, swinging his sword in an arcing motion. Mel easily stepped out of his reach, moving much faster in plate armor than any soldier Aramis had seen before.

As the soldier's momentum took him forward, Mel thrust his own blade out, striking the soldier in the thigh. His sword pierced straight through the soldier's armor, his leg, and through the back of the armor.

The man gargled in pain, dropping to a knee. Mel withdrew the blade and turned to the other three soldiers, who thought to rush him. Mel gripped the hilt in both hands and held the sword up before him. A dazzling light blinded the guards. They staggered forward, trying to shield their eyes from the glow.

One of the soldiers reached out toward the light. He screamed as his hand was instantly incinerated. Turning, he also fled. The other two dropped their weapons and knelt before Mel. "I surrender!" one of them said.

"As do I," the other chimed in. Mel lowered his sword and the light faded, leaving the hall darker than before.

"Take your captain and retreat." The soldiers rushed to their feet and over to the man clutching his leg. They dragged him by the arms and took flight down the corridor. Mel returned to the wall and after a moment of searching pushed on a stone that was barely sticking out from the others. The floor shook as the wall trembled visibly and then slid into a hidden panel.

Then he lifted the prince effortlessly off the floor and over his shoulder and entered the tunnel. Aramis's mind was reeling. What did he just witness? He looked around and noticed the walls were not made of stone like the dungeon but were carved directly into the dirt.

Everything was pitch black except for Mel's armor.

It radiated a faint luminescence. In the middle of the back plate, right below Mel's neck, was a symbol etched into the armor. A closed hand with an eye in the middle of it. It didn't strike any chords with Aramis; he'd never seen it before.

After roughly a hundred yards, the tunnel ended, and they were walking in the open landscape surrounding the castle walls. It took a moment for his eyes to adjust to the brightness. The sun was nearing the middle of the sky. Just as Mel had said, the Stalwart River flowed nearby.

Mel walked over to a small copse of willow trees on the bank of the river and set Aramis on the ground. The air shimmered briefly, and then Mel's armor was gone. The two stared out at the river in silence. Aramis looked at the man he had been friends with for two years, still trying to comprehend everything.

"How did you do that?"

3

SHE SMELLED THE SMOKE BEFORE she saw it.

The pungent stench that assaults the nostrils and clings to your clothes long after the smoke is gone. Jovanna stepped out of her stone and mud house and looked around to glimpse what was burning. Nothing she could see.

Tiny gray flakes of snow began to fall. She held out her hand to let some of the flakes collect in her palm. They were warm.

Her eyebrows rose in curiosity. Snow wasn't warm. She ran her index finger through the flakes and they smeared across her skin. It wasn't snow.

It was ash.

Jovanna looked to the edge of the village and noticed a crowd had gathered. Deciding to see what was happening, she walked down the dirt path that wended its way through the small village. The place felt deserted. She was used to large cities so densely packed with people that it was hard to walk without bumping into others.

She welcomed the change and the solitude, as she didn't really care for people. As she reached the edge of the village where the people had gathered, she could see massive clouds of smoke in the distance. She avoided the multitude and stood off to the side by herself.

She could hear the people murmuring, but she didn't bother to listen. They could be a superstitious lot. She scanned the horizon and saw the black clouds were billowing up from beyond the border of Talvaard.

"The fires of war," his voice startled her, though she did well to hide it. Jovanna looked at him and shrugged.

"Talvaard is without a king, and many are trying to take the throne by force. Several of the generals are using their armies to their own advantage."

"Jerik, I don't know why you bother my ears with your petty trifles. You know I don't care." She turned from him and began walking back toward the village.

"If you don't care," he called out to her, "then why are you still here?"

Jovanna ignored him and continued walking. She found his constant barrage of information annoying. The old man acted like he knew everything. The ash was falling thicker now. The war for the throne was none of her concern. This village was located in the Deadlands, not Talvaard, and she found it highly doubtful that the battle would go beyond Talvaard's border.

Jerik had saved her life, true. In her reckless attempt to use the dragon's sphere to gain power, she had frayed the magic. The result had been a potent explosion that had almost killed her.

Jerik was an enigma to her. He was old, ancient even. He led the Guardians, an unknown band of people who worked unseen to keep the balance in the world. He had used his power to save her and brought her to this remote village where he lived among the elven tribes of the Deadlands.

Jovanna spotted Velent, the chieftain's son, returning from a hunt. He didn't look happy. He stepped wide of her as he passed by, an elven form of snubbing someone.

"Careful," she said loudly. "You wouldn't want to offend the wrong person." He stopped mid-stride and puffed his chest out defiantly, glaring at her. She returned his gaze with equal ferocity. She rested her hand on the hilt of her sword, tapping her finger on the pommel.

He looked like the rest of the elves she had seen. Lithe and tall, with long brown hair and black eyes. His arms were covered in tattoos. They weren't for decoration, Jovanna knew. They were weapons, every one of them. From the time an elf could walk, they were tattooed with magical symbols and taught how to use them.

She enjoyed toying with him. He was too honorable to fight her, but he was open about his hatred for her. Elves hated all humans, especially sorcerers. Finally, he spat in her direction and continued on his way. A few others were with him, and they all cast her distrustful glances.

If it weren't for Jerik, they would likely try to kill her. She returned to her house and stood in the doorway. There were only a few stone and mud houses in the village, usually reserved for the important people of the village like the Tribe Chief. Perhaps that was another reason Velent disliked her so much. She had one of the best homes in a village that was not her own.

The other homes were made of wooden poles and animal hides. Jerik had told her that this was because the elves used to migrate from place to place. They were fairly sturdy, but sometimes wind storms would come through and a few elves would have to rebuild their tents.

A horn sounded in the distance. Jovanna looked toward the origin. Whoever had sounded the horn was too far to be seen yet, but they had made their intent to enter the village known.

Several warriors, including Velent, went running toward the sound. He was full of pride. Jovanna smirked. He reminded her of herself at times.

Half an hour later, Velent and his warriors returned, escorting a robed figure and a procession of elves. Jovanna's curiosity piqued, she watched as they walked along the path through the city, heading to the Tribe Chief's home.

She spotted Jerik heading her direction. She closed her eyes in irritation. "Jovanna," he said, "come with me."

"What do you want, old man?" she growled.

"The Tribe Chief has called a meeting and he has requested my presence."

"And?"

Jerik's face grew serious. "Something out of the ordinary is occurring. I'd like you there as well."

She stared hard at him for several moments, then nodded in silence. "I will come," she answered. She followed him to the center of the village. Once a month, the entire village would gather and have a feast.

A large tent had been erected for the occasion. The next feast would be held in two days. The elves were already gathering under the tent as they approached. Jerik led her through the crowd and to a table that had been set up for the Tribe Chief. Tanil was there already with his war advisors.

Jovanna had only seen Tanil a few times, usually from a distance. He wasn't as open about his hatred for her as his son was, but he only allowed her to stay because of Jerik. For reasons unknown to her, Jerik was highly esteemed by the elf leader.

Jerik sat at the table with Tanil and the others, but Jovanna chose to stand behind them, leaning against one of the thick poles that held the tent up. The old man didn't ask much of her outside of his constant talking, so the fact that he asked her to attend this meeting bothered her. Did he think something was going to happen?

The villagers parted as the robed elf and his entourage came to the tent, escorted by Velent. He sat beside his father. The visiting elves were not offered chairs as they were not the hosts. Guests were not treated in the friendly manners that humans showed to one another. Another thing Jovanna liked about the elves; they were rude. Unlike Cygnus.

Cygnus. She hadn't thought about him in months. He was the leader of the wizard city Palindrom, and one of the few people that Jovanna didn't hate. She didn't like him, but he had taken her in and tried to teach her how to control her magic. In the end, however, even he feared her.

She realized suddenly the entire tent had gone silent. According to elven custom, the visitor would speak first. If the Tribe Chief decided he liked what the visitor said, they wouldn't kill him. Jovanna liked such brutality. It displayed power. Jerik said it was barbaric.

The robed elf's men had brought a large chest with them. "The contents of this chest are a gift to the village," he said. Tanil nodded once, the sign that what had been spoken was agreeable.

One of the visiting elves opened the chest. The villagers began murmuring all at once. Jovanna squinted. It was full of food. At any other time, this would not have meant anything. Yet this was not an ordinary time. They were experiencing a drought.

The Deadlands was mostly desert. Very few plants grew there, but the ones that did served as the food source for the elven tribes. The rains had come less frequently than in past years, and crop raising was difficult enough *with* the rain. The crops were barely producing enough food to feed the village, so some of the warriors had taken up hunting.

Jovanna had seen earlier the results of that endeavor. Velent and his men had returned with only a few quail and a malnourished addax. It seemed that the drought was affecting the animals of the desert as well.

"This is a generous gift," Tanil said. "All the tribes are dealing with the hardship of the drought. Where did this food come from? And why do you bring it to us and not share it with your own tribe?"

The robed elf waved his hand at the gathered villagers. "Are we not all Elves of the Tribe? We may live in different villages, and we may war against each other, but why should we not band together in this time of great difficulty?"

Tanil looked impressed. Jovanna could see Velent wasn't so easily convinced.

"There is more where this came from," the visitor said. "Much more. And it can be easily had. We only need to go out and retrieve it."

"And where is this food?" Velent said. Tanil scowled at his son. "Don't disgrace the gift," the Tribe Chief commanded. Velent sat back in his chair and folded his arms. "We are not beggars, father."

The robed elf nodded his head. "I take no offense at the question. I would have the same reservations if I was in your seat." The elf began speaking to the crowd. "Who is responsible for our troubles?" he asked. "Who drove us from our homes and into the Deadlands to fight for everything?"

"The humans!" one of the villagers shouted.

"Exactly!" the visitor said. "The humans drove us from our

homes and took our lands. They pushed us into this wasteland and grow fat off the land that is rightfully ours." The robed elf turned his attention back to Tanil. "The food is in the human lands. In *our* lands. It is time we unite and take back what is ours!"

Jerik gave Jovanna a look of alarm. The villagers started talking excitedly.

"What must we do to get this food?" Tanil asked.

"Swear your allegiance to me. Give me authority over your warriors and I will ensure the provision of your people."

"We reject your offer," Velent said, shaking his head. "What you ask for is foolish."

Tanil slammed his fist onto the table. Everyone turned their eyes to him. "Velent, you are not Tribe Chief. If you speak out of turn again, I will banish you from the tent."

Jovanna could see Velent was fuming. He kept his mouth shut, however.

"It sounds easy, but what you propose is unachievable," Tanil said. "Perhaps if more tribes were behind this cause, I would consider—"

The robed elf cut him off. "Every tribe has committed their warriors to me. You are the last tribe remaining."

"Impossible," Tanil replied. "The tribes have never been united, even before we were driven to the desert. Where is your proof?"

The visitor snapped his fingers. The elves who had traveled with him stepped forward, each one reciting their name and their tribe. When they finished, Jovanna had counted one elf for each of the major tribes. Tanil was quiet for a moment. "And if I refuse to commit?"

"That would not be wise, for you or your people."

Velent bristled at the threat. "Father," he said in hushed tones. "Do not let him strong arm you into this. He could be lying."

Tanil ignored his son. "I will do as you say, so long as you promise my people will be taken care of." Velent stood up, his chair tumbling over behind him. "I will not bow to anyone but my father," he said.

"Velent, sit down!" Tanil shouted, outraged. Velent did not obey. He pointed to the robed elf.

"Warriors, seize him!" Several elves detached from the crowd and stalked toward the visitors.

The robed elf glowered at Velent. "You should reconsider your actions, *boy*. You don't know who you are angering."

Velent didn't answer. The warriors closed in and attempted to grab the visitors. Jovanna was amazed at the quickness of the robed elf's men. They unsheathed their swords and fought back against the warriors. Chaos ensued.

The war advisors leaped over the table, attempting to help their warriors subdue the visitors. The robed elf's men were cutting the warriors down left and right. Tanil seemed lost for a moment, then drew his own blade and flipped the table over. He and Velent joined the fray.

Jovanna found it all very amusing. They were fighting over something that was impossible. Elves invading human lands? She laughed at the thought. Jerik retreated beside her.

"This is not good," he said to her. She snorted.

"They will fight it out and the winner will get what they want. Such is the way of things."

Jerik shook his head. "You don't understand."

Be that as it may. She didn't care, either.

Tanil fell to the ground, wounded. Velent touched one of his tattoos and the ink flared to life with blue light. A thunderous *boom* shook the ground. One of the robed elf's men fell to the ground, charred by the magical explosion. Velent went flying backward as the robed elf countered back with his own spell.

One of the visitors stood over Tanil. With a nod from the robed one, the elf stabbed his sword into Tanil's throat, killing him.

Velent staggered to his feet, crying out in anguish. The robed elf went in for the kill. He raised his sword and thrust it forward.

A clang of metal sounded.

Jovanna's sword was a blur of motion. Her blade weaved a dangerous path through the air, parrying the blow of the robed elf. She knelt down and spun around, her foot lashing out and connecting solidly with a kneecap, sending the elf sprawling onto the ground as his leg gave out.

She leveled the blade with his throat. Lifting her left hand up, she called the magic to her. She 'saw' the magic floating all around her and commanded it to obey her will. Tendrils of black smoke began to rise from her hand, snaking through the air like tiny serpents.

The lithe lines of smoke angled down toward the elf, slowly wrapping around his legs. The magical haze tightened its grip on him as it tangled around his entire body, immobilizing him. Her eyes flickered momentarily, and the smoke began to change color to a reddish hue.

The elf grunted in pain as the smoke began to burn his flesh. She urged the tendrils to burn more intensely. The elf looked at her and she could see hatred boiling within him.

"*Sadaka lae nash!*" the elf shouted. The tendrils of smoke burst apart, scattering into the air. He struggled to his feet and snarled at her. His hood fell back, revealing his face. Jovanna thought she had seen him somewhere before.

He rolled his sleeve back and touched one of his tattoos. It came to life with blue light. He began to shimmer, then a popping sound filled the air and he was gone, leaving his men behind.

Jovanna laughed, thrilled with the excitement of battle. "Weakling!" she hollered. "He fled like a scared—" her words halted as she turned to see Jerik slumped up against a wooden tent pole.

He was dead.

4

Twelve Years Ago

SHE WATCHED THE DOG FROM a distance. Had it caught her scent? She couldn't know. She hadn't seen any other kids today. That was odd. Usually, there were a few others who walked this same section of the dump. They could have died. It wasn't out of the ordinary. The dump was a place of hard living, fighting for food, and always trying to stay warm at night.

She pulled her handmade dagger out of her belt just in case. She looked it over, making sure it was sharp enough to puncture flesh if she had to fight. She had made it out of a bone she found. By rubbing it against a rock, she had given it a fairly spikey point.

The dog perked its ears and she held her breath. She watched as the mutt sniffed the air and turned its attention elsewhere. She breathed out deeply and watched the dog until it disappeared among the mounds of trash. Only when she was sure it was gone did she come out of hiding. She still didn't see any other children. Shrugging, she continued searching through the trash for scraps.

She didn't know what city she lived in, but she knew it was big. The amount of trash in the dump told her that. The dump was massive, stretching as far as she could see in every direction. It was located on the southern end of the city, next to the slums. If only she lived in the slums. One could dream.

"Jovanna!"

She whirled around, pointing the dagger towards the voice. She sighed with relief when she saw it was only Danica. "You scared me," Jovanna said indignantly. Danica skipped over to her. She was always so happy.

"Sorry," she said. "I've never seen you scared before. You are the bravest kid I've ever met."

"*Psh*," Jovanna slapped the air and shook her head. "Just because

I don't look scared doesn't mean I'm not scared on the inside. You find anything today?"

"I found this," Danica said, pulling a leftover piece of bread out of her pocket. She held it up for Jovanna to see. There were obvious teeth marks in it. She always wondered why people threw perfectly good food away.

"You are lucky," Jovanna said, smiling. "I haven't found anything yet." She turned and continued looking. Sometimes she touched things that made her shudder, but you had to look everywhere if you hoped to find something edible.

"Have you been to the pond today?" Danica asked, humming a tune as she followed Jovanna.

"No," she answered, realizing suddenly that she was pretty thirsty. The pond was the most dangerous place in the dump. It was the only source of water, and you had to be careful how much you drank. It would make you sick, causing stomach cramps so bad it would immobilize you, usually resulting in the dogs getting you.

Thankfully Jovanna had never gotten sick from the water. She was careful about not drinking too much, even though she wanted more. "Have you seen any others today?" she asked Danica. There was a pause.

"Now that you say that, I haven't. They could be dead."

"That's what I thought earlier," Jovanna said, pushing aside something wet and smelly. She scrunched her face in disgust but was rewarded with finding a piece of bread like Danica's. Whatever the wet smelly stuff was, it had gotten on the bread a little. "I need to go to the pond to wash this off," Jovanna informed Danica. "I'll see you later?" she asked.

Danica shrugged. "I'll come with you."

"Are you sure?" No one ever went to the pond twice. It was dangerous enough just trying to go once. She nodded. Jovanna led the way through the hills of trash, twisting and turning like giant snakes laid out in the sun. Snakes were a rarer occurrence in the dump, but Jovanna had come across one before. It was the best meal she could remember.

They walked for a long time. Every time they passed one of the safe areas—mini caves dug into the trash mounds or pieces of wood turned into shacks—they called out and glanced inside to see if any other kids were inside. Oddly, there weren't. Jovanna began to worry something bad, something very bad, must have happened.

The pond was surrounded by a tall circular wall of trash with one way in. Jovanna paused cautiously at the entrance and peered around the wall. No dogs. No kids, either. "It's safe," she said to Danica. They walked toward the water, glancing around the towering walls to make sure there weren't any animals hiding. Especially dogs. The dogs were vicious.

They approached the edge of the pond and Jovanna dipped her bread in and pulled it out quickly, then rubbed the nasty stuff off. It looked better so she took a bite out of it. It was a little moist from the water, but it was better than going to sleep hungry. "One day we are going to live in the slums," she promised Danica while chewing.

Danica was humming that tune she always sang. "That day will be great," she replied, her smile enveloping her face. A commotion rang out across the water. Jovanna snapped her gaze toward the noise. There, at the very back end of the pond, was a pack of dogs and a group of kids.

"What's happening?" Danica asked, squinting to see.

Jovanna was trying to determine that herself. "Let's get a closer look."

"I don't know … I think we should leave." Danica sounded scared. Jovanna didn't blame her. She didn't like the idea of being anywhere near a pack of dogs, but if they were fighting over food …

"Come on," Jovanna said. "I'll protect you." Danica nodded hesitantly. They walked along the edge of the pond slowly, not wanting to draw attention. After several minutes, they got close enough to see what was happening.

A deer carcass, freshly killed, was the object of the fight. The kids were fighting the dogs for the food. And they were losing. Jovanna could see several small bodies lying on the ground, dead or dying. This was bad. "It looks like they need help," Jovanna said.

Danica shook her head. "We need to leave. We can't stay here."

Jovanna was debating what to do. Help the other kids drive the dogs back for the food, or run. Her instincts told her to run, but she didn't want to abandon the kids who needed help. The last few kids gave up the fight. They turned and fled, some of them scrambling up the hills and others running toward Jovanna and Danica.

"Let's go," Jovanna said, pushing Danica in front of her. She trotted backward for a few steps, watching the dogs. Some of them didn't stay with the deer. They were following the kids.

"Run!"

"Our character is constantly tested. The most difficult tests happen all at once."

—The Prophet of Edria

5

ARAMIS DIPPED HIS MANGLED HAND into the river. The water was surprisingly cold. He pulled it out a few seconds later after his hand had numbed. He rested it on his leg and let the air dry his skin.

"You aren't really a noble from … wherever you said then, are you?"

Mel nodded. "I am of noble blood, yes. And that is my family's estate. I have not seen them since I joined the order, though. I came here under the instruction of the Prophet."

"Who is the Prophet?" Aramis asked.

"He is the head of Edria's following. He alone receives divine counsel from her and guides the rest of us in her will."

"And Edria is …?"

Mel sighed. "Have you paid so little attention to what I have said? She is the Goddess of Knowledge."

Aramis held his hand up and inspected his broken fingers. At least the pain was manageable now. Before … Aramis shuddered. Jarn was a cruel man.

"The priests of my order can heal your hand," Mel informed him. "It would be wise of us to head there now, considering our current situation. If anyone sees you, they'll be sure to alert the guards."

"I can't go like this," Aramis replied, waving at himself. "I look like a vagrant. I need shoes and a shirt, at least. These pants will make do if I can wash the blood out of them."

"Of course, my Prince. I will go immediately and find you something."

"How are you going to do that?" Aramis asked. "You can't exactly go into the city. The guards will be looking for you as well.

`243

You assaulted soldiers. That's a serious crime unless you have forgotten?"

Mel frowned and tapped his chin with his index finger. "Blast. I had a perfect pair of Cantabrian albarcas and a brown silk tunic that would make you the envy of everyone. If neither of us can be seen, how do we get you something to wear?"

Aramis tensed as he heard a noise that sounded like a carriage. "Guards?" he asked, rising quickly to his feet. They were off the road, but the trees they were resting under were in plain view of anyone passing by.

"I don't think so," Mel answered, peering through the low hanging branches. "It would appear to be a cart. Yes, it is. And a woman is pushing it. We should stay here until she passes, just in case."

Aramis nodded in agreement. He watched as the rough looking cart trundled into view. A woman dressed in what appeared to be dirty rags stitched together walked behind it, pushing the cart with stooped shoulders. A hood covered her head and she walked barefoot.

A homeless woman, Aramis supposed. It seemed like the woman was going to pass by, but then she stopped when she reached the thicket of trees he and Mel were resting under.

She stood there, motionless. Without turning to look in their direction, the woman said: "Ah, Prince Aramis. And Melchiades. I knew he would guard you well. A shame about your father. I rather liked him."

Against his better judgment, he called out to the woman. "You knew my father?"

"My Prince," Mel whispered, shaking his head.

"Don't worry about me, Melchiades. I have no desire to see Aramis harmed." The woman turned her heard toward them. A dirty cloth covered her eyes, and Aramis realized she was blind. "I knew your father, though he did not know me. But that is not important."

She slid open a door on the top of the cart and rummaged through it. Finally, she pulled something out. Walking slowly and using a staff for support, she joined them under the shade of the willow trees. She held a bundle out for someone to take.

Aramis stepped closer and accepted it hesitantly. Unrolling it, he realized it was a shirt wrapped around a pair of shoes. "Thank you," he said gratefully. "How did you know I needed these?"

"Some things don't require sight, my boy."

"I am indebted to you. Mel, please pay her for these items."

She shook her head. "I don't want your money. They are a gift. You two must leave here quickly. A company of soldiers travel this road looking for you and will pass by shortly. Listen to me carefully. Trust Melchiades, for he will not lead you astray. The new king will not rest until he finds you."

"What new king? I am the heir." Aramis shook his head. "What are you talking about?"

"You will not understand everything now, but revelation will come in time. Now hurry, before the soldiers come." She turned and walked away, leaving Aramis troubled by her words. She reached her cart and continued pushing it along the road.

"We should cross the river," Mel said, interrupting his thoughts. "It might aid us in losing our pursuit. Then we will travel to my temple. You will be safe there. And perhaps my order can discern who the assassin was."

Aramis sighed. "I don't like the idea of leaving my people without a leader, but until I clear my name I have little choice in the matter."

"Thinking like a king already," Mel smiled at him.

Aramis decided not to put on the clothes the woman had given him until he dried off from crossing the river. Mel led the way, jumping onto exposed rocks to keep from getting soaked. About halfway across the river, they ran out of rocks. Mel turned to him. "Looks like we will have to get wet after all."

A *whirring* sound filled the air, followed by a splash. They turned simultaneously to see a group of five soldiers at the edge of the river behind them. They all had crossbows brandished and aimed.

"Go!" Mel shouted, grabbing Aramis by the shoulder and shoving him. "Get to the other side!"

Aramis didn't have much choice as the momentum from Mel's shove sent him flying into the cold water. Aramis instinctively sucked in his breath, along with some water, and started coughing. He ignored the burning in his throat and started swimming. He almost dropped his clothes. He glanced over his shoulder to see if Mel was following. The air rippled around him and that strange armor formed out of mist.

Aramis snapped his gaze forward and kept swimming. Mel would be fine. He reached the other side and sloshed out of the water, shivering. Even though it was summer, the water was freezing. He looked back at Mel again.

The soldiers were trying to shoot him down with their crossbows. Mel had summoned his sword and was deflecting the bolts out of the air. An occasional *clink* sounded. "Mel!" Aramis shouted. "Come on!"

Mel deflected two more arrows and then turned and leaped. Aramis expected him to sink like a rock, only he didn't. In fact, he didn't even appear to touch the water at all. Mel was running, his metal-clad feet barely rippling the surface of the water. Aramis stared, awestruck.

"Fancy trick," Aramis said as Mel stopped beside him. Melchiades grinned proudly. The air shimmered and then his armor was gone. An arrow slammed into the sandy ground at their feet. They exchanged looks and started running.

Several times Aramis stepped on rocks and other sharp objects. He cried out a few times as pain lanced through him, but kept going. They had to get out of range of the crossbows. They continued running for several minutes before stopping. They were both breathing hard and Mel was sweating.

Aramis noticed he wasn't cold anymore. He sat down on the ground and inspected the bottoms of his feet. There were numerous small cuts and sand clung to his skin. He brushed them off and put the shoes on. They were wet, but soft and felt good on his aching feet. He stood back up and put the shirt on as well. "Which way to the temple?" he asked.

Mel wiped the perspiration from his forehead and nodded to the east. "It's a two-day journey to Kaldore on foot. Perhaps we can find a carriage that will take us, or at least rent some horses."

"Let's do it quickly then. Before word gets too far that we are fugitives."

"Good point, my Lord."

—

Aramis leaned against the wall, arms crossed. He stared out a window, watching the clouds float lazily across the sky. In the distance, he could make out the sounds of a bustling town. The view was amazing, but he didn't recognize it. He suddenly realized he didn't know where he was.

He turned his attention to the room he was in. It was similar to his personal chambers in the castle, yet it was slightly different. Everything seemed to be in the right place, only ... it wasn't. He couldn't quite put his finger on it, but something was very wrong.

His left arm began to itch. He absently scratched it, then yelped in pain. There on his forearm was a black cross. "What the ..." he muttered softly. It was roughly the length of his middle finger and as wide as two.

He ran his finger along the shape and the flesh began to squirm under his touch. An intense fear made his stomach lurch. The black cross on his arm began to melt, small drops of black liquid falling to the floor.

There was no pain, just the incessant itching. The black drops began to drip faster, quickly pooling at his feet. He tried to rub the blackness off his skin but it seemed stuck, as though a part of his very flesh. Aramis watched in amazed shock as the black pool of liquid began to shift and take shape.

The cross disappeared as the last few drops fell from his arm. He staggered back from the shifting pool, his mind telling him to run. His body wouldn't obey him. A dark robed form rose from the black liquid of the floor.

The air in the room seemed to chill. Aramis could feel the hairs on his body stand on end. The figure turned toward him. The light in the room dimmed considerably and Aramis couldn't make out any of the person's features.

"I see the world cloaked in flame," the voice that came from the man was unearthly. It gave Aramis the impression of evil things scurrying in the darkness. Dead things. "And a sword will swiftly follow. My sword."

The figure was suddenly standing before him and the stench of rotting flesh reached his nostrils. He gagged, covering his mouth and nose with his hands.

"Who are you?" Aramis breathed.

"Mordum, God of the Dead."

Aramis startled awake, screaming and clutching his left arm in pain. Melchiades was standing over him, the concern evident on his face.

"My Lord," he asked hesitantly. "Are you well? I heard you screaming from the other room."

Aramis writhed in pain. His arm was burning like hellfire.

"Let me see it," he vaguely heard Mel say. He heard other voices as well and saw other people enter the room, men dressed similarly to Mel. He didn't know what he was doing or what was happening.

Brief images flashed through his mind. Men trying to hold him down. Mel's penetrating eyes staring at him. All swirled together with the haunting images of his dream.

And then the pain was gone. His mind cleared and he realized that he was tied down to the bed. Mel stood nearby, slowly flipping through pages in a book.

"What happened?" he asked.

Mel looked at him, offering a wan smile. "I wondered when you would come to. Forgive me for rapping you on the head, but after you struck the second priest, I had to do something."

"You knocked me out?" Aramis asked, surprised.

Mel nodded. "We have a lot to talk about. Why didn't you tell me you bore the mark?"

Aramis was confused. "The mark? What mark?" He tried to move but his bindings held him fast. "And untie me, will you?"

Mel complied with his request. Aramis sat up and ran his hands through his hair. "Now, what are you talking about?" Mel pointed to his arm. Aramis followed his gaze and his eyes widened in horror. A black cross, identical to the one in his dream, was on his left arm.

Aramis jumped up off the bed. "That was in my dream! Where is he?" He looked around the room frantically, but Mel was the only one in the room with him.

"Your dream? You dreamed of this symbol?" Mel asked.

"I wouldn't call it a dream so much as a nightmare." Aramis related the disturbing details. Mel listened in silence, seeming thoughtful.

"I remember something else," Aramis said. "The assassin who killed my father, he pointed at me and said something I didn't understand. I … I think that's when my arm started burning. Everything was so chaotic and fast, I honestly can't remember."

"I assume you don't know what this symbol is then, do you?"

Aramis shook his head. "I've never seen it before."

"This is the symbol of Mordum, the God of the Dead. The same figure who spoke to you in your dream."

"Why is this god's symbol on my arm?" Aramis asked.

"Why indeed," Mel replied. "I will need to speak with the Prophet about this. Perhaps he knows the answer. You should get some rest while I wait to speak to him. You look …"

"Horrible?"

"I was going to say tired, my Lord."

Aramis smiled at his friend. "I will try. Wake me when you know anything."

"Immediately," Mel said with a flourished bow before leaving him.

"Always the aristocrat," Aramis muttered. He looked around the room again to make sure the dark figure really was only a part of his dream, then he climbed back into the bed and closed his eyes.

He didn't sleep much.

6

ARAMIS SAT ON A STONE bench in the hallway, waiting on Mel. While he didn't get much rest, he did feel more refreshed. The church had a bathing room which he had taken full advantage of. He'd shaved and cleaned up, as well as washed the blood from his pants. Laying in a bed had been a welcome reprieve from the cramped carriage they had ridden in to get to the temple.

Now he waited impatiently for Mel to finish speaking with the Prophet. Most of the other priests seemed to keep their distance from him. He first thought was that it was because they knew he was the king, but Mel informed him it was because of the mark on his arm. Apparently, Mordum was the sworn enemy of Edria.

Aramis didn't care about their religious politics. He just wanted the thing removed and his hand healed, which still no one had done. He needed to hunt down the man who had killed his father so he could clear his name and claim the throne.

The words of the blind woman from the castle still bothered him. Who was she talking about when she said 'the new king'? The nobles might be petty and fight amongst themselves, but none of them would try to usurp the throne. Or would they?

His troubled thoughts were interrupted as a door opened and Mel stepped into the hallway. He stood there for a moment and covered his face with his hands. Mel appeared more troubled than Aramis felt. Mel lowered his hands and stopped midway, seeming surprised to see Aramis. "What are you doing here?" he asked.

"I thought I would wait here for you," Aramis answered. "Is there a problem?"

Mel shook his head. "Of course not," he answered, his entire demeanor changing. "I was simply curious. Come," he beckoned Aramis with his hand.

Aramis rose and followed Mel down the corridor and out into the open courtyard of the church. Priests were moving in all directions, most of them carrying parchments. They wove their way through the bustling courtyard and out into the city of Kaldore. The church of Edria was located inside the city, surrounded by a short wall that was more for decoration than any sort of defense.

"What did the Prophet say?" Aramis finally asked. "Is he going to remove this mark?"

Mel didn't answer immediately. "He said he is not able to."

"Who can?"

"He doesn't know if it *can* be removed. The mark of Mordum is given to his agents when they swear their devotion to him. A commitment to Mordum is for life, and his followers carry the mark until they die." They stopped beside an abandoned building, its windows and doors boarded up.

"I'm not a follower of this Mordum," Aramis said indignantly.

"I know that," Mel replied, "But the Prophet does not. He won't allow anyone to heal your hand until you agree to something first. Something that will prove you are not an agent of Mordum."

"Are you jesting with me?" Aramis asked.

"I wish that were the case, my Lord. Things have changed dramatically, it seems. There are many things unfolding not just in your kingdom, but in others. The Prophet believes these events are all linked to Mordum. His followers are moving quickly to secure important positions all over the lands. I had hoped the Prophet would take my word for your testimony. Unfortunately, since I was not in your father's room with you when the assassin struck, he cannot trust you based on my word alone." Mel sighed and leaned back against the building.

They both sat in silence, watching the townspeople pass. "I suppose whatever he requests of me shouldn't be too difficult. If my arm wasn't defaced with this mark, then he would believe me. Wouldn't he?"

"I don't know. He will not ask anything easy of you, that I am sure of. He did not tell me what your task would be, he only told me to see what your answer would be."

Aramis chewed on his lower lip. "What other option do I have? I cannot go back to the castle until my name is cleared, and I can't do that so long as my father's killer is walking freely. I need proof I didn't do it. Tell your prophet I will do it."

One of the townspeople approached them pushing a wooden cart. Aramis assumed it was a vendor coming over to try and sell them something. He was about to tell the person they weren't interested when he realized it was the blind woman from the castle.

"Prince Aramis," she greeted as she reached them. She halted pushing the cart. "I see you two escaped the soldiers. Good thing I warned you." She smiled at them.

Aramis stared at the cloth that covered her eyes. "You aren't really blind, are you?" he asked.

"Of course I'm blind," she cackled. "Why would you think otherwise?"

"You recognized us back at the castle. And just now you said you 'see' we escaped the soldiers. And how did you get here so fast? We rented a carriage and got here yesterday. There's no way you pushed that cart all the way here in so short a time."

The lady continued to smile, but she reached up and removed the cloth. Aramis' mouth dropped. Where the woman's eyes should have been were two empty sockets. "You see?" she asked. "I am as blind as it gets."

"But how …?" Aramis trailed off, dumbfounded.

"I told you before, some things don't require sight." She tied the cloth back in place, then reached into her cart and shuffled through it. Aramis and Mel exchanged looks but didn't say anything. Finally, she pulled out a dagger. She held it out for Aramis to take. "You'll need this. It's the only thing that will work."

Aramis accepted the weapon. He turned it over in his hands. It had a plain wooden hilt. The blade itself was only a few inches long and seemed likely to rust soon. He looked to Mel who shrugged in response. "I'll need it for what?" he asked.

"You'll see in time," she answered nonchalantly. "I must be on my way now. Remember what I said about Melchiades?" she asked.

"Trust him," Aramis answered. She nodded once and continued pushing her cart.

"There's something really odd about that woman," Aramis said as he slid the dagger into his belt. Mel watched her closely as she left.

"I couldn't agree more."

—

A few hours later, Aramis was summoned to speak with the Prophet. Mel escorted him to the same hallway they had previously been in. His friend knocked on the door and another priest answered. He looked to be the same age as Mel. They entered into a small room with no chairs or decorations of any kind. Aramis waited with Mel while the other priest disappeared through another door.

"He's going to let the Prophet know you are here. The first time someone meets him, it can be a little nerve-wracking. He can be … overzealous."

Aramis wasn't worried. He grew up in the king's court. After a few minutes, the priest returned and led them into the Prophet's chamber. The room was windowless, but candles were everywhere. Aramis assumed there must have been hundreds of them. They gave the room an eerie yellowish-orange glow. He could smell something in the air. Probably incense.

Behind a large wooden desk stood the Prophet. He didn't look how Aramis had pictured. He was tall, with broad shoulders and a muscular frame. He had black hair, or at least it appeared black in the lighting. Aramis couldn't tell. He wore robes similar to Mel's, though they were much more richly decorated. A large gold chain hung from his neck with a pendant of a closed hand with an open eye in the center. He'd seen that symbol etched on the back of Mel's armor; the symbol of Edria.

"Welcome Prince Aramis," he greeted formally. Aramis bowed in respect. "Please sit down. We have a lot to talk about." There was only one chair in front of the Prophet's desk. Aramis looked to Mel, who motioned him to take the seat. Aramis did so. He leaned back and tried not to inhale the smoke from the candles on the desk.

If the Prophet noticed his discomfort, he didn't say anything. "Melchiades says that despite the fact that you wear the mark of Mordum, you are not one of his agents. I'm a logical man. If you don't belong to Mordum, why do you have the mark?" He leaned forward, the shadows of the candlelight wavering along his face.

"I do not know for certain how I got it, but I have not devoted myself to Mordum, let alone any other god. I am not a weakling to rely on fairy tales to get me through life."

He looked at Mel. "No offense." Mel nodded, knowing Aramis didn't put faith into anything other than what he could see.

"What I do know is that my father was killed by a man who managed to scale the castle walls despite the fact that they are warded against magic. He said something to me I didn't understand, and then he simply disappeared into thin air. I haven't even had time to properly grieve my father's passing. I am a fugitive in my own kingdom for a crime I didn't commit. I've come to hear your request of how to prove that I am not a follower of Mordum, not to sit here as though I am on some sort of trial when I could be searching for the assassin who killed my father!"

Aramis ended his tirade, suddenly feeling like a fool. The Prophet could give him the opportunity he needed to clear his name, and he just yelled at the man. His emotions had gotten the better of him. He was about to apologize when the Prophet sat back and smiled.

"Your father certainly raised you to speak like a king. I understand your position, but you have to understand mine. Let me explain." The Prophet stood up and walked over to a table in the corner of the room. Mel nudged Aramis and nodded toward the table. Aramis stood and joined the Prophet. "This is a map of everything that has ever been explored. My predecessor had it commissioned for missionary purposes. Today it serves me as a means to track the enemies of my goddess."

The Prophet pointed to Talvaard. "We know that a follower of Mordum wages a war here in disguise, but we have yet to figure out who it is. Here," he moved his finger to the Deadlands, "another is trying to organize the elven tribes under one banner. We don't know why, but I'm not as concerned about that." He pointed to Oakvalor. "Here is your kingdom. The king is murdered, by *you* according to the word spreading, and you bear the mark of Mordum.

"His followers have been dormant for years. Now they are moving to secure entire cities. In Talvaard, they are moving to secure an entire kingdom. Aside from the fact that Mordum is Edria's enemy, this is cause for concern even for those who don't believe in fairy tales," he said, looking directly at Aramis. "Mordum is God of the Dead. He seeks to destroy life and anything that is good. If whatever he is planning comes to pass, I can guarantee that we will all suffer the consequences."

"What does all of this have to do with me?" Aramis asked.

"As of right now, I believe you are the agent of Mordum in Oakvalor. So unless you can give me proof that you are not, I have no other choice but to assume I am right."

Aramis considered the implications of what the Prophet was saying. "What do you want me to do to prove that I'm not?"

The Prophet turned back to the map and pointed to the Viss Mountains. "There is a shrine to Mordum in these mountains. Once a year, his followers gather there to collect blood that comes out of the shrine. When they drink it, it gives them power. I don't know where the blood comes from or how it gives his followers power, but we do know the time for the next collection is coming. I want you to retrieve this blood and bring it back to me."

Aramis frowned. "What are you going to do with it? And why can't your priests get it for you?"

"Fair questions," the Prophet said. "My spies tell me that some kind of ritual is going to happen, and the blood from this shrine is one of the keys to the ritual. If you are not truly a follower, you will have no qualms about getting this and bringing it to me. As to why my priests cannot gather this blood, that is because only those who have the mark of Mordum can enter the gate surrounding the shrine."

"What if they realize I'm not one of them and they try to kill me? This doesn't seem like a fair deal."

The Prophet chuckled. "Who said this was a deal? You are in a bind, Aramis. I could execute you as a follower of Mordum, or turn you in for crimes against the country. You have a tough decision to make, but it is your decision."

"Suppose I do this task and I am successful, thus proving I am not a follower of this god Mordum. What benefit do I get from this that will help me clear my name?"

The Prophet stared at him intently. "You will have the backing of Edria and her church. I will issue an edict declaring our belief in your innocence, and I will provide you with anything you need to catch the real assassin.

"What say you?" the Prophet asked.

Aramis scratched his chin. "I will do it," he decided.

7

Twelve Years Ago

JOVANNA FOLLOWED DANICA TO THE first safe area, a small cave dug into the trash. She didn't see any of the other kids now. They all ran in different directions. She could hear the dogs barking not too far behind them.

"We won't be able to fend them off here," Jovanna said as Danica was started to climb through the entrance. "The opening is too big. We need somewhere that only one dog can come in at a time if they find us."

Danica hesitated. She was scared and just wanted to hide. Jovanna didn't fault her for that. But they had to be smart about it. If you didn't think smart, you didn't live long. Jovanna grabbed Danica's hand and pulled her out of the cave, dragging the younger girl behind her. She kept her bone dagger in her free hand, clutching it tightly.

Her mind raced through the many places they could hide. Which one would be best? The dogs were getting closer. She didn't have much time to choose, and she had even less time to get wherever she chose. And then she had an idea.

"Faster!" she yelled at Danica. She veered to the left, towards where she found the bread. The smelly wet stuff she had encountered, if they rubbed it on themselves, would hinder the dogs from being able to smell them. The idea of rubbing that nasty stuff on her skin was repulsive, but desperation called for options that weren't normally considered.

They reached the area fairly quickly. Jovanna continued pulling Danica behind her as they climbed the steep hill of garbage. "Here," she said breathlessly. "Roll around in it." Jovanna pointed.

Danica had a look of utter disgust on her face. "No way," she said defiantly. "I don't want that on me."

"Do you want the dogs to find you?"

Danica looked over her shoulder to where the dogs would be coming, then back to the slime. She closed her eyes, pinched her nose, and fell face first into the smelly stuff. Jovanna did the same, rolling around and feeling the slime cover her skin. Her body involuntarily shuddered at the feeling.

"Gross, gross, gross," she heard Danica whispering.

"Quiet!"

Danica stopped talking and Jovanna listened intently. She didn't hear anything. Perhaps the dogs had lost their trail. Jovanna decided, to be safe, they would wait for a while before moving. She lay there in the slime, listening. She felt like forever had passed before she finally lifted her head to look around. *No sign of the dogs.*

She turned to Danica to let her know it was okay to move, but the girl had fallen asleep. Jovanna smiled at the sight. Danica's blonde hair was stained a brownish green color from the slime. Her tattered clothing barely hung to her body. Where the material had completely ripped, she had tied it back together with small knots. Danica was already living in the dump before Jovanna came to call it home.

Jovanna had been here two years now. She couldn't believe how much time had gone by when she really thought about it. Two long, grueling years of fighting merely to survive. At least at the orphanage, she was guaranteed real food. Not much, but it was still more than she found now.

The orphanage.

Before the dump, she lived at an orphanage for a few weeks. Before that, she had a real family. Her parents had loved her. That was before …

No.

She pushed the thoughts from her mind. She dared not think about that time. She slowly got to her feet, trying to be as quiet as possible so as not to wake Danica. She stood there in silence, looking across the dump. She didn't see or hear any sign of the dogs. She sighed and tried not to breath in the smell of the slime covering her.

She would be forced to wash in the pond. She hadn't taken a bath in several weeks. It was hard to find a safe time to do so. She slid the bone dagger into her belt and climbed down the hill. She wouldn't leave Danica unprotected, but she needed to find more food. She had dropped the bread she found when they fled the pond.

Jovanna started picking through the trash. People threw lots of things away. Every once in a while she would find a coin or two. When most of the other kids found coins, they would go to the slums and spend them on food or clean water.

Not Jovanna. While it was tempting to use them, especially when she couldn't find anything to eat, she saved them. She hid them across the dump, always careful not to put too many in one spot. She also hid them in spots that didn't get explored much.

Once she had enough coins, she was going to buy a shack in the slums. She was only eight, true, but several children had their own shacks. Either their parents had died, leaving them what little they owned, or their parents had simply abandoned them. No one really cared what happened in the slums. They cared even less about what happened in the dump.

She spotted something shiny and reached for it. Before her fingers could reach it, she heard a scream. She spun around, her heart suddenly racing. Her eyes scanned the hill.

There.

Danica was running from a dog. Not just any dog. The dog she saw earlier before Danica met up with her. The mangy mutt easily overtook Danica, snapping at her heel and tripping her in the process. Jovanna sprinted toward them, her skinny legs burning from the effort of trying to run through the garbage that seemed to try and suck her down.

Jovanna growled in frustration and used her hands to aid in her climb. She finally reached Danica. She was in a frantic fight with the dog. It was all snapping teeth, growls, and blood.

Lots of blood.

Jovanna jumped into the fray, using her bone dagger to stab the dog several times. The animal's growls turned to cries of pain. The dog tried to turn and bite her, but she jumped backward out of the way and kicked the dog in the jaw. The dog yelped in response but attacked her still.

She fell to the ground as the dog slammed into her. She momentarily freaked out. She hated not being in control. The dog's nails raked across her flesh, opening wounds along her arms. Jovanna pushed her left arm up to try and block the dog while angling her right arm to the side.

She screamed in pain as she felt the dog clamp down on her arm, the animal's teeth piercing her skin. She tried to keep her focus. She lifted her free arm and swung as hard as she could, bone dagger leading the way.

She was rewarded with a cry from the dog as well as the sensation of something warm spraying against her skin. The dog released her arm and ran, leaving a trail of blood behind. Jovanna lay there breathing heavily. She could hear her heartbeat in her ears. Was that normal?

Relief flooded over her as she realized that the cuts on her arm weren't very deep. That was good. It could have been much worse. She struggled to her feet and saw Danica laying very still.

Danica!

She had almost forgotten the girl she was trying to save in her frantic fight with the dog. "Danica, it's okay. The dog is gone. I stabbed him pretty good." She still didn't move. "Danica," Jovanna said as she knelt down beside the girl and grabbed her shoulder. She rolled the girl onto her back. Her heart fell into her stomach.

Danica's throat was ripped open. Blood covered the entire front of her body. Jovanna grit her teeth against the pain. She stood up and looked around. There was still no sign of the dogs from the pond. But the fresh scent of blood would easily draw them. *Well,* Jovanna thought, *they won't be making a meal out of this girl.*

Jovanna grabbed Danica's feet and pulled the girl's lifeless body behind her. There was a place nearby where the kids buried their dead. The dogs never went around it for some reason, which is why they picked the spot for their graveyard. Jovanna was angry at that stupid dog. Angry that another person had been robbed from her. Angry that life was so hard.

Warm tears spilled down her face. She cried for her fallen friend mostly. But she also cried for herself. She cried the entire time she pulled Danica's body behind her, the entire time she dug a hole in the graveyard for Danica's body, and the entire way back to her shelter. She cried until she finally fell asleep.

And that was the last time she cried.

8

DUSK HAD FINALLY ARRIVED. JOVANNA wanted nothing more than for the day to end. She stood a short distance from the hut that Jerik had made his home. Two guards were posted at the doorway of the mud and stone building, mainly to keep curious children away. None of the elves dared to enter the makeshift tomb. They considered it a bad omen to stand in the presence of the dead.

They did, however, walk by and pause momentarily in front of the doorway. One at a time, everyone in the village—or so it seemed—stopped in silence, paying tribute in their own way to the man. Jovanna was conflicted. Death came to everyone at some point. That was a fact she had come to acknowledge long ago. And she didn't really care for the man. Yet Jerik's death bothered her. It was like a parasite eating at her mind.

She kept reminding herself that he had saved her life and so she felt she owed him a debt of some kind. And now he was gone. If you owed something to another, did death break the debt? She didn't know the answer to that. She didn't know what she owed him, either.

So she just stood there staring at the darkened doorway for what felt like hours. She barely noticed when the ash stopped falling. Eventually, all of the villagers had paid their respects and went back to their normal routines. Even the guards left their post after night claimed the sky. A part of her wanted to go in there and look at him one last time. The other part of her wanted to burn the building down and forget she had ever met the man.

A voice inside told her this was what it meant to care. She scoffed at the thought. She didn't care about anyone or anything. She started to turn away and go to her own house when she heard shouting coming from the Tribe Chief's home. It sounded like Velent. She cast another glance to Jerik's house, then made her way toward the commotion.

When she reached the Tribe Chief's house, she expected to find an argument of some kind. She was disappointed when she saw otherwise.

"We must not let this traitor get away with his crimes," Velent was saying. She peered into the doorway. The leaders of the warriors and some of the tribe's elders were gathered in a circle, listening to Velent speak. Some of them were nodding their heads, others were shouting aggressively in agreement.

"I issue a formal declaration of war on the tribes responsible. I don't care if every tribe is gathered under one banner. I will go to the grave seeking justice."

Jovanna thought he was a fool. But as he continued with his speech, Jovanna began to understand what he was doing. By default, he was the new Tribe Chief. However, anyone could challenge him if they felt he was failing in his duty as the leader of the tribe.

He was bringing them to his cause, and by doing so, was earning their support to lead the tribe. Maybe she was wrong. Perhaps he was only slightly foolish.

"And what if we lose?" one of the elders spoke up. Immediate silence fell among the elves. "What then?"

Velent acknowledged the elder elf with a nod of his head. "It is a risk we must take. If we don't strike back for this crime, they will return again."

"Perhaps," the elder said. "What happens to our village if we lose? If all of our warriors are killed, what of our women and children? They will be defenseless against the other tribes. You know what will happen," he said ominously.

"I do," Velent said softly. "I have considered this already. And I have also put a plan into place should that be the case. Our people will be safe. I vow it."

Jovanna leaned against the wall beside the door and half listened to the rest. Velent went over his plan to track down the tribes responsible and what the villagers should do if they were to lose. He dismissed them and ordered them to get their rest. She waited until everyone left before stepping into the doorway.

"What are you doing here?" Velent demanded angrily.

Jovanna ignored his question. "I heard you've declared war on the other tribes," she said casually, looking at the few items that decorated the house.

"That's none of your concern," he answered. "So I ask again, what are you doing here?"

"It's no secret that we can't stand each other," she said. "But there is one thing we can agree on. The death of your father and of Jerik must be dealt with." Velent continued to glare at her but he didn't say anything.

"I want to go to war with you."

"You are not fighting with us," Velent replied. "You are not an elf. You don't belong here."

Jovanna wanted to strangle him. "I want to be here less than *you* want me here, trust me. But if I do not fight to avenge Jerik's murder, how would I honor him? Stand by and do nothing?" Though the elven tribes were barbaric, they adhered to a strict code of honor. Jovanna appealed to that quality. "He saved my life," she reminded him.

"He saved many lives," Velent answered.

She scowled at him. *Impetuous brat.*

"Tradition forbids it. And unlike my father, I will not betray our customs. Out of respect for Jerik, you can stay in the village. For now. But I will not let you go to war with us. Even if you were of the tribe, our women do not fight. They tend to the children and the chores. Only men go to war."

And to think that she thought he was clever. "I can fight better than any of your men. And I can cast any spell you can. Stop giving me petty excuses. I'm willing to put my hatred for you aside to achieve a common goal. Can you not do the same, *boy?*"

She took satisfaction in seeing Velent's jaw stiffen. "I. Refuse." His tone implied finality. But Jovanna was stubborn. She crossed her arms and stared him in the eyes.

"Jerik saved my life," she reiterated. "I will go and avenge him.

I have more right to do so than you. He was not an elf either. He was a man."

Velent shook his head in frustration. "You do not know what you speak of." He motioned toward the door. "Now leave."

Jovanna pushed him aside with her shoulder as she left. She wanted to punch him in the face. He could deny her the right to fight with them all he wanted, but he couldn't stop her from fighting the tribes herself. She hesitated as she passed Jerik's house. What would he do? She knew what he would say. He would have tried to dissuade Velent from war.

She was not Jerik. She grew up fighting for everything she needed. War was her life. If he had thought to change her, he was more foolish than Velent. She continued toward her house. She smiled as she began forming a plan. Velent would let her go to war if he didn't *know* it was her.

This was going to be perfect.

—

Jovanna was up before the sun rose. She had packed what few belongings she had into a small sack. It was made of long reeds tied together; a gift from one of the few elven women who spoke to her. It had a strap attached to it for carrying. She slung the strap over her shoulder. It felt heavier than it looked.

Grabbing her sword, she sheathed it in the left side of her belt. She doubted Velent would notice her sword was different than those of his warriors'. She had used a spell to change her appearance. She didn't have a mirror to check, but her illusion should have given her the visage of a young elven male. She wouldn't be able to speak, as even magic had its limitations.

She went back over the plan in her mind. She would join Velent's ranks as they marched out of the village and fight beside them against the other tribes. If the battle looked to be going ill for Velent, Jovanna would retreat and go her own way. If the battle went well, she would continue with them. She waited at her doorway and listened as the elves marched through the village.

They marched quickly and quietly, perhaps to keep from waking the rest of the village. She waited until the last warrior passed her house, then she stepped out onto the road and followed the small army. She couldn't see clearly enough to get a correct count, but she guessed Velent only had fifty warriors at his disposal. She had seen battles won with smaller forces, but they usually boasted cavalry. Elves didn't ride horses though, so the battle could go either way.

Every elf was tattooed from the neck down, making them all potent weapons. But if what the visitor had said was true, he had united the other tribes under one banner. There was something about that elf that didn't seem right. She couldn't figure it out, but that didn't really matter. He would fall to her blade as easily as her previous enemies had.

The elf in front of her looked over his shoulder at her and did a double take. Jovanna gritted her teeth, thinking her illusion had faded prematurely.

"I thought I was bringing up the rear," he said.

She shrugged her shoulders in response. It would be easy to keep from speaking while they marched, but she'd be forced to speak at some point. By then Velent wouldn't have any other choice but to let her fight.

"What do you think about this rumor?" he asked her. He wasn't looking at her, but she knew he had directed his question at her. She remained silent, hoping he'd just leave her alone.

"No one wants to talk about it," he continued, "but we should consider if it is true. If this elf has united the tribes, he has done a mighty thing. 'Who can stand against an elf? No one. Who can stand against all elves? No one.'"

Jovanna recognized that quote. Jerik had told her its meaning. Supposedly an ancient Tribe Chief from one of the clans had said that in a speech to rally his warriors. Elves saw themselves as the favored race above any other, despite their destitution and harsh living conditions. The elf continued to ramble, but Jovanna didn't pay him any attention.

She stared at the vastness that stretched out before them known as the Deadlands. It had been aptly named. The desert was an unforgiving place. There were more creatures that could kill with a single bite here than any other place she had been to. It was quite possibly on par with the dump she spent some of her childhood living in. Perhaps the only difference was that in the Deadlands there was more to eat, even with the drought.

She had lost track of how long they traveled, but they stopped when the sun was nearing the middle of the sky. All of the elves took a break, drinking water from skins and eating meager rations. Jovanna drank some water but refused to eat anything. She fought better on an empty stomach.

They rested for only a few minutes and then they were up and moving again. They didn't travel more than an hour when they stopped again. There was murmuring among the elves.

"We've found a village," the elf in front of her said, still not looking at her. He paused. "It appears to be empty."

Jovanna smirked. The elf must have known Velent would declare war and had the villages retreat somewhere safe.

"He knows we're coming," she said aloud to herself. The elf looked at her quizzically.

"What?"

Jovanna shook her head. She needed to be more careful. The elf turned back around. They waited a few more moments and then continued marching. Every half hour, almost like clockwork, they came across an empty village.

"It seems the rumor must be true," the elf said. "No tribe spaces their villages this closely together. Not even during an alliance."

She had been thinking the same thing. Her pulse quickened at the anticipation of battle. They had passed through several villages now. They couldn't be far from whatever trap their enemy had set. And she knew they were walking into a trap. It was too obvious. Perhaps Velent knew that as well. Yet he still led them onward. She had to admit that he certainly didn't lack courage.

Energy began to thrum through her body as they continued. Something was going on ahead. She could feel the magic pounding against her flesh like the sound of war drums. She noticed the magic was erratic, not flowing rhythmically like it normally did. This was definitely a trap.

Jovanna unsheathed her blade, wanting to be ready. The elf in front of her looked at her oddly, but she didn't care. She scanned the landscape but didn't see anything out of the ordinary. Yet the magic continued to beat against her flesh. It was almost becoming painful. The elf in front of her broke away from them, pointing to a small patch of cacti.

"I'm going to relieve myself," he said.

She nodded and continued following the others. A few moments later, the elf returned. They entered another abandoned village, similar looking to the others. The magic was pulsing so strongly now Jovanna thought it might rip through her flesh.

She stopped walking and looked at the huts around her. They were made of the same materials as the ones in Velent's village. Nothing out of the ordinary. She stepped into one of them. It had a bed and some chairs made of reeds, but nothing more. She left the hut and walked to the next one, followed by the next one. The pulsing was getting stronger with every step she took. She had a feeling it was coming from one of the huts.

She entered the next hut. There, sitting on the bed, was an elf. His breathing was quick and shallow and he was covered in sweat. The tattoos on his skin were glowing fiercely. And he wasn't wearing any clothes. Not even a loincloth.

That didn't faze her, but his odd behavior did. That and the pulsing magic was coming from his body. His feverish eyes turned to her. They were bloodshot and had started to cloud over.

"What's wrong with you?" she asked softly. His body jerked wildly as he attempted to stand. Jovanna backed up, not sure what he was doing. Finally, the elf managed to get up, and with wild uneven movements, he made his way towards the door.

She continued to back up and exited the hut, watching him warily. She realized that some of the elves had noticed the naked elf and had come to investigate.

"What's wrong with him?" one of them asked her. She shrugged.

She honestly didn't know, but the fact that his body was burning with energy wasn't a good sign.

One of the elves ran back to the others, probably to fetch Velent. Within moments the entire army had turned around and come back. Velent walked up to the man and touched his shoulder. He quickly pulled his hand away.

"His skin is on fire!" he said, clenching his hand. "Where are his clothes?"

No one spoke. Velent turned to the elf that had fetched him. "Where did you find him?" The elf said something softly in reply that Jovanna didn't hear.

The elf's tattoos began to pulse. His breathing remained shallow, but it was slowing down rapidly. His eyes were now completely covered in a thick milky substance. Velent called for one of the elders who made his way through the crowd of confused warriors.

"We must leave, now!" the elder yelled.

Velent stopped the elder with his hand. "What do you mean we have to leave? What's wrong with him?" The elder started ranting. Jovanna didn't understand most of it because he was talking too fast. She heard the word "stone-skin", which meant nothing to her.

The elf dropped to his knees and Jovanna noticed blood was starting to drip from his eyes. She had never seen *that* happen before. The elder pushed through the warriors and ran away quickly. She watched him run until she could no longer see him, then she looked back to Velent.

He was still investigating the naked elf. Jovanna could feel the magic thundering in her ears now. She vaguely heard something and looked to her right. The elf who had been marching in front of her was looking at her with concern.

She gave him an odd look. He pointed at her. She raised her hand and waved it, bidding him to say something.

"Your ears," he said.

She reached up and touched one but didn't feel anything. She looked at her fingers, thinking her ears might be bleeding with the pounding of the magic. Nothing. She looked at him questioningly.

"They are melting," he added.

A thunderous *boom* sounded and the next thing Jovanna knew, she was lying on her back staring up at the sun. Her ears were ringing and a foul smell was assaulting her nostrils. She sat up for a moment—just long enough to see the devastation—and fell back down.

Everyone was dead.

9

ARAMIS STARED THROUGH THE BLACK gates that guarded the shrine of Mordum. He was hiding beside Mel in the woods that surrounded the shrine, waiting and watching. The Prophet said it was reported that the blood would come out of the fountain at midnight.

They had barely found a caravan to travel with. Although the war with Talvaard was at a stand-still, most people still didn't travel across the border. Using a crudely drawn map, they had navigated the mountain trails to the shrine. They had seen the caved-in entrance of the tunnel Calderon had supposedly defeated Orlek in.

They'd been watching for over an hour and had yet to see anyone. It was almost midnight. Aramis looked to Mel. "It's almost time. I should get in there. Who knows how long the blood will be available in the fountain."

Mel summoned his armor and sword, the air rippling with mist around him. "I can't enter through the gates, but I can keep others from going in. Be careful, my Lord."

Aramis walked over to the gate entrance. He took another look around and pushed the door. It swung open on silent hinges. *It's well maintained,* he thought. After he stepped through the gate, it swung shut behind him with a soft *clang*. He stood perfectly still, half expecting an army of Mordum's priests to come from every direction.

Nothing.

Stepping slow and quiet, he walked around the area looking for the fountain. Although the sky was clear, the moon didn't seem to illuminate anything. Everything was bathed in shadows. Trees looked like gnarled creatures, hanging vines looked like claws reaching to whisk him away into the darkness. He was about to go back when he saw a faint glow coming from a ring of trees. He approached cautiously.

Peering through a gap in the trees, he saw the glow was coming from a pile of neatly stacked rocks. They illuminated a rectangular stone roughly five feet wide by five feet tall. In the center was a carving of a horned creatures head. Its mouth was open in a silent roar and water poured from it into a round metal bowl. Circling around the trees, he entered the small clearing.

His arm began burning as he neared the fountain. He rubbed it unconsciously. If people came here to get the blood, where were they? Aramis knelt down in front of the shrine and looked into the metal bowl. The water was crystal clear. He didn't see a drain, so where would the water go once the bowl was full? He touched the ground expecting it to be damp. It was dry.

"Hmm," he muttered softly. "That's odd." He stood back up and examined the rest of the fountain. It was relatively plain except for the carved head. It was made from a shiny black rock, possibly obsidian. The eyes sparkled red. He leaned in closer and realized the eyes were rubies. They were a decent size, probably worth a small fortune. A rustling sound caught his attention.

Aramis pushed himself up against the trees that ringed the clearing and looked through one of the gaps. He didn't see anything, but he heard muffled voices. A sudden panic shot through him. He started wondering why he agreed to do the Prophet's work in the first place. He had to remind himself that he was trying to clear his name. The Prophet was the first step.

He turned back to the fountain when he heard the water sputtering. Water still came out of it, but it was tinged red. It continued to sputter for several moments before a thick red liquid replaced the water.

Blood. Aramis knew that's what he had come to collect, but part of him didn't believe blood would actually come from a fountain. It surprised him. He shook his head and pulled the wineskin he brought from his belt. Sudden shouts broke out across the clearing. Aramis hurriedly held the skin under the fountain, collecting the blood. He filled it most of the way and then capped it. He wrapped the strings through his belt, ensuring they were tight so the bag wouldn't come loose and fall.

He could hear the sounds of battle now. Mel was surely fighting the followers of Mordum who had come to gather the blood themselves. Aramis sprinted towards the gate. He didn't have a sword, but he was well trained in hand to hand. A movement to the left, from the corner of his eye, caught his attention. He didn't pay it any heed; he just kept running. And then a hissing sound filled the air. He looked over his shoulder just in time to see something large crash into him.

Snapping jaws tried to maul his face. He covered his head protectively with his arms, attempting to roll away from whatever it was. Sharp claws raked across his arms as the thing tried to get at his head. Aramis started swinging his fists wildly. One of his blows connected, hitting something hard and scaly. The thing hissed loudly and backed away. He scrambled to his feet, the wounds on his arms burning like fire.

It was too dark to tell what was attacking him. All he could see was a big shadow. It was coming back at him. He took off running back toward the fountain. The creature was right behind him. Whatever it was, it was quick. He heard the thing's jaws snapping behind him. He almost tripped and fell as he reached the ring of trees.

He entered the clearing and picked up one of the glowing rocks in each hand. It was the closest thing he had to a weapon. He stood there, thinking his time on the earth may be about to end. The creature slowly entered the clearing. The glowing stones revealed a large head covered in scales. Aramis immediately recognized what it was.

A phiebus.

Dangerous creatures, they were distantly related to dragons. They resembled lizards but were massively larger. The one staring at him now was huge. He guessed it to be the size of a horse. Its scales were diamond-shaped and as black as the shadows of the shrine. He had seen only two in his lifetime. One from a distance as a boy. The other he had hunted with his father. Supposedly the species was on the brink of extinction, and for good reason.

Aramis felt as though his heart were pounding in his head. When his father and he had hunted one, they had several soldiers to help them and narrowly avoided being killed. Aramis knew he was overmatched. He stepped back as the phiebus lowered its head. The scales of the creature's neck began to glow red. Aramis turned and threw himself to the ground as a blast of fire exploded through the clearing.

He scrambled to his feet and ran as fast as his legs would go, still clutching the stones in his hand. The creature followed him, hissing and snapping. Aramis turned and threw one of the stones. It smacked the phiebus in the nose and only seemed to anger the creature further. No wonder they had not seen any priests or guards. The creature alone could handle almost any intruder.

He ran toward the gates. In the back of his mind, he knew he wasn't going to make it. The phiebus would catch him and maul him to death. He could make out Mel, his armor glinted in the moonlight, and saw he was busy fighting off several figures. Mel wouldn't be able to help him either since he couldn't enter the shrine.

Aramis tripped on some roots and fell face first. His head hit the ground hard and he lay gasping for breath. The phiebus was on him quick, clawing and biting. As soon as he gained his breath back, he rolled onto his back and slammed the glowing stone into the creature's head repeatedly. It didn't even seem to faze it.

The phiebus tried to bite his hand which caused him to drop the stone. He cursed and tried to get out from under the creature. It slammed a clawed foot onto his chest, pinning him down. He fought to free himself, but the creature was incredibly strong.

His mind raced frantically, trying to figure out how he could escape. The phiebus watched him squirming and he realized the creature was toying with him. He raised his leg and kneed the beast in the stomach. He may as well have tapped it on the shoulder for all it accomplished. Something fell beside him. He moved his head, trying to see past the phiebus's claws. The dagger the old blind woman had given him. It lay in the dirt, having fallen out of his belt.

Aramis hadn't even considered the small blade. It certainly wasn't long enough to pierce the creature's thick scales. What other option did he have? He struggled to reach the dagger with his right arm. An odd sound drew his attention to the beast's neck. It began to glow red again. Apparently, it was bored with him.

He felt the wooden hilt of the dagger with his fingertips. Stretching his arm out as far as he could, he grabbed the dagger and stabbed it toward himself, striking the phiebus's claw that had him pinned. A blinding white light flared to life. He closed his eyes and turned his head away, but his vision had already been seared. The weight of the claw lifted off of him. His eyes were watering so much he almost couldn't open them.

The phiebus had backed away, hissing and scratching at the ground. Aramis got back onto his feet. The powerful glow was coming from the blade of the dagger. He shielded his eyes and picked it up from the ground, having dropped it when the light burst forth. The phiebus continued hissing at him as it backed away. He didn't have time to wonder about the blade. He could hear the sounds of fighting still raging at the gate and knew he had to help Mel.

Turning his back to the creature, he was about to head to the gates when he heard the phiebus coming back at him. He turned around, holding the blade out as if to ward off the beast. It stopped, dropped its head, and bellowed out a breath of fire. It took him by surprise and he braced himself as the blast of fire enveloped him.

Only he didn't feel the heat. Nor did he smell smoke. The flames sputtered and died as they reached him, fading out of existence. The beast hissed and leaped through the air, landing in front of him. It stared down at him menacingly and opened its mouth again. Aramis looked at the glow coming from its neck. The reddish light illuminated a small spot where one of its scales was chipped, leaving the skin exposed.

Without thinking twice, Aramis took the opening. He lunged forward and thrust the dagger into the beast's neck. Fire spewed out of the wound, igniting the dry grass and leaves on the ground. He yanked the blade free and staggered back. It looked like liquid fire was pouring from the phiebus's neck, burning everything it touched. The beast roared in pain, piercing the air with a high-pitched shriek. Aramis clapped his hands over his ears. It was so loud!

The fire began to burn the creature itself. The thick black scales melted from the heat. The phiebus walked forward sluggishly before slumping onto the ground. Shouts drew his attention back to the gates. He sprinted that way, feeling his belt to make sure he still had the wineskin of blood. It was there, though the cap had come loose and some of it had spilled out. He replaced the cap as he ran, but kept the dagger out.

Reaching the gates, he pulled them open and stepped out. Mel's back was to him and he was fighting an orc. An orc! Aramis thought his father's patrols had killed them all or driven them off after the battle outside Palindrom when Orlek had been defeated. He saw three bodies on the ground, all orcs. Apparently, they hadn't all been driven off. Mel swept his blade out in an arc, pushing the orc back.

He seemed to have everything handled. Aramis saw torches in the distance heading their way. "We've got company!" he yelled. Mel didn't acknowledge him other than to quickly dispatch the orc, severing its head from its body.

He turned to Aramis, running a hand through his hair and wiping sweat from his brow. "These were just scouts," he said, waving at the bodies. "They tried to go into the shrine."

"I thought only those with the mark of Mordum could enter?" Aramis asked.

Mel knelt down beside one of the bodies and lifted the orc's arm up. He pointed. Aramis had to get closer and lean in to see. A black cross, just like the one on his own arm. "So they've aligned themselves with Mordum? That doesn't make any sense. Orcs worship their chiefs as gods."

"Cut the head off a snake, does it not still move?" Mel asked.

Aramis nodded in agreement. "They're getting closer. We've got to get out of here."

Mel pointed to the wineskin at his belt. "Is that the blood?" Aramis nodded. "What happened to you? Are you all right, my Prince? You've got blood on you." Aramis gingerly rubbed the scratches from the phiebus. Though they had stopped bleeding, they were still painful.

"There was a phiebus guarding the shrine."

"Nasty creatures," Mel said, shaking his head. "I'm surprised you survived to tell the tale." He motioned to the east. "Down the mountain," he said. Aramis didn't argue. He wanted to get as far away from this place as he could. He wasn't sure if it was the scratches or the cross, but his left arm was burning intensely. They trotted off at a jog. Aramis kept looking over his shoulder to see if the orcs had picked up their trail. It didn't appear that they had.

After an hour, they reached a flat area where they stopped to rest. "Climbing down the mountain is much easier than going up," Aramis said as he leaned against a boulder. He accepted a canteen from Mel and drank deeply. Mel sighed as he looked out over the landscape.

"What is it?" Aramis asked.

"To think that I bathed in lavender before we left, only to be covered in sweat and orc blood. It's utterly depressing."

Aramis laughed at the absurdity of that. "You're ridiculous." He took another drink and passed the canteen back to Mel. Some rocks clattered down the mountain from above. Both of them turned and looked.

"There," Mel pointed. An orc.

"They did follow us," Aramis groaned. "I don't think we can make it down the mountain without engaging them." Mel remained silent, watching as more orcs appeared above them. Another figure joined them, standing much shorter than the orcs. "Is that a man?"

"I think so," Mel answered. "I can't be sure from this distance. If it is a man, it's surely one of Mordum's priests. They were probably coming to collect the blood. We need to keep moving."

They continued downward, treading carefully so they didn't cause a rock slide or trip on anything. They didn't stop again. They couldn't afford to, not with the orcs closing in on them. After several hours, they had almost reached the bottom of the mountain. The sun was beginning to rise on the horizon, bathing the sky in brilliant reds and oranges.

Aramis looked back to see how far the orcs were. They were closing the gap. With the sun coming up, Aramis was able to more clearly see their features. They were tall and muscular, with varied skin colors. Some of them were gray skinned, but most of them had a pale green hue to their flesh. They wore steel breastplates covered in spikes and tattered clothing underneath. They wielded large battle axes and hammers. Jutting up from their lower lips were two large canines, roughly three or four inches in length.

The shorter figure kept pace with them which surprised Aramis. Orcs were stronger and faster than men, usually being able to travel three times the distance in the same amount of time. Mel tapped him on the shoulder to get his attention and handed him a small spyglass. Aramis took it and looked at the orcs through it. He counted at least fifteen. Then he looked toward the man. It *was* a man. And Aramis recognized him.

He lowered the spyglass and clenched his jaw.

"My Lord? What is it?"

Aramis stared hatefully up the mountain in silence. His breathing intensified. He would have crushed the spyglass in his grip if it weren't made of metal and glass.

"The short one up there," he said.

"That's my father's killer."

10

"YOU ARE CERTAIN?" MEL ASKED. He took the spyglass from Aramis and looked through it himself. Aramis nodded stiffly. "I'd recognize his face anywhere. I'm going to kill him." He stepped forward as if he would fulfill that pledge then and there.

Mel gripped his arm. "This isn't the place or the time," he said softly. "I know your pain, my Lord. I do. But you'd go up against orcs and a priest of Mordum with nothing but a dagger?"

Aramis stared up the mountain for a moment longer and then turned to his friend. "You are right. I cannot allow my hatred to cloud my judgment. But I *will* have my revenge." Aramis pointed at the man and glared. He didn't know if the man could see the action or not, but he swore he heard laughter echoing down behind him as they continued their trek.

They climbed over rocks and stepped over fallen trees. It was difficult trying to move quickly without tumbling down to their deaths. The orcs were getting closer. Aramis thought he could hear their heavy breathing.

"We need a new plan," Mel said between labored breaths. "We can stand and fight, but they have the high ground to their advantage. We might reach the bottom, but they'll be able to outrun us on the flat ground."

Aramis didn't have any ideas. He was struggling just to keep his pace. Fighting certainly wasn't an option; he didn't have a suitable weapon.

They walked around a massive boulder and Aramis paused. "We've got to keep moving," Mel said. Aramis looked at the boulder, then down the mountain.

"I'm getting an idea now. We can hide here and wait until they pass us. Once they do, we can push this rock down and crush them."

Mel wiped sweat from his forehead with the back of his hand. "What if it misses them? Or if they realize it's a ruse?"

"Do you have a better plan?"

Mel looked up the mountain at the approaching horde. "No. But we'll need to make sure they are in the rock's path. I'll continue down further and draw their attention. You push the rock down."

Aramis was shaking his head before Mel finished speaking. "You could also be caught in its path. And I can't push this rock myself. It's got to weigh at least a thousand pounds. I'll need your help to do this."

Mel held out his hand and summoned his sword. The silver blade materialized from mist, glinting in the light of the morning. He began cutting away at the bottom of the enormous rock, causing its balance to become precarious.

"That should be enough for you to easily push it yourself. I'm going to draw them down into its path. It's too risky for you to do it. I'm much more protected."

"You think your armor can keep you alive through an avalanche?"

Mel summoned his armor and pulled the face plate of his helm down. "Only one way to find out," he said. Before Aramis could argue further, Mel leaped away, jogging down the rocky landscape. Aramis knelt down to the right of the boulder, waiting for the orcs to pass. He counted them silently as they ran down towards Mel, who stood in a battle stance awaiting them.

The black-robed priest jogged past, taking up the rear position of the line. As soon as he passed, Aramis scrambled uphill to the backside of the boulder. He placed his hands on the rock and pushed as hard as he could. It didn't budge. He growled in frustration and pushed again. The dirt beneath his feet shifted and he had to make a walking motion to keep traction. Despite the fact that Mel had cut away most of the rock that held the boulder in place, it remained solidly stuck.

Aramis stepped back and kicked the boulder. He also threw himself bodily against it, possibly bruising his shoulder. He was sweating from the exertion. Clanging metal filled the air and he knew

the orcs had engaged Mel. He had to find a way to move the rock
and quickly. He turned to place his back against the rock and saw the
priest standing there.

Aramis's eyes widened and he reached for the dagger at his belt.
The priest spoke a word and Aramis was bound in place, unable to
move. His muscles strained against an invisible force.

"You have something that belongs to me," the assassin's voice
said. He stepped close to Aramis and took the wineskin filled with
blood from his belt. "You also killed Mordum's pet. He is not
pleased with you. The quicker you let the mark consume you, the
easier your life will become."

Aramis tried to speak but nothing came out. He could still
breathe, but his vocal cords obeyed him as well as his muscles did;
not at all. The priest pulled his hood back and Aramis was greeted
by the familiar face of the man who murdered his father. His vision
hazed as his rage boiled over. Despite his raw emotions, he still
couldn't break free of the spell. He vaguely heard the sounds of
fighting. Mel needed his help and yet he was useless.

"The new king is searching for you. He will kill you when he
finds you. I wonder how angry he would be if I took that joy from
him?" The priest continued talking, seemingly more to himself than
to Aramis. "We serve the same god, but we all have different
interests, you see?" He tapped his chin as if contemplating
something. "I shall not kill you yet. But I will kill your friend."

The priest placed his foot on the boulder and pushed. The rock
went rolling. He made it seem so easy. Then he physically turned
Aramis around. It went tumbling wildly down the hill, bouncing and
causing a landslide. Aramis watched in mute horror, hoping Mel
would be able to escape. The massive rock crushed everything in its
path. After a few minutes, the dust settled and Aramis could only see
the mangled bodies of orcs. He couldn't see Mel; hopefully, that was
a good sign.

Without saying anything else, the priest continued walking down
the mountain. Aramis remained paralyzed until he could no longer
see the priest in the distance. As the spell wore off, his muscles began
to ache. He slumped down onto his knees, his entire body shaking.
How could anyone stand against a man who could stop you with a

single word? After a few minutes, Aramis stood back up and slowly made his way toward the bodies. He had to know.

Many of the orcs were nothing more than bloodied lumps. He had to look away lest he vomit. There was no sign of Mel. He searched all around the devastation left behind from the avalanche. He was ready to give up his search when something shiny caught his eye. It was sticking up from some loose dirt. He knelt down and realized it was a hand. Well, it was a gauntlet. Aramis grabbed it and pulled.

The dirt fell away to reveal the armored body of Mel. "Thank the gods," Aramis breathed. He paused. Did he really just say that? Pushing the thought away, he pulled Mel's faceplate up. His eyes were closed, and his skin was covered in sweat, but he seemed all right. "Mel? Mel, can you hear me?"

A long, low groan was Mel's reply. Aramis sighed in relief. "Can you move? I can help you up, but I don't want to move you in case something is broken."

Mel's eyelids blinked rapidly multiple times before they finally opened fully. He met Aramis's gaze and said, "The only thing that's broken is your sense of style."

Aramis laughed. "You're a fool, you know that? I'm surprised your armor held up to that."

Mel forced himself up out of the dirt and got to his feet. He surveyed the area, nodding to himself. "You did it," he said. "You crushed them with the boulder. What about the priest?"

"I didn't push the rock. I couldn't. It was too heavy for me. The priest pushed it down after he took the blood." Mel looked to Aramis's belt. "He cast a spell on me, I think. I couldn't move or speak. All I could do was watch." Aramis shook his head forlornly. "He's taken the blood and he's gone to who knows where. What do we do now?"

"We find him," Mel said resolutely. "We find him and we take it back." One of the orcs stirred and Aramis drew his dagger instinctively. Mel shook his head. "Leave him. We should get moving. We've got to find his trail."

Aramis hesitated, finding it odd that Mel didn't want him to kill the creature. He sheathed the dagger back at his belt. "Let's be off," he said.

Mel dismissed his armor and they made their way down the rest of the mountain. With no one pursuing them, they were able to travel at a slower pace and reserve their strength. After an hour, they reached the main road that wound its way through Oakvalor.

"It's unlikely we'll pass anyone this close to the mountains," Mel said as they walked. Aramis nodded in silence. At least the road was paved and relatively flat. His legs were still burning from the descent of the mountain. The scratches on his arm were itchy, but he tried to ignore it. The blood had dried and wasn't dripping down his arm anymore. Now that he thought about it, his hand didn't hurt.

He held his broken hand up and made a fist. Then he wiggled his fingers. He started laughing and Mel looked at him quizzically. "My hand," Aramis said. "It's not broken anymore. I hadn't realized it in all the chaos. Did you heal me?"

Mel shook his head, frowning. "It's the mark. As time goes by, other things will begin to happen."

"Like what?" Aramis asked, still flexing his hand.

"I've read it's different for everyone. Some people gain powers, others go insane. Mordum is a cruel god and shows favor to few. Let us hope we don't have to find out what it will do to you."

"The priest must have some serious power. I struggled to push that boulder and couldn't do it. It seemed like he moved it without much effort. And his eyes looked strange."

Mel stopped walking. He tilted his head. "What do you mean? What about his eyes were strange?"

"They were black," Aramis answered.

"A templar," Mel said softly. Aramis didn't hear him. "A what?"

"A templar," he repeated. "They are the elite of Mordum's forces. I've never encountered one before, but I have heard stories. The Prophet battled one a few years ago. He managed to kill the templar, but it wasn't easy. They are said to be gifted with many dark powers and are almost impossible to defeat. The Prophet only managed it by the power of Edria."

Aramis took it all in. He would still get his revenge. Given this new information, he wasn't sure how, but that wasn't going to deter him.

"Brookhaven is the nearest town," Mel said, changing the subject. "We should make it there by nightfall. We can eat and get some rest. Then we can decide what to do in the morning." Aramis voiced his agreement with the plan and they continued walking.

When they finally reached the town, the sun was just setting. Aramis found the place welcoming. Children ran through the streets, heading home for dinner after a long day of playing. People were closing down their shops. The only places that seemed to stay open were the inns and a single bar. The only difference between the two was the bar didn't have rooms to rent.

They rented a room from the only inn that had a vacancy. Mel insisted they go to the bathhouse to wash up before getting anything to eat. Aramis was so exhausted the only thing he wanted to do was sleep. He was too tired to argue with Mel, so they ended up at the bath house. Sitting in the hot water relaxed his muscles and Aramis had to concede that Mel's idea had been a good one.

As they bathed, the attendants took their clothes and washed them. Though he was still sore, Aramis felt refreshed after the bath. The attendants also bandaged their wounds and scrapes for them after applying a healing salve. He almost felt like he was back at the castle.

It reminded him that he had a duty to his people. They couldn't remain leaderless. The petty nobles would plunge the kingdom into civil war, similar to Talvaard's current state. He also kept thinking about what the blind woman and the templar had said. A "new" king. Had someone usurped the throne? What kind of chaos was the castle in? There were so many things he didn't know.

Aramis went back to the inn and claimed one of the empty tables. He didn't think it was likely anyone would recognize him this far from the capital, so he didn't bother to conceal himself. The barmaid came to take his order, but as hungry as he was he wanted to wait for Mel. After thirty minutes of waiting, he was about to get up and go looking for his friend when Mel walked into the inn.

He was smiling as he made his way over to the table. "It's about time," Aramis said.

"I'm sorry for the delay, my Lord. I was enjoying an amazingly talented woman's hands."

Aramis raised his brow quizzically. Mel's face flushed in embarrassment. "I should clarify I meant a massage. I was enjoying a massage. Took the pain right out of my neck."

"I'm starving," Aramis said, "and you are getting your back rubbed? I could have eaten and gone to bed already."

Mel's eyes widened. "I'm sorry! If I'd have known you were waiting on me to eat, I'd have skipped the massage until after our meal." Mel waved the barmaid over and they ordered some food and wine. It didn't take long for her to bring their order. As they ate, Aramis noticed that Mel kept looking at the door every time someone entered the inn.

"Waiting on someone?" Aramis asked curiously.

"I'm merely being cautious," Mel answered. "We can't talk about it here, but I learned some interesting things from the bathhouse girl." They finished their meal and Mel led Aramis outside, much to his displeasure. He just wanted to get some sleep. They walked to the edge of the town before Mel would answer any of his questions. Even then, Mel kept a close watch at any passerby with an intensity that probably made the strangers uncomfortable.

"Mel, I'm exhausted. Please get on with it already." Aramis stood with his arms folded.

"I'm sorry, my Lord. I have to be sure we aren't being watched. The girl seemed a little too open about what she knew. It appears the priest of Mordum came through here not too long before us." That piqued Aramis's interest. He tilted his head and waited for Mel to continue.

"He scared several of the townspeople pretty well. He came through long enough to eat, without paying, and left. The town guard seemed to know who he was because they were too frightened to approach him about the unpaid bill. When I asked the girl if anyone knew which direction he headed, she said the local blacksmith saw him go west, riding off on a horse the likes of which he'd never seen before."

"Is that it? You snuck around and looked at everyone as if they were a criminal over that bit of information?" Aramis shook his head.

"As I said, I was being careful. She was very willing to talk about the priest despite the guards being afraid of him. She could be a spy."

That could be true, but Aramis doubted it. "So he went back the way we came from? We didn't pass anyone on the road. The Viss Mountains stretch the entire border of my kingdom all the way to the Deadlands. He couldn't have ridden a horse—" Aramis cut off his words, remembering how the priest had climbed the walls of the castle.

Mel nodded, probably thinking the same thing. "So he headed where? To Talvaard? Why would he go west?" Aramis asked.

Mel shrugged. "I've been pondering the same thing. I will send word to the Prophet and see what information he can provide."

"How are you going to do that? We don't have time to wait for a courier to go to Kaldore and back."

"Edria has given us other means of communication," Mel replied. "We can communicate through prayer. We don't do it often, as it is taxing on our strength. I will pray before we retire so I will have time to rejuvenate. It bothers me that he went west. Aside from another follower of Mordum being in Talvaard, I cannot discern why he would head that way. There is constant division in Mordum's ranks, so I don't believe they are working together. There is only one way to find out," Mel said.

Aramis unfolded his arms and rubbed his face. "We must travel to Talvaard," he said, groaning inwardly.

"Precisely," Mel answered.

—

After they returned to the inn, Aramis went to his room to get some much-needed sleep. Mel went to his own room, deeply troubled by the events of the day. Kneeling before the bed, he withdrew a medallion from under his shirt.

Holding it in his hands, he focused his mind and reached out through Edria's connection. He waited only a moment before he heard the Prophet's words in his mind.

Melchiades, he greeted, *I trust all is well?*

I wish it were so, Mel answered. *We have crossed paths with a templar. He could have killed us both easily, but he spared Aramis. He may believe he killed me, but Edria's blessed armor kept me safe. Aramis was able to retrieve the blood, but the Templar took it. According to people in the town we are in, he headed west. What is in the west that would send him that way?*

There was a pause. *There are rumors that Mordum has an outpost somewhere on the edge of Talvaard. None of our agents have been able to find the place if the rumor holds true. What of the prince's progression? Has the mark begun to take over his mind?*

Not that I have seen, Mel said. *He appears to be holding it off. He is strong of mind. I don't think the mark will take him easily. The faster we can retrieve the blood, the faster we can get him back to you. I do hope you can find a way to remove the mark. Have you found anything yet?*

Melchiades, listen carefully to my instruction. Edria has abandoned the prince. He bears the mark of Mordum. Our goddess refuses to aid him in any way. Let him help you retrieve the blood and then wash your hands of the man. That is the will of Edria.

Mel was taken aback, so much so that he almost lost the connection. He shook his head in disbelief. *What are you saying? Edria would never abandon someone in need. Are you sure you heard her correctly? Surely this is not the will of the goddess!*

Calm yourself, the Prophet said, *You allow your emotions to cloud your mind. One man is not worth the cost of the world. We do what is right and true for the sake of humanity. Perhaps I should have assigned another to watch over the prince. Your friendship with him is hindering your ability to obey Edria. Do as I have commanded and return to Kaldore in haste.*

The connection severed. Mel opened his eyes and put the medallion back. He trusted the Prophet above any man, but this did

not seem right. It twisted his gut and made him feel ill. He numbly
climbed into the bed and lay on his back, staring up at the ceiling.
He silently pleaded to Edria, asking her to help Aramis.

He eventually fell asleep, hoping Edria had heard his prayers.

11

IT WAS HARD TO BREATHE.

Jovanna *forced* breath into her lungs. Her ears were ringing loudly, but at least the magic wasn't pounding at her anymore. She continued to lay there until she could somewhat breathe again. She got up slowly. She was surprised to see several elves up and moving. She thought for sure they had all died. As she looked around, she saw that many of Velent's warriors *had* died.

Gruesomely, some of the elves had been blown apart completely and their limbs lay far from their bodies. There was nothing left of the elf who had been glowing. She walked over to the group of elves who had survived. Of Velent's fifty men, only half had survived. And some of them probably wouldn't be able to walk. She hoped her illusion had endured the magical blast.

She noticed the elf who had been talking her ear off the entire march was among the group. He nodded toward her as she joined them. She nodded back. One of the elves was tending a wound on Velent's arm. He was yelling at everyone, but Jovanna didn't know if it was from the blast or out of anger. He glanced at her when she walked up but turned his attention back to the elf he was yelling at. Apparently, her illusion was still up.

A horn sounded in the distance. Everyone turned toward the direction it sounded from and drew their weapons. Jovanna reached to her belt and grabbed air. She looked down and remembered she had been carrying her sword when she was flung to the ground. She spotted her sword in the sand close to where she fell. She retrieved it and rejoined the elves.

She could make out a large force in the distance. Most likely it was their enemy coming to meet them. Velent began giving orders and directing his men to take positions in hiding. They were going to try and ambush the enemy. Jovanna hid on the backside of one of the huts, out of view from the road. And then they waited.

Roughly twenty minutes later, the enemy entered the village. Jovanna counted at least a hundred warriors. A few of them had skin color different than the others. She thought it odd that she had never seen that before, but she had only been among Velent's tribesmen. She scoured their ranks, hoping to find their mysterious leader among them, but she didn't see him. She did see the elder who had run away. Part of him, anyway. His head was impaled upon a wooden shaft and carried at the head of the army.

A whistle sounded; Velent's signal. She waited a moment and watched as chaos unfolded among the enemy warriors. Velent's men had surprised them. She joined in the fray, cutting down several elves quickly. They were no match for her skill with the blade. She risked a glance at Velent and saw him fighting ferociously despite the wound to his arm.

The initial shock had worn off and the enemy warriors formed into small organized groups. Velent's men had managed to take down a third of the warriors, but now they were hard pressed. They were still highly outnumbered. Two elves came at Jovanna. She leaped backward out of their reach and swung her sword horizontally. She missed and one of them charged her. He landed a solid punch to the left side of her face and she staggered back.

She growled in anger and spun her blade out in front of her in a weaving pattern. She was quicker than he was, and she managed to push him back and put him on the defensive. The other elf was one that had a different skin color. He stepped out in front of her, putting his body in the path of her blade. She smirked as she put more strength behind the swing.

The blade smacked into him and bounced off, leaving her hands throbbing. She managed to keep her grip on the blade and was surprised to see him still standing. Her surprise escalated when she realized her blade had not even nicked his flesh. He came at her, swinging an elven pole-sword at her. It was a primitive weapon, consisting of a wooden staff with a six-inch blade on each end.

She easily deflected his move. He grabbed the weapon in both hands and was pulling it back toward himself. Stepping forward, she brought her sword up and over in an overhanded chopping motion and sliced the wooden staff in two. Unfazed, the elf wielded each piece like two swords. Jovanna saw an opening and thrust her sword forward, attempting to hit him in the stomach. Again the blade bounced off his skin with nothing to show for it.

Backing away, she watched him intently, trying to discern what kind of magic was keeping her sword at bay. She didn't sense any spells other than his tattoo magic. She wondered if it was possible that a tattoo could produce such a strong spell. She didn't know much about the elven tattoo magic; they were very secretive about it. She also couldn't figure out a way around the spell. It was as though his skin had been transformed into a layer or rock.

She remembered then that the elder who ran away had said something about "stone-skin". She needed to find out what it was. She spun around and threw her leg out, slamming it into the elf's ankles and knocking him from his feet. Before he could get back up, she jumped over him and cut down the other elf. Then she jogged over to a group of Velent's warriors and took up a position next to them.

The elf who had marched in front of her was in the group as well. He moved to stand beside her. "Stone-skin," he said, motioning to the elf she had knocked down. He was back on his feet. She looked at him and shrugged.

"You must be mute."

She nodded. That would keep her from having to speak.

"Stone-skin is a tattoo our people used to use when we fought against the humans. Some of the elders said that the knowledge of this tattoo was lost, but somebody has found it. They think it is the Uniter."

Jovanna scoffed. They came up with names and titles for everything.

"It's a dangerous tattoo to get. It doesn't work on everyone. Either it makes the skin change, or you die. The elders believe this is what happened to the elf we found. His body rejected the tattoo and it destroyed him."

Jovanna stared at the elf with the stone skin. How could she counter the tattoo if it was in his skin, and his skin was now as hard as stone? She wouldn't be able to cut it. She wished her illusion could mask her voice so that she could ask questions. She would have to make due.

She stared at the magic that floated through the air. The particles swirled around the elf, like miniature flashing lights. Why were they doing that? As she continued to stare, she noticed that while the magic was swirling around him, some of the lights were disappearing. It looked as if his body, or more specifically his tattoo, was siphoning the magic.

She watched a few moments longer. That's exactly what his tattoo was doing. She looked to the elf standing beside her and grinned, then ran out to battle the elf again. He didn't say anything to stop her. They charged each other and she used her sword to deflect his two blades. She needed to get close; dangerously close. She dipped down under one of his swings and spun up behind him. She lifted her leg and kicked him hard in the back, flinging him forward.

To his credit, he didn't fall. She growled and closed the distance. He turned to face her and she managed to knock one of the blades from his grasp. She switched her blade to her left hand and locked her sword against his remaining blade. Then she held her right hand above the tattoo that was sucking in the magic. She focused on the swirling lights and commanded them to obey her.

The tattoo was strong, but her will was stronger. The magic stopped flowing into him. His body stiffened and his jaw clenched. She balled her hand into a fist and "pulled" the magic away from him. He gasped aloud and dropped to one knee. She kept her concentration, willing the magic to keep away from him. And it obeyed.

The color of his skin began to change to a normal hue. She knew the change had to be painful because he kept grunting and crying out. When she felt his skin had become normal enough, she released her control on the magic. Gripping her sword in both hands, she spun a complete circle and easily lopped off his head. Blood splattered and the head thudded into the dirt.

A cheer rang out from Velent's warriors. Jovanna raised her sword in the air and bellowed a war cry. Then she charged the nearest group of enemies, cutting through their midst with abandon. Velent's warriors followed her example, and though they were outnumbered, they fought more fiercely than their enemy. Jovanna took down another stone skin elf similar to the way she handled the first. It seemed to have put the fear in them as Jovanna heard the elves call for a retreat with their horns.

Velent's warriors let out another cheer and started to pursue the enemy before Velent ordered them to stay put. He told his warriors to burn the dead and assemble themselves at the edge of the village. Then he stalked over to Jovanna and stopped in front of her, staring intently into her eyes.

"I declined your request to fight with us. So tell me, why are you here?" He glared at her. She assumed he realized who she was by her spellcasting. Elves only used tattoo magic.

"I'm here because I want to avenge Jerik. Stop wasting my time with questions to which you already know the answer."

"You disobey me and then you mock me? I should have you put to death."

She laughed. "Try it. I dare you." She tightened her grip on the hilt of her sword. "If it wasn't for me, you'd have lost this battle. You've lost half your warriors as it is. You can't deny you need my blade. Not without sounding like a foolish brat."

"You'd have me look like a weak leader by allowing a woman, a *human* woman no less, to fight with our men?" He spat on the ground at her feet.

"I can keep this illusion for weeks, *elf*. And I don't need your permission to fight my own enemies."

They locked stares. Finally, Velent cursed and stormed away. Jovanna watched him go, knowing she had beaten him. Now that she knew how to kill the elves with stone skin, Velent would need her too much to send her away. She had pushed him into a precarious position. Despite their hatred for one another, she knew he was a good leader when it came to battle. At least he had that in his favor.

She knelt down next to the elf she had decapitated. His skin had completely turned back to its normal color. She examined the body, making note of tattoos she had never seen before. There were at least a dozen of them. The tattoo that had given the elf stone skin appeared to be made from a different type of ink, as well.

A puddle of blood had formed at the neck where his head had once been. Jovanna stared at it, reminded of a time long ago. She turned her attention back to the tattoos. She would need to study these new ones. One could not defend against an enemy if one did not know about their strengths. She used her sword to cut the elf's skin off, rubbed it in the dirt to dry the blood, then rolled the skin up and tucked it into her boot.

She stood up and surveyed the rest of the carnage. Bodies of the enemy tribe littered the abandoned village. She smiled at the death around her.

It had been a good day so far.

12

Fourteen Years Ago

SHE WAS TURNING SIX.

Normally her parents would get her a small frosted muffin from the local bakery and present it to her on her birthday. Her mother would sing her a song that her mother had sang to her when she was a child, and her father would give her a speech about the importance of getting older and learning something that would make her a valuable member of the community.

Jovanna's father was a farmer. They had the largest field of wheat in the region. Her father didn't make enough to be wealthy, but they never went hungry either. Her mother helped with the planting in the early spring, but she normally spent her time sewing clothing that would be sent to the castle for the nobles. Since the styles in the court seemed to change as often as the weather, her mother had a steady stream of work to keep her busy.

Their house was small compared to the other farmers' homes, but her father had made sure to have a sewing room so her mother could work from their home and not have to travel into town for work. Her mother would get up with the sunrise and sew for hours, stopping long enough to make lunch and then sewing until it was time to prepare dinner.

Her father would come home dirty and tired, but always smiling. He would greet her mother first, giving her a gentle kiss and then sweep Jovanna up into the air and tell her about the latest snake or gopher or other creature that he had killed in the fields. He would clean up and then they would eat dinner as a family.

That's how most days went. Sometimes her father would come home drunk, and she didn't like to think about those times. Her birthdays were always different. Her father would skip working the fields and take her to town, letting her peruse the new items in the shops and buying her one thing that she liked most.

When they returned home, her mother would have spent the day sewing her a new dress or a fancy looking shirt. She would eat the frosted muffin and go to bed feeling like the most important person in the world. She looked forward to her birthday every year for those reasons. And her birthday was always like that. At least, they were. This one would be much different.

Jovanna stared out the window of the orphanage, watching the other children play outside. She sighed and began pacing around the room, counting her steps. She walked from the window to the door and counted sixty steps, then walked from wall to wall and lost count twice before counting one hundred and twenty steps. She did this several times every day, usually getting the same numbers. Sometimes a few of the other kids would ask her to come outside with them, but she ignored them.

She didn't like other kids. In fact, she didn't like other people. They all treated her differently like she was some kind of oddity. It was probably because of what happened to her parents. It didn't matter to her what they thought. What happened had happened and there was nothing that could change it. Was she upset? Of course. But if she had learned anything in her six short years it was that being upset didn't change anything.

When she first arrived at the orphanage, one of the other children asked her what brought her there. She tried explaining the events that led to her arrival, but the girl screamed and ran from the room before she could finish. Then she was scolded later by one of the adults for telling lies and trying to scare other children.

Jovanna shook as her head as she thought about it. She wished it were all lies. She wished it were all some story she had read in a book and not the reality of her life. Her mother always told her, "If you don't like how life is going, then change it." And that's exactly what Jovanna was going to do.

She was going to run away from the orphanage.

It had only been a couple of months, but she couldn't stand it any longer. There were too many kids crammed into the room. There weren't even enough beds for everyone. Not that Jovanna cared about that so much. She just *really* didn't like people. And here in the orphanage, she was surrounded by them. She loved the open fields of her family's wheat farm. She enjoyed the company of the wildlife and the floating white lights that seemed drawn to her.

She still saw the lights, even as she paced the room, but it wasn't the same. It hadn't been the same since …

She stopped pacing as she noticed one of the other children standing in the doorway staring at her.

"Do you want to come outside?" the girl asked.

Jovanna ignored her and began pacing the room again. The girl didn't leave. Usually, when she ignored them, they would leave. After a few minutes of watching Jovanna pacing back and forth, the girl began doing the same thing.

Jovanna stopped. "What are you doing?" she demanded.

The girl stopped as well. "I'm counting. That's what you are doing, right? I can tell by the way you are walking around that you are counting your steps. It's sixty-two steps from the window to the door and one hundred and eighteen from that wall to this one."

Jovanna just stared at her.

"I know because I counted them when I first got here. My village was burned down by some thieves and my parents didn't make it out of the house in time. What happened to your parents?"

"I don't want to talk about it," Jovanna said. She started pacing again. The girl copied her.

"It helps, you know. Talking about it. I still cry sometimes because I miss them, but talking about them helps."

"I killed them," Jovanna said. "Is that what you want me to say? I killed them and they are never coming back. And no, it doesn't help me to talk about it. Nothing helps except the lights!" She hadn't realized it, but she was yelling and had clenched her fists. The girl looked frightened. She looked like she was about to say something, but instead, she turned and fled. Jovanna gritted her teeth and walked to the window. She watched the girl run to one of the adults. The same woman who had scolded her before. The woman looked up at her.

"Great," she muttered as she turned from the window.

After they had eaten dinner and been sent to their beds, Jovanna lay in the darkened room staring at the ceiling. She had it all planned out already. She would wait until everyone was asleep and then she would get up and sneak down the stairs. The orphanage didn't employ guards, so she didn't have to worry about getting past anyone.

She just had to get a key from one of the adults so she could unlock the main doors and get outside. She figured all of that would be pretty easy except for getting the key. There were five adults who helped care for all of the orphans. Jovanna had thought long and hard about which one to try and take the key from. She had finally decided to take it from the adult who had scolded her earlier.

She lay there for as long as she could bear. She got up off the floor. She considered taking the blanket with her, but she wasn't sure how she'd carry it. It was twice as long as she was and she would need to carry food. She hesitated a few more seconds and left it, heading out of the door and into the hallway. It was completely dark except for a single candle that stayed lit through the night. Jovanna blew it out as she passed.

The adult's room was downstairs next to the pantry. Jovanna took that as a sign that she had made the right choice. She would get the key, grab some food, and escape into the night. Some of the boards creaked as she walked. Each time it happened, she would pause mid-step and wait. Perhaps it seemed louder to her since she was trying to be quiet.

She reached the door and waited. Her heart was hammering in her chest. What would happen if they caught her trying to sneak out? Would they punish her? And if they did, how bad would it be? Jovanna swallowed hard and twisted the door handle, pushing it open carefully. A candle burned on the nightstand next to the adult's bed. She was propped upright on her pillows with a book in her hand. For a moment, Jovanna thought the woman was awake.

Then she noticed that the woman's eyes were closed. She shook her head, suddenly realizing the absurdity of what she was doing. She almost gave up and went back upstairs. She thought of her mother, though, and that gave her some strength. She walked slowly and quietly to the nightstand. The key was laying there, gently reflecting the candlelight. The candle rested on a small, thin metal stand. It was probably worth something.

Using her left hand, she laid it on the key and slid it across the wood. The soft scraping sound woke the woman, and she drowsily looked at Jovanna.

"What are you doing?" she asked, frowning.

Jovanna panicked. She couldn't stay in the orphanage. She hated people. She especially hated *these* people. They took her from her farmhouse and brought her to this horrible place. Dozens of scary scenarios played out in her mind. Her eyes widened as the woman sat forward, becoming more awake. "Why are you in here? Did you have a nightmare—"

Crack!

Jovanna smacked her across the face with the metal candle holder. She watched in horrid fascination as blood and hot wax splattered across the wall. The woman's body slammed back onto her pillows and she lay very still.

Dread washed over her as she realized that she had probably killed the woman. She dropped the candlestick and backed up slowly, her eyes watering up. What had she done? First her parents, and now this woman?

Turning to the door, she ran straight past the pantry and to the main doors. She struggled to get the key into the lock. Her tears were making it hard to see clearly. Finally, she managed to undo the lock. She pulled one of the doors open and stood there, suddenly terrified. Where was she going to go? She hadn't thought that far ahead.

She heard something behind her. She didn't wait to see who it was. She ran as fast as she could. She passed through the yard where the other children played, past the houses and shops that lined the streets. She kept running, not going in any specific direction. Her mind raced. Where could she go? No one would want her. She could go to the slums. She heard that many kids lived there on their own.

Jovanna headed in that direction, her small bare feet slapping against the cobblestone road. As she got closer, she realized that if the others at the orphanage knew she killed the woman, they would come looking for her. The town guard might even come looking to apprehend her.

She stopped in the street, breathing heavily. She looked back toward the orphanage, and then to the slums. She would need to hide. Not forever, but long enough that they would stop looking for her. There was one place they wouldn't be able to find her. She changed direction and started running again.

A few minutes later she reached the place. It looked much more frightening in the dark. She gritted her teeth and tried not to be afraid. Then she ran into the place that she would now call home.

She entered the garbage dump.

13

EVERYTHING WAS GRAY.

Aramis looked out over a desolate landscape. Dry grass and dead trees covered the terrain. He wondered briefly where he was, and when he tried to remember how he got there, his mind went blank. He was standing on a hilltop, looking down into a small valley. And everything was shaded in a gray hue. Even the shafts of sunlight that filtered through the clouds seemed to be devoid of any real light.

From his vantage point, he saw that a stream ran through the valley to the far right. He was thirsty, and so he made his way down the hill and toward the water. He noticed a slight breeze was blowing because brittle leaves tumbled across the ground and flitted about in the air. Oddly he couldn't feel the wind at all.

As he neared the stream, he noticed that the banks were littered with fish, all dead. Some had already begun decomposing. A few were nothing more than bones. The water flowed at a gentle pace, belying whatever sinister thing that had ended the fish's lives. Aramis was much thirstier than he had first thought. His throat was parched. He gazed into the water, unsure if he should try to drink it.

"A little shouldn't hurt," he said to himself. Kneeling down, he cupped his hands and filled them with water. It was neither warm nor cold against his skin. Indeed, he couldn't even tell that the water was in his hands other than the fact that he could clearly see it was. He lifted it to his lips and took a sip. It was salty and tasted like copper. It reminded him of a time when he was younger and had put a coin into his mouth.

He opened his hands and released the water, shaking his head at the foulness. He rubbed his wet hands along his arms. The black cross started to itch. He scratched at it absent-mindedly, gazing into the water of the stream. Something about the water seemed odd, besides the nasty taste. The texture of it seemed thicker than what it should have been. His hands felt sticky. He looked at them, and though everything was gray, he could immediately tell it was not water.

It was blood.

Aramis gagged and spit to clean his mouth out. It did little to comfort his mind. He turned from the stream and his arm began to burn. He looked at the cross and saw the skin was starting to bubble up, like a pot of water that was beginning to boil. Only the bubbles didn't dissipate, they moved along his arm toward his fingers and began to drip onto the ground. They looked like circular black bugs spiraling down onto the ground.

Somewhere in the back of his mind, he knew this felt similar to something else he had seen, but he couldn't place it. The skin itched and burned like fire. He gritted his teeth against the pain. The last few bubbles of black skin dripped from his fingertips to the ground and he rubbed the painful spot on his arm where the cross had been.

The black liquid moved along the ground of its own accord, flowing into the stream and mixing with the blood. A figure took shape from the blood, rising up out of the stream and stepping onto the banks. The wind picked up, ruffling their clothes and whipping the figure's hood off his head. His face was gaunt and unnaturally pale. His head was nearly bald, with only a few wisps of hair remaining and a scraggly goatee hung down from his chin. His eyes were sunken deep into his head, the pupils devoid of color.

Despite the fact that the man seemed ready for the grave, he radiated a sinister power that made Aramis's flesh crawl. "Who are you?" he asked.

"I have many names, but you know me as Mordum." The man's lips barely moved, but his voice echoed across the landscape. With blinding quickness, Mordum was suddenly standing mere inches from him. The smell of decay assaulted Aramis and made his eyes water.

"Their blood calls to me night and day," Mordum said. "And soon I shall answer." Aramis didn't know what he was talking about. He would have asked, but he feared if he stopped holding his breath he might inhale some disease from the man.

"The faithful continue to gather. When the moon is high, and all have been gathered, I shall sweep over the earth like a plague. None can stop the coming of death!"

Mordum grabbed Aramis by the throat and held him up off the ground, choking him. Aramis struggled to break Mordum's grip, but he was too strong. Mordum's hand was intensely cold against his neck. His vision began to blur as he struggled to breathe. Then Mordum released him and he fell backward, seeing everything in slow motion. And then he hit the ground.

—

Aramis awoke, kicking and swinging. It took several moments for his mind to figure out where he was. He was lying in his bed at the inn. He was breathing heavy and covered in a thick sheen of sweat. He slumped back against the pillows and sighed in relief.

It had seemed so real to him. He didn't think it wise to try and go back to sleep, so he got up and walked over to the window. It was still dark. He wasn't sure what time it was. He grabbed his shirt from off the floor, apparently having taken it off in his sleep. He pulled it over his head, threw on his boots, and left his room. He headed down to the tavern area.

All of the chairs had been placed on top of the tables and the barmaid that had brought their food was mopping the wooden floors. Two men, drunk judging by their boisterous conversation, sat at the bar sipping from their mugs. The barmaid paused in her cleaning.

"Can I get you anything?" she asked.

Aramis shook his head. "No, thank you. I just need some fresh air."

"You're pale as chalk," she said. "Are you ill? There's a doctor at the edge of town if you need one."

Aramis tried to smile reassuringly. "I'm not sick. Just bad dreams. I'm going to step outside." She nodded and went back to mopping. He walked to an area that didn't appear to have been cleaned yet and exited through the door.

The streets were empty, which he expected at this hour. Every twenty feet or so, a lantern hung from a lamp post or off the side of a building, providing light with which to see. The sky was cloudless and Aramis figured even if there weren't lanterns, he probably would have been able to see clearly by the light of the moon.

The roads were all paved with cobblestone. Aramis's great great grandfather was responsible for that. He had paid for all roads in Oakvalor to be paved so that trade could be improved. Some of his detractors claimed it was really done so the king could move his armies about the realm faster. Aramis knew it was actually due to the first reason.

While he preferred spending his time with the soldiers outdoors, he did study many topics at the direction of his tutors growing up. He read several biographies of people from his lineage, as well as their personal journals. He obviously never met the man, but judging by the thoughts he recorded in his journal, Aramis knew him to be a good and just ruler. Just like his father.

Tears stung his eyes at the thought of his father. He didn't hold them back. He wondered how his mother was holding up. The funeral had probably already happened, and he couldn't even attend it because he was running around the kingdom like a criminal. The young spoiled prince in him wanted to feel sorry for himself, but the growing kingly part of him knew there would be time to grieve later.

He stopped walking when he reached a darkened building that appeared to be vacant and sat down on the steps of the porch. He stared up into the sky at the moon, silently praying. And then he laughed at himself. He didn't believe in the gods, any of them, and yet here he was giving lip service to any one of them that would listen. Aramis had often debated with his religious tutor.

He was adamant that the gods did not exist. He attributed "miracles" to natural events that couldn't readily be explained. His teacher would always counter with, "If you don't believe in the gods, why do you always pray to them when you are in trouble?" He always denied that he did, but deep inside he knew his tutor hit the sword on the shield.

Why indeed?

A noise on the road ahead of him drew his attention. A familiar wooden cart came rolling into view. The blind woman he had met previously was pushing it along the street. She slowed her pace as she neared him.

"Prince Aramis," she greeted.

"Lady," he returned. He couldn't remember her name. As he thought about it, he couldn't remember her ever giving him her name. "What are you doing out this late? Granted this town seems safe enough, but aren't you afraid vagabonds might try to rob you or your goods?"

The woman cackled loudly. "I have no fear of highway robbers," she answered. "What I have cannot be stolen, only given." He doubted that, but he didn't say it. "How do you travel from place to place so fast?" he asked.

"I'm afraid I don't know what you are talking about," she laughed again. Aramis shook his head in defeat. "You talk cryptically every time I see you. I pray one day you will give me a straight answer."

"That's something you are doing more often," she said with a grin.

"Praying or wanting a straight answer?"

Her answer was another laugh. Aramis grunted and shook his head in frustration. He didn't know why he humored the crazy old woman. She hobbled around to the side of the cart facing him and leaned against it.

"Do you still have the dagger I gave you?" she asked.

"I do," he said. He didn't have it on him currently, but it was in his room at the inn.

"I assume it helped you at the right time?"

More of her confusing talk. "It hasn't. Actually—" he stopped. It had been a huge help in his fight with the phiebus back at the shrine. "How did you know?" he asked.

"Know what?"

"When you gave it to me, you said something about it being the only thing that would work. I used it to kill a phiebus. I've hunted them before with my father. The fire of their breath can easily melt steel. The dagger wasn't damaged at all." He stared at her intently. "Are you a seer?"

"Something like that," she laughed again.

"Seriously, I want to know. Who are you?"

"You are not ready for that," she said, her tone growing solemn. "But your friend is close," she added.

"Mel?" he asked.

The woman nodded. "I told you before, Aramis. Revelation will come in time."

Aramis sighed loudly. "I came out here to get some air and clear my mind. Every time I see you, I walk away with more questions than I started with. Can I ask you a question without you giving me an indirect answer?"

"I will do my best," she answered.

"You mentioned something before about a new king. Do you know if someone has usurped the throne in my absence? I obviously haven't heard much being on the run. I would appreciate anything you know."

The woman was silent for a moment. "The new king is your brother."

Aramis scoffed. "I don't have a brother. I'm the only child, excluding my dead sister."

"That you know of," she replied.

"That's ridiculous," he said, rising from the stairs. "I would know if I had a brother." He started to walk away, headed back towards the inn.

"He was banished before you were born," the woman said. Aramis paused. It sounded insane. A brother? Why would his parents have hidden this from him? It seemed unlikely. He turned to face her.

"My parents were older when they had me. I was hailed as a miracle child. Why would that be said of me if I had an older brother?"

"Who told you that your birth was miraculous?" she asked.

"Everyone," he answered.

"Your parents told you this?"

He hesitated. "Perhaps. The nobles said it constantly when I was younger."

"Why would the nobles tell you that but not your own parents? Consider that."

Aramis shook his head and turned his back to her. "I wanted a straight answer," he growled.

"I gave you one. Revelation will—"

"Come in time," he finished for her. Then he stalked angrily back to the inn. He looked over his shoulder to make sure she wasn't following him. He didn't see any sign of her or her cart. Good, he thought. The woman infuriated him. Her riddles, it seemed, had become lies.

He entered the inn to find everyone had retired. The barmaid had left a single lantern lit on one of the tables to provide enough light for him to navigate to his room. He made a mental note to thank her in the morning. He got back to his room and threw himself onto the bed. All he wanted was to clear his name and take care of the kingdom his father had worked to make a better place. Eventually, he fell into a fitful sleep.

—

The next morning, Aramis got up and performed his ablutions. When he was finished, he went to Mel's door and knocked. When no answer came, he shrugged and went down to the tavern area. He found his friend already seated at a table. Aramis joined him.

"Good morning, my Lord," Mel greeted. Aramis nodded his head in acknowledgment and looked around the tavern. There were a few people scattered throughout, most of them eating breakfast.

"Have you ordered yet?" he asked Mel.

"I have," Mel answered. "I heard they serve some of the best potatoes in the kingdom. I ordered us both a plate with eggs and some bread. I hope that is suitable?"

Aramis nodded. "I'm starved," he said. He looked around again to make sure none of the people in the tavern were paying attention to them. He leaned across the table and lowered his voice. "I had another vision."

Mel stiffened. "Let me see your arm," he said. Aramis placed his arm on the table for his friend to inspect. Mel stared intently at the mark and finally shook his head.

"I'm not sure, but it might be a shade darker than it was. Time is always against us, it seems. We need to leave as soon as we are done eating. What happened in the vision?"

Aramis was about to answer when the barmaid delivered their food. She set two large plates down. Aramis's mouth watered at the sight of the steaming potatoes. The eggs looked just as appealing. He looked at the barmaid and smiled. "Thank you for leaving the lantern for me last night. I appreciate it."

She scrunched her face up in confusion. "I would say you are welcome, but I didn't leave a lantern out. When I left, this place was as dark as a cave. What do you want to drink?" she asked them. Mel asked for wine while Aramis ordered water. She left and returned a moment later with the drinks. She set them on the table and left to greet two men who had entered the tavern.

They both began eating. Mel made several odd sounds that Aramis took as compliments to the taste of the food. He talked as they ate, relating his dream to Mel. He also told her about how the blind woman met him on the road when he went to clear his mind.

"There's something about that woman that puts me on edge," Mel said. "She knows too much to be blind."

Aramis nodded in agreement. "I know. You saw what I saw, though. Her eyes are missing from her head. I think she is a seer. I read about them in my studies. Some of them don't need eyes to see. They have some kind of power that produces images of their surroundings in their minds. I asked her if she was one, and she said 'something like that'."

Mel tapped the table with his finger. "That could explain it."

Aramis ate the last bit of food on his place and pushed it to the center of the table. Mel had already finished his and they both stood up. Mel placed a few coins on the table and they left the tavern.

"I tried to get some horses, but none of the stables had any that could make it up the mountain. We'll have to go on foot until we get to Talvaard."

"Can our luck get any worse?" Aramis asked.

"I'm sure it's about to," Mel replied.

"Why do you say that?"

"Because we're being followed."

14

THE PALE LIGHT OF THE sunrise lit up the sky, making the immense cloud formations boiling out of the east seem that much darker by comparison. A storm followed them, traveling slowly, but inexorably. Some of the smaller clouds had broken away and had begun to pelt them with rain.

Aramis and Melchiades had continued out of the village and onto the path through the mountain on foot. They were being tailed by two people, though they did well to keep hidden. Mel had noticed the two follow them out of the inn. They didn't appear to be hostile. Their followers could have attacked them once they left the city, but so far they simply continued to follow them up the mountain.

"Who do you think they are?" Aramis asked. He was covered in sweat from the arduous climb. He kept wishing that a caravan would pass by and offer them a ride. He knew it wasn't likely. He paused for a moment to wipe the sweat from his face. He could tell that the uncovered areas of his skin were getting too much sun.

"I'm not sure. My first guess was Mordum's followers, but they'd have made their move already. We'll just have to keep going and see if they reveal themselves. Be ready, my Lord."

Aramis nodded in response. Unlike their trip to Mordum's shrine, at least now he had a sword. Mel had purchased it for him before they left. They continued their trek up the mountain, hoping to find someplace to take shelter before the main body of the storm hit. Mel informed him that flooding was a dangerous possibility where they were. They picked up the pace.

After an hour of climbing, they managed to reach the mountaintop right as the storm's fury crashed down upon them. The wind ripped furiously at their clothes and the driving rain pelted their skin. Aramis thought the raindrops felt like needles stabbing at him. Within minutes, tiny streams of water began running past them, carving paths through the dirt. Lightning flashed among the clouds and ground shaking thunder followed soon after. He faintly heard Mel say something over the thunder.

He shielded his eyes and looked at Mel, who stood hunched over bracing himself against the wind. He pointed and said something Aramis couldn't make out. He shrugged and followed his friend. The dirt under his feet had quickly become thick mud. It sucked at his boots, threatening to pull them off. His legs burned from the exertion.

The ground suddenly gave way and he fell forward, landing hard on his right shoulder. He cried out more in surprise than pain and struggled to get back up. The wind, rain, and mud made it almost impossible. He was so tired and his energy was flagging. Strong hands grabbed him and pulled him up. It was Mel. "I found a cave!" he shouted loudly, trying to be heard over the storm.

"Lead the way!" Aramis shouted back. They didn't walk far before Aramis saw the dark outline of the cave's entrance to their left. They angled themselves toward it, fighting against the wind that seemed likely to throw them down the mountain. They finally managed to stagger into the cave. Aramis slumped to the jagged rocky ground, exhausted.

Mel summoned his sword and walked further into the cave, disappearing into the darkness. A few moments later, he returned. Aramis looked up and Mel had his finger pressed against his lips.

"There's a bear in there," Mel said softly, motioning with his hand. "And she has cubs. If we stay quiet, we shouldn't bother them too much. The storm should pass by quickly judging by the power of the wind."

Aramis nodded wordlessly and unsheathed his sword. He set it beside him just in case. They sat resting in silence for several minutes before Aramis heard something. Instinctively, he grabbed his sword and stood up. Mel did the same. They positioned themselves on either side of the cave and away from the entrance. They didn't have to wait long before two figures staggered in.

"I swear they came this way," one of them said loudly.

Aramis looked to Mel and they both nodded. Simultaneously,

they jumped from the shadows and each pointed a sword at one of the men. The one who had spoken yelped in surprise, brandishing his own blade astonishingly quick.

"Hold," the other figure spoke. From the tone, Aramis knew it was a man. His companion lowered his sword. "Prince Aramis, is that you?"

Aramis recognized the voice, but he couldn't see well enough in the gloom to determine if he recognized the man's face. "Who's asking?"

A soft glow suddenly illuminated the cave. Aramis saw the light was coming from Mel's sword. His friend was full of surprises. His eyes widened in shock when he realized who the strangers were. "Lord Bavol," he said. "What are you doing here?"

Lord Bavol was an older man, with short white hair and pale blue eyes. He stood nearly the same height as Aramis but was a bit overweight. His stomach hung out over his belt. His clothes were stained from travel and he was dripping from the rain.

"Prince Aramis! Thank Zevea I found you!" The two men bowed low. "We've been scouring the entire country it seems. The court is in turmoil. The nobles are at odds, and there is a man claiming to be the new king!"

"Calm yourself," Aramis demanded, holding a hand up. "Slow down and tell me what is happening."

Bavol nodded. "I apologize, my Prince. Everyone knows the king is dead. Many rumors circulate the court, mainly that you killed him to take the throne. The nobles are divided. Some believe this tale, and some do not. I belong to the latter group."

"I appreciate your loyalty," Aramis replied. "You are right, I did not kill my father. He was assassinated before me as I struggled to defend him." Aramis's jaw tightened just thinking about it. He struggled to hold back the tears.

"We have had our differences in the past, but I would never believe you would have killed him. A few of the nobles agree with me, but many more have their doubts. The new 'king' isn't helping the matter. He's spewing accusations against you. He uses the fact that you are in hiding as his proof of your guilt."

Aramis fumed angrily. "Who is this man who claims to be king? I am the heir to the throne, and I am in hiding because I was being tortured in the dungeon like some sort of criminal!" Aramis stabbed his sword into the cave's floor. No one spoke. Aramis cupped his face in his hands and groaned, then looked back to Bavol.

"The man claims to be your elder brother. I don't trust him, though. He doesn't look respectable. He has some shady consorts as well. They all have a tattoo on their arms."

"A black cross?" It was Mel who spoke.

Bavol nodded. "Eric here was the first to notice and pointed it out to me. They are strange men and everyone seems to be afraid of them. My Prince, you must return to the castle and remove this charlatan."

"He can't," Mel said. "The guards are searching for us. What do you think would happen if he revealed himself? If they didn't kill him, they would lock him up. He cannot return without proof that he did not kill his father. That's why we are in hiding."

"He's right," Aramis chimed in. "I can't return. Not yet. We came across my father's assassin yesterday. We are trailing him. When I return, I will have proof."

"I'm afraid proof may not be enough, my Lord," Eric said. "The man has taken command of the army. This man will not forfeit the throne simply because you have proof that you didn't kill your father. You will need allies."

Bavol bit his lower lip. "Eric has a point; one I hadn't considered until now. If he controls the army and he doesn't intend to give up the throne, you'll have to take it by force. You will need your own army to do that."

"I will not make this kingdom a war-torn land like that of Talvaard," Aramis stated. "I grew up with the soldiers who served my father. I know where their loyalty lies, and it is not with some fool."

Mel cleared his throat. "My Prince. If this man consorts with the likes of Mordum's followers, the soldiers may not recognize you. Some of Mordum's priests are known to be able to control the minds of others. It would be wise to consider that this may end in violence."

Aramis considered Mel's words. He didn't want everything his father worked so hard to sustain to come crashing down in blood. Yet he couldn't control that outcome if he planned on taking his rightful place as king. "We will cross that bridge when—"

A loud roar echoed throughout the cave suddenly. They all turned to see a massive bear charging towards them. Aramis yanked his sword out of the ground and was about to charge the beast when Mel pushed him out of the way. He watched as Mel ran forward and slammed his magical blade into the ground. The air rippled around the sword and began to glow faintly. The bear slammed into the barrier and roared in frustration.

Mel turned around and shrugged. "I didn't want you to kill her," he said simply.

"Where can we get more of him?" Bavol asked in awe.

Aramis chuckled. "He follows Edria. His goddess is an enemy to Mordum. It's difficult to explain, but we will eventually have his order to aid in our fight against Mordum."

They watched the bear stalk back and forth in front of the barrier, occasionally growling at them. It was silent for a few moments and then Aramis spoke. "Lord Bavol, I need you to go back to the court and sway as many of the nobles as possible to our cause. I will find allies where I can, and when I return we will remove this man from the throne."

"I will do everything I can, my Prince. Allow my servant Eric to go with you. He will help you with anything you need."

"I thank you for the offer, but I fear he will only slow us down. He is not a soldier and where we travel will be dangerous. Keep your servant with you. Eric will serve our cause better in the court than on the road with me." Aramis looked out of the cave's entrance. "The storm is letting up. Lord Bavol, you should go now. Mel and I need to get back on the road as well. We have many things to do, and time is quickly passing."

"May Zevea watch over you," Bavol said. He bowed low and turned to Eric. "Let us be on our way." They left the cave and headed back down the mountain toward Oakvalor.

"We have one problem," Mel said.

"What?"

"The bear. Once I remove my sword, the barrier will fade. We'll have to run like never before."

Aramis nodded in agreement. "So be it," he said.

Mel grabbed his sword, turned, and they ran as fast as they could.

—General Garrick

15

ARAMIS FOUND TALVAARD TO BE not so unlike his own kingdom. Having grown up his entire life knowing they were at war with their neighboring kingdom, he had always assumed the place was … different. But what he found was that the people were just like his own. They tended their fields, worked various jobs, and went about their daily lives.

Aside from the many battle-destroyed sites that littered the land, he couldn't tell the difference between the two kingdoms. He had heard rumors that the kingdom was engulfed in civil war, but what he and Mel encountered was much worse than something written in a report.

The first few towns they came across were nothing more than burned out husks. They had seen only a few people in those places, and none of them would answer their questions, let alone look at them. The horrors of war were being revealed to Aramis in a very real way. Aramis had decided that although they were on a time-sensitive mission, they would help the people of Talvaard where they could.

In one of the towns, they had spent an entire day digging graves and helping bury the dead. Once they were finished, they were treated by some of the townspeople with a bath and warm food. Aramis was surprised that Mel didn't complain about getting so dirty and said as much.

"Simply because I enjoy the aristocratic way of life, doesn't mean I don't also enjoy doing good. I am a priest of Edria for a reason, my Lord."

"I didn't mean to offend you, Mel. I was only jesting with you."

"You did not offend me. I can understand why you would think that, however. I do enjoy the court probably more than I should."

The next morning as they were getting ready to head out, they were greeted by one of the townspeople.

"Morning, gents. I've got a message for you from the general who oversees this town. He'd like to meet with both of you."

Aramis was wary. They had already lost a good deal of time, and he didn't want to get drawn into the political battle being waged in Talvaard. "I'm afraid we must get back on the road. Can you tell the general that we were in a hurry and perhaps on our way back through we can meet with him?"

"I could do that. But you may want to make time to meet with him now. He wants to thank you for helping us. General Garrick is a man of honor. He has always defended our city from vagabonds and orc raiders. His army is now stretched thin trying to defend so many from the other generals who simply want to take the throne. He tried to stay out of the battles, but the others continued to attack his province. It took the blessing of the townsfolk to get him to join the fray."

Aramis listened intently. This General Garrick sounded like a man whom he could trust. He looked to Mel for advice, but Mel only offered a shrug as if to say 'it's your decision'.

"We will go now," Aramis decided.

The man smiled. "Great! Follow me. He arrived in town just this morning after receiving news that our town was sacked." The man led them to one of the few buildings left mostly unscathed. Aramis couldn't tell what kind of building it was. Two thin posts hung above the entrance, but the sign that should have been hanging from them was missing. Aramis assumed it had been knocked off during the town's attack, but it was impossible to be sure.

The man led them into the building which turned out to be a tavern. It was dark inside except for a few candles and lanterns. The windows were covered with dark sheets that managed to blot out almost all of the sunlight.

"Wait here," the man said. He made his way to a table where several armored men sat. They hadn't waited long before the man returned and directed them to the table. As they approached, one of the men stood up to greet them.

His plate armor was a deep onyx color. It was also covered in dents and scrapes. Aramis thought he could see spots of blood as well. The man's face was a dark tan color, and his hair was almost as dark as his armor. He smiled as they approached the table.

"Thank you for meeting with me. I hope this will not delay you too much?"

Everything about the man exuded a sense of dignity and humility. His bearing was that of a strong leader, but his voice was soft. The man almost reminded him of his father.

"It's no trouble," Aramis replied. "We do have pressing business, but it can wait."

The man nodded. "These men are my Captains. I don't mean to be rude, but they are about to leave with their orders. You are all dismissed." All five Captains stood up and left the tavern. "Please sit," Garrick bade them. They both did as he asked. "Would you like anything to eat or drink?"

"No, thank you," Aramis answered. "Your people have taken care of us already."

Garrick smiled again. "Good. I've asked you two to meet with me because the people of the town told me how you helped them. I am indebted to you. When I heard that the town was attacked, I rode all night to get here."

A young girl approached the table and set a wooden cup down in front of Garrick. He took a sip and looked to the girl. "This is perfect, thank you." The girl curtsied and disappeared into the kitchen.

"As a man who strives to protect my people, I have many agents in many places. As such, I know a great deal more about people than they know about me." Garrick took another drink from his cup. "So tell me, how do the Prince of Oakvalor and his servant come to be in Talvaard?"

Aramis's mouth gaped in surprise. He wasn't sure how to answer. The man seemed trustable, but how much should he reveal? He was thankful when Mel spoke up.

"We are on a quest to retrieve something that was stolen from us."

"I see," he said, frowning. "And these thieves are in my province?"

"Most of them were killed in a rockslide in the Viss Mountains. The one who stole from us escaped. We are not sure where he is exactly. We only know he came through the mountains and crossed into Talvaard. Perhaps you may have seen him? He wears robes and has a black cross tattoo on his left arm."

"I'm sorry, but I have not seen anyone like that. You must be Melchiades, correct?"

Mel tilted his head in a bow. "I am."

Garrick looked to Aramis. "Do you trust Melchiades?"

"With my life," Aramis answered.

"Very well. We can speak freely then. I know the rumor in Oakvalor has spread quickly that you have killed your father. There is always a seed of truth in a rumor, but I would rather hear it from the one who was there."

Aramis cleared his throat. "My father is dead, but I did not kill him. The man we are searching for didn't just steal from us, he is also my father's assassin."

"I am sorry to hear that," Garrick said. "Your father was a good man."

"You knew my father?" Aramis asked.

"I did not meet him directly, no. But I did correspond with him by letter when my own king was alive. They were working on a peace treaty by marriage … and I'm sure we all know how that went." Garrick shook his head sadly.

"Yes. My sister was killed and both of your princes died."

Garrick nodded. "The people of my country haven't even had proper time to grieve the loss. The other generals and some of the nobles began fighting over the throne immediately. It has become brother against brother, family against family."

"I fear that my own kingdom will look like this," Aramis said softly.

"What do you mean?" Garrick asked.

"I've been accused of murdering my father and a man has usurped the throne in my absence. I'm trying to track down the assassin to prove my innocence, yet this false king is adding to the rumors about me. The longer it takes me to find this man, the more damage is done. I fear my own kingdom will fall to pieces as yours has."

"You have a hard road before you; that is true. Tell me though, why did you help the people here? Our kingdoms have been at war for longer than anyone can remember. You are searching for an assassin and you probably could have tracked him down by now, so what made you stop and give time you didn't have to these people?"

"I saw in them my own people," Aramis answered. "I've grown up believing the people here were cruel and wanted only to fight. I've seen otherwise. These people just want to live their lives in peace as my own do. Helping them bury their dead was the least I could do to make amends for my forefathers' mistakes."

"You will make a good king," Garrick said. "I appreciate what you have done here for my people. In return, I will do something for you. Though I have not seen this man you spoke of, I do know a place where people with these tattoos congregate. I will give you a map to this place."

"You do more for us than we have done for your people," Aramis said. "This will put us one step closer to proving my innocence."

"I believe you are innocent. I would like to propose something to you. You don't have to decide now. The war here will be coming to an end soon. If you will give me your support, I will give you mine. Make a public endorsement in favor of me being king of Talvaard, and I will help you get your throne back."

"I'm sorry, but I don't understand how my endorsement of you would help. Technically we are enemies. If anything, I would think the people here would see that as a bad sign."

Garrick nodded. "Let me try to explain. I did not want anything to do with this war. But at the urging of my people, I fought back against the others who were doing nothing but terrorizing their own kingdom. The men you saw earlier, my Captains? They were generals fighting against me not long ago. I defeated their armies and took their cities. Now they follow me without question. I have reunified the majority of the kingdom. There is only one who continues to fight. He is a violent man, prone to drunkenness.

"If I can show the people that our long-time enemy Oakvalor has given me the blessing to rule and backs me with support, I will be able to unify the entire country back under one banner. No more civil war, no more pointless fighting. The only man left causing strife may even surrender without any more bloodshed. I desire peace and my people desire peace. That is all I want."

Aramis digested everything. It made sense. "So all you want me to do is say I approve of you being king? That seems much less effort than it does for you to help me get my throne back. I feel like I would owe you something I cannot repay."

Garrick waved his hand. "Nonsense. We both want what is best for our people. All I ask is that we help each other bring peace and stability back to our kingdoms. Once we have accomplished that, we can finally create the peace treaty that has been a long time coming. As I said, you don't have to answer now. Think about it and let me know when you come back through with the proof your people need. If I am not here, you can leave me a message here at this tavern and I will get it."

"May I speak with my friend in private?" Aramis asked.

"Of course," Garrick said.

Aramis and Mel rose from the table and retreated toward the entrance. Aramis was thinking through everything. It seemed the right course of action, especially since it would give him the military support he would need to take his throne back if it came down to it. "What do you think, Mel?"

"It is your decision, my Prince. I would not want to sway you one way or another."

"I think I should do it. The man seems honorable and level-headed. You said yourself that we should be prepared in the event that I have to take the throne by force. He has an army that he is willing to lend me. This is an opportunity to not only get support to take the throne back but also to end the conflict between our two kingdoms."

"I see it the same way. I just didn't want to sway your opinion if you were against the idea. Though he didn't say he would lend you his army. He only said he would help you. You may want to clarify that point."

They walked back to the table and took their seats. Garrick took a drink from his cup.

"I fear the man who usurped my throne will not leave without a fight. Does your support include your army, if it is needed?" Aramis asked.

"I will give you anything I can to aid you. Supplies, men, weapons. Whatever you need."

"Then we have an agreement," Aramis said. He reached across the table and grabbed Garrick's hand.

"Agreed," Garrick said with a smile. And they shook hands. "I will need my messengers to carry the letter of your support to every city. Can you provide a letter now?"

"If you have parchment and ink, I can pen it before we leave."

Garrick summoned the young girl from the kitchen and told her what he needed. She left and returned shortly after, bringing several pieces of parchment, a quill, and an inkwell. Aramis wrote out a letter of support and signed it. He slid the paper to Garrick, who read it and nodded in satisfaction.

"Excellent. I asked the girl to have one of my Captains bring the map I told you about. He should be here in a moment."

They didn't wait long before the man arrived and delivered the map. He handed it to Garrick and left. Garrick unfolded it and looked it over, then gave it to Aramis.

"The black square is our current position. The line that leads west is the road you will need to take. It is a long journey even by horseback, so make sure you have all of the supplies you need. The people will provide you with whatever you need. I believe there is a carriage if you need one. With that said, may you find success. I look forward to seeing you again, King Aramis."

Aramis and Mel had been fortunate enough to find the carriage. Judging by the map, it would take them several weeks to reach their destination. The place Garrick described was on the edge of Talvaard, close to the unmapped regions beyond. They loaded the carriage with enough food and water for two weeks. Aramis wanted to take more, but there was only so much space.

"We can find game to hunt if we run low on food," Mel said. "According to the map, there aren't any cities that far west. Just forests and flatlands."

A week into their journey brought bad news. They were both sleeping when the carriage jostled about harshly, waking them up. Aramis could hear the driver cursing. "We'd better see what happened," he said. They stepped out of the carriage into a rainstorm. Within moments they were drenched.

"What happened?" Mel asked the driver, using his hands to keep the rain out of his eyes.

"The blasted wheel hit a rut and cracked in two," the driver answered.

"Is there a replacement?" Mel asked.

The driver shook his head. "No. If I can't repair the wheel, I'll have to head back and get one. It could take a couple of weeks if they have to build a new one." Aramis looked to Mel helplessly.

"When will you know if you can fix it?" Mel asked.

"As soon as the rain lets up. I can't apply anything while the wood is wet. You two should get back in the carriage and wait. I'll let you know."

Not knowing how they could help, they did as the driver said and climbed back into the carriage. "This isn't good," Aramis said. "If he can't fix the wheel, we will lose even more time. It's taking too long to get there as it is."

"I know, my Lord. We should have a plan in the event that

repairing the wheel isn't going to work. We could take the horses and continue on. They can carry more than we can on foot. Aside from that, I don't see many options that don't put us farther behind. We're also assuming the templar is going to this place Garrick mentioned, but we don't know that for sure."

Aramis covered his face in his hands and rested his back against the soft cushions. "This isn't happening," he muttered. "Mel, tell me this isn't happening. Tell me this is all a horrible dream."

"I wish that I could, my Lord."

Aramis didn't know how much time had passed, but the door to the carriage opened and the driver peeked his head in. "I'm sorry, but I'm unable to repair the wheel. I'm going to head back to town and see about getting a replacement. You're welcome to come along, or you can wait here if it suits you."

"I think we will stay here," Mel said. "But you may want to bring some horses back as well."

"Why?" the driver asked.

"Because we are taking these ones. Don't worry about coming to get us. We'll be back when we are finished with our business."

"Very well. Safe travels to you." The driver shut the door.

"Looks like we better get packing," Mel said. Aramis nodded wordlessly. They exited the carriage and saw the driver had already started walking back toward the town. Mel unhitched the horses and Aramis began loading their supplies. They packed more food than water, as the map showed a few streams and rivers located along their route.

They mounted the horses and continued west, following the map and taking note of points of interest and traveled until dusk, then made camp next to a stand of trees. They ate a small meal and took turns keeping watch as the other slept. In the morning, they continued on. The same routine followed until the days had blurred into weeks.

After almost a month, they finally came across signs of people. A few scattered campsites at first, then makeshift shelters. They traveled warily, looking everywhere to make sure there were no guards or scouts. Their food supply had exhausted weeks ago and they relied on berries and small animals to hold them over. Being on the road so long had made them irritable. The signs that they were almost there gave them some excitement.

"According to the map, there is a clearing on the other side of these trees. In the clearing is where the followers of Mordum are supposed to gather," Mel said.

"We're almost done with this madness," Aramis growled.

They dismounted and tied their horses to one of the trees. Aramis grabbed his sword from the saddle and sheathed it as his side. They walked quietly through the woods, trying to avoid stepping on anything that might make a sound.

Suddenly the world went upside down. Aramis cried out in surprise as he and Mel were hanging above the ground in a net. They struggled but were unable to free themselves. Giving up, Aramis looked down to see how they had managed to walk into this trap.

And standing there looking up at them was his father's killer.

—Prince Aramis

16

Fourteen Years Ago

JOVANNA STARED AT THE FLOWERS that seemed to represent every color one could imagine. Vibrant reds, oranges, blues, and purples that came in all sizes and oddly beautiful shapes. The flower shop was one of her favorite places to visit in the market.

She never bought any of them, though her father would bring them to her mother sometimes, usually after they had argued about something. As she walked around the shop, she noticed a flower she hadn't seen before. It was tall and bright yellow.

"What is this one?" she asked the lady who owned the shop.

The owner came around the desk she was standing behind to take a look. "Ah," she said with a smile. "That's a day lily."

"I've never seen one before. Did you just get it?"

"Yes, it arrived today. They don't naturally grow in this part of the country. I'm going to see if I can change that. How's your mother doing?"

Jovanna shrugged, still staring at the flower. "She's well. She and father had another fight last night. I'm guessing he'll come by here to get her some of these. It's how he says he's sorry." The owner nodded and went back to her work behind the desk. "I'm going to head home now. Mother will get worried if I'm not home before my father."

"Give your mother my regards," the owner said.

"I will," Jovanna answered as she left. She walked along the cobblestone paved streets, enjoying the sights and smells of everything as was her custom. Being the only child of a poorer family, she wasn't expected to do much. Jovanna had tried school, but she didn't like it. She wasn't like the other children and didn't feel like she fit in. Since schooling was free, her mother didn't complain too much.

"I want you to be smart as well as happy," her mother had said when she found out Jovanna wasn't going back to the school. "Going to school may not make you happy, but it will make you smart. They'll teach you things you won't learn otherwise."

"You didn't go to school. And neither did father. Why should I?"

"So that you can be successful in whatever you decide to do. So that if you leave this town, you can go anywhere you want."

Jovanna laughed. "Why would I want to leave? You and father have never left. And I wouldn't want to leave you anyway."

Her mother had simply shaken her head and said, "You'll understand when you are older."

She didn't understand adults. They didn't like to have fun and they were always so serious. Didn't they know they were kids once too? As she passed the bakery, the scent of freshly baked bread greeted her. She breathed in deep, savoring it. Jovanna continued along the road until it became a dirt path. Her house was on the outskirts of the town.

As she entered the house, her mother was coming out of her sewing room. "I was starting to wonder where you were," her mother said. "You are usually here earlier."

"I was at the flower shop," she answered. "The owner got a new flower in and it's beautiful!" Her mother smiled at her enthusiasm.

"Carina is too busy for you to be bothering her every day."

"I don't bother her. I just look at her flowers."

"Did you see your father while you were there?"

Jovanna shook her head. "I told her he'd probably come by to get you flowers because you had a fight."

"Why did you tell her that? Please don't repeat those things. And how did you know we argued? You were asleep."

"I told her because it's true. And I was asleep until I heard father yelling."

"Just because it's true doesn't mean you have to say it," her mother admonished.

"Really?" Jovanna beamed.

"You know what I mean," her mother said, pointing her finger playfully. "Now go get ready for dinner. Your father will be home any minute."

Jovanna ran to do as she was told. Since she hadn't played in the dirt with any of the other kids in town, she really didn't need to wash her hands. She took her shoes off and changed into her sleeping clothes. When dinner was finished she would go to bed, so she liked to be prepared.

After she had changed, she met her mother in the kitchen and sat down at the table. Her mother placed a bowl in front of her that was steaming. She looked in the bowl: mashed potatoes, gravy, and small pieces of meat all mixed together. She blew on the food several times before she went to take a bite.

"Don't eat yet," he mother said. "You need to wait for your father."

"Yes mother," Jovanna groaned. She was hungry and didn't want to wait. She snuck a few bites while her mother wasn't looking. A few minutes later, her father arrived. He came in and went to clean himself up, then came into the kitchen. He threw himself into the chair he always sat in.

"What's wrong?" her mother asked.

"The crops are bad this year," father responded. He rubbed his face with his hands and closed his eyes. "It's going to be a rough year."

"Last year was rough but we survived," mother replied. She placed a bowl before him and then sat down at the table with her own bowl.

"I'm tired of just *surviving*," father said. "For once I would like things to go well for us and to enjoy life." He took a bite of his food and chewed in silence.

"Things will get better," mother said, smiling at him. "Things can only get better."

Her father slammed his fist onto the table. "Stop being so positive!" he yelled. "Things are horrible. They've been horrible and they are only going to stay that way! If you think your comments are helping, they aren't. Just shut your mouth."

Jovanna could tell her mother was trying to hold back her tears. The rest of the meal was oppressively quiet. As she went to her room to go to bed, she realized her father didn't bring any flowers back. "But he always brings flowers," she whispered to herself. She fell asleep troubled.

—

The next morning, she woke to find her mother sewing and her father had gone to work the fields. Everything seemed like normal. She shrugged and left the house, walking to the market area to see what new things the merchants had.

She made her normal rounds, checking out the jewelry and clothing vendors. She loved spending time in the market and the time always seemed to pass by so quickly. Before she knew it, it was almost time to head home. She stopped at the flower shop and took in the sights and smells. Carina was watering some flowers that looked like they weren't doing so well. She greeted Jovanna and continued working.

"Did my father come by yesterday?" she asked.

"He didn't," Carina answered without looking up. She was pulling dead leaves off some of the flowers. "Perhaps he forgot."

"Father never forgets to bring flowers," she answered. She stood before the day lily, admiring its beauty. "He should bring her this one. It will make mother's day. It's so beautiful," she said wistfully. Carina looked at her thoughtfully. She came over to stand beside her.

"It is beautiful," Carina agreed. She put the flower into a smaller vase and handed it to Jovanna. "Take it to your mother."

Jovanna shook her head. "I don't have any money," she said.

"Don't worry about that," Carina answered. "Just take it to her. If you think she will love it, then she should have it. This will be our little surprise."

Jovanna's smile encompassed her entire face. "Really? Thank you! You are the nicest person I know!"

Carina smiled. "No, thank *you*."

Jovanna left, holding the vase tightly so that she wouldn't drop it. When she finally reached her house, she hid the flower from her mother and waited for her father to get home. When he did, she noticed that he hadn't brought anything back for her mother again.

She decided to surprise her mother with the flower by making her think that her father had brought it. While her father cleaned up for dinner, she brought the flower into the kitchen and placed it on the table while her mother wasn't looking.

Father entered the kitchen and sat down tiredly in his chair. He looked at the flower on the table but didn't say anything. Her mother brought their plates to the table and paused when she saw the flower. She smiled and finished setting the plates down.

"How was the work today?" mother asked.

Father grunted in reply. That usually meant he was too tired to talk about it. They ate in silence again like the night before, only this time it wasn't awkward. She saw her mother smiling at the flower while she ate. Her father was looking at it also. For some reason, Jovanna didn't like the way he was looking at it. After she had finished eating, she went to her room. She fell asleep happy to know that she made her mother smile by bringing the flower home.

Yelling woke her up. She sat up in her bed, wondering why her parents would be fighting again. She slipped out of bed and quietly stood outside their bedroom. They were standing on opposite sides of the bed. Her mother's face was streaked with tears and her father looked angry.

"Tell me who it was," father demanded.

"I told you already," mother sobbed. "There isn't anyone."

"Then where did the flower come from?" he asked.

"I don't know," mother answered. "I thought you had brought it for me."

"You are lying," father said. "Tell me who he is."

Jovanna wasn't sure what they were talking about. Were they fighting over the flower? Jovanna bit her lip in worry. She didn't want to get in trouble for it. She only tried to make things better.

"I'm not lying," mother said. "I really thought you brought it for me."

Father glared at her and clenched his fist. Jovanna had never seen him so enraged before. "Stop lying to me," he said through gritted teeth. "I didn't bring it for you."

Her mother began weeping uncontrollably. "I'm not lying to you," she said brokenly. "I swear to you there isn't another man. I love you."

Her father stormed quickly across the room and grabbed her mother, slamming her violently into the wall several times. "Don't you dare say that to me after what you've done!" he screamed madly. Jovanna backed away from the door, frightened by what she saw. Father slammed her into the wall one more time before letting go of her. Her body slumped lifelessly down the wall and onto the floor, leaving a trail of smeared blood.

"Get up," father said. The anger in his voice seemed to have lessened, replaced by something else. Was it … worry? "Get up," he said again, gently this time. He kneeled down beside her and touched her face. "Please wake up," he said. He shook her a bit before becoming frantic.

Jovanna turned and fled back to her room. She hid under the blankets and cried bitterly. She cried until she eventually fell back to sleep.

When she woke up, it was morning. She slowly got out of bed and looked around the room. She had the scariest dream. Leaving the room, she went into the kitchen. Her mother hadn't made breakfast yet. That was odd. A feeling of dread came over her as she walked toward the sewing room. She hesitated, then pushed the door open. It was empty.

She went to her parents' bedroom and opened the door. Lying on the floor was her mother's body. She gasped.

It wasn't a dream at all!

She cried as she ran to her mother's body. Her skin had become pale. A puddle of blood surrounded her, most likely from the wound on the back of her head.

She ran from the room, looking for her father. "Father!" she screamed. "Father!" The house appeared to be empty. She opened the front door and found her father. His lifeless body hung from a rope attached to the awning of their porch. She screamed in horror.

—

When her father didn't show up at the fields for work, some of the other workers came to the house to see where he was. Upon finding his body, the entire house became a place of chaos. The workers had found Jovanna in her room wrapped in a ball crying hysterically.

The city guard was called in to investigate and clean up the bodies. They tried to get Jovanna to talk about what happened, but the only thing she said was, "I killed them."

"She's traumatized," one of the guards told another. "It's highly doubtful she actually killed them. It looks like the man killed his wife, then hung himself. The poor girl."

A few hours later, someone from an orphanage came and took her away from the only home she had ever known.

"One is left with the horrible feeling now that war settles nothing, that to win a war is as disastrous as to lose one."

—General Garrick

17

JOVANNA WATCHED THE ELVES FROM the vantage of a small hill. The sun was setting but still burned brightly, causing her to sweat more than she cared to. Velent and his warriors were in similar positions along the hilltop. The enemy appeared to be finishing setting up their camp and preparing to settle in for the night. Jovanna had seen many war camps in her time, and this one was no different.

Tents made of animal hides were sprawled out in all directions. At one of them, several elves were being tattooed by some elders. Another tent served as the meal area and had a small line of elves gathered. This force was much larger than the one they encountered in the village four days previously. Even though they were massively outnumbered, Jovanna counted the number of Velent's warriors.

Eighteen.

She turned her gaze back to the war camp. Eighteen against close to what looked like a thousand. They wouldn't even likely put a dent in those numbers. All she needed was to find their leader, the one who was responsible for Jerik's death. She would kill him and then … and then what?

The thought made her freeze for a moment. What would she do after she avenged the old man who had saved her life? She forced the thought from her mind. That wasn't important right now. She could hear Velent instructing his warriors.

"Once the night is upon us, we will sneak into their camp. Tent by tent, we will kill as many as possible. We must not be seen or caught. In one hour, we will meet back here. If you aren't here, I will assume you are dead or dying. Am I clear? Good. Take your positions."

He didn't bother giving her any direction. She didn't need it either way. She continued scanning the tents in the waning light, looking for anything that resembled a command post. Eventually, the sun was gone and she still hadn't found it. "I'll search them all if I have to," she muttered to the darkness. She waited and watched as the guards switched out. It was time.

She made her way down the hill as stealthy as possible, pausing here and there to make sure she wasn't seen. It was dark, but the elves had a perimeter of torches and the moon was shining brightly. She got past the first two guards easily. They were playing a traditional elven game called *dueling*. The game was played with several small sticks that had various symbols inscribed on the ends. Each player would then throw the sticks down and hope that two matching symbols landed on each other.

Jovanna thought it was a waste of time as the winner didn't get anything. At least the humans knew how to properly gamble. They were so focused on the game they didn't notice her slink by in the shadows. She entered a large tent and found two elves sleeping. She quickly slit their throats and slipped out, looking for another large tent. She saw several, but none of them housed the leader. After killing thirty elves, she was starting to get frustrated. The war camp was large and only semi-organized.

She was about to make a rash decision and cause a commotion to see if she could draw him out when a horn split the air suddenly. It was followed by another, and then a third one. The camp burst to life and warriors began running toward the western side of the camp. She cursed, knowing that Velent or one of his warriors had probably been caught.

Jovanna waited until she didn't see any other elves before leaving the tent she was in. She jogged through the camp, trailing a few of the warriors. She rounded a tent and almost bumped into a group of them. She quickly entered another one of the tents to keep from being seen.

Cutting a slit in the back of the tent, she looked out to see what was happening. It looked like the entire camp had gathered. She couldn't see enough to know if one of Velent's men had been caught or not. She heard someone talking loudly, but she wasn't able to hear what was being said.

"What's going on?" one of the elves asked.

"War council," another answered.

"How do you know?" the first one asked.

"I can hear him speaking," the other answered.

"You got Wolf Ears?"

The other elf nodded.

Jovanna's face scrunched in confusion. *Wolf Ears?* She hadn't heard of that tattoo before. She made a mental note to research it.

"He says we leave at first light to invade the human cities," Wolf Ears said.

The other smiled. "Good. It is time we take our lands back."

She listened to their conversation a little longer and then decided she needed to get moving. As she moved to leave the tent, she realized that one of the beds was occupied. She went in for the kill before she noticed the elf was already dead. She grunted softly, knowing Velent's men would be somewhere close by. The tent opened and an elf stepped in.

Giving little thought to it, she pushed the dead elf to the edge of the bed and laid down in his place. Immediately she felt the warm blood soaking through her shirt. She shuddered as a memory came back to her, the darkest part of her childhood. The elf who entered the tent brought her back to the present.

"You didn't go to the council," he said. It sounded more like an accusation than a question. She didn't respond.

"Tairu won't stand for rebelliousness. You know better than I what he will do to those who stand in his way. Make sure you are ready in the morning. We march for Talvaard." He climbed into his own bed. Jovanna waited until she heard him breathing evenly, then she got up. So the elves *were* marching into the human kingdoms. And who was this Tairu?

She had not heard the name before. She considered the possibility that Tairu was their leader. He appeared to instill fear in these warriors. Jovanna hadn't spent long with the elves, but she did know that fear was not something they generally showed. She decided that Tairu must be the leader who had united the tribes. She left the tent and wandered the camp a little longer, still looking for the command post. Since the horns had woken everyone up, however, it was much harder moving about the camp. She finally decided to leave and meet back with Velent and his men.

Jovanna made her way out of the camp and back up the hill to where they had been before. Velent met her as she crested the hill. "You were down there longer than an hour."

"I wasn't aware I had instructions," Jovanna replied. "You didn't seem eager to share your plan with me, so I did what I felt was prudent."

"I knew you were listening," he said, his tone revealing his growing impatience.

"Did you learn anything?" she asked.

"What?"

"I don't like repeating myself," she answered.

Velent scowled at her. "No. We didn't."

"I figured as much. When I heard the horns, I thought for sure you or one of your warriors had slipped up and gotten caught."

He spat at her feet. "*Please*. You aren't half of what my weakest warrior is. *I* thought *you* had messed up down there."

"Do you want to test that statement?" she asked, resting her hand on the hilt of her sword.

He ignored her threat. "Did *you* learn anything?" he asked mockingly.

"You know I did," she said.

"Lies."

"Have you heard of an elf named Tairu?" she asked casually, looking up into the sky.

"That isn't funny," he replied.

Jovanna noticed a change in his demeanor. "What do you mean?"

Velent continued to glare at her.

Jovanna was curious now. "I honestly don't know what you are talking about. I've never heard the name until tonight." She thought for a moment he didn't believe her and would walk away. After a bit of silence, he responded.

"Tairu was a powerful warrior of my tribe," he began hesitantly. "His tattoos were strong … his skill with weapons was unparalleled. He quickly gained favor in the tribe and was elevated to War Chief. Our tribe became highly respected and another Tribe Chief offered his daughter to Tairu for his wife. The woman refused him, so Tairu killed her. As is the custom, when one tribe affronts another, the offended tribe can declare war. Instead of doing that, the Tribe Chief told my father to banish Tairu and there would be peace."

"That doesn't seem like a fair trade. A daughter for a warrior? I know women aren't as valued as men in the tribes, but it was his daughter." Jovanna knew there was more to the story. "The chief demanded that to strip your father of his prized warrior, didn't he?"

"That may have been part of his reasoning," Velent replied, "but it was fair. Tairu was my brother, the eldest of us. One family member for another."

"Why didn't I know this already?"

"Other than the fact that you are a *human* and it is none of your concern?" Jovanna could tell he was forcing the sarcasm. "When someone is banished, they are forgotten. Their name can never be spoken again. This is why."

Before she could say anything, he turned to walk away. "Velent," she called after him. "The army down there is marching for Talvaard at first light." He just kept walking. She shrugged and looked out at the war camp. She needed a way to get near Tairu.

—

After a few hours, Jovanna headed back into the camp. The excitement of the warriors had finally subsided. She found a tent with only a single warrior and killed him. She was careful not to get the blood on his clothes. She managed to remove his shirt and replace her own dirty one. She hid the body in another tent and waited for morning.

As the sun crested the horizon, horns rang out across the camp. It was time to get moving. Jovanna rubbed the sleep from her eyes. She had intended to stay up through the rest of the night in case something happened. Apparently, nothing had. She drew her sword and looked at her reflection. Her illusion was still holding up.

She left the tent and fell into step with the other warriors as they began forming into ranks. Her stomach growled and she wondered if the elves would eat breakfast before they began their march. They waited for almost an hour as all the warriors got into their positions. As soon as the stragglers had joined the multitude, other elves began breaking down the camp.

At first, she thought the elves were captives, but then she saw that they were women. *I thought Velent said women don't go to war,* she thought. Whoever this Tairu was, he was obviously going against tradition. Other groups of women ran through the ranks of warriors handing out food. Jovanna was given two dry biscuits and a cooked lizard. As soon as she choked it down, the elves began marching.

Jovanna analyzed their skills and methods as they traveled toward Talvaard's border. They certainly weren't trained like men were. Everything she had seen in the armies of men was seriously lacking here. But the elves had something the humans didn't. Tattoo magic. Their spells were some of the most powerful magic she had ever beheld.

Outside the walls of Palindrom, as the dragon possessed prince was leading his armies, she had witnessed a single elf obliterate the soul of the dragon. If the humans thought they were up against tribal barbarians, they had a rude awakening coming.

They marched most of the day and didn't take many breaks. Jovanna guessed they had traveled a substantial distance when they paused at the outskirts of a large city. Protective walls surrounded the place and she wondered how the elves would break through the defenses. In the distance, she could see the guards on the walls looking their way. She wondered briefly what they might be thinking.

An order was shouted from one of the formation leaders and several elves sprinted toward the city. Jovanna watched curiously.

As the elves neared the walls, some of their tattoos began to glow. They threw themselves into the walls and they exploded. Her eyes widened in surprise. Why would they sacrifice their warriors to break through the walls? As the smoke and debris cleared, she saw the elves had blown holes in the walls.

Commotion rang out in the city and Jovanna realized the elves hadn't sacrificed themselves after all. They had merely used their tattoos to blast through the walls.

"Clever," she said to herself. It wouldn't work every time, especially once the humans learned of the trick. They would cut the elves down from the walls with crossbows or ballistae. But for now, it worked. The captains shouted and the ranks of elves surged toward the city. Jovanna tried to hang back so she could find where Tairu was.

It was impossible to weave through the mass of bodies and she was forced forward with the army. Other elves worked to make the holes in the walls larger so the warriors could get into the city faster. Jovanna tried desperately to remove herself from the flow, but she was forced into the walls as well. The city's guards had gathered at the blasted portions of the walls and were fighting with the elves trying to enter.

Jovanna drew her sword as she was forced toward the guards. It was utter chaos. The clash of steel and the screams of the dying filled the air. Blood had already begun to cover the streets and Jovanna almost slipped. She stepped over the bodies of the fallen and tried to evade the guards. They were overcome with adrenaline and were hacking and slashing wildly, careless of the safety of their fellows.

Jovanna managed to get to the outer edge of the elvish line, but a group of guards came running from the inner part of the city to join the fray. They were coming right at her. Jovanna considered every option. Unfortunately, there weren't many. If she released her illusions, the elves would try to cut her down because she was human. If she kept the illusion, the guards would try to kill her because she was an elf.

Something inside her broke and she rushed forward, attacking the guards. She demolished their ranks and cut through them with ease. She hacked arms off and crushed kneecaps with her foot. She sliced through helmets and armor, killing with an animal like ferocity.

When her blood lust finally abated, she stood in the midst of a pile of bodies, both elves and men. Her body heaved as she breathed hard and surveyed the damage. She had taken a few cuts along her arms and legs, but nothing serious. The elves had overrun the city and the humans were on the run.

Jovanna knelt beside one of the guards and pulled his helm off. She felt a horrible wrench in her gut as she saw the guard couldn't have been older than fifteen. His face was covered with blood, but she could still see the look of terror on his face. And she had killed him. She turned her head and vomited, sickened by what she had done.

"What's wrong with me?" she growled. She had never shied away from battle or death. Why was this any different? *He's just a kid*, she thought, answering her own question. She stood up and staggered through the carnage to lean up against one of the buildings nearby. She took several deep breaths and tried to calm herself. She didn't like this feeling. She *hated* this feeling.

She looked up as a group of elves entered the blasted walls. She recognized some of them as the formation leaders. One of them walked with a different bearing. He projected strength and authority. It looked like the elf she had battled with when Jerik was killed. She knew without a doubt this was Tairu.

She wiped the sweat from her face. They weren't even looking her way. *This is it*, she thought, *this is where he dies.* She gripped the hilt of her sword tightly and walked calmly toward him.

18

ARAMIS STRAINED AGAINST HIS BONDS, but it was no use. The ropes were cutting into his wrists and he could feel that his hands were sticky from the blood. Directly across from him, Mel was in a similar situation. They were each tied to a tall wooden pole. He looked over to his friend and thought he was sleeping, but then he noticed Mel's lips were moving.

"Why is he praying at a time like this?" Aramis whispered to himself. He looked around the courtyard they were in. There were several of the wooden poles sticking up out of the ground, but he and Mel were the only prisoners. A few of the poles were stained red from what Aramis assumed was blood. The courtyard was on the outer edge of the temple complex.

Aramis had been surprised to find that the location of Mordum's followers wasn't a camp as he had suspected, but a small city. At the northern end stood the massive building made of dark gray stone that served as a temple. It was foreboding and Aramis found it to be nightmarish. Ghoulish creatures decorated the outside. The entire place radiated evil. The temple was backed against a series of hills too small to be considered mountains. The front area was a decently sized courtyard, surrounded by a short brick wall.

Outside the courtyard was the city proper. When they were being dragged through the streets, Aramis had seen both houses and shops. It was a self-sustaining city, full of people. Women and children wandered the streets freely. All of the men, it seemed, were priests of Mordum who remained secluded inside the temple.

As he looked around, he noticed a group of priests coming towards them. He braced himself, ready to fight the moment they cut him loose. They passed by him, dragging a man in their midst. They tied the man to one of the poles and continued on toward the temple. Aramis was surprised the man was even breathing.

"The priests must have beaten him badly," Mel said.

Aramis could tell that as well. The man was covered in blood and bruises. "I wonder who he is, and why they brought him here?"

Mel shrugged. "There's no telling when it comes to the followers of Mordum."

Aramis tried to get his hands loose from the ropes again. He grunted in pain as they ripped his skin open. He gave up again and sagged against the pole, defeated. Mel was staring at him. "We're going to die here, aren't we?" he asked.

"Of course not," Mel answered. "Edria will aid us."

Some of the priests that brought the new prisoner returned. One of them was carrying a curved sword. They approached the battered man and began to question him.

"Where is he?" one of them asked.

The man groaned lowly. Aramis wasn't even sure the man was conscious. They began to punch the man and slam his head back against the wooden pole. He cried out weakly.

"What is wrong with you?" Aramis shouted. "Leave him alone!"

The priest carrying the sword glanced over at him momentarily but turned his attention back to the prisoner. They pointedly ignored his protests. After several minutes of continued abuse, the priest with the sword finally pushed the other priests out of the way. In one deft movement, he lifted the blade and hacked the man's arm off at the shoulder.

Blood went everywhere. The poor man didn't make a sound. The priest continued to cut the man's limbs off one at a time. His other arm, then each leg. Aramis vomited. He was no novice to battle and had seen his fair share of injuries, but this was careless murder.

The priest cut the robes that bound the man and his body fell onto the ground. The other priests gathered the limbs and carried them back to the temple. The remaining priest walked over and stood before him. Aramis could see the blood dripping from the priest's sword. He met the man's eyes, sickened.

The priest lifted his sword as if to strike him. Aramis closed his eyes and waited to die. His hands were suddenly free. He opened his eyes, confused. The priest grabbed him by the back of his shirt and forced him toward the temple.

Aramis was about to fight, but when he looked over at Mel, his friend subtly shook his head. He considered the fact that they were in the middle of a city controlled by Mordum and decided not to fight or try to run. The priest placed the tip of the sword against his back and led him through the courtyard and into the temple.

As soon as they entered the stone building, Aramis was assaulted by a horrid smell. He had smelled something similar once during a battle. A rotting corpse had been left on the field in the sun. He tried not to gag. The priest guided him through a long hallway and into a room that Aramis would have thought was from a nightmare. Blood covered the floor and was splattered on the walls. He noticed the priest treading carefully behind him, careful not to slip in the mess.

Aramis considered running for a brief moment but decided it wasn't worth the risk. Where would he go? He was trapped in the stronghold of Mordum's followers. They exited the bloody room through one of several doors and entered a narrow hall. It would have been difficult for two men to walk beside each other in the small space. They entered another room with severed limbs laying on tables of various shapes and sizes.

He was beginning to realize just how morbid these people were. Exiting that room as well, the priest stopped outside another door.

"Wait here," the priest warned, his glare promising torture if he was disobeyed.

Aramis didn't answer but stood rubbing his sore and bloodied wrists. The priest knocked twice before pushing the door open and disappearing within. Glancing around the hall, Aramis saw the priests weren't much for decoration, except for the blood and body parts. The priest opened the door and motioned for Aramis to enter.

He hesitated for just a moment, unsure of what might greet him inside this room. He stepped in and was immediately taken by surprise. The walls were covered with beautifully woven tapestries of vibrant colors, the floors covered with thick, plush rugs. A massive bookcase covered the back wall of the room, overfilled with books. The priest gave him another look of warning and left the room.

Aramis couldn't believe the wealth displayed in the place. A large desk sat in front of the bookcase and he suddenly realized there was someone sitting at it. The room was well lit, which provided him a perfect view of the man.

The first thing he noticed about the man was his bald head. It seemed to gleam in the lamplight. He wore a black cuirass with the symbol of Mordum—the upside-down cross—in silver on the left side of the chest. He sported a long horseshoe mustache that reached a few inches off his chin. As the man looked up at him, Aramis felt the tattoo on his arm tingle. He resisted the urge to scratch it.

"I've been waiting for you," the man said. His voice was deep and baritone.

"That's news to me," Aramis answered dryly.

The right side of the man's face rose in a smile. He stood up from his desk and put his hands behind his back. "Allow me to introduce myself. My name is Ilias. Mordum told me you were coming." He pulled the sleeve of his left arm up to reveal the symbol of the god. It was similar to Aramis's own tattoo, but Ilias's had a sword behind the cross. "I am the Prophet of Mordum," Ilias said.

"Then you are responsible for my father's murder?" Aramis growled angrily.

Ilias frowned. "I'm afraid I don't know what you're talking about. Who is your father?"

Aramis didn't believe the man. "My father was the king of Oakvalor."

"You are *him*," Ilias said softly. "'And behold, He shall come from a royal bloodline.'"

"What are you talking about?" Aramis asked.

"You are the promised one of Mordum," Ilias answered. "Long ago, he walked the earth in a mortal body. He seeks to do so again and he has chosen you to make this happen." Ilias shook his head in disbelief. "You must feel honored."

Aramis laughed. "I don't believe in any divine figure," he said.

"And I certainly haven't been chosen for anything beyond my own choices."

"It doesn't matter whether you believe it or not," Ilias chided. "It is the truth. Truth is not dependent upon belief or faith, it simply *is*."

"Regardless, I will never aid a murderer. If you lead those who follow Mordum, then you are responsible for my father's murder."

"I assure you I don't know what you mean. Why would I have killed your father? For what purpose or to what gain would I do such a thing?"

"You tell me. Your assassin killed him. I saw it with my own eyes. And then he cursed me with this!" Aramis yelled, pointing at his tattoo.

Ilias regarded him silently for a long while before responding. "Was this assassin wearing anything that caught your eye? A pendant of some sort?"

"I don't remember."

"Hm. How did he curse you with that tattoo? Tell me exactly what happened."

Aramis related the events of that horrible night. He described how he saw the man scaling the castle walls, his attempt to protect his father, and the murder. As he finished the story, he found his anger had subsided and was replaced with sadness. *I miss him so much,* he thought.

"Have you seen this man since then?" Ilias asked.

Aramis nodded. "Twice. Once in the Viss Mountains. My friend Mel called him a—" he tried to remember the word—"templar?"

"When was the second time you saw him?"

"He's the one who brought us here as prisoners," Aramis answered.

Ilias's face became like stone. "I see. Tell me, what were you doing so far from Oakvalor if you don't serve Mordum? This is his city, after all."

"I was hunting down my father's killer." Aramis didn't bother to mention he was also trying to retrieve the blood from the shrine. "And the trail led me here. Mel and I got caught in some traps in the woods."

"This place is a highly guarded secret. Surely someone told you where this city was. Who was it?"

Aramis shook his head. "No one told me anything. I didn't even know a city was out here. We just followed the assassin."

"I don't believe you," Ilias said. "Though that matters little. Mordum told me you were coming and that you would be the one to ensure he walks the earth again. Whether this is by your own choice, or by Mordum's will, I know it will come to pass. However, I cannot allow you to leave the city. And I cannot allow your friend to live."

Aramis stepped toward him. Ilias smiled as he touched his tattoo and Aramis froze in place. It was a strange feeling not being able to control his own body. He struggled with everything he could muster to no avail.

"You see," Ilias said, "as the Prophet of Mordum, I am given authority over everyone who bears the mark. I can *make* you do anything I desire, even if it violates your conscience. Show me reverence."

Aramis felt the muscles in his legs work of their own accord, moving and bending until he was on his knees before Ilias.

"You will kill the priest of Edria with your own hands," Ilias said malevolently. "Repeat it to me."

Aramis fought desperately to keep his mouth shut, but he heard the words come out of his mouth anyway. "I will kill Melchiades." As soon as he uttered them, deep inside he knew that Ilias really was going to make him kill his friend.

—

An hour later, Aramis was led out into the courtyard of the temple. When he saw that Mel was there as well, guarded by several priests, he knew the situation did not bode well. Ilias was there also, seated beneath a small pavilion. The priest leading Aramis took him to the center of the large area, directly across from Mel. Many of the priests gathered around the area, forming a wall around Mel and himself with their bodies. After they had enclosed the entire area, Ilias stood up.

"Brothers! Listen well. We have in our midst one of Edria's own warriors. How does he dare enter our holy city? His fellows murder our faithful, trying to snuff us out. And then he enters this place trying to do the same! Yet I declare to you that it will not work. Mordum himself fights on our behalf!" A cheer rang out from the gathered priests.

"To prove our god is stronger than Edria, we will have her pawn fight one of our faithful!" Aramis watched Mel standing resolute, outwardly seeming unfazed by the entire thing. Aramis hoped that Mel wasn't freaking out on the inside like he was. "Priest of Edria, summon your blade!"

Mel crossed his arms in defiance. Judging by the look on Ilias's face, Aramis could guess he wasn't pleased.

"Suit yourself," Ilias said. "You'll summon it if you want to live. Let the faithful one of Mordum step forth!" Aramis felt his muscles disobey his mind as he walked forward and lift his hand in salute to the Prophet.

Mel's arms uncrossed and slowly came to rest at his sides. He turned his head curiously, wondering what was happening.

"Aramis, the chosen one of Mordum, has honored our god by pledging to kill this vile intruder!" Another cheer rang out. "Choose your weapon!"

Aramis didn't want to choose a weapon. And he certainly didn't want to fight Mel. Yet his body was under the control of Ilias, and he could only watch helplessly. He walked over to one of the priests and took their sword, then returned to the center.

"Kill him!" Ilias shouted.

Aramis walked closer to Mel, swinging the sword in front of him in small 'X' shapes. He could feel his muscles loosening from the effort. He tried to shake his head or say something, to do anything that would warn his friend.

"I won't fight you," Mel said to him as he got closer. Aramis tilted his head to each side until it cracked, then did the same with his back. He lunged forward, stabbing towards Mel's stomach. His friend easily slapped the blade away with his hand as he leaped out of the way. "I'm not going to fight you," he said again, the confusion evident in his voice.

Aramis didn't bother trying to respond. He couldn't do anything to thwart Ilias's hold over him. He turned to the left and swung again, narrowly missing Mel's right arm. Ilias must have been getting impatient with Mel, for Aramis's attacks became faster and more furious.

Mel continued to dodge and evade the attacks, but Aramis could tell it was getting harder for him not to engage. Aramis scored a strike to his leg, opening a large gash in Mel's flesh. Mel grunted in pain and finally summoned his sword. Aramis felt fear rise within him. What if Ilias had his way and he killed Mel? Or if Mel, in self-defense, had to kill him? He didn't see any good outcome to their situation.

"I don't know what you are doing," Mel panted, "but I will not fight you. I will die if need be to ensure you live."

If he had control of his body, he likely would have teared up at Mel's loyalty. *I'm sorry*, he thought, wishing Mel could hear him. And then he rushed his friend, swinging the sword in a powerful arc. Mel brought his own blade up and blocked the blow, then pushed his arm out wide, throwing Aramis's sword from his grasp.

Aramis quickly retrieved the blade, thankful that Mel didn't take the advantage and try to strike him. Many men could be loyal, but when it came to life and death, loyalty usually went out the window. He had known Mel long enough to know that he was more honorable than anyone he had met, but their friendship had never been tested like this.

Trust Melchiades, for he will not lead you astray. The words of the old blind woman echoed in his mind. Aramis did trust him. He trusted Mel like a brother. So it came as a surprise when Mel attacked him. Aramis staggered back, deflecting the attack. Mel didn't let up and knocked Aramis to the ground. He put the point of his sword to Aramis's throat.

"Your champion has been defeated," Mel said to Ilias.

Ilias laughed. "You fool, this isn't a duel. This is a fight to the death."

Mel removed the blade from Aramis's neck. "I won't kill him," he said.

"You *can't* kill him," Ilias replied.

Before Mel could move, Aramis forced himself up and threw himself against Mel's blade. It punctured the skin of his neck and Aramis could feel the blade sever his windpipe. He coughed and choked as blood filled his airway. He slumped back onto the ground and saw the horror on Mel's face.

I'm dying! His mind screamed at him. His vision began to fade as he struggled to breathe. He finally had control of his body, but there was nothing he could do to save himself. He closed his eyes as he felt death sweep over him.

And then he opened them. He could breathe again. He reached up to his neck and felt nothing but smooth skin. "What—" he was about to say 'happened' before he felt the control of his body slip out of his grasp. He stood back up and retrieved the sword that had fallen out of his hand. Mel was staring at him incredulously.

"Mordum is God of the Dead," Ilias stated loudly, "and therefore Aramis cannot die unless I allow it. Now kill that Edrian scum!"

Aramis launched himself at Mel, trying to strike him in the chest. For some reason, Mel had yet to summon his armor. They continued back and forth, trading blows with one another and both receiving cuts and scrapes. Aramis lifted his sword up high to bring it down for a killing stroke when Mel's blade came at him suddenly, slicing the tattooed skin of his left arm.

He felt Ilias's hold break immediately. He flung the sword down and staggered away from Mel, raising his hands in surrender. "It's me!" he yelled. "It's me! Ilias was controlling me! I'm sorry for attacking you!"

Mel summoned his armor, the air shimmering with mist as it formed. "I figured something was going on when you cut my leg," he said. "I don't see any other option than to fight our way out."

Aramis nodded and picked his sword back up.

"Kill the priest and take Aramis captive!" Ilias commanded. The wall of priests began to close in around them. Aramis surrendered himself to the fact that although he didn't kill Mel, these priests certainly would. They were seriously outnumbered. Aramis readied himself.

A horn sounded in the distance. The encroaching priests hesitated, glancing around uncertainly. A second horn sounded, this one closer and louder than the first.

"What's that?" Aramis asked, casting a brief glance at Mel.

"I'm not sure, but it sounds like Orcish war horns."

A priest came running from the city area, shouting for the Prophet. He reached Ilias, panting and out of breath. "They're coming," he said.

"Who is coming?" Ilias demanded.

"Orcs!"

Ilias turned to look at Mel and Aramis, seeming to struggle internally with some decision. "Forget the priest," he commanded. "Defend the city! An army of orcs approaches!"

The priests quickly scattered, heading toward the walls that protected the city's borders. Ilias continued to stare at Aramis.

"We've got to get out of here," Mel said.

"We can't leave without the blood," Aramis replied.

"Any ideas where it might be? We don't have much time."

"I'm sure the priests will be busy with the orcs for a while," Aramis said, turning toward the temple. "It has to be in there."

"I'm not worried about the orcs," Mel said. "I took a chance at slicing your tattoo, but from what I saw a moment ago, it's not going to be long before your skin heals itself and Ilias takes control of you again. We need to be long gone before that happens."

"Wait, you didn't know for sure it would work?"

"Of course not. How could I?"

Aramis shrugged. They ran towards the temple and entered to find the halls empty. Apparently, all of the priests were present for the fight. They began searching through every room they encountered. Many of them seemed to be lodgings for the priests.

"In here!" Mel called out. Aramis left the room he was searching and ran to where Mel was. It was the room with the severed body parts on the tables. On one of them was the wineskin they had used to collect the blood from the shrine.

Aramis grabbed it and they ran back into the hall, trying to navigate their way back out of the building. "What are they doing in that room?" Aramis asked. "It looks like something out of a nightmare."

"There's no telling with Mordum," Mel answered.

They escaped the building and ended up back in the courtyard. Ilias was nowhere to be found. They made their way toward the city area. The sounds of battle could be heard in every direction. Women were screaming and children were running through the streets, trying to find somewhere to hide.

They turned a corner and almost ran into a large orc. The orc cut down a priest and turned to face them. Aramis brought his sword up and was about to charge the creature when Mel stopped him. The orc nodded at Mel.

"I see you are still following your god," the orc said.

"And I see you are out for revenge for your kin," Mel answered.

The orc growled. "These priests will feel the fury of my anger for their betrayal!"

"I pray that you will get what you seek, my friend. Can you point us to the way out?"

"I can show you the way out, but this one must stay with me," the orc said, pointing to Aramis. "He wears their brand on his arm."

"He's not a follower," Mel said. "He was cursed by the Templar who betrayed you on the mountain. He's with me."

Aramis thought the orc was going to refuse to let him leave, but then he bowed his head. "I trust your judgment. Follow the road that leads to the east. It will take you out of the city. Fight well, my friend."

"Thank you," Mel said. They turned to leave, only to find the templar from the mountain blocking their way.

"Out of the way!" the orc roared. "He's mine!"

Aramis and Mel both stepped aside quickly as the massive creature charged the priest. As they crashed into each other, Aramis and Mel took advantage of the distraction and quickly ran past them, continuing down the road.

"I hope the orc doesn't kill the priest," Aramis said between breaths. "I want to be the one to kill that murderer."

"He won't," Mel replied. "The templar will crush him, so we don't have much time. We need to get as far as we can before he catches up to us."

Aramis looked down at his arm as he felt the tattoo on his skin begin to itch. The skin was healed.

19

ARAMIS AND MEL RAN ALONG the worn path, weaving among the trees. Aramis kept one hand clutched against the wineskin of blood at his waist to ensure it didn't come loose.

"We've got to hurry," Mel huffed.

"I'm moving as fast as I can," Aramis replied. His lungs and his legs were burning. The fact they hadn't eaten anything wasn't helping either. He could feel the dry blood from his wrists on his palms and fingers. "I'm afraid we aren't going to make it," he said. "It's too far."

"We have to try," Mel answered.

Aramis thought he could faintly hear hoof beats behind them. "They've noticed our escape. We can't outrun horses. We've got to find some place to hide."

"I agree, my Prince. But I don't see anywhere worthy of being called a hiding spot here in the trees."

Aramis knew Mel was right. It didn't look good for them. The path suddenly veered right and led them out of the trees and onto the main road. He cursed their luck and stopped running. Mel stopped beside him. Aramis looked back and could see a lone horseman riding his way through the trees.

"It took us over a week to get here by carriage and horse, Mel. I don't see a way out of this."

"Not for both of us," Mel answered.

Aramis looked to him, confused. "What do you mean?"

The air rippled as Mel summoned his sword. "We both can't get away. One of us will need to be a diversion."

"Mel, you said yourself that very few have defeated a templar. Don't put your life at risk on account of me."

"Once they catch us, they'll kill me anyway. If I can give you time to get away, then you at least have a chance of getting the blood to the Prophet. We cannot allow the blood to fall back into their hands. Go, Aramis."

"I'm not leaving you," Aramis said defiantly.

"You have to. There is more at stake here than one man's life. You have to go. Use the mark to aid you. I know I've been telling you to fight the sway of Mordum, but the power of his curse may offer some help. Go."

Aramis didn't move.

"Go!" Mel screamed. The horseman reached the road. Aramis looked from Mel to the templar. He didn't feel right about leaving his friend behind. In the army, they taught that a soldier should never be left behind. Aramis knew what Mel said was true, however. If Mordum walked the earth as a man, Hell would come with him. There *was* more at stake than one man's life, no matter if it was his friend or not.

"Go!" Mel screamed again.

Aramis grit his teeth in anger. There was no other option. He turned and fled.

—

Mel watched over his shoulder as Aramis sprinted off. He nodded in grim satisfaction. "Goodbye, my friend." He turned to face the templar, who had dismounted and was approaching deliberately.

"He won't get far," the templar said. "After I destroy you, he will be next. You cannot stop Mordum." The templar pulled his hood back and held his hand out, summoning his own blade. The air hissed as the black blade came into existence.

Mel got into his battle stance, holding his sword up before him. He watched the templar carefully. Though he had never fought one of Mordum's Knights before, he had learned enough from the Prophet's tales to know they could be very powerful.

The templar leaped forward suddenly. He was much quicker than Mel expected, but he was able to parry the attack. He launched into his own attack, twisting his blade about and striking the templar's armor twice, resulting in two jagged lines on the otherwise flawless armor.

The templar laughed. Lightning flickered along his blade and he struck Mel's shoulder. It bounced off the plate harmlessly, but the shock made Mel flinch involuntarily. They exchanged several blows, weighing each other's weaknesses. Mel knew immediately that he was outmatched. He had to injure the templar or hold him off long enough for Aramis to get a decent head start. He knew it wasn't likely.

—

Aramis ran as fast as he could, which wasn't very fast. He was exhausted, hungry, and sore. He looked back several times, but he couldn't tell what was happening. Why did Mel have to be so blasted righteous? Giving his life so Aramis could *try* to escape. It wasn't even a guarantee. He fought back the tears as he thought of the violent end Mel would likely meet at the templar's hands.

He slipped on a rock and twisted his ankle, tumbling down onto the ground. He grunted in pain. He'd had worse injuries before, but if he couldn't walk on it, he certainly wouldn't get far before the templar reached him. He got up and took a few steps, gritting his teeth in agony. His ankle burned like fire.

Use the mark.

Mel's words echoed in his mind. Aramis looked at the tattoo, disgusted by it. The mark of the god responsible for everything that had gone wrong in his life the last few weeks might be his only chance at survival. The irony wasn't lost on him.

Mel said before that the mark had all kinds of effects on people. He was wary of trying to use it. He could just as likely go insane as he could gain power that others could only dream of. The most obvious problem was that he didn't even know how to use the tattoo. Did he just need to touch it? Or did he will it to work?

"I've got to try something," he said to himself. He closed his eyes and focused on the tattoo. He pictured it in his mind and willed it to let him walk without pain. He opened his eyes and took a step. His ankle screamed in rebellion and he almost fell again. He kept his weight off of it as he tried everything he could think of to try and activate the tattoo. Finally, he touched it with his finger. He felt … *something* … run along his arm.

It was a strong tingling feeling that threatened numbness, like the time he was almost struck by lightning on the castle walls. The air had thrummed with electricity. It was almost the same.

Almost.

There was something different about this feeling. With the lightning, there had been the fear of dying. Not with this. This felt good. *Really* good. It called his name, begging to be released. So he released it. Power flowed through his body, overwhelming him. His body convulsed violently before he lost his sight.

There was nothing but darkness.

—

Mel was struggling just to defend himself. He parried the attacks as fast as he could, but he was getting sluggish. It must have been obvious, for the templar began attacking faster. He prayed to Edria for strength, but none came. There was nothing but a disturbing silence. And then the realization struck him. Edria had abandoned him. That knowledge was worse than the fact that he knew he would not survive this battle.

If it was his time to die, then so be it. But he couldn't bear the thought that his goddess had forsaken him. Was it because of Aramis? Was it because he had decided in his heart not to obey the Prophet about leaving the prince to die? If so, he didn't understand. All life was sacred. How could Edria forsake him for refusing to let an innocent man die?

He tried to push the thoughts from his mind. The templar thrust at him. Mel barely deflected the blow and was surprised when the templar followed through with a vicious kick to his knee. His leg buckled, but thankfully he didn't go down. He brought his blade up and to the left, going for an attack in the opening the templar left. Too late, Mel realized it was a ruse. The templar's blade plunged into his stomach, slicing through his armor, flesh, and bone before ripping out through his back.

He gasped in shock. His own sword slipped from his hand and fell to the ground at his feet. The templar jerked the blade forward roughly, forcing Mel to stagger backward. He clutched his stomach as the templar withdrew his sword from his body. Black dots ringed the outside of his vision. Blood poured freely over his hands. Oddly, he thought to himself that he needed to sit down. But the thought didn't make any sense, because he knew he was battling for his life.

Suddenly he was on his back staring up into the sky. It was so *blue*. He'd never noticed before how blue it really was. Then he saw the templar looking down at him with a wicked grin.

"Now your friend dies," he said.

And then he no longer saw the man. He heard the sound of a horse galloping away. Something in his mind told him that Aramis was going to die, but for some reason, he didn't care. He wanted to care, but he just … couldn't.

He was bleeding to death. He couldn't see anything now, but he was sure he had his eyes open. As he exhaled for the last time, he thought he heard the sound of a merchant's cart.

And then he died.

—

Release me.

Aramis looked to where he heard a voice calling faintly. It was coming from the other side of a large wooden door. As he walked toward the door, he realized he was back home at the castle. The door was to his father's room. He put his hand on the handle, then hesitated. What would it be like to walk back into that room?

He gritted his teeth as tears stung his eyes and opened the door. His father stood there, gazing out the window. Aramis stopped mid-step in confusion.

"My son," his father's voice greeted him.

"Father?"

"You sound surprised," his father said without turning around.

"I … I saw you die," Aramis said softly.

"You must have dreamed it," his father replied.

Death cannot contain me.

"What?"

"I said you must have dreamed it."

"What did you say after that?" Aramis asked.

"I didn't say anything, son. What's going on with you? Are you feeling well?"

Aramis felt confused. He looked around the room for anything that seemed out of the ordinary. Everything seemed normal. Had he really dreamed everything? Was his father still alive? He hoped it was true.

"Father, what happened last night?" he asked.

"What do you mean?"

"What happened last night? Do you remember?"

"Of course I remember. Are you drunk, boy? We were out riding after our hunt."

Aramis stared at the man who seemed to be his father. "We didn't go riding, or on a hunt," he replied. "We had a feast."

His father didn't answer. Aramis stepped closer and laid his hand on his father's shoulder. A sharp coldness ran up his arm and he cried out in surprise. His father turned around, only it wasn't his father. The man's face was pale and thin.

"Mordum!" Aramis exclaimed, stepping back from the man.

Release me.

"I am your father."

"No!" he yelled. "You cannot fool me with your tricks!"

"I have given you a new life," Mordum said. "I have taken away the sting of death. And now I will give you power among men. They will see your deeds and know your power comes from *me*. Now go."

Aramis backed away and reached to his belt for his sword. The scabbard was empty.

"Go. Go forth and *release me!*"

Aramis turned to flee and saw that he was on the road. He looked around frantically, fearing Mordum was there as well. He was alone. In the distance, he could see someone coming. He couldn't be sure, but he thought he could also see a horse. The templar.

He prepared himself for the pain as he tried to start walking. There was no pain. He rolled his foot around and put his full weight on his hurt foot.

Nothing.

He didn't have time to contemplate the sudden change. He started running, trying to gain ground on the approaching horseman. He knew it was foolish to think he could outrun a horse, but what other options did he have?

He ran as fast as he could. And that's when he noticed it. Everything was flying past him speedily. Aramis looked over his shoulder and didn't even see the rider. He slowed to a jog. He'd only run for a few minutes, but it seemed like he had covered a lot of distance.

I will give you power among men.

Aramis wondered if that was a good thing. If it gave him the ability to escape and take the blood to the Prophet, then perhaps there might be some good in wielding Mordum's powers. He increased his speed and watched as the scenery flew by. At this rate, he'd make it back in half the time.

—

After three days, Aramis finally reached the city. He was drenched in sweat and covered in dirt. None of that mattered to him. He had the blood from the shrine and the Prophet would now give him the support he would need to begin clearing his name. He would not let Mel's sacrifice be in vain. He entered the church's compound and was greeted by a small group of priests.

"I need to see the Prophet," he informed them.

One of the priests held his hand up as if to block him. "The Prophet speaks with the people of the city during the weekly service. He's currently unavailable."

"That's great," Aramis said impatiently. "I'm not here for that. He sent me on a mission with Melchiades."

"A mission?" The priest looked at his cohorts. "I'm not aware of any mission. What exactly did he send you off to do?"

Aramis pulled the wineskin from his belt. "To retrieve this blood from the shrine of Mordum."

All of the priests began talking at once. The one who had spoken commanded silence from them. "My apologies," the priest said. "I'll take you to him immediately. Follow me." The man led Aramis into the building, the other priests falling in behind them. He recognized the hallway to the Prophet's office as soon as they turned down it.

"Wait here," the priest said before entering into the room. He returned and held the door open for Aramis to enter.

The Prophet was standing by the map table, looking expectantly at him. "You've brought the blood?" he asked. There was an excitement to his tone that wasn't lost on Aramis.

"I have," he answered.

"This is good news. Where is Melchiades?"

"He …" words failed him. He swallowed hard and tried to speak again, but nothing came out. Finally, he simply shook his head.

"I see," the Prophet said somberly. "His sacrifice will not be forgotten. Melchiades was a great man, ardent in his faith. He will be greatly missed."

Aramis could only nod in agreement.

"Where is the blood?"

Aramis held the wineskin out to him. The Prophet gingerly accepted it and set it on his desk.

"I'm grateful that you managed to retrieve the blood, and I know it cost you a lot to do so."

"I trust you will give me your support in trying to clear my name?" Aramis asked.

The Prophet stood tall and looked Aramis in the eyes. "I'm sorry, but I cannot do that. You wear the mark of Mordum openly on your skin. The fact that you returned with the blood so easily tells me that you truly are a servant of Mordum. Escort Aramis to the dungeon." He motioned to the other priests. They obeyed quickly and grabbed Aramis by his arms.

"What are you doing?" Aramis demanded. "You said if I got you that blood you would help me!"

"About that," the Prophet said, "I lied. Take him now."

Aramis struggled to get free, but the priests dragged him out by force. They pulled him through the church's halls and finally down the stairs that led to the dungeon. He continued to struggle against them, but it was no use. He was outmatched. They tossed him into one of the cells and locked the door. He shook the bars of the gate.

"You can't do this!" he screamed. "You can't do this to me!"

No one was listening.

*"Order is not pressure which is imposed on society from without,
but an equilibrium which is set up from within."*

—General Garrick

20

GARRICK WAITED UNTIL HIS WIFE was asleep to move. He gently kissed her forehead before rolling off the bed. They had left a window cracked and a cool breeze wafted through the opening. He grabbed a robe from the closet and covered his nakedness.

Making his way to the study, the few guards he passed lowered their heads in reverence to him. He had worked hard and given much to help the people of Talvaard. Thanks to his men—who had bravely fought against the tyranny of the others—and to Aramis, tomorrow he would be king. The details of the coronation were being planned by the court chamberlain, with a little help from his wife.

He hoped she would get pregnant soon. Now that the kingdom was reunited, life would return to normal and he could focus on the good of the people and raising a family. He smiled as he imagined what his children might look like. His sons would be strong like him, his daughters beautiful like his wife. All that he had worked for was certainly worth it.

Garrick entered the study to find that the servants had already prepared it for him. A desk made of cedar sat to the left. To the right, numerous bookstands lined the enormous room with books on every subject imaginable. He was thankful that the kings before him had been learned men, choosing to be educated not only in war. He walked among the stands, reading some of the titles on the books.

A History of Talvaard.

The Book of Faith.

The Sayings of Kings.

The Persecution of Mages.

He decided suddenly that he would make plans to read every book in the study. It might take him the rest of his life, but it would be a great accomplishment. He walked to the table and sat down. Two silver bowls, one on each side of the desk, were filled with glow stones. They glowed a faint bluish color. Often cheaper to use than candles or lanterns, the stones were usually found in the same mines as gold. Although stones had been found in almost every color, the predominant hue found was blue. No one was quite sure why the rocks gave off the light, but many offered varying conjectures.

A decently sized stack of papers had been placed on the desk, all needing to be signed. Grabbing one of the quills on the desk, he dipped it into an inkwell and was about to sign the first paper when he paused. There was no telling what the documents might contain, so he began reading. He found many of them disagreeable and placed them to the side. The others he signed and placed in a separate pile, then he went back to the others. He crossed out lines he didn't agree with and added things he thought should be included.

By the time he was finished, several hours had passed. His eyes were burning from reading so long, but otherwise, he wasn't very tired. He knew it was well after midnight. Perhaps it was his excitement over the coronation, but he simply couldn't sleep. He grabbed the two piles of papers and left the study. A young man in the robes of a monk was standing outside the door.

"Good evening, Your Majesty," the monk greeted.

"I've not been crowned king yet," Garrick replied. "But I appreciate the sentiment."

The monk smiled and bowed his head. "My apologies. Is there anything I can do to serve you tonight?"

Garrick held out the papers. "These have been signed and are ready to be issued. These ones here need to be re-written and brought back to me."

"Re-written, Your Maj—" the monk paused momentarily before correcting himself, "My Lord?"

"Yes. I don't like what they propose, so I've made changes and want them fixed. I will not sign anything until I have read it and agree with it."

"That is wise, my Lord. I will deliver them and pass along your message." The monk took the papers and disappeared down the hall.

Garrick rubbed the back of his neck. Staring down at those papers so long had put a crick in it. He wandered along the hallways, pausing to admire the many statues and tapestries that decorated the palace. Eventually, he entered the throne room where he would listen to petitions from the people and the nobles. He surveyed the design etched in the floor and wondered if it signified anything.

The vaulted ceiling rose sixty feet above him. Support pillars were spaced every ten feet, outlining the main walkway through the chamber. Two giant alabaster statues of winged men standing at attention flanked either side of a door located in the middle of the far wall. Portraits of regal men, the kings of the past, were spaced along the entire chamber. Garrick spent time staring at each one. He wondered what each man's character had been like. He was only slightly familiar with the reign of the older kings. Perhaps he would read some books that recorded the events of their reign.

He made his way to the door flanked by the statues and entered it. He found a hallway large enough for two carriages to comfortably pass through. There were a couple of doors but they were all locked. He made a note to investigate the hall when he had the keys to the doors. He turned around and went back into the throne room.

The events of the day were starting to wear him down. He returned to his room to find his wife still sleeping. He returned the robe and climbed back into bed, kissing his wife on the forehead again before laying on his back. He closed his eyes.

It seemed as if he had just drifted off when he heard something. Garrick's eyes snapped open and he sat straight up in the bed. He looked to his wife. She was still sleeping. Had he really just fallen asleep, or had it been several hours? He looked around the room, trying to figure out what had woken him. Someone knocked at his bedroom door.

In his tiredness, he forgot he was naked and opened the door. The hallway lights had been dimmed for the night. He was greeted by a guard and one of his captains. "My King," the Captain bowed. "I hate to wake you, but if it wasn't urgent you know I wouldn't."

"Of course. What is wrong?"

The Captain glanced at the guard, then back to Garrick. "Perhaps you'd like to get dressed first?"

Garrick looked down at himself. "Excuse me," he said. He shut the door, retrieved his robe, and then stepped out into the hallway. "Report Styrmir."

Styrmir pulled a rolled parchment from his waist and read it to Garrick. "The northern border was attacked and three cities have been destroyed. Two of them were smaller villages, but one was a decently fortified city. Hundreds are feared dead. Most of those who escaped made it to the closest city, a few of them managed to get here to report it."

Garrick listened intently. "Who is behind the attack? If someone is trying to rebel against my rule, I will banish them from Talvaard."

Styrmir shook his head. "No, it wasn't any of the generals. The report says it was elves."

"Elves?" Garrick was dumbfounded. "From the Deadlands?"

Styrmir nodded grimly. "Yes. I didn't believe it at first, but when more than one of the survivors had the same story, I requested a report from Captain Ghottard in the north." He held the parchment up. "This is the official report. According to best guesses, it sounds like the elves had a large force, possibly in the thousands."

"Has Captain Ghottard mounted an offensive?"

"No, sir. He wants to, but he doesn't have enough men. He seems confident that he can hold the city if they attack, though he is requesting reinforcements."

"The elves are still in the area?" Garrick asked, still trying to wrap his mind around it.

"They are. They've set up camp a few miles from Ghottard's city."

"How many men does he have available right now?"

"Five hundred, maybe. I've ordered two battalions of three hundred each to march immediately. Obviously, it will take them a few days to get there. Is this sufficient, or should I send more?"

Garrick folded his arms across his chest. After giving it some thought he said, "That should be sufficient. The elves are barbarians. They don't have the defenses or weapons we do. I don't know how they took a fortified city, but they won't be doing it again. Thank you for bringing this information to me. It is troubling indeed."

"I knew that you'd want to be informed immediately. We finally have peace in the kingdom. We don't need it shattering now."

"I agree," Garrick said. "Thank you again." Styrmir bowed and left. The soldier guarding his door saluted Garrick with a hand to his chest. Garrick returned the salute and went back into his bedroom. He was deeply troubled. Why would elves be attacking his cities? He noticed his wife was sitting up in bed.

"What's wrong?" she asked sleepily. "Why aren't you in bed?"

"Nothing is wrong, my love. Styrmir brought some important news. He's handling it, but he wanted to inform me."

"Okay," she said. "Come back to bed then."

"I will in a moment. First I must pray. Go back to sleep, my beauty. I'll be back shortly." She laid back down among the pillows and rolled over. He left the room and made his way back to the study. The monk who was there before must have retired for he wasn't to be found. Garrick entered the chamber and closed the door behind him. There didn't appear to be a locking mechanism, but he didn't expect many people to be up so late.

He sat at the desk and pulled the left sleeve of his arm up. The flesh was smooth and tan. He scratched at the flesh about an inch above his wrist until a small piece of skin came up. He pinched the skin and pulled slowly but firmly. As the skin was removed, a dark tattoo began to take shape. Garrick pulled a rectangular piece of skin off, roughly five inches long by two inches wide. He set it on the desk and looked it over.

It wasn't skin at all, but a fabric type of material. It had been dyed to match his skin color and he held it in place using an adhesive liquid. It was a clever design he had commissioned a few years ago. Placing his index and middle finger on the tattoo, he closed his eyes.

"Mordum, hear my prayer …"

THE END OF BOOK 2

THE VALIANT KING

"Like sand in the hourglass, so does time elude our grasp."

—Garrick

1

A LIGHT BREEZE BLEW IN from the east, causing Garrick's cloak to stir slightly. He closed his eyes and breathed the cool air in deep then exhaled slowly. He opened his eyes and saw the sun was just beginning to rise, bathing the dark sky in soothing reds and pinks. The beauty of the heavens was almost enough to forget reality.

Almost.

Garrick turned his gaze to the fields outside the castle. As far as he could see, makeshift tents blotted out the scenery. Here and there he could pick out movement among the camp as they slowly awakened.

He considered, as he had many times since their arrival, why they were here. Thousands of them, slowly encroaching into his kingdom. From the corner of his eye, he noticed one of his scouts approaching.

"My Lord," the man said as he drew near before dropping down on one knee.

"Please rise," Garrick answered, turning away from the elvish army. "What do you have to report?"

"Their numbers are growing. More elves show up every day. We haven't been able to get close enough to find their leader's tent yet, but we are working on it. It's not easy to slip past their guards. Magic and whatnot."

Garrick nodded. "I understand. Do the best you can. That's all I ask." He turned back to the fields. After a few moments, he realized the man was still standing there. He turned to him, raising his eyebrows questioningly.

"You didn't dismiss me, my Lord."

"My apologies," Garrick replied. He nodded toward the elvish army. "Why do you suppose they are here?"

The scout shrugged. "I'm not sure. Perhaps they want their land back."

"Excuse me?"

"You know, from the old stories? Supposedly the elves lived in these lands before humans pushed them into the desert. Maybe they want their land back." The man shrugged again.

"It's definitely something to consider," Garrick said. "Thank you. You are dismissed." The man bowed low and left.

Garrick rubbed his chin as he considered what the scout said. Perhaps the man was right. It had been a long time since he had heard those stories of history. Was there truth to them? He didn't know. He would definitely need to research it.

An explosion shook the ground beneath his feet.

"And so it begins again," he muttered. It had been two weeks since he arrived, bringing fresh reinforcements to help stem the tide of elves overrunning his cities. They were using their strange magic to create holes in the walled cities, enabling their warriors to storm through and massacre his people.

After three cities had fallen, he mustered as many men as he could and made his way to the battlefront. He'd sent runners to the outer cities, calling on his generals and their men to follow suit. They were slowly starting to arrive.

Once he had witnessed how the elves were getting through the defenses of his cities, he had placed archers on the walls and ordered them to cut down the elves rushing the walls.

And it had worked. The elves finally stopped trying to breach the walls. The last two days had essentially been a stalemate with neither side attacking the other. Garrick ran to where a group of soldiers had gathered.

"What's happening?" he asked.

"One of them rushed the wall, but Tarn here shot him down right before he hit it."

"Excellent job, Tarn. Was it just the one?"

"Yes, sir."

"They're testing us, probably to see if we are still paying attention," Garrick said.

"That's what we were thinking, sir."

"Keep me posted. If anything happens, I want to be alerted immediately."

"Will do, sir."

Garrick left the wall and headed down the steps, walking toward the main keep. The generals who had arrived late last night were supposed to be gathering there now. A messenger waved him over.

"There's a battalion roughly a mile out," he said breathlessly.

"I appreciate the update," Garrick said. The messenger sprinted off, likely to deliver more news elsewhere.

He entered the keep and made his way to the appointed room. Silence ensued and everyone in the room bowed as he entered.

"Thank you for making haste," Garrick said. "Please be seated." After everyone had found a seat, he also took a seat and then briefed them on the current situation.

"What has brought them to our doorstep?" Rycroft, one of the generals, asked.

"That is the question, isn't it?" Garrick motioned to one of the guards standing nearby. The man came over and unrolled a map that was on the table. He placed four small stones onto the map, one at each corner.

"This is a map of the area. Our position is marked with the green square here," Garrick pointed to a spot on the map.

"Our enemy encampment is here in red. The last two days have been silent. Before that, they had men rushing the walls and using their magic to blow holes in the stone. Our archers put a stop to that."

He ran his finger from the enemy camp north to the Deadlands. "This is the route they are taking to arrive here. Every day more of them turn up. The curious thing is that they are all men."

"What do you mean?"

Garrick looked to Rycroft. The man was intelligent when it came to tactics on the battlefield. He was one of the few who had given him a run for his gold when he was working to unify the generals. It seemed so long ago, but only a few months had passed since Garrick was crowned king.

"They are all men. No women or children are among the camps. Curious, is it not?" Some of the generals muttered to themselves.

"Where do you suppose they are?" Garrick asked.

"Perhaps they are still in the Deadlands?" again, Rycroft answered.

"Perhaps. Assuming they are, who do you suppose is protecting them?"

Again, murmurs filled the room.

"If all of their warriors are coming here, it seems likely there is no one protecting their women and children. Which opens a possibility of us ending this battle, or at the very least, postponing it long enough for us to rally more soldiers here."

"What are you suggesting?" Caidan, one of the younger men, asked.

Garrick rose from his chair and clasped his hands behind his back. His eyes looked from one general to the next, moving around the table and finally stopping at Rycroft.

"I am suggesting that we send a contingent of men into the Deadlands to find their women and children."

Instead of the murmuring, there was only silence. "Make no mistake, I am not proposing that we massacre them. We are not barbarians. But I believe if we can find them, we can use them to our advantage."

Caidan ran his left hand over his bearded face. "What's the plan, then?"

"I need a volunteer to take a few men and follow the route the elves are coming from. You'll need to act as scouts. Follow the trail and find their source, or at the very least one of their camps. Ensure there are women and children, then send one of the men back here with the location. I'll dispatch soldiers during the night and the scout will lead them to the camp."

"What then?" Rycroft asked.

"Then, depending on the situation here, we'll decide what our next move is. I understand you'll all need time to think it over. Take the rest of the day and sleep on it. I'll need to know who is volunteering by tomorrow at first light. Are there any questions?"

"Yes," Caidan said. "We know their men have magical tattoos. What of their women? Do they have them as well?"

"That we are unsure of," Garrick answered. "I have scribes searching every library for information on our enemy. That is one of the questions I am looking to have answered."

"What other information are you looking for?"

"I am looking for the truth," Garrick said. "I'm sure you all know the stories."

"What stories are you referring to? Their magical prowess? Their deadly homeland? Their—"

"Where they originated from," Garrick interrupted Caidan. "I'm talking about the stories of where they came from. There are some stories that say parts of Talvaard and parts of Oakvalor used to be home to the elves until humans pushed them into the desert."

"Those are childish fairy tales," Caidan scoffed. "They're used to scare children into obedience." His next words were said with a mocking tone: "'Do as you are told so the elves don't come for you and drag you off into the Deadlands as punishment for their banishment.'"

"Perhaps you are right," Garrick replied. "And perhaps you are wrong. We don't know if they are fairy tales or if they are historical truths. Until we do, I suggest everyone keep an open mind. Suppose it is true. Suppose that our ancestors did indeed push them into the desert. Why do you think they would be here, after all this time, attacking our cities?"

"Revenge?" Rycroft suggested.

"Precisely. What if they have come to take their land back?"

"That's preposterous!" Caidan barked.

"Is it?" Garrick asked.

"You're serious?" Caidan said, seeming to realize that Garrick was posing a genuine theory.

"Absolutely. Keep an open mind. Your people are pushed from their homes. They are possibly struggling to survive in a foreign land. Eventually, they grow in strength and they are constantly reminded of what happened to them. What do you think it would lead to?"

"I suppose it's possible," Caidan confessed hesitantly.

"That's all I'm suggesting," Garrick replied. "That it is possible the stories are true. And if they are, I don't see this being a short battle."

"You think this will turn into a siege?" Caidan asked.

"No. They will not stop until they succeed. I am sure this will turn into a war."

The generals exchanged looks.

"That's all I have for now," Garrick waved dismissively. "I ask that you all meet here again in the morning. Until then, see to your men and get what rest you can. Dismissed."

Garrick turned and left the room, likely leaving his generals confused. He tried not to let it bother him. He was just as confused about the motive of the elves himself.

He noticed soldiers running toward the northern wall. Shouting filled the air. He stopped one of the men running by.

"What's going on?" he demanded.

"The elves, my Lord! They're rushing the walls again!"

Garrick dismissed the man with a nod and ran toward the stairs leading to the battlements. He bounded up the stairs two at a time and rushed to the wall. Down below, a group of elves were running toward the castle.

Arrows whistled through the air, some striking the ground around them. A few of them hit their mark and the elves staggered and tumbled to the ground. Caidan and Rycroft came and stood on either side of him, watching the spectacle.

"I thought they stopped attacking the walls with the archers up here?" Caidan asked.

"They did," Garrick answered. "I don't understand this foolish move."

The remaining elves stopped their approach and began lifting their fallen comrades. Garrick assumed they were going to remove their bodies from the battlefield. Instead, the elves used the bodies as shields and continued their trek toward the castle.

"Take them down!" Garrick shouted.

More arrows filled the air. The few elves remaining were quickly killed and a cheer roused from the archers. Garrick watched the encampment. There was no reason to celebrate.

The elves had proven somewhat intelligent in their attacks against the walls. It seemed out of place for them to attack now, knowing their warriors were at the mercy of his bowmen. An unsettling feeling crept into his stomach.

"Something's not right," he muttered.

"What's that?" Rycroft asked.

"Something's not right. They wouldn't attack like this. Not with the archers up here." His mind began racing through scenarios. He looked toward the archers and whistled. One of them jogged over.

"Captain, have some men sweep the walls. Tell them to keep their eyes sharp."

The man nodded and left, his pace much faster than before.

"What do you think they're doing?" Caidan asked.

"I'm not sure, but I think they're creating a diversion."

As if to prove him right, a horn sounded from the eastern side of the castle. Garrick sprinted in that direction, Caidan and Rycroft following close behind him.

Before they were halfway there, an explosion sounded and the castle walls shook violently. Garrick leaned up against the outer wall to keep his balance.

"They've hit the wall!" he shouted.

As soon as the shaking settled, he stood up straight and continued running to where a crowd of archers had gathered. He reached the area just as they let off a volley of arrows. Garrick looked down to see a charred spot on the wall and the body of an elf lying nearby.

"He got right up to the wall before we knew he was even approaching," one of the bowmen said. "We hit him right before he made it."

Garrick saw a small group of elves approaching slowly. "There," he said, pointing to their position.

"They're out of range, but we'll hit them hard as soon as they get close."

Garrick nodded and watched their advance. "Why aren't they running?" he asked to no one in particular.

"What do you mean?" Caidan asked.

"They normally rush the walls. Why are they walking?"

Everyone remained silent. After what seemed like an eternity, Garrick heard the captain shout an order.

A stream of arrows whistled through the air. Garrick squinted his eyes, thinking he was seeing things. It looked as though the arrows had bounced off the elves.

"What happened?" he asked.

"I'm not sure," Rycroft said uncertainly, also squinting into the distance.

"Draw!" The captain shouted beside him. The archers knocked their arrows to their bowstrings and pulled the strings back.

"Loose!"

Another torrent of arrows showered down among the elves. They were still too far away to be certain, but Garrick again thought the arrows had fallen harmlessly off them.

"Someone get me a spyglass," Garrick ordered. A moment later the Captain handed him one. Garrick pulled on the end of the spyglass, extending it as far as it would go, then placed it to his eye and located the elves.

"Draw! Loose!"

He watched carefully as the arrows descended upon them. This time, there was no mistaking it. The arrows *were* bouncing off them.

"Impossible," he breathed.

"What is it?" Caidan asked. "What's happening?"

Garrick handed him the instrument. "The arrows … they're, they're ineffective," he said, not wanting to say it aloud. Caidan used the spyglass and watched as another volley of arrows filled the air.

"By the Divines," Caidan whispered in awe. "They're bouncing right off them!"

"Draw! Loose!" the Captain shouted again.

Garrick considered telling them to hold their arrows, but he wasn't sure if that was the right decision. If it were some sort of spell, would it eventually wear off as the arrows continued to hit their invisible shield? He looked to the captain and could tell he was thinking the same thing.

"Keep firing," Garrick commanded. The captain nodded.

"What does this mean?" Caidan asked. "I've never seen anything like this."

"Neither have I," Rycroft chimed in.

Garrick remained mute. He didn't know what it meant, and he didn't like it. The tattoo on his forearm began to itch. Subconsciously he rubbed at it. It was covered by a thin piece of material that looked like his skin and was held in place with sticky resin. Besides that, it was hidden beneath the sleeve of his shirt.

What is this threat, Mordum? He prayed mentally. He glanced at his generals from the corner of his eyes. No one knew he was a follower of Mordum. Not a single soul. Not even his wife knew. He despised keeping secrets from her, but this was different. This could destroy everything he had worked to build and protect.

He turned his attention back to the elves. They were much closer. He didn't need the spyglass now to see that the arrows had no effect.

He watched as the arrows struck the elves innocently and then fell to the ground like twigs.

They looked different from the other elves. There was something odd about their skin color. Garrick frowned as he studied them.

And then he realized the danger. Located in the center of the group of elves, hunched down and hidden by their odd skinned brethren, were more elves. Just like the others who rushed the walls. His eyes widened in understanding.

"Captain, in the center! Aim for the center of the group!"

The captain looked intently at the elves and then snapped his gaze to Garrick, the fear evident in his eyes.

Garrick pointed toward the elves. "Aim for the center, Captain!"

The man shook his head as if waking from a dream and started directing the bowmen. Arrows filled the air again, raining down among the elves. Garrick began formulating plans if they should break through the wall.

Once the wall was compromised, it would be hard to keep them out. He had read the reports from the previous city that had fallen. The elves would throw themselves into a group of soldiers and use their explosive magic to destroy men as easily as they destroyed stone.

He turned to Caidan and Rycroft. "If they break through the walls, we have to do everything we can to hold them off. Seal the hole if possible." His generals nodded their understanding.

The wall shook as an explosion rocked the ground below. Garrick and his generals pressed themselves up against the wall. Several more explosions went off and the wall shuddered intensely. The Captain was still directing the bowmen.

Garrick waited a few moments before looking over the wall again. Several of the elves lay dead, full of arrows. The odd skinned ones began stacking the bodies up against the wall. He watched as the arrows continued to assail them, all to no good. They continued to bounce off harmlessly.

A horn sounded from the north. Before Garrick could turn his attention that way, hundreds of elves suddenly came into view. They were sprinting across the field toward the wall. He looked about frantically, trying to figure out what they were doing.

He looked back down at the elves stacking bodies. Realization dawned on him. With no time to shout a warning, he watched in horror as one of the elves leaped through the air toward the pile of bodies.

A brilliant light blinded him. Garrick's eyes watered up as an explosion jolted the wall, much harder than the others. He lost his footing and fell to the hard stone. He blinked his eyes rapidly, trying to clear his vision. Rycroft was standing over him.

"Are you all right?"

Garrick nodded. He accepted Rycroft's arm and stood up. Shouting erupted below and Garrick realized the elves had blown a hole in the wall. He looked over the wall's edge and saw hundreds of elves running toward the breach. He knew what he had to do. He considered alternative options, but he knew none of them were guaranteed to work. They had to close the opening and seal the hole.

He turned to Rycroft and Caidan. "You two are in charge. Do your best to keep them from overtaking the castle. If it comes down to it, pull back and regroup at the closest city on this route. That's likely their next target. There's a battalion less than a mile out. Make sure they know to divert there as well."

"What are talking about?" Rycroft asked.

"Just do as I command," Garrick answered sternly. "We don't have time to debate."

"Yes, my Lord." Rycroft looked questioningly at him.

"What is it?" Garrick asked.

"What are you going to do?"

Garrick clenched his jaw. "I'm going to crush them."

He climbed atop the wall and watched as the mass of elves coalesced on the breach. He looked back to Rycroft and Caidan, nodded once, then leaped off the wall.

2

RELEASE ME.

Aramis startled awake, kicking off the thin piece of cloth that served as a blanket. Though his prison cell was dark and cold, his skin was burning and he was covered in sweat. Ever since he tapped into the power of the tattoo, it seemed as though his visions were more real.

"Another nightmare?"

The voice came from the cell across from his. Aramis didn't bother responding. He didn't know who was also being held prisoner, and he didn't care. He just wanted out.

Sitting upon the stone slab that was his bed, he rubbed his hands over his face. He considered how the Prophet of Edria, the leader of Mel's order, had betrayed him. He shook his head, knowing Mel would have been crushed by it.

"Oh Mel," he sighed, thinking of his friend. The man had willingly stayed behind to face a templar of Mordum in order to save Aramis's life. A sacrifice, it seemed, made in vain by the Prophet's treachery.

Grinding his teeth in frustration, he began pacing his cell. It wasn't very large. He guessed it to be six feet wide and ten feet long.

And it was always cold. He figured the dungeon must be underground because the walls and floor were cool to the touch and there were no windows. He couldn't tell if it was day or night. The little bit of light available belonged to a single torch a few cells down. It illuminated almost nothing, but Aramis had quickly realized it wasn't meant for the prisoners.

Eventually, he stopped his pacing and sat on the floor, leaning his back against the wall. He yawned and pondered how many days he had been locked in the cell. His thoughts wandered to how his people were faring. The nobles had always relied so heavily on his father.

From his conversation with Lord Bavol, the nobles seemed divided on their loyalty to this new king. Aramis still didn't believe the man was his brother. He would need a lot more proof than the word of a blind seer and the whispers of the court.

A scratching noise drew his attention. He held his breath and listened intently. It was coming from the edge of his cell. Rising slowly, he stepped over to his bed and continued to listen. It was definitely coming from somewhere close.

He knelt down and crawled to the left corner of the cell. The scratching got louder. He thought at first it might be a rat, but as he felt around on the floor, his hand bumped something smooth.

Hesitantly, he felt around the smooth object and picked it up. He realized the scratching was coming from inside whatever he was holding. A soft cracking sound echoed in his cell. He dropped the thing as he felt it move in his hands. He wished he could see what it was. Looking at his arm to where he knew the tattoo of Mordum was, he wondered if it would be any help.

Aramis had tried to use the tattoo to escape his cell shortly after being thrown into it, but nothing had happened. Other than his ability to run faster, he hadn't discovered any other powers from the mark.

He placed his fingers on the tattoo and closed his eyes, willing the tattoo to bless him with sight in the dark. Not sure if it worked or not, he opened his eyes and gasped slightly. It *had* worked! Somewhat, at least. He couldn't see perfectly, but he could see vague shapes.

The bed, the outline of the stones of the floor and walls, and the egg-shaped item that was moving. He squinted his eyes and leaned forward.

Suddenly a phiebus leaped at him. He shouted in surprise and scrambled back. The creature was quick and leaped on him, scratching and biting. Aramis used his hands to shield his face and rolled onto his stomach, trying to protect himself.

He lay there for a moment, waiting for the creature to jump on his back. Nothing happened. Rolling onto his side, he looked to where the phiebus was. Only it wasn't there. And neither was the egg. None of it was real. Aramis slowly got to his feet. Were the visions happening while he was awake now?

"Are you okay over there?"

It was the man in the cell across from him again. His first instinct was to continue to disregard the man. But if he was going to be here indefinitely, he might as well pass the time with someone.

"I'm fine," he answered.

"Ah, you can speak. I was beginning to wonder if you were mute until I heard you shouting."

"I'm not mute," Aramis smiled as he talked, "I was ignoring you."

The man laughed. "Ha! Honesty is my favorite attribute in men. I appreciate that."

Aramis laughed as well, the feeling of hopelessness fleeing momentarily. He tried to use the power of his tattoo to see the man, but that ability must have also been part of his vision, for it didn't work.

"So what did you do to get thrown down here?" the man asked.

"It's a long story," Aramis answered, not wanting to think about it.

"I don't know about you, but all I've got is time."

Aramis considered the man's words and knew he was right.

"I was betrayed," he said softly. Aramis started talking, telling the man everything he had been through the last few weeks. His father's murder, the man who tortured him thinking to get a confession of the murder, and the Prophet's betrayal. The more he talked about it, the less it stung.

"My friend Mel threw himself into the path of danger to let me get away. He was a loyal companion. A hero."

"Did he die?" the man asked.

"I'm sure he did. He stood against a powerful force."

"I'm sorry that you've gone through so much in such a short

time."

"Thank you," Aramis said. "What about you? How did you end up down here?"

"I'm in exile," he replied. "And the Prophet didn't like what I had to say."

"Why are you in exile?"

"My homeland was attacked and I had to flee to survive."

"I didn't think you were from Oakvalor. You have an odd accent."

"No, I am not from Oakvalor. My home is far from here."

"I'm sorry you've lost your homeland. For what it's worth, if you make it out of here, I welcome you to Oakvalor. You are more than welcome to build a new life here."

They continued talking until one of the priests brought food. Aramis's stomach growled and he realized he didn't know how long had passed since they fed him last. The priest was carrying a tray which he set down on the floor.

Grabbing a bowl off the tray, he then unlocked the cell door and kept Aramis at bay with a sword. He knelt down and placed the bowl on the floor inside the cell, keeping a wary eye on Aramis.

"I'm not going to do anything," Aramis said.

"I don't trust your words, vile scum of Mordum," the priest retorted as he closed the door and re-locked it. Picking up the tray, he left without another word.

Aramis picked up the bowl and sat on the edge of his bed. His mouth watered from his hunger. He raised the bowl to his lips and began to drink whatever was in it.

It was definitely watered down. A few pieces of what he assumed was meat were tough and hard to chew. He paused suddenly when he realized the guard had not given the other prisoner any food.

"Hey," he called out, pausing a moment when he realized he didn't know the man's name. "The guard didn't leave you anything, did he?"

"No," came the answer.

"Would you like to share mine?"

"I appreciate the offer, but no thank you."

"Are you sure?" Aramis asked. "I don't mind."

"I am sure," the man answered. Shrugging, Aramis finished off what remained and left the bowl by the door.

"What do they call you?" Aramis asked.

"My name is Tael. And yours?"

"Aramis," he answered. "It's nice to have someone to speak with."

"I agree," Tael said.

"I think I'm going to rest now," Aramis informed him.

"Enjoy," Tael replied.

"I'll try," Aramis laughed as he laid on the hard bed of stone.

—

Aramis slowly opened his eyes, waking for the first time from a sleep that was not riddled with nightmares. He sat up and noticed that the bowl he set by the door was gone. He didn't remember hearing the gate open. He must have been in a deep sleep. He stretched and began to perform his exercise routine. He did several sets of pushups and sit-ups, pushing himself until his muscles burned with the exertion.

"A fit body equates to a fit mind," as one of his father's generals always said. He didn't know when he might get out of the cell, but that didn't mean he shouldn't be ready when he did get out. He assumed Tael was sleeping, for the man wasn't trying to talk his ear off again.

The sound of footsteps caught his attention. Aramis stepped up to the bars of his cell and peered out. A group of priests was approaching. They stopped in front of his cell and one of them unlocked the door.

"The Prophet wants to see you," the one with the keys said.

Aramis shrugged and stepped out into the hall. The priests formed a circle around him and led him through the dungeon to the stairs that spiraled up into the main portion of the temple. As they climbed the stairs, Aramis's thought ran wild with what the Prophet might want. Regardless of what it was, he would refuse.

As they reached the door that led into the temple, the light blinded him. He stopped mid-step, shaking his head and blinking back the tears that overwhelmed his eyes. The priests didn't appreciate the abrupt stop and pushed him, causing him to fall onto the floor.

One of them kicked him several times in the side. He grunted under the force of the priest's blows and tried to block the kicks with his arm. Finally, the priest stopped and the others grabbed him, lifting him roughly onto his feet.

Aramis felt as though fire was burning inside his ribs. He gritted his teeth against the pain and tried to move at a pace that kept the priests from shoving him. They turned down a long hallway and he immediately knew where he was.

They stopped at the Prophet's door and led him inside. The room was the same as it was the first time he had been in it. There were no windows in the chamber, just several candles on the desk. And standing behind the desk was the traitor himself.

Aramis didn't bother to hide his hatred for the man. He glared openly at the Prophet. If his look bothered the man, he did well not to show it. He stood with his hands clasped behind his back. His black hair gleamed slightly in the light of the candles. The priests pushed Aramis forward until he was standing a few feet from the desk.

"Prince Aramis," the Prophet greeted. "I hope you are enjoying your stay here." Some of the priests snickered at the comment.

"What do you want?" Aramis asked tiredly.

"Is that any way to speak to your host?"

Aramis spat on the desk. One of the priests smacked him across the back of his head. His anger flared but the priests held him too tightly for him to do anything. He growled in frustration.

"Come now," the Prophet said, "do not act like an animal. We are civilized men here. Let us talk together as such." He walked slowly over to a small table and motioned Aramis to come near. When he didn't budge, the priests moved him by force.

Aramis recognized the map on the table. It was the same one he had seen previously when the Prophet had tricked him into retrieving the blood from the shrine. There were several red pins at random points.

"Those pins represent Mordum's agents," the Prophet remarked, as though reading his thoughts. "We have yet to discover the agent in Talvaard, but I am certain it won't be much longer. The elves of the Deadlands have launched an attack along the northern border of the kingdom."

The Prophet ran his finger along the map. "As the new king diverts his forces to the border, it will leave them vulnerable for attack. That is when I believe the agent will make his move."

Aramis wondered why the Prophet was telling him this. He couldn't care less about the agents of Mordum with the exception of one: his father's assassin. And he was likely the cause of Mel's death as well.

"Here in Oakvalor we know Mordum's agent is you. And since we have you as our guest, there's nothing you can do to further the cause."

The Prophet picked up a pin from a small wooden bowl at the edge of the table and pressed it into the map. This pin was green and was located in the Deadlands.

"My priests have found the whereabouts of the next item Mordum's followers are searching for. We don't know *what* it is, but we know where it is kept."

Aramis stared at the pin. He knew what was coming. The Prophet was going to ask him to retrieve it, perhaps because the only way in was to have the mark of Mordum. He smiled slightly, taking pleasure in the fact that the Prophet would not get his way this time.

"Have you ever been to the Deadlands?" he asked.

"What reason would I have to go there?" Aramis answered.

"It was merely a question." The Prophet shrugged and continued speaking.

"The Deadlands is an unforgiving place. Its borders stretch from the length of Oakvalor past Talvaard. No one has mapped its end. Some speculate that the Deadlands have no end; that the desert stretches on for eternity." The Prophet chuckled to himself.

"Anyway, it is also the home of the elves. They are barbarians at best, marking their bodies with magical symbols and waging war against one another. My priests are still determining what has brought them forth to attack the human settlements. King Garrick certainly has a lot on his—"

"Can you spit it out already? I'm assuming there's something there you want? Something you think I'm going to *fetch* for you?"

The Prophet stared at him. "Straight to the point, I see. Very well. Located in the Deadlands far to the north is a place known as Red Mountain. At the top of that mountain is a building. Within lies what I seek. It is there you will go and find it."

Aramis shook his head. "No, I won't. I will not do anything for you. I did what you asked once and it brought nothing but the death of my friend. Then you imprisoned me. I refuse."

The Prophet was grinning. "You seem to be mistaken," he said. "I'm not asking you to go. My priests are taking you there. Your will in this matter is pointless."

Aramis felt his stomach churn. He considered the fact that it might be easier to escape while out in the open. That was a small light at the end of the tunnel, he supposed. He still didn't like the fact that the Prophet thought he would do whatever the man ordered.

Time to play along.

"How am I to get something if I don't even know what it is?" he asked.

"You will find out when you get there. The item is guarded by a powerful sorcerer. The sorcerer will know what the item is."

"And he is just going to give it to me?"

"Of course not," the Prophet answered. "You have to earn it. I only have so much of the details, but you have all of the information I have. My priests will take you to get cleaned up and you will leave first thing in the morning."

Aramis considered arguing further but decided against it. There was no use. Now he needed to figure out how he was going to escape.

"I have a request."

The Prophet's eyebrow rose in curiosity. "You aren't in any position to ask for anything." He paused. "But I will consider it."

"I only ask that you give me my dagger. Honor my request as a favor to Mel's memory."

The Prophet seemed taken aback. "The rusty piece of junk you were carrying? That's what you ask for?" The Prophet laughed.

"I would have figured you'd ask more than that, especially in honor of Melchiades's memory." He shook his head, still laughing.

"Very well. Make sure he gets the dagger before you set out tomorrow," he instructed one of the priests. "Now take him away from me."

As the priests led him out of the chamber, Aramis began forming his plans.

He has no idea what that blade can do, he thought to himself. It had pierced the scales of a phiebus. And soon, it would cut his bonds and he would be free.

—Adamar

3

ADAMAR'S FOOTSTEPS ECHOED THROUGHOUT THE hallway as he walked toward the throne room. His freshly-polished boots clacked loudly against the stone floor, reminding him of a time long ago. A time when he had run through this very hallway as a boy. The walls were covered with beautiful tapestries and massive murals. His father certainly had good taste. Before Adamar had the templar kill him, anyway.

His two bodyguards followed behind him, flanked on either side. They were as silent as shadows. Other than the occasional ruffle of their robes, he would never have assumed they were there. As he approached the large doors that led to the throne room, the soldiers standing nearby hustled to open the doors for him. They saluted as he passed.

The chamber was crowded with the nobles. As soon as they noticed his presence, a hush fell over the room. He made his way to the throne at the back of the room and sat down, his two guards moving to the shadows behind the giant chair. Adamar tilted his head to either side until he felt his neck crack, then drummed his fingers on the armrest.

He had always admired the throne as a boy. It was elaborately decorated, with the backing of the chair carved to resemble a large Oaktree—the namesake of the kingdom. It was finally his. And all he had to do was kill for it. He smiled as he felt a great sense of achievement settle over him. He realized the nobles were all staring at him, waiting for him to speak. He motioned for the herald to come closer.

"Are the generals present?" Adamar asked.

The herald, a young boy of fifteen, nodded vigorously. "Yes, my lord."

"I'd like to hear from them first."

The boy bowed low and then turned to face the crowd. Cupping his mouth with his hands, he shouted, "The King requests the generals!"

Three men separated from the crowd of people and came forward, stopping at the bottom of the three stairs that raised the throne above the main floor. They bowed as well.

"What word?" Adamar asked.

The generals glanced at each other hesitantly before one of them spoke up.

"Nothing yet, King Adamar. The patrols are still searching, but they have yet to even find a trail. It's possible he has fled the country."

Adamar snorted in derision. "I highly doubt that. The traitorous coward is probably hiding. Have the patrols continue to search for him. I want him brought to me immediately when he is found."

"Of course," the general replied. One of the other generals cleared his throat. Adamar recognized him with a wave of his hand.

"King Adamar, some of the soldiers have gone missing."

"Missing? Were they killed?"

"I don't believe so," the general answered. "It seems they have abandoned their post."

Adamar leaned forward. "How many?"

The general swallowed nervously before speaking. "Twenty, including one of the Captains."

Adamar stood up. "I hereby declare deserters to be punished with death!" he thundered. "Anyone aiding a deserter will also be put to death. Is that clear?"

The crowd of nobles nodded or voiced their assent. Adamar sat back down and dismissed the generals. He waved the herald back over.

"You can run down the list in normal order now."

The next few hours were filled with boredom as he entertained the nobles' petitions. Petty land disputes, tax reports, the mundane things of running a kingdom that he didn't really care to do.

He'd have to find someone to do these things for him so that he could concentrate on more important matters. Such as finding his brother.

Aramis would be a pain in his side until he was found. Adamar hadn't decided if he wanted to kill him or lock him in the dungeon for the rest of his life. Although the templar had cursed Aramis with the mark, Adamar believed he would still prove to be problematic in the grand scheme of things.

Besides that, he now had reports that Ilias, Mordum's appointed Prophet, was demanding Aramis be kept alive because he was the chosen one to bring Mordum into the mortal plane.

Adamar scoffed at the notion. Obviously, Mordum would choose someone more suitable for the task. Someone like himself, or the templar. Someone strong and decisive, who took action without waiting around for specific directions.

After all, the blood from the shrine had been stolen from Ilias's temple, proving that the Prophet himself was inept. On top of having the soldiers looking for Aramis, he now had several patrols looking for the blood in case Aramis had left it with someone he trusted.

If he could track down the blood and retrieve the other two items needed, that would ensure his rise to Prophet. Yes, he would be second only to Mordum himself. The thought thrilled him.

Long after the nobles had left, he still sat on the throne musing about his rise in power. Servants eventually came and lit the candles, signaling night had come. Breaking his reverie, Adamar stood and left the chamber, his guards falling into step behind him.

"Is everything ready?" Adamar asked aloud.

"Yes," one of the men answered.

Adamar nodded in response. He walked through the twisting hallways and stopped at one of the many doors that ran the length of the wall. Pulling a small chain out from the neck of his shirt, he produced a small key.

Removing the chain from his neck, he slid the key into the opening on the door and turned it. A soft click sounded and he pushed the door open and entered the room.

It was faintly illuminated by a few candles. When one of his guards shut the door behind him, the candle flames flickered briefly. The shadows danced wildly in response, reminding him of the night he had committed himself to Mordum's service.

The room was sparsely furnished. A large chair, fashioned after the throne, sat at the back of the room. Directly behind the chair was a window that he'd had covered with a thick black cloth. He'd always been more comfortable in the dark. That had probably been one of the many warning signs to his parents.

On the ground a few feet from the chair was a large silver bowl. It gleamed occasionally in the candlelight. To the far left stood a rectangular table. Its only adornment was a wooden carafe and chalice.

Adamar walked to the table and looked inside the carafe. It was full to the brim with water. Partially unsheathing his sword, he ran his right palm along the sharp side of the blade. Pain lanced through his hand as it cut deeply into his flesh.

Lifting his hand over the carafe, he let the blood drip into the water. Awkwardly using his left hand, he re-sheathed the sword. He counted the drops of blood as they left his hand and hit the water. When the appropriate number had been reached, he pulled his hand away and pressed it against his leg.

He'd forgotten to bring something to bind it with and didn't feel like ripping his shirt. Pressing his palm hard against his leg for good measure, he removed his hand and grabbed the carafe. Careful not to let any of it spill, he brought it to the silver bowl.

Kneeling slowly, he poured the contents into the vessel. Once it was empty, he returned the carafe to the table, grabbed the chalice, and went to sit in the chair. Placing his hand over the chalice, he let the wound on his palm continue to drip.

His vision began to blur and he realized in the midst of everything, he'd forgotten to eat. The loss of blood was making him feel lightheaded and he feared for a moment he might pass out.

The dizziness was momentary and eventually passed. Placing the cup on the ground, he knelt down in front of the bowl and began whispering softly; chanting the words he had memorized like a fiery brand in his mind:

"Bind the light,

bind my soul,

use this knight,

to make you whole."

Adamar felt the air in the room immediately chill. A sound that reminded him of someone exhaling filled the air and the light of the candles was snuffed out. A presence, dark and sinister, filled the room around him.

"Rise, my servant."

Adamar stood up and looked into the corporeal face of his lord and master.

"Mordum," he managed to utter. The name filled him with power and his body shuddered. Suddenly lacking any control over his body, he fell backward into the chair. The room echoed with a screech as the chair's legs moved along the stone floor a few inches.

"Have you found my blood?"

It took a moment for Adamar to gain control of his body. The power of Mordum was intoxicating. It burst through every part of his body. He clenched his fists as he tried to keep the power within him, but it was no use. The power receded and he sat in the chair, weakened and frustrated.

"I am displeased to inform you that I have not found it yet," Adamar answered. "I have several patrols searching day and night for it."

Adamar could feel Mordum's anger as though it were something palpable. The feeling faded quickly.

"Very well. What of the other items? What of my bones and my ashes? Have your scribes found where they were hidden?"

"Not yet, but I am confident that they are getting close. As they scour through the history books, it becomes more and more evident that those who hid your body intentionally do not mention the locations.

"As we speak, they are looking through a book with a detailed account of your previous … defeat." Adamar waited for a mental barrage of pain, but it never came and so he continued.

"This account is much more detailed than any others they have come across. It mentions the place they brought your body and what they did to it. To you. I am sure this account will name where they hid your bones and your ashes."

"What of your brother? Have you found him yet?"

"No."

"He evades even my eyes. I can feel him drawing closer to the Mark. It will not be long before his location is known to me. Continue searching. Do not summon me again until you have news that will please me."

"Yes, my master."

"There are glorious rewards for you if you succeed."

"I want the Mark," Adamar said, his tone almost begging.

"The Mark will come when I am ready to give it to you. Your faith continues to strengthen. Persist in the ways that I have called you and you will surely find pleasure. But if you fail me …"

"I will not fail," he said adamantly. "I will do anything necessary to ensure your return."

"Good."

Adamar moved from the chair to the floor and grabbed the chalice. He held it up to Mordum and kept his eyes lowered. He felt Mordum take the cup.

"The only thing sweeter than the blood of my enemies is the blood of my servants."

The chalice clattered to the floor and Adamar felt Mordum's presence withdraw from the room. He grabbed the cup and stood up on shaky legs. His hand hadn't stopped bleeding and he was feeling weak again.

He managed to put the cup back on the table and stagger over to the door before he collapsed. The door opened and his two guards stepped in and picked him up, then carried him to his personal chambers.

They had servants bandage his hand and change his clothes under their watchful eyes. They dismissed the servants and placed Adamar into his bed. One of them stood by the door and the other sat in a chair next to the bed.

As Adamar floated in and out of consciousness, he was vaguely aware of his bodyguards. Mordum's words became a litany in his mind, repeating them over and over.

But if you fail me ... but if you fail me ... but if you fail me ...

Though Mordum was God of the Dead, Adamar knew Mordum loved him. And he would give his soul to prove his devotion to his god.

4

THE AIR RIPPED AT HIM furiously, as if it were angry that he was flying through it. His clothes billowed about wildly and he found it hard to keep his mouth shut. The air hissed around him suddenly as he summoned his armor. It formed out of mist, slowly taking shape over his body. It was black as night with an upside-down red cross emblazoned on the breastplate.

Garrick hit the ground on one knee. The armor protected him, but he still felt the jarring force of the sudden stop. The ground beneath him shattered like pottery pieces. Dirt and stone debris filled the air.

After a moment the air cleared. He expected to be overrun by elves already. Then he realized there was complete silence. Elves stood staring at him dumbfounded. Beneath his helm, Garrick grinned wickedly.

He summoned his blade and the familiar hiss filled the air. It had been a while since he had summoned his armor and blade together. The feeling of power coursed through his veins.

Without warning, he charged into the elvish ranks, slashing and gutting anyone near him. After their initial shock wore off, the elves began to mount a defensive. They were too wary to get close enough to strike him, so he pushed into their defenses, forcing them to fight him.

Most of them carried crudely made swords and they shattered under the force of his blade. They came at him with spears and he easily sheared the tips off. His blade separated limbs, cut throats, spilled intestines and seemed as eager to drink his enemy's blood as a demon.

His armor was by no means invincible, and neither was his body. His arms began to grow heavy with exhaustion. He was drenched in sweat and blood covered his helm, making it hard to see.

Something heavy crashed into him from behind. He almost tripped and fell, but managed to get his feet steady. Then he turned and thrust his sword into the gut of the elf he assumed had struck him.

In the left corner of the slit of his helm, he could see more elves rushing toward him. He risked a glance behind him to see if his men had managed to seal the hole in the wall.

He could see several soldiers struggling to push back some of the attackers. He noticed that they were the odd skinned elves whose skin had deflected the arrows. He struck down another three elves and then rushed toward the breach.

He threw himself bodily into one of the elves and grunted in pain. It was like running into the castle wall. The elf turned to face him and Garrick swung his blade diagonally, using both arms to try and cut him from shoulder to hip.

His blade *clanged* in his hand and he almost lost his grip on it. Garrick was surprised to see that his sword hadn't even nicked the elf's skin. The elf smacked his own sword against Garrick's shoulder which didn't do any damage but sent him reeling backward. His armor and blade were blessed by Mordum himself. How could elven magic stand against Mordum's power?

As he considered the question, the elf came at him, slashing haphazardly. Garrick could tell he didn't have any formal training. His form lacked any discipline and he held his blade awkwardly.

Garrick lifted his own blade and slammed it against the elf's, snapping it in half. Then he launched a vicious kick at the elf's kneecap. It felt like he was kicking a boulder. Pain shot through his foot and he staggered back, trying to keep from putting pressure on it.

The elf grinned at him and began touching some of the tattoos on his arms. The symbols he touched began to glow with a faint bluish light. Garrick began to backtrack slowly but the elf closed the gap, striding toward him confidently.

Hands grabbed him from behind and he struggled to free himself. Within seconds he was surrounded by elves. They knocked his legs out from under him and forced him to the ground. He stared up at the approaching elf, his tattoos glowing brighter now.

Garrick's struggling was useless. The elves were holding him down. Sweat pooled around his eyes. He tried shaking his head to keep it from blinding him. The elf stretched his arm out toward him. Garrick gritted his teeth and tried to prepare himself for anything. Lightning flickered along the elf's fingertips.

Mordum help me!

Suddenly the elf's arm jerked to the side, the lightning from his fingers flying through the air into the group of elves holding Garrick down. He quickly snapped his visor up so he could see clearly and was greeted by a woman fighting with the elf.

He rolled onto his side and got to his feet. He snatched his blade from the ground and watched the woman. She gripped the elf by the shoulder and held her hand over his arm. He wasn't sure what she was hoping to accomplish, but then he noticed the hue of the elf's skin changing. It slowly turned from the grayish color to a light tan color, resembling more closely the other elves he had seen.

"Take his head!" the woman shouted at him.

"What?" he asked, confused. He was trying to figure out what she was doing and hadn't expected her to speak.

"Cut his head off!"

Garrick pushed the confusion to the back of his mind and with an easy swing of his sword removed the elf's head from his shoulders. The woman released her hold on the elf's body and it slumped to the ground. She was covered in blood but it didn't seem to affect her. She ran toward the breach and grabbed another one of the gray-skinned elves.

After a few moments, she commanded him to take his head. Garrick and the woman followed the same pattern for the remaining elves with the gray skin. When they had cleared the area, the men inside began sealing the hole in the wall. Garrick motioned to a large group of elves coming toward them.

"We've got company," he said.

The woman didn't bother looking. "Is there another way in?" she asked.

"On the other side of the castle. There's a hidden entrance in the wall. If we can get there without drawing attention to it, we can get in."

They sprinted off and ran along the wall, Garrick in the lead. While he knew there was a hidden door, he couldn't remember exactly where it was. The castle had one tower and he knew it was located on the same side, but it was intended to blend in and he wasn't entirely sure he'd spot it. His breath came in short gasps and he was drenched in sweat. He dismissed his blade so he could focus solely on running.

Garrick ran a few feet away from the wall and looked up, trying to locate the tower. They were roughly a hundred feet past it. He scanned the wall, looking for anything that might give an indication as to where the door was. He didn't see anything.

"Where's the door?" the woman demanded.

"It's here," he answered, still looking. "Somewhere."

"You don't know where your own secret entrance is?"

Garrick turned to her. He didn't like her tone.

"This isn't my castle," he said briskly. "This is my general's castle."

She grunted in response and walked to the wall, running her hands along the stones. Garrick looked back the way they had come and could hear the elves coming. They didn't have much time.

He ran over to the wall and started searching. He looked for loose stones, handholds, anything. And he found nothing. Just as he was about to give up and search further down the wall, he heard the woman give a triumphant shout. He jogged over to her.

"I've found it," she grunted as she pushed against the wall. "This stone has a mark on it."

Garrick looked closely and saw she was right. Etched lightly into the stone was a mark that looked like a keyhole. It wasn't deep enough to be an actual keyhole, but it looked just like one. He pressed his shoulder against the wall and helped the woman push. The wall didn't budge.

"The elves will be coming around the corner any minute," he said.

Suddenly the wall shifted inward and began sliding to the right. Garrick stepped back and watched as the section of wall disappeared into the rest of the wall. There stood Rycroft and several armed men.

"My lord," Rycroft said, the relief evident in his voice.

"General," Garrick greeted. "The elves are closing in."

Garrick let the woman go first, then he followed. The soldiers pushed the section of wall back into place. On either side of the section were two "U" shaped steel bars sticking out. The soldiers dropped a large wooden plank into them.

"The door opens from the inside?" Garrick asked.

Rycroft nodded. "It's intended to be an escape route." The general led them out of the tunnel and into the courtyard. Garrick dismissed his armor and it disappeared in a swirl of mist. Everyone stared at him but he ignored their unvoiced questions. He ran his hands through his sweat filled hair.

"Is the breach sealed?"

"Uh … yes, sir. That section of the wall is obviously weakened, but it will hold for now. The engineers have given us the news that they are low on the supplies needed to fix it properly."

"We need to keep the elves away from the wall," Garrick said.

"What do you propose?"

That was a good question.

"Arrows have proven ineffective. Hitting the gray-skinned ones is like hitting a stone wall. I nearly dropped my sword when I struck one of them."

He looked at his hand and flexed it. It was a little sore, but otherwise undamaged.

"Stone skin," the woman said. Garrick and Rycroft turned to her. He had almost forgotten she was there.

"Excuse me?" Rycroft said.

"Stone skin," the woman said again. "That's what it's called.

Their ability to deflect your arrows with their skin. It's a tattoo some of them have. It makes their skin like stone."

"How do we get around it?" Rycroft asked.

"You don't," she answered.

"*You* did it," Garrick pointed out. "You did something that changed their skin color. What did you do?"

"That's none of your business," the woman replied.

Garrick frowned. *I really don't like this woman.*

"I helped you get inside to safety. The least you can do is tell me how we can defeat them."

"Fair enough," she answered. "Are you a wizard?"

Garrick shook his head. "No."

"Are you?" she asked, turning to Rycroft.

"No," he answered.

"Then there is nothing you can do. Even if you were wizards, there is a very specific ability I have that few other wizards possess. It allows me to see magic."

"I have seen magic before," Garrick said.

"That's not what I mean," the woman answered. "I mean actually see magic. The …" she seemed to struggle for the right word, "specks of … magic that makes up a spell."

Garrick thought she looked flustered. "How does that help you?"

The woman sighed. "I can see how the tattoo works and I can control the magic flowing to it. I can't destroy the tattoo, but I can weaken its power enough to inflict bodily harm."

"She could help us," Rycroft said.

"She's only one person," Garrick pointed out. "There are thousands of warriors outside these walls. Who knows how many of them have this stone skin? There's no way to gather that information."

"Who says I would help you anyway?" the woman said disdainfully.

"You are bound by the laws of our kingdom to help the king in any way you can," Rycroft retorted.

"He's not *my* king, he's yours."

Rycroft eyed her closely. "You aren't from Talvaard?"

She snorted. "Of course not. When is the last time your kingdom has seen a wizard?"

Rycroft remained silent for a moment. "She's from Oakvalor," he said, glancing to Garrick.

"I assumed as much," he said. "And as such, she's a welcome guest. If you don't want to help us, I understand. My authority has no sway over you. But I can assure you that if the elves manage to push through further into Talvaard, they will do the same in Oakvalor. The people of your kingdom will suffer the same tragedies."

The woman rolled her eyes. "You're assuming I care."

Garrick tilted his head curiously. "Who are you? What's your name?"

"Jovanna," the woman answered. "My name is Jovanna."

5

THE NEXT MORNING, ARAMIS AND ten priests left the temple and headed north toward the Deadlands. The temple of Edria was in the city of Kaldore, which was a two-day journey northeast from Oakhaven, the capital of the kingdom. While Aramis had never been to the Deadlands, he knew the boundaries and landscape of his country.

To get there, they'd have to travel through the countryside where the majority of the people were simple farmers, then through the Tylhem Forest. Aramis remembered hearing stories from some of his teachers about the forest.

Some said it was haunted, and others that a mystic race of beings called it home. It had interested him as a child, but as he considered it now he found it to be foolish.

The priests rarely stopped to rest. When they did, it was to relieve themselves and eat something quick. Aramis had attempted to escape a couple of times using the power of the mark to run with quickened speed as he did when running back to the temple.

Unfortunately, it didn't work. At first, he suspected it meant the mark wasn't working, but he later determined it was the shackles they had put on his wrists. Something about them seemed to negate the power of Mordum's mark.

He began to study each of the priests, watching their mannerisms and how they held themselves. Although they didn't seem to have official titles, he quickly discovered who the leader was. It was obvious by the man's demeanor. He issued orders subtly and dictated their pace and their breaks. The others appeared to be lowly apprentices, perhaps just the "muscle" for this trip.

Other than pushing him when he started lagging, the priests ignored him for the most part. He didn't bother trying to talk to them, instead spending his time thinking about how to get away and where he would go if he managed to succeed.

Perhaps he would head to Talvaard and ask Garrick to assist him. He remembered that the Prophet mentioned Talvaard being under attack by the elves. If that were true, Garrick had his own problems to worry about.

Aramis sighed in frustration. He felt so lost and helpless without Mel. His friend had been a wise advisor, someone he could trust and rely on. Now … he bit his lower lip forlornly.

The farther north they traveled, the warmer the air got. He knew that once they entered the forest the heat would be much worse. As they passed through a small village, some of the priests broke away from the group to resupply their provisions.

The rest of the group continued to the outer edge of the town and waited for the others to return. After roughly twenty minutes the others met back up with them. One of them pulled the leader to the side and conversed quietly with him. Aramis attempted to get closer without being noticed. He only heard bits and pieces of the conversation.

"That's what the farmer claimed," one of the priests said.

"When did they pass through here?" the leader asked.

"Yesterday. They didn't interrogate anyone, but they made it clear who they were looking for. Seems they shook the townsfolk up a little. They don't see soldiers often."

The leader nodded. "They're looking for him …" he trailed off as he noticed Aramis looking at them. "Find us somewhere to stay for the night, preferably somewhere out of sight."

The priest nodded and left to do as he was commanded. Then the leader came over to him.

"It seems the soldiers of the king are out here looking for you," he said to Aramis.

"To arrest me for a crime I didn't commit, I'm sure," Aramis replied.

"Fortunately for you, the Prophet still has need of you. They won't find you. At least not for now." He walked off before Aramis could reply.

Aramis considered how this new information would impact his escape attempt. It was possible he could elude both the priests and the soldiers if he got away, especially this far out.

A little while later, the group headed to a barn to spend the night. The town was so small and visitors so few that the town didn't even have a proper tavern or an inn. They would all have to sleep on the floor of the barn. Despite the fact that there was a thin layer of hay on the ground, Aramis still found it uncomfortable. The priests took turns keeping watch.

He lay there staring at the rafters of the barn, unable to sleep. It seemed like hours passed before his eyes started to get heavy. As he closed them and began to drift off in the darkness, a sound outside startled him. He sat up and looked around. The priest keeping watch must have heard it as well, for he seemed on edge and kept looking out into the night. Aramis heard it again. He thought it sounded like a gentle thump against the side of the barn.

The priest at the door hesitated for just a moment before he stepped out of the barn and into the blackness of the night. Aramis looked at the other priests. They all appeared to be sleeping. Just as his muscles tensed and he decided to get up and make a run for it, the priest appeared in the doorway. Aramis slumped back against the ground.

Blast it, he thought. The priest took up a new position at the door and stared out into the night.

Heaving a sigh, Aramis tried to get back to sleep. It took him a while because of his sudden excitement at the possibility of escape. Eventually, he finally drifted off back into sleep's embrace.

—

Aramis woke to one of the priests nudging him with his boot. He grunted and slapped the man's foot away. Rolling onto his side, he realized everyone was awake and moving except him. He got up and stretched before brushing strands of hay off his clothes. Aramis noticed the priest was still standing there.

"You done, Your Highness?" the priest said sarcastically as he performed a mocking bow. When he realized Aramis wasn't going to say anything in retort, the man handed him a small bread roll and an apple.

"Here's your breakfast. If you get thirsty, there's a horse trough outside."

Aramis took the food and left the barn. It was after sunrise already. The sun had probably been up for almost an hour, possibly two, if his guess was correct. He ate his breakfast fairly quickly, not realizing how hungry he was. Then he walked over to the horse trough.

It was a long wooden box filled with water. Aramis dipped his hands in, flinching at the coldness. He wasn't expecting that. He noticed small bits of foam floating in the water. It was probably horse saliva.

With a shrug, he held his breath and dipped his head into the box. He came up sputtering and coughing. The cold had caused him to inhale sharply, and he sucked in some water.

Laughter broke out behind him and he turned to see some of the priests looking in his direction. He gritted his teeth in anger and tried his best to ignore them. He let the water drip dry from his hair and face.

As the priests were collecting their meager belongings and getting ready to head out, Aramis noticed one of them was standing off to the side, looking out into the woods. He watched the man curiously, wondering what he might be looking at. He made a subtle motion with his hand, so subtle that Aramis almost wondered if he saw it at all. Then he turned and joined the other priests. He was keeping his head down.

Aramis found the actions odd but gave it no further thought. He didn't care if the priests were crazy, as long as they didn't bother him any more than they already were. He walked over to where they were gathered.

He must have missed a conversation between them because as he reached the group, they began to walk north without orders from the leader. Two of them took up positions beside him. One of them was the man who had acted oddly.

He looked at the priest and noticed the man was staring at him. When they made eye contact, the priest winked at him. Aramis scrunched his face in confusion and looked away. The man had probably spent too long as a priest.

When was the last time any of these men had seen a naked woman?

They continued their trek north, leaving the small town behind and nothing but farmland as far as they could see. They walked for several hours before stopping for a short break. Aramis slumped down onto the ground and pulled his boots off and began furiously rubbing his feet. His feet were sweating profusely and his skin was beginning to rub on the soles of his boots painfully.

He watched the leader of the group and knew that he'd force them to continue walking. He surveyed the landscape as he continued rubbing his feet. A few hundred feet ahead was a small copse of trees. Aramis heard the leader and one of the priests talking.

"Is that Tylhem?" the priest asked.

The leader shook his head. "No, but I think we are close. Maybe a mile past those trees there—if this map is correct."

"Why would the map be incorrect?"

The leader pulled a rolled parchment from his robes and unfurled it.

"Because it's fairly dated."

Aramis saw him point to something on the map. Then he rolled it back up and stuff it back into his robes.

"What of the rumors?"

The leader scowled. "I don't believe in folklore."

"Every rumor has a seed of truth to it," the other priest countered.

"Be that as it may," the leader replied, "that will not stop us from entering the woods. Let's get moving. The faster we can get to our destination, the faster we can get back to the temple."

Aramis put his boots back on and stood up. His feet were sore, but there was nothing to be done. The tattoo on his arm didn't seem to help with soreness, only open wounds. The other priests got up and started walking again. The two who were guarding him took up their positions again. Aramis began limping along as best as he could.

As they continued their trek, the pain turned from a dull soreness to excruciating before finally numbing his feet completely. His steps became sluggish. He ground his teeth in annoyance. One of his guards shoved him from behind.

"Keep up," he growled.

Aramis managed to keep from falling. He turned and shot a murderous look at the priest. He guessed it must have caught the man off-guard because he hesitated. Someone touched his arm and he snapped his gaze to them.

It was his other guard. He smiled disarmingly and nodded with his head to keep moving. Something about the man's attitude calmed Aramis's anger and he reluctantly continued.

They walked for about ten minutes. Aramis's pace was steadily slowing, but the priest who pushed him didn't say anything. They were nearly to the grove of trees when the leader motioned for them to stop.

"We're going to camp here for the remainder of the day until morning. At sunrise, we'll—"

His words were cut off as an arrow ripped through the back of his shoulder, spinning him in a violent circle. Chaos broke out among the priests as more arrows rained down among them, striking the ground around them as well as the priests. Cries of pain and fear filled the air.

The guard who had smiled at him removed his robes and threw them to the ground, then grabbed Aramis's arm and pulled him toward the trees. Aramis struggled against the man's grip and tried to escape.

"Stop fighting, my Lord!" he yelled. "Follow me!"

His words confused Aramis. Only his loyal subjects called him

Lord. Pushing his reservations aside, he stopped fighting and followed as fast as he could. They broke through the tree line and when he saw who was firing the arrows, realization suddenly dawned on him. They stopped running after they got a decent distance into the woods.

Aramis slumped to the ground, pressing his back against the trunk of a tree. He could feel his heart racing and he tried to catch his breath. He looked around the wooded area and saw several men in armor, all of them wearing his family's crest and colors. These men were soldiers of the crown. He felt greatly relieved until he remembered what he'd overheard the day before.

These men have been looking for me.

He felt worms of fear squirming in his stomach.

"They're going to take me back to the castle in chains," he breathed to himself.

He had to run while they were occupied with the priests. He rose to his feet and turned to head further into the woods when he noticed the man he had followed was standing there, his blade drawn.

"It's good to see you," the man said with a smile.

"Is it?" Aramis asked, his tone revealing his suspicion.

"Yes, sir. We've been looking all over the countryside for you. The Captain wanted to find you before anyone else. Ah, here he comes now."

In a quick movement, he cut the shackles that bound Aramis's hands. Aramis assumed they must have been old, for they broke easily under the man's blade.

He turned to an unexpected but familiar face. Kaldrick approached with a wide grin.

"My King!" he greeted loudly before embracing Aramis in a tight hug.

"What in Hell's name are you doing way out here?" Aramis asked in surprise, returning the man's embrace.

Kaldrick was impressively strong and his hug crushed the breath from his lungs. The captain released him when he started coughing.

Aramis backed up a step and appraised the Captain.

It had been a few months since he had seen the man. He didn't look much different. He was as tall as Aramis, though much more muscular. His upper arms were as thick as some of the branches that littered the ground around them.

His hair was black and cut short, almost to the point of being shaved. He was wearing a hauberk without the sleeves, supplemented by bronze lamellar. The lamellar consisted of small platelets that were punched and laced together in horizontal rows, adding more protection to the torso. Aramis liked the look of it.

"We're out here looking for you! Been searching a few weeks now. You have no idea how glad we all are to have found you. The man who has usurped your throne has patrols out at all times trying to hunt you down. I was praying I would find you first."

"He'll get suspicious when you don't check in," Aramis warned.

Kaldrick laughed heartily. "I'm sure he's more than suspicious now," he replied. "We deserted our post. I'm sure there's a bounty on ours heads same as yours."

Aramis shook his head. "You need to go back. I don't want anything to happen to you men because of my situation."

Kaldrick waved his hands in the air. "I won't hear it, my Lord. We are loyal to the end, regardless of how that end may turn out. If we die, we will die fighting for a cause we believe in. No one left unwillingly, I assure you of that."

Aramis knew there was no sense in arguing with him. The man was as stubborn as they come, which added to his battle prowess. He had sparred with the captain a few times and Kaldrick never once bowed out, no matter how exhausted or injured he was. Truth be told, Aramis was glad to have him.

"Very well, Captain. How many men do you have with you?"

"There are twenty of us," Kaldrick answered.

Aramis nodded, considering again what he had thought about many times since leaving the temple. One of the soldiers approached, handing a water skin to Kaldrick. The captain took a long drink and handed it to Aramis. He drank a couple of mouthfuls and poured some onto his head. The chilled water ran through his hair and down his face and neck, cooling him off.

"What was the plan assuming you found me?" Aramis asked.

Kaldrick shrugged and rubbed the back of his neck, slightly embarrassed. "I didn't think that far ahead to be honest. Nevertheless, we are at your disposal. What did you have in mind?"

Aramis took another drink from the skin and handed it back to the soldier who brought it.

"Are the priests dead?" he asked.

Kaldrick looked to the soldier for the answer. The soldier put the stopper in the water skin and shook his head.

"No, sir. The majority of them have fled, but there are a few wounded that they left behind."

"Thank you …" Aramis paused expectantly.

"Jonn, my Lord."

"Thank you, Jonn."

The soldier bowed and left. Kaldrick stared at Aramis intently. "I see your wheels turning, sir."

"One of the wounded should have a map on him. I need it."

"I'll retrieve it myself," Kaldrick said.

"I'll come with you. I have a message for him to take to his prophet."

They left the woods and walked to where three bodies lay in the grass. The soldiers had gathered around them awaiting orders. They all bowed as Aramis approached. He looked to each of the bodies.

One of them lay very still and Aramis wondered if the priest was dead. He tried not to think about it and knelt beside the priest with the map. The arrow that punctured his shoulder was at an odd angle. It looked quite painful. His robes had a pool of blood near his thigh.

Aramis lifted the cloth up to take a look. It wasn't as bad as it seemed. The skin had a clean cut that was probably from an arrow that had grazed him.

"You'll live," Aramis informed the priest. "When you get back to your temple, I want you to deliver a message to your prophet. Tell him I'm not a fool. I know what god really holds his allegiance, and it isn't Edria. It's Mordum."

The priest's face scrunched up, but Aramis didn't know if it was from the pain or his words.

"If you don't believe me, consider why he wants the items that will bring about Mordum's entrance into this world. Also consider why he isn't bothered by the death of Mel, one of Edria's most faithful." Aramis paused at this, fighting back his emotions. He clenched his jaw and spoke through gritted teeth.

"Tell him I will retrieve the next item, but he will *never* see it!"

Aramis snatched the map from the priest's robes and stood up. He looked around at all of the soldiers and finally settled his gaze on Kaldrick. The captain raised his eyebrows in expectancy.

"Leave the priests here. If they die, so be it."

"Yes, my Lord."

Aramis walked back towards the woods and Kaldrick fell into step beside him. They walked in silence for a few moments before Kaldrick spoke.

"Why didn't you order them killed?"

Aramis considered the question.

Why indeed? he wondered.

There were numerous reasons at the tip of his tongue, but he settled with the one that made the most sense to him amidst his whirling emotions.

"They are not the reason I am out here as a captive. They are following the orders of someone above them, someone who holds a position of power. They are culpable for their actions, obviously, but I cannot blame them for following orders. Killing them would not make me any better of a king, nor would it satisfy my anger and hurt."

Kaldrick remained silent, but his demeanor told Aramis that he approved of his reasoning. He hadn't noticed it before, but the air in the woods was humid, overwhelmingly so. He began sweating almost immediately. Aramis let Kaldrick take the lead.

As they made their way further into the woods, Aramis noticed a small camp was set up. Tents were strung up between the trunks of large trees. In the center of the camp was an enormous tree stump that had been converted into a makeshift table.

When they reached the stump, Aramis unrolled the map and laid it on the surface. He used a few small stones to hold the parchment down and examined the map. The priest was right: the map *was* outdated. The numbers in the lower left corners of the map marked the year it had been drawn. It was almost a hundred years old.

Kaldrick held out a biscuit. "Hungry?"

Aramis accepted it and ate without tasting it. He stared intently at the map, considering his next course. Finally, he pointed to a square symbol on the map.

"Have you ever been to the Deadlands?" he asked.

"I have not," Kaldrick answered. "There's nothing out there worth seeing. At least that's what everyone says."

"I need to go there. Here, specifically. It's some sort of castle or fortress. This map indicates that it is at the top of Red Mountain. Ever heard of it?" He looked at the captain.

Kaldrick shook his head. "No. Why do you need to go there?"

"It's a long story," Aramis sighed. "I don't expect you and your men to come with me, but if you do I will tell you everything on the way."

"I've always wanted to travel," Kaldrick said with a grin.

"I appreciate your loyalty," Aramis replied. "I have to warn you that this journey will be perilous."

"All journeys are in their own way," the captain said.

Aramis turned his attention back to the map. He eyed the path the priest had chosen. It seemed the best course, so he decided they would continue following the route.

"This forest here," he pointed, "have you ever heard of it?"

When the captain didn't answer, he looked up. Kaldrick had a troubled look on his face.

"What is it?" Aramis asked.

"Well, it's …" Kaldrick looked down at the map. "I can't read."

As he considered it, Aramis wasn't surprised. Most soldiers were only trained for battle, not academics. Only those from wealthy families typically paid for both. Aramis shrugged.

"No matter. It's called Tylhem Forest. I overheard some of the priests talking about it. They seemed overly superstitious about the place."

"I've heard stories," Kaldrick said. "Most of them as a child. It's rumored that the place is filled with druids, though nothing has ever been confirmed."

"What's a druid?" Aramis asked.

"Old men of magic. They usually keep to themselves. Supposedly they prefer the company of animals to other men. Harmless unless provoked." Kaldrick shrugged. "That's all I know. And most of it is hearsay."

"Our path takes us through it," Aramis said, waiting to gauge the captain's reaction.

Kaldrick merely nodded.

"Will the men have an issue with it?"

"Some of them may be a little wary, but they'll be fine."

"Good. We leave in the morning before it gets too warm."

—

Aramis walked toward the woods, his men following behind him. It was silent. A disturbing silence, devoid of the normal sounds of the night. Not even the creatures that came awake in the dark were making noise.

Aramis was walking across an open field. The tall grass swayed gently from a breeze he couldn't feel. Not far ahead he could see the tall, dark silhouette of trees rising up from the landscape. As he drew close to them, he could hear a voice drifting on the wind.

"Do not enter."

A robed figure stepped out from the tree line. He held his hand up before him, warding the way. Aramis stopped and looked back. His men were no longer there. He wondered where they went and how they left so suddenly. The robed figure pointed back the way Aramis had just come from.

"Do not enter these woods."

"We only want to pass through," Aramis replied, confused.

The trees swayed suddenly under a strong wind. The figure stepped back into the trees, disappearing from Aramis's view.

"You have been warned."

Aramis's eyes snapped open. He was burning up and covered in sweat. He got up and pulled his shirt off, then left his tent and walked to the outer edge of the camp where he noticed a fire was burning. He sat down on a large rock next to the fire and stared into the flames, considering his dream.

It was different than the others. The figure had warned him not to enter the woods, but it wasn't the oppressive dreams he normally experienced since having the mark of Mordum. He looked up when he heard someone approaching. It was Kaldrick.

"Can't sleep?" he asked quietly.

Aramis shook his head. "I had a disturbing … dream."

"That makes two of us," Kaldrick said.

Aramis's heart quickened in his chest. "What? What did you dream about?"

"Barmaids that weren't loose women," Kaldrick said with a snort, shaking his head.

"I've never even heard the like before. Must be all the time we've spent outside of civilization." He sat down on the ground beside Aramis and stretched his legs toward the fire.

Aramis felt a huge sense of relief. He feared that Kaldrick might have experienced the same vision-like dream he had. He looked at the mark on his arm. The black cross stood out in stark contrast against the color of his skin.

"Are you a religious man?" Aramis asked.

"Not really," Kaldrick answered. "I know there are forces or powers or whatever out there that we don't understand, but that doesn't mean I follow them. What about you, my Lord?"

Aramis opened his mouth to answer the question, then hesitated. He really wasn't sure that he was religious, but he had seen things that could not be explained.

"I've always said I didn't believe in divine beings," he said, "but recent events have caused me to re-evaluate that belief. I know there are gods, but like you, I have not chosen to follow any of them."

Aramis traced his index finger along the dark shape of the mark and felt the pull of its power. It was tempting to fall into the power it offered, but he knew it was nothing more than a façade. Mordum offered nothing but death and destruction. If there was such a dark force as Mordum, then certainly there must be a power on the side of good.

He considered Mel's goddess Edria. The Prophet was evil, but did that mean that Edria was evil as well? Or was it possible that the Prophet had simply turned away from her path?

Given how Mel had modeled his life, Aramis highly doubted that Edria was evil. He leaned back on the rock and looked up into the sky. The foliage of the trees blotted out most of the heavens, but he could see a few stars twinkling against the black sky. He heaved a long sigh and stood up.

"I'm going to try and get back to sleep," Aramis said. "We've got a long road ahead of us."

Kaldrick nodded. "I'm not far behind you."

Aramis returned to his tent and eventually fell asleep.

—

Aramis woke to the sound of voices and the clattering of metal. Apparently, the entire camp was awake already. He rolled out of bed and put his shirt on, then grabbed his boots from the corner of the tent and slipped his feet into them. The balls of his feet were still sore from walking the day before, but he knew they had to get moving. There was no time for weakness. Not now.

He stepped out of his tent and was surprised to find Kaldrick and his men had packed up almost the entire camp. Aramis looked at his own tent and decided to take it down. He knelt down and just as his hand touched the rope that was staked into the ground, he felt a hand on his shoulder. He looked up to see Kaldrick smiling and shaking his head.

"Don't worry about the tent," he said. "The men will tackle that. You need to get some food before we pack up the cooking supplies." Kaldrick motioned toward the front of the camp, close to where the fire had been the night before.

"You'll get no argument from me," Aramis answered. He stood up and went to see what was left. He was greeted with smoked sausages and a leg from a turkey. The soldier in charge of cooking informed him that they had been lucky and found a group of the feathered birds that morning.

Aramis thanked him and ate as he watched the soldiers break down his tent. He downed the sausages pretty quickly and bit into the turkey leg. It had an odd taste to it. It wasn't a bad flavor, but it wasn't all that great either.

"Beggars can't be choosers," he muttered to himself and took another bite. The men moved quickly and efficiently to break down the tent. Before he had finished eating they had it completely packed up and ready for their march.

Aramis stripped the leg of the majority of the meat and then tossed the bone into the brush. He licked his fingers before wiping them on his pants, then went and relieved himself. After washing his hands and face in a small pool of water he had come across, he met up with Kaldrick and unrolled the map he had taken from the priest.

"We're still agreed on the path through Tylhem?" Aramis asked.

Kaldrick nodded. "Yes, my Lord. Some of the men are a bit skittish, but not enough to bail out."

"Good to hear. Well then, let's get moving."

Aramis was surprised at the organization of the men under Kaldrick's command. With little guidance from him, they collected their belongings and began marching out of the woods. They headed north toward Tylhem Forest, moving at a decently quick pace.

Scenes of his eerie dream kept running through his head. He tried to ignore them, tried to think of something—*anything*—other than the mysterious man who had given him an ominous warning, but it was useless.

They traveled for a while, walking across flat grasslands. There was a gentle breeze blowing which helped to make the heat of the day tolerable. In the distance, not more than a quarter mile, Aramis could make out an expanse of trees. Judging by the distance they had traveled, he felt certain it was Tylhem. That and the fact that the forest seemed to stretch across the horizon.

The map he carried had given a large amount of space to mark the forest, but Aramis had assumed that whoever had drawn the map was being generous. Now that they were closing in on it, Aramis didn't think the mapmaker was even close.

Kaldrick called for a break, and they all stopped a few feet from the boundary of the forest to drink water and rest their legs. After a few minutes of rest, Kaldrick called two men over and gave them instructions to scout out the front of the forest. They trotted off into woods, disappearing among the thick underbrush.

"They are decent at scouting," Kaldrick said as he approached.

"I trust your judgment," Aramis replied. He lowered himself to the ground and then lay on his back, blotting the sun out with his hands. "How long before they come back?"

"Ten, maybe fifteen minutes. I told them to do a quick run through of the area, nothing too detailed. We haven't seen any signs of life this far north, so it's unlikely we'll run into anything other than wild animals."

"Sounds good," Aramis yawned. His eyes were getting heavy.

Now that he thought about it, he felt fairly exhausted from the march. "I'm just going to lay here a minute. Rest my eyes a little."

Kaldrick nodded.

Loud screams split the air and Aramis quickly sat upright, his heart pounding in his chest. The men were running towards the woods. Aramis scrambled to his feet, trying to figure out what was happening.

"Where's everyone going?" he shouted to no one in particular.

"Women!" one of the soldiers yelled. "There are women in there!"

Aramis scanned the tree line but didn't see anything. He looked for Kaldrick but didn't see him. The man must have already entered the woods. As he started toward the forest, a powerful wind picked up, making the tall grass weave violently. It whipped his clothes about wildly and his shirt made a flapping noise. Thunder rumbled in the distance. Aramis picked up his pace as he saw the last soldier disappear in the brush.

He entered and tree line and pushed into the thick brush. It was noticeably darker in the forest. The wind rustled the foliage overhead. He could see the branches swaying from the force of the wind. And then he heard the shouts.

They were faint at first, but as he continued deeper into the woods, they became louder. Aramis lowered his head as he walked, trying to keep the thin branches of saplings out of his face. Finally, he broke through the brush and was surprised to find a path. It was well worn and had signs of recent footprints.

Kneeling down, he studied the prints and recognized the familiar shape of boots. The men had come this way. As he followed the trail that wound through the woods, the shouts he heard earlier were gone.

It was silent, with only the occasional sound of the wind moving through the treetops to let him know he hadn't gone deaf. He followed the path deep into the forest. It wasn't just a long walk. It was hot and humid, making his shirt stick to him.

A while later, he entered a small clearing. Small shacks were spread out among the trees, but he didn't see anyone. Upon further investigation, he realized the buildings weren't shacks at all.

They were made up of tree roots, extending from the ground to make small home-like structures. He glanced into a few of them. The contents were fairly basic: beds, tables, and chairs—all made of tree roots and vines.

The path he followed into the clearing picked back up on the far side the small residential area. Aramis continued following the trail, still not hearing much other than the wind. Tree branches creaked ominously and the leaves seemed to whisper at him. An eerie feeling began to worm its way into his gut.

The path wound between trees and under low hanging branches. Insects bit at his exposed arms, raising small itchy bumps along his flesh. He thought he could see things moving among the shadows. He walked for a lot longer than he cared to, wondering just how far into the woods the path went. Just as he was about to turn back, the path dumped him into another clearing, this one smaller than the first.

The glade was one of the oddest things he had ever seen. It was almost a perfect circle, ringed by large, thick trees. The ground was flat and dark brown, devoid of any grass or leaves.

And then he saw the body. There, lying in the middle of the clearing in a puddle of blood, was Kaldrick. Aramis ran to his still form and knelt down beside him. He was breathing. Aramis sighed in relief. That was a good sign. Kaldrick was covered in blood, but it didn't seem to be his own. Kaldrick's eyes fluttered momentarily before finally opening.

"What happened?" Aramis asked softly.

"There were women," he answered weakly. "Naked as newborn babes. We chased after them, but I don't have any idea why. Something I can't explain came over me. It came over us all. And then … and then …" he shuddered and shook his head.

"Easy now," Aramis said. He looked around the clearing, but there were no signs of the other soldiers.

"We have to leave," Kaldrick whispered urgently.

"Why? Where are the others?"

Kaldrick lifted a shaky hand and pointed to one of the trees that ringed the glade.

Aramis stared in confusion. "What is it? I don't—"

And then he saw it. The tree had a face. Aramis rose and got closer. It was definitely a face. There was also something oddly familiar to it. It kind of looked like …

Aramis backed away from the tree quickly when he saw the face move. It was one of the soldiers. He could see the vines and bark of the tree had covered the man almost entirely. One of the man's hands was uncovered and his fingers twitched spasmodically.

The tree was eating him. A feeling of dread came over him when he heard a familiar voice behind him. He turned around slowly to find the man from his dream standing over Kaldrick.

"I warned you not to come here."

—Prince Aramis

6

Eighteen Years Ago

"DO IT QUICKLY AND QUIETLY."

The written words echoed in Osen's mind as he watched the young man that was celebrating at the bar. The tavern was somewhat dead for the night compared to the normal flow of people that visited the run down establishment. Considering what he had been tasked with, he considered that a blessing. Fewer witnesses.

Osen felt the heavy bag of gold at his waist. It was enough to secure his future for the rest of his days. He could buy an estate somewhere quiet and never work again. And all he had to do was kill someone. He had killed before, of course. Usually in back alley brawls, and once when he robbed someone. That one had been an accident.

His attention shifted from the drunken revelers to the barmaid serving them. His eyes widened in surprise when he saw that she was pregnant. She wasn't too far along judging by her size, but her stomach stuck out enough that it was noticeable. He swallowed hard. No one had told him the person—the *woman*—he'd be murdering was pregnant. He felt a flush of anger at the lack of information.

Snatching his mug off the table, he drank the rest of the ale. He wiped his mouth with his forearm and rose from the table. He tossed a few of the gold coins onto the table after a long look at the pregnant barmaid. Shaking his head, he left the tavern and walked around to the stables where he'd left his horse.

"I'm a killer, but I'm not killin' no baby," he muttered to himself. He considered tossing the gold into a ditch but decided not to. No one would know if he didn't go through with the job seeing as how he'd never actually met his employer. They had exchanged letters in random locations and Osen was always careful to ensure no one saw him.

He retrieved his horse from the stable boy and led the mare out of the stable. He was about to mount up when he felt the call of nature. Slipping the reins around a wooden pole next to one of the watering troughs, he walked into the shadows at the edge of the tavern and relieved himself. When he turned around, he was startled to find two men standing there.

"If I hadn't just gone, you boys would have scared the piss outta me," he said with a nervous laugh.

"You aren't thinking of leaving, are you Osen?"

Osen took a step back and tried to make out their faces in the dark. "Jace?"

"Not quite," the other figure spoke. "Did you kill the barmaid?"

"N-not yet," Osen stuttered. "I was just checkin' on mah horse."

"Good. I'd hate to think you were going to run off with my money without completing the job you *willingly* accepted."

"Now hold on. No one said anything about killin' a baby."

"You weren't asked to kill a baby. You were asked to kill a woman."

"Yeah, but she's preg—"

"I'm well aware of what she is," the man snapped irritably. "Get in there and kill her."

"In the middle o' the tavern?" Osen asked dumbly.

"If you have to," the man answered. "Or bring her out here. Either way, just get it done."

Osen nodded and stepped around the man. He wasn't completely sure, but he thought he saw the glint of metal as he passed the larger of the two men. Gooseflesh covered him as he considered what he was about to do. Leaving his horse tied to the pole, he made his way back around to the front of the tavern. For a brief moment, he considered running off into the night. It was the cowardly part of him, he knew. For some reason though, he had a feeling he wasn't going to be alive much longer.

He stepped back into the building and went back to the table he had been sitting at. His empty mug and the coins he'd left were gone.

He sat down and began thinking of how he was going to get out of his situation. He didn't want to kill an unborn baby. He took no issue with killing a woman, but a baby? Absolutely not. He knew then why they had offered so much money for the job. How many others had turned it down?

"I'm sorry, I thought you had left."

Osen jumped at the words and looked up to see the barmaid. "What?"

"I thought you had left, so I cleaned up the table. Want me to bring you another drink?"

"No thanks," Osen managed to say. "I won't be here much longer."

"Ok." The woman smiled and left to another table.

After seeing her up close, Osen realized she was younger than he thought. She couldn't have yet reached twenty years. If he had doubts before, they had doubled now. She was younger than his daughter. Granted he'd not seen her since she was born, but he'd kept track of her age as the years passed. How would he feel if someone snuffed her life out?

He slammed his fist onto the table. The room went quiet and he realized everyone was looking at him. Some of the looks he got were curious while others were of concern. He ignored them and began tapping his fingers on the table. He didn't see any other way out.

"Screw it," he muttered to himself. Standing back up, he walked over to the barmaid as she was cleaning off a table.

"I need to talk to you," he said, trying not to speak too loudly.

"Sure," she said as she looked up from her work.

"Not here. Somewhere … private."

"Ah," she said with a knowing grin. "I would, but I'm spoken for. I don't think he'd appreciate me double-dealing on him."

"What? No, not that." He glanced around the room and lowered his voice. "There are two men outside who are here to kill you."

If his words scared her, she didn't show it. She continued wiping off the table, then gathered up a couple of empty mugs and made her way toward the bar. Osen followed her. The woman set the mugs on the end of the bar where an older man retrieved them and disappeared into the kitchen.

"I think you're drunk and need to sleep it off," she said.

Osen shook his head. "I'm not drunk. They …" his mouth suddenly went dry. Why was he going to tell her anything? What was it to him if someone killed her? He didn't know her and it was none of his concern. But he knew it was wrong.

"They hired me to kill you," he blurted out. He quickly looked around to see if anyone had heard him. The revelers made it hard to hear anything and no one appeared any wiser.

"I took the job because o' the money." He grabbed the bag from his waist and opened it, showing her the contents. "I came here ta kill yah, but I din't know ye was with child. I tried tah leave, but they met me out back. They mean tah see yah dead."

Perhaps it was the tone of his voice, but she looked like she believed him. Her face had gone pale and her hands were shaking.

"I'm going to help yah get out," he said. "I won't be killin' no baby, and I won't be lettin' someone else do it neither."

She nodded and removed her apron, tossing it carelessly onto the counter. She went into the kitchen and came back a moment later carrying a travel sack. Osen led her out of the tavern, pausing as they stepped outside to let his eyes adjust to the darkness. He put his finger to his lips and walked quietly toward the road that wound through the small town. The woman followed him, but she kept her distance. They followed the road for about twenty minutes before breaking the silence.

"Is there somewhere safe ye can go?" he asked.

"I can go home," she answered.

"I dun't think that's a good idea. They may know where ye live. What about ye'r man? Does he live nearby?"

When she didn't answer, he looked over his shoulder to see if she was still following him.

"There is no man," she said. "This baby is the result of a bad decision."

Osen didn't know what to say so he changed the subject. "Where are we going?" he asked.

"My house isn't much farther. Just beyond the trees there."

He had no idea what he was going to do after he got her to her house. He didn't want to stick around, but he also wasn't excited about leaving her alone. It didn't appear that anyone had followed them. As the woman had said, her house wasn't far. It was small and shabby. Not that he was judging. His bed was usually the floor of a bar. She took the lead as they got closer.

When they reached her doorstep, she lit a lantern that hung on a hook next to the door. Using the flame of the lantern, she lit a candle and entered her house. Osen turned and surveyed the darkness around the house. He didn't hear or see anything out of the ordinary, so he followed her into the house.

The candle lay on the floor, sputtering. His heart began to pound and he drew his dagger. Looking into the shadows, he saw the woman lying face down on the ground. Had the men followed them after all? He warily reached down and picked up the candle. Shining it into the shadows, he didn't see anyone. Kneeling beside the woman, he shook her.

"Hey … are ye ok?" he whispered.

She groaned. Relief flooded him. He'd feared she was dead. She rolled over slowly.

"Adamar?" she asked.

"Adamar?" Osen repeated confusedly. Then he realized she was looking past him. Dread filled him as he rose to his feet and turned around. The two men from the tavern stood in the light of the candle.

"Good evening, Tasia," one of the men said. "It's been a while."

Osen held his dagger out threateningly and stood over her.

"Don't hurt her," he said.

"I don't want to," the man responded, "but unfortunately, I don't have any choice in the matter. You see, the child she carries is mine.

And I can't have illegitimate kids running around when I become king."

"King?"

"Yes. Now if you don't mind, please kill her."

Osen looked from the prince to the woman. Her face was contorted in a fearful expression. The prince wanted him to kill someone? From what he'd heard of the king, that didn't seem like something he'd condone. He struggled internally, unable to decide what he should do. Something hard struck the back of his head and his legs stopped holding him up. He fell onto the floor and watched in horror as the bigger man in armor drove his sword through the woman's stomach.

She screamed in agony. Osen burst into tears and began sobbing uncontrollably. The prince pointed at him and said something he didn't hear. The other man jerked his sword out of the woman and came at him. The last thing he saw was the prince smiling in delight.

7

GARRICK WRAPPED A CHUNK OF bread in a cloth and stuck it into his pack. He'd already packed cheese and a few apples as well. Slinging the pack over his shoulder, he left the pantry and made his way through the castle hallways. None of his men had volunteered to go to the Deadlands, so he'd decided to go himself.

It was a risk in many ways, but he could not think of any other option. None of the generals had really voiced much opposition. This concerned him mainly because he had worked hard to reunify the kingdom and feared that the men would tear it apart in his absence. With the threat of elven invasion, however, they might stay focused. All he could do was hope.

He entered the courtyard and was greeted by all of his generals. They regarded him in silence and he wondered what they all might be thinking. Nothing ill-intentioned, he hoped.

"I will send word back as soon as I find their women and children," Garrick said. "I expect to find this place still standing and not overrun by elves. Whatever it takes, you must work together to keep our people safe."

A few of the men nodded their agreement. Garrick looked to each of them in turn, his gaze lingering longer on those whom he didn't fully trust.

"My King," Rycroft spoke. "Please take an escort with you."

Garrick shook his head. "No. The more people traveling together, the more likely we are to be seen. We need to enter the Deadlands with no suspicion from the elves. I will take one soldier to send back word with me as we discussed."

He thought Rycroft would argue further, but he didn't. "Where is Kelvin?"

"Here I am, my Lord."

Kelvin was handpicked by Garrick. The man was strong and well versed in battle. And he was devoutly loyal. Garrick knew if he got into a rough situation, Kelvin would be a great ally. He also knew he could trust Kelvin to get word back to them once they found the elven camp in the Deadlands.

"Let's get moving then," he said. The generals followed Garrick and Kelvin to the concealed passageway that led out of the castle. He slid the door open and stepped out. He glanced around to make sure there were no elves present, then he turned to the men. "Wait until you see my signal to create the diversion."

Kelvin stepped out of the doorway and the generals closed the door again. Now that Garrick knew where it was, it was a little easier to see the outline of the door amidst the wall. He jogged around the castle toward the eastern side where he hoped to use the coverage of some woods to hide their journey. A few miles of walking and they'd be out of Talvaard and enter into the Deadlands. He'd never been there before, but he knew it would be radically different than the grasslands that surrounded him now.

It was still early and the sun had yet to rise. Garrick paused at the edge of the castle wall and peered into the gloom. He could make out the shapes of tents and see their campfires, but he did not see any movement. He waited a moment longer, then sprinted across the landscape toward the trees. Kelvin followed close behind him, the sound of their steps dulled by the tall grass.

While they ran, Garrick turned around and jogged backward. He made a whistling noise that resembled the sound of a bird. A few seconds later, the sound was returned. He turned back around and continued running.

They reached the grove of trees without alerting the elves. Garrick paused for a few minutes to catch his breath, then headed north. He took care of where he stepped, not wanting to snap twigs or make loud noises. The faster they could make it to the desert without interruption the better, but he also knew that stealth was important. At least until they were far enough away. By now his men should have been raining flaming arrows down among the elven camp.

It took them several hours, but they eventually reached the edge of Talvaard's borders. The tall grassy plains slowly started to transform. Here and there large patches of sand splotched the landscape until finally, they could see the desert stretch out before them. There was nothing but sand as far as Garrick could see. Large hills that stretched for miles across the horizon cropped up from the flatter ground. They stopped to eat a light lunch. They had passed a stream earlier and had filled their canteens with fresh water.

"Drink light to conserve your water," Garrick instructed Kelvin. "Who knows when we might see water again out there."

"Yes, sir."

"Are you ready for this journey?" Garrick asked.

"I am, sir."

Garrick turned his gaze over his shoulder and took a long look at Talvaard. He thought about praying to Mordum and asking to keep his people safe but thought better of it.

Why would the God of the Dead protect the living?

They set off at an easy pace, but it didn't take long before Garrick was drenched in sweat. The sun was in the middle of the sky and there wasn't a cloud to be seen. The desert air was dry and suffocating. His throat became parched and his mouth felt like it was made of cotton. He continuously spat foamy saliva out and drank sparingly of his water.

He began to wonder if he had made the right decision. From all he had read, the Deadlands was aptly named. There were slithering creatures that could kill a man with a single bite. Getting overheated in the dry air could cause hallucinations. There was the possibility of dying from thirst.

All of these facts floated around in his mind, mingling with the thoughts of his people. He thought about his wife back in the capital of Talvaarin. She was safe there for the time being. If the elves pushed further into Talvaard, there wouldn't be anywhere safe for anyone. His steps became slower the longer they traveled. It became a monotony in the back of his mind:

Left leg. Right leg. Left leg. Right leg.

He looked back to check on Kelvin and could see he was

struggling just as much as himself. Their eyes met and Kelvin nodded. Garrick returned the nod and they kept walking. That was another reason he chose Kelvin for this task—he was stubborn. He would push himself to his breaking point before giving up. Garrick admired that trait in men. Not so much the stubbornness, but the ability for a man to be able to control his body with his mind.

Garrick was having trouble keeping track of how much time passed. Other than the position of the sun in the sky, there was nothing to indicate they were even moving. They trudged uphill and down. Several times they had to stop and dump the sand from their boots. The grains rubbed against the bottom of his feet, scouring the skin off. He wasn't bleeding, but it was a bothersome pain.

They stopped and set up camp as the sky began to darken. Garrick was surprised at how quickly the temperature dropped as the sun descended. Kelvin began setting up their tent. He'd offered to carry it along with his pack for which Garrick was thankful. He'd had enough trouble carrying his own pack and trying not to collapse from the heat. There was no wood to make a fire, so they ate a meager dinner and retired into the tent.

As Garrick lay down, he knew his face had been burned from the sun. His skin was sore and hot to the touch. He felt extremely dirty as his sweat dried.

"This is going to be a long walk," Garrick whispered to himself.

"Yes, it is," Kelvin answered.

Garrick chuckled softly. They hadn't talked much at all the entire day. He was tired and wanted to get to sleep, but felt obligated to talk with his traveling companion.

"How are you holding up?" he asked.

"I've seen worse days," Kelvin answered.

"Me too," Garrick said. "Are you married?"

"No, sir."

"Is there a woman you fancy?"

A moment of silence. "Yes, sir."

"You can stop calling me sir."

"Yes, sir … er, O … okay."

"Does she know?"

"Know what?"

"Does she know that you fancy her," Garrick clarified.

"I don't know," Kelvin answered. "I've had a few gifts delivered, but I never let her know who was responsible for them. I'm trying to work up my nerve."

"That's the mystery."

"What's that, sir? I mean … Garrick."

Garrick smiled in the darkness. "That men like us can go into battle with nerves of steel, fight off our enemies, take a life if necessary. Yet when it comes to approaching a woman, we sputter and make fools of ourselves."

"I thought I was the only one," Kelvin admitted.

"Nonsense. You should have seen me when I began courting my wife. I was like a frightened dog running from its shadow."

They both laughed at that.

"You should tell her you like her," Garrick added. "Once this is all over."

"I think I will," Kelvin said.

"I think I'm going to sleep now."

"Me too."

Reminiscing of the early days with his wife, he fell asleep with a smile on his face.

—

Garrick awoke to the world spinning around him. He grunted as something heavy slammed into him. He realized it was Kelvin. The tent wrapped around them and Garrick could hear the sound of the tent flapping wildly. They tumbled over each other several times before coming to a jarring halt.

Managing to escape the tent through a tear in the fabric, Garrick crawled out to a nightmare. The wind was blowing so hard that sand had filled the sky and blotted out the sun. The stinging sand quickly blinded him and he covered his face with his hands. He heard Kelvin start cursing and figured the man was in the same predicament.

His eyes were watering which made matters worse. The sand was now encrusted around his eyes. Dropping to his knees, he placed his head between his legs and resigned himself to wait until the storm passed.

Eventually, the wind died down enough that he was able to start cleaning the sand from his face. His eyes, ears, and even his nose were caked with it. Using the last of his water and the hem of his shirt, he was able to remove the majority of it. Finally able to see again, he found Kelvin had wrapped himself in the tent. He helped the man untangle himself from it.

Working together they attempted to break down the tent. In the process, they found it had been ripped in several places.

"It's almost unusable," Kelvin remarked.

"I agree," Garrick replied, kneeling down and studying a long tear in the material. It was almost a foot long.

"We don't have anything to patch it with, but maybe we can salvage some of it."

Garrick generally tried not to let things get to him, but he was starting to feel the weight of their task. He stood up and eyed the position of the sun.

"I'd say it's mid-morning," he guessed. "I'm out of water and we now have no shelter from the elements. We're only a day's march into this blasted place and already we're at a disadvantage. Not to mention we have no idea what direction we should be searching in."

Kelvin remained silent.

"This place is bigger than I imagined it to be." Garrick heaved a sigh and stared at their surroundings, trying to decide what to do.

"Sir," Kelvin said.

"I told you yesterday you don't have to call me that."

"Sir," Kelvin repeated, his tone more urgent. "Don't move."

"What?" Garrick froze mid-turn. "What is it?"

And then he heard it. An odd rattling noise and a hissing sound.

"It's a snake," Kelvin answered, speaking softer. "And it's right beside you."

Garrick shifted his head slowly and looked down. The snake was coiled up, its tail flicking back and forth faster than his eyes could keep up with. It was less than two feet away from his left leg. He feared if he tried to move away, it would strike him. Eyeing the distance, he suddenly had an idea. He lifted his hand a little. The snake tensed and for a moment Garrick thought it was about to come flying at him. Fortunately, it didn't move.

He didn't realize he was holding his breath until he felt the pressure building in his lungs. He forced himself to breathe normally, then he summoned his blade. The air hissed as it formed. He blinked and almost missed seeing the blade fully form, slicing the snake's head off. Its body began floundering about. He leaped away and dismissed his blade.

"That was close," he said. He looked to Kelvin and saw the man staring at him.

"What was *that*?"

Garrick smiled disarmingly and shrugged. "I've been blessed."

"Blessed?" Kelvin asked.

"You could say that."

"Blessed with a black blade of Mordum? Where is your mark?"

Garrick's heart began pounding. "What?"

Kelvin's gaze hardened. "So it's *you*. You are Mordum's agent in Talvaard. How … how could you betray your own people?"

"You are mistaken," Garrick answered, holding his hands up.

Kelvin shook his head. "You seemed so honorable, so respectable. I should have seen through your act."

"I am not whatever it is you think I am," Garrick said. "I've never followed the tenets of Mordum."

"Yet you summon one of his blades? The evidence against you is not good."

Garrick watched as the air around Kelvin began to shimmer with mist. Gleaming silver armor shaped around him and a long silver blade formed in his hands. On the right side of the breastplate, Garrick recognized the symbol of Zevea: a sun with outstretched wings. The Goddess of Light.

"Prepare to meet your dark god," Kelvin said. He lifted his blade and approached threateningly.

"Blast it," Garrick muttered as he summoned his own armor and blade. He brought his blade up and took a defensive stance.

"I don't want to fight you," he said.

"Then you will die quickly," Kelvin replied.

Garrick braced himself as Kelvin charged him. The blades clashed together with a loud *clang*. Garrick didn't want to fight his own soldier. He stayed on the defensive, parrying Kelvin's thrusts and back-stepping. He could tell by Kelvin's body language that he was starting to get angry. Garrick knocked Kelvin's blade aside and threw himself to the ground, rolling away to put some distance between them.

He got back on his feet and brought his sword up. Just as Kelvin began to rush at him, a loud cry startled both of them.

"STOP!"

They both turned to see an unexpected sight. An elderly woman pushing a wooden cart. Wrapped around her eyes was an old dirty bandage. Garrick stared in confusion, even more so when Kelvin dropped to his knees and lowered his head.

"Who are you?" he asked.

The old woman smiled.

8

ARAMIS STOOD MOTIONLESS. THE MAN from his dream was *real*. The man didn't move, but he was standing uncomfortably close to Kaldrick. He wore loose fitting-brown robes that had a hood pulled over his head. He didn't seem very tall.

"What have you done to my men?" Aramis asked, slowly walking toward the druid.

"I haven't done anything to them, Prince Aramis."

"How do you know my name?" Aramis ceased walking.

"I know much more than your name, but that is not important. I warned you not to come here, and yet you still entered these woods."

"It was a dream," Aramis replied. "*You* were a dream."

"Yet here I stand."

"What's going on? What happened to my men?"

"Come with me and I will explain everything."

Aramis eyed the druid warily. He certainly didn't trust the man. He pointed to Kaldrick. "Step away from him."

The druid did as he asked and backed away from him. Aramis strode forward and helped Kaldrick to his feet.

"Don't trust him," Kaldrick said.

"I don't," Aramis answered.

"I'm not asking you to trust me," the druid said. "I'm asking you to follow me and to listen."

Aramis debated whether or not he should. If he refused, would the druid cast some spell on him? Perhaps turn him into a tree as well? He didn't know anything about druids, whether they were good or evil. He glanced back at the tree that seemed to be eating one of his men not thirty feet away. He made his decision.

"Lead the way," Aramis said.

The druid turned and led them along the path through the woods. He led them deep into the forest. Aramis gradually noticed a difference in the air. It was cooler and the sounds of birds and other animals filled the air. He hadn't realized it before, but he hadn't heard any sounds earlier. There was something about this part of the woods that seemed more … lively.

The path took them to a small wooden bridge that crossed over a gently flowing river. The druid led them across the bridge and the sound of voices filled the air. They entered a glade similar to the one Aramis had found earlier, with small huts made of vines and tree roots spread out along the clearing. Aramis saw men, women, and even a few children present. They were all busy, some cooking at small fires outside their huts, others carrying firewood, and still, others carrying baskets of fruit and vegetables.

"What is this?" Aramis asked curiously.

"This is our home," the druid answered.

"I saw another clearing like this one, but it was empty."

"Yes."

The druid didn't elaborate, and he didn't press the man. The people of the village took notice of Aramis and Kaldrick, but they didn't stare or point like other places Aramis had been. The druid led them to a long table that was being set up for a meal.

"Leave your friend here," the druid said.

Aramis frowned. "I will not leave him alone."

"He will be taken care of, I assure you. You can rejoin him shortly."

Aramis didn't want to leave Kaldrick, but he didn't sense any danger from these people. He looked around the village. The people were going about their normal duties and not paying them any attention. He leaned in close to Kaldrick and lowered his voice.

"I don't like the idea of leaving you here alone, but I don't think these people will do anything. Can you stay here while I talk with the druid?"

"They are different than the others," Kaldrick replied. "I'll be fine."

"The others?"

"The ones that …" Kaldrick shuddered and refused to say anything else. He sat down at the table.

"Help yourself to the food," the druid said, his tone comforting. "The meal will be ready soon." He motioned for Aramis to follow him and they walked to one of the huts. This one was slightly larger than the others. Aramis hesitated for a moment before following the druid into the hut.

The inside of the place was nothing like what he expected. The floor was made of smooth marble. The walls were covered with tapestries and paintings that had exquisite detail and the ceiling was painted with a beautiful mural of the night sky. There were hundreds of stars and they almost seemed to glow as though they were not merely painted on.

"How—"

"It is an illusion," the druid answered before Aramis could finish speaking. "It reminds me of what I left behind for the life I have now."

"You weren't born a druid?"

The man laughed. "Not many are born into this life," he answered. "Most of us got tired of the cities, the crowds of people, the hectic pace of life passing too quickly. No, most of us have chosen this life after forsaking the places we once called home."

Aramis was stunned. *Why would anyone want to leave civilization for this?*

The druid retrieved two wooden cups from a cabinet and poured some sort of colored liquid into them. He handed one to Aramis. When he didn't drink it, the druid smiled.

"It's just wine."

Aramis waved the cup under his nose and sniffed. It smelled sweet. He took a sip and was pleasantly surprised by the taste. It made his tongue light up with pleasure.

"It's good," he said. "Very good."

The druid set his cup down and pulled the hood back from his head. Aramis guessed the man to be in his fifties, possibly late forties. He was mostly bald, with only a thin ring of white hair that rounded his head above the ears. His eyes were a striking dark blue. His skin was a light tan color.

"So what happened to my men?" Aramis asked. He still wanted to know what was going on.

The druid picked up his cup and took a drink. "Before I can explain that, I must tell you some other things first. I've been living here as a druid for over twenty years. The ring of trees where you found your friend, that is a sacred place for us. It's been a sacred place for as far back as any of the druids can remember. We believe that Edria, the Goddess of Light, once walked in that very place."

Aramis finished off the wine in his cup. He was familiar with Edria and nodded. The druid refilled his cup.

"We go there to pray each day. Recently the area has taken on a different feeling. Dark whispers drifting on the wind that bespeak wicked sayings. Things in the shadows scurrying just outside of your view. Unnatural things." The druid made a sign in the air.

"I'm sorry, but I don't have time for a history lesson," Aramis said. "I've got something important that I need to do. The longer I'm held up; the more danger everyone faces."

"I know well the danger that presents itself," the druid replied. "For it is dwelling here in our forest."

"What do you mean?"

"You are familiar with Mordum?" The druid pointed to the tattoo on Aramis's arm.

Aramis rubbed at his arm. "I'm not a follower if that's what you are asking."

"You'll get no judgment from me," the druid replied. "Who a man chooses to serve is his own business. I merely asked because I noticed his mark on you and thought you might know what has happened to our forest. Our sacred place has been infected by Mordum. Something is happening in the realm of the gods, though what exactly no man knows. Unfortunately, we mortals are caught in the middle."

"What do you mean Mordum has infected the forest?"

"Do you remember the trees you saw earlier?"

"How could I forget?" Aramis said. "It was eating one of my soldiers."

The druid nodded. "That is part of the blight Mordum has caused. The forest itself turns against us. The village you first encountered that was empty … we had to flee that area. We've had to come here to this clearing. And yet the darkness of Mordum spreads further into the woods every day. Before long, we will have to flee this area as well." The druid finished his wine and set the cup on the table.

Aramis digested the man's words. While these woods were on the very edge of his kingdom, it was still part of his realm. What could he do for these people? How could he possibly help them against a god? *What would Mel do?* He downed the rest of his wine and set the cup down. The druid went to refill it, but Aramis shook his head.

"I need to keep my head clear," he said. "Have you tried using your magic against this blight?"

"Yes, though it hasn't done much. Mordum is God of the Dead. There is no force stronger than death, I fear. We managed to push the blight back at first. At least it appeared that we had. But it spread much more quickly than I thought possible. The darkness corrodes our spells, disintegrating them into oblivion."

"Do you know where it started?" Aramis asked.

The druid nodded. "I have a good idea," he said. "It's not far from the sacred ring of trees. There is a black patch of grass. One of the children noticed it after things started changing. We tried healing spells on the grass, but we might as well have been throwing dirt on it for all it accomplished."

Aramis massaged his hands over his face and rubbed his eyes. He was exhausted. He looked at the druid, considering his next words.

"If there were a way to stop the blight, what do you think it would be?"

The druid scoffed. "If I knew that, we'd have already stopped it."

"I'm sorry," Aramis said, waving his hands in the air to mollify him. "Let me rephrase it. What is the opposite of death?"

"Life," the druid said without hesitation.

"Exactly. If Mordum can use the power of death to bring destruction to the forest, there must be a way to reverse it. Or at the very least, combat it."

"With what? Our magic is no good against his power."

"With the power of life."

The druid frowned. "If you are talking about human sacrifice, you are out of your mind."

"That's not at all what I'm talking about," Aramis replied. "I'm talking about using the power of life, not taking someone's life. There has to be some sort of spell that creates life."

"It's not a spell," the druid said. "That's called being a god."

"I'm not talking about *creating a life*. I'm talking about harnessing the power of life. Is there nothing like that you are aware of?"

The druid was silent for long moments. "Nothing that I can think of. I'll consult with the others and see if they know of anything. But even if there is a spell that powerful, how would it work? The one who casts it has enough trouble keeping the spell going. Where would they harness enough energy to combat death and power the spell?"

"Can spells feed off of people?"

"Yes, but that's dangerous. Take too much, and the person will die. It is forbidden among the druids to use another's energy."

"There are always exceptions to rules," Aramis replied.

The druid shook his head. "I don't like it. I will not risk the life of one of my people to try something we don't even know is possible."

"You won't have to."

"What are you talking about?"

"I will let them use my life force."

The druid stood speechless. He moved his mouth as if to answer or offer up some sort of argument, but no words came out.

"I know the risk," Aramis said. "And regardless of it, your people are citizens of my kingdom. I will do what I must to aid you. If it doesn't work to save your home, at least I tried. I cannot leave you in a time of need as if it doesn't bother me."

The druid finally collected himself. "You have your father's heart."

"I appreciate that," Aramis said. "Have you heard the news of my father?"

"We don't get many visitors," the druid replied with a smile.

"Of course," Aramis said, feeling stupid for having asked. "He was murdered."

"No!" The druid was aghast.

"It is true," Aramis said. "I was there. An agent of Mordum killed him. I tried to stop him, but I was no match for him. I found out later it was one of Mordum's knights."

"A *templar*," the druid said in awe. "I have heard of these men if men are what they are. I am surprised you are alive to share this tale."

"He cursed me with this mark," Aramis said, pointing to the tattoo. "It is always difficult trying to explain that I am not one of his followers because of this thing."

"Why?" the druid asked.

"Apparently his followers receive the mark when they choose to follow him, and it is a lifelong commitment."

"I see."

Aramis sighed heavily. "I need to get some rest."

"Of course," the druid said. "You can rest here in my home.

Dinner will be ready soon. I'll confer with the elders and see what I can find. Do you need anything?"

"No, thank you."

The druid left the hut. Aramis looked around the place. The illusion of the place was so realistic. There was a single chair that formed out of the wall. It appeared to be formed of a tree root and shaped to look like a chair that laid back. Aramis sat down on it and laid back. It was surprisingly more comfortable than he thought it would be. He closed his eyes and thought about what lay before him.

His life had been so simple a few short months ago. He'd never imagined life would take him where he was now. An exile in his own kingdom. His father murdered. His best friend dead. He was suddenly aware of how alone he was. Everything had been so crazy the last few days, he hadn't had time to think. Now his thoughts assailed him. The same images kept running through his head. His father dying before his eyes. Mel standing in the road prepared to give his life for him. His thoughts turned to Lord Bavol, one of the nobles in the court.

Aramis wondered how he was faring in his attempt to gather support for Aramis to take his throne back from the man who had usurped it. The old blind woman had said the man was his brother. Aramis still had his doubts about that. The truth would be known soon. And if the man was his brother, Aramis would never accept him. There had to be a good reason why his parents would have never told him about having a brother. According to Bavol, the men who served him had the mark of Mordum. Was the usurper a follower of Mordum as well?

Aramis could feel the welcoming darkness of sleep coming over him. He fought it at first. It wasn't a good idea to let his guard down among people he didn't know. Eventually, he stopped fighting and gave in. His dreams were twisted and dark. He saw his home engulfed in flames, his people massacred in the streets. And then he was in the forest standing in the sacred tree ring, watching his soldiers being consumed by the trees.

He walked out of the ring and saw a patch of black grass. As he approached it, the ground around the grass began to move erratically, as though it were liquid. He knelt down and placed his finger on the ground. His entire arm disappeared into the ground. He quickly pulled it out. His arm was clean. No dirt; nothing. His mind couldn't understand what was happening. He stood up and placed his foot in the same spot. His leg up to his knee disappeared into the ground. He pulled it out and noticed the thing as he did with his arm.

It was clean. No dirt, no grass. He stared at the black grass in confusion. An arm grabbed him on the shoulder and started shaking him. He cried out in surprise and tried to pull away. The shaking grew more insistent. Aramis tried to push the arm off. He couldn't see who it belonged to. When he tried to look, the person's face was just a shadow. The arm started pulling him forward, dragging him toward the grass.

Aramis's eyes snapped open. Kaldrick stood over him, a hand on his shoulder, shaking him. "My Lord?" he said questioningly. "Are you okay?"

Aramis looked around and realized it had all been a dream. He sighed in relief. "I'm fine," he answered. "I was having a nightmare. There was this black grass that …" he trailed off.

"What is it?" Kaldrick asked.

Aramis quickly got up from the chair. "I think I know how where to find the cause of the blight."

"The what?"

Aramis realized Kaldrick had no idea what he meant. "Where is the druid who brought us here?"

"I haven't seen him. Why?"

"I need to find him. Come on." Aramis left the hut, walking at a brisk pace. He looked around the clearing but didn't see the man. A woman walked by carrying a small basket.

"Lady," Aramis called out. "Where is the man who lives here?" He motioned to the hut behind him.

"I think he's talking with the elders."

"Where can I find them?"

The woman nodded toward the path that led into the woods. "I saw them go that way. They may have gone to the sacred tree ring."

Aramis sprinted to the trail. He hoped he wasn't too late.

—

Aramis and Kaldrick arrived at the ring of trees and found the druid elders conversing quietly. Aramis was out of breath and had to calm his breathing before he could speak. His calve muscles were burning fiercely and his throat was dry. He looked over at Kaldrick. Other than the fact that he was sweating profusely, he would never have known Kaldrick just ran through a humid forest. Aramis approached the druids and was about to call out to the man he'd talked with earlier, only to realize that he still didn't know the man's name. The group of men turned to greet him.

"Prince Aramis," the man he'd spoken to earlier addressed him. "I have bad news. None of us know of any spells like what you described."

"I had a dream … or a vision. I'm not sure which. But it does not bode well. Show me the patch of black grass."

"It's over here," the druid led him outside the ring of trees to a grassy area. Most of the grass was a vibrant green. Fallen leaves and twigs littered the area. In the center of the grass was a circular dark spot that stood out in stark contrast. If Aramis didn't know any different, he would have thought it was nothing but ashes. He stepped forward but the druid blocked him with his arm.

"This place gives off a foul aura," the druid said. "It may not be safe to get any closer."

"I have to see something," Aramis replied. He pushed gently past the druid's outstretched arm and knelt down right outside the dark splotch. He held his breath as he reached down and poked the ground with his finger.

Nothing happened.

He pulled his hand back. It was clean. He exhaled in relief. Yet he was also frustrated. Where did the blight originate? He'd thought for certain his dream had been some sort of sign. He stood up and turned back to the druid.

"I thought I would find something here," he said, shaking his head. "I don't understand."

"What did you hope to find?"

"In my dream, this was a portal of some kind. When stepping on the ground, it sucked my leg into it." He turned back and stared at the grass. A feeling of dread slowly came over him. The hairs on his arms stood on end. He began backing away.

"What is it?" the druid asked.

"I don't know," Aramis answered. "I have a bad feeling about this place." The tattoo on his arm began to tingle. He tried to ignore it.

And then the black grass erupted into the air. Aramis cried out in surprise and jumped back quickly. A large creature climbed up out of the ground. Its skin was a shiny gray color, reminding Aramis of metal. It was manlike, with two legs and two arms. It had no hair on its head. Its eyes were like snow with bloodshot lines snaking through the white. Its teeth were jagged and looked razor sharp. The druids began chanting in a strange language.

The creature moved much quicker than Aramis expected. It ran at one of the druids and swiped at him with its clawed hand, cutting a deep gash into the man's neck. Blood spurt from the wound uncontrollably. The druid clutched at his throat as he fell to the ground, writhing in agony. The chanting of the other druids quickened.

Aramis was about to turn and flee into the woods when he saw Kaldrick charge the creature and tackle it to the ground. He suddenly felt foolish. If he ran, he was nothing more than a coward. He said he wanted to help these people, and at the first sign of danger, his first instinct was to run. That should not be the character of a leader. Especially not a king. Aramis drew the small dagger he had used to kill a phiebus with and charged into the fray. Kaldrick and the creature rolled back and forth, pummeling each other with blows.

He waited until they rolled around and the creature was on top, and then he plunged the dagger into the creature's back. It jerked away and growled in pain, causing Aramis to lose his grip on the hilt. The creature knocked Kaldrick in the head once more, got up, and turned to face Aramis. Suddenly the chanting came to an abrupt stop. In a move of stupidity, Aramis turned to see why they had stopped. And then the creature was on him, knocking him to the ground and scratching his arms and chest with its claws.

The scratches immediately began to burn and itch. He struggled against the creature, trying to get back to his feet. Suddenly he was free. Aramis scrambled to get up. He looked around frantically, trying to see where the creature was. And then he saw it—fighting with another creature. The new creature looked like a tree in appearance. It was covered in bark and had small, thin branches coming off of its body with tiny green leaves sprouting along the branches. Though it resembled a tree, it had legs and arms that looked humanoid. Aramis watched in fascination as the two creatures battled viciously. Kaldrick startled him when he limped up beside him. Aramis jumped and then laughed nervously.

"You scared me," he said, shaking his head.

"I didn't intend to. Are you all right?" he asked with concern.

Aramis looked down and noticed his arms were slick with blood. He hadn't even noticed. Using his hand, he wiped the blood off his left arm. The cuts were already healed.

"I'm fine," he answered. "What about you?"

"I'm a little banged up."

They sat in silence as the two creatures continued to fight. The tree looking creature appeared to be winning. It grabbed Mordum's gray creature by the throat and lifted it into the air. It kicked at the tree creature's chest, cracking some of the bark.

Aramis tore his gaze away and looked for the druids. He saw them gathered around their fallen comrade. He walked over to them quietly. The man he had been speaking with since arriving into the woods had tears in his eyes, but he remained fairly composed.

"I'm sorry," Aramis said, looking down at the dead druid.

"Jared was still young," the druid lamented.

Aramis didn't know what to say to that, so he didn't say anything. He wasn't much for religion, but he offered up a silent prayer for the man to whoever might be listening. Aramis's attention was drawn back to creatures.

"What are those things?"

"I don't know about the creature that came out of the ground," the druid replied. "The other one is an elemental. They are powerful creature wrought of magic and nature. In the past, we have used them for manual labor, but according to history they have been used in times of war."

"I thought druids were peaceful?" Aramis asked.

"We are. There are times, however, when peace does not solve problems. There are times that call for war, though we find them to be rare."

The elemental slammed Mordum's creature into a tree, pinning it in place with one of its massive arms. With the other, it grabbed the creature by the head and began twisting it. The creature struggled frantically. A crack filled the air and the creature slumped lifelessly. The elemental tossed the creature to the ground and stood there unmoving.

"I wonder if that creature was the cause of the blight," Aramis questioned.

"I suppose we shall find out soon," the druid answered.

"My throat is on fire. Is there a stream anywhere nearby?"

The druid pointed. "That way there's a shallow stream that flows all the way through the forest."

Aramis nodded and walked the direction the druid had indicated. He passed Kaldrick and motioned him to follow. "There's a stream this way if you're thirsty?"

Kaldrick followed him, his pace hindered somewhat by a slight limp. After a few hundred feet, Aramis heard a noise. It sounded like wind blowing through the treetops, but it turned out to be the stream. It flowed to the north, twisting and turning along the landscape. They stopped at the edge of the bank and Aramis knelt down. He splashed water onto his arms and washed the blood off. Then he cupped his hands together and dipped them into the water, quickly bringing them up to his mouth. He drank the water and immediately spit it out.

It was one of the foulest things he'd ever tasted. He spat several times, but it didn't help. He vomited into the stream. The taste was still in his mouth, but not as strong. He stared into the water and noticed a thin oily film floating on the water.

"What is it?" Kaldrick asked, stepping away from the water's edge.

"I think the stream has been affected by the blight," Aramis answered as he stood back up. "Gods that was nasty. Let's get back to the druids. Hopefully, they have better water in the village."

As they were approaching the ring of trees, he could hear shouting. He picked up his pace and realized it was the druids shouting. There were several of the gray-skinned creatures attacking them. The elemental was busy fighting three of them. Aramis looked back and saw Kaldrick was doing his best to keep up, but his limp was throwing him off. Kaldrick motioned for him to go ahead.

Aramis sprinted toward a group of creatures around one of the druids. He leaped into the air and stuck his leg out, slamming into one of the creatures with a jarring impact. The creature fell to the ground roughly. Aramis remembered he'd left his dagger in the back of the first creature and ran toward its body. One of the creatures stepped in front of him, stopping him short. It swung its arms at him, trying to rake him with its claws. He narrowly avoided the strikes and feigned going to the left, then went to the right and ran past the creature. He reached the body and yanked his dagger out of its back.

He turned to face the creature. It came at him quickly, clawing at him haphazardly. One of its claws gashed him on the shoulder. He jabbed the dagger into the creature's chest. On any normal man, it would have been a death blow, striking the heart. But the creature just roared in anger and grabbed onto his arm, dragging its claws across his flesh. Aramis's eyes widened as he saw how deep the creature cut him. He could see tendons and the white of his bone.

Fear engulfed him. He didn't think the tattoo would be able to heal that. As he stared at his arm, he saw the skin begin to close. Relief flooded him. Within seconds the wounds had closed fully, leaving only the wet blood on his skin. Aramis pulled the dagger free and stabbed it into the creature's neck. Black blood gushed from the cut in its chest and neck. His hand was covered in it. Jerking the blade out, he staggered backward out of the creature's reach. Though it had received two mortal wounds, it didn't appear to deter the thing at all. It came at him still.

Kaldrick rammed into the creature from the side, using his shoulder to knock it into a tree. Aramis ran over and together they punched, kicked and stabbed the creature until they were sure it was dead. Aramis turned to survey the scene around them, his breath coming in heaving gasps. The creatures had killed one of the druids. He lay in a pool of blood, covered in gashes. The three fighting the elemental were ripping pieces of its bark off. Aramis wasn't knowledgeable when it came to magic, but he was certain that the elemental wasn't going to last much longer.

He ran over to help the remaining druids who were being attacked. He glanced over to where the black grass was as he ran and saw five more of the creatures coming up out of the ground. At this rate, they would be quickly overrun and have to flee the area. How far would the creatures chase them? Would they follow them to the village?

Aramis growled in frustration. He was starting to feel helpless. All he had was a short dagger and it didn't do much damage to the creatures. He reached the druids and helped drive one of the creatures back, stabbing it several times with the dagger. Again, the wounds seemed not to faze it much. Aramis pushed the creature to the ground. He leaped on top of it, grabbed a rock from nearby, and bashed it into the creature's head over and over.

After it stopped moving, he dropped the rock and stood back up—only to be knocked painfully to the ground. More of the creatures leaped onto him. He was pinned down and could barely move. Intense fear gripped him as he realized he wasn't in control of the situation. Between flailing limbs, he saw more of the creatures running to join the fray from the direction of the black grass. They were sorely outnumbered now.

He struggled to move his arms. The weight of the creatures on him made it impossible. His heart was pounding in his chest. He could feel the creatures flaying his skin off. Everything seemed to slow down, but he didn't know if it was his imagination or from the loss of blood. He closed his eyes and prepared himself to die.

Summon your blade.

The words entered his mind, cutting through the chaos around him. Within seconds, he had an entire conversation with … himself? His conscience? He didn't know and didn't have time to figure it out.

What?

Summon your blade.

What blade?

The Blade of Mordum.

How? I don't know what that is.

Focus.

On what?

On the power flowing through you.

It might drive me insane.

Insanity is better than death.

Is it?

You tell me.

Aramis snapped his eyes open. He had no idea what was happening inside his mind, but he focused on the power of the tattoo. A hissing sound filled the air and he noticed his hand was wet. He assumed it was blood. One of the creatures screeched wildly and flung itself off of him. He looked to his hand and saw a gleaming sword. Silver runes ran down the length of the blade. The tip of it was covered in a thick black liquid. He realized it was blood. Blood from the gray-skinned creature.

Using strength he didn't realize he had left, he drove the sword into the creatures atop him, slicing limbs off with ease. Within moments he was free and managed to get to his feet. His arms were healing, the deep wounds closing before his eyes. He looked at the carnage around him and was perfectly calm, perfectly in control of his thoughts.

The elemental lay defeated on the ground, looking like nothing more than a twisted tree. The druids were surrounded. They were chanting and holding their hands up. It looked like they had erected some sort of shield around themselves. It probably wouldn't hold for long. He could see sweat pouring down their faces and he knew they were exhausted.

Kaldrick. He found the man attempting to fight off two of the creatures. He was covered in blood, his own and that of the creatures. Aramis knew the man's strength was failing him by the way his body moved. Aramis walked toward the creatures and cut them down effortlessly; their heads rolling onto the ground, their black blood splattering the grass around him. Then he strode to the druids and began dispatching the creatures. They turned to fight him, but he was too quick; much quicker than they were. Limbs and heads flew in all directions as he dealt death with abandon.

He cleared the entire clearing of the creatures. The scene was so surreal; he almost didn't believe his eyes. Their bodies lay strewn all over. He saw the two druids who had been slain. So much death. The druids stopped their chanting and their shield faded from sight. Aramis glanced to where the creatures were coming up from the ground. He saw a hand rising from the hole. There were would be more, no doubt. Would they ever stop coming?

"Thank you," the druid said as he approached Aramis. "You saved our lives."

"Not all of them," Aramis said softly.

"Death comes to us all," he replied.

An idea formed in Aramis's mind. He had no way of knowing if it would work, but he had to try something to stop the hellish creatures from continuing their killing.

"Not always," Aramis said. He looked to Kaldrick as he limped over. "Stay with the druids until I return. I don't know how long it will be. Maybe hours, maybe days."

"Where are you going?" Kaldrick asked.

"Into the pit of Hell," Aramis answered. He walked toward the hole in the grass. Another one of the creatures was struggling to climb out. Aramis casually lopped off its head with a swing of his blade. He looked down at the hole, wondering what he might find below. He would never normally do something so insane. He held his sword up and studied the runes. It was Talvaarish for all he knew.

Had summoning the blade given him the calmness he was experiencing? He didn't know.

He held his breath. And then he stepped down into Hell.

9

GARRICK MULLED OVER THE OLD woman's words as he sipped water from his canteen. They were still hard to believe. She had given them new canteens of water, and a new tent, before pushing on through the desert with her wooden cart.

He marveled at how she had survived out here, especially being blind. He looked at Kelvin. The man was ignoring him. Garrick sighed. At least the man wasn't intent on killing him now.

"I'm sorry," Garrick said.

Kelvin looked at him but remained silent.

"For not telling you."

Kelvin turned away.

"I'll explain everything if you let me. There is a reason I bear the Mark, and it is not what you likely think. I am not one of his mindless pawns."

"Tell me," Kelvin answered. He did not turn around.

"Very well. Please know that you will be the first person to hear this. Not even my wife knows about this."

That seemed to get Kelvin's full attention, for he finally turned to face Garrick. Their eyes met and Garrick thought he sensed a change in Kelvin's eyes. A small change, but a change nonetheless.

"The Mark of Mordum can bring many different abilities, much like your goddess's blessing. It can also bring madness."

"I already know this," Kelvin said.

"Most people of faith do. However, you must be chosen by Mordum to receive the Mark. Usually, these people are already on a path of destruction. Murderers mostly. A few already claimed by madness and the occasional liar. By their actions, Mordum chooses them. It is rare that anyone would ever willingly choose to take the Mark."

Garrick took another sip of water.

"I was young …"

———

Garrick was up before sunrise. He dressed quietly in the dull reddish light provided by the hearth. His mother was still asleep and he didn't want to wake her. Stepping out of the house, he walked over to a barrel that held rainwater and splashed some on his face. He ran his wet hands through his tousled straight black hair several times. Checking his reflection on the water's surface, he decided his hair would just have to do.

The air still had a chill to it. He ran back into the cabin and grabbed a heavy cloak and threw it over his shoulders, then ran back outside. In his anxiousness, he almost forgot to close the door. He walked with a quick pace down the dirt road that winded through the small town. He could see puffs of his breath in the pre-dawn air.

The small town was quiet and still. The people were sleeping off the exhaustion from the previous day's work. Garrick had worked hard as well and was still tired, but his excitement at the return of his father and the other members of the town was too much to allow him to sleep. They had been gone a week, hunting and foraging in the woods for supplies to last the winter.

As the eldest of the town's kids, Garrick was naturally the leader. As such, his father charged him with helping to manage the town while the men were gone. That meant he was responsible for keeping the younger children in line and helping tend to the chores. Several of the cabins needed minor repairs and the perimeter of the town needed to be watched for bears and roaming packs of wolves. A lot of work, but Garrick didn't mind it. He was almost sixteen, which meant he was almost considered one of the men. Next year, when the men went out again, Garrick would be old enough to go with them.

"Where are you going?" a voice called out.

Startled, Garrick stopped and looked around. He realized quickly the voice was not directed at him. Pale candlelight flickered in the window of his friend's house. The voice belonged to Aela's mother.

"I'm going to greet father when he returns," Aela answered.

Garrick stood in the road and waited. They had planned to walk together to the top of the hill outside the town and watch for the men to return.

"It's dangerous out there," her mother said. "And the sun isn't up yet."

"I'll be fine," Aela protested. "The sun will be up soon and I'm not going alone. Garrick is waiting for me."

"Oooh," her mother said. "Go ahead, then. I don't want to hear about any kissing in the woods, though."

"Mother!" Aela screeched.

Garrick chuckled. A few years ago, he would have been disgusted at the thought of kissing a girl. That was something only adults did. Now, with manhood speedily approaching, he found that he liked looking at Aela more and more. She was younger than him, but she was blossoming into a beautiful woman. Though she was younger, she was slightly taller. He was barely above five feet and she was roughly four inches taller than him. He was dismayed when he didn't grow taller over the summer, but his father assured him that his height would come with time. Apparently, it ran in the family.

Aela stepped out of the house. The candlelight gave the appearance that she was glowing, like some otherworldly creature. She peered into the gloom. There was a gentleness to her, a softness that he had once viewed as weakness but now viewed as strangely distracting. Her hair was brown and smooth, thick enough to lose a hand in. It bounced around her shoulders with a charming ruggedness. Her eyes were a rich and clear blue, like two great lakes soaking in the world and reflecting her every mood. When her eyes showed sadness, he felt a sting in his heart. When they showed joy, his body danced on the clouds.

Her lips were big and full. Most of the boys in the town often made fun of Aela for her lips, saying that if she wanted to, she could whisper in her own ear. Garrick had no desire to taunt her when looking at her lips. He sensed their softness and found them so very inviting.

"I'll be home for lunch," Aela told her mother.

"The woods are dangerous in the dark," her mother warned, trying to dissuade her one last time.

"I'll be fine," Aela replied dismissively. Then she walked out to the road to meet Garrick.

"You're late," he said.

"I'm early," she insisted. "And I'm sleepy."

Garrick shrugged and led her with a swift pace. Despite her complaints, she kept pace with him and even passed him at one point. They left the town behind and began their ascent of the hill. Aela stopped and looked back, pointing to the sky.

"The stars," she said breathlessly.

Garrick turned to follow her gaze and smiled. Stretched across the sky were many different colored stars, all shining brightly against their black canvas. They stared in silence for a long while, neither speaking nor moving. Staring at the vastness of the sky, Garrick suddenly felt very small. The grandness of the stars overwhelmed him and though he felt small, he knew that he was a part of the vastness. A small, insignificant part, but a part nonetheless. He felt a strangeness in the atmosphere. It flooded him with heat and he vaguely felt the name "Mordum", though he didn't know why.

The sensation passed and Garrick turned to Aela. He was about to say something when he realized she was immersed in the same feeling as well. He suddenly felt very close to her, as though they were sharing a very private moment together.

He watched as she slowly drifted back to reality, the moment forever seared into Garrick's remembrance. He had a sudden urge to kiss her, but he resisted it. Barely.

"What?" she asked.

Garrick looked away, embarrassed by the feelings he had. Aela was his friend, of course, but she was a girl. Anything more than friendship was terrifying.

"Garrick?" she asked. "What's wrong?"

"Nothing," he replied abruptly. "Let's go. The sun will be up soon." He started up the hill at an intense pace, a few times even having to bend down and use his hands. He crunched through the thick layer of fallen leaves, the noise seeming louder than normal in the silence. Aela paused and watched him, confused at his abruptness. A smile found its way on her face and her cheeks began to blush. She suspected she knew the feelings Garrick was fighting. They were the same feelings she had fought earlier in the year. She had gained victory in that battle by accepting her feelings for Garrick. Every time she saw him, her stomach fluttered as though full of butterflies. She hoped he would find the same victory she had.

She caught up to him as they reached the peak of the hill. The valley below was dark and ominous, even though she had often ventured into the wooded place. The entire world seemed to be still. There were no birds chirping, no tree branches swaying, not even a hint of a breeze.

They sat down together, separated only by Garrick's confusion over his emotions. He tried hard to ignore her, but she stared at him intently which caused him to shift uncomfortably. She hid her amusement and looked away from him, down to the town behind them. She could pick her house out by the faint light in the window from the candle she had lit.

Looking back to the sky, she saw the stars were fading from sight. She could still make out some of the colors, but the odd feeling she had experienced was gone. As the sun rose, she began to see more of the town and even discern the different houses.

"They should be back today," Garrick said.

Aela hoped he was right. She missed her father when he was gone.

They sat in silence for several hours. The sun eventually brightened the world around them, making it easier to recognize their surroundings. In the valley below, Garrick could now make out the ancient trees—mostly evergreens and pines. The dew on the ground reflected the morning light in dazzling sparkles. A small stream could be seen meandering its way down into the valley and further out, further than Garrick could see. During the heat of the day, he knew he'd be tempted to strip off his clothes and go for a swim.

He saw Aela looking at him from the corner of her eyes and he turned away, blushing.

"From this height, we should spot them easily," Aela said.

Garrick was glad she wasn't staring at him openly now. He'd decided if she did it again, he would kiss her. Curse his inhibitions. He noticed movement down in the valley.

"There!" he said suddenly, pointing.

Aela looked to where he was pointing and could faintly see the men traveling through the forest. They jumped to their feet and began talking excitedly. The hunters would return with deer, elk and anything else they could catch. Garrick's patience quickly faded and he ran down the slope, trying to angle himself so that he'd intercept the returning men.

From the hilltop, the way down seemed easy and open. Going into the dense forest, Garrick quickly remembered how easy it could be to get lost. He looked back over his shoulder for Aela and saw she wasn't far behind him. He almost ran into a massive pine tree when he turned back around. As he zig-zagged through the tree line, he quickly lost Aela. They had to call out to one another for a short while in order to find each other. Then they argued for several minutes about which direction they should travel.

Being the natural leader, Garrick determined the best option would be to keep the sun at their backs since that's where it was when they were on the hilltop. Aela nodded her agreement, trusting in Garrick's instincts.

He wove his way through the thick trees, picking leaves off some of the trees as he walked. Autumn was well under way, and the leaves of the deciduous trees had already changed colors. Reds and oranges and yellows bathed everything around them. Garrick checked behind him frequently, keeping a closer eye on Aela. He picked up his pace when he heard the voices of the returning men.

Aela pushed past him suddenly, bursting into a clearing. The startled men drew their weapons, ready to defend themselves. Garrick stopped dead in his tracks and Aela screamed in surprise. The men began scolding them both, but Garrick barely heard them. Some of the men were carrying poles with animals strung on them.

His eyes went to each one, seeing a deer on one, an elk on another, and finally … his eyes widened in surprise—and fear.

—

It was mid-afternoon by the time Garrick and Aela led the procession of hunters into the town. As the townspeople saw what the men had returned with, a crowd had quickly gathered and several people began asking questions. The reactions of the people ranged from curiosity to fear.

"Is it a goblin?" asked one woman.

Some of the younger children peered at the creature while they cowered behind their parents.

"I'm not sure," answered Kadin, Garrick's father.

Garrick had seen many things living on the edge of civilization, but he had never seen anything like this creature before. He had taken up a position next to the dead creature as though he were guarding it. He inspected it for the hundredth time, taking in every detail he could.

It was humanoid, but that was where the similarity ended. Its flesh was a distinct murky green color. He had noticed over the last few hours that the color was beginning to change, slowly fading to an ashen color. Its face was shaped like that of a man, but it had two elongated canines protruding from its mouth. A thin layer of black hair covered its entire body from the neck down. And it smelled. Badly.

"It's not a goblin," a man from the crowd answered. Garrick looked up to see the old man Len. The people moved out of his way as he limped forward. He stopped a few feet from the corpse and eyed it intensely.

"It's an orc," he said finally.

People began murmuring among themselves.

"How do you know that?" Kadin asked.

"I've seen them," Len answered and pat his leg. "This limp was caused by one of them."

Garrick turned his complete attention on Len, not wanting to miss any information. Normally he ignored the old man, just like most of the townsfolk. Now, however, he had everyone's attention.

"It was years ago. Myself and a few others were out by the Viss Mountains hunting. We had come across a group of them. Ugly brutes. They attacked us and we fought back. We outnumbered them, which is the only reason I'm standing here now. They were aggressive fighters and gave us a run for our gold if you know what I mean. Anyway, before they ran off, one of them struck me with its blade. Cut a deep gash in my leg. The other hunters had to carry me home. I thought for sure I was going to bleed to death."

Garrick recognized the look on his father's face as one of doubt. As other people chimed in with their own stories—rumors of orcs and goblins in other outlying towns, someone claiming to have been captured by a giant (and other less believable things)—Garrick began to realize they were just seeking attention.

Eventually, the interest died and the crowd dispersed. In less than half an hour, everyone was back to their normal duties. Garrick, however, was not to be deterred. He searched out Aela and gathered the children of the town. He took them out to the hilltop where he and Aela had spotted the hunters earlier that morning.

"Everyone has seen the orc?" he asked.

General agreement echoed back from the kids.

"Orcs are like deer. Where there's one, there's more."

Aela flashed Garrick a questioning glance as if to say "what are you talking about"?

"I heard Len talking about them with my father after everyone left. He says that these creatures are vicious. They travel in groups and they are always looking to kill humans."

Some of the children gasped in terror and looked around as if they would hide immediately. Others set their faces in scowls, looking prepared to fight.

"Since we have one of their dead friends, I think they'll come looking for its body."

"What does that have to do with us?" asked Aela.

Garrick tried not to be irritated. He thought that out of everyone, at least she would take his side in what he was going to propose.

"The adults are too busy preparing for the winter to worry about setting up guards to watch the borders of the town. So I have decided to step up to the task myself. I will coordinate everything, but I can't do this alone. I need help. From all of you."

Garrick got mixed reactions from the kids. Some of them were eager to volunteer, but most of them wanted nothing to do with it. In the end, he had only 5 kids volunteer, not including himself and Aela. After the kids had headed back to the town, Garrick began walking the perimeter of the town, doing some math in his head. Aela walked with him, though she remained silent.

"With only seven of us, we've got limited options. One of us can work all day, but that may not work well. If they are on the north side of the city and the orcs come from the south, they would never know and the town would be overrun. I think our only option is for all of us to work every day. We'll be fairly spaced out, but it's all we can do."

"You do realize we aren't trained soldiers," Aela said.

Garrick nodded. "Yes. That's unfortunate, but we'll just have to make do with what we've got. There's an endless supply of wood around us, so we can sharpen some tree branches into spears."

Aela laughed.

Garrick stopped walking and turned to face her. She was starting to make him angry. "What is so funny?"

"You are," she answered. "You remind me of your father. Taking charge, planning everything. Have you spoken to him about this yet?"

"No," Garrick said, losing much of his confidence. "I wanted to have everything in line before I brought it to him. That way, he'd have no other option but to agree with it."

"I don't think that's how it works," she replied.

Garrick suddenly realized that they were alone. Not only that, but she was very close to him. Too close. He looked at her lips. They looked so soft, so …

"Garrick!"

He turned to see one of the kids, a boy named Kiernan, come running towards them. His pace slowed as he neared them and Garrick could see the boy was struggling to catch his breath.

"Your father is looking for you," he said. "He asked me to find you."

"Thanks for letting me know," Garrick replied. His eyes went back to Aela. She was smiling at him. "I'll see you later," he said. She nodded and he made his way back to the town. He found his father in the tavern seated with a few other adults next to the fireplace.

"Father," he said as he joined the group.

Kadin waved his hand and the other adults got up and went to another table. Garrick took one of their seats and looked his father in the eyes.

"I just heard an interesting rumor," Kadin said.

"What's that?"

"I heard you are trying to put together some guards."

The tone in his father's voice made him slump down in his chair. His father wasn't going to let him do it.

"I was going to have everything planned before I told you," Garrick said.

"That's commendable," Kadin replied, "but unnecessary. The leaders of the town have already discussed the matter. We will set the watch for the borders of the town."

"What about the things that need to be done for winter?" Garrick asked.

"We are going to take shifts. Some of us will do the work, some of us will guard the borders. We will do what we have to."

"I could—"

"No," Kadin said before Garrick could finish. "Preparing for winter is more important than playing soldier. We will likely freeze or starve to death before we'd be attacked by orcs."

Garrick bit his cheek angrily.

"I need to you help around the town like you normally do, but I need you to pick up more responsibility. With some of the adults on guard duty, we'll be shorthanded."

Garrick blinked slowly. He knew his father was wise, but he was tired of being seen as a child. He was almost a man and he wanted the adults of the town, especially his father, to see him that way. He decided he would do what his father asked without complaint. He would work extra hard and prove himself.

"Yes, father. I understand."

Kadin regarded his son thoughtfully. "Thank you. I know you likely don't agree, but I appreciate you doing it anyway."

Garrick gave a grudging nod of his head.

—

Eventually, the excitement died down. After a few weeks, with no sightings of any kind, the people of the town began to find the guard shifts unnecessary. Every day Garrick heard more and more complaints from the adults. And every day, when he asked his father for the responsibility of the watch instead of cabin repairs, the resistance in his voice faded.

Garrick had finished his work for the day and went to the tavern. When he walked in, he found his father standing at the bar talking with another of the town's leaders. They were deep in discussion when he walked up and tapped his father on the back.

Kadin turned around and smiled at his son.

"Father, I'd like to take over the watch today." He'd repeated the words so many times over the last few weeks, he'd almost gotten tired of saying them.

"Done," his father said.

Garrick's face lit up in surprise. He knew his father was becoming less resistance to the idea, but he was still shocked when his father agreed.

"Really?" Garrick asked.

"Yes, really." Kadin handed him a parchment with a crude drawing of the town on it. His father pointed to various points. "This is where we're currently keeping a watch. You should keep to these areas. The adults will no longer take shifts after today, so you are limited to whoever volunteers from the children. Make sure everyone is well armed. Speaking of," his father paused as he unwrapped something on the bar, "take this."

He handed Garrick the family sword. Garrick swelled with pride and gingerly took the sword from his father. It was old. The blade had specks of rust on it and several notches along the edges, but it was a *sword*.

"I expect a daily report from you," Kadin said sternly. He knew that his son desperately wanted to be seen as a man. If he acted as though this was not a serious matter, it would crush something in his son. He would never forgive himself if he did that.

"Yes, father." Garrick raced off to gather his "soldiers".

"Do you think that's a good idea?" the man at the bar asked.

"Why not?" Kadin answered. "He finds value in protecting others."

"I mean letting the children roam about the forest. It's dangerous out there."

"It can be. If the orcs come, they'll be safer in the woods than they will be in the town. We have no defenses. No wall to hide behind. We have more farming tools than we do weapons."

"True."

"But let's be serious. Orcs attacking the town?" Kadin snorted.

"Lest you've forgotten, we encountered a band of them while we were hunting."

"I know, but that was thirty miles from here. There've been no reports from any of the other towns about anything out of the ordinary. I think it was a chance meeting out in the wilds."

The other man shrugged.

—

The patrol began the next day, with the five volunteers, Aela, and himself walking the edges of the town's borders. While the majority of the adults stopped taking shifts, there were two teenagers, older than Garrick, who went deeper into the woods each day to do their own patrol.

Garrick knew them fairly well and knew that although the two were entrusted with the more important patrol sweep, his group was just as important. If the two caught sight of the orcs, they would rush to the border and find Garrick, who would then alert the town. Garrick knew that were that to happen, he'd be considered a hero.

He didn't take charge of the guard duties for that reason, however. He wanted to make sure everyone was safe. In order to ensure that, he needed to be in charge. He needed to be the one to make decisions, quick decisions, that would help to avoid danger to the people of the town. His spirit was soaring as he was one step closer to being considered a man.

As the days came and went, the weather began to change. Colder winds began to blow in from the south, causing the patrol to have to end earlier in the evening. One of the boys in his group was eight and his mother complained incessantly if he wasn't back before dusk. Garrick knew their time was growing short, but he didn't want to acknowledge it.

Two weeks passed by uneventfully. The patrol had dropped to three, including Aela and himself. Garrick kept at it, covering as much of the borders as he could by himself when Aela had to go home. Once Aela was no longer able to patrol with him, there would be no point and he knew his father would call upon him to start helping around the town again. Winter was almost on them and there was still much to do.

"It's time for me to get home," Kiernan said. His words broke Garrick's contemplations. He waved the boy off.

Garrick stabbed his sword forcefully into the ground.

"What's wrong?" Aela asked.

"What do you mean?" he replied.

Aela recognized the frustration in his voice, though he made an attempt to seem nonchalant. She stepped closer to him.

"Their parents are calling them home because no orcs have been seen," Aela said gently. "That's a good thing."

Garrick rolled his eyes.

"Do you disagree? Would it be better for orcs to overrun our town and likely kill everyone?" She realized immediately that she had wounded his pride. He likely hadn't thought of that, and even if he had, what could a small band of kids do to defend against orcs?

"I'm sorry, I didn't mean that what we've been doing is unimportant. It is. But maybe it is better that we patrol and find nothing. Winter is setting in. Do you know how hard it would be to defend a town that is unprepared for the cold?"

"Do you?" Garrick retorted.

"No," Aela answered without pause. "But my father does. And so does yours. They have enough to worry about without the threat of orcs."

Garrick sighed. He knew she was right, of course. She was always the sensible one. He didn't really know what he'd expected. Eventually, it would be too cold to patrol. Once the snow began to fall, it would be even less likely that orcs would come this far.

"I suppose you are right," Garrick conceded.

Aela reached out hesitantly and grabbed his chin in her hand, turning his head to face her. "You are a natural leader," she said softly. "You will do great things."

"I—"

She stopped him from speaking by covering his mouth with her hand. It was then that Garrick realized how close they were. Her face was inches from his. He was suddenly hot. He could feel his skin flush with heat. His heart started beating fast.

Aela closed the gap and moved her hand, pressing her lips against his. She *kissed* him. His eyes widened in surprise, then fear, then pleasure. He almost pushed her away. A year ago, he would have. Not now. He realized that he was ready for it now. Did she know he was ready? She must have. They'd spent the majority of the day together for the last few weeks. She knew him better than anyone else. She knew him better than he knew himself some days.

He slowly slid his arms around her and pulled her closer. She pressed against him and he could feel the curves of her body. He experienced a moment of panic. He didn't know where he should put his hands, or better yet, where he shouldn't put his hands. All he knew was that he didn't want the kiss to end and that he wanted something more, but he didn't know what that might be. He realized at that moment that he loved Aela.

That thought scared him and he broke away to catch his breath. She stared at him, smiling brightly. He stared back at her, into her eyes and the fear melted away. Garrick leaned toward her, his hands gently touching her face, and kissed her. She pushed herself against him. Their clothes were suddenly a hindrance. Garrick moved his hands from her face to her neck, caressing her soft skin, before moving down her arms and onto her hips. The kiss became less gentle and more urgent. His hand brushed the outside of her thigh and she opened her mouth, giving a soft moan. She surprised him when her tongue touched his lips. It was soft, inviting him …

And then the moment was destroyed by a horrified scream. The two broke apart, startled. Garrick turned toward the town. Smoke was rising from one of the buildings and countless forms were rushing into the town.

Orcs.

Thousands of orcs. They had finally come.

10

AN ACRID SMELL FILLED ARAMIS'S nostrils. He coughed involuntarily, trying not to breathe through his nose. Everything around him seemed to ripple, as though he were looking at a mirage from far away. It made his eyes water if he stared in one spot for too long. And everything was gray. Not that there was much to see. A barren landscape stretched endlessly before him in all directions.

There was no plant life, no trees, nothing. He thought the ground was dirt until he knelt down and grabbed a handful of it. It was a thick powdery substance. He brushed it off on his pant leg. He looked up and surveyed what he assumed was the sky. It was hard to tell the ground from the sky, for each one was the same dull gray color. Aramis didn't see any of the creatures. He found that odd, as they had been pouring through the hole above ground.

Where did they come from? He wondered.

His words echoed across the landscape. The sound startled him. He hadn't spoken the words out loud, yet they were audible. He stood in silence and eventually the echo faded. Guessing as to which way was North, he started walking. His steps caused the dusty ground to sink beneath his feet and send small clouds of the stuff into the air.

The air still smelled, but he was getting acclimated to it. He considered turning back after several minutes but quickly discarded the thought. He needed to find the source of the blight—of the creatures—and destroy it. He trudged on for what felt like hours. The sun wasn't visible, but the temperature was uncomfortably warm. He wasn't sweating though, which was a dramatic difference from the forest. The air above was humid and made him sweat between his legs, which gave him a rash.

He saw something ahead. At first, he thought it was his

imagination. But as he got closer, he realized that the tower was very real. At least a hundred of the gray-skinned creatures stood guard, an equal number on either side. He halted his approach and brought his sword up defensively. The creatures had to have seen him by now, but they weren't moving. He resumed walking toward the tower but kept his pace slow, watching the creatures intently.

The tower wasn't enormous. Aramis guessed it to be about three stories high. It was simple in design and there were windows on each level. He stopped a hundred feet from the tower. The creatures still hadn't budged.

"Come in," a heavy voice boomed from the tower.

Aramis shied back a few steps. The voice was loud and piercing. The tattoo on his arm began to burn. He rubbed it with the hilt of his sword and slowly made his way closer. In the center of the tower was a doorway with no doors. He hesitated at the threshold of the doorway for a moment, glancing to the creatures. They paid him no attention, so he stepped inside. Aramis touched the surface of one of the walls. It was made of the same gray powder as the ground, but it had been hardened and was sturdy.

A single, plain staircase wound its way upward along the wall. The frames where the windows were had no glass and was open to the air outside. Aramis followed the stairs with his eyes, but he couldn't see where they led. There was nothing else of note. He began climbing the stairs. By the time he reached the top, his legs muscles were burning fiercely. Where the stairs ended there was a small platform. He walked across the landing and through a doorway.

Aramis entered a large circular room. At the back of the room stood an upraised throne on a large dais. At the end of each armrest was a human skull. And seated on the throne was an enormous beast. Aramis felt the hairs of his neck stand on end at the sight of it. He'd never seen anything like it, not even in his nightmares.

The beast's head was that of a large cat he'd only seen pictures of. Its upper body was massive and muscular and reminded Aramis of a bull. Its arms ran down the length of the armrests and it had human hands. The lower body was feathered and its feet had talons several inches long, all of them razor sharp.

"Kneel, servant of Mordum."

The voice of the beast was deafening and shook the foundation of the tower. Despite his fear, Aramis did not bow. He merely stood staring at the dreadful thing before him. How could something like that even exist?

The beast stood up and Aramis involuntarily dropped to his knees, his sword clattered onto the floor. Its very appearance exuded a tremendous power. The beast's talons clacked against the floor as it walked toward him. It took everything he had to keep his bladder from despoiling his pants. The beast towered over him, making him feel extremely small. It lowered its head and sniffed his hair, then snorted. The beast's breath was hot and putrid.

"What has brought you to my domain? Is it time?"

"Time f-for w-what?" Aramis asked haltingly.

"Is it time for Mordum to release me onto the world? My slaves have infected the home of the druids as he commanded. Is it time now for my wrath to be poured out?"

Aramis could only shake his head in reply. The beast growled.

"Then why are you here, servant?"

Aramis couldn't speak. His mind screamed the response: *I'm here to stop the infection of the forest!* The words echoed within the tower as if he spoke them aloud. The beast laughed. It was a terrible sound and made Aramis tremble. It leaned down and sniffed at him again, longer this time. The beast's pupils turned to slits.

"You haven't submitted to the Mark yet," it said slowly. Realization must have dawned on the beast. *"Crafty mortal. Foolish mortal."*

The beast circled around Aramis, eyeing him with its feline gaze. Aramis had never even heard of such a creature. *Mind over body*, he reminded himself. If he could focus his mind, then he could control his body. He looked away from the creature and down at his sword. He hadn't even realized he'd dropped it. The creature continued to stalk around him.

The creature said he unleashed the plague on the forest.

Aramis steeled his nerves. He grabbed his sword and stood up, then turned to face the creature. He almost lost control of his mind as fear spread through his body. He knew the creature could tear him limb from limb without a second thought. He brought the blade up and stepped toward the beast, quickly swinging the blade in a horizontal strike.

The creature was faster than he expected and it back stepped the swing easily. It laughed and lashed out at him with its clawed leg. The talons cut deep gashes along his leg. Aramis cried out in pain and staggered back. He tried not to put weight on it. The tattoo on his arm itched and he watched as the gashes healed before his eyes. He turned his attention back to the creature.

"That's an interesting talent you've got. I wonder if it will reattach your head to your body?"

The creature roared savagely and came at him full speed. Aramis tried to bring his sword up, but the beast crashed into him and they tumbled to the floor. His hand slipped from the hilt of his blade and he dropped it again. The creature wrapped one of his large human hands around Aramis's neck and began squeezing.

Aramis felt his windpipe crush under the power of the creature. His eyes bulged wide from both the pain and the lack of oxygen. He experienced an intense fear as he didn't feel the power of the tattoo healing him. He desperately tried to pull the creature's hand away. It was futile. His body started to twitch spasmodically.

Your dagger.

The same subconscious voice he'd heard earlier. His vision was beginning to blur and he was having trouble understanding what was happening. Without thinking, his right hand retrieved the rusty dagger from his waist. With his last bit of energy, he tried to stab the creature in the chest. He lost all feeling in his body.

His vision went black. He couldn't hear anything. Aramis knew he was dead. Yet if he was dead, how was he still able to think? And then his mind went blank.

—

Aramis groggily opened his eyes. He lay there unsure of where he was. His head was throbbing with annoying pain. Sitting up took an enormous effort. As soon as he saw his surroundings, everything came flooding back to him. The creature that had tried to kill him was lying slumped against the wall in a pool of blood.

At least, he assumed it was blood. It wasn't red like his own. It was black. Just like the gray-skinned creatures he'd fought in the forest. He looked around, trying to determine what or who might have killed the beast. There was no evidence of anyone else having been in the room. His dagger lay next to him. It was covered in the same black blood.

He sheathed the dagger back at his waist and stood up, making a mental note that he'd need to clean the dagger when he got out from … wherever he was. His sword lay a few feet away. He wondered if he had to will the sword to disappear to make it go back to wherever he had summoned it from. He heard footsteps coming from outside the room. Several pairs of footsteps, judging by the sound. Aramis forced himself onto his feet. Other than the minor headache and feeling exhausted, he was unscathed.

Just as he picked up his sword from the floor, a group of the gray-skinned creatures entered the room. They stopped and looked from the dead creature to Aramis, then back to the creature. One of them shrieked. The sound pierced Aramis's skull painfully. He clenched his eyes shut and shook his head. When the creature stopped, Aramis realized they were all staring at him. And then he heard more footsteps, only this time they sounded like they were running.

Aramis considered his options quickly. They were coming in the door he entered, so he couldn't go that way. He could try fighting his way out, but it didn't seem likely he could defeat an army of the creatures. While he may not die, it was possible they could overpower him and keep him from escaping. Aramis didn't like the idea of spending the rest of his life as a prisoner.

He glanced around the room. There was only one option. He ran towards one of the windows and jumped. As he plummeted toward the ground, he realized he was a little higher above the ground than he thought. Apparently, the tower was higher up than it looked from outside. He landed onto the powdery ground with a grunt and narrowly avoided injuring himself with his own sword.

Most of the creatures were pouring into the tower, but some of them noticed him. They ran towards him, shrieking wildly. Aramis struggled momentarily to dismiss his blade. He had no idea what he was doing. Finally, the air hissed as the blade disappeared in a swirl of mist. He hoped he could get out of this place the way he had entered it. He sprinted in the directions he'd come from, dodging past the creatures as they neared him.

They chased after him. He looked over his shoulder and saw that the other creatures had realized he was fleeing and they began pouring out of the tower. Some of them stormed out of the doorway, and others leaped from the windows. It was a scary sight. Aramis focused on the power flowing through him from the tattoo and fell into it.

The landscape blurred around him as he ran with increased speed. The creatures were far behind him now, but they were still chasing him. As long as he could get to the portal and get out, he would be fine. He ran for several minutes before he slowed his pace and forced himself out of the tattoo's power. Looking around, he couldn't tell where the portal was that he entered from. The gray landscape all looked the same.

He felt like he was walking in circles. It wouldn't be long before the creatures caught up to him. Aramis was starting to get worried. What if he couldn't get out of this place? He growled in frustration and continued looking for anything that was different. And then he found a single leaf. He knelt down and examined it. It looked like the leaves from the forest. The portal had to be close. He looked straight up and saw a small black spot above him.

Aramis assumed it must be the portal. The grass in the forest had been black. The only problem he had now was how to reach it. It swirled about three feet above him. He wracked his brain for ideas. Not far in the distance, he could see the creatures coming.

He only had one idea. And it had to work. He summoned his sword and stabbed it into the ground. It sunk a foot deep. He shook his head, hoping it was long enough. Aramis placed one foot on the cross guard of the hilt and used it to jump into the air. His hand missed the portal by mere inches. He was so close. He did it again, trying to jump higher. Again, he missed by only a few inches. He had enough time to try once more before the creatures were on him.

He took a few steps back and got a running start, then stepped onto the cross guard and leaped into the air. The fingertips of his right hand made it into the portal. Aramis didn't know what he was touching, but he gripped it with all his might. It was soft and damp. As he hung there in the air, he guessed he was holding onto dirt or wet grass. He honestly wasn't sure which. The creatures were swarming below him, trying to grab his dangling legs.

Aramis moved his feet around, trying to stay out of their reach. He dismissed his sword so the creatures couldn't use it against him. He lifted his other arm and reached into the portal. With both hands gripped firmly, he tried to lift himself up. His arms were burning and his hands were cramping up. He considered himself to be in fit shape, but he simply couldn't lift himself. He started to laugh softly at the futility of his situation. Not much longer and he would lose his grip and fall.

He focused his mind on the tattoo. He could feel its power pulsing. He closed his eyes and tried to force his will onto the power. His mind struggled against the power as he tried to bend it to his will. Aramis wanted the strength to lift himself up. He focused only on that thought, putting everything he had into it. The tattoo began to itch. He felt a renewed feeling enter his body. He tried again to lift himself out of the portal. His progress was slow but steady.

Finally, he pulled himself completely out of the portal and threw himself onto the ground beside it. He released the power and immediately felt extremely drained. Every muscle in his body burned. He could feel his arms trembling. Looking around, he saw he had escaped back into the forest. He laughed again, this time in relief. No one would ever believe where he'd been or what he'd done. His head rolled weakly to look at the portal. He wondered when it would close.

What if it doesn't? he thought. Dread filled him as he entertained the thought. What if the portal didn't close and the creatures started coming out of it again? He had to find a way to close it; but how? He could barely move. He was utterly exhausted. He fought a losing battle to keep his eyes open.

No.

Aramis would not pass out before he closed the portal. He immersed himself into the power of the tattoo once more. It was harder this time. The power was like a river flowing away from him. He tried to catch it, but he was too slow, too sluggish. He wrestled against the impending darkness of sleep and tried to grab the power.

He felt it faintly slip through his fingers. He tried harder, using what he had left in him. He managed to get a weak hold on it. He bent the power to his will and forced it to close the portal. He felt like he was struggling with an immovable wall. The portal wouldn't budge. Aramis was losing control of the power again. He could feel it slipping from his hands.

Reaching deep inside, he grabbed hold of his own spirit and fed it into his willpower. The portal grew smaller. It was only a fraction of a movement, but it gave him the hope he needed that he could close it completely. Something latched onto his physical arm. It startled him and almost broke his concentration. He pulled more from his spirit and forced the portal closed. He heard a pain filled yelp as it shut completely. Releasing the power of the tattoo, he pulled more of his spirit and fed it into his body to give him strength.

He opened his eyes and found everything was blurred. He blinked several times until his surroundings came into focus. He still felt weak. And he felt … different. It wasn't a bad feeling, but it wasn't good either. He felt almost as if he were missing something. Some part of him on the inside. He shrugged the feeling away and forced himself to get up. He could rest later. Glancing around the clearing, he didn't see Kaldrick or the druids. They had probably gone back to the village.

Aramis looked to where the portal had been. The grass was a dull gray color. Laying in the center of the circle was part of one of the creature's arms. One of them had almost escaped before he closed it. He rubbed his face tiredly and made his way to the trail that led to the druid village. He couldn't wait to get some sleep.

11

ADAMAR STOOD IN FRONT OF his bedroom window, staring out at the sprawling city of Oakhaven. He was feeling good today despite the previous night's mishap. Watching the people below go about their daily lives, he told himself that they were beginning to love him.

He'd been hard on everyone initially, but for good reason. They were used to the weakness of his father. The man had essentially let the nobles run the kingdom. They needed to see that he was not weak like his father. And so he had been forceful with many of the nobles to show his dominance.

He didn't turn around when he heard the servants enter his chamber. They were there to set up his extravagant breakfast. Now that he was king, he dined on sumptuous food, had more gold than he could spend, and lived in a magnificent castle. He had Mordum's favor, his enemies feared him, and soon his god would bless him with the Mark. All he needed now was a wife, and he already had someone in mind.

Turning from the window, he walked over to the table the servants had set. Plump grapes—both green and purple—several different kinds of cheese, and fresh bread were all arranged in a neat pattern. Grabbing a few of the grapes, which had conveniently been pulled from the stems already, he popped them into his mouth. As he chewed them, he found they were very juicy and sweet with only a slight tang.

In the corner of his eye, he could see one of his templar guards standing in the shadows near the door. He motioned to the table.

"Hungry?"

The man shook his head. Adamar shrugged and ate a few more grapes. At first, he'd thought it odd that his guards rarely spoke, but as the years had passed he had gotten used to it. They'd been his guards since the day he accepted Mordum's offer. He shook his head thinking back on that day. It seemed like ages had passed since then, and at the same time, it felt like it was only a few days ago.

Pouring himself a glass of sweet honey wine, he sniffed the expensive liquid and enjoyed the taste on his tongue after he drank some. Walking back over to the window, he continued gazing out at the city as he sipped the wine. A servant came in and laid his clothes out on the bed before quietly excusing herself. He finished off the wine and then changed his clothes.

Grabbing a robe from the closet, Adamar draped it over his clothes. It was white trimmed in gold. And it was long, almost brushing the floor. In the center, where his back was, the Oaktree symbol of his kingdom was stitched in a vibrant blue. He checked his appearance in a mirror and then left the room, striding through the hall.

Servants and soldiers alike averted their eyes as they passed him. He smirked. Whether it was out of reverence for him or fear of his guards, he didn't know. Either way, they were honoring Mordum whether they knew it or not. He left the main keep and turned his direction toward the home of one of the nobles. As he got close, he was greeted by servants. They threw rose petals on the ground in front of him as he walked. The nobleman met him at the edge of the property.

"King Adamar!" he hailed as he bowed low.

"Lord Bavol," Adamar returned.

"I see you've come to call on me?"

"Of a sort," Adamar said. "I've come to talk to you about your daughter."

Bavol's face, for just a split second, betrayed him. Adamar made a mental note of it for later.

"My daughter?" Bavol asked, smiling widely.

"Yes. I am in need of a wife, and I have seen her around the court. She is a beautiful creature. She hasn't been promised to anyone, has she?"

"Uh, no. No, my lord, she hasn't."

Adamar smiled. "Good. Is the lady home?"

"I'm afraid not, m'Lord. She's out gallivanting as women do. I'm sure you know what I mean. Anyway, I will let her know you came to see her."

Adamar nodded, studying the man. He decided he didn't like the man. He'd need to be replaced, preferably with someone more willing to hide his emotions. Yes, he would definitely need to be replaced.

"I expect to be married at the end of the week," Adamar informed him. "An escort will be here then to bring her to the castle."

Bavol bowed low in subservience. Adamar eyed the nobleman's property and then turned and left.

—

After Adamar left, Lord Bavol glanced down both directions of the street and retreated into his home. He ordered the servants to start packing up the house. When they stared at him in confusion, he waved them off.

"Hannah!" he called out. "Hannah!"

His daughter came down the stairs from the second floor.

"Yes, father?"

"It's time," he said.

Her face and shoulders slumped.

"Now?"

"Immediately," he answered. "Adamar came calling for you. I told him you weren't here, but he's made his intent to take you as his wife quite clear."

"Has there been any word from Aramis?" she asked hopefully.

"Not yet," he answered.

"It's been months," she said, her words hinting at what they both feared.

"I know, but do not worry about such things. We have to get somewhere safe."

She nodded and ran back up the stairs.

Bavol called for a servant. He had the woman pen a letter, dictating to her what he wanted it to say. He would have written it himself, but he was too nervous to keep his hands steady. After the letter was finished, he called for a runner.

"Take this letter to the king of Talvaard," he instructed.

"My lord?" the man asked.

"You heard me. Guard this letter with your life. You must deliver it to the king himself. I do not expect a reply, but if he gives you one, don't bring it here. Go to the cabin. You remember where it is?"

The man nodded.

"Good. We'll be there until I feel it is safe enough to come back here. I cannot stress enough the importance of this letter's delivery."

"I will deliver it," the man answered.

"Do not fail," Bavol said.

The man bowed low, tucked the letter in his shirt, and sprinted off.

"For the sake of the kingdom, do not fail," Bavol whispered to himself.

—

Adamar was interrupted by a knock on his door later that night. In the middle of undressing, he waved to the guard by the door. He opened it and a soldier entered and bowed low.

"What is it?" Adamar asked though he was certain he knew the answer.

"Lord Bavol has left the city."

Adamar snorted.

"Coward. No matter. Are they being followed?"

"Yes, my lord. His daughter is also with him."

"And a liar. Lord Bavol is a disgrace to this kingdom. He will have to be dealt with."

"Your orders, my lord?"

"Nothing for now. Inform me as soon as you discover where he's going."

The soldier bowed again and left.

"Why do men run from their fate?" he asked aloud.

As expected, neither of his guards answered. Pushing the thought from his mind, he made his way over to the bed.

"What do you think?" he asked.

The sheets moved and two women looked up at him questioningly.

"Why do men run from their fate?" he repeated.

"Perhaps they can't … handle it," one of them said seductively, arching her brow.

Adamar smiled at her.

"Can you handle it?" he asked as he climbed into the bed.

"Let's find out," she purred.

12

"I'M SORRY TO HEAR THAT," Kelvin said quietly. "I never knew any of that."

Garrick nodded. "It was a long time ago."

"You still haven't told me how you got the Mark."

"I'm leading up to it. Once I saw the orcs pouring into the city, I could only think of one thing."

—

Aela screamed and sprinted down the hill toward the town. Garrick would have stopped her, but he was frozen with fear. His mind told him to do something, but he didn't know what to do. He had never been in battle. He'd never even seen a battle.

Somehow he gained control of his mind and followed Aela's path down the hill. Halfway down a large orc intercepted him. The ugly creature raised a crudely made spear. Garrick tried to slow his pace and almost tripped. He lifted the sword his father had given him and rolled his wrist, causing the blade to move in a circular motion and knock the spear out wide.

As Garrick ran past the orc, he swung the sword up and around, turning himself in a complete circle, and slammed the blade against the orc's head. The creature jerked awkwardly and slumped to the ground. Garrick was surprised how easy it was to kill the thing. He continued running down the hill and into the town. Chaos was everywhere. Many of the townspeople were dead, lying broken and bloody in the streets.

Garrick looked frantically for his parents. He ran to a spot between two houses, slipped into the small space, and peered around the corners. There were no defenses, so the orcs had taken the entire town before the people were even aware of what happened. Sounds of fighting drew his attention and he saw his father and several others had formed a defensive ring around some of the women and children.

They were surrounded by orcs. Garrick almost considered joining them, but he knew it was a lost cause. The orcs were making short work of the men. Garrick watched in horror as one of the orcs stabbed forward with a spear, striking his father in the chest. Blood poured freely from the wound when the orc pulled the spear back.

Garrick turned his head, not wanting to believe what he saw. Soon after, the screams of the women and children filled the air and he knew that the men had fallen. He needed to escape the town, but he also wanted to find Aela. She was likely dead, but he had to hope for something good. He made his way cautiously through the town, running and ducking into hiding spots wherever he could.

As he neared Aela's home, he recognized the shouting of her mother's voice. Hope filled him and he ran to the house, only to find three orcs ripping Aela's mother to pieces. He gagged as one of them ripped her arm off. He turned to flee and saw Aela struggling against a pair of orcs. Fighting to ignore his fear, he ran over to help her. Before he could reach her, one of the orcs grabbed her by the hair, jerked her head back, and stabbed her in the throat with a wicked looking dagger.

"No!" he screamed.

The orcs turned their attention toward him. They ran at him, hollering something in their guttural language he didn't understand. His parents were dead, and now his friend. What else did he have in the world to live for? He wanted to throw his sword down and let them kill him. He wanted to die.

But his instinct for self-preservation wouldn't allow him to. Garrick brought his sword up and tried to knock away their spears. He'd never been trained with a sword though, and his attempts were weak. The orcs quickly outmaneuvered him and one of them struck him in the face with the butt of his spear.

Garrick reeled backward and landed on his back. He could feel the warm flow of blood pouring from his nose. His vision was blurred from the tears in his eyes. He blinked rapidly, trying to clear them. His hands scrabbled around desperately trying to find the hilt of his sword, but it eluded him. His hand came to rest on a rock, and he gripped it tightly.

One of the orcs stepped over him and leaned down. Its foul breath reminded him of a long-dead animal he had once encountered in the woods. Drops of saliva dripped from its mouth, landing on his neck. He gritted his teeth and swung as hard as he could. The rock in his hand connected solidly with the orc's temple. A loud *crack* sounded and the orc staggered back, howling in pain and outrage. Garrick scrambled to his feet and saw his sword. It was at the feet of the second orc, who was coming right at him.

Garrick grabbed the first orc's spear and swung wildly, smacking the orc in the head and neck several times. The creature growled at him. Garrick realized he was probably annoying it more than he was hurting it. He tried to stab the tip of the spear into the orc, but it was wearing what appeared to be armor made of bone. It kept the spear tip from doing any damage.

The orc grabbed hold of the spear and yanked it from him. Garrick let go of the weapon and sprinted past the creature, sweeping the sword up quickly. The first orc had recovered from his hit and was also coming at him now. Garrick's nose was still bleeding and he was starting to feel lightheaded. It was an odd feeling. He shook his head, hoping to stop his sight from fading. He had nothing left to lose.

He charged the two orcs, hacking and slashing haphazardly. They didn't seem too worried about him and didn't put up much of a defense. He was quickly losing his strength and energy. Changing tactics, he swung the sword low and tried to take out their legs. He struck one of them hard, but the dull blade didn't even break the skin. It still caused a considerable amount of pain, for the orc howled in agony. The other orc circled around behind Garrick. He was trapped between the two creatures with nowhere to go.

Something inside—some instinct—told him to drop down. He threw himself to the ground immediately. Above him, a spear from one orc struck the other. Where Garrick lacked the strength to penetrate the orc's bone armor, the first orc's force was enough to not only puncture it but also to stab straight through the second orc's flesh and out its back.

The creature dropped to the ground, dead. The other orc shouted something that Garrick assumed was a curse. The orc kicked him hard in the back. Garrick slammed into the ground face first. He grunted from the impact and rolled onto his back. The orc had its dagger gripped tightly and lunged toward him. Without thinking, Garrick raised up his sword. He missed the creature's chest and abdomen, but the orc's groin became impaled on the blade.

An unearthly cry of pain filled the air that made Garrick shudder. The fight was gone from the creature as it held itself and dropped to its knees. Garrick wanted to flee, but he knew it would be foolish to leave without his blade. He risked a look around. The entire town was ablaze. Dead bodies, both orc and human, littered the ground. The screams had all but stopped completely. No other orcs had noticed him yet, but he knew it was only a matter of time.

He kicked the orc in the face and felt the crunch of bone beneath his foot. The creature fell onto its back and Garrick grabbed the hilt of his sword and yanked the blade free. To his surprise, the orc was still alive. He considered killing the creature but instead started running for the tree line. He made it without being seen, at least as far as he knew.

As he ran, he ripped a piece of cloth from his shirt, rolled it up and stuffed it into his nostrils. He ran until the town was far behind him and his legs threatened to give out, then he stopped his frantic pace and slowed to a walk, continuously looking over his shoulder to see if he had been followed. He was exhausted. And thirsty. Those needs tugged at the edge of his mind, but they were kept at bay by the burning of his lungs and muscles.

His breath came in short, quick gasps. He was drenched in sweat and could feel it dripping down his skin. The sun was beginning to descend. Somehow he was aware of the fact that night was approaching and he needed to find shelter. He needed water too. Ahead, he thought he saw the outline of a cave among the trees. He angled his steps toward it and collapsed at the entrance.

It wasn't a cave at all. It was a door. He laid down on the soft ground and stared at the huge wooden door. He was going to pass out. He could feel it coming. His vision began swimming. The last thing he remembered before he fell into darkness was a large cross. Upside down.

—

Garrick awoke with a pounding headache.

He lay still for a moment, trying to figure out where he was. Shafts of starlight peeked down at him through the foliage above. Shakily, he rose to his feet. A massive wooden door stood before him. It seemed to cover the entrance of a cave and was hidden by the surrounding trees. Two torches, placed on either side of the door, burned low.

He looked back and tried to remember how he got there. In a whirlwind, it all came back to him. He vomited. Somewhat. There wasn't much to come up. Garrick became acutely aware of his hunger and thirst. Seeing no other options, he knocked on the door. It was sturdy and his knock barely made a sound. He knocked harder, pounding his fist on the wood as hard as he could. Throbbing pain filled his hand. He was about to kick the door when it opened suddenly. Not all the way. Just a crack. Enough that he was able to push it open.

Thoughts of his ransacked town and dead parents could not hold his mind as he crossed the threshold from the forest into a grand entrance hall. He gaped in disbelief.

The hall was enormous. Torches spaced the wall at regular intervals, providing enough light to see the splendor around him. High above, the ceiling was shrouded in darkness. He had never seen anything so spacious in his life. The effort to create such a wonder boggled his imagination.

Magnificent tapestries lined the walls between the torches, depicting scenes of battles between armored knights—some in silver, others in black. The details woven into the fabric were staggering. Hundreds of colors captured his eyes, unfurling stories he had never heard. Racks of weapons and suits of armor were placed below the torches, the light seeming to dance off their metal surfaces.

Garrick walked slowly down the hall, his attention diverted in every direction. At the end of the hall was a huge rectangular table. His house was smaller than the table was long, making him wonder who had taken the time to craft it. Certainly, no mortal hands had any part of it.

At the very end of the table stood a tall chair. As he walked nearer, he realized there was a figure sitting in it.

"I'm sorry for coming in uninvited," Garrick said. "My town was attacked by orcs …" his voice, and his emotions cracked.

"What is your name?" the figure asked. The voice was masculine and deep, echoing through the hall.

"G-Garrick," he answered.

"Garrick. Do you know what your name means?"

Garrick shook his head mutely.

"It means 'one who rules by the spear'. You said your town was attacked. Where are the survivors?"

"I think I'm the only one," he said. His throat was dry and he was nervous. He couldn't see the figure's face, only a shadowy form.

"You are strong. I feel it in the air. It radiates from you. Do you want vengeance upon those who have destroyed your town?"

The question took Garrick by surprise. Did he want vengeance? He struggled with the answer. To deal out punishment on the orcs who killed his parents, his precious Aela. What would it accomplish? Would he feel any less dead inside? He didn't know the answer. He struggled in silence for a long while. The figure waited patiently.

"No, I do not want revenge." He finally said.

"Hm."

"I want the power to keep it from happening to anyone else."

"I can give you power," the figure said. "And you can use it as you will. There is only one thing I require in exchange."

Garrick tilted his head questioningly.

"When I call upon you, you shall answer. And you shall carry out whatever task I give you."

"What will you ask of me?" Garrick questioned.

"That is not for you to think upon. I offer the power you seek. What is your answer?"

"I will do it," Garrick answered.

"Come, kneel before me."

Garrick did as he was instructed. Even as close as he was, he still could not see the figure's appearance.

"Swear your loyalty to me."

Garrick hesitated for a moment, then said, "I am loyal to you."

"Stretch forth your arm," the figure commanded.

Garrick lifted his right arm.

"No, your left arm."

Garrick switched arms and held his left arm out. The figure grabbed hold of him and an intense cold shot through his arm. He groaned softly and the pain seemed to intensify. The middle of his forearm began to burn, but the rest of his arm remained freezing.

The figure let go of him and the cold diminished, but the burning on his forearm remained. He pulled it back and looked at his skin in the torchlight. A cross, upside down and black as night, marred his flesh. He looked up at the figure questioningly.

"You now bear the Mark."

"What mark is it?" Garrick asked.

"The Mark of Mordum."

"Who is Mordum?"

The torches flickered and went out, leaving Garrick in darkness.

"I am," the figure answered.

The torches flared back to life and the figure was gone.

Garrick wondered if he had made the right decision.

—

"I don't know what to say," Kelvin said quietly, his tone somber.

"You don't have to say anything," Garrick replied. "Just know that not every man is what he seems on the outside."

Kelvin nodded mutely. A long while passed before either of them spoke again. "What happened after you received the Mark?"

Garrick rubbed his hands over his face, stopping briefly to scratch the skin beside his ear. "I left the place. I later learned that it was one of Mordum's abandoned temples. There was more food and water than I could ever consume there, but it was lonely. I stayed for a few days, then traveled west. My hometown was on the fringes of the kingdom, far from the larger towns of Talvaard. I walked for days before ending up on the steps on some nobleman's house.

"He was a good man, though. Took me in and cleaned me up. I told him what happened to my town. He wasn't surprised. Apparently, several other towns on the edge of the kingdom had experienced similar fates. What few survivors came through repeated the same story. He sent word to a friend of his that served as a general under the king at the time. The general took a legion out to investigate. They tracked down some of the orcs and slaughtered them. He also offered to help rebuild the towns that had been destroyed, but the king refused to finance it."

Kelvin shook his head in disbelief.

"I hated him for it. I don't now, but I did then. I guess I had to blame someone for what happened. Although I had the Mark, I didn't know what it did or how to use it. I joined the king's army to learn how to use a blade and one of the generals took an interest in me. He mentored me and taught me everything I know about war." Garrick smiled fondly at the memories.

"Sir," Kelvin said.

"I told you to call me Garrick."

"Sir," Kelvin repeated, his tone more urgent. "Look!"

Garrick turned to where Kelvin was pointing and saw a large formation of elves coming toward them. There were too many to count, but Garrick guessed there were at least a hundred.

"They are moving too fast for us to make a run for it," Garrick said.

"Where would we go? We're surrounded by desert for miles."

"True," Garrick replied. He stood up and brushed the sand from his pants. He looked back to Kelvin. "There's only one option," he said. "We have to fight."

Kelvin stood up and nodded.

They both summoned their armor. The air hissed loudly. Garrick summoned his blade and looked at Kelvin's silver armor, glinting radiantly in the bright sun. He turned his gaze back to the approaching elves.

"Who would have ever thought?" he asked.

"Ever thought what?"

"That a templar of Mordum and a priest of Zevea would ever be fighting together instead of themselves?" he said with a laugh. When he didn't hear Kelvin say anything, he looked over at him just in time to see the pommel of Kelvin's sword coming straight for his face.

The blow struck him hard and he dropped to his knees, the world spinning around him. He wanted to say something, but his mouth didn't work. He looked at Kelvin through watery eyes.

Kelvin's face was impassive, unreadable.

"I'm sorry," he said.

Garrick scrunched his face in confusion. Kelvin struck him again and he fell unconscious into the sand.

Kelvin knelt beside him and tried to ignore the sounds of the elves coming. He closed his eyes, placed his hand on Garrick's chest, and began to pray.

13

ARAMIS WALKED INTO THE VILLAGE tiredly and looked for the druid he had spoken with. He saw several people but didn't recognize any of them. Making his way to the center of the village, he saw Kaldrick. The man hadn't noticed him yet. He was talking with one of the druids. He also had a travel sack strapped to his back. As he neared the two men, Kaldrick noticed him.

"My Lord?" he asked, several emotions shadowing his face.

Aramis raised a hand in greeting, too tired to speak.

Kaldrick wrapped him in a strong hug. Aramis didn't try to fight him off. He was too exhausted. Kaldrick released him and looked him over.

"You look rough," he said with a grin.

Aramis looked to the druid. "The creature that caused the plague has been killed," he said.

The druid stood silent for a moment. "I am not one to take pleasure in death, but this news does indeed lift my spirits. How did you kill it?"

Aramis honestly didn't know. Everything was hazy. "I'm not sure," he answered. "I have never seen anything like it before. It seemed to be made up of a few different animals."

The druid's eyes widened. "Can you describe it to me?"

"It had the head of a large cat, the body of a bull and the feet of a bird."

"A chimera," the druid breathed. "You defeated a chimera? Alone?"

Aramis shrugged. "I can't remember what happened," he sighed. "I hate to be rude, but I am in desperate need of some rest."

"Of course," the druid replied. "My apologies. Come with me. You can sleep at my house."

Aramis and Kaldrick followed the druid.

"What's the bag for?" Aramis asked Kaldrick.

"I'm sorry, my Lord. When you didn't return, I feared you were …" he trailed off. "I was getting ready to leave."

Aramis's confusion was evident on his face. "I've only been gone a few hours," he said.

"You've been gone a full week to the day," the druid chimed in.

Aramis's mind reeled in shock. "A week?" How had he been gone that long? It certainly didn't feel like it. Perhaps that was why he was so tired. He followed in silence, digesting the information. The druid led them to his home, the same place Aramis had been to earlier. He allowed Aramis to rest in his bed and left him alone with Kaldrick.

"I am glad to see you, my Lord."

Aramis smiled tiredly and nodded. "I am glad to see you as well. I feared that I would never escape that place." He closed his eyes. The druid's bed was very comfortable.

"What happened?"

When Aramis didn't answer, Kaldrick realized he was asleep. He turned and quietly left the room.

—

He opened his eyes. Confusion overwhelmed him as he didn't recognize anything around him. He had fallen asleep in the druid's home, yet he was lying on a cold stone floor. He sat up and inspected his surroundings. He was either in a castle or a dungeon. The ceiling, walls, and floor were all made of the same smooth stone.

Pushing himself up off the floor, Aramis realized his hands were covered in dirt. He brushed them off on his pants and noticed the entire floor was covered in a thick layer of dust. There were no footprints or anything else indicating anyone had brought him here or that he had made his own way into the room. The outline of where his body lay was the only spot not covered with dust.

Aramis didn't find anything of interest in the room. He left through the only doorway and wandered along the halls. There were no torches or light of any kind, yet he was able to see decently well. He passed by a few rooms that were similar to the one he woke up in. Those rooms, as well as the hallways, also had a layer of dust covering the floors. That gave Aramis the idea that no one had been in the place in a very long time.

The end of the hall split left and right. Aramis paused, not sure which direction he should go first. He started to go right. The tattoo on his arm began to itch. He stopped and changed direction. He followed the hall until it ended. Two large wooden doors stood closed before him. He pushed one and struggled with it for a few moments before it creaked open. He checked the hinges and saw they were rusted from disuse.

He stepped into the room and stared in surprise. Ghostly figures were everywhere. Some sat at long tables looking through papers and writing, others were walking from one table to another, conversing with other people. They were all dressed in the same clothing, white hooded robes with blue sashes around their waists. On the right side of the chest was a symbol stitched into the material: a sun with outstretched wings.

Aramis had never seen it before. At the back of the room stood a man with his hands behind his back. He was dressed the same as the others, but the symbol on his chest was different. It was two swords crossed over each other. He didn't recognize that one either. He wondered what he was seeing. He could see the mouths of the people moving, but he didn't hear any words.

His tattoo was burning strongly. He rubbed at it and walked further into the room. The people reminded him of the priests of Edria, though none of them wore her symbol.

"What are you doing here?"

The voice startled him and he turned to see the man at the back of the room looking at him.

"I don't know," Aramis answered. "What is this place?"

The man ignored the question and continued to stare at him. Aramis walked through the room and came to stand before the man.

"I don't know how I got here. What is this place? Who are you people?"

"You are supposed to be guarding the body."

Aramis frowned. "What?"

Another figure stepped up beside him and Aramis realized the apparition wasn't talking to him, but to the other ghost.

"My apologies, Prophet. I left the body in the hands of capable men until I return. He has yet to move. I believe he is completely immobilized, if not dead."

"Explain to me how the God of the Dead could possibly be dead himself?"

Aramis realized they were talking about Mordum.

"I am not in familiar territory, so I apologize for any presumptions I make."

The Prophet sighed. "No, I must apologize to you. I am weary. This war has exhausted us all, and now that we are close to victory, I am struggling to ensure the safety of the world. It is a heavy burden."

"I can't imagine," the other priest replied. "I take no offense at your words. Have the others found the answer yet?" The priest turned to regard the others working at the tables.

"Not yet," the Prophet answered. "Tael has told me that the answer lies in one of these manuscripts. I fear time is against us, however. The longer it takes to find the answer, the more opportunity Mordum has to break the spell."

Aramis recognized the name Tael, but he couldn't remember where he'd heard it before.

"I understand. I will return to my post. I merely wanted to know how the search was going." The priest left and the room became quiet again. Aramis went over to one of the tables and looked at the papers that littered the surface. They were covered in writing, but he couldn't read the script. He assumed it was another language.

"I think I've found something!" one of the priests shouted. He was sitting at one of the further tables.

"Bring it to me," the Prophet said.

The priest scrambled up from the table and ran to the Prophet, a single parchment in his hand. He handed it to the Prophet. Aramis walked over to them and looked at it over the Prophet's shoulder. Again, he didn't recognize the language that flowed across it, but he did recognize a symbol on it. The black cross of Mordum was penned at the top.

"Is this it? Is this what we've been looking for?" the priest asked.

"I believe it is," the Prophet answered, relief evident in his voice.

A ragged cheer rang out from the other priests in the room.

"What do we need to start with?" the priest asked.

The Prophet's eyes scanned back and forth over the text. "We must burn his body."

"That seems easy enough."

"Not quite. We must burn his body on his own altar using wood from the sacred trees of Tylhem Forest. Then his bones must be separated from the ashes using a Holy Blade. The bones and the ashes need to be kept away from one another."

"We will begin the preparations now. Where should we send his bones?"

The Prophet seemed to consider the question for a long while. "Take the bones to Red Mountain in the Deadlands. We will entrust them to the wizard. As for the ashes …" Aramis tried to hear the next part, but everything began to fade from his vision.

His eyes opened and he found himself back in the home of the druid.

—

"I know what Mordum's followers want from the Deadlands," Aramis said as he practically ran into the druid. He wasn't sure how long he'd slept, but it didn't seem long. The sun had yet to set and the people were still going about their normal duties.

"I wondered if you would ever wake," the druid replied with a friendly smile.

"What do you mean?" Aramis asked.

"You slept through the remainder of yesterday, all through the night, and most of today."

"I did?" Aramis was shocked. He certainly felt rested, but he didn't feel like he'd spent that much time sleeping.

"You did," the druid confirmed. "But you mentioned something about Mordum?"

"Yes. I had a dream or a vision. I'm not sure which. What I saw, if it was real, explains a few things. What do you know about Mordum?"

The druid shrugged. "As much as anyone else, I suppose. He is the God of the Dead. His followers are very powerful. Or insane. Or both."

"Has he ever walked the earth as a man?"

"Ah," the druid nodded, "you are referring to the Dead Epoch?"

"The what?" Aramis wasn't sure if the druid had asked a question or was stating a fact.

"The Dead Epoch. Historians say it was a dark time for the world. They say Mordum walked the earth in the form of a mortal man. His armies came close to devouring the entire world. The other gods stepped in and gave man what they needed to stop him."

Aramis had never heard that before. He'd heard of the Lord Aio several years ago, but that religion had all but vanished, especially after the Five Islands were destroyed by Orlek. It was said of the Lord Aio that he was a god who came and walked among men as well.

"That seems to match what I saw," Aramis said. "There were men who looked like priests. Two of them had a conversation about

Mordum's body. They stopped him somehow, and they were trying to find a way to banish him. They needed to burn the body using wood from your sacred trees."

The druid's face lit up with interest. "That would explain why he targeted our forest."

"Yes. They separated his bones from his ashes and the bones were sent to the Red Mountain in the Deadlands."

"That's north of here," the druid said. "What about the ashes?"

"I don't know," Aramis lost some of his excitement. "The vision faded before I could hear where they might be."

The druid stroked his goatee. "It's whispered a powerful wizard lives on Red Mountain. I don't know if there is any truth to it or not."

"The men in my vision mentioned a wizard," Aramis said. "How long ago was the Dead Epoch?"

"Hundreds of years," the druid replied, shaking his head. "I don't know the exact amount."

"How could a person, even a wizard, live that long?"

The druid merely shrugged again. "Magic can prolong one's life, but there's no telling how long. Death is inevitable for even the most powerful."

"I need to leave immediately," Aramis said, the excitement coming back into his voice. "Where is Kaldrick?"

"He went to the stream to get some water."

"I appreciate you taking care of him. And thank you for your hospitality. I'm in your debt."

"Nonsense," the druid said. "You killed the creature that brought the plague on our home. Even now I feel its foulness fading. If anything, we are indebted to you. If you ever need anything, call on us."

"I may soon call on you to honor your word."

"Please do. In the meantime, take whatever supplies you need for your journey." They clasped hands and shook, then Aramis turned and left to find Kaldrick. It didn't take long to find him. He was returning from the stream and they met at the wooden bridge.

"It's good to see you alive," Kaldrick said.

"It's good to feel alive," Aramis replied. "We need to leave immediately. We've got to get to Red Mountain before Mordum's followers do."

"I'm waiting on you," Kaldrick laughed.

They filled two packs until they were bursting at the seams with food. The druids gave them fresh bread, fruits, cheese and some strips of venison. Aramis was eager to get moving, so they expressed their thanks to the druids and left just as the sun was setting. They lit torches and walked all through the night. They stopped for a short time in the morning so Kaldrick could take a nap and then they continued on, Aramis leading the way with determination.

He was glad that Kaldrick didn't complain about the pace he set. After all, they had been through, Aramis knew it would probably have done them both some good to rest a few days. Something inside told him to keep moving, though. He didn't know why, but he felt the need to get to Red Mountain as quickly as he could. Perhaps Mordum's followers were on their way there just as he was.

"I have a question," Kaldrick asked as they trekked through the forest.

"Ask away," Aramis replied. He wiped sweat from his brow with the back of his hand. He couldn't understand how the druids lived in the forest, especially not with their thick robes. Aramis felt like he would die from sweating and he wasn't even wearing armor.

"When we were fighting those creatures, I saw you fall. I thought those creatures had killed you. There was blood everywhere. And then … you got up and you had a sword. You don't have a scratch on you. You slaughtered those creatures easily. How? Where are your battle wounds? And where is the sword you had?"

Aramis wasn't surprised by the questions. He had a few of his own. The problem was he had no one to get answers from.

"I thought I was dying," he began slowly, trying to recollect the details. "I was buried under those creatures and I could feel them ripping my skin off." He shuddered as he remembered the feeling.

"It's a little foggy after that. All I remember is I opened my eyes and felt the hilt of a blade in my hand. This," Aramis pointed to the tattoo on his arm, "has connected me to a power that I can't explain. It heals me when I get injured. And it allowed me to … create a sword? I'm not sure how it works."

"So you are like a god?" Kaldrick asked curiously.

"Far from it," Aramis replied acidly. The words came out sounding hateful. "Sorry," he said. "I don't mean to be rude. It's just … it feels like I am nothing more than a pawn on a chess board and some god is controlling my future."

"We may indeed be pawns to higher powers, but that doesn't mean we don't make our own choices. They may be able to influence us, but ultimately we make our own way."

"True," Aramis agreed.

"Can you make the blade appear only when you are in trouble? Or can you make it appear on command?"

"That's a good question," Aramis said. He was curious himself. He stopped walking and focused on the power flowing through his tattoo. He summoned the blade. The air hissed and mist formed around his hand. Within seconds, the blade had fully formed.

"Now that," Kaldrick breathed, "is amazing."

Aramis nodded in agreement. He dismissed the blade and the air hissed as it disappeared. "That's good to know," he said. "I *can* summon and dismiss it on command." He continued walking.

"What about the creature you saw in the portal? How did you kill it?"

"I don't know. It was massive, bigger than anything I've ever seen."

"Bigger than a phiebus?"

"Much bigger," Aramis said. "I've never felt fear so intensely before. It crushed my neck with one hand." His hands instinctively went to his neck, feeling for any defects that might not have been healed. His skin was flawless. "I can't remember anything after that. When I came to, the creature was dead in a pool of blood. My dagger had some blood on it, but I don't know how I could have killed it. The dagger is old and rusted. It's not even that sharp."

"Maybe your tattoo power helped?"

"Maybe," Aramis said. He was unconvinced. Something wasn't right about that encounter, but he had no idea what.

"I wonder what the desert is like," Kaldrick asked, changing the subject.

"We're about to find out," Aramis answered.

After two days, they reached the end of the forest. Flat grassland stretched out before them. A full day of travel and they began to see patches of sand. They rested for the night and continued on early in the morning. The Deadlands was unlike any place either of them had ever been.

—

Two rough, terrible weeks later they reached what was unmistakably Red Mountain. They had run out of water only a few days into the trek and had quickly learned that it was better to travel at night than during the day. It was much cooler and allowed them to travel faster and farther without the danger of overheating. During one night, they had stumbled upon a small rocky expanse. The smooth flat rocks had water sitting on them. It had been warm and had an odd taste, but they drank it anyway. They had lost two days as they stayed there long enough to recuperate. It took four days from there to finally reach Red Mountain.

"We're here," Kaldrick said, his voice a little coarse. "We finally made it."

"And yet we've only just begun," Aramis said. They gazed up at the mountain top. He could faintly see the outline of a building. "We've got the climb to the top."

The mountain rose up from the desert landscape, tall and almost completely vertical.

"Great," Kaldrick said, heaving a sigh. "Let's get this over with."

Aramis scratched his jaw and eyed the cliffs of the mountain. The stubble growing on his face was starting to irritate him. He'd thought about summoning his blade to shave, but he didn't want to risk cutting his face in the middle of the desert.

"This isn't going to be easy," he remarked. "There doesn't appear to be any handholds."

Kaldrick's response was a muted grunt.

Aramis studied the mountainside, eyeing everything that resembled a crevice in an attempt to determine the best area to scale up. Deciding on his course, he stepped up to the cliff and gripped the stone with his hands. As he was about to lodge his foot into a small fissure, he heard a voice that didn't belong to Kaldrick. He turned to look and was greeted by the sight of a dozen men—all shirtless— with spears leveled at them both.

One of the men, the one who Aramis assumed had first spoken, said something in a language he didn't understand and thrust the spear forward menacingly. Aramis let go of the cliff face and put his hands up nonthreateningly. The man said something else and motioned with his spear toward Kaldrick.

"I don't understand," Aramis said, shrugging his shoulders. He tried to make his facial expression look confused.

The man repeated himself and when Aramis just stood there, one of the other men grabbed him and roughly shoved him over beside Kaldrick. The armed men started talking to one another, pointing at Aramis sporadically. At one point it seemed to get heated between two of the men. One of them finally seemed to yield, and the man who had spoken to Aramis appeared to win the argument. The men proceeded to bind Aramis and Kaldrick's hands behind their backs with strips of leather, then took up positions in front and behind them.

"I wonder who these people are," Aramis whispered to Kaldrick.

One of the men jabbed him painfully in the ribs with the butt end of his spear. Aramis took that as a sign to keep his mouth shut. The men led them around the west side of the mountain to a set of steps carved into the mountainside. Aramis laughed and shook his head. If it weren't for these men, he and Kaldrick would likely have killed themselves trying to climb up the steep cliff.

The steps were jagged and rocky, forcing him to take care where he stepped. The stairs wound steadily up the mountain. In a few places, the rock had broken and most of the stair was missing. Since he was bound and couldn't use his hands, his captors had to assist him. It was obvious the walkway was rarely used. Aramis was certain where they were being taken, but he didn't know why they would take him exactly where he wanted to go.

It took the better part of an hour before they reached the plateau. Aramis was surprised to find the ground was smooth and looked like it had been polished. The ground was the same red color as the rest of the mountain, but there were black flakes scattered amidst the red as well. It reminded him of the snowflakes he had seen once as a child. He wanted to bend down and get a closer look, but he figured one of the men would strike him again.

They halted suddenly. Aramis couldn't see anything past the men. They were taller than he was and they walked shoulder to shoulder. The thought occurred to him that these men might be soldiers. The more he studied their body language, the more he came to realize they were highly disciplined. They wore loose-fitting white pants and black leather boots. Their skin was a dark tan hue, but it seemed natural and not related to being in the sun.

The men parted and stepped to the sides. A figure dressed in white robes approached them. Aramis couldn't tell if it was a man or a woman until the figure spoke. He spoke the same language as the bare-chested men and they conversed for a few moments before the robed man stepped closer to Aramis.

"What are you doing here?" he asked. He spoke without any hint of an accent. "They say you touched the holy mountain."

"My apologies," Aramis answered. "I didn't know it was holy."

The man waved his hand dismissively. "Why are you here?"

"We've come here in search of something."

"What?"

Aramis hesitated. From the vision he had, it seemed as though the priests had sent the bones of Mordum here to be protected. Would they simply allow him to have them? Would they try to kill him for coming to their holy mountain?

"Well?" the man's tone indicated his impatience.

"The bones of Mordum."

The man stiffened. An awkward silence ensued, then the man turned and stalked away. Their guards stayed put but exchanges glances. The robed man disappeared into the massive doorway of a fortress. Aramis hadn't even noticed the building, likely because the soldiers had blocked his view. It was an imposing structure, towering into the sky hundreds of feet.

Its gray stone walls stood in stark contrast to the red landscape of the mountain. The large entryway had two massive wooden doors. One of them was ajar. Aramis noticed thin vertical apertures spaced along the upper section of the walls. He recognized them as arrow slits. He couldn't tell if anyone was manning them.

After a few minutes had passed, he saw the robed man was coming back. Judging by his demeanor, he was more irritated than before. Stopping a few feet away, he motioned at them with his hand.

"Come on, then," he snapped. Then he turned and began walking back toward the fortress.

Aramis and Kaldrick quickly followed after him. They entered through the door and stepped into a spacious and open chamber. A cool breeze tickled Aramis's skin. A dozen braziers, evenly distributed, ran along the walls to his left and right. He passed an empty divan as they continued further into the room. They walked on soft, thick rugs that were so colorful, they reminded him of some rare birds he had seen once. The man took them to an oversized pillow. Two shirtless men—looking rather bored—stood on either side, fanning the person on the pillow with poles that had giant feathers on the ends.

"Wait here," the man instructed them. He knelt beside the pillow and whispered something to the figure. There was a whispered argument.

"Now!" the figure on the pillow shouted. It was a woman.

Aramis's interest grew as the man stood up and shooed the men away. All three of them left the chamber. The woman rose from the pillow, slow and graceful. The first thing Aramis noticed was that she was almost naked. She wore a thin, sheer loincloth of white material which left little to the imagination. Her breasts were uncovered and Aramis had to fight desperately not to stare at them. Stealing a quick glance, he saw they were round and naturally buoyant. Her skin was a bronzed hue and her eyes were a vibrant green. Her hair was long and reached down past her shoulders, so blonde it was almost silver. Her wrists and ankles glinted with silver and gold bands.

"Well," the woman said, her voice smooth as honey. "What brings you to my home?"

Aramis stuttered on his response, finding it hard to focus. Kaldrick cleared his throat next to him. He'd almost forgotten the man was there. He opened his mouth but no words came out. The woman sighed and spoke a word he didn't understand and couldn't remember. A purple robe flittered down from the ceiling and she grabbed it from the air. She slipped it on but didn't tie it shut. Her body wasn't as revealed, but Aramis still found it enticing.

"I-uh," he stammered. Shaking his head slightly, he started again. "I've come here looking for the bones of Mordum."

Her sapphire eyes seemed to pierce his very soul. She studied him intently for a long moment. "Assuming they were here, whatever could you want with them? I'm sure they are nothing more than dust."

"It's a long story," he answered.

"Well, it's a good thing I have nothing but time." She smiled at him. "Take off your clothes. Both of you."

Aramis and Kaldrick exchanged glances.

"Don't be fools," she said with a laugh. "I've got plenty of men around here to satisfy my needs. Your clothes are filthy and I will not allow them to touch anything in here. I'll have them laundered and patched. I'll have some other clothes brought for you."

The thought of clean clothes was enough to make him strip down. They both stood there naked, feeling awkward. The woman looked them over and made a noise in her throat.

"I think you should both be bathed as well. You look dirtier than your clothes." She snapped her fingers and several attendants rushed into the room. She nodded toward Aramis and Kaldrick and the servants pulled them out of the chamber, down an enormous hall, and into a room with pools built into the floor. Some of the servants were women and they took them to separate pools and washed them with soft sponges.

Aramis tried not to let his thoughts get the better of him, but he ended up being aroused. The servants acted as if they didn't notice and finished washing him. They rinsed him off with buckets of clean, but cold, water. The chill air in the fortress chilled his skin, giving him gooseflesh. The women dried him off and led him into another room where they gave him fresh clothes to wear.

Leading him back out into the main chamber, he saw a table and benches had been set up. Bowls of fruit, bread, and cheese had been set out. Kaldrick joined him, clean and freshly dressed as well.

"Talk about service," Kaldrick whispered with a grin, nudging Aramis in the ribs.

"It's like being back in the palace," he answered.

"Come and sit," the woman said. Aramis was startled to see she was seated at the table. There had been no one there a moment ago. He obeyed, seating himself at the left side of the table. Kaldrick sat at the right.

"Help yourselves," the woman said, motioning to the food.

Kaldrick did just that, stuffing grapes and cheese into his mouth at the same time. Aramis ate more conservatively.

"Who are you?" he asked the woman between bites.

"You can call me Vashah," she answered. "You couldn't possibly pronounce my real name."

"Your real name?"

Vashah smirked at him. "Who do you think I am?"

Aramis shrugged. "I honestly don't know. A druid in the Tylhelm Forest said that a wizard lived here."

"You've been to the forest, have you?" she seemed overly

curious.

"Yes," he answered slowly, eyeing her suspiciously.

"I'm surprised they let you, considering the mark you openly wear on your arm."

Aramis subconsciously rubbed the tattoo. "He wasn't very judgmental."

"That's a surprise. Things must have changed in the last few hundred years." Vashah saw the face Aramis made when she said that. "What do you know about wizards?" she asked.

"A little. They have a city in my kingdom where they are free to study."

"Palindrom," Vashah said.

"You've been there?"

"Of course not," she said disdainfully. "They are not wizards. Sure, they may be able to cast magic, but they are not *true* wizards. True wizards are much more powerful and live much longer than normal humans. There aren't many of us left." She said the last part wistfully, almost sad.

"You are not here to discuss such things though, are you? Tell me your story."

Aramis finished chewing a bite of bread, then related the events of the last few months. He told her everything he could remember. The murder of his father, his torture in the dungeon, his rescue and Mel's magical armor. He even told her about the blind woman he'd encountered on the road several times. His trip to the shrine of Mordum in the mountains was easy to describe. He hadn't forgotten how the dagger the blind woman had given him had saved his life.

Vashah asked a few questions about the shrine. He answered them and then told her about his trek into Talvaard, his meeting with Garrick, and their capture at Mordum's city. He told her of the Prophet's betrayal with hesitation. She listened intently, seeming to devour his every word. He also shared his fragmented memory of his fight with the chimera. She asked more questions about the chimera than anything else.

"That's an interesting tale," Vashah said when he finished.

"You seem surprised by some of it."

"Of course. I don't exactly have the ability to leave this place whenever I want."

"You're a prisoner?" Aramis asked.

"Yes and no. I'm not a prisoner in the sense that someone keeps me locked up in here. I am a prisoner to responsibility." Vashah paused, seeming to consider her words.

"I know the bones are here. I saw them in a vision."

Vashah tilted her head curiously. "A vision?"

Aramis nodded. "I saw a gathering or priests. They were searching for a way to destroy Mordum's body."

The room went quiet except for the sound of Kaldrick eating. Vashah stood and walked to the far end of the chamber. A tall window allowed sunlight in. Aramis rose slowly and joined her at the window. The view was magnificent. The desert stretched out as far as he could see. Here and there he could see the landscape rise and fall in some places.

"I was told by Edria that a messenger would come one day to claim the bones of Mordum. She didn't describe him. She only said I would know him by the mark he carried. I know you bear the mark of Mordum, but I don't understand why Edria would want one of his followers to claim his bones." She turned to face him. Her lips were full and red. Aramis had the overwhelming urged to kiss her. He pushed the thought away.

"I'm not one of his followers," he said. "I was cursed with this mark."

"Have you summoned the armor?" Vashah asked.

"No," he said. She seemed relieved. "I have summoned the blade."

"So you haven't fully accepted the mark. That is good. I have never taken sides with any god, but I've never been able to stomach Mordum or his slaves."

"I'm trying to keep his followers from getting the bones. They already have the blood from the shrine."

"What of the ashes? Have the followers found them?"

"I don't think so," Aramis answered. "I don't know where they are either. The vision ended before I could hear where they sent them."

"A pity," she said. "The priests didn't entrust me with that information." She looked back out the window. "You are more than welcome to have the bones."

Excitement flooded through Aramis. "Really?"

"Yes. There is a catch, however."

"What kind of catch?" His enthusiasm lowered.

"You'll have to retrieve it from the Nexus."

"What is the Nexus?"

"It is a dangerous place designed to protect the bones. Powerful creatures and magic guard them. The pathways around the Nexus are like a maze, each one leading to something different. Only one of the paths lead to the center, the Nexus, where the bones are kept."

"I went into a hellish place and fought a chimera," Aramis said. "Is it worse than that?"

"Much worse," Vashah answered.

"How do you know? Have you been there?"

"No. I designed it."

After they had finished eating, Vashah had her servants take them to different rooms for the night. Aramis had fallen asleep almost immediately. He awoke and was startled when he didn't remember where he was. As his mind slowly became more aware, he remembered the trek through the desert and that they had made it to their destination.

Rolling out of the plush bed, he made his way to the door. As soon as he opened it, he was greeted by servants. They swirled around him, taking off his borrowed clothes and replacing them with his clothes. They were soft and smelled of lavender. The holes had been patched with such skill, he almost couldn't tell where they had been. The servants led him to the main chamber. Vashah and Kaldrick were already at the table eating breakfast. Aramis sat down with them and grabbed an apple from one of the bowls.

"Where does all this food come from?" he asked.

Vashah smiled at him. "What sort of wizard would I be if I couldn't conjure up anything I want?"

Aramis shrugged. He didn't know much about magic.

"As soon as you are ready, I will take you to the Nexus. Your friend will have to stay with me."

"What do you mean? Why can't he go with me?"

"Only someone who bears the mark of Mordum can enter," Vashah answered.

"If you are trying to protect the bones from being taken by one of his followers, why would you only allow someone with his mark to enter? Doesn't that defeat the purpose?"

"The Nexus is designed to be a death trap," Vashah said with a laugh.

Suddenly Aramis wasn't so sure about everything. He'd seen the power of Mordum's templars and didn't have any doubts that they could defeat anything thrown at them. They had powers given to them by a god. What could a wizard conjure to stop the power of a god? Aramis could summon a blade, but he was nothing compared to a templar. He didn't know if he had the strength to complete this task. He realized Vashah and Kaldrick were staring at him.

"Are you sure about this?" Kaldrick asked worriedly.

"No," Aramis said, "but if I don't get them, it's likely Mordum's followers will get them. And we can't let that happen."

"Everything in the Nexus is deadly, but there are two creatures especially that you should be wary of," Vashah said. "The Lamia and the Jackalwere."

"What are those?" Kaldrick asked.

"The Lamia are half snake, half human creatures. Their upper body is the human part, and the rest is a snake. They are quick and clever. If you see one, run the other way. A Jackalwere is a doglike creature that walks on two legs. Their claws are wickedly sharp and their teeth contain venom that can paralyze you within seconds. Both of these creatures are drawn to the power that flows through the tattoo."

Kaldrick looked at Aramis, the concern evident on his face. Aramis digested the information, trying not to let it worry him. He wasn't afraid of the fact that he had to go in alone. No, that did not worry him. He'd gone into the shrine by himself to get the blood. This was different because he was afraid of failing. If he failed, his kingdom would remain in the hands of the usurper. Only the gods knew if they'd be taken care of. His father's killer would go unpunished. Mordum would take on human flesh and bring war across the world.

Aramis steeled his nerves and forced his mind to control his emotions. Failure was *not* an option. He smiled at Kaldrick to calm him down.

"I'll be fine," he added.

Kaldrick looked doubtful for a moment, then nodded. He didn't say anything further as they continued their breakfast. Aramis knew he needed to eat so he'd have enough energy to do whatever he needed to survive, but he wasn't really hungry. He finished off the apple and picked apart a bread roll, not really eating much of it. Convincing himself he was ready, he stood up.

Vashah snapped her fingers and her servants came running. They cleared the table off with quiet, quick efficiency. Aramis admired their hard work. *If only the servants in the castle were half as skilled,* he thought.

"Follow me," Vashah said. She led them out of the main chamber and down the hallway where their rooms were. They continued to the end of the corridor, then turned left. They went down a massive spiral staircase carved of the same stone as the rest of the fortress. When they reached the bottom, torches suddenly burst into life, lighting up a small room with a single door. It was plain and unadorned.

"This is the door to the Nexus," Vashah announced. "I'll need to shut the door quickly to ensure nothing escapes. As soon as you are ready, I will open it for you.”

Aramis inhaled deeply, preparing himself mentally. He tilted his neck to the left until it cracked, then repeated the motion for the other side. He walked over to the door and held his hand out, summoning his blade. The air hissed as it formed in his grasp. He looked to Vashah and nodded.

The wizard closed her eyes and began chanting softly. Runes on the door began to glow with a soft white light. The ground began to tremble slightly as the door began to open. When it had opened a quarter of the way, Vashah opened her eyes.

“Go now!”

Aramis sprinted through the opening and was plunged into darkness.

14

ADAMAR SAT AT HIS DESK reading through financial ledgers when a knock interrupted him. He looked up from the mass of numbers and nodded toward one of his guards. The robed templar moved noiselessly to the door and opened it. A sweaty and breathless messenger stood in the doorway.

"Enter," Adamar said as he went back to studying the numbers.

The messenger walked in and kneeled down beside the desk.

"Rise," Adamar said with an air of boredom. He was focused on the ledgers. Something about the numbers from the tax collectors wasn't right, but he couldn't find the error. He went line by line, tallying the numbers with an abacus. He eyed the page and began to get irritated.

The messenger rose to his feet. He waited for the king to look at him. When he didn't, the man glanced to the templar. Receiving no sign from him either, the man decided to deliver the message.

"King Adamar, I have news regarding the bones of Mordum."

Adamar turned his full attention on the messenger. The intensity of his gaze caused the man to stumble over his words.

"Speak!" Adamar commanded angrily. The messenger took a deep breath.

"Your spies have located the bones of Mordum."

"Where?"

"The Deadlands. Far to the north at a place called Red Mountain."

"The Deadlands?" Adamar stood and walked over to a large table at the back of the room. Spread out on the surface were maps of every size and shape. He eyed the distance and began estimating the time it would take to get troops there.

"I have a battalion that can make the trip in six days. Seven including the time it takes to dispatch orders to them."

"There's something else, my Lord."

"Yes?" he asked, still staring at the maps.

"The spies also indicate your brother has made an appearance."

"Where?"

"He's at Red Mountain as we speak."

"What?" Adamar spun around swiftly. "What is he doing there?"

The messenger shrugged. "That was not in the report."

Adamar turned back to the maps and slammed his fist down onto the table. "Call for my generals!" he yelled.

"My Lord," the messenger continued, "the report was delivered today, but the general who received it initially from the spies has already ordered his men to march on Red Mountain."

"That's a bit of excellent news," Adamar said, the news calming him somewhat. "When will they arrive?"

"According to the general, they should arrive at the mountain today. Tomorrow at the latest."

Adamar took in the information. The man responsible needed a promotion. "Is there anything else?"

"No, sir."

Adamar walked back to his desk and sat down. A servant poured him a glass of wine, which he downed in a long drink. He looked back at the ledger and immediately found the error. He looked to the messenger who was still standing there, waiting to be dismissed.

"How many shops are in the market?" he asked.

The messenger's face contorted in thought. "I believe there are one hundred shops."

"Exactly one hundred?"

"Yes, my Lord."

"Thank you. You can go."

The messenger left the room. Adamar looked to the templar who had opened the door. "Find the bookkeeper for the market district. He's been stealing from me," he said. The templar bowed and headed for the door.

"I want you to kill him," he added as an afterthought. "And bring me his skull."

The templar tilted his head in acknowledgment.

Now that he'd found the error, he adjusted the totals. Satisfied everything matched up correctly, he signed the ledger and closed the book. The servant who poured his wine refilled the glass and collected the stack of ledgers on the desk and carried them off.

Adamar was close to having the bones of Mordum and yet somehow his blasted brother was one step ahead of him. He should have killed the brat when his mother was pregnant. Adamar drummed his fingers on his desk, contemplating what he would do if his men failed to secure the bones. There were three items he needed to bring his dark god into a fleshly body, and he didn't have any of them.

At least I know where two of them are, he mused. *It could be worse.*

They were the key to securing his Mark. He wanted the Mark more than anything he'd ever desired. He needed it. Desperately. He drank the wine and pushed the thought from his mind. Standing up, he left the private study that was attached to his bedchamber. Servants quickly gathered around him and pulled his clothes off, replacing them with armor. It was made of gold and silver, more for ceremony than for actual use. They worked quickly and efficiently, using oiled cloths to remove any smudges.

Adamar admired his own appearance in a tall mirror once they had finished. The armor glinted like a stunning jewel. The majority of the breastplate was silver. Etched into the metal were large decorative symbols in gold, and the edges of his bracers and greaves were trimmed in gold as well. He turned and left the room, his remaining templar bodyguard falling into step behind him.

He was going out to the barracks to see his troops and ensure their loyalty to his cause. Initially, he'd lost a large number of soldiers. They were loyal to his brother, so he didn't mourn their departure. There were a few dissenters who stayed and tried to cause trouble. They loudly voiced their opinions and spread rumors like wildfire. Adamar had them flogged. When they continued with their opposition, he had them killed.

For the most part, the nobles had welcomed him with open arms. He had received lavish gifts from all of them. He knew it was a show. If anyone else had taken the throne, they would have done the same thing. He didn't let it bother him. The nobles were dependent upon the king for their land and their status. Likewise, he was dependent upon them for their support and the taxes they paid. Were they to band together and rise against him … he pushed the thought away. They were not the warriors they thought they were. Besides, he controlled the kingdom's military. If they did rise up, he would quickly crush their rebellion.

Adamar exited the castle and made his way to the barracks. The barracks consisted of six large buildings, all within the castle's protective walls. They were square in design with two stories. The first floor had a kitchen and a massive dining area where the men ate in shifts. The second floor, accessible from within the building as well as without, housed the rooms where the men slept. Each building could comfortably house five thousand men, seven thousand if comfort wasn't an option. Unfortunately, two of the buildings sat empty, the result of the recent departure of soldiers loyal to Aramis.

A messenger met him halfway to the first building, waving his arms wildly. His shirt was a little too big for him and his sleeves rippled as he waved, reminding Adamar of flags blowing in the wind.

"My Lord," he called out shrilly. "My Lord! The generals asked me to inform you of their location. They've gathered outside the walls for training drills. They've asked that you meet them there."

Adamar stopped mid-stride, turned, and headed toward the castle gate. He hoped this wasn't some attempt to irritate him. He didn't like changes without proper notifications. His bodyguard followed along quietly.

Leaving the castle behind, he made his way to the fields where the soldiers were training. The sight of twenty thousand men in military formation was stunning. As a boy, he'd always wanted to ride at the head of an army, leading his troops into battle. Now that he was king, he would get his opportunity. As soon as he had the favor of the common people, he would lead his army in Oakvalor and expand his kingdom.

"My Lord," one of the generals greeted as Adamar approached. "My apologies for not sending word earlier. This was a last minute decision."

"Understandable," Adamar replied. "Don't let it happen again."

"This was a one-time mistake," the general said.

"Show me what you are doing out here."

The general motioned to his peers. They began issuing commands to young men, who in turn relayed the messages to men holding large flags. Those men, called flag bearers, then began waving the flags in specific patterns.

"Those patterns were used to inform the soldiers what they should be doing," the man said. "It's much quicker than sending runners into the field."

"How so?" Adamar asked.

"Once fighting commences, there isn't much order. You're as likely to strike a friend as you are an enemy. The runners can get killed or turned around and unable to find the captains. So instead we use these flag patterns to send messages."

"Does it work?"

"Well ..." the general paused. "We don't know yet. We've not used it in an actual battle, but in these training sessions it works very well."

Adamar nodded and watched as the formations split and changed directions as the flags waved. "I like it," he said. "Whose idea was this?"

The general cleared his throat. "Prince Aramis's."

"I see." Adamar frowned. As much as he wanted his brother dead, he had to admit that the idea was clever. "A good idea is good whether it comes from a fool or a wise man. Continue using the patterns. I want this system perfected in the next six months."

"Yes, my Lord. A question, if I may?"

Adamar nodded.

"What's in six months?"

Adamar smiled. "The expansion of my kingdom."

He turned and walked away, leaving the general to figure out his words alone. Adamar returned to the castle and retired to his personal chamber. The armor was beautiful but stifling. It was a good thing it was only for show. He'd never be able to fight in it for all the sweating.

He sat down on a pillowed chair and relaxed, flipping through a book he'd found in his father's wardrobe. Most of it didn't make any sense, just scribbled drawings and half-written sentences. A servant brought him some wine and fruit to tide him over until dinner was prepared. He must have dozed off, for he startled awake when his head began slipping sideways.

He cleared his throat and looked around the room. It was empty except for his lone bodyguard. He wondered where the other one was. He should have killed the bookkeeper and returned with his head already. Maybe he'd gotten lost in the market.

Adamar was about to close the book he'd been looking through when something caught his attention. He rubbed the sleep from his eyes and lifted the book up closer to his face. The half sentences that caught his attention said:

Deep below lies a secret ...

Sent long ago to keep it ...

Black and gray and sifted ...

Behind red stones shifted ...

Adamar read the words again several times. His heart began to beat excitedly in his chest. These words were referencing the ashes of Mordum. The third key to bringing the dark god into a mortal body.

"Yes!" he shouted aloud.

The templar looked at him.

"The ashes of Mordum. I know where they are!"

The templar gave him a questioning look. Adamar found the man's lack of speech irritating. "They are here," he said.

The templar looked around the room.

"Not *here*. Here," Adamar waved his hand, encompassing the castle. "When I was a child, I saw a room deep in the dungeon. I used to hide there and make the servants find me. One of the walls had red stones in it. I don't remember the design, but I remember the color. It reminded me of blood."

The door to the chamber opened suddenly and the other templar walked in.

"It's about time," Adamar snapped. "What took you so long? Nevermind that," he said, shaking his head, "we need to get down to the dungeon." Adamar noticed the templar was carrying a severed head.

"When I said bring me his skull, I didn't mean bring it to my bed—" the words died on his lips. The severed head wasn't the bookkeeper's. It was the templar's. Adamar's eyes widened in surprise.

The other templar had already noticed. The guard had summoned his armor and blade and was rushing toward the imposter. Adamar quickly scrambled to the edge of the room, moving to stand in front of the window.

Tossing the head aside, the imposter removed the templar's robes to reveal an older man in silver armor. Adamar immediately recognized the insignia on the breastplate as the symbol of Edria—a closed hand with an open eye in the center. How had the priest killed his guard? Mordum's knights controlled fearsome powers.

"Kill him!" Adamar screamed in fury.

The priest of Edria lifted his hand and summoned his blade. A blinding light filled the room and a thunderous *boom* shook the floor. Adamar's fury quickly changed to fear. Armor and blades from the gods hissed when summoned. The only difference was …

"The Prophet," Adamar whispered. Only a Prophet's blade created such a spectacle. He'd never seen one, but he'd heard stories of Mordum's Prophet summoning his. Flashes of black lightning and blue flames.

"I've come for a reckoning!" the Prophet of Edria shouted. "Your dark god may have killed my precious Edria, but I will make the tally even!"

The templar and the prophet collided in a clash of blades. Adamar stood transfixed, watching the battle unfold before him. He didn't know what he should do. The templar would kill the prophet. Wouldn't he? Adamar looked to the discarded head and had his doubts. He turned to the window and pushed on it. The glass pane pushed outward easily. Adamar looked down. He was hundreds of feet above the ground. He looked back at the battle. They seemed fairly matched. Hopefully, he wouldn't have to jump. He'd never survive, but it was better than dying at the hands of the Prophet.

Soldiers appeared in the doorway and attempted to apprehend the Prophet. He cut them down without a backward glance. He appeared to have the advantage as he was driving the templar back. Adamar climbed onto the ledge. His hands were sweating profusely and his legs were involuntarily shuddering. He flexed his leg muscles, trying to regain control of them.

More soldiers spilled into the room. Suddenly the Prophet inhaled sharply. Adamar struggled to see what was happening. The templar's blade was covered with blood. The Prophet staggered back, clutching his stomach. Turning his hate-filled eyes on Adamar, the Prophet lifted his blade and spoke a word. A blinding light filled the room and then the man was gone.

Adamar jumped down from the ledge and was quickly surrounded by soldiers. The templar was covered with sweat and blood, but none of the blood appeared to be his own.

"You almost killed him," Adamar said. "You defended my life."

The templar merely bowed his head in reply.

"How did he get inside my castle?" he asked aloud. "Double the guard. No, triple it! I want every soldier on duty!" The soldiers scrambled out of the room to comply. Once they were gone, servants came in and began cleaning up the mess from the fight.

Adamar slumped into the pillowed chair. This was exactly why he needed the Mark. What if the Prophet had managed to kill both of his templars? He could have been killed. He slammed a fist on the arm of the chair in frustration and anger.

"How dare Edria's followers come here and try to kill me!" he shouted. He ordered one of the servants to bring him some wine. After he'd consumed a few glasses, his nerves had calmed. He sent a messenger to retrieve one of his generals. Half an hour later, the general appeared in the doorway.

"Gather some workers," Adamar commanded. "I need them in the dungeon for a project. Bring some of your men, too. No one sleeps until this project is done."

The general bowed and left.

—

It was in the early hours of the next morning when the workers managed to remove the red stones from the wall. Looking at it now, Adamar realized that the stones had been arranged in the symbol of Mordum. Once the workers cleared the way, he ordered them out of the room. Then he ordered the soldiers to kill them.

"I don't want anyone knowing about this," he explained to the general.

Adamar grabbed a torch from a sconce and stood in front of the demolished wall. He held the torch out in front of him, expecting to see something magnificent holding Mordum's ashes. Instead, he found a long hall that stretched into darkness.

"Grab some torches," he ordered the soldiers. "We're going in."

15

THE DOOR SLAMMED SHUT BEHIND him with a thunderous crash. Aramis stood frozen in place, expecting an army of creatures to suddenly attack him. After what seemed like an eternity, he slowly let his guard down. As his eyes adjusted to the gloom, he realized that he was not in complete darkness as he had first thought.

The ceiling glowed with a faint light. It provided just enough illumination to see by. Aramis looked around and noticed that the walls and floor were crafted from dull bronze colored stones, all interconnected to one another. He estimated the distance between the walls to be about six feet—plenty of room to defend himself.

Keeping a tight grip on the hilt of his sword, he cautiously began to walk forward. He stopped immediately when he felt the stone under his foot shift beneath his weight. Inches ahead, arrows flew forth from holes in the walls. The bolts struck the stones with such force that they lodged tightly in place. Aramis stood in shocked surprise. He knew Vashah said that the place was designed to kill, but he hadn't expected anything dangerous in the entrance.

He decided to take Vashah's warning more seriously. He began testing every stone he stepped on, pressing his weight on them and leaning back to avoid being struck by anything that might come from the walls. It was impossible to judge the passing of time, but he felt like it was taking too long to make any real progress. Concluding he was being too cautious, he picked up the pace and only tested the stones every tenth step.

When he finally reached the end of the hallway, he came to a forked path. There were three hallways before him: left, right, and one straight ahead that appeared to descend. He looked down each hall, trying to decide which way to go. Vashah said the place was a maze. If he went the wrong way, there was no telling how long it would take him to backtrack and get back to where he was now. *If* he could make it back.

He recalled an old saying:

The left-handed path is for the wicked.

Aramis chose the hall to the right.

In the distance, he could hear what sounded like howling. Trying to step as lightly as he could, he followed the hall for a long while. It twisted and turned, but he did not encounter any side passages. Eventually, the hall widened and connected to a large room. Aramis paused at the edge of the hall, testing the stones by pressing his blade on them and applying pressure.

Satisfied there were no traps, he stepped into the room. It was oval in shape and had two doorways, one to the left and one straight ahead. He decided to continue going straight when he saw something move at the edge of his vision. He froze immediately. He turned his head slowly to see what had moved. A rat, a very large rat, skittered along the edge of the wall.

Exhaling the breath he didn't realize he was holding, Aramis took a step just as a larger shape on four legs entered the room from the doorway to the left and snapped the rat up in its mouth. He heard the sickening sound of bones crunching. The larger shape finished off the rat and lifted its nose into the air, sniffing. Aramis started moving slowly.

The shape stood up on two legs and Aramis saw the glint of red eyes. It was covered in dark brown hair and had two ears standing straight up on the top of its head. Its outline was similar to a man's, but its face was elongated. Torn, dirty bandages were wrapped around its forearms and calves. A tattered material served as pants. It lifted its head and howled loudly.

Aramis sprinted for the doorway and heard the creature take up the chase behind him. The howl was likely a call to its fellows. He needed to find a defensible position, and quickly. He dared not look over his shoulder but he could hear the creature right behind him. Suddenly he threw himself to the ground. The creature tripped over him and landed on the ground in front of him, snarling.

Aramis got back on his feet and ran his blade through the creature's back. A pitiful whelp filled the air, reminding him of a dog. He twisted the blade and jerked it out roughly. Blood pooled around the creature as it struggled weakly to move. Howling echoed off the walls from the room behind him. He ran down the hall, all regard for safety lost.

He felt a stone shift under his foot and grunted as something struck him in the ribs. Gritting his teeth against the pain, he kept running. He could feel something warm and wet running down his skin. *Blood,* he thought. The hall started to become narrow. It was hardly noticeable at first, but as he went further it became obvious. He felt like the walls were steadily coming closer, threatening to crush him.

Finally, he stopped. The space was too narrow. He measured the gap with his hand. From the tips of his fingers to the end of his palm, where his wrist was. He shook his head. It would be too close, especially if it narrowed anymore. He considered going back until he heard the sound of the creatures. He wasn't sure, but it sounded like they were coming closer.

Cursing his luck, he dismissed his blade and forced his body into the narrow gap. He had to suck his stomach in and turn his head sideways. He started to get scared when he felt like he was stuck.

I don't want to die like this.

A sudden howl startled him. The creature was right behind him. More howls followed. He realized there was more than one. Many more. He tried to suck in his stomach even more, but there was nowhere else for his body to squish. He felt something touch his arm and involuntarily gasped.

The creature went wild. It started scrabbling at the narrow gap, trying to reach him. Aramis felt the creature's claws rake his arm. Pain lanced up his shoulder. He pushed himself into the gap further, trying to put more distance between himself and the creature. He recalled Vashah's description of a Jackalwere and assumed that's what he was facing.

It was relentless. He could hear the others growling and snarling. He started to panic when he couldn't move any further. The walls were crushing him. He could only take small breaths. Blood flowed openly from his ribs and his arm. His vision began fading. Aramis stopped fighting and gave himself to the darkness.

—

Aramis looked at his reflection in a large pool of crystal clear water. His hair was a dark gray. His face had many wrinkles, some of them tugging at his eyes. He looked exhausted. The sound of someone approaching grabbed his attention and he turned to see who it was.

A woman who reminded him of an older Hannah smiled at him as she flipped through the pages of a book. She stood a few feet from him and was wearing a beautiful dress. Pearls and other beads of semi-precious stones created a dazzling pattern across the front of the bodice.

"Who are you?" he asked.

The woman laughed playfully. "I'm your wife, silly. Even after all these years, you can still make me smile with such little effort."

Aramis stared at her, confused. He looked around and noticed they were in a garden. Carefully sculpted shrubs in the shapes of mythical animals dotted the cobblestone walkway that surrounded the pool. The pool was perfectly square and had a large statue of a knight in the center. The knight was holding his sword up high, saluting some unseen deity. Water sprayed elegantly from the pommel of the blade, creating a rainbow among the drops of water as they fell.

Looking up, he saw the spires of a massive castle reaching high into the sky. The garden seemed to be located somewhere in the center of the castle around him.

"Where am I?" he asked.

Again, the woman laughed. "Are you okay?" she asked. "You look tired. Perhaps you should retire for the afternoon? I'm sure your son can handle the courtly duties while you rest." She closed the book. The cover looked familiar to him.

"My son?" he asked.

As if following some cue, a young man entered the garden from a doorway in the castle wall and approached them.

"Father," the man greeted.

Aramis stared at him. He was handsome, with short cropped brown hair. His eyes were a dark green and his skin was a bronzed color. His clothes were made of expensive materials. Aramis also recognized they were the colors of the kingdom; Oakvalor's colors of royalty.

"How old am I?" he asked curiously.

The woman and the young man exchanged glances.

"Father," the man said quietly. "Are you well? Should I call the physicians?"

"My love," the woman said, "I'm worried about you. Are you ill?"

Aramis shook his head. "No, I'm fine." He saw the concerned look in their eyes. "I'm just jesting with you." He smiled to make it convincing.

The young man seemed satisfied, but the woman continued to stare at him worriedly.

"Well if you don't need me, I'm going on a hunt with the nobles," the man said. "Lord Bavol insists that I go with them."

"Lord Bavol? He's still alive?" Aramis asked in surprise.

The young man laughed. "Everyone says that. He claims he's the oldest man in Oakvalor, but he also claims he's seen a golden phiebus." The man shook his head, chuckling.

"Have you seen your sister?" the woman asked.

"Not in the past hour. I saw her at breakfast, though. She said something about going to the barracks."

"I wish you'd put a stop to this," the woman said indignantly.

"She doesn't listen to me," the man returned. "You know that."

"I'm talking to your father," the woman said.

Aramis looked from the man to the woman. He was married and had two children? What was happening?

"What is she doing at the barracks?" he asked.

The woman threw her hands up. "It's as if you aren't aware of anything today," she said exasperatedly. "Your daughter goes to the barracks every day and trains with the soldiers. It's not proper for a woman. Especially not for a princess."

Aramis looked to the man for an explanation, but the man only smiled.

"I'll leave you two to discuss that," he said with a laugh, then turned and walked away.

Aramis turned back to the pool and stared at his reflection again. He looked as old as his father was when he was killed.

"All I'm asking is that you to talk to her," the woman said. She was beside him now.

Aramis turned to her. Only she wasn't there. The beautiful garden was gone too, replaced by a dead landscape. He looked into the pool. It was empty. The castle walls had vanished. The only thing the same was the pool.

"Which of these do you prefer?" a voice behind him asked.

He turned around to see a robed figure, a hood pulled low over his face.

"What's happening?" Aramis asked.

The figure motioned to their surroundings. "This is the future. One of many that could be."

Aramis stared hard at the figure. His skin began to crawl and the terrible smell of death filled his nostrils. "Mordum."

The dark god tilted his head in acknowledgment. "This is the future if you fight my will. The glimpse you saw of your wife is what the future holds if you bow to my will."

"I'll never bow to you," Aramis said, spitting at the figure.

"You will bow," Mordum answered. "Whether willingly or by force."

Aramis stepped toward the god threateningly, then dropped to his knees in agony. He clutched at his arm where the Mark was.

"Who are you to defy a god?" Mordum asked harshly. "You are nothing. Your life is nothing compared to the eternity I have lived. This world will burn."

"Men stopped you before," Aramis gasped through the pain.

Mordum ignored the comment. "You will obey me." He pointed at Aramis and the skin around his tattoo burned hotter. Aramis collapsed onto the ground, rocking back and forth. And then Mordum was gone. After a few minutes, the pain subsided.

Aramis lay there cradling his arm. He looked at his skin, expecting to see it burned. It wasn't. But the veins in his arm were black. He felt sick. He also felt as though a fire were burning under his flesh. The dark power of Mordum flowed through him, filling his mind with twisted thoughts. He was going mad.

And then he remembered something. The book the woman had been holding. He knew why it was familiar. It was his father's.

—

His eyes fluttered open. To his great displeasure, he was still stuck. He gingerly touched his side with his injured arm. The bleeding had stopped and the wound was closed. That was a small relief. Judging by the dried blood on his arm, he assumed it had healed as well.

Aramis could hear the Jackalwere still scratching at the walls behind him. It wasn't as frantic as before. He tried to push himself forward and failed. The creature's interest was captured again and it tried harder to reach him.

He played through his vision. Why was Mordum so bent on having his loyalty? He didn't know. A disturbing thought entered his mind then. If he summoned his blade, he could cut some of his flesh off to get through the narrow space.

The thought almost made him gag. Was the Mark going to drive him mad? He remembered Mel telling him that while some of Mordum's followers received power, many of them went insane. As he considered the thought, it started to become more appealing. He was stuck. Behind him was a room full of creatures bent on killing him. He didn't know what was ahead, but it had to be better than the alternative.

He summoned the blade with his right hand and the air hissed as it formed. Aramis twisted the blade around until the tip of the blade was pointed toward him. Closing his eyes, he placed the blade against his stomach.

One, two, three ...

He pushed the blade hard and felt the metal bite into his flesh. Agonizing pain assaulted his body. He screamed aloud. He vaguely heard the creature's behind him howling. His body began trembling uncontrollably. He managed to press the sword in a downward motion, cutting the front of his stomach off. He felt blood pouring down the front of his body. So much blood!

Removing the chunk of flesh allowed him to push through the narrow space. Not far ahead, he could make out an opening. He dismissed the blade and slipped forward along the wall. The pain was so intense he thought he might pass out again, but he could also feel the healing power of the Mark kicking in.

A little further ...

Aramis slipped through the opening and fell onto the ground. He was covered in blood. Pulling his torn shirt up, he saw with horror the gaping wound. He could feel vomit trying to rise up his throat. He swallowed hard, trying to keep it down. After several unbearable minutes, the Mark had healed him. His skin had completely grown back. He desperately wanted to sleep. His mind and his body were beyond exhausted.

"I can't," he whispered to himself. "I have to get—"

A sound to his left made him pause. He turned his head slowly. A Jackalwere lay curled up asleep a few feet away. He sat up slowly and quietly and his heart almost stopped at what he saw. The room he was in was full of sleeping Jackalwere. He silently cursed the gods. He looked for an exit and found three. None of them were as close as he would have liked, but at least there was a way out.

He moved as quietly as he could, pausing when his clothes or his boots made noise. He was roughly twenty feet from the nearest doorway but it felt like an eternity away. He heard one of the creatures make a snorting noise. He stepped around their sleeping forms, carefully checking to ensure he didn't step on their hair. From the corner of his vision, he saw the glint of red eyes and froze mid-step. It was smaller than the others and watched him curiously, huddled behind two other still forms.

These things are breeding in here?

Aramis stood still, waiting to see what the creature was going to do. When it didn't move or make a sound, he thought it might be sleeping with its eyes open. He placed his foot on the ground, not watching where he stepped and heard the yelp of a creature. The room became a flurry of motion as the Jackalwere scrambled up to see what the commotion was.

Aramis summoned his blade and removed the head of the creature he stepped on. He managed to kill two more before the creatures realized what was happening. He was quickly surrounded. They lunged at him, trying to cut him with their wickedly sharp claws. He managed to cut some of their paws off, but there were too many. He was struck several times and they backed him up against a wall. Claws raked across his flesh from all directions and he was quickly covered in gashes and scratches.

He fought to ignore the burning their claws left behind. He knew there was no escape this time. There was no hope. He swung his sword in a wide arc, driving the Jackalwere back momentarily. One of them came at him as his sword passed and he lifted his left arm up to block the creature's swipe. As he did, he noticed that his arm was covered with black lines. The Mark was burning fiercely. He could feel the dark power welling up inside him.

Aramis closed his eyes and let the power flow freely. He was immediately energized. Mist started swirling around him and the creatures drew back in confusion. Aramis was confused as well, but he used the distraction to cut down several more of the Jackalwere.

The air hissed and he felt something closing around his body. He looked down and saw black armor forming around his body. The creatures, having overcome their confusion, came at him with fury. The armor felt weightless and he was able to maneuver as easily as if he weren't wearing any. He reached up and pulled the visor of his helm down. It limited his vision a little, but it protected his face from their claws.

Even though he knew the Mark continuously healed his wounds, he didn't know if it had a limit to its power. If he lost an eye, would the Mark be able to replace it? If he was stabbed in the heart, would it keep him from dying? He allowed his mind to wander as he hacked and slashed his way through the creatures, making his way toward the closest doorway.

One of the creatures began howling, its tone different than the previous howls he had heard. The others took notice too, as they began to start acting nervous. Their heads shifted around and they sniffed at the air. He killed a few more as they began moving in different directions, abandoning the fight. Aramis didn't question his luck and ran toward the exit.

He stopped quickly as soon as he saw the reason for the Jackalwere's reactions. A large snake slithered into the room. It was the size of a horse. Aramis realized it wasn't actually a snake. At least, not all of it. The upper part of the slithering creature was humanoid. It looked like a woman, with long blonde hair. Its skin was pale and had its breasts exposed. From the stomach down it was covered in scales. Its tail swayed back and forth behind it.

Aramis brought his sword up and blocked its tail as it came flying straight at him. The force made him stagger backward. Several of the Jackalwere rushed the snake-human, scratching at it with their claws. He remembered Vashah mentioning this creature as well. A Lamia, she had called it. He watched as the Lamia used its tail to smack the Jackalwere away. One of the creatures slammed into the wall and fell to the ground, unmoving.

He looked toward the other two doorways. Most of the Jackalwere had fled through them, but he didn't see any other option. He sprinted across the room. Quicker than he would ever have imagined, the Lamia shot across the room and intercepted him, slamming its thick, powerful tail against his shoulder. The blow sent him spinning in circles and he crashed to the ground, his armor clattering loudly.

Using his sword, he pushed himself onto his feet and turned to face the creature. In the doorway, he saw three more of the snake-humans slither into the room, crushing and flinging Jackalwere as they entered. The one in front of him whipped its tail around his legs and spun him about, wrapping its thick tail around his entire body. He dropped his sword as the Lamia squeezed him tightly, crushing the air from his lungs. His vision exploded with stars and he thought he could feel his ribs cracking. He was vaguely aware of more snake-humans entering the room.

Just as he thought his chest was going to collapse, a blinding light filled the room. The Lamia used its human hands to cover its eyes, shrieking in a piercing tone. The light was intense, illuminating every corner of the chamber. Aramis felt its grip on him loosen slightly. He sucked in a deep breath and closed his eyes against the light. It blinded him still.

A burning smell filled the air and he gagged as he recognized the scent of burning flesh. He fell backward unexpectedly, landing in something soft. He tried to open his eyes, but the intense light made them water. He blinked several times to clear them but it was no use. And then everything went silent. He wasn't sure, but it seemed like the light began to dim. He heard the sound of footsteps coming toward him. He quickly wiped the tears from his eyes. His vision was still blurred, but he saw the outline of someone standing over him.

As his vision cleared, the features of the figure—a man—started to become visible. The man was wearing silver armor. A symbol was etched into the breastplate: a burning sun with outstretched wings. He'd never seen it before. When he looked upon the man's face, his heart skipped a beat. He stared in shock, unable to speak. There was no mistaking it. His voice failed him several times before he was finally able to speak.

"Mel?"

16

JOVANNA FOUND THE CASTLE'S LIBRARY to be larger than she expected, especially for a place on the edge of civilization. Tall bookcases lined the chamber, creating aisles that reached from one side of the room to the other.

Jovanna stopped at one of the many empty tables and tossed several rolled parchments onto it. The library was vacant with the exception of two robed men, both of them much too old to be of any help with the battle that raged outside the walls. Apparently, they'd been left to themselves.

"Can I help you with anything?" one of the men asked as he approached her.

Her first thought was to ignore him, but as she looked around the library, she quickly realized it would be hard for her to find what she was looking for on her own.

"Yes, actually. I'm looking for anything on the tattoo magic of the elves."

The man raised a brow in curiosity but didn't question her.

"I also need a quill, an empty vial for ink, some parchment, bandages, and a small metal container that I can burn something in."

"That's quite a list," the old man said. "You aren't planning on burning anything in here, are you? Many of these books are very old and could easily catch fire."

Jovanna stared at the man as if he were some sort of odd creature.

"Of course I'm going to burn something in here, you old fool. But I'm not going to be burning anything next to the books. Now go and get me what I need."

The man hesitated, but at the deadly gaze she settled on him, he quickly left. He returned a few minutes later with everything she requested. She unrolled one of the scrolls and saw the old man's eyes widen in shock when he realized that the scrolls were made of flesh and not parchment. He set the items on the table and left without a word.

Jovanna smirked at his reaction and continued working. She traced the outline of the tattoo onto a piece of parchment. Then, using the edge of the quill, she cut into the flesh along the outline of the tattoo that marked the patch of skin. She set the extra skin aside and put the tattooed portion into the metal bowl. Calling to the magic that was floating around her, she commanded it to heat the bottom of the bowl.

A burning smell began to fill the air. She sifted the charred skin in the bowl and was pleased to see the ink pooling at the bottom. Once the skin was completely burned, she poured the ink into the vial. She followed the same process for each of the rolled pieces of skin, four in all.

Once she had collected all of the ink, she looked at the items on the table and noticed that the man didn't bring her any books. She growled in frustration and got up. After several minutes of searching for one of the men, she gave up and started searching the rows of books herself. They were well organized, but most of them were covered with a thick layer of dust. She saw familiar titles from her days in the wizard city Palindrom, but many more titles that she did not know.

A Lineage of Kings.

Languid Poetry.

She walked a few aisles over and continued her search.

The History of Talvaard.

Tattoo Origins.

She stopped and pulled the book out, brushed the dust off the cover, and flipped through the pages. After a few minutes of scanning through the pages, she concluded the book would not be helpful. She placed it back on the shelf and continued looking.

Three shelves down she found another book. *The Tenth War*. She frowned, trying to remember where she'd heard the title before. She couldn't remember. She pulled the book out and started flipping through it. She carried it back to her table and sat down. It was a detailed account of the Tenth War, a time of bloody history in the kingdom of Talvaard. The narrator was part of the war and present for most of the fighting.

We never expected it to happen, she read. *The slaves had been so useful to that point, it hardly seemed like they would rebel. They were well treated and taken care of, so why would they rise against us? None of us knew the answer. We all were fearful, however. We had given them positions of trust, so they knew everything about us. They knew our secrets.*

It finally came to war. The slaves united behind one of their own. He was intelligent and charismatic. None of us were quite sure whose slave he had been, but that mattered little. He convinced the others, the few slaves who still trusted us and wanted peace, to turn aside from our kindness and to raid our cities. The first few raids were expected. We had assumed it would happen due to their anger. When the attacks didn't stop, that's when we knew it was much more serious than we had first believed.

The leader of the rebellious elves, who had named himself Tairu, mounted attack after attack on the undefended towns and villages.

Jovanna stopped reading. "Tairu?" she muttered. "It couldn't be the same …" the thought gave her pause. Was it possible that it was the same elf? Elves were long-lived compared to the humans, but how long-lived exactly? She calculated the years and shook her head. "He would have to be over a thousand years old," she said aloud. She kept reading.

The magical tattoos our wizards had given them quickly became a curse to us. They used them to slaughter us. Some of the elves had learned to alter the original purpose of the tattoos and they changed them into something destructive. They were able to blast through stone walls and deflect arrows with their skin.

Jovanna sat back in her chair. She didn't believe this was a coincidence. She'd lived among the elves for a few months and none of them had the stone skin tattoo. She'd never seen them blast through stone walls until she witnessed their march on the first walled city they had attacked. She turned the page and saw a symbol drawn on the top right. She'd seen it before. She closed her eyes and tried to remember where. It was recently. In the first city, the elves had attacked. When she saw Tairu.

She'd just killed a kid. She hadn't known he was a kid. He was dressed in armor and helping to defend the city from the elves. She had tried to break away from the rushing army, but she couldn't. She'd been forced into the city and had to make a decision. So she had killed the human guard. Shortly after, Tairu entered the city with a few personal guards.

She had drawn her sword and stalked toward him. She encountered his guards first. She slew them easily and swung her sword at Tairu, thinking to decapitate him. Her sword had merely clanged against his skin. She'd realized then that he had the stone skin tattoo, but his flesh was a normal color. It wasn't like the other elves whose skin had turned a grayish hue. She tossed the sword and their battle became one of magic.

Lightning bolts, waves of fire, and other magical attacks filled the air. Upon their first encounter, she had almost killed him. Fighting with him the second time led her to believe she'd only caught him off guard in their first battle, for he was very skilled at using his magical tattoos. They seemed evenly matched in power, neither one gaining an advantage.

If it weren't for several of his warriors joining the fray, she might have seen which of them was the better. She quickly became outnumbered and had to flee. During one of his attacks, he had come close enough that she could have landed a blow on him. Were she not focused on defending against his attack, she would have struck him bodily. She remembered that now. She had thought for a brief second of hitting him in the throat.

His throat. That's where she had seen the tattoo in the book. Jovanna opened her eyes. She looked at the symbol on the page again. Yes, she was sure of it now. The Tairu who incited a rebellion a thousand years ago was the same Tairu attacking people today.

"Where has he been for the last thousand years?"

She also wondered how he had lived that long. Elves were known for their ability to live a long time, but a thousand years was a stretch even for an elf. Many questions plagued her, but she pushed them from her mind. She'd come here with a purpose. Jovanna rolled her left pant leg up and set her ankle across the knee of her other leg. She placed the paper with the outline of the tattoo on her calve. Unsheathing a small dagger from her waist, she stabbed through the paper and into her flesh.

Her eye twitched from the sting, but she continued. She traced the blade along the outline on the paper, creating shallow scratches on her skin. Once she was finished, she removed the paper and eyed the shape. Blood seeped from the dagger marks, but not much. Taking the quill and the vial full of ink she'd removed from the skin, she dipped the quill in the vial and began filling the scratches with it.

As she worked, she could feel the magic working under her skin. The ink began to fuse with her blood, binding them together with a magical connection. Jovanna felt exhilarated. She always felt powerful when casting spells, but this was something entirely different. She could see the magic in the air, hovering over the tattoo as she applied the ink.

Once the vial was empty, she used the bandages the old man had brought to wrap the tattoo. Unrolling the next piece of skin, she followed the same process. She did that for all six of the tattoos she collected. She tattooed all of the designs on her legs. When she finished the last one, she stood up and stretched.

Her body thrummed with power. It raged within her, seeking an escape. How the elves managed to refrain from using the magic for so long, she didn't know. She felt compelled to use it right there, to unleash its power and destroy everything in her path. But she didn't.

She needed to test the magic. The elves tattooed themselves from head to toe with runes. They each had different effects, but they were all designed for war. The longer the elf kept from using the magic, the more powerful it became. She tried to imagine what the elders in the elven tribes felt like. All that power boiling under the surface, ready to be poured out.

Jovanna left her mess for the old men to clean up, but she grabbed the book and took it to the room she'd been given. She tossed it on the bed and made her way to the courtyard. The sounds of battle could be heard. The elves had attacked the walls every day since Garrick's departure. Arrows from both sides flew through the air. Blasts shook the ground as the elves continued to breach the walls with their explosive magic.

How would she get outside the walls to test the tattoos? Then she remembered the secret entry that Garrick had brought her through. Everyone was occupied with the fighting at the walls, so she doubted anyone would see her. She jogged to the door and paused in front of it. Once she opened it, she wouldn't be able to close it. It could only be opened and closed from the inside.

Jovanna didn't care. She pushed the door open and slipped out. Excitement welled up in her as she made her way around the castle toward the fighting. The magic clawed at her from the inside, trying desperately to get free. Her hands began to tremble involuntarily. She rounded the corner of the castle wall and entered the chaos. Elves were charging the wall. Arrows filled the sky and the humans were tossing large rocks from the wall. Some of them hit their mark and crushed the charging elves, blood splattering in every direction.

A few elves caught sight of her and ran toward her. Her heart was beating rapidly in her chest. Her hands continued to shake. The magic demanded to be loosed. It demanded to be used. Jovanna watched as the elves drew nearer, focusing on the one at the front. Time seemed to slow down. Every step he took seemed to take an eternity.

Her body raged against her mind. She flushed so hot that she was cold, so cold that she was hot. Her flesh felt like it was on fire and steam began to waft from her clenched hands. She kept her focus on the lead elf.

Five steps.

The magic was almost uncontrollable.

Four steps.

She couldn't wait anymore.

Three steps.

It was going to kill her.

Two steps.

Flames leaped off her skin.

One step.

She exhaled and released the magic.

THE END OF BOOK 3

THE RESTORED KING

1

GARRICK OPENED HIS EYES.

His head was pounding with a powerful headache and the front of his face felt swollen. He blinked a few times and stared at the unfamiliar ceiling above him. *Where am I?* he wondered.

Hearing movement to the left, he turned his head to see an old man in robes. The man was standing beside a closed door that looked like it was made of gold, his arms crossed over his chest. His robes were white and trimmed in silver. Garrick squinted and thought the man was looking at him, but he wasn't sure.

With great effort, he pushed himself up to a sitting position and looked around the room. It was fairly large and had beds that were spaced evenly throughout. Garrick counted six in total, including his. The other beds were empty, their sheets pulled tightly in place and tucked under the edges. The walls appeared to be white marble striated with blue and black lines. Alternating triangular tiles of teal and blue created an interesting pattern on the floor.

Garrick reached up and began rubbing his temples with his index fingers, hoping it might help relieve his headache. It didn't. The old man at the door hadn't moved the entire time, though Garrick suspected the man was watching him like a hawk.

"Where am I?" Garrick finally asked. His voice sounded odd and nasally. Was his nose broken?

"The Temple of Zevea." The old man's response was so quiet, Garrick almost didn't hear him.

"How … how did I get here?" he asked. Fear clenched his stomach. He tried to remember what might have happened, but it was a dark blur in the back of his mind. The old man didn't answer. A few moments later, the door swung open and a familiar face greeted him. It was Kelvin. He was dressed like the old man in the same flowing robes.

"Come with me," he said.

"Why am I here?" Garrick asked.

"I'll explain on the way. Follow me."

Garrick stood up on shaky legs. He hesitated, fearing his legs might give out on him. When they didn't, he took a few steps. Satisfied, he walked out of the room and followed Kelvin. The man's robes billowed around him as he walked at a brisk pace. Garrick kept up as best as he could. The hall they walked through was identical to the room he had just left. Every door they passed was gold and glinted in the strange light that came from spheres hanging at various intervals.

"How did we get here?" Garrick asked as they walked.

"You don't remember?"

"No."

"Well … it's probably best that you don't. I knocked you out."

Garrick's face scrunched in confusion. "Why?"

Kelvin cleared his throat. "I apologized before I did it, if that means anything to you. I didn't mean to hit you as hard as I did, but I managed to break your nose." They continued walking in silence before Kelvin spoke again. "There was an army of elves coming toward us. We had nowhere to go and you were ready to die fighting. I'm blessed by Zevea with a unique talent. I can … travel … far distances in mere moments."

"What does that have to do with hitting me?"

"The power only works with one conscious person. It's a blessing for those called to hunt down agents of Mordum. We can travel with someone, but they can't be conscious."

"Why not?" Garrick asked.

"It would kill them. We are not invincible with our armor, and I did not feel like dying. So, I took the only other option I could think of. And I brought us here."

"Where is here, exactly?"

"The location of this temple is a closely guarded secret. I'm afraid I cannot tell you … my Lord."

"I see."

They stopped at the end of the hall in front of two tall golden doors. Garrick wondered if they were really made of gold. Kelvin easily pushed them open.

"Not real gold," Garrick muttered to himself.

"It's real gold," Kelvin replied. "The gold is only a coating over the wood beneath. If they were full gold, I doubt I'd be able to budge them. Even with my armor."

Garrick nodded in silent agreement and they stepped into the doorway. The room they entered was no differently designed than the hall or the previous room. Several robed priests stood guard along the walls that led toward a raised floor. In the center of the rise sat an unadorned throne. As they approached, Garrick could tell the chair was old. The wood was smooth from wear. It had a tall back and two armrests. It was lacquered and seemed to shine when the light hit it just right.

Sitting on the throne was a woman. As soon as Garrick noticed, his entire focus rested on her. She was one of the most beautiful women he had ever seen, and he had seen many. Her hair was brown and spilled down over her shoulders, the ends reaching her waist. She sat straight with perfect posture, reminding Garrick of many of the nobles in his court.

Kelvin stopped right before the raised floor and bowed low. Not wanting to be rude, Garrick did the same. The faint smell of lavender reached his nose. His eyes met hers for long moments. Neither said anything. Garrick felt as though he could stare into her eyes forever and never grow weary of their green depths.

"King Garrick," she finally greeted. "It is good to finally meet you face to face."

"My Lady," Garrick replied. "I would honor your name, but I do not know it."

"You may call me Laracova," she paused, "Prophet of Zevea."

Garrick's fear returned. Why would the rival Prophet of Mordum summon him? He glanced uneasily between Laracova and Kelvin. Nothing about their attitude or posture seemed hostile. Still, he had a bad feeling.

"How can I be of assistance to you?" he asked.

"Please, calm your emotions," Laracova said. "I can sense your chaotic feelings and they are disturbing my calm. You have nothing to fear from me or anyone else here."

Her tone did calm him somewhat. "My apologies," he said. "I'm sure it is obvious whose mark I bear, though I do not follow his ways. I am curious to know why I am here."

Laracova smiled at him disarmingly. "Kelvin did what he thought was the best course of action, given the situation. While I may disagree with him, the point is moot since you are already here within our walls. I did not ask him to bring you here," she said. Leaning forward, she motioned him closer.

He took a few steps closer, but did not step onto the stairs that led up the platform.

"I want to be of service to you," she said. "I know the peril your kingdom faces. The elves are a formidable enemy. I offer you the strength of our warrior priests."

Garrick considered her words. "Why?" he finally asked.

"I have heard tale of your honor," she answered, glancing briefly to Kelvin. "You care for your people as a good king should. I had my doubts about your intentions, especially when I learned you were one of Mordum's servants." She held up a hand to still his argument. "Yet Zevea has commanded me to assist you regarding this matter. While we may only see the outside of men, the gods see the inside."

That truth resonated within him. "Indeed they do," he said.

"Once the elves have been dealt with, my priests are to report to Oakhaven."

"The capital of Oakvalor?" Garrick asked. "What's in Oakhaven?"

Laracova stood from her throne and descended the steps. "Come, walk with me in the garden."

She led the way out of the chamber, and Garrick fell into step beside her. Kelvin followed behind them, though he kept a respectful distance.

"What do you know of Mordum's intent? Does that mark give you insight into his mind?"

"No," Garrick said. "I have not received anything other than the armor and the blade."

"A pity," she said. "While the gods know the thoughts of men, they do not know the thoughts of gods. Zevea has told me that something is coming. Darkness. War." The hall they walked through split to either side and she turned them to the right. A door, plain and unadorned, led them outside. Walking down a few flagstone steps, they entered the garden.

It was a large area built in terraces along the sloping face of a mountain. Garrick tried to guess their location by the landscape, but quickly gave up. The scenery was as foreign as the elves at his gates. Ornamental shrubs and ponds surrounded small tinkling fountains. Orchids and roses and trailing vines covered stone archways. Paths led between carefully carved hedges and into shady grottos. The garden, exceedingly beautiful, served several functional purposes as well. In the center of the top level, where they were standing, was a large ornamental pond. The aura of tranquility struck Garrick immediately. It was quiet except for the occasional chirping of a few multi-colored birds.

"This place is breathtaking," Garrick said softly, fearing that his words might somehow impact the peace of the garden.

"Thank you," Laracova said. "Its beauty is deceptive. This garden is a fortification. Tunnels run the length of each terrace, with grated openings in strategic locations. It allows us the advantage of being in all places at once."

Garrick nodded, admiring the beauty of the garden as well as the hidden function of it. *She must trust me,* he thought. *Why else would she share that secret?*

She led them to the pond in the center. A few large coy fish swam lazily. A short pillar held a silver bowl atop it. Reaching into the bowl, Laracova grabbed a handful of bread crumbs and tossed them into pond. The fish fought each other for the pieces, disrupting the calm surface of the water.

"The pond reminds me of the world," she said. "The surface is calm from the outside, but underneath there is turbulence. And every so often, that turbulence affects the surface. I think it is evident to all of us in faith, but the gods are at war. Mankind is about to be brought into the conflict, with or without our consent. Mordum seeks a mortal body to wage his war here among us."

"I've heard the rumors," Garrick acknowledged. "How much truth there is to them, I don't know."

"In every rumor, there is a seed of truth. Yet they are more than rumors, Lord Garrick. Even now, Mordum's servants seek out the remains of his previous body. War is on the horizon. Where do you stand, I wonder?"

Garrick wondered that himself. He would do whatever he had to in order to protect his people. If Mordum's plans included keeping Talvaard safe, then his lot was with the dark god. And if Mordum's warpath were to consume his kingdom … Garrick paused the thought in his mind. Would he—*could* he—stand against Mordum? He bore the god's mark, after all. And he has seen the Prophet take control of men with the mark, watched as men with no inhibitions killed and destroyed their own loved ones. He rubbed at the thin material that hid the mark.

"I will do what is right," he finally answered.

Laracova stared at him with a piercing gaze. "I'm sure that you will. I have heard that you allied yourself with the prince of Oakvalor."

"I have," Garrick said. "His support was pivotal for my claim to the throne. As such, I am in debt to him."

"Then you shall march to Oakhaven as well?"

Garrick looked at her, confused.

"One of Mordum's servants currently sits on the throne in Oakhaven. From what my priests tell me, he has made it an all-important mission to bring Mordum into our plane of existence. He must be stopped. I hear that the prince you call your ally is on the path, ready to stand in the way of Mordum's goals. He walks a dangerous road and there are few strong enough to offer him aide. So, I ask again. You shall march to Oakhaven?"

"I will do what I can to help," Garrick answered evasively. "Right now, my sole concern is for the safety of my people. Once we drive the elves back, I can focus on helping others."

"I understand," Laracova said. "As I said, you have the support of my warriors. They are ready to travel when you are."

"Thank you." Garrick watched the fish cease their fighting. They resumed swimming, moving about the pond slowly.

Laracova gasped and clutched at her chest. Garrick reached for her as she collapsed, saving her from hitting her head on the ground.

"What's wrong?" he asked worriedly.

Her face blanched in terror, then softened into sadness. "Something has happened," she whispered.

"What? What is it?"

"Death, so much death." Her eyes roamed back and forth, as though seeing something other than his face. Her eyes widened.

"Your people," she gasped. "They are in danger!"

"No one loves a warrior until the enemy is at the gate."

—Melchiades

2

KESWICK LOOMED BEFORE ARAMIS AND Melchiades like a mountain.

Gray stone walls, taller than anything Aramis had ever seen, stood vigilant guard around the port city. It was supposedly second in size only to the capital of his kingdom. Judging by the massive stretch of coastal land that the city covered, Aramis wouldn't be surprised if the city of Keswick was larger. Spaced every few yards a guard tower rose from the wall. Aramis wasn't sure, but he thought he could see shrouded figures atop them. A massive portcullis, wide enough to comfortably allow four carriages through side by side, was halfway down.

"That's odd," Aramis said. "Why would the gate be closing so soon?"

Mel shrugged. Exchanging glances, they both urged their mounts to pick up the pace. As they approached the gates, Aramis noticed several heavily armed guards moving to intercept them. Slowing his horse down to a smooth trot, he raised his hand and hailed them.

"What's your business in Keswick?" one of the guards asked when they stopped.

"We're looking to book passage on a ship."

"Where are you headed?"

Aramis raised his brow, but answered anyway. "Down the coast. Near the Five Islands."

"Oakhaven?" the guard asked.

"Does it matter?" Aramis replied. His patience was beginning to fail and he made it evident in his tone. The guard didn't appear to be bothered by it.

"I'm sorry, sir. Standard procedure. I'm sure you understand?"

"Interrogating people is standard procedure? Since when? Keswick has always been an open city. Has something changed that I'm not aware of?"

The guard pulled his helmet off. Aramis saw the man was young; possibly no older than sixteen winters. A scar ran the length of his face on the left side. The path of mottled flesh barely missed his eye. His hair was black and he had bright blue eyes. Aramis wondered when the boy had been conscripted into the military.

"A lot has changed, I'm afraid. The city has experienced a lot of tragedy recently. The Lady of the city has taken extra precautions to ensure that tragedy stays minimal. I apologize if you feel like I am interrogating you. Unfortunately, the Lady isn't allowing just anyone into the city these days."

Aramis looked past the guard and into the city. It seemed normal. He could see traders in the market offering their wares. People walked about freely. He frowned.

"My friend and I are only looking to book passage on a ship headed for Oakhaven, or anywhere close to it. I've got urgent business there and I cannot delay. Is the harbor still open?"

"Yes, but not for much longer. No ships are permitted to leave port after sundown. If you don't make it onto a ship before then, you can find lodging at one of the inns near the docks. They're older buildings, but fairly priced considering recent events."

"Thank you," Aramis said. "I appreciate the information. You mentioned the Lady of the city. What of her husband? Lord Abriel?"

The young man's face betrayed his emotions long enough for Aramis to deduct that something ill must have happened.

"News doesn't travel well lately," the guard answered solemnly. "Lord Abriel is no longer among the living. Did you know him?"

"Not personally, no. I met him once and we spoke briefly. I'm sorry to hear of his loss. He was a good man."

The guard didn't say anything. Aramis suspected the young man was trying not to cry. *The people of the city must have loved him*, he thought.

"You may want to hurry if you expect to leave the port tonight," the guard finally said.

"Thank you again," Aramis said. The guards moved out of his path. He urged his horse forward and Mel followed him.

They dismounted after entering the city and began looking for a place to leave their horses. Mel spotted a stable to the left and they headed toward it.

"Something bad has happened here," Aramis said quietly. He glanced over at Mel. His friend nodded but didn't respond. He quickly realized why. The people they passed were eyeing them suspiciously. Some of them even stopped to stare.

"Do you think they recognize me?"

"Let's discuss things somewhere more ... private," Mel answered.

"Good idea."

They sold their horses at the stable for a poor price. The owner told them he had an overabundance of horses and no buyers. He apologized but didn't seem to care if they were pleased with his offer or not. Aramis accepted the offer, mostly because they didn't need to bring the horses on their journey. It'd cost them a small fortune to ship the animals and their funds were limited.

By the time Aramis and Mel reached the docks, sundown had come and gone. They'd gotten turned around and lost their general sense of direction. Hundreds of people packed the streets and by the time they found someone willing to point them to where they should go, the sky had already darkened. There were a few ships in port, but the area was devoid of any life.

They chose the closest inn to stay at. The sign above the door read *The Compass.* Inside, the place was crowded, hot and loud. Everyone in the place appeared to be a sailor. All the tables were taken so the two squeezed through the mob and made their way to the bar.

"What'll ya have?" the barkeep asked.

"A room for the night would be great," Aramis answered.

"You're in luck. I've got one left. Mostly lads from the sea renting tonight. Two gold for the room. You want anything else?"

"Food," Mel chimed in. "Can you have it delivered to our room?"

The doubtful look on the barkeep's face changed when Mel laid another gold coin on the counter.

"I'll have it up shortly," he said with a toothless grin.

"I appreciate it," Mel answered.

"Room's the last door on the right, second floor."

"Thank you," Aramis said. He led the way through the crowded inn to the stairs and up to their room. Mel paused in the hallway and made sure no one was following them, then stepped into the room and shut the door. It was dark except the moonlight coming from the sole window. Using matches that were on one of the side tables, Mel lit a few candles. The room brightened considerably.

"What do you suppose happened here?" Aramis asked.

"I haven't the faintest idea, my Lord," Mel answered. "It's obvious it was something bad. Particularly so to close a fortified city down at night. Keswick has the largest standing army outside of the capital."

"I know." Aramis walked over to stare out of the window. He could see men lighting the lanterns that lined the cobbled streets below. Other than the distrust of the guards at the gate and some of the people in the streets, the city seemed normal.

"Well, we are stuck here until morning regardless. I say we eat and get some rest. We have plenty to do once we get back to Oakhaven."

Mel nodded in agreement. He could hear footsteps in the hall. A loud knock echoed throughout the room. "That must be the food," Mel said. He opened the door to find a half dozen guards, all armed and armored. They pushed their way into the room. Mel stepped to the side to get out of their way.

"What is the meaning of this?" Aramis demanded.

"Is this them?" one of the guards, the apparent leader, asked.

The guards parted to let a young man come through. Aramis realized it was the scarred young man from the gate. He glanced at Aramis and Mel quickly and then lowered his head. He mumbled something Aramis couldn't hear.

"Speak up," the leader said.

"Yes," the young man answered.

"You're dismissed."

The young man turned to leave and cast a glance back at Aramis. The look on his face was apologetic. Aramis kept his face as impassive as he could despite his annoyance. There was no telling what sort of trouble was about to ensue.

"I will ask again," Aramis said calmly. "What is the meaning of this?"

"Your presence is requested," the leader finally answered. "If you will." He motioned toward the door.

Aramis looked to Mel. His friend nodded ever so slightly.

"Very well," he said.

The guards escorted them down the stairs, through the crowd, and out of the front door. The streets were mostly empty now; only the occasional drunk passed them. Although there wasn't much light, it was obvious that they were being led toward the direction of the castle. As they turned down various roads, Aramis noticed that some of the buildings were damaged. He had a suspicion that a battle had happened recently.

Roughly a quarter of an hour later, they entered the courtyard of the castle. It was large and open, with gray statues of armored men in various places. As they approached two large doors that led to the inside of the castle, he noticed a large group of guards. They were lined up on either side of the doors and looked uneasy. Several of them kept looking back toward the gatehouse Aramis had just entered through.

Their escort led them into the castle and left them in a small, unfurnished room.

"Wait here," the leader said.

Once they were alone, Aramis informed Mel of his observations.

"I noticed the same things," Mel replied. "Perhaps there has been a rebellion?"

"Perhaps," Aramis acknowledged. He ran his hand through his hair and scratched the back of his head. "I can't think of anything else that might have the city on edge, but even that doesn't make sense. Why lock the city down only at night? If there was a rebellion, guards would be walking the streets continuously. I didn't notice additional patrols. The common people are still going about their business as usual."

Before Mel could respond, the door opened and a nicely dressed young man stepped into the room. His clothes were made of expensive materials and by the way he held himself, Aramis figured he was of noble birth.

"Please follow me," the man instructed.

Turning on his heel, he walked out at a quick pace. Aramis and Mel followed him, surprised at the man's stride. They traveled down a long hall and entered a massive dining room. A table, roughly twenty feet long, was covered with dishes of exotic foods. The smells made Aramis's mouth water.

"Smells heavenly," Mel said quietly.

"Mm." Aramis grunted. He expected the man to seat them at the table, but they continued past the table and out of the room into another hall. This one was much shorter and only had one door. The man knocked on the door twice, paused, and then knocked again three times. The door swung open on silent hinges and the young man waved them in.

The first thing Aramis noticed was the bed. It was enormous, with four large posts at each corner that supported a canvas that draped over the entire bed. Incense filled the air, but there was no smoke. The young man bowed, then turned and left the room.

Aramis glanced around. Everything in the room led him to believe this was a bedroom for a noble. Large sturdy pieces of furniture were positioned throughout the room. Expensive combs, bejeweled mirrors and other garish things decorated every available surface. They appeared to be alone in the room. Aramis walked over to a desk that sat in front of a large window. Papers, piled in neat stacks, sat atop the surface.

Perusing them led him to believe they were reports. He saw the word "Warlock" scrawled on many of them. He was about to read one of the reports when a noise drew his attention away. A hidden panel in the wall slid to the side and a woman with two armored guards entered the room.

Aramis had only ever seen Lord Abriel's wife once, but he recognized her immediately. Her beauty was a thing of legend. Despite being in her later years, her beauty still captivated men of all ages. Aramis tore his gaze away from her long enough to see that Mel's mouth was hanging open. Aramis laughed and stepped toward her. One of the guards quickly drew his sword and went into a defensive stance.

"Peace," the woman said.

Gods, thought Aramis, *even her voice is perfect.*

The guard hesitated for a moment, but finally sheathed his weapon.

"My Lady," Aramis greeted. His voice faltered and he had to cough to clear his throat. "My Lady," he said again, bowing.

"Good evening," she replied. "Please, call me Lynessa. I am sorry to have brought you here the way I did, but I didn't see any other option."

"No need to apologize," Aramis managed to say. Words seemed to have fled from his vocabulary. "I must mention that we would have come if you had called upon us."

"I'm sure you would have. Unfortunately, I didn't have time to be proper. You are a wanted criminal. Word of your deeds has reached far. You are fortunate that some of my men recognized you. There are others who would have turned you in already."

"Let me guess," Aramis said as he folded his arms defiantly, "you want me to do something for you or you'll turn me in yourself?"

"You wound me, my Prince. Do you think I am like the beggars, seeking only what I may gain from others? No. I have a petition."

"A petition?" His defiance quickly melted.

"Indeed, but I'm being a terrible host. Are either of you hungry? Or thirsty? I can have a servant fetch something for you?"

"Some wine would be nice," Mel said.

"I agree," Aramis chimed in.

Lynessa grabbed a bell from one of the tables and rang it. Within seconds, a female servant rushed into the room. "Wine for our guests," she said. The servant curtsied and left.

"The matter I'd like to talk about is … delicate. Normally I would host you in the dining room, but I desire privacy in this matter. I'm sure you understand?"

"Of course," Aramis replied.

"Good. I'm not entirely sure how much you know about our recent events, but terrible things have happened."

"I have heard that your husband passed away. I'm sorry to hear that."

"Abriel was murdered," Lynessa said.

Aramis's eyes widened in shock.

"I had debated keeping it a secret from the people. He was loved by everyone, and I didn't want anyone taking rash actions. Before we could deliver the news, something else happened."

The servant returned, bearing a tray with tall glasses. She handed one to Lynessa, then to Aramis and Mel.

"Thank you. You are dismissed for the evening. If I need anything, I'll have one of my guards attend to it."

The servant bowed her head and left. After a few moments, Lynessa motioned to the door. The guard who had drawn his sword on Aramis left the room and returned a moment later.

"She's gone," he said.

"Very good. I—"

The second guard suddenly threw Lynessa to the ground. Aramis was confused until he saw the glint of steel in his hand. The guard drew his hand back to drive the dagger into her, but the first guard threw himself bodily into the other man. The two rolled around, struggling against one another. Aramis quickly helped Lynessa to her feet and stood protectively in front of her.

One of the men screamed in pain and stopped struggling. The man who tried to kill Lynessa stood up and rushed Aramis. Barely thinking about it, he summoned his armor. The air hissed loudly as the armor formed around him from mist. Just as his armor finished materializing, the man struck him with the dagger. It made a clanging sound as it slid off his breastplate.

Aramis grabbed the man's wrist and twisted it sharply. The man gasped and the blade clattered to the ground. Mel was there suddenly, grabbing the man from behind and locking him in a chokehold. The guard flailed and attempted to fight back, but it was futile. Swiftly rendered unconscious, Mel dropped him to the floor a moment later.

"What is going on?" Aramis said. His pulse was pounding in his head.

"It is as I feared," Lynessa replied. "He has infiltrated my personal guard."

"Who has?"

"The Warlock."

"Who is the Warlock?" Aramis asked.

"Please, we must tend to Cardon first. Can you find one of my servants?"

"I'll go," Mel offered. He hurried off.

Aramis dismissed his armor and knelt beside Cardon. A small pool of blood had formed near the man's shoulder. He gently lifted the man's arm to get a better look. The dagger had pierced him in the armpit and blood was flowing freely from the wound. Aramis ripped the hem of his shirt off and pressed the cloth against the wound. Cardon groaned.

"Will he survive?" Lynessa asked worriedly.

"I've seen men survive much worse. He'll be fine so long as we can stop the bleeding." Aramis was growing worried the longer that Mel was gone. The cloth was already soaked with blood.

"Perhaps I should go find help," Lynessa suggested.

"No," Aramis said immediately. "If your personal guard has been compromised, there's no telling how many of your servants are also assassins in disguise. Mel will get help."

As though hearing his name, Mel came flying into the room with a group of servants trailing him.

"Out of the way!" a deep voice cried out.

An older man pushed his way through the servants and knelt at Cardon's other side. "He's turning pale. Where's the wound?"

"In the armpit," Aramis answered. "I'm trying to halt the blood flow, but it's not going so well."

"Give me your shirt," the older man said. "And get out of the way."

Aramis took it off without hesitation and handed it to the man. The man wrapped the shirt under Cardon's arm and tied a tight knot.

"We've got to take him to the infirmary," he demanded. "Any longer and I can't guarantee he'll live." The servants broke into action. They lifted Cardon and carried him out of the room while the older man shouted orders.

Aramis looked at Lynessa. "Are you all right?" he asked.

"I'm fine. A little shaken, but I'm fine."

"What should we do about him?" Aramis pointed to the unconscious assassin. "He won't be out forever."

"I'll take care of him," Mel said. He walked over and grabbed the man by his legs, then dragged him out of the room.

Aramis sat down on the floor. His hands were covered in Cardon's blood, so he tried not to touch anything. He realized Lynessa was staring at him.

"So, it's true," she said softly.

"What is?"

"That you bear the mark."

Aramis sighed. "Yes, but it is not what you may think."

"Explain it to me," she said. "My husband was murdered by the Warlock. And he has the same symbol."

Mel entered the room then, followed by more servants. They began cleaning the blood from the floor. One of them began washing Aramis's arms. He tried to protest, but the servant ignored him. Once he was clean, another servant brought him a shirt. It was dark blue and made of a thin material. He put it on and got back on his feet.

After the floor was cleaned, the servants departed. They had done such a good job that Aramis would never have known anyone had almost died.

"May I speak to your prince alone?" Lynessa asked Mel.

He nodded and closed the door behind him as he left.

"Tell me," she said.

Aramis explained everything. As many times as he had told his story, relating his father's death never got easier. After he had related all the details, including his escape from Red Mountain, they sat in silence.

"It sounds like you have suffered as I have suffered," Lynessa finally said. "I trust you."

"It gives my heart gladness to hear it," Aramis replied. "Why did you bring me here?"

"I need your help. The Warlock murdered my husband. I've had the city guard searching for him since it happened, but they have been unsuccessful so far."

"You mentioned something else happened?"

"Yes. I would not have believed it if I had not seen it myself. At night, the dead come alive."

Aramis waited for her to explain. When she didn't, he asked, "What do you mean?"

"There is a graveyard for the nobles not far from here," Lynessa said. "Every night since Abriel's death, the dead rise from their graves and attack the city. I know the Warlock is behind it, but I haven't figured out how."

"You want me to find him."

"If you can. I've heard many rumors concerning you lately. I don't know how much of it is true, but anything you can do would be greatly appreciated."

"I wouldn't know where to start," he said.

"The graveyard will be the best place. I will give you whatever you need. Soldiers, money, anything."

"I would love to assist you, but I'm afraid I can't. There is something much bigger at work and I need to find my father's killer. I can't reclaim my throne if I can't prove I didn't kill my father."

Lynessa closed her eyes and lowered her head, crestfallen. "I had hoped … I don't know what I had hoped," she whispered sadly.

Aramis felt terribly guilty. He considered what she had said. If this Warlock was one of Mordum's agents, it wouldn't hurt to try and track him down. He would certainly need Mel's help, though.

"Lynessa," Aramis said softly, "I will help you."

She lifted her head and met his eyes. He could see tears had started to slide down her face. Even in her sadness, he found her beautiful.

"If you find him, I will reward you with anything you ask. I will publicly swear my loyalty to you as King."

"I will do what I can," Aramis replied.

Lynessa leaned in uncomfortably close to him. He could smell her perfume. Staring into her eyes, he had the sudden urge to kiss her. She must have had the same idea because she moved in even closer. They were mere inches from one another. Pushing his nervousness aside, he was about to kiss her when someone knocked on the door. The interruption broke the moment and Lynessa pulled back.

The door opened and Mel poked his head inside. "You need to see this, my Lord."

"What is it?" Aramis asked, still staring at Lynessa. His heart was thudding against his chest.

"The dead. They're … not dead. They're attacking the city."

"A man is never too weak or wounded to fight if the cause is greater than his own life."

—Aramis

3

ASH.

Jovanna stood on a blackened field. As far as she could see, there was nothing but a smoldering, charred landscape. Scorched bones littered the area. The smell of burnt flesh—and death—filled her nostrils. It was overwhelming. She dropped to her knees and vomited.

Inhale. Exhale.

Jovanna repeated the words in her mind and her body obeyed. She wiped the back of her hand across her lips and spat the vile taste from her mouth. She was stronger than this; *better* than this. She staggered to her feet and immediately felt her strength drain from her. It was all she could do to remain standing. Tremors ran through every muscle in her body. It was a weakness like she had never experienced. A pounding ache in her head reverberated behind her eyes.

The weakness was undeniable, yet she also felt *powerful.* She had done something no one else had. She had used the elven tattoo magic. Her, a human, able to wield both elven magic and human magic. She smiled as the implication slowly came into focus.

She stood and waited for the dizziness to pass. The rushing torrent of magical energy that had left her and caused the destruction that she gazed upon was great indeed, though it left her feeling sick and weak. She would need to learn to control it better.

As her vision returned to normal, Jovanna noticed the elves had regrouped across the field. They were preparing to attack, forming ranks and putting their archers at the rear of their force. She needed to recuperate.

Jovanna tried to turn and retreat to the fortress, but her muscles would not obey her. She stood there, frozen. She was confused. Then she thought maybe one of the elves had cast a spell at her. Closing her eyes, she sent her senses out. Nothing. She could feel the humming of the elves' magical tattoos, but aside from that, there was no other magic in effect.

She opened her eyes and looked down at her legs. They trembled slightly from weakness, but there were no wounds she could see that would keep her from moving. Her confusion turned to anger as she tried harder to move. Had the tattoos she'd inked caused an issue? She watched the magic floating around her calves. Everything seemed normal. Then again, to her knowledge, she was the first human to use the elven magic. Perhaps there was a good reason why humans didn't use it.

The book. She remembered reading in the book that humans had given their elven slaves the tattoos. There was no mention of whether the humans had used them as well. Jovanna sighed in frustration.

A single braying trumpet sounded from the fortress behind her. She turned her head—she had some control—and her eyes widened in shock. The front half of the castle had been blown apart. Had she done that?

The army of elves came across the field at a run, shouting insults and defiance to their foes. Arrows from both sides arced into the skies, forming a canopy of death above the heads of the armies, who came together with a resounding crash. Not far from the fighting, she was trying desperately to move. No one had noticed her. Yet.

Then she saw Garrick, the king of Talvaard, look her way. She had saved his life when the elves were assaulting the walls. Like some fool, she had watched him leap off the castle walls into the midst of the elves, single handedly fighting them off while his men repaired the breach the elves had created.

She watched as combat became hand to hand. The archers on both side were now effectively useless. The two armies were locked together in a bloody embrace. After several moments, she saw the human line of defense break.

Their order and discipline quickly dissolved and chaos ensued. Then, faintly, she felt something in the air. It was magic, she was sure, but it was not like anything she'd experienced before. There was something … *old* to it. She twisted her head in every direction, but she didn't see the source.

Her attention returned to Garrick once she noticed he was fighting one of the elves with the stone skin tattoo. He was fighting a losing battle. She'd helped him once; now he was on his own. And then suddenly, she could move again. Whatever had held her still just dissipated. Jovanna surveyed the battle. There was nothing she could do. Until she learned to control her new magic, everyone was at risk of being killed by anything she cast.

Just as she decided to run, she saw him. His black robes billowed around him as he stalked through the battlefield. She watched as with barely a touch, he made men collapse to the ground as though they were dead. Her eyes narrowed when she realized it was Tairu.

She unsheathed her sword and ran towards him.

4

ARAMIS WATCHED THE AMASSING CROWD of corpses from behind the castle's courtyard gates. They shuffled in random directions in what appeared to him to be laziness. Mel stood at his side, a look of disgust on his face. They'd both had their fill of a delicious meal and changed clothes. They were each wearing thin black cloaks over plain brown tunics and black breaches.

Mel had initially scoffed at the plain clothes, but knowing they would likely be covered in blood and the gods knew what else, he had finally acquiesced.

"It's odd," Aramis said. "They don't seem like they are all that dangerous."

"Don't be fooled," one of the nearby guards said. "They only act like that when the Warlock isn't among them. When he is, they become very formidable."

"Formidable would be an understatement," one of the other guards chimed in. "I've fought formidable men before. These things can't die. They're much more than formidable."

"Have either of you seen the Warlock?" Aramis asked.

"No," the first man said.

"I have," said the second. "It was only a glimpse, but that was enough to raise the hackles on my neck. Creepy looking fellow."

"What did he look like?"

"Hard to say," the guard said. "He was wearing a long robe and his face was covered with a hood."

Aramis frowned. "A man in a robe whose features you couldn't see made you uneasy?"

"Of course not," the man bristled. His face flushed with anger. "There's something about his presence that was…" the man grasped at the air as if he could grab ahold of the word he was searching for, "… dark. Evil."

He knew the feeling well. When he'd faced the chimera in the woodland home of the druids, the very air seemed to be sucked from his lungs. The creature's presence was overpowering. Aramis nodded in understanding. He looked around the courtyard and surveyed the demeanor of the guards. Although the gates were closed and barred against the dead, they all seemed anxious. Their hands gripped the hilts of their swords and their eyes darted from shadow to shadow.

"What about the townsfolk?" Aramis asked. "How are they safe outside these walls?"

"The dead act like this normally, so they are safe within their homes or other buildings. The first few nights they came alive was different. They were smarter."

"Smarter?"

"Yes. They knew how to enter buildings, they carried weapons. They had *purpose*. It was as if they had someone commanding them, guiding them to where they should be. I know it sounds odd, but you'd have to have seen it to understand."

Aramis looked to Mel, who only squinted out into the darkness. "What do you think?" Aramis asked. "Should we make our move tonight?"

Mel reached up and tapped his chin with his right hand. "The idea of walking among these disgusting things is appalling." He sighed dramatically. "Yet I suppose the quicker we take action, the quicker we can be done here and move on to our intended destination."

"Agreed," Aramis said. He turned to the guard. "Open the gates."

"What?" The guard looked like he might run off in fear.

"We need to get out there and find the Warlock. Open the gates."

The guard hesitated, looking from the corpses outside the gate to the castle.

"Don't worry," Aramis said. "We won't let any of them breach the wall. We don't even need to open it much, just enough for us to slip out."

Aramis thought the man would deny the request, but he nodded. He waved to the other guard who came over and helped him lift the bar from the gates. Opening the gate just enough to fit his body through, Aramis stepped out among the dead. Mel followed quickly, then pushed the gate back in place. The two guards replaced the bar.

"Good luck," one of them said. "You're going to need it."

"Thanks."

Aramis summoned his blade. The air hissed as the black metaled weapon formed in his hand. Mel did likewise, the silver blade standing in stark contrast to his own. They began making their way through the undead, dodging the corpse's slow-moving attempts to grab at them.

"It's hard to imagine these things actually fighting," Aramis said over his shoulder to Mel.

"I agree, my Lord. The idea that these things could have anything resembling intelligence is … doubtful."

They stopped at the end of the street. It continued straight and forked to the left and to the right. The area was devoid of any of the dead. The street lanterns had been lit and they had plenty of light to see by. The buildings in this area looked similar to the ones they had passed by earlier. Signs of fire, broken windows. Aramis placed the tip of his sword in the cobbled ground and balanced the blade against his leg, then pulled out a piece of parchment.

"This map shows the graveyard should be down the street to our right. A few hundred feet, if that."

"The Lady seems taken with you," Mel said unexpectedly.

"What?" Aramis turned to his friend.

"I can see it in her eyes," Mel added. "She fancies you. She's twice your age, surely, but she likes you. Do you not see it?"

"Oh, I see it," Aramis answered. "She probably would have kissed me if you hadn't walked in earlier."

"If I may be direct, my Lord?"

"You know you can," Aramis said with a laugh. "You've never asked permission before."

"Do not toy with her emotions. If you do not feel the same way about her as you do about Hanna, I would avoid anything other than our current business with her."

At Hanna's name, Aramis pulled the pendant she had given him out from beneath his shirt. It glimmered faintly in the light of the street lanterns. He hadn't thought of Hanna in a while.

"Of course I don't feel the same way," Aramis finally said. "They have two completely different personalities. Lynessa is beautiful and strong. Especially in the wake of her husband's murder. Trying to deal with grief and run a city … I can only imagine what she is going through. Hanna though … Hanna is more than someone whose looks I admire." He placed the pendant back beneath his shirt and rolled the parchment back up. He slipped it into his belt and picked up his sword.

"That's good to hear, my Lord. I fear that her attraction to you may simply be part of her grieving. Freedom changes people."

"Freedom? I wouldn't think the loss of someone beloved to you to be freedom."

"Perhaps freedom was the wrong word. Loneliness, maybe? The lack of love changes people. It makes us do things we would never do otherwise. Certainly, you understand this?"

"Yes," Aramis lied. He knew what Mel meant, of course, but he couldn't say he understood how it *felt*. He didn't like talking about his feelings anyway. "This way," he said. They went to the right and walked for a while in silence. The further they traveled, the less the street lanterns illuminated anything. It was like a dark haze was pulling the light into its depths. Ahead, Aramis saw the small stone wall and steel gate that marked the entryway into the cemetery.

"There," Aramis paused and pointed. "That must be it. It fits the description."

"Something feels wrong here," Mel said.

Aramis looked around them, expecting to see more of the corpses. Everything was quiet. The flame of the lantern to their right flickered sporadically before suddenly dying. They were left in complete darkness except for the pale moonlight that filtered down through the thick murky clouds above. They exchanged glances.

"Eerie," Aramis said. The sound of his voice seemed loud and out of place. Without another word, Aramis headed toward the gate. It swung open on silent hinges. Apparently, it was well kept. Large stepping stones, surrounded by small pebbles, led them into the cemetery. The footpath was only a few feet wide. On either side of the path, manicured grass stretched out before them. A dense fog blanketed everything. It was so thick Aramis could only see a few feet in any direction.

"This seems like a bad idea," he whispered.

"I couldn't agree more, my Lord," Mel whispered back.

As they continued along the path, they began passing gravesites. Most of them had been disturbed, the grass and dirt having been heaved up off the wooden caskets below the ground. Aramis's senses began to play tricks on him. He thought he saw movement within the shadowy fog, but when he peered toward the movement, there was nothing there. Whispers called out to him, but when he stopped walking, he heard nothing.

"Is it just me, or does this place seem *alive?*" he asked.

"That would be one way to describe it," Mel answered.

The path circled around a large fountain. Gray stone benches were placed on the edges of the pathway, close to the grass. The base of the fountain was round and made of the same gray stone as the benches. An angelic statue stood guard in the center of the fountain, holding a sword in one hand and a shield in the other. Water sprayed mist like into the air from the tip of the blade.

"What is that?" Mel asked.

Aramis turned his attention to where Mel was pointing. A mass of shapes slowly materialized out of the fog. As they came closer, he realized they were corpses. They weren't like those outside of the castle, however. These corpses didn't shuffle around. They walked like normal men and they were armed with swords and axes.

Aramis summoned his armor. He could hear the air hissing around him as Mel did the same. With a sudden quickness, the dead charged them. Aramis brought his sword up in a sweeping arc as one of them came within range. The powerful stroke cut through the creature's rotting flesh easily, but stopped as it struck the dead man's ribcage.

The blow hardly affected the thing. It growled at him and brought its own sword up to strike him. Throwing himself backwards to avoid the blow, he had to let go of his own blade. The dead man came at him, swinging its sword back and forth like an untrained thug. Aramis easily maneuvered himself away from the swings. When he saw an opportunity, he lunged forward and grabbed the hilt of his sword and yanked hard. A cracking noise filled the air and the blade came free. No blood rushed from the wound. He deflected the man's next few strikes and scored a few of his own.

"How do you kill someone who is already dead?" Aramis shouted. He risked a glance over at Mel and saw he was busy fending off two corpses.

"I haven't figured that out yet!" Mel shouted back.

Swinging low, Aramis succeeded in hacking off one of the man's legs. It threatened to fall over, but managed to stay upright. It began hopping toward him. Aramis was unpleasantly surprised to see the limb stand up and reattach itself to the man's stump. It came at him as if nothing had happened.

Gods, he thought, *this was a terrible idea. I don't even know how to fight these things!* Then he thought about Lynessa and her look of disappointment. He couldn't let her down. He wouldn't. With a loud cry, he swung with all his might and removed the dead man's head. The corpse continued to stand for a moment before toppling to the ground. He watched for a moment to see if the thing would get back up. It didn't move.

"Cut off their heads!" he yelled to Mel.

He watched as Mel spun about in a circle and, with an amazing flourish, both corpses had their heads lopped off.

"You've got company!" Mel shouted.

Aramis turned to find three of the dead men running at him. He growled in frustration and rushed to meet them head on. Though they were obviously untrained, he was outnumbered. He went on the defensive, parrying their strikes. They kept him so busy fending off their attacks that he couldn't get his own strikes in. He began to back pedal, slapping their swords away as he struggled not to trip over himself. His back suddenly slammed into something hard. Glancing back, he saw it was Mel.

His friend was fighting a pair of dead men. Being so focused on the fight, he almost didn't notice the mass of corpses that were joining the fray. It was slow at first. Two and three here or there, but then they started appearing in droves. They were quickly surrounded. Only a small circle of space kept the dead at bay.

Aramis could feel his arms getting heavy. His breathing was getting labored and sweat was dripping down his chest and back. As his defenses began to falter, his armor started taking more hits. Clanging filled the air as the dead men's blows rained down on him. He could hear Mel grunting in pain behind him.

A breeze blew through the cemetery, causing the fog to swirl in random directions. To his right, Aramis caught sight of a small stone building. Two torches were lit on either side of the doorway. He wasn't completely sure, but he thought the door was ajar. And then he had a desperate idea.

"I think I see a defensible position!" he shouted. "We need to clear a path to *my* right. Can you manage it?"

"Yes," Mel answered. The word came out more as a gasp.

Aramis managed the knock the sword out of one of his attacker's hands, then quickly decapitated him. "Let's go now!"

As one, they turned in the direction of the building and forced their way through the crowd of dead men. Arms and legs got hacked off as the two used the last of their strength to push through the bodies. When they finally broke free, they sprinted to the building and crashed into the stone door. It barely moved. Placing his shoulder against the door, Aramis pushed with all his might. It moved an inch. Mel joined him and they shoved their weight against the door.

With slow momentum, the door finally swung inward. The two men ducked inside and tried to force the door shut. The dead men were quickly closing the distance. Aramis cried out in pain as his muscles threatened to disobey him. He put everything he had into his last shove. The door slid closed with a soft clunk, leaving them in a faintly lit corridor.

Aramis slid down the door, his backside resting on the floor. His exhaustion was complete. There wasn't a muscle in his body that wasn't screaming for relief. Against his better judgement, he dismissed his sword and his armor.

For long moments, the only sound was their heavy breathing. Aramis was burning up. He was soaked with sweat and his clothes clung frustratingly to his flesh. He met Mel's gaze and managed to grin.

"You owe me for this one, my Lord."

Aramis laughed. The absurdity of their situation was obvious. If they could escape the place before daylight, it would be a hard fight all the way back to the castle. If they waited out the night, assuming they survived, they would have to do it all over again the next night.

The air hissed as Mel dismissed his own blade and armor. They sat quietly, each trying to catch their breath and find what rest they could. As their breathing became normal, Aramis thought he could hear something echoing throughout the corridor. It was faint and sounded like singing. He was about to dismiss it as his imagination when Mel looked at him.

"Do you hear that?" he asked.

"I think so," Aramis answered. "It sounds like singing."

"Why would anyone be singing?"

They must have come to the same conclusion at the same time as they both said in unison, "The Warlock."

Aramis pushed himself to his feet and held a hand out to Mel. They locked hands and Aramis leveraged his weight backwards to help Mel onto his feet. They walked cautiously down the corridor, stepping lightly. The hallway ended abruptly with stairs leading down to a lower level. Aramis took the lead and made his way down the stone steps, Mel right behind him. After roughly twenty steps, they found themselves in a small antechamber.

Small spheres of light hovered at random along the room's walls. Old paintings, worn and unrecognizable from time, covered the walls. A once lavish rug, now frayed and faded, decorated the floor. To their left and their right were doorways that lacked any sort of door. Straight ahead, a rotting wooden door hung on rusted hinges.

Glancing through both doorways provided nothing useful. They were dark and from what he could tell, were empty. Aramis could now hear the singing more clearly. But it wasn't singing; it was chanting. It drifted into the chamber from behind the door.

Aramis summoned his blade. He held off on calling his armor. He wanted the element of surprise, and if he entered the room creaking and clanking about, he surely wouldn't have it. Approaching the door, he paused in front of it and listened. The chanting was in a language he did not know. Raising his eyebrows at Mel, he nodded toward the door. Mel shrugged.

Gritting his teeth, Aramis pushed gently on the door. It creaked softly as it partially opened. Cursing the hinges in his mind, he waited. The chanting didn't stop. Not wanting to press his luck, he squeezed himself through the opening. The door creaked again when his shoulder pushed against the door. His anger getting the better of him, he pushed the door completely open. Surprisingly, no sound came from the hinges.

Of course, he fumed.

They entered a large, circular room. Spheres of light, identical to the ones in the previous chamber, illuminated everything with their soft light. The walls and floor were made of marble. The ceiling arched overheard, a dome supported by delicate columns. Embedded in the walls of the room were row after row of glass chambers, chambers intended to hold bodies. Many of them were empty, but others were occupied. From the light of the spheres, Aramis could see aged corpses inside. *A mausoleum,* he realized.

Rows of benches lined the room from left to right. They were separated by a walkway down the middle that led to a raised platform. Upon the platform was a long slab, and in front of that slab stood a robed figure. His back was to them and he was bent over the slab. Aramis inched into the room, treading lightly. Kneeling behind one of the benches, he waved Mel in.

Mel entered the room and knelt behind the row of benches across from Aramis. They watched the figure in silence. Aramis suddenly noticed that atop the slab lay a corpse. The figure continued chanting softly.

"What should we do?" Aramis whispered.

Mel's face scrunched in thought, and after a moment he shrugged.

Aramis looked around the room. Besides the door they entered, there was only one other located to the right of the platform. The chanting stopped. Aramis froze, not even daring to breathe. The figure left the room. Without having any sort of plan, Aramis sprinted across the room, holding his sword up before him. He stopped just shy of the door and peeked through the doorway. A narrow hallway, roughly fifty feet long, ended abruptly with a stone wall. There were no other doors, yet the figure was nowhere to be seen. He turned to see Mel examining the body on the slab.

"This one is fresh," Mel said softly.

Aramis joined him and looked at the body. He gasped. "That's Lord Abriel. Or, it was."

"Where's the Warlock?" Mel asked, looking toward the doorway.

"I don't know. There's nothing but an empty hallway through there."

Mel frowned. "I don't like this," he said. Then he summoned his armor.

Aramis shuddered. An intense feeling of dread crept up his back and the tattoo on his arm began to burn furiously. The hovering spheres of light were unexpectedly snuffed out, leaving them in darkness. Aramis summoned his armor. The air hissed as it formed.

"I should have known the Lady would send her minions looking for me," a deep voice echoed in the room.

A dull red light broke the darkness. The robed figure stood on the other side of the slab, holding a black wooden staff in his left hand. The light shone from a small crystal on the tip of it. His robes were as black as the staff. A hood was pulled low over the top half of his face. Judging by the lower part, Aramis guessed the man was young.

"I did not expect a fellow follower of Mordum, however. Are you here with orders? No? I didn't think it likely."

Aramis tried to move, but his muscles wouldn't obey him. His eyes darted to Mel. He seemed frozen as well.

"A neat trick, isn't it? Not when you are on the receiving end of it maybe, but no matter. So, what to do with intruders …" the man tapped his chin with his index finger. He smiled. "I know."

Leaning down, he began a whispered chant in the corpse's ear. Aramis's skin tingled. The air grew cold, so cold that Aramis could see his breath. Despite the spell the Warlock had cast, he shivered. He could feel the warmth leaving his body. And just as suddenly, the cold was gone.

The Warlock stood back up, the same smile on his face. The body of Lord Abriel began to spasm, here and there at first, but growing in frequency. Abriel's mouth opened and he exhaled loudly. His eyelids opened and Aramis saw nothing but black where the whites of his eyes should have been. Abriel sat up. A wave of foul smelling air hit Aramis's nostrils. The signs of decay had already set in.

"I think I'll leave you two here to get acquainted with the previous lord of the city. I've got people to terrorize and I'd rather not be late."

The Warlock stepped around the slab. "It's a pity the Prophet wants you kept alive," he said to Aramis. "Though there are others who … don't care as much. Like your brother. Personally, I don't see the resemblance. You can judge for yourself soon enough. Goodbye, gentlemen."

The Warlock faded from sight. As soon as he was gone, the spell of binding ended. Aramis staggered back from the slab. The soulless body of Abriel turned his dead gaze on them. He got off the slab and took shaky steps toward them. Aramis and Mel backed away but took defensive positions.

"I don't know what he's planning, but we've got to stop him," Aramis said.

"I agree, my Lord, but I fear we have troubles of our own now."

Abriel raced toward them, his arms swinging wildly. Aramis threw his sword in an upward arc, cutting off Abriel's left arm at the elbow. That hardly stopped him. He slammed bodily into Aramis and they tumbled to the floor in a mass of blows. Mel jumped in and grabbed Abriel by his tattered shirt and pulled him off Aramis. Pushing Abriel back, Mel brought his own blade across and cut Abriel's head cleanly off his shoulders. The body dropped lifelessly onto the ground.

Mel offered his arm to Aramis and helped him back onto his feet. They stared down at the corpse. Aramis wondered if it was truly that easy. After a few minutes had passed, and the body still hadn't moved, Aramis figured it was safe.

"I don't feel right leaving the body like this," Aramis said.

"What do you mean? What are we supposed to do with it?"

"I think this place is used for putting the city's nobles to rest. I'd hate for someone to come down here and see their previous lord cut to pieces. Let's put him in his ..." he waved to the glass chambers embedded in the walls, "coffin thing."

Mel sighed. "Yes, my Lord."

They found that a small placard with each person's name and house was placed below the chamber that the body rested in. They found Lord Abriel's easy enough as the placard for his name was made of gold. Several minutes of struggling later, they had placed the lord's body, severed arm and head in his chamber and closed the glass paned door.

"Now we must fight our way back to the castle," Aramis said. "Gods, this night just keeps getting better and better."

They backtracked their way to the stone door that sealed the outside world out. No sound could be heard from the other side, so they took the risk of pulling the door open. They were greeted with silence and an empty cemetery.

"Do you think we should get back to the castle?" Mel asked.

"I think that would be a good idea."

They ran the entire way. Aramis fumbled with the map as they ran, navigating them to the correct street. Once they reached the street that led to the castle, Aramis could hear a commotion. They sprinted the remainder of the distance to the gates and found the castle swarming with the dead.

"I bet the Warlock is in there somewhere," Aramis said.

"I know he is," Mel replied, pointing with his sword. The robed man was striding across the courtyard, headed for the castle doors.

"I'll see you inside," Aramis said. Mel nodded to him.

Aramis began cutting his way through the mass of dead, trying to push his way through to the castle. He had to stop the Warlock before he got to Lynessa. Her guards were hard pressed to provide a decent defense. The courtyard was overrun and they were highly outnumbered. Aramis managed to break through the line of dead in time to witness a handful of guards rushing the Warlock.

The Warlock used his staff to block the sword strikes of the guards. He began chanting loudly and waved his hand at the closest guard. The man began screaming and clawing at his own face. Aramis watched in disgust as the man's flesh began melting off his body. The guard dropped dead to the ground a moment later. Aramis tried to close the distance to help the guards.

He was too slow. The Warlock dispatched the other soldiers in a similar fashion and disappeared into the main keep. Aramis growled in frustration. He could feel the power of his tattoo pounding in his body. He denied the temptation to use it.

Entering the keep, he found a scene of chaos and death. Servants and soldiers alike lay dead. Blood was on the walls and the floor. Booted footprints smeared the blood in places. Aramis had to force himself not to vomit. All these innocent people were dead because of Mordum and his servants. Gritting his teeth in anger, he stalked through the room and navigated his way through the confusing halls of the unfamiliar castle.

He encountered a few skirmishes, mostly small groups of soldiers driving the dead back from the inner rooms. Aramis avoided these as much as possible, searching furiously for Lynessa. He managed to find the dining area they had eaten in earlier. After getting turned around a few times, he finally found Lynessa's private chambers. She wasn't present, but the secret door she had emerged from was ajar. Pulling it open, he charged into the darkness.

After a few seconds, his eyes adjusted to the gloom. Torches, too few for adequate light, revealed a narrow corridor. The ceiling was inches above his head and it was only wide enough for one person to pass through at a time. Aramis walked down the hall. He kept his sword up before him, ready for any surprises. The beginning of the corridor was made of stone, but as he continued it became hardened dirt.

"This place was carved into the earth," he muttered to himself.

Ahead, he could see the corridor curved to the left. He slowed his pace as he approached. He could hear voices. He peeked around the bend. The hall opened into a large room. Several other corridor and stair cases were scattered around the room. Apparently Lynessa had an entire series of secret passages in the castle. As he inched closer, he could see the robed figure of the Warlock. He was standing over someone … *Lynessa!*

"It seems a pity to kill you," the Warlock said to her. "I could use a queen to help me manage this city. Among other things, of course. Beauty like yours shouldn't be wasted … but the Prophet was very clear on this matter."

"Please," Lynessa pleaded, "I will give you whatever you want. Please don't kill me."

"As enticing as that sounds, I'm afraid it won't do you any good. If I want something, I take it. Your husband's life, your city, and now … your throne."

"Not if I can help it," Aramis said as he entered the chamber.

"Aramis!" Lynessa screamed in relief.

"The exiled prince," the Warlock said with a tone of boredom.

"I'm not as easy to kill as you presume," Aramis said.

"I wasn't trying to kill you," the Warlock replied with a laugh. "I was merely trying to slow you down. How did it feel, anyway?"

"How did what feel?" Aramis asked, spinning and twisting his sword around in front of him. He was ready to end this already.

"Why, cutting up the lord of the city. Did you know that he was down in the mausoleum?" the Warlock asked Lynessa. "He went down there to desecrate your dead husband's body."

Lynessa looked at Aramis with uncertainty. Aramis glared at the Warlock.

"You know that's a lie," Aramis said. "Stop talking and fight me."

"Fight you?" the Warlock asked as he pulled the hood of his robe back. Aramis had been right. The man *was* young, perhaps only a few years younger than himself. The Warlock set his staff on the ground and removed his robe. The staff remained standing upright and the Warlock placed his robe on it. He wore black leather boots, black breaches, and a loose fitting black tunic with no sleeves on. He took a few steps toward Aramis with his arms outstretched. Aramis could see the mark of Mordum on his forearm.

"I fear that what is about to happen will not be so much of a fight as it will be a slaughter." The Warlock laughed maniacally.

"Tough words," Aramis said. "Prove them with your actions."

"Fair enough." The air hissed as armor formed around the Warlock from mist. A wicked looking blade formed in his hand. It was completely different than Aramis's own blade.

They stood staring at each other in silence. Aramis was confident he could take the Warlock if their fight was only with blades. If the man used magic, he'd be at a sore disadvantage. He glanced to Lynessa. She was sitting on the ground with her knees pulled up against her chest. Even dirty and forlorn she was breathtaking.

The Warlock came at him in a blinding rush. Aramis forced his attention to the man and brought his sword up defensively. As their swords clashed, a multitude of black sparks filled the air and their blades disappeared with a loud hum. They staggered back from each other in confusion. Aramis tried to summon his blade back, but nothing happened. He still had his armor. That was something, at least.

"Mordum certainly has a sense of humor," the Warlock said. "Looks like we must settle this with magic."

Aramis cursed the god of death in his mind. Feeling for the power of his tattoo, he was surprised to find it was gone. Frantic with fear, he focused all his willpower into finding the power. He could feel it, barely. There was some sort of barrier around the power. When he tried to grab at it with his will, it slipped away from him.

"Having trouble?" the Warlock cackled. "This will be fun."

An intense, searing pain erupted in Aramis's torso. He gasped and collapsed to his knees, clutching at his chest. His breath came in short wheezes. His body shuddered from the pain. Any thought of trying to summon his power quickly fled his mind. The burning sensation spread down from his chest into his stomach, all the way down to his legs. His body jerked involuntarily with spasms. He thought he could hear laughing. In the chaos, a voice spoke to him inside his mind. It was somehow familiar to him. It broke through the pain enough for him to understand it.

Focus.

I can't, his mind groaned.

Focus! Pierce the veil that hides your power.

How?

Focus.

And then the voice was gone. Aramis writhed in agony. In the haze of his vision, he could see the Warlock moving toward Lynessa. Tears of pain filled his eyes and he knew in that moment he was going to fail her. She would die while he laid there powerless. He clenched his eyes shut. He couldn't bear to watch.

There, in the darkness of his mind, something flashed. Something small, but sharp. It was silver and triangular, like the tip of an arrow. *The tip of an arrow*. Aramis grasped desperately at it, trying to pull himself away from the pain. Clutching it with everything he had, he drove it into the slippery wall around his flow of power.

A small crack.

He stabbed the wall again. The crack, almost imperceptibly, widened. Striking the weakness repeatedly, he could feel it growing larger. It became like a spider web, branching out in every direction. The searing pain threatened to break his concentration. He drove the edge as hard as he could into the crevice.

The wall threatened to collapse. The power of Mordum began to flow through the gap. Slowly at first, but then it began to pour through. It rushed through the wall, tearing it apart. The power invigorated him. Aramis breathed in deep. The searing pain was suddenly snuffed out by the power. Regaining control of his body, he opened his eyes and saw the Warlock strike Lynessa in the head with his staff.

"No!" he screamed. He reached toward the Warlock and the power flowed from his hand. It was like a thick, black river flowing through the air. It struck the Warlock in the back, flinging him forward. He crashed into the wall with a groan.

Aramis stood up. He had never felt the power so strongly, so *powerfully.* His arms began to tremble. It threatened to overtake his willpower. He forced himself to control it, to bend the power to his will. It took tremendous effort, but he managed to keep it in check. The Warlock got up and staggered toward him. Aramis crafted a shield of power and kept the Warlock at bay.

The power wanted him to drain the Warlock. Faint wavering colors danced around the man. The colors jerked away from his shield as if in fear. Somehow, Aramis knew the colors were the Warlock's soul. With one hand, he reached out and grabbed one of the waves of color. He gripped it tightly and the Warlock cried out in agony. In a quick, sudden movement he yanked the color.

Blood began flowing freely from the Warlock's nostrils. He coughed several times and bloody spittle flew forth from his mouth. The knowledge that he was killing the Warlock suddenly revealed itself to him. A sinister smile crept onto his face. This was power! This was what it was like to have endless power at your disposal.

Aramis drew near to the Warlock. He sent a powerful kick into the Warlock's knee. With a snapping noise, the Warlock dropped to the ground. The lower part of the man's face was covered in blood. He smiled up at Aramis, but not in defiance. Aramis wanted to crush the life from him.

"Welcome … to … m-madness," the Warlock uttered softly, still smiling.

The words immediately sobered him. Aramis stared around in confusion, not realizing what he was doing. He saw Lynessa lying a few feet away. The Warlock lay at his feet, choking and laughing at the same time. He dismissed his armor and pulled the rusty dagger from his belt. Kneeling besides the Warlock, he held the blade over the man's neck.

"Madness," the Warlock uttered again. He repeated it over and over between his coughs. The word sent chills down Aramis's spine. With a suddenness that surprised himself, he cut the Warlock's throat. Blood spurted from the wound immediately and the Warlock jerked. Aramis watched as the life slowly left the man, then he closed the Warlock's eyes.

He took a few steps toward Lynessa's still form. An intense weakness overcame him and he staggered briefly before collapsing to the ground. The last thing in his mind before unconsciousness took him was how cold the floor was.

5

GARRICK DROVE HIS HORSE AS fast as it would carry him, pushing it to its limit. The landscape whirled by him in a flash. Whatever Laracova had seen, it was terrible enough to urge him to leave immediately. She'd promised her priests would follow quickly. Kelvin had used his power, after knocking him unconscious again, to take him as close as possible to the fortress they'd set out from.

Not knowing what awaited him, he rushed to get there quickly. His people were in danger, she had said. He knew it had something to do with the elves. Had they breached the walls again? He could only guess. The horse was foaming at the mouth. He'd found the beast roaming freely with no rider, yet saddled and ready for battle. It hadn't shied away when he'd approached it. And so, he took it.

As the fortress came into view, he could see smoke rising into the sky. He fought to push the fear down, to keep a clear mind. The distance felt like an eternity as the horse's pace began to slow. After a quarter of an hour, the horse finally stopped altogether and collapsed. He didn't have time to worry about the beast. He sprinted onward, closing the distance.

The nearer he got, the more the damage became apparent. Where there had once been grass was only ash. Bodies littered the area, some of them still smoking. A trumpet sounded. Whether from his fortress or from the elves, he couldn't tell. Sweat drenched his clothes. He slowed his pace as he rounded the side of the fortress. Garrick came to a dead stop when he saw the extent of the damage. The front section of the wall was gone. There were no signs of siege machines. No loose stones to show that it had been knocked down. The entire wall was simply missing.

Scattered cries echoed from the men inside the fortress. Across the way, at the edge of the blackened landscape, a large force of elves dashed across the open field. With the fortress now open to them, the men had little chance of fending them off. He noticed someone standing in the field. From the distance, he didn't recognize who it was.

Another trumpet sounded. Waves of men poured out of the ruined fortress, forming ranks across the open gap. Swordsmen grouped together in tight knit squads and archers lined up behind them. Garrick's heart swelled with pride as he witnessed the product of their training. He summoned his armor and his blade and ran to join them.

He recognized Rycroft's voice shouting orders and directing the men. Garrick changed direction and headed toward his general.

"What happened?" he asked as he neared the man.

Rycroft's face brightened in surprise. "My King!" He bowed low.

"Quickly! What happened here?" Garrick repeated.

Rycroft pointed toward the lone figure out in the field. "She happened. It's the girl that helped you when the elves broke through the wall. I don't know what she did, but she used magic and … this," he waved at the devastation. Garrick frowned. *She caused all this,* he thought.

"Hold your positions!" Rycroft shouted.

Garrick saw the elves were advancing quickly. They didn't have time to talk. He nodded to his general, then took a position next to a group of soldiers. He pulled his helm down and prepared himself. The seconds felt like eternity as they passed. His adrenaline began surging as the first of the elves met their line. A war cry went up as a chorus from the elves and more trumpets blared.

The two forces met in clattering press of shields and a ringing of swords. The sounds of metal impacting metal were punctuated by shouts of challenge and screams of agony. Here and there, explosions sounded and the ground shook as the elves unleashed their devastating magic.

Garrick kept his gaze straight ahead, studying his enemy as they came rushing at him. He ignored the chaos around him as their defensive line shattered. Soldiers abandoned their formations, behaving as individuals instead of a unit.

Two soldiers veered toward him. He used his body as a shield against the first, feeling the force of the elf crash into his armor. His armor protected him and caused the elf to go flying backwards as he struck Garrick head on. The second elf fell to his blade quickly. Garrick stabbed his blade into the neck of the first elf as he stepped over the shocked warrior.

Another elf wielding a longsword swung at him. Garrick parried the elf's blade with the flat of his own sword, so ferociously that the elf wavered in his stance. Pressing his advantage, Garrick braced himself and swung his sword into the elf's head. A wave of blood and gore washed over him as the blade sheared through flesh and bone, cleaving half of the elf's face off.

Garrick plunged his sword into another elf, piercing his thin armor. The elf screamed. Garrick kicked the warrior, then turned to face another elf. The sounds of battle filled the air, making it hard to hear any one sound over another. Screams of the dying, the clash of steel, and magical explosions were everywhere. Garrick fought with all he had, knowing that if the elves breached their line and reached the ruined fortress, their main line of defense against an invasion would be broken.

He swung his sword at another elf, but his blade bounced harmlessly off the elf's skin. Garrick cursed, remembering the last time he encountered one of the stone skinned elves. The only way he knew to overpower them involved magic, and he was no wizard. He risked a glance to Jovanna, the woman who had found a way to defeat the elven magic. He needed her help.

He launched himself into a furious offensive, hoping to push the elf close enough to the woman to get her assistance. He scored several hits that would have killed anyone else. The elf's skin turned his blade aside every time. Since the elf had no concern for his safety, his plan quickly crumbled. The elf pressed his own attack, driving Garrick back towards the failing line of defense.

Three more elves joined the fray. Not only was he now outnumbered, he also couldn't kill half of his enemies. He focused his attention on the two elves who did not have the stone skin spell.

He took several blows from the other two, but he had to slim their advantage. Garrick managed to cut one across the stomach, spilling his blood and organs. The other elf seemed to be more trained in battle and put up a better fight.

Garrick cursed in frustration. He knew they were losing. He stepped over more of his own men's bodies than he did those of elves as he back peddled from their attacks.

A trumpet split the air. Garrick couldn't turn his attention away from his enemy. He was on the defensive, mostly trying to keep from getting struck. He caught a flash of silver in his peripheral. Then another. His enemies halted their attack long enough for him to turn and see that Zevea's priests were beginning to arrive. The air pulsed in random spots as their forms magically appeared on the battlefield. As soon as they became visible, the priests charged toward the elves, bolstering the line.

The sight of added numbers, priests with magical armor and blades no less, gave Garrick hope that they could turn the tide. He amped up the energy of his attacks, throwing himself bodily into the elves to drive them back. He managed to force them where he wanted, but realized Jovanna was gone. Garrick twisted his head left and right, trying to spot her. She appeared to have vanished.

His only advantage gone, he gave up the fight and ran, trying to put distance between himself and the stone skin elves. Garrick noticed that Zevea's priests also had trouble fighting them. Despite wielding god-blessed weapons, they were useless against the elven magic.

The line was holding now. Garrick saw the soldiers regrouping. The archers, protected by the line of swordsmen, were firing arrows over their heads and into the elven ranks. It was working for now, but if they couldn't find a way to kill the stone skinned elves, they would quickly lose the stalemate.

And then something caught Garrick's attention. A black robed elf. He stood amidst the battle, unperturbed by anything happening around him. He walked along the bloody field, touching human soldiers as he passed by them. The men crumbled to the ground, writhing in agony.

Garrick grit his teeth and stalked toward him. As he closed in on the dangerous elf, he saw something else that shook his faith. When the elf raised his arm to touch another soldier, the sleeve of his robes fell back to reveal an upside down black cross. The Mark of Mordum. Confusion, then anger, filled him.

Why was Mordum leading an attack against one of his own followers?

He charged the elf, raising his blade and attempting to strike him down in one blow. His aim was off, though he didn't know how. His sword glanced off the elf's robe. It was like striking a shield. For the hundredth time, Garrick cursed the elven magic.

The elf pointed at Garrick with one hand and touched one of his tattoos with the other. A great gout of flames rushed through the air towards him. Garrick could feel the heat before the conflagration reached him. He dove out of the way, rolling and coming back up onto his feet. The two stared at each other.

"What are you doing here?" Garrick demanded. "We are both servants of Mordum."

The elf pulled his hood back and smiled. "I'm not here for Mordum's cause," the elf answered. "I'm here for my own." The elf touched another tattoo and a jagged fork of white lightning zig zagged towards him.

Garrick lifted his blade up and deflected the bolt into the sky. He knew the elf held the advantage. Aside from whatever gift Mordum had given the elf, he also had the tattoo magic. Garrick decided then that he needed wizards of his own.

The two circled one another. Garrick leapt into the air, raised his sword up and swung down hard. The elf lifted his arms up in an "X" shape, blocking the blade. Garrick scurried back in case the elf decided to launch his own attack and saw that while he had not struck a mortal wound, the elf's forearms were bleeding. That gave him hope that his enemy could be killed.

Suddenly, Garrick felt his feet leave the ground. He flew backwards a short distance and crashed to the ground on his back. He struggled to rise as he watched the elf come closer. A glow surrounded the elf and he raised his arm up. Garrick saw a flickering orb swirling in the palm of the elf's hand. Garrick flinched as the magical ball suddenly grew blindingly brighter.

From his peripheral, he saw a shadow rush by. Jovanna knocked the elf's arm aside as he released the magic. The radiant globe struck the ground a few feet away from Garrick. The concussive force shook the ground and rattled Garrick's armor.

Tairu's face was locked in a look of disbelief. Jovanna swung her sword at him, attempting to strike the elf in the chest. The blade deflected at the last moment, and Jovanna could feel the magic of the spell that protected him as it flared to life.

She summoned her own magic. It flooded her senses and she almost lost control of it again. At the last second, she forced her will on the flow of energy and cast a shower of fiery darts at him with a wave of her hand. They fizzled out of existence as they neared him. She was impressed. His magic was strong.

Jovanna staggered back as Tairu cast his own spell at her. A wave of cold air swept toward her, freezing everything it touched with tiny crystals. She summoned a shield of flame in front of her. The two elements crackled with bright flashes as the spells negated one another.

Garrick stood up and began circling around Tairu, hoping to flank him. The elf saw him and turned himself at an angle so that he was facing both of his enemies.

"Surrender," Garrick demanded. "You can't hope to win this battle."

Tairu laughed, but his gaze didn't waver from Jovanna. "I don't need to win. I have already set events in motion that cannot be stopped. Even if I fall in battle, my cause will carry on."

The air flashed and crackled as Jovanna and Tairu threw spells at one another. Garrick had to shield his eyes with his arm to keep from being blinded.

"I can feel your strength," Tairu said to her as their magical barrage faded. "The tattoos enhance it, but you are strong without them. Why are wasting your talent with *them*?" he sneered. "Join my cause and no one can stop us."

"Enough talk," Jovanna growled. She jabbed her blade toward him. Tairu backed up out of her range.

"As you wish," he mocked with a bow. "Let's end this!"

A harsh wind picked up as he summoned the magic of every tattoo on his body. All of the symbols burst into life, glowing a faint blue.

Garrick could feel the air humming. The ground around the elf split with small cracks. Not sure if his armor could protect him from what was about to happen, he sprinted towards the castle. *Let the wizards duel it out,* he thought. *I'll fight flesh and blood.*

Jovanna channeled the magic around her into a spherical barrier. She doubted it would hold up against the onslaught, but anything that could help her get close enough to him would be better than nothing at all.

Tairu released his magic. Streaks of red fire, bolts of blue lightning, and many other magical attacks that Jovanna couldn't name struck her shield. Her strength quickly faded and the barrier flickered, almost dissipating completely. She fought to keep the shield up as the attacks crashed into it.

For a split second, a thin veil of space amidst the magical bombardment opened. She glimpsed the magic that fueled Tairu's spells, a rushing torrent of energy that churned around him. She seized the opportunity. Closing her eyes, she envisioned the flow of magic and threw everything she had at it, trying to form a barricade around the elf.

Jovanna could feel the darkness of unconsciousness clawing for her. As the magic howled around them, she unwillingly dropped to her knees. The magic whirling around Tairu began to slow. She could sense him fighting against her, trying to battle her will with his own.

She felt the magic pulse once and opened her eyes. The magic blinded her and tears stung her eyes, running freely down her cheeks. A blazing white light was all she could see as the magic shuddered, flared and with a roar, shattered and exploded into a thousand fragments. An inhuman shriek tore from Tairu's throat and the elf burst into flame.

Jovanna collapsed onto the ground.

Dying wasn't at all like she thought it would be. It felt more like being sleepy. The absence of fear, pain and regret was comforting.

I will assist you, a voice in her mind said.

Jovanna briefly felt magic, old and powerful. And then the last of her strength faltered and everything went black.

6

HE WALKED ALONG A DESOLATE road that wound its way through a dead valley. The dry grass, yellows and browns, crunched beneath his feet. In the distance, smoke rose lazily into the sky. He didn't know where he was; he only knew he had to get somewhere he couldn't remember.

He felt nothing. His muscles did not tire; his skin did not sweat; he was neither hot nor cold. He walked for what seemed like days, though he could not tell the passage of time. He did not see a sun or a moon in the sky, though the atmosphere seemed to always be illuminated.

After an eternity, he drew close to the source of the smoke. An abandoned town. Most the buildings were blackened husks. The smoke was filtering up into the air from the chimney of the only intact building. He walked to the building and paused at the doors. The place appeared to be a temple. He felt drawn to it. This was the place he needed to be.

He pushed the door open and stepped inside. It was dark. A few scattered lanterns, all of them sputtering into death, provided a dim flickering glow. Several empty tables and chairs filled the room. In the far corner of the room, one table was occupied. A figure was sitting in the shadows. He walked to the table and stood before it.

"I knew you would come," a female voice said. He didn't recognize it.

"Why am I here?" he asked.

"You are broken," the voice answered.

"I don't understand."

"There are many who don't."

He paused. The answers were cryptic and confusing. "Please explain."

The woman laughed. "They are all impatient like you. You are broken. Your mind has been severed. It happens to most of you."

"Most of who?" he asked.

"The servants."

"What servants?"

"My, my. You are a bit slower than the others. The servants of Mordum."

"I'm not one of them," he said.

"Do you bear the mark? Do you summon the blade and the armor? Do you call upon the power that flows from the mark? Then yes, you are one of them."

That made his stomach lurch. "I use the tools for my own means. That doesn't mean I obey him."

"You are here, aren't you? Only those Mordum commands can come to this place."

He looked around the room. There was nothing to indicate the place was different from anywhere else. "Where am I?"

"You are here."

"Where is 'here'?"

The woman leaned forward into the light and smiled. "You are in the place between life and death."

"I'm dead?" he asked, panicked.

"Not quite. Mordum doesn't let his servants out that easy."

"So, I'm alive, then?"

The woman pursed her lips. "That's not quite true either. You are in the middle of the two, dangling precariously. Only the strong make it out of here, if that's what you want to call it."

"What do you mean?"

"Once you've been here, you're never the same."

"How so?"

"Do I look like a sage? I cannot give you all of the answers."

"Who are you?" he asked.

"I'm a sentinel. I guard the path to death."

"How do I get out of here?"

"Through the door you entered."

"No, I meant—" he sighed. "How do I get out of this place? Not this building. This place between life and death?"

"You have to die."

"What? You said only the strong get out."

"I did. Death is not for the weak. It is for the strong. Death brings clarity. Power. Wisdom. And ... madness. Most cannot handle it."

"I've heard that before," he said. When he tried to remember where, his thoughts grew muddled.

"I'm sure you have."

"Someone said it. I-I can't remember who." He shook his head as if that would help clear his mind.

"Be that as it may. It's not important." The woman stood up and came around the table. She was shorter than he was. Her face was one that time had aged beyond years. She wasn't ugly, but she wasn't attractive either. When he looked into her eyes, he saw nothing but his own reflection.

"Brace yourself," she said. "This is going to hurt."

By the time he realized she was holding a dagger, she had already plunged it into his chest. He expected there to be pain, but there was nothing. She hesitated, then she pulled the blade out and stabbed him again. Still, there was nothing. They stood there for a moment before she finally pulled the blade out.

"Interesting," she said.

"What is?" he asked.

"Apparently Mordum has ... different plans for you." She sheathed the blade at her hip. She stepped closer to him and kissed

him. It was a deep, passionate kiss. He was so taken aback, he merely let it happen. As he regained his wits and tried to pull away, he couldn't. And then she began to blow into his mouth.

The air was heavy and began to choke him. He fought to push her away, but they were locked together at the lips. In her eyes, he saw himself struggling. He saw a shadow pass between them. His vision darkened and his strength failed him. And then he was falling. He fell through the floor and into darkness.

—

Aramis opened his eyes. He was lying in a bed, an extremely comfortable bed. He sat up and rubbed his bleary eyes. He groaned. Every muscle in his body ached. He felt as though he'd been struck with hundreds of stones.

"You're awake."

The voice startled him. He looked around confusedly. A veil covered the bed. He could make out the shape of someone, but he couldn't tell who it was. The veil parted and Lynessa peeked in.

"Lynessa? What … where am I?"

"You are in my personal chambers," she replied.

"What happened?"

"You killed the Warlock. You must have passed out. When I came to, you were out cold and the Warlock was dead, his throat slit. I called for my guards and had them bring you up here."

Aramis rubbed the side of his face. The thin stubble of hair was prickly against his hand. A dull ache pounded at the base of his neck. He'd killed the Warlock? The haziness of his thoughts blotted out all the details, but he did remember bits and pieces. He'd used his dagger to cut the man's throat. He'd saved Lynessa's life. Relief flooded him.

"What about Mel? Is he …"

"He's fine," Lynessa said. "He refused to leave your side. It took a few hours, but I finally convinced him to leave. I told him I would watch over you as well as he would."

Aramis chuckled. "He's very devoted."

"That's an understatement. He's loyal to the core of his being. His loyalty is not blind, though. Nor is it forced. His loyalty is a sincere bond pledged out of respect and gratitude. That says a lot about his character, but it speaks volumes more about yours."

Aramis shook his head. "I'm no different than anyone else."

"That's not true. You risked your life for my people. And for me." She pushed through the veil and climbed onto the bed. "You saved my city. You saved *me*." She crawled to him on all four. Aramis was suddenly aware that she was only wearing a very thin robe, so sheer as to be transparent. His face flushed and he looked away. She pushed him down and straddled him.

"Lynessa, I—"

"Shh," she said as she placed her finger on his lips. "You are a hero, Aramis. Now enjoy your reward."

—

The next morning, Aramis awoke feeling refreshed and well rested. The silk sheets felt good against his bare skin. He rolled over to find that Lynessa was gone. He sat up and tried to peer through the veil. As far as he could tell, there was no one in the room. He felt around under the sheets for his clothes but couldn't find them.

Aramis rolled out of the bed. Atop a side table, a neatly stacked pile of clothes was laid out. His boots had been cleaned and polished and set next to the clothes. As he finished getting dressed, he heard a soft knock at the door.

"Come in," he said. He slid his boots on and ran his hands through his hair. The door opened to reveal a servant.

"My Lord," he greeted formally, bowing at the waist. "My Lady asked me to deliver this to you."

The servant entered the room and handed him a letter. "She's asked that you not read it until you've left the city."

Aramis raised his brow in question, but the servant either didn't notice or didn't know what to say. Aramis tucked the letter into his belt. "Thank you. I'd like to have a letter sent to the Lady. Can you do that for me?"

The servant nodded. "I'll get the items you need. I'll return shortly, my Lord."

After the man left, Aramis found a tall mirror on one of the walls and checked his appearance. *I need to shave,* he thought. Whoever had picked the clothes he'd been given had a good fashion sense. He was wearing a dark green tunic and a pair of brown trousers.

"My King." Mel's familiar voice greeted him. Aramis turned from the mirror to see his friend standing in the doorway. "I'm glad to see you are well."

"I'm fine," Aramis said with a smile. "I heard you wouldn't leave my side."

"I never will," Mel said.

The servant returned with a parchment, an ink jar and a quill. He laid them on a table and sat down. Aramis turned his thoughts to the words he wanted to leave with Lynessa. He knew what he wanted to ask her. He cleared his throat and dictated the letter to the servant. When he finished, the servant sealed the letter.

"Please make sure she gets this," Aramis said in a serious tone. The servant bowed and left. Aramis checked himself in the mirror one more time. "We should be able to book a ship now," he said. "I'm sure Lynessa has lifted the city restrictions. Hopefully the people here can return to some semblance of normal life."

"Most of the corpses have been moved back to the cemetery," Mel said. "What happened down there, anyway?"

"I'm not sure," Aramis replied. "It's all a haze. The only thing I clearly remember is killing the Warlock."

Mel stepped in close. "It was foolish for you to attack him alone. He could have—" Mel stopped short.

"Could have what?" Aramis asked.

"What's wrong with your eyes?" Mel asked, changing the subject and peering closely.

"What do you mean?"

"They look black. Not noticeably, but … I can see a change."

Aramis frowned and looked back in the mirror. He didn't know what Mel was talking about. There was nothing wrong with his …

Mel was right. It was faint, but there was a black tinge to the whites of his eyes. "*Gods*," he breathed. "What is that?"

"I'm afraid I don't know, my Lord." Mel frowned.

"Well, it's not obvious. Hopefully it doesn't get worse. Come," he led Mel out of the bedchamber. "We've got to find a ship."

7

ARAMIS AND MEL FOUND A ship heading down the coast and booked passage for a reasonable price. After several minutes of Mel complaining about not getting the food they had paid for, they returned to *The Compass*. The barkeep from the previous night was there preparing for the day's business. He paused in his work upon seeing them.

"I don't much mind ruffians in here, but I won't stand for trouble from anyone that's been escorted out by the Lady's guard."

"I completely understand," Aramis replied. "Though I think there may be some confusion. We were summoned to the Lady for a task, not because we are in trouble."

The older man eyed they warily. "What d'ye need then?"

"We paid for a room and food," Mel chimed in. "And as you are aware, we didn't receive either."

The barkeep glared at them and pointed above the bar. Aramis noticed a sign that read: *No Restitution*.

"I see," Aramis said. "Perhaps I can explain what happened?"

"I'm sure that ye can," the man said, "though ye won't find an audience." With that, the man stomped off behind the bar and disappeared through a door.

"Well," Mel huffed, "I don't think I've received such horrible treatment before in my entire life."

"You exaggerate. You were killed by a templar, remember?"

"Don't remind me," Mel said.

They turned to leave and found the way blocked by one of the city guards. "What now?" Mel muttered.

The guard stepped into the inn and removed his helm. It was the scarred young man from the gate. He knelt at Aramis's feet and bowed his head.

"Please, rise," Aramis said.

The man stood up. "I want to apologize for squealing."

"There's no need," Aramis replied.

"I feel like I betrayed you somehow."

"Nonsense. You were following orders. I respect that."

"Even so, you are my king. I should have warned you, at least."

"You are forgiven of whatever you believe you did wrong," Aramis said. "Are you on duty?"

"No, sir. Well, not on guard duty. I work here with my father in my off time."

"You should talk him into changing his policy," Mel said, nodding to the sign over the bar.

The youth rolled his eyes. "He's a stubborn one. What does he owe you?"

"Don't worry about it," Aramis said. He gave Mel a look.

"Can I get you anything before you leave? I assume you are sailing out today now that the port is open?"

"Yes, we leave within the hour. Some breakfast wouldn't be too much, would it?"

"Of course not," the youth said. With a grin, he walked to the back of the inn. "Have a seat," he called back at them.

Shrugging, Aramis picked a random table and made himself comfortable. Mel sat across from him. They stared at one another in silence. The youth came back a few minutes later with two plates of food. He set them down, then went back to the bar and returned with two mugs of ale.

"You want anything else?" he asked.

"No, this is perfect. What's your name?" Aramis asked.

"Jarrod."

"You obviously know me. This is my friend Melchiades. I call him Mel."

"It's an honor," Jarrod said. "I've never met a king before. Do you mind if I sit with you?"

"By all means," Aramis said between mouthfuls of food.

"What brings you all the way to Keswick?"

"We need to take a ship back to Oakhaven."

"I know that. I mean, what are you doing so far from your castle? Oakhaven is hundreds of miles from here. What brings you so far from home?"

Aramis and Mel exchanged glances. "It's a long story," Aramis replied. "I don't think we have enough time for me to tell it in full."

"I heard about the king, your father. I'm sorry to hear what happened."

"Thank you. I have been searching for my father's killer. That's what has brought me out here. Have you heard of Red Mountain?"

Jarrod scrunched his eyes as if trying to remember something. "Possibly," he said after a moment.

"It's in the Deadlands. There is a wizard there who was guarding something I needed. That's where we were before we came here to Keswick."

Jarrod's face lit up in excitement. "You went to see an elven wizard?"

Aramis shook his head. "No. She was a human wizard."

"Is she dead?"

"No," Aramis said, taken aback. "Why?"

"You said she *was* a human wizard. I just thought ..."

Aramis nodded. "Ah, yes. No, she is not dead. If not for her, Mel and I might have been."

"What happened?" Jarrod asked.

Aramis looked to the bar and eyed the hourglass. "We might have enough time. I had arrived at Red Mountain ..."

"Mel?" Aramis asked. *I must be dead,* he thought. The smell of charred flesh assailed him. The dead Lamias were unrecognizable except for their tails, some of which writhed among the ashes. Mel reached out his hand, offering his assistance. Aramis accepted it hesitantly, still unbelieving.

"Hurry, my Lord. We don't have much time."

"How?" Aramis asked.

"I'll explain later. Come." Mel pulled Aramis to his feet.

Aramis grunted. His entire body was sore. He eyed himself and saw that his armor had cracks in various places. He wondered if he had struck his head on the ground. Certainly, Mel couldn't be here. How could he be? How would he have gotten inside of the Nexus?

Mel led the way through the maze of corridors. There didn't appear to be any pattern to his navigation. "Do you know where you are going?" he asked.

"I do," Mel answered. "My goddess has shown me the way."

"Did Edria bring you back from the dead as well?"

Mel stopped walking and turned to face him. "No. Edria is …" Mel's face slackened in sadness.

"What is it?"

"Edria is dead."

Aramis was confused. "How is your goddess dead? Aren't gods immortal?"

"It would appear that is not the case."

"How did she die?"

Mel swallowed hard, the struggle not to cry evident on his face. "Mordum killed her."

Aramis was stunned into silence. Things were more serious than he'd thought. Mel turned and resumed his pace.

"I faced the templar, but I was outmatched. I've never feared death until that moment. When he struck me a killing blow, I thought I had failed you. The fight was so quick, I was certain that he would have caught up to you. How did you escape?"

"I surrendered to the mark," Aramis answered.

Mel nodded. "I figured as much. As I lay dying, I heard singing. I thought I was imagining it. I wasn't." The sounds of pursuit echoed into the corridor. Mel quickened his pace. "Zevea, the Goddess of Light, welcomed me when I died. She told me of Edria's demise and asked for my allegiance. She promised to avenge Edria's death and to restore my life."

They stopped at the end of a long hallway. A wooden door blocked the way. Behind them, Aramis heard the howling of Jackalwere growing nearer. Mel motioned to the door. "I cannot follow you inside. There is something more powerful than the magic of mankind guarding this door. I will wait here for you."

Aramis stared at the door. He was tired and sore. Every move he made caused his muscles to scream at him. He guessed that the bones of Mordum were somewhere beyond that door. He feared he didn't have the strength to continue. His resolve was like steel, but his body threatened to rebel against him. He was aware of Mel's eyes on him.

"Why did you decide to come back?" he asked. "You were free of this life."

"I was not free of responsibility."

"Responsibility to what?"

"To the world. To the people who were still here. If Mordum succeeds, everything will be gone. I could not continue through eternity knowing that."

Those words gave Aramis a boost of strength he didn't know he had. He summoned his blade. The familiarity of its hilt reassured him. He could do this. Nodding to Mel, he pushed the door open and stepped inside.

Darkness enveloped him. The ceiling did not glow like it did outside the room. The blackness felt tangible, like a thin layer of material that parted and swept around him. Aramis had the feeling that something was watching him. A chill crept through his armor and he shivered. The walls around him shuddered from an unseen force. As he continued forward, he held his left hand out in front of him so that he didn't run into anything.

Fire leapt into life directly ahead of him. A large brazier was the source of light. Behind it, the flickering flames illuminated a figure seated on a throne. He stepped forward slowly, his grip on the sword tightening. As he drew near, he gasped.

The figure on the throne was his father.

He knew that is was an illusion, but it seemed too real. His face was identical to the last time Aramis had seen him. The royal crown rested on his head in the exact place his father always wore it. He was sitting straight, but upon seeing Aramis, he leaned forward.

"My son, is that you?" he asked. Even his voice was the same. Aramis's heart fought against his mind, wanting to believe that his father was truly alive.

"You're not real," Aramis whispered.

"Am I not? Then how do you suppose I am here?"

"I …" he did not have the answer.

"Tell me, my boy, why have you come here? Do you not know that this place is a trap?"

"I know," Aramis said. "The wizard told me what this place is."

"And yet you came anyway?"

"Yes."

His father nodded slowly. "You were always brave. Nothing like your brother."

"My brother?"

The older man sighed and Aramis realized how aged his father looked. "There are many things I wanted to tell you. Some of them, such as this, I kept from you for your protection. I was going to reveal it to you before I died. At least, I intended to. Come closer." His father beckoned him.

Still unsure, Aramis kept his guard up, ready to strike. He inched closer. His father waited patiently as he took his time.

"I will not harm, my son. That is not why I am here. But *they* will." He nodded toward the darkness. Aramis looked to the edges of the firelight and saw shadowy figures moving about.

"What are they?" Aramis asked.

"Twisted creatures. Servants of the god of the dead. Never mind them," he said. "There is something you must know. Your brother is a vile man. The atrocities he committed are the reason I banished him from the kingdom."

"What did he do?"

"Many terrible things, all of them done in fear. I told him that he would not inherit the throne if he did not stop his dallying with the common people of our realm. He had many illegitimate children. He had them all killed, even those who had yet to be born." Tears trailed down the old man's face.

"Your mother was heartbroken, both at his actions and my decision. She was pregnant with you when it all came to light. Your brother had been angry. He's angry still, and he will not rest until he finds you."

"He won't have to," Aramis said. "I will take back the throne. By force, if necessary."

"It will not be an easy task," his father said. "Adamar is clever as a serpent and he has found favor with Mordum. You will need strong allies to fight the coming battle."

"I'm afraid," Aramis said.

"I know, my son, but you must persevere. If you fail, Mordum's darkness will sweep over the world."

"Is there no one else who can bear this burden?"

"Possibly," his father replied. "I am not gifted with visions of the future. Mordum has his gaze set on you, though I do not know why. My time here draws to its end. There is one more thing I must tell you. There are three things Mordum seeks. His blood, his bones, and his ashes. His blood you know of, his bones are here in this room, and his ashes are hidden beneath the castle."

"What castle?"

"Your castle. In the dungeon, there is a secret network of tunnels. Melchiades knows the entrance. The ashes are buried there. If your brother hasn't found them yet, he soon will. You must stop him from completing the ritual that will allow Mordum to take human flesh." The image of his father began to dissipate.

"Father, I don't know if I can do this. It's too big!"

His father smiled, and then he was gone. Before the flames in the brazier went out, he saw two things. The bones of Mordum sitting on the throne, and the shadows alive with movement. Aramis sprinted to the throne.

—

"My Lord," Mel interrupted. "We must be going if we plan to make it to the ship."

Aramis checked the hourglass at the bar and knew Mel was right. They could still make it if they hurried. "I'm sorry, but I must be on my way. Thank you for the food."

"Wait," Jarrod pleaded. "What happened? Did you get the bones?"

Aramis glanced to Mel who shook his head. Not seeing any danger in telling the boy, Aramis smiled. "I did. After fighting off the creatures that waited in the shadows, I escaped the room. Mel and I made it out of the Nexus to find that one of Mordum's armies was attacking the wizard's domain. My friend Kedrick was killed, but with the aid of the wizard, we were able to get away." A look from Mel cut Aramis's retelling short. "I'm sorry, but we must be going now."

"Thank you," Jarrod said. "I wish you luck on your journey."

"I appreciate it. We'll need everything we can get."

After Aramis and Mel left, Jarrod cleared the table and went to the back of the inn. He washed the dishes and helped his father start the fire in the kitchen's stove. Once the workers arrived and he was satisfied his father had ample help, Jarrod left the inn. He walked a few streets northward and turned down an alley. Glancing around to make sure he wasn't followed, he knocked on the backdoor of one of the dilapidated buildings.

The door partially opened and a robed figure peered out at him. "Is it done?" the man asked.

"It's done," Jarrod answered. "I put the poison in their food. He and his priest friend ate all of it."

"Well done," the man said.

"One more thing. He told me they have the bones."

"You have more than earned your reward." The man opened the door fully. Jarrod stepped inside and the man closed the door behind him.

"Prepare yourself to receive the Mark."

8

SHORTLY AFTER LEAVING PORT, ARAMIS became ill. It began as a minor stomachache, but quickly progressed. He gripped the worn wooden frame of his bed and vomited into a bucket. Mel hovered around him like a distraught mother, but there was nothing he could do.

"Perhaps," Aramis choked, "I ate something that didn't agree with me."

Mel shrugged helplessly. "I don't know, my Lord."

Aramis laid back on his bed. His lips were chapped and felt like they were burning with fire, while his mouth was dry and tasted of the vile acids of his stomach. He was light headed from the heaving. His vision swam before him and he thought for a moment that he might pass out. He held onto consciousness, however, and looked to his friend. Mel had a worried look on his face.

"I need some fresh air," Aramis croaked.

"The windows don't open," Mel answered. "I've already tried them. I can carry you out on deck, if you feel up to it?"

Aramis debated with himself for long moments before nodding his head. Mel helped him out of the bed. Aramis placed his arm around Mel's neck and the two staggered from their cabin to the open deck above.

The smell of saltwater and the sound of waves lapping against the hull greeted them. Aramis breathed in deep, trying in vain to make the stench of vomit leave his nostrils. They passed the Captain on their way to the railing.

"Put me down," Aramis said. Mel helped him to sit on the deck with his back to the rails. The Captain walked over to them.

"Gods man," he said. "You look like a demon from Hell."

"I feel like I'm in Hell," Aramis replied. The roof of his mouth felt like dried leather and the light headedness had been replaced with a splitting headache. He closed his eyes and enjoyed the mild afternoon breeze that blew across the deck.

"That's the worst case of seasickness I've ever seen," the Captain muttered to Mel.

"I don't think that is what he's suffering from," Mel replied softly.

"It's not the plague?" the Captain asked alarmingly. He took a step back.

"No, not at all. I've seen something like this before, years ago. It was poison."

"Poison?" the Captain said.

Mel nodded. "Deadly nightshade, if all of the symptoms hold true."

The Captain stared at Aramis in concern. "He needs help, and soon. I'd wager he'll be dead in a day, two at the most."

"Not if I can help it," Mel replied. The Captain clapped Mel on the shoulder and then strode away.

"You know I can hear you," Aramis said. "The wind carries quite well down here."

"I know you can."

"If I die—"

"Don't," Mel interrupted. "You are not going to die."

Aramis sighed. The two remained silent.

"Did you hide the bag?" Aramis cracked his eyes at Mel.

"I did. It's under a loose floor board beneath your bed."

Aramis noticed one of the sailors nearby taking an interest in their conversation. He opened his eyes fully and stared at the man. The sailor met his gaze momentarily before turning away. Aramis was too tired and give it any thought.

"I think some sleep will help me," he said. Mel helped him to his feet and took him back below deck and placed him in his bed. Aramis knew Mel wouldn't leave his side, so he didn't bother telling him to go. He closed his eyes and darkness overtook him.

Dry, brittle grass crunched beneath his boots. A few feet away, he could see a fountain that showered water droplets into a small pool. He suddenly realized he was thirsty. He walked to the fountain and knelt beside it, reaching his cupped hands in. Scooping the water up, he drank some. It burned his mouth and his throat.

Instinctively, he spat it out and flung it from his hands. Before his eyes, the water turned colors. It became black and oily. A shadow moved beneath the surface of the water. Aramis stood up and back away warily.

The shadow slowly lifted from the water. It had the form of a man, yet it had no defined features. The shadow stepped out of the pool. Whatever it touched quickly turned black and oily like the water that had spawned it.

Aramis tried to summon his blade, but nothing happened. The shadow approached him. Aramis backed away, only to be stopped by something tall and flat. He risked a glance. It was a wall. It stretched the length of his vision. He turned back to the shadow.

Its arm reached out toward him. Dark, oily water dripped from its fingers. It grabbed him and he screamed in agony. A searing pain shot through his body. He gasped and tried to push the shadow's hand away, but his hand slipped through the shadow. He couldn't touch it!

The shadow's other hand gripped his throat and began to squeeze. He choked and struggled, but the shadow did not relent. And then he died. He knew the feeling. It was familiar to him. Although he was dead, he was still aware. The shadow dropped him to the ground.

Aramis felt the life come back into him. He pushed himself up and stood before the shadow. This time, it did not touch him. Hesitantly, Aramis reached out and touched the shadow. It immediately collapsed upon itself and splashed to the ground.

Aramis awoke to screams and smoke. He sat up and immediately noticed he no longer felt ill. He was, however, extremely weak. His cabin door was open and Mel was missing. Summoning his armor and sword, he staggered feebly out of the door and up onto the deck.

Chaos was everywhere. Sailors were battling each other. The clash of steel filled the air. Aramis quickly spotted Mel. He was back to back with the Captain and they were surrounded. Aramis summoned his blade and lurched toward them. The ship swayed erratically. A quick glance revealed that no one was manning the tiller.

A sailor intercepted him mid-deck and engaged him. Aramis lifted his sword to parry the man's attack, but he was exhausted and offered a sloppy defense. Had he not been protected by his armor, the sailor would likely have ended the fight quickly.

His muscles screamed in reproach as he struggled to keep the sailor's blade at bay. The ship swayed hard to port and Aramis slipped, falling to one knee. The sailor managed to keep his balance and struck Aramis in the chest with his blade. The sword clanged off his breastplate and Aramis focused all his strength on swinging his own sword in a horizontal arc. His blade cleaved through the sailor's first leg and halfway through the other.

The sailor screamed and dropped to the deck, blood gushing freely from both extremities. Aramis's vision blurred from the exertion. He tried to move his body with the swaying of the ship as he waited for his vision to clear. As soon as it did, he saw the Captain get struck down by one of the sailor's. From his vantage point, he couldn't tell if it was a mortal blow or not.

The sailor he'd maimed continued screaming, rolling around the deck, washing the boards with his blood. Aramis rose to his feet and as he passed the fallen man, he drove his blade through the man's throat.

"Shut your mouth," he muttered to himself. He forced his burning muscles to obey him and made it to Mel's side.

"What are you doing?" Mel shouted as he struck a sailor in the nose with the hilt of his blade. His armor glittered brilliantly in the sunlight.

"I'm helping," Aramis answered. He attempted to block a blow from another sailor, but the force of the sailor's swing knocked Aramis's blade from his grasp. Mel whipped his blade around and stabbed Aramis's assailant in the stomach. The sailor collapsed backward, falling to the deck and holding his wound.

"You are too weak to be of help, my Lord," Mel said.

"What's going on?"

"Assassins," Mel answered. "Agents of Mordum."

"What are they doing here?"

"I have my suspicions, but I'm not sure. I think they are looking for the bones."

Aramis nodded. He suspected as much. "I can't tell friend from foe," he complained.

"Just kill anyone that attacks you," Mel said. "Can you check on the Captain?"

Aramis looked to where the man had fallen. A puddle of blood had pooled around him. Aramis knelt beside him and examined his wound. He'd been gashed across his chest. It wasn't mortal, but it was deep. Aramis retrieved his sword and cut the Captain's shirt off. Using the material like bandages, he covered the wound and tied it tightly around the man's chest. He groaned as Aramis worked. *That's a good sign,* he thought.

He slumped to the deck beside the Captain, holding his sword across his lap. He couldn't put up much of a fight in his state, but he was determined to defend the Captain from further harm. Within a few minutes, Mel and the few remaining loyal sailors had taken back control of the ship. Mel made his way back over to him.

"How's the Captain?"

"He's not in immediate danger, but he may get an infection. Does anyone know how far we are from the closest harbor?"

Mel consulted with one of the sailors and returned. "Two days sailing with a strong wind and a full crew. There aren't many of them left, though."

"Unless there's a healer on board, the Captain won't make it two days."

One of the sailors began shouting and pointing. Mel looked and shook his head.

"What is it?" Aramis asked.

"We've got a bigger problem," Mel answered. "We're close to show and we're about to run aground."

A splintering crash shook the entire ship and sent everyone sprawling. Although Aramis was already sitting, he fell flat and went sliding across the deck, slamming hard into the main mast. The wounded captain slid across the deck and would have fallen into the sea if it weren't for Mel. He managed to grab the captain's boot and hung on with all the strength he had as they tumbled along the deck.

The ship immediately listed and tilted starboard. The remaining sailors scrambled madly, dashing in different directions. A few moments later, as Aramis struggled to his feet, one of the sailors appeared from below deck.

"She's taking on water!" he yelled. "Abandon ship!"

Gods, Aramis groaned, *could things get any worse?*

He staggered weakly toward Mel and the captain. Mel started toward him with a worried look on his face. "No," Aramis shook his head. "Help the captain. I'm all right. I just need some rest."

Mel hesitated but aided the captain anyway. Mel lifted the man easily. "I don't think I can tread the water with extra weight," he said. "We'll need to get him on one of the boats."

They headed to the side of the ship where the sailors had gathered. They were lowering a boat with a few men into the water with a system of pulleys. Once it was safely on the water, the men in the boat pushed away from the ship and began paddling toward the shore.

"Everyone in the boat," Mel said to the few sailors left aboard the ship. "I'll lower you down, but you need to take the captain."

The men climbed into the boat and helped pull the captain over the railing. They eased him down onto one of the benches. Mel motioned for Aramis to get into the boat.

"You can't lower it yourself," Aramis said. "I'll help you."

"You can barely stand, my Lord. I don't think you'll be much help."

Aramis would have argued, but he was too exhausted to think. He nodded and climbed into the boat. Mel lowered the boat easily enough until the last four feet, when he lost his grip on the ropes. The boat dropped with a sudden jerk, slamming into the water. The captain groaned. The sailors waited to move the boat until Mel had leapt off the ship and into the water. He swam near and they pulled him into the boat.

As they paddled away, the timbers of the ship creaked and groaned like some kind of large animal that was slowly dying. Close to half an hour later, they reached the shore. Aramis waited to depart until the sailors had moved the captain out of the boat, mostly because he didn't know if he had the strength to.

He waved away offers of help and stepped out of the boat. He had the distinct feeling of falling before he saw the ground rushing up to meet him.

—

Aramis awoke feeling warmth against his skin. He turned his head toward the source and saw a small fire burning. The smell of something cooking made his mouth water. He grunted as he sat up and looked around. Mel was tending the fire and cooking. A few of the sailors sat around the fire, staring blankly into eternity. The captain lay a few feet away, his breathing shallow and uneven.

"We've got to help him," he said, but his words came out as nothing more than a croak. Mel looked at him and frowned.

"I'm afraid there's nothing we can do," he said softly. "If I could heal him, you know I would."

Aramis watched the wounded man in silence. *I can't stand to see anyone die,* he thought. *How am I going to kill my own brother if it comes to that?*

His thoughts were interrupted when Mel handed him a piece of wood with some sort of pinkish meat on it.

"Fish," Mel said, as if reading his mind.

"Thanks." Aramis ate in silence, watching the captain the entire time. The sun was quickly descending and the temperature was beginning to drop. "How long was I out?" he asked.

"A few hours," Mel answered.

Aramis sighed. He didn't know exactly where they were, but he knew they were still a long way from Oakhaven. It would take them weeks to reach on foot, even longer once they got closer to the castle. His brother was sure to have troops patrolling the entire kingdom. He glared at the fire, cursing the gods for ruining his life. Everything had been perfect. He had no need to worry about being king for many years because his father had been in perfect health.

But now … everything had changed. Even if he took the throne back from his brother, life would never be the same. It could never be the same. He looked over to see Mel staring at him.

"Are you well?" Mel asked.

Aramis nodded. "Physically, I'm fine. Mentally? I've got a lot on my mind."

The sailors finished their meals and worked to pull the boats further up the beach, intending to use them for beds. After they had settled down for the night, only Aramis, the captain and Mel remained by the fire.

"I don't know if I can do this," Aramis said suddenly.

"What do you mean?"

"All of this." Aramis waved his hand. "I don't know if I can do what I need to. What if my brother refuses to give me the throne? What if I must take it by force? Many innocent people will die for something that won't affect them."

"Tell me, my Lord, how does this not affect the people? The one who sits upon the throne has more to do with the commoner's lives than you may realize. He dictates the taxes, appoints the nobles, commands the generals and the armies. If the wrong man rules the land, do you not think that his decisions, good or ill, will affect the people?"

Aramis knew Mel was right. He had learned a lot from his father about being a king, even though he never thought he'd have to worry about kingly responsibilities for several years. "How can I kill my brother?"

"How could your brother have your father assassinated?"

"That's different," Aramis said.

"Exactly my point," Mel countered. "What your brother did was evil. What you will do, if you do it, will be justice."

"It's not about justice." Aramis paused. "It's about the reckoning," he whispered. "I want him to pay for *everything* he's done. I want to kill him, but I fear that if I take that path, I may never come back from it."

Neither spoke for long moments. "What are the sailors going to do? Are they coming with us?" Aramis changed the subject.

"No," Mel shook his head. "I spoke to them while you were unconscious. They're going to head back up the coast and try to find work on a new ship."

"What about the captain? What do we do with him? We can't travel far with him in his condition."

"I think the sailors will take him when they go."

Aramis rubbed the stubble on his chin. "It's my fault."

"My Lord?"

"The shipwreck. It's my fault. Mordum's agents are after me. If that were not the case, these people would be alive and sailing."

"Possibly," Mel said. "All men die at some point."

"They shouldn't have had to die early." Aramis lay down and stared up at the sky. "I'm going to sleep."

"Good idea, my Lord."

At some point, his eyes got heavy and he drifted off to sleep. He awoke the next morning when the sun was shining on his face. Groggy and sore, he sat up. Mel was still asleep, but the sailors were nowhere to be found. And they had left their captain behind.

"Blast them," Aramis muttered as he rose to his feet. He grabbed a water canteen that lay by the fire and drank deeply. The cool liquid soothed his parched throat. He relieved himself near the lapping waves and came back to check on the captain.

He was dead.

From what he could tell, the captain had been dead for a few hours. His skin was pale and his limbs had stiffened. Aramis kicked at the sand in anger. A noise startled him and he turned to see a familiar old woman. Her eyes were covered by a stained cloth and she was pushing a wooden cart that creaked as she walked.

"How …?" Aramis was at a loss for words. He hadn't seen her in a long while.

"How what, boy? How am I here?" she stopped pushing the cart and laughed. "I've told you before," she said. "Revelation—"

"Will come in time," Aramis finished for her.

"Took you long enough," the old woman cackled.

Aramis shook his head. "You say that it will come in time, yet I have more questions now than when we first met."

"Such is life for mortals. Come here, my boy. I will give you some knowledge."

Aramis stepped closer to her and she rested one hand on his shoulder and one on the side of his head. Aramis's vision swam and then he was looking upon a vast black ocean, only it didn't ripple like normal water. As he struggled to understand what he was seeing, tiny pinpricks of light began to sparkle across the black surface.

Suddenly, he felt very small. The black ocean wasn't an ocean at all, but the dark vastness of the sky and the tiny lights were a multitude of stars. Aramis staggered back, breaking free of the old woman's touch.

"What … what did I see?" he asked.

"An impression. I can only show you a glimpse, lest you fall into madness."

"I don't understand."

The old woman cackled gleefully. "Your mind is a fragile thing! It can only accept so much. To show it more would drive you to insanity."

"It was like …" Aramis struggled for words. "Like seeing the sky and the stars, but not from here. From above, looking down."

The old woman smiled and nodded. "Exactly."

"Holy Goddess!"

Aramis turned to see Mel staring in wonder. His friend took a few steps, then knelt before the old woman. In that moment, Aramis realized something he had overlooked, though he couldn't recall noticing it before. When Mel had first found him in the Nexus, his armor had a new symbol—a sun with outstretched wings, the mark of Zevea. The old woman's cart had the same symbol etched into the wood on the sides. As though scales had been removed from his eyes, Aramis suddenly had an epiphany.

"You're … a goddess, aren't you? You are Zevea?"

"In the flesh," the goddess answered.

"I'm confused. I thought the gods were immortal beings that lived … up there?" Aramis motioned to the sky.

"We did, but now we walk among you in flesh and blood. We live as you live, but we too can die as you die." Her face turned sad.

"How?"

"It is not easily explained, but I will try. Long ago, before the stars were born, there were five of us. Alandren, the god of strength. Edria—" the goddess paused at the name, "the goddess of knowledge. Tael, the god of valor, whom you have met before. Mordum, the god of the dead. And myself, the goddess of light. We five created this world and the races that live upon it. We sought to create a balance in the expanse. There was only darkness before creation. I created the sun, the moon, and the stars. Alandren created the world, Edria created the races, Tael gave them strength to survive, and Mordum set the limit of their lifespan.

"As the people flourished, we five made an agreement. We would bless those who devotedly sought us, giving them armor and weapons. In return, their faith strengthened us. We also agreed never to directly interfere with the events of this world. But one of us did not keep this arrangement."

"Mordum," Aramis said knowingly.

Zevea nodded. "Yes. He broke the agreement and came to the world as a mortal, but with all his godhood. He tried to gain more power for himself. He thought that if the people saw him in the flesh, they would know he existed and would believe in him, their faith increasing his power."

"But faith is believing in what you cannot see."

"You are correct, but Mordum did not want to see reason. He was full of greed and malice. As he killed and rampaged across the lands, his power grew because of the souls he was taking. Thankfully, with our guidance, mankind was able to stop him."

"Or did they? It seems like he's causing a lot of chaos in the world right now."

"That he is," Zevea said. "When he was defeated the first time, we allowed a part of ourselves to empower the tools needed to stop him. What we did not know at the time was that in doing so, we lost our immortality."

Aramis considered some of the other religions that he had heard of, gods and goddesses not named by Zevea. "What of the other gods that people put their faith in?"

"We five were the originators of creation," the goddess answered, "but other minor gods came to our world. Though they were gods, they were not as powerful as us, and so we did not fear anything they might do within the world. That may have been one of our mistakes. The god who came to the world and called himself the Lord Aio inspired Mordum's betrayal."

"The man who battled Orlek?"

"The same."

Aramis digested her words. He had difficulty believing them. He'd never been a man of faith. He believed only in what he could see. During his journey, however, he'd found that there were many things that he could not explain.

"One of the other gods you mentioned. Tael. You said I've met him before?"

"Indeed. When the Prophet of Edria imprisoned you, he was there as well. He spoke to you."

The memory came back to him and he laughed at the absurdity of it. "A god was stuck in a prison?"

"Of course not," Zevea scoffed. "He could have left at any time. He stayed because he wanted to discern your character."

"Why?" Aramis asked.

"There is much more at stake than you reclaiming your throne. The gods are at war. Mordum has killed Edria, and he seeks the remaining three of us that still live. This is not a battle for a throne, Aramis. This is a battle for mankind. If he kills us, there will be nothing and no one who can stand in his way. Tael wanted to know if we could trust you, if you had the strength to deny the dark power that Mordum offers his followers."

"Did I pass his test?" Aramis asked brusquely. "I'm glad to know that the people's decisions don't matter, that our lives are just some pawns on a board that you gods play with." Aramis turned away from her, angry. Mel still knelt before her. That made Aramis even more angry. "What are you bowing for?" he demanded. "She's mortal, just like you and I. There's no reason to be worshipping her."

"She saved my life," Mel replied quietly. "That templar killed me. I was dying on the road and she saved me. She gave me my life back. That may not be worthy of anything in your mind, my Lord, but it is in mine."

His sudden guilt outweighed his anger. He shook his head in frustration. "I'm sorry. You know what I meant."

Mel said nothing.

Aramis turned back to Zevea. "What do we do, then? How do we defeat Mordum?"

"You will need the items that his followers have been collecting. The blood, the bones, and the ashes."

"Ashes?"

"Yes. They are the ashes of Mordum's body when he walked the world previously. When these items are mixed and the body of one of his servants is offered freely, Mordum will take over control of the body, destroying the soul of his follower."

"Where do we find them?"

"Your brother has already found them. They were hidden beneath the castle at Oakhaven."

"Great. We only have the bones."

"You have the blood *and* the bones," Zevea said.

"No," Aramis argued. "The traitor prophet has the blood."

"Edria's prophet is not a traitor. He was protecting you."

"By throwing me into prison? I must be missing something."

"You were bent on revenge for the death of your father. You were not strong enough to face Mordum's templar. You still aren't. He was protecting you from yourself."

"I don't believe it," Aramis growled. "Either way, I'm going to get the blood from him, even if I have to kill him."

"I don't think that will be necessary," Zevea kept her sightless gaze on him. "With Edria dead, his power is no more. He used the last of it to launch an attack against your brother and his guards. His armor and his blade are gone."

"I can't imagine the feeling," Mel said. He was standing now, shaking his head.

"So he has to find new weapons," Aramis said dismissively.

"When you've had the blessing as long as I have, you will understand. When you have the armor and blade, you can feel the closeness of the gods. If that presence was gone," Mel stared off into the distance. "You'd feel different. It would be like a piece of you were missing."

Aramis wondered if he'd feel that way once the mark of Mordum was no longer a curse upon his body. He imagined he would feel free again, but as he considered it more, he wondered if it would be worse not feeling the power. *Gods,* he thought, *I'm actually thinking of keeping the power. I've got to deny the temptation.*

"I will do what I can to stop Mordum," Aramis said, making his final decision. "But know that I do not do it for the sake of the gods. I do it for the people who suffer with you meddling in their lives."

If his words bothered her, she did well to hide it. "Good. I have something that will help you on your way. It will speed your journey." Zevea opened the top of her cart and reached inside. She dug around for a moment before pulling out two small objects. She handed one to each of them.

Aramis held up and inspected it. It was a wooden figurine of a horse. It was intricately carved, with all the details of a real horse. "What am I supposed to do with this?" he asked.

"You will summon the spirit of the animal that is bound to it. Put it on the ground and speak the word *'Capall'*. The spirit will come to you and take you wherever you need to go."

"'Capall," Aramis repeated. Suddenly he felt a strong vibration in his hand. The wooden figurine trembled in his hand. He tossed it to the ground on instinct, which saved him from injury. As it fell through the air, the figure of a large horse materialized. The figurine landed in the sand next to the horse. Aramis stared in awe and surprise. The horse was identical to the figurine.

"Next time, make sure you place it on the ground first. I'd hate to see you get crushed by a few hundred pounds."

Mel placed his on the ground and repeated the word. Within moments, another horse had materialized.

"They can travel longer than a horse of flesh, but they still must rest. They are spirits, so they will need to return to their realm. To dismiss them, you must say *'dhíbhe'*. If you run them too long, they will dissipate on their own, whether you are still mounted or not."

"Thank you, Holy Goddess," Mel said with a bow. "We appreciate these gifts."

"Will you be there when you are needed?" Aramis asked Zevea. "When we confront my brother?"

"I will be near," she answered. "You will need all the help you can get if you hope to stop Mordum."

Aramis turned to Mel. "Let's be off then. Maybe we can find a town to eat at. I don't really care to eat more fish."

Mel chuckled. "I agree, my Lord."

"Until we meet again," Zevea said. Then she continued pushing her cart along the beach.

Aramis mounted the spirit horse and pressed his lower legs tightly against the horse. He urged the horse forward, holding onto its mane with his hands. He let the horse walk until he felt secure, then urged the horse to speed up. He looked over his shoulder and saw that Mel was not far behind.

If the gods thought to use him like a tool, they had a rude awakening coming. He refused to be pawn in their game.

They rode for nearly an hour in silence before they saw signs of life. Several people walked along the road ahead of them, headed in their direction.

"We should keep our guard up," Mel suggested. "I know we are far from Oakhaven, but I would not underestimate the reach of Mordum's servants." Aramis nodded wordlessly in agreement.

As they neared the group, it became evident there was nothing to worry about. The people were dirty and appeared to be carrying everything they owned. They moved to the side to allow the horses by. Aramis stared at them as he passed, wondering how they had come to look so pitiful. They continued following the road and eventually left the people behind, only to encounter another group in a similar condition.

Eventually, the road was crowded with people. Most of them looked like farmers or traders and almost none of them spoke. The air about them radiated hopelessness. Some of the people led livestock while others carried or herded small children.

"I wonder where these people are coming from," Aramis said with a glance to Mel.

"Hail," Mel called out to one of the farmers. "Where are you going? And where do you come from?"

The haggard man walked next to a woman whom Aramis assumed was his wife. Two younger girls, likely his daughters, stayed close by his side.

"We're going anywhere that will take us," he answered. "And we've come from Ravencliffe."

"Why are all these people on the road with you?" Aramis asked.

"Haven't you heard? The town has been raided and burned." The man's wife choked up and started to sob quietly.

"By who?" Aramis asked.

"The king."

Aramis stopped his horse. "What are you talking about?" The man backed away warily. "I'm not going to hurt you," Aramis said. "What do you mean the king raided the town?"

The farmer ran his dirty hand through his even dirtier hair. "I don't know how you haven't heard," he said. "The king has been terrorizing everyone. He's looking for the prince that murdered his father. When his soldiers were told that no one knew where he was, they destroyed everything." The farmer placed his arm around his wife comfortingly. "We've lost everything we've known. So, we're leaving to find a new place to start over. But I'm afraid that no matter how far we go, those soldiers will just continue to follow us."

"I'm sorry to hear of your troubles," Aramis said. A deep hatred was boiling up within him. How could his brother do such terrible things to the people that he was supposed to serve? He reached into a pouch on his belt and pulled out a few coins. "It's not much, but please, take it."

The farmer stared at him. "Who are you?" he asked.

"Someone who cares," Aramis answered.

"You might need it," the farmer said. "The soldiers have set a blockade outside of the town. They are charging for passage, in or out."

"Take it," Aramis insisted. "I'll be fine."

The farmer hesitated for a moment, then accepted the money. "The gods bless you!" he called out as Aramis nudged his horse onward.

"The gods can go to Hell," Aramis muttered under his breath. Once they got clear of the people on the road, Aramis spurred his horse and thundered down the road. Mel followed suite. He could tell from Aramis's demeanor that he was beyond enraged. *Zevea help anyone that gets in his way*, Mel thought.

9

IT WAS NEARING NOON WHEN they reached the rolling hills that marked Ravencliffe's borders. Aramis reined in his horse, jerking on the bit so hard that the animal grunted. Ahead, the smoke of the burning town hung in a thick haze and some of the buildings were still aflame. Aramis watched the thatched roof of one of the buildings give way in a shower of sparks. A few feet away, a copse of oddly swaying branches caught his attention. As the smoke swirled, the truth became clear. The trees were gibbets, and a dozen bodies hung from their branches.

His anger burned as hot as the flames around him. He stood in his stirrups and surveyed the rest of the town. Spotting a large gathering of people, he nudged his horse in their direction. As he got nearer, he counted four guards. Two were standing idle, while the other two were harassing people trying to pass. A long line of people stretched down the road, all of them trying to flee somewhere safer. The guards were extorting money, goods and even livestock as passage fees.

A few people were allowed to pass through the blockade at the cost of all the money they had on them. The guard stopped a woman with two small children.

"Please," she begged. "I don't have anything to pay with. I've lost everything." Behind her, the ill-clad children clutched at her and huddled together.

"I don't believe you, wench! Now pay the fee."

"That or you can trade one of the children," the other guard said. "I like children," he added with a leer. He reached toward one of them and the woman screamed.

"Get away from them," Aramis said. He summoned his blade and the air hissed as it formed. The crowd gasped and backed away from the blockade.

The guard who had reached for the child turned to face him. "Well, well. A rogue on a horse. Likely stolen, too. Mind your business, fool."

"Get away from them," Aramis repeated. He heard the air hiss behind him as Mel summoned his own blade. He moved his horse forward until he was between the guards and the helpless woman.

The guard drew his sword. "This is none of your business." The other guard drew his blade as well, but the two standing idle only had their hands on their pommels.

"I've just made it my business," Aramis said. "I suggest you and your fellows remove this blockade and get back to the castle."

"What are you going to do?" The guard sneered at him. "You're outnumbered."

"Is that so?" Aramis asked as he summoned his armor. The black metal formed around him and it felt different this time, stronger, more powerful. The guard exchanged uncertain glances with his fellow and then swallowed hard.

"You'll have to kill us all," he said. The other two guards unsheathed their swords and advanced toward him.

"With pleasure," Aramis said. His ebony blade glinted in the sun as he brought it down hard. The child-loving guard brought his own sword up to block, but it shattered under the force of Aramis's blow. Aramis wheeled his horse around, knocking the backside of the animal into the man. He staggered backwards and landed on the ground. As the horse came about, Aramis leveled his blade and swung horizontally, catching the other guard at the neck, just under his helm. The blade cleaved through bone and sinew. The guard's head dropped to the ground, followed quickly by his body. The other two guards slowed their advance, approaching cautiously.

Strike them, a voice bade him. *Strike them down.*

His heart was drumming in his head, pounding loudly in his ears. His hand clenched tightly around the handle of his sword. He swung out of the saddle, landing on the ground with a heavy thud. The guards, thinking they had the advantage, rushed him. He cut them down with little effort. He'd experienced the blood rage of battle before, when adrenaline coursed through his veins. Yet this feeling was something different, something darker.

He turned his attention to first guard who was still on the ground, not quite recovered from the horse hit. Aramis stalked toward him.

"Please," the man said, "I'm sorry. I was only following orders!"

Aramis barely heard the words. He closed the distance and placed the tip of his blade to the man's neck. "Beg for mercy," Aramis said.

The guard was terrified. A puddle formed under the man as he urinated on himself.

"Mercy!" he cried out. "Please, give me mercy!"

The tattoo on his arm began to pulse. Aramis could hear voices whispering, but he couldn't make out the words. Images flashed through his mind in a whirlwind. Death and destruction, visions of Mordum and his servants plunging the world into darkness, Oakhaven burning. The one that finally broke him was Hannah. Her body lay strewn on a roadside, naked and battered. A man he didn't recognize laughed as he tossed a coin onto her dead body.

Then the images were gone. Aramis shook his head, trying to clear the things he had seen from his mind. The guard stared up at him, trembling in fear. "Please," he whispered. "Mercy."

Aramis drove his blade through the man's throat. He made a choking sound as blood poured from the wound and out of his nose and mouth.

"Death," Aramis vaguely heard himself say, "is mercy."

—

"You didn't have to kill him," Mel said quietly. Sunset had come and they sat around a small fire. They had dismissed their spirit horses for the night and made camp outside the town of Ravencliffe. Most of the refugees had continued on, but a few had stayed. They had thanked him countless times, especially the woman he had rescued. The people had also offered him gifts, the only things they had with them. He'd gently refused, knowing they needed more help than he did.

"Yes, I did."

He picked up a stick and poked at the coals, then threw a few small branches into the fire. "He would have done it again to someone else."

"How do you know that?" Mel asked. "You could have scared him enough to make him leave that life behind."

"Doubtful," Aramis replied. "Those inclinations are bound deep in the heart. It would have taken the power of a god to change him. And the only god he seemed want to follow was Mordum."

"So, you are judge and executioner? Can you see into the hearts of men now?"

Aramis felt the tattoo on his arm burn. He looked at Mel. His friend stiffened. "What is it?" Aramis asked.

"Your eyes. They're worse."

Now that he mentioned it, Aramis noticed that his eyes did feel dry. "Must be the smoke," he said. "I think it's drying them out."

"No, they are getting darker. The blackness … it's noticeable." Mel summoned his sword and offered it to him. Aramis took it and tilted the blade at an angle, using the firelight to see the reflection of his eyes. Peering back at him were two large black orbs. Aramis dropped the blade and stood up. His heart started pounding and he looked around in panic. *My eyes! What do I do?* His mind screamed.

Mel's voice cut through the fear. "My Lord, please sit down."

Aramis tried to calm himself. He sat back down and stared into the fire. *The power is changing me,* he thought. He could feel Mel staring at him. *What does he think of me now? What happens if this power takes control of me? Will Mel kill me?*

As much as he tried to convince himself that Mel would never try to, the thought nagged at him. "I'm going to sleep," Aramis said. He left the fire and laid a few feet away after taking his shirt off to use as a pillow. Not long after, he heard Mel put the fire out. Aramis stared up at the stars, his thoughts tormenting him worse than any physical pain could. His night was sleepless.

The next morning, despite being exhausted, Aramis's mood improved. He could feel the beginning of a headache, likely from not sleeping. His muscles ached and he didn't want to get up, but he knew that time was something they lacked. He sat up and looked for Mel. His friend was cooking breakfast. He put his shirt on and walked over to the small crowd that had formed around Mel. A couple of refugees were talking with him.

"It's worse the further you go," one of the men said. "The new king is a tyrant."

Some of the other nodded their ascent.

"Anyone who tries to fight back is punished. I've heard stories. Someone told me their brother was taken to the dungeons and tortured. They took a bucket of rats and placed it on his stomach, then put hot coals on the top of the bucket. Once it got hot enough, the rats tried to escape."

The man paused. "They burrowed through his flesh."

Mel remained silent, but Aramis saw the disgust in his friend's eyes.

"I go to stop him," Aramis said.

The people turned to see who spoke.

"Who are you?" the man who had been speaking asked.

"Aramis, prince of Oakvalor." There was a moment of silence before a few of the people began to kneel.

"Hold on," the man said. "You don't know this man from a beggar in the streets. How do we know he's really the prince? From what I hear, he murdered his father for the throne. He's the reason we're in this mess."

"I am the prince, but I did not kill my father." Aramis turned his arm to display the tattoo on it. "I was cursed by the god of the dead with this mark. The man who claims to be king is my brother, banished long ago for dark crimes. He's responsible for my father's death, not me."

The man eyed Aramis, his uncertainty evident.

"I will make him pay for everything he's done. I will restore everything he has destroyed. Your homes, your crops, everything."

"You can't bring back the dead," the man said, his tone softer.

"No, I can't," Aramis replied. "I lost my father to an assassin's blade. I know the sting of loss. I know too, the anger that burns beneath the grief. I will do everything in my power to right the wrongs he has committed. I swear it."

"I don't know if you are really the prince or not," the man said, "but I can hear the conviction in your words." He looked around at his fellow refugees. "I'll follow you."

The people in the crowd began to voice agreement, pledging their loyalty to him. "Please," he interrupted. "The path I walk is a dangerous one. I would never ask any of you to put yourself in peril."

"You didn't ask," the man said. "We volunteered. He may have killed your father, but my daughter was killed by his men on his orders. I will take up my sword and fight in her memory."

Aramis considered the man's words and knew he could no more deny the man's right to revenge than he could deny bread to the hungry. "If only I had a few thousand more men like yourself," Aramis said.

The man straightened with pride. "I don't know about that many, but if you are looking for men who want to fight against that tyrant, I know a few. I'll get word to them."

"Thank you," Aramis said. "Gather anyone you can find willing to fight, and meet me in ten days outside of Oakhaven."

After they ate breakfast and the refugees had departed, Aramis summoned his spirit horse.

"It's a few days' ride from Oakhaven," Mel said. "Why did you tell them to wait so long?"

"We're going to make a stop along the way," Aramis answered.

"Where at?"

Aramis mounted his horse and adjusted his position in the saddle until he was comfortable. "We're going to the Temple of Edria."

—

The scene that greeted them when they reached Kaldore two days later gave Aramis pause. At least a hundred refugees crowded the city. So many makeshift tents littered the streets, there was no room for wagons to pass by. Not that there were any wagons to speak. Trade, it seemed, had all but halted. Several priests roamed among the people, handing out meager portions of food and spare clothes and blankets.

Seeing the plight of his people added to the hatred for his brother that was already on the verge of boiling over. They pushed their way through the crowds and made their way toward the temple. Aramis felt a nervousness building within him as they got closer to the temple grounds. He remembered the betrayal of the Prophet. Although Mel had explained the Prophet's actions, he still felt the bitter sting of treachery when he thought of the man.

They only saw a few priests within the courtyard of the temple. Aramis assumed that most of them were out in the city, doing what they could to ease the troubles of the people. The large wooden doors were wide open, allowing free passage in or out. Mel took the lead and navigated through the various halls to an all too familiar door.

Aramis thought he saw the shadows flicker with life. Dark whispers filled the air around him. Distracted by them, he didn't notice that they had entered the Prophet's chamber until the man's voice echoed through the space.

"Melchiades?"

When he'd first met the man, he had been impressed. Now, Aramis barely recognized him. The Prophet's once muscular frame was now on the flabby side. His hair was disheveled and unkempt and his jaw had the faint beginnings of gray hair. The pendant he normally wore around his neck, a closed hand with an open eye in the center, lay on his desk.

"I thought you were dead," the Prophet said. He came around the desk and hugged Mel. "Had I known you were alive, I would have sent you help." As he broke the embrace, the Prophet seemed to notice Aramis for the first time.

"Ah, Prince Aramis. It does my heart good to know you are safe."

"No thanks to you," Aramis said. Mel shot him a look of disbelief, but Aramis ignored it. "I'm here for the blood."

The Prophet nodded. "I figured as much. Adamar has only sent one patrol here to try and claim it, but they did not find it so easy to overcome an old man." He chuckled. "I may not have my powers anymore, but I can still wield a blade."

"What news from Oakhaven?" Mel asked.

"Not much," the Prophet sighed. "The only visitors we get are refugees, and the only stories they have all sound the same. Death and destruction. You are free to anything you need, if we have it. There isn't much left. How did you survive the templar?"

Aramis felt his anger growing the longer he stared at the Prophet. He hated the man.

"I didn't. The templar mortally wounded me and I died, but Zevea brought me back."

"Zevea?" The Prophet's eyebrows rose in surprise. "Perhaps you can tell me the tale?"

"I'd love to, but perhaps another time. We still have a long journey ahead of us, and time is short."

"Of course," the Prophet waved his hands. "Please, follow me."

The Prophet led them through the temple to a room Aramis did not remember seeing previously. Withdrawing a key from the folds of his robe, he unlocked the door and directed them inside. The room was empty except for a small table in the corner of the room. Atop the table was a familiar item Aramis immediately recognized.

Blood. Blood. Blood. The dark voices began whispering the word repeatedly. It got faster, almost frantic. Aramis's heartbeat quickened in his chest as he got closer to the table. Aramis assumed it was his imagination, probably from his lack of sleep lately. Then his tattoo began to itch. He resisted the urge to scratch it. Mel reached for the wineskin that held the blood.

"No," Aramis said sharply. Mel and the Prophet exchanged glances.

"I'll take it." Aramis grabbed the wineskin from the table and strapped it to his belt. "We should get moving."

"Yes, my Lord."

"A word, if I may," the Prophet said.

Aramis shrugged. "Make it quick."

The Prophet looked to Mel. "I'd like to speak with him alone."

Mel frowned but nodded and left the room.

"The power is changing you, isn't it?" the Prophet asked.

"What do you know of power, priest? Your god is dead." Judging by the pained look on the man's face, Aramis knew he had struck a nerve. *Good,* he thought. *Let him suffer.*

"I know that Mordum uses the Mark to control his servants. For some, the power is too much. It brings madness. I can see the stain in your eyes, Aramis. The power is controlling you. Mel can see it, but I know he hasn't said anything. He doesn't want to confront you, but he must if you continue to get worse."

Aramis clenched his jaw. Deep down he knew the Prophet's words rang with truth, but something kept him from accepting it. A dark shadowy wall pushed the words from him.

"I may not have the gifts of my goddess anymore, but I can feel the darkness of Mordum radiating from you. You must fight the darkness!"

A torrent of hideous visions assailed Aramis. The dark whispers intensified and he staggered back, shaking his head. The Prophet stepped toward him, concern etched on his face. Suddenly, Aramis unsheathed the rusty dagger Zevea had given him and he plunged it into the Prophet's chest. The man's eyes widened in surprise. He opened his mouth as if to speak, but nothing came out.

Again, the voices whispered. *Again!*

Aramis jerked the dagger out and stabbed the Prophet again. The man fell to the floor, but Aramis's hatred was not satisfied. He knelt beside the Prophet and jabbed him with the blade over and over. When he finally stopped, he had no idea how long or how many times he had stabbed him.

His breathing was heavy and the muscles in his arms burned. Wiping the dagger clean on the man's clothes, he sheathed the blade. He considered hiding the body, but immediately discounted the thought. There was nowhere in the room to hide him, and Mel stood in the hall. *They'll blame it on the soldiers,* he told himself.

He looked himself over as best as he could to make sure there was no blood, then he left the room. Mel was leaning against the wall a few feet down the hall.

"Let's go," Aramis said.

"Where's the Prophet?" Mel asked.

"Praying," Aramis answered. "He said he wished he could go with us, but his duties here will not allow it."

Mel stared at him for a long moment. Aramis returned his gaze. "Come," Aramis bade and began walking. Mel fell into step beside him.

"Now that we have the blood, we must find the ashes," Aramis said. "The bones are still safe."

"How do you know?" Mel asked. "Didn't Vashah hide them with magic?"

"Yes," Aramis replied. "Vashah hid them, but I can feel their power. I know exactly where they are."

They left the temple and walked along the streets. Aramis knew time was something he severely lacked, but he wanted to make sure his people were being cared for. They spent the next hour talking with the refugees and helping the priests bandage wounds. Aramis listened to their terrible stories and would have wept with them, but no tears would come. Many of the people stared at him as if he were some sort of wild animal. He kept forgetting that his eyes had grown dark. After they saw his goodwill, their stares became less fearful.

"It's time," Aramis announced after they had finished putting together a few tents for a family of farmers. "It is time to go to Oakhaven. I want to do more for them, but I can't do that until I have reclaimed my father's throne."

"I fear we will not have enough men if it comes to war," Mel said later as they rode toward the capital. They saw less refugees the closer they got. Aramis had seen the road once before when it was bustling with traders coming in and going from Oakhaven. Now, it was desolate. Aramis wondered if anything would ever be the same.

Not if I die, he thought. He looked at Mel from the corner of his eye. The man had been his friend for years and had willingly given his life to protect him. Aramis considered his actions at the temple. He'd killed the Prophet, someone that Mel was close to. He searched his feelings, but he didn't find guilt. He did feel bad for Mel, knowing that at some point, he would learn of the man's death. It would be rough on him, but Aramis knew Mel was strong enough to get over the loss.

Something fell into his lap. Aramis looked down and saw that it was the pendant Hannah had given him. The chain had broken. Grabbing the chain before it fell, he wrapped the pieces around his belt. The beautiful woman's image came to his mind and he wondered where she was and if she were safe. He wondered, too, how her father had fared in drumming up support from the nobles for his cause.

"My Lord," Mel's voice shattered his thoughts. He looked to where Mel was pointing. A large contingent of soldiers was coming their way.

"Looks like we've lost the element of surprise," Aramis said as he summoned his armor and blade. The air hissed as Mel summoned his own. As the soldiers closed the distance, Aramis noticed they were all wearing the mark of Mordum as their insignia.

"I've got an idea," he said to Mel. "Dismiss your armor and your blade." After a moment of hesitation, Mel did as Aramis instructed. "Now hand me your reins."

Aramis pointed the tip of his blade at Mel. He slowed their horses to a stop as the soldiers hailed him.

"What's this?" one of them said as he pulled off his helm. He was clearly the leader, likely a captain. Aramis didn't recognize him. He had the typical short haircut of a soldier, but his face had distinct features that implied his noble birth. Aramis guessed he was the son of one of the nobles.

"I'm taking him to the king," Aramis answered. "Been searching for this dog for weeks, but I've finally caught him."

"Good work. I'll have some of the men escort him to the castle."

"That won't be necessary."

The captain leaned forward. "And why's that?"

"The king sent me specifically to track him down. If I wasn't the one to bring him back, I'd probably get the noose."

The captain eyed him suspiciously. "What's your name? And who do you report to?"

Aramis had no idea how the priesthood of Mordum was structured, but from everything else he had seen, it was similar to the other orders. He decided to bluff.

"That's not your place to ask, captain." Aramis dismissed his armor and displayed the Mark for him to see. The man's eyes immediately filled with fear.

"My apologies," the captain said quickly. "I didn't know you were one of them."

"Them?" Aramis asked.

The captain stammered. "Them, uh, one of the king's protectors."

Good to know, Aramis thought. "No harm done," he said.

The captain put his helm back on and bowed in his saddle. "We're looking for people who are trying to leave with the king's property. Have you seen anyone on the road?"

"Yes," Aramis lied. "A small group, about ten of them, were headed west toward Talvaard."

"Thank you," the captain said. He barked orders to his men and they rode off.

Once they were no longer visible, Aramis gave the reins back to Mel. "It seems my brother has Mordum knights as protectors."

"Why would a servant of Mordum need protection?" Mel said rhetorically.

"I think we'll find out soon enough."

They used the prisoner ruse twice more as they neared Oakhaven, but each time it was harder to pull off. Although the soldiers they encountered seemed fearful—reverent even—when he displayed the mark, they became more insistent about taking his "prisoner" themselves.

"The servants of Mordum, while they all seek to fulfill his purposes, have their own agendas. They will lie, cheat and kill anyone, including fellow servants, to gain Mordum's favor," Mel said after they left the most recent group of guards behind.

"Seems like chaos to me," Aramis remarked.

"When everyone is following the same delusion, with different intentions, chaos is sure to abound."

Aramis pondered Mel's words in silence as they continued south toward Oakhaven. It was nearing sunset and they still had several miles to cover, so Aramis decided they should stop soon and setup camp.

"If I may make a request," Mel said. "I'd like to stay at an inn."

"Do you think that's wise? We're close enough to be recognized by anyone working for Mordum."

"We could disguise ourselves," Mel suggested. "We're dirty and it's obvious to anyone that we've been on the road a while. Besides, I haven't gone this long without a bath in years."

Aramis shook his head, but he was smiling. "Ever the aristocrat," he chided jokingly. "Fine, but we need to keep out of sight as much as possible. If we get caught, everything we've worked for was in vain."

Mel's face went serious. "I won't allow us to be caught now, not after everything you've faced to get here."

They stopped for the night at a small village half a day's ride from Oakhaven. The sun had passed beyond the horizon and a breeze picked up. Aramis could smell rain coming. Dark clouds blotted out the moon and stars, making it hard to see more than a few feet ahead. Only a few lanterns had been lit and the wind made them sputter; their faint light flickering and causing the shadows to dance erratically.

Aramis eyed the dark shapes suspiciously. He felt like he was losing his mind lately. Seeing things in the shadows, hearing voices that weren't there … but the grim visions were the worst. In the back of his mind, his thoughts always went to Hannah. Was the vision he saw real, or was it some evil joke sent from Mordum? He had promised himself that he would marry her. If she were dead … he pushed the dismal thoughts away.

They found an inn down one of the side streets. No lanterns were lit, but the sound of music and boisterous conversation drew them in. The place was fairly full considering the current crisis that enveloped the kingdom. A fire burned in the hearth, tinging the air with the sharp smoky incense of too-green wood. Another smell, roasting pig, made Aramis's mouth water. Both scents were more pleasing than the others that wafted through the air: mercenary sweat and spilled food and drink that had been left for who knew how long.

"*Ugh*," Mel muttered beneath his breath. "It's too hot for a fire, especially with all these people. The heat is unbearable."

Aramis noticed that almost everyone looked like a mercenary. *No wonder the place is packed,* he thought. *They have no reason to be fleeing.* There was a small table in the corner available, so they sat there and waited for the barmaid. It took longer than Mel liked, and he huffed his indignance a few times, as though anyone other than Aramis could hear him. Finally, a young girl with sinuous sun-lightened hair that spilled down past her breasts came to serve them. She was wearing a flowing brown skirt that reached her knees and a cloudy white, almost transparent blouse that left little to the imagination. She leaned onto the table and made no attempt to hide the clear view of her cleavage through the V of her blouse.

"Drinks?" she asked with a grin.

Aramis didn't reply. He stared at her, his dark eyes catching her watery blue ones and holding them. Faint lines edged away from her eyes, though from exhaustion or worry, he didn't know. Her eyelashes were thick with kohl, the lids covered with a deep shade of purple. It reminded him of the nobles at court, who covered themselves with ridiculous shades of color, always trying to outdo one another. Finally, he looked away, and the woman blinked and shook her head as if to rouse herself from a dream. Her ample breasts swayed with the motion.

"I'll take a drink, and some food," Mel said. "We'll also need a room for the night," he added.

The woman looked at Mel as if just noticing him for the first time. "You're a handsome one, aren't you?" she said. Mel blushed, and she continued flirting with him. "Anything else you'd like? Anything you see that you might *want*?"

Mel looked away and caught Aramis's gaze. Aramis remained impassive to the exchange.

"You're both handsome," she said. "Your friend doesn't smile much, hm?" She made a soft huffing sound, angling her breath up with her lower lip, causing her collection of curls that hung over her forehead to flutter and resettle. She sauntered away and came back with a tray, her ample hips swinging. She placed two mugs of beer on the table and looked at Mel.

"Need company for the night?" she asked.

"I'd love some company," Mel replied, winking at her with one eye. "Unfortunately, I don't have much money."

The woman frowned with puckered lips. "Pity. I bet we could start a fire hotter than the one in this room." She flounced away to another table, flirting with the patrons there as well.

Aramis was scanning the room, looking for anyone that might appear to be a soldier of Oakvalor. The last thing they needed was to be recognized by someone. As he finished looking over the room for the second time, he noticed one man who stood out from the crowd. He definitely wasn't a mercenary, though he was too well dressed to be a refugee. He kept fidgeting, making Aramis think he was nervous. He decided it would be a good idea to keep an eye on him.

The barmaid returned with two plates of food and refilled their drinks. Aramis knew if he drank too much more, he'd begin to lose his focus. He continued to glance at the man occasionally.

"I think he's waiting for someone," Aramis said.

"What?" Mel replied through a mouthful of food.

"The man at the table there," he nodded with his head. "I think he's waiting for someone. We may want to watch him for a bit. There's something … odd about him."

Mel finished his food and leaned close to Aramis. "Should I go talk with him? See if I can get anything out of him?"

Aramis studied the man closely. His clothes were from the Oakhaven court. At least, the current style that was in fashion before he'd left. He didn't have the bearing of a noble. A servant, perhaps?

The door to the inn opened and a man dressed in riding clothes entered. He swept the crowd with his gaze and then headed toward the fidgeting man. He sat down and the two began speaking. They were too far away for Aramis to hear their conversation.

"I'll be back," Mel said. He made his way toward the two men, but stopped within earshot and pretended to flirt with the barmaid. After a few minutes, Mel came back.

"I don't know who they are, but they know Lord Bavol," Mel said quietly. That perked Aramis's intrigue.

"Could you hear what they were talking about?" he asked.

"Somewhat. The lady certainly has a way with words. Anyway, the better dressed man is a servant to Bavol, I believe. From what I could make out, the rider delivered a letter to the king of Talvaard."

"Garrick?" Aramis asked. "I didn't realize he'd been coronated yet." He shook his head. "We're behind on current events. That could bode ill for our journey."

"Perhaps. The other man, the messenger, he said he had a return letter for Lord Bavol. He didn't say what it contained. He's concerned, though. Apparently, he was supposed to meet Bavol somewhere, but it didn't appear he was there, or had ever arrived."

Aramis felt his heart drop into his stomach. *The vision …*

"Gods," Aramis sighed. "He was our key to the nobles. Without him, we don't know who is on our side." He rubbed his face.

"Maybe," Mel said, then paused. "Maybe we could speak to them. Figure out where they were supposed to meet. That might provide some clues as to where Bavol might be if he ran into trouble."

"They could be spies," Aramis said.

"That's true, though I don't believe so. They both seemed genuinely concerned for him."

Aramis steepled his fingers and stared at the two men in silence, biting on his lower lip. "I think it's worth the risk," he finally said. "The information Bavol has is pivotal to our next move. We don't have much time, though. We've only got a few days left."

"Until what?" Mel asked, confused.

Aramis smiled, the first time in a while. "While we were in Keswick, I sent a message to Lynessa."

"I vaguely remember that," Mel said, nodding.

"She promised me anything I needed if we helped her with the Warlock. I asked her to send her armies to Oakhaven."

Mel's surprise was sincere. "I had no idea!"

"I know," Aramis said. "I figured the less people who knew about it, the more of a surprise it would be to my brother when her troops showed up."

"Her armies alone should suffice if it comes to violence," Mel said excitedly. "Then there's the refugees who band together."

"And the druids," Aramis said. "I instructed Lynessa to send word to the druids as well."

"You didn't tell me about any druids."

"It was after … you were gone. Anyway, I helped them as well. They don't want war and they won't use their magic to harm anyone directly, but their help will be an invaluable defense against Mordum's dark magic."

"I must confess something," Mel said. "I will follow you anywhere, to any danger. You are my friend, my brother. But I had my doubts about whether or not we could do this. Now," Mel's eyes lit up, "now, I think we have a chance."

"That makes two of us," Aramis said.

10

THE MESSENGER WAS THE FIRST of the two to leave. Shortly after, the other man followed. Bavol's men had stayed at the inn long enough for Aramis and Mel to take turns cleaning up while the other watched them to make sure they didn't leave.

They paid the barmaid and left the inn. The air had gotten cooler since their arrival, and it was a nice change to the stuffy inn. The servant didn't appear to be as nervous. He walked with a purposeful stride down the cobbled road, not paying any attention to his surroundings. *He's not concerned with safety,* Aramis noted.

The man walked for a quarter of an hour, still seeming oblivious to his pursuers. He kept turning down different side streets and even began to whistle a melody. Aramis was taking care to try and be aware of their surroundings, but his main focus was on the man they were following.

"My Lord," Mel whispered suddenly. "We're going in a circle."

Aramis looked around and realized they were passing the inn they had left earlier. The hair on his arms began to tingle as he realized the trap.

The man stopped walking and turned to face them. He continued his whistling a moment longer, then smiled mischievously.

"A couple of rogues, then? Seeking to cut my throat and take my purse?" He folded his arms across his chest. "You'll find more than you bargained for here."

Several men, armed and armored, stepped out of the shadows between the buildings.

"I think there's been a misunderstanding," Mel said, holding up his hands. "We just want to talk with you."

"Right," the man said. "I won't fall so easily to your highwayman tricks." He nodded at one of the men. He drew his sword and began to approach.

"I'm looking for Lord Bavol," Aramis said. "You're one of his men, aren't you?"

The man tilted his head in curiosity. "And you are?"

Aramis looked to Mel, then back to the man. "Aramis, rightful king of Oakvalor."

The man unfolded his arms and looked around. "You'd best be keeping that information quiet," he said. "Sheath your blade, Sergid. He's an ally. Let's go somewhere safer to talk."

He led them to one of the dark buildings a few spaces down from the inn. The man made sure no one was watching them, then led them inside. They paused in the doorway as he lit a lantern. The dim light illuminated what Aramis thought was someone's home.

"The people who lived here left a few weeks ago," the man said. "We've been using it for our network." He hung the lantern from a hook in the ceiling and motioned them in. The man he'd referred to as Sergid closed the door and took up a position in front of it.

"You can't be too careful these days. Especially with that despot Adamar on the throne."

Adamar, Aramis thought. *So, that's his name.*

"So I've heard," Aramis replied. "I've encountered a number of people on the road. Their stories are all similar. What's your name?"

The man bowed low. "I am Larson," he answered. "Humble servant to Lord Bavol and commander of his house guard."

"You fooled me back there," Aramis said. "Watching you at the inn, I assumed you were an anxious type."

"All part of the ruse," Larson grinned.

"How'd you know I was watching you?"

"Not all of those men were soldiers. At least, not ones loyal to Adamar. One of them caught your interest in me and gave me a hand signal. Pretending to be a bumbling servant was easy. I'm glad you weren't a rogue. We've had to kill too many of them." Larson frowned.

"I'm glad you aren't a spy," Aramis replied. "Do you really not know where Bavol is, or was that part of your ploy as well?"

"I wish it were," Larson answered. "He's been missing since he and Hannah left Oakhaven. They were supposed to go into hiding at a cabin he owns a few hours from here. According to the last missive he sent, Adamar had taken an interest in Hannah."

Aramis felt bile rise in his throat. He forced himself to swallow it. The gruesome images from his vision flooded his mind. Her mutilated body lying on the side of a road. A man he didn't recognize tossing a coin onto her body.

"Was there a specific road they would have taken?"

"We've checked every road out of Oakhaven," Larson said. "No sign of them. They would have taken a wagon, and we haven't seen any signs of passage near the cabin. It's almost as if they simply disappeared. We're all worried."

Aramis knew the feeling too well. "I think I might know where you can check, if you haven't already." He recalled the image of the road her body lay beside. There was a tall stone marker a few feet ahead, though it did not have any engravings or signs. "There's an old hunting path that branches off the main road heading north."

Larson shook his head and looked to Sergid. They both shrugged.

"It was one of my father's favorite places to hunt. All of the nobles know where it is."

"Can you draw a map of it?" Larson asked. "I'll have my men search it."

"I can do better than that," Mel chimed in. "I'll lead them there."

"I didn't get your name," Larson said to him.

"Melchiades, but most people just call me Mel."

"It's an honor," Larson said. "Is the path far from here?"

"A mile, maybe."

"Please, go with Sergid and show the men where this road is. If we can find them, I hope they are alive."

"A storm is coming in. Maybe we should hold off until morning?" Sergid asked.

Larson nodded. "True. I wouldn't want you getting lost in the night. Can you take them in the morning?"

Mel glanced at Aramis.

"We've got pressing business. I was hoping to reach Oakhaven tomorrow."

"How did you plan to enter the city?" Larson asked. "Adamar has it locked down tighter than a prison in Talvaard."

"That's where we needed Bavol. He was working to rally the nobles to our cause. I was hoping to get there without bloodshed. I was also hoping to take the throne back without war."

"Those are some high hopes, if I can be so bold. Adamar has the nobles by the balls, some by fear and others by loyalty. Some of them remember him when he was younger."

"Then what do we do?" Aramis asked.

"We can get you into the city," Larson said. "But what are your plans once inside? I don't think you can trust anyone, especially the nobles."

Aramis didn't know what he planned to do. He'd put all of his thought into getting there alive, he didn't think about what he'd do if he succeeded. "I'm … not sure," he said. "I know that doesn't sound promising, but it's been Hell just trying to get here. Do you have any suggestions? You've obviously been in the city. Where should we stay? We've got to setup a place of operations. I've got an army headed this way."

"An army, you say? How large?"

"Lady Lynessa from Keswick is sending her troops to aide us."

Larson whistled. "That's great news. You're definitely going to need it. Adamar has those black robed priests that follow him around. They give me the chills. There's also been a lot of rumors that there's some sort of ceremony that's going to happen soon. We haven't been able to get the details, but it sounds like a big deal. Lots of mercenaries are showing up, too.”

“Gods,” Aramis growled. “This is getting more difficult to fathom by the minute.”

“Sorry,” Larson shrugged. “I’m just giving you the facts. Once we get you into the city, I think it would be a good idea for you to only travel at night, and only under guard.”

“Won’t having guards be conspicuous?” Aramis asked.

“Don’t worry about that. No one will be any wiser. I’m sure you both are exhausted. There’s beds upstairs. I suggest you get some rest. Tomorrow will come faster than you want it to.”

“Thank you,” Aramis said. “I appreciate everything.”

“I’m just doing my duty to the crown,” Larson said. “We’ll keep the house guarded. Get some rest. Until tomorrow.”

“Until tomorrow,” Aramis said.

—

Aramis was plagued by nightmares. Each time he awoke— drenched in sweat with his heart rapidly pounding in his chest—he would convince himself to go back to sleep. And each dream was worse than the last. Every one of his senses were affected by the dreams, making them seem so real that he woke himself from crying out. After waking from the last nightmare, he realized that sunset was not long in arriving.

He used a hand mirror and a razor he had found in the room to shave his face. No matter how dirty and sweaty he got on the road, he hated the feeling of an unshaven face the most. After he finished, he stared at his reflection for a long while. He scrutinized every inch of skin. It had only been a few months since he’d fled his home, yet he seemed to have aged by many years. Bags under his eyes did little to help. And his dark eyes were like two black pits in his head. The sight unnerved him. He flung the mirror at the wall, shattering it. The floor was littered with shards of glass.

"My Lord?"

Aramis turned to see Mel in the doorway. He hadn't heard him come in. "Yes?"

"The men have prepared breakfast, if you are feeling hungry."

"I'll be down shortly," Aramis said.

"I'm going to show Sergid and a few others where the trail is. I'll be back as quickly as possible."

Aramis nodded. "I'll meet you in Oakhaven, then. Larson is taking me there today. We need to prepare for what's coming."

Aramis knew that Mel didn't like the idea of them traveling separate. The look on his face made that evident. But they both knew, too, that there was little choice in the matter. Lord Bavol had important information.

"Don't do anything rash," Mel said, only half-jokingly.

Aramis grunted in reply. After Mel left, Aramis went downstairs and ate a small meal. Although he was hungry, he just didn't feel like eating. Larson showed up shortly after and gave him a change of clothes. Aramis hadn't realized how dirty and torn his own were despite cleaning them the night before. The clothes were a drab shade of brown and made of cheap material.

"You'll stand out less," Larson explained. "We want as little attention on you as possible."

Aramis didn't argue. The sooner he was in the city, the better. He assumed they would have ridden horses, but Larson thought traveling on foot was a better idea.

"It's easier to hide without a horse," he said. "Patrols are everywhere."

It took a few hours to reach the city. They would have arrived earlier, but a large group of soldiers had caused them to take a roundabout approach to the city. Aramis assumed they would enter the city through the main gate with some sort of disguise. Instead, Larson led him to a sewer grate on the side of one of the walls. Larson glanced around, then lifted the grate up and motioned Aramis to get in the tunnel.

"Hurry," he said.

Aramis obeyed and climbed inside. The tunnel was small, only four feet high. He had to crawl on his hands and knees. He heard the gate close behind him.

"Where does this lead?" Aramis asked.

Larson laughed. "I don't think you want to know."

A few feet in and Aramis's hands touched something wet and slimy. A foul smell assaulted him. "Gods, please tell me we aren't in the sewer."

"We're not in the sewer."

"Then, where are we?"

"The sewer. I told you that you didn't want to know."

"Yeah," Aramis muttered.

Larson squeezed by him and guided their crawl. After a hundred feet, they reached a large open chamber lit with torches. Aramis was glad they didn't have light in the tunnel. There was no telling what he might have touched.

"I found this place shortly after Adamar took the throne. We haven't explored all the tunnels. Some of them are caved in. But this one leads out of the city. We use it to get in and out without being noticed. We'll wait here until nightfall, then we'll go up to the city."

"Up?" Aramis asked, looking toward the ceiling.

"Yes. This room is underground. There's a ladder against the far wall there," Larson pointed, "that leads into an alley between some shops."

"What do we do until then?"

Larson shrugged. "Make yourself comfortable?"

Aramis spotted a cot. "Is that clean?" he asked.

"Yes, I had one of my men bring it here earlier."

"Good." Aramis climbed into it and propped his arms behind his head. The minutes ticked by slowly. Larson pulled a dagger from his boot and began sharpening it with a whetstone.

Sssk, sssk, sssk. Pause. *Sssk, sssk, sssk.* Pause.

Aramis's eyes began to grow heavy. His long night of terrible dreams had finally caught up with him. He vaguely heard Larson continue to sharpen his blade. *Sssk, sssk ...*

His eyes opened and he felt someone touching his shoulder. He snapped his head up and reached for his attacker, only to realize it was only Larson.

"Sorry," Larson said. "I didn't mean to startle you. It's time."

"It's dark already?" Aramis asked, surprised. That was the first time he'd slept without having a nightmare.

"Yes. I was going to wait until I'd heard from Sergid, but no messenger has arrived yet. I'll take you up. There's a tavern you can use at night. The owner was loyal to your father and he's given us his blessing to use it. During the day, you'll need to stay here. Your sleeping routine will have to change for the next few days."

"What sleep?" Aramis said with a chuckle.

"How long before your army arrives?"

"If Lynessa sent them when I asked? Three days, maybe four."

Larson tilted his head and squinted his eyes, muttering calculations to himself.

"If they don't kill or capture the patrols on their way in, Adamar will know they're coming before they get close. The element of surprise will be lost and he'll be prepared to fight. I'll send a runner to pass the word to the army."

"Good idea," Aramis replied. "I honestly hadn't thought of that."

"Well then," Larson motioned toward the ladder. "After you."

They climbed up and opened a grate like the one on the outside of the walls. The grate opened and closed without a sound. *Larson must keep it oiled,* he thought. The night air was warm. The alley they came up into was quiet and dark except for the rats and other denizens of the night that scurried in the shadows.

Larson closed the grate and then motioned for Aramis to follow him. They paused at the end of the alley, then Larson casually stepped out into the main street and glanced around. Satisfied all was clear, he nodded to Aramis. The two walked a block north, toward the castle, and stopped at the building on the corner of the street. A newly painted sign swung above the doorway. It read: *Kingsway Tavern*. Aramis found the name funny in an ironic way.

They entered the building and found that it was empty with the exception of the owner, who stood behind the bar.

"Larson," he greeted with a nod. He was wiping a glass with a rag.

"Albert," Larson replied, "this is Aramis."

Albert set the glass on the counter, tucked the rag into his belt, and came around the bar. He stopped a few feet from Aramis and knelt on one knee.

"My Lord," he said humbly, "as I served your father, so I shall serve you. Anything you require is yours. Merely say the word."

"Thank you, Albert. Please, rise."

Albert stood back up. "Business has been slow lately, so I was just doing some cleaning. Do you need anything?"

"Yes," Aramis answered. "Ink and paper, if you have any."

"Of course." Albert disappeared behind the bar and returned a moment later carrying parchment paper, a quill, and an ink vial.

Larson cleared his throat. "We may want to keep you out of sight. In case anyone decides to come in for a drink."

"Take any room you want," Albert said.

Aramis accepted the items from Albert and headed toward the stairs that led to the rooms. Larson followed. Aramis picked a room at random, checking to make sure it had a desk. He took a seat and began scribbling onto the paper.

"What are you writing?" Larson asked.

"A letter to my brother."

"I'm sorry?"

"He doesn't know where I am. I'm going to send him a letter with false information. I'll need one of your men to deliver it to the castle."

"Do you think that's wise?" Larson asked.

"If we can divert his attention elsewhere, the army can get here with little notice."

"I suppose …"

Aramis finished writing and blew on the ink to make it dry faster. "Can you get someone to deliver it tonight?"

"I'll take care of it," Larson said.

The next morning, while Aramis and Larson were eating, a messenger came into the underground makeshift camp.

"Sir," he said to Larson. His breathing was labored.

Larson stood up. "What is it?"

The messenger shook his head, tried to speak, and fell silent. His eyes became watery.

"What happened?" Larson asked, the worry in his voice evident.

"Dead," was all the man managed to say.

Larson glanced back at Aramis. "I'll be back." He left with the messenger.

Aramis could only guess at what might have happened. He finished his breakfast and then summoned his sword and armor and began practicing his sword fighting. Before he'd left in exile, he would practice with the soldiers. While he wasn't the most skilled, he could certainly handle himself in most situations. And his magical armor and sword didn't hurt either.

A quarter of an hour into his practice, he had worked up a sweat. While his armor was practical, there was only one flaw: ventilation. His body heat was trapped inside the metal encasing, making him burn up more than other types of armor he'd worn. He stopped to drink some water and Larson returned.

"What happened?" Aramis asked between mouthfuls of cold water.

"The messenger who was here. His brother was killed last night. His head was removed and set on a pike outside the castle. His body was hung by the feet above the castle's main gate."

"Gods," Aramis said, shaking his head. "For what?"

"For delivering your message," Larson said softly. "Whatever was in it, your brother did not take it well."

Aramis slumped to the floor, dropping his water. The wooden cup clattered to the floor and the water splashed his legs. "I never …" he sighed. He opened his mouth several times to speak, but words failed him.

"Don't blame yourself," Larson finally said. "Adamar is a cruel man."

"We cannot use that excuse to justify all of his atrocities," Aramis replied. "This ends. Now."

11

ARAMIS WAS SPRINTING TOWARD THE castle, his anger overriding his good sense. He'd outdistanced Larson when the man had tried to stop him. The man meant well, but Aramis knew there was only one way to stop Adamar. He had to kill him.

The main gate was shut. Aramis pulled his helm down midstride, lowered his head, and ran as fast as he could. He slammed into the gate with the force of an ox, bending the metal barrier and sending it crashing open. Several guards stood nearby. As he breached the walls, they all gaped at the spectacle, unsure of what was happening.

One of them snapped out of the shock and drew his blade, then charged him. Aramis summoned his own blade and met the man head-on. Their blades clashed together loudly. The guard issued a curse. Even with his armor, Aramis felt the vibration in his arm. He fought like a man gone mad, lacking all self-control. His practiced moves and footwork were drowned by his sheer ferocity and wild strikes.

Aramis quickly had the man on the retreat. The man attempted to feign left but slipped on a loose rock and Aramis had him, driving his onyx blade into the man's stomach. He violently ripped the blade free, then met his next attacker.

A peal like thunder shook the courtyard and Aramis realized someone had sounded the alarm. He noticed black robed men streaming from the castle, heading towards him. Pure rage and something darker inside him took over. He howled like an animal and swung his blade in any direction his arm would go. Blood splattered his armor and covered the ground, bathing the stones with a slickness he found hard to navigate.

He hardly noticed the flash of light in the corner of his eye before he felt himself flying through the air. His senses disoriented, he didn't know what was happening even after he crashed hard into the castle wall. Aramis struggled to his feet and was quickly surrounded. His breathing was labored and his muscles burned like fire, but he refused to give in to exhaustion. He swung his sword and severed someone's arm at the elbow. Another swing caught a man in the face, splitting him open from his ear to his cheek.

He saw one of the black robed men standing among the crowd of soldiers that had surrounded him. Aramis lunged toward him and tried to cut him down, but his blade turned at the last moment and struck the ground harmlessly. Aramis growled and swung again with the same result. So focused on trying to strike the man, he was taken completely by surprise when something heavy struck him in the head.

He staggered from the blow and his legs became wobbly. His muscles rebelled against him and he collapsed to the ground.

"Don't touch him!" he heard someone shout. And then he was laying on his back, staring up at the sky. An unfamiliar face knelt over him.

"Impressive, little brother. Though I must admit, it was foolish. Whatever you were trying to attempt …" Adamar frowned. "Well, let's say it was a wasted effort." Adamar looked to someone who Aramis could not see. "Bind him, gag him, and take him to my quarters. Do not leave him alone. If he escapes, your life is forfeit."

Before Aramis realized he was being lifted, his vision went dark. At first, he thought he had passed out. He quickly realized that someone had placed a sack over his head, as he was fully aware of being moved and could hear his guards talking, though the sound was muffled. A door creaked open and the sack was removed. He found the method of his transport to be ludicrous, considering he had grown up in the castle and knew every room.

He immediately recognized his father's chamber. The terrible memory of his father's assassination flooded him, overwhelming his senses. His guards set him roughly into a chair and bound his arms and legs. One of them grabbed a cloth and forced it into his mouth, then tied it in place. He glared at them.

I'll get free, and I will kill all of you! He screamed the thought in his mind as he struggled to break his bonds. One of the robed men entered the room and came to stand in front of him.

"Dispel the armor," he said. His voice was a deep baritone and didn't fit the face that stared down coldly at him. Aramis hardened his eyes in an attempt to show his disobedience.

"Dispel your armor or I will dispel it for you."

Aramis huffed through his nose. He dared the man to try.

Perhaps knowing Aramis would not be complicit, he touched Aramis's forearm and leaned down, placing his face within inches of Aramis's. "I warned you," he said softly.

An intense pain shot through his body. Had he not been bound to the chair, he would have flailed about wildly and fell to the ground. Unable to move, it made the pain that much harder to bear. A muffled noise was all that escaped him through the gag. Then his armor disappeared in a swirl of hissing mist.

He breathed furiously through his nose as the pain receded. The robed man stood back up and straightened his hood. "Now then," the man said. "Tell me where the bones are."

Aramis bit the cloth in anger and frustration. He refused to be a pawn to Mordum or his servants. The robed man's eyes stared at him intently, studying him.

"I understand," the man said. "You are rebellious by nature. No matter. I shall just have to break your will. I can do it, you know. I have broken many men's minds. It's never an attractive sight, madness. It changes you, makes you into something that is neither human nor animalistic, but something in between. If you force my hand, I will do it."

Aramis knew by the look in the man's eyes that he wasn't lying. He saw darkness in the man's eyes, but not the darkness that had consumed his own. A different darkness, but no less real. Yet he knew if he gave up the location of the bones, any chance of stopping Adamar and Mordum would be impossible. He hardened his gaze. *No,* he thought, *I will not give him anything willingly.*

The man shrugged, turned, and left the room. Aramis looked at the guards. He didn't recognize them. They were probably men his brother recruited. If he could escape his bonds, he knew he could deal with them easily enough. Since his armor was gone, the ropes were not as tight. He kept his eyes on the guards as he began to wriggle his arms, trying to pull his wrists through the ropes. Just as he almost had one arm free, the robed man came back into the room.

He was carrying a glass orb that glowed faintly with a red hue. White tendrils floated around within it, their motions slow and lethargic. There was something about the orb that grabbed his attention. He tried to look away, but he couldn't. His eyes remained fixed on the orb and his thoughts became fuzzy. And then he found himself floating on a sea of red. Wispy clouds floated above him, churning lazily. He felt groggy, as though he had just woken and not gotten enough sleep. Everything around him moved in slow motion.

"Hello?" he called out. The word disappeared into the distance. There was no echo, no reply, nothing. And then he heard the dark whispers. They said terrible things. He covered his ears with his hands to blot out their voices, but it didn't help. The whispers intensified. They sounded angry. They demanded things from him. Things that he knew he shouldn't give them. He fought back against the voices, denying them. That only angered them further.

Suddenly, one of the cloud wisps came for him. It changed direction from the rest of the clouds, moving down towards him. It was slow, but Aramis found that when he tried to move, it was like being stuck in molasses. His movements were sluggish and the cloud easily caught him. It wrapped around his head, but he didn't feel it touch him. And then the things he knew he shouldn't give flew freely from him mind.

"No!" he cried.

The dark whispers laughed. And then he had the sensation of falling.

"What is *he* doing here?" an angry voice demanded.

Aramis blinked several times, trying to clear his mind. Something had happened, but he couldn't remember what. He shook his head, fighting against the fuzziness. The world around him swam momentarily, then came into glaring focus.

The robed man held the orb, but there was no color swirling within it. It was clear and empty. Then he saw his brother, Adamar, for the first time. He stood as tall as Aramis but he was thin by comparison. Fine-boned and long-fingered, he cut a handsome figure in the opulent court clothes that he was wearing. Light blue eyes under long lashes were as pretty as any maiden's, and his classic, even features reminded Aramis of sculptures he had seen. Were it not for his evil actions, Aramis guessed that the ladies of the court would have vied for his attention. Yet for all his beauty, Aramis sensed a vulnerability in him.

"I don't like repeating myself," Adamar said, his tone icy.

"We thought you sent him," one of the guards answered.

The robed man smiled condescendingly. "I was just leaving," he said. He looked to Aramis and tilted his head. "Thank you for the conversation." He started to leave, but Adamar blocked his path.

"What are you doing here?" he asked. "And why do you have that with you?" Adamar pointed at the orb.

"The Prophet asked me to gather some information," the man answered. "And so I have."

"What information?" Adamar demanded.

"I'm afraid I can't say. You can ask the Prophet, if you'd like. I do need to be on my way," the man said. "The Prophet doesn't like to be kept waiting." Adamar stepped out of the way with a growl. The robed man, his face smug, left the room.

"I don't want to see him around this prisoner again. Is that understood?" Adamar's face was flushed red with anger. The guards nodded uneasily.

"Let him hide behind Ilias's power. Once I have gained the Mark, it is *I* who shall rule Mordum's servants!"

No one spoke and no one moved. Finally, Adamar walked over to Aramis and removed the gag. Aramis inhaled deeply, relieved to breath better.

"Tell me, Aramis, why you are here? Certainly, you know that you have signed your own death warrant?"

Aramis studied his brother before answering. "I am here to reclaim the throne that you have stolen."

Adamar laughed. "Stolen? I am the eldest of us. I am the rightful heir to the throne. You are *nothing.*"

Aramis could see that there was a deep-seated rage within Adamar. He wondered what happened to him, wondered what he had experienced to make him full of so much hatred. Aramis knew that anything he said would fall on deaf ears.

"I don't know where you've been all these years," Aramis said, "but I am heir to the throne. It is known to everyone in this kingdom by royal proclamation." Aramis shook his head. "You have no legitimacy other than the *claim* that you are the heir. You have nothing but your word. And the word of a killer is worthless."

Adamar's eyes lit up with a burning fury and Aramis had the fleeting thought that perhaps he'd gone too far. He didn't care. Whether they were brothers by blood or not, Aramis hated him. He'd killed their father and there was nothing that could quell his own hatred for Adamar.

"Leave us!" Adamar shouted. The guards scrambled to flee the chamber. The last one to leave slammed the door shut behind him. Adamar paced back and forth across the chamber in front of Aramis.

"I understand from the Prophet that you are the chosen vessel for Mordum's return," he said as he paced. "Tell me, *brother,* what did you do to catch our dark god's attention?"

"I serve no god," Aramis spat. "Least of all Mordum."

Adamar paused to look at him. "I held the same delusion once," he said. "Over the years, I have learned otherwise." He began pacing again. "The gods do they as please, choosing us for service when they see fit. Assuming you live beyond today … give it time. You'll see things as I do."

"I will never see things as you do. You are a tyrant. I've seen the destruction your troops have brought upon the people. Your people. How could you?" Aramis asked, his voice rising to match his anger that threatened to boil over.

Adamar sighed. "You don't understand, do you? I thought you'd have figured it out by now. Seen the signs." Adamar walked over to a table that sat in the corner, adorned with a few crystal glasses and a bottle of brandy. He poured himself a glass and looked at Aramis from over his shoulder. "Would you like some? The servants found it in the pantry, hidden behind some flour. Apparently, father had a secret stash and was keeping the best stuff for himself."

Aramis glared in response.

Adamar shrugged and downed the entire glass. He refilled the glass and then resumed his pacing. "I'm going to be honest with you. As such, I expect you to do the same service to me. Can you agree to that?"

Aramis remained silent.

"I'll take your silence as consent, then. Where do I start?" he asked aloud. "How about from the beginning, as far I know it to be true. You and I are brothers, but only half. We share the same father, but my mother died after contracting the plague. Father spiraled into a depression after that. A long, deep darkness that consumed him. Have you ever experienced anything like that? I suppose you haven't. But I have." Adamar took a sip from the glass.

"I was ten when death took her from us. She was beautiful. Her passion for life was unrivaled. I think that is what father loved most about her." Adamar paused for a long moment before continuing. When he spoke again, Aramis could hear a strangled emotion in his voice.

"I tried to help him feel better, but nothing worked. The servants told me to be patient, that he needed to grieve and that once enough time had passed, he would find some normalcy. As the years passed, I began to doubt that was true. Those years were difficult, to understate it. I was passed from one servant to another, servants who barely noticed my existence. I was tutored and trained as I should have been, but not having father's attention was …crushing."

Aramis thought he saw Adamar wipe a tear from his eye.

"When I was sixteen, father met your mother. Somehow, she managed to pull him out of his depression. He came alive again, enjoying the things he had forgotten for so long. Well, most of them.

Father doted on his second wife the way he never had time to do with me. After a few years, she became pregnant with you. My disdain and jealousy doubled when I heard the news. I was already jealous of your mother for the attention father gave her, attention that I never received.

"The thought of a half-brother getting the charming life I never experienced was too much. When it comes to kings, second sons are … disposable, only needed in the event that the heir dies prematurely. Second sons never feel the weight of the crown, nor the dangers of kingship. I digress." Adamar drank the rest of the brandy and returned the glass to the table.

"Why are you telling me this?" Aramis asked. "Are you trying to justify your evil by blaming our father's grief for your childhood? That it didn't go the way you wanted it to? Please, spare me! That's life. Nothing ever goes the way you plan."

"You are right, my brother. You are too right."

Aramis knew that he should hate Adamar, but he was finding it hard to keep that hatred burning the more he heard.

"Yet I am not trying to justify anything. The things that happened, happened. There was nothing that anyone could have done to change that. But," Adamar came to stand in front of Aramis and looked him in the eyes. Aramis could see that his eyes were watery and red. *Is he crying?* Aramis thought. "father and I didn't agree on many things, least of all … you. When you were born, the physicians thought you were blind. Your eyes had a milky substance that could not be cured. Father suggested …"

Adamar sighed and bowed his head. "Father suggested that you be put out of your misery. Since you weren't going to be heir, he felt that he would be doing you a service, keeping you from facing the difficulties of life without sight. I disagreed."

Aramis didn't want to believe it, but … something in Adamar's tone made him consider the words closely.

"What happened?" Aramis asked.

Adamar looked at him. "I told him you weren't blind. I didn't know for certain, but I thought I had seen your eyes following me a few times. It was only a suspicion, but one that ended up being proven. Unfortunately, it took an action on my part that father found unforgivable."

"What did you do?"

"Nothing to warrant his wrath. I merely committed a few acts that shined an undesirable light on me. Father cared about how people saw him too much. He didn't like the negative attention from what I did, and so … he banished me. That forced him to keep you alive. Thankfully, one of the physicians found a cure for your eyes. It turns out you weren't blind after all."

Wait, Aramis thought. *He ...*

"You saved my life?" Aramis asked, his voice a whisper.

"I wouldn't go that far," Adamar said.

"No," Aramis suddenly understood why he'd never heard of his brother. "No, you did save my life. If you hadn't been banished, father would have followed through. I would be dead."

Adamar nodded.

Aramis was overwhelmed with emotions, but then his suspicion returned. "What about what you've done to our people? To our father?"

Adamar knelt in front of him. "Lies, all of it. I would never have father killed. We may not have been close, but he was my father the same as yours. The Prophet, unbeknownst to me, sent an assassin to kill father. I didn't know, I swear it."

"Then why did you claim the throne?"

"The Prophet told me that father had removed my banishment and had requested that I return. He tricked me," Adamar said harshly. "I had no reason to doubt him. When father exiled me, I had nowhere to go. Ilias found me. I was starving, living on the streets in Talvaarin. I fled our kingdom because everywhere I went, people shunned me. No one would give me work. I even begged on the corners for spare coins. People spat on me and cursed me. I …"

Aramis felt himself welling with emotions. Confusion, anger, disappointment. So many that he couldn't fully feel any single one over the other. "I'm sorry," he said. "I'm sorry that you went through that."

"It wasn't your fault," Adamar replied. "I did what I did for the right cause. I never anticipated father banishing me, but that doesn't change why I did what I did. Given the same situation again, I wouldn't choose any differently. The things I experienced helped make me who I am today."

"So, you came here thinking that you were going to be reunited, only to find that father had been killed?"

"Yes," a tear slid down Adamar's cheek. "I arrived after he'd been killed, but before the funeral. I was told that you had killed him. I didn't know you or your character, so I assumed it to be true. I had the guards sweep the city for you. They never found you. I assumed that you had fled, and that was proof of your guilt."

"I was being held as a prisoner in the dungeons," Aramis said. "I was tortured and told to admit that I had killed our father. I didn't kill him, and I refused to admit anything like that."

Adamar stood up. "You were in the dungeon the entire time?"

"Until my friend rescued me."

"Melchiades, right? Yes, I was told he had helped you murder our father." Adamar shook his head in disbelief. "They lied to me," he muttered. "They lied to me!" he repeated, shouting it. "Ilias had our father killed and blamed on it you. I can't believe it. Why would he do that? I trusted him. He was like a second father to me."

"From what I've seen and experienced at the hands of Mordum and his servants, I'm surprised you want the Mark. They are all dark and twisted people."

"No, not all of them," Adamar said. "I've come to see that corruption has indeed filled Mordum's ranks, but it wasn't always like that. Not until recently. Something has changed, but I don't know what. Mordum told me to find you, to keep you safe. The Prophet said Mordum wants to take human form and that he has chosen you as the vessel. You must feel so blessed."

"Blessed?" Aramis said. "Gods, no. I didn't want this blasted mark to begin with. A templar cursed me with it."

"That's odd," Adamar said. "Mordum only gives the mark to those who ask for it. I believe you, but … I don't understand. That's not possible."

"Did they tell you that, too?"

Adamar's shoulders slumped. "I'm sorry, Aramis. If I'd have known they weren't what they said they were …"

"What do we do?" Aramis asked.

"What do you mean?" Adamar replied.

"The man who had the orb. He did something to me. I'm not sure how, but he forced my armor to dispel. And I think he found out where the bones are."

"The bones of Mordum?" Adamar's sudden excitement worried Aramis.

"Yes," he answered. He watched his brother carefully as he related how he got the bones. Adamar was excited, but not in a way that justified his initial worry.

"So, you have the blood and the bones? That is good. I have the ashes. Where are they? We need to keep them out of Ilias's hands."

"The blood is back at my hideaway. The bones are hidden by magic, but I can get them. We may have a problem, though."

"What?"

"The man with the orb. I think he knows how the bones are hidden. I'm a little confused as I think about it, but I think he pulled the information from me. Everything is muddled."

"Then we need to hurry. There are different types of crystal spheres like that, but there are some that can rob a man of his wits. It's possible he used it to get what he wanted out of you. He's probably going to find the bones as we speak."

"Can't you send your men to stop him?"

Adamar shook his head. "He's a higher rank than I am. If my men even obeyed that order, he'd have them killed. No, we've got to do this ourselves." Adamar unsheathed a dagger from the folds of his tunic and cut Aramis's bonds. "He's templar and he's very dangerous. Tell me where the blood is and I will retrieve it. You go get the bones."

"I don't think that's going to work," Aramis said as he stood up. He rubbed his bruised and scraped wrists. "There's a network of men loyal to our father who have it. If they saw you, they would kill first and ask questions later. I'll get them both and bring them to you. Where should we meet?"

Adamar rubbed his chin, thinking. "There's a house in the city. It's secluded and abandoned. I can slip you out of the castle, but the rest is on you."

"What about you?" Aramis asked. "What are you going to do?"

"I'll keep Ilias and the others busy."

"What if they ask where I am?"

"I'll make something up. Don't worry about me. Come on, we've got to hurry." Adamar opened the door to the room and stepped into the hall. Two guards stood on either side of the doorway. "Their prisoner says there is another man here in the castle. Go, find him. Bring him to me alive!"

The guards sprinted off. Adamar walked both ends of the hall to make sure they were alone, then he waved for Aramis to follow him. Adamar led Aramis to the end of the hall and into an empty room on the right side. He closed the door behind him. "There's a passage in this room that leads outside the castle walls. You'll need to find a way back in as the door only opens one way. I'm sure however you got into the city will work for you again. Meet me at the end of District street. You'll know the building when you see it. The windows are boarded."

Adamar pressed a stone and a section of the wall shifted back and to the left, revealing a narrow staircase. Aramis grabbed a torch from the wall. "It was odd finding out I had a brother. I didn't believe it at first. It's even more odd meeting him after all this time." Aramis smiled. "I like it, though. I'll see you in a few hours. Together, we'll stop this darkness before it's too late."

Adamar embraced him in a hug. "Be safe, my brother."

“I will.” Aramis nodded, then stepped into the tunnel and disappeared into the darkness. Adamar pressed the same stone and the wall slid back into place.

Mordum was right. That was easy.

12

IT TOOK ARAMIS LONGER TO escape the castle than he thought it would. The tunnel branched off in different directions, all leading to caved in chambers or dead ends. By the time he finally found the exit that led outside the city, he had gotten turned around and backtracked several times.

The sun was setting and the sky was painted with beautiful colors. Aramis felt hope for the first time since his father's death.

I have a brother!

The knowledge that his brother was merely deceived and being used by the gods as he was offered some comfort. Finally, someone who understood what it was like to be a pawn in a game you couldn't control. His excitement made him want to rush, but he knew he needed to stay out of sight. Just because his brother was on his side, didn't mean that fighting Mordum's servants would be any easier.

He walked around the outskirts of the castle for half a mile before he found the sewer entrance that Larson had shown him. The grate was wet with fresh waste that had been dumped. Aramis grit his teeth. Even that could not dampen his joy. He lifted the grate and climbed inside. He made his way carefully through the tunnel to the chamber they'd been using as a hideaway. As soon as he stepped into the room, he was greeted by several faces.

"Aramis!"

He turned to see Hannah. His heart fluttered down into his stomach and he realized in that moment just how much he loved her. He embraced her tightly and held her close for a long moment, breathing in her scent and feeling her soft hair and skin. It felt like a dream.

"I'm so glad you're all right," she said. "Larson told us you went to kill Adamar. I was afraid you'd been captured."

"I was," Aramis said, releasing her. "But I escaped."

"How?" Mel asked. He stepped through the small crowd of people.

"Adamar let me go."

Everyone in the room went silent.

"What do you mean?" Larson finally asked.

"He's not what we think he is," Aramis said. "He's been deceived by Mordum's prophet. He's not responsible for any of this."

"My Lord," Mel said gently. "He's trying to subvert you. We know he's responsible. Everything we've seen ..." Mel had a troubled look on his face.

"I know how it looks, but he's not the decision maker. He's not behind any of this."

"What about your father?" Larson asked.

"Mordum's prophet tricked him. He sent the assassin, not Adamar. I know it sounds crazy," Aramis said. "But I believe him."

"It is crazy," Mel said. "The fact that you would believe him is even more concerning. Think about it, my Lord. Think. Why would he tell you all that? Why would he let you go? He wants something from you."

"No," Aramis said, shaking his head. "He's telling the truth. I saw it in his eyes. He said we need to keep the blood and the bones out of the Prophet's reach. He's got somewhere safe we can hold them until we defeat the Prophet and his men."

Aramis realized everyone was staring at him as if he'd gone mad. "What?" he asked. "What is it?"

Larson shook his head. "I can't trust the word of someone who willingly follows the god of death. I've seen things that can't be reconciled to this ... information."

Aramis was confused. He wished he could take the things he saw and put them into their minds. If only they had seen and heard what he'd seen, they would know. "If you don't believe him, that's fine.

That's your choice. But I do, and I am going to take the blood and the bones to him."

Aramis went to grab the wineskin that held the blood. Mel stepped in front of him and placed a hand on Aramis's chest. "My Lord, I can't let you do this. We've worked too hard to get here. We can't just hand everything over to him."

"Of all the people," Aramis said softly. "I would have expected you to back me. Get out of my way. I'll finish this. I'll end this darkness myself."

Mel didn't budge. His eyes were pleading. *He's trying to trick you,* a voice whispered in his head. *He doesn't want you to succeed.*

"Move," Aramis warned. Mel stood resolute. "I said move," Aramis said again. "You can't handle it, can you?"

"I'm sorry?" Mel asked, confused.

"You can't handle the fact that this war is coming to an end. Your entire life's mission has been to fight against Mordum. If he's defeated, you wouldn't know what to do with yourself, would you?"

"My Lord, think about what you are saying. I never wanted war in the first place. Can't you see that Adamar has you fooled? You are going to give him everything he needs to bring Mordum back into this world. *Please*, tell me you see the truth."

Aramis did see the truth. "Move," he said again.

"I cannot let you do this."

Mel's betrayal stung worse than anything he'd ever felt. Aramis's eyes watered with tears. "I knew it," he said. "I knew you would do this, but I thought maybe ..." Aramis clenched his jaw and steeled his emotions. "I thought maybe you'd value our friendship more than the lines in the sand. You know I don't want this. But I have no choice."

Aramis pushed Mel away, then summoned his armor and his blade. The air hissed, echoing off the walls of the chamber. The others gathered scrambled out of the way. Hannah backed up, shaking her head in disbelief. "What happened to you?" she asked, horrified.

Her disgust wrenched his heart, but he knew that she didn't understand. He could forgive her of that. Mel stood protectively in front of the wineskin. *That,* Aramis thought, *I can never forgive.*

"Please, my Lord. Aramis," Mel said, shaking his head. "Please don't do this."

"I am your king," Aramis said coldly. "And you will address me as such. Get out of my way or I swear by the gods I will cut you down."

When Mel didn't move, it enraged him. The dark whispers began filling his ears, urging him to strike him down. They told him things that Mel had thought about him. His rage took over and he charged Mel, swinging his blade in a downward chop, seeking to cleave him from shoulder to hip. Mel's surprise was splayed across his face. He managed to summon his own blade in time to block the strike.

Aramis heard Larson and his men draw their own blades. "Traitors, all of you!" he snarled. "You will all regret this!" he screamed. He turned on Larson's men. One of them came at him, waving his sword wildly. Aramis quickly sidestepped and tripped the man as he passed. He tumbled to the ground. Another man began to circle around him, trying to flank him from the rear.

With a growl, Aramis threw himself into the others, kicking, punching and even jabbing with the hilt of his blade. His anger told him to kill them, but something else kept his hand from following through. He knocked several of them unconscious and broke a few noses. Larson dropped his blade, the fear evident on his face.

Aramis turned back towards the wineskin to find Mel still guarding it. He'd summoned his armor and stood in a defensive position. The whispers urged him on. He stabbed forward with his blade, attempting to pierce Mel's armor. Mel knocked his sword aside, but didn't counterattack.

Fine, let him die a coward!

He stepped close to Mel and thrust a few strikes at him, testing his defenses. Mel blocked them all easily. Aramis felt his tattoo burning. The power called out to him. It wanted him to use it, to unleash it against Mel. His anger, the whispers, the call of the Mark … they overwhelmed his senses. He closed his eyes and unleashed the dark power welling within him. A blast of black lightning shot forth from the tip of his blade, striking Mel in the chest.

Mel staggered back from the force, landing heavily against the table and smashing it. The wineskin fell to the floor but didn't burst. Aramis screamed with all of his might. The dark power flowed out from him and black flames consumed everything near his sword. The cot and the broken table flared, giving birth to a fire. Mel rolled out of the flames and got back to his feet. Still, he would not attack.

Aramis sent a torrent of black flames at Mel, bathing him in a shower of darkness. The fire seemed to have no effect on him. He charged Mel again, this time ramming him with his shoulder. The two went down in a clash of metal. Hannah scream. Aramis ripped Mel's helmet off and punched him in the face several times with his armored fist. Blood splattered his armor and Mel's body went limp.

Aramis got up and walked through the fire he'd created and grabbed the wineskin. He realized Hannah was trapped by the fire. He ran to her and wrapped his body around hers, then stepped through the flames, using his armor as a shield for her. He knew the fire would end up consuming the entire room. He didn't care. He glanced at the men who lay unconscious on the ground. Larson was trying to pull one of them toward the exit tunnel. Mel's body still lay unmoving.

They'll see, he thought. *In this life or the next, they will see I was right.*

He led Hannah out of the burning chamber using the ladder that led into the alley above. She was shaking uncontrollably. Aramis reached out to touch her face and she flinched. He drew his hand away. *So be it.*

She met his eyes briefly. He smiled at her, but he could see the fear in her eyes. He'd become something else entirely to her. She would see. She would see just like the others would see.

He left her in the darkened alley, alone. He dismissed his armor and blade as he walked toward District street.

—

Aramis found the house easily enough. It was the only building on the street that seemed out of place. Everything else was in good condition and well taken care of. The boarded windows hid any light that might be shining within.

The door was unlocked and opened with a soft creak. The main room was alight with a fire burning in a stone hearth. The walls showed signs of age and the floor squeaked as he made his way toward the figure standing in front of the fire.

"Brother," he called out.

"Aramis," Adamar replied. "Did you bring the items?"

"I brought the blood."

Adamar turned from the fire to face him. "What of the bones? Did the templar get them?"

"No," Aramis said. "They are still hidden by the spell. I can get the magic to release them anywhere I am."

Adamar stared at him. "What happened? You look like you ran to get here."

"It's nothing," Aramis answered with a shrug. "It doesn't matter."

Aramis knelt on the floor and drew his rusty dagger. He cut a circular shape into the wood and crossed through it with an intricate set of lines. After he finished, he sheathed his dagger and closed his eyes. Feeling the power of the Mark flowing through him, he channeled it toward the symbol he'd cut. The air rippled in front of him briefly before a brown sackcloth appeared. Cutting off the flow of power, he snatched the bag up just as the symbol burst into flames. They seared the floor and then quickly diminished.

"The Mark gives you magic?" Adamar asked curiously.

"No. Well, not that I know of. The spell was cast by a wizard. She told me how to unlock it."

Adamar eyed him greedily. "I've begged Mordum for the Mark," he said softly. "Yet he makes me wait for it."

"You shouldn't want it," Aramis replied. "It's brought me nothing but death."

"So where is the blood?"

Aramis produced the wineskin from his belt.

"The blood, the bones, and the ashes," Adamar said with awe. "I knew it would be me. I knew I would be the one to perform the ritual and bring him back."

"What are you talking about?" Aramis said. "We're hiding these from the Prophet until we can kill him. Then we need to find a way to destroy them."

Adamar laughed. "No, little brother. I will not keep Mordum from what he desires. I couldn't even if I wanted to."

Aramis took a step back towards the door. "I am going to stop the plague that is Mordum from spreading."

"I don't think you are going anywhere," Adamar said.

Rough hands grabbed him from behind. He dropped the wineskin and the bag as he struggled against his attackers. He saw a glint of steel and then felt a stinging pain on his arm. He managed to glimpse his arm and saw that his tattoo had been cut.

"Hurry," Adamar commanded. "The Mark will heal. Get him to the ceremony. Quickly!"

Aramis was struck in the back of the head and then there was only darkness.

"To abandon a friend to the darkness would be an assault upon my conscience."

—Melchiades

13

WHEN HE AWOKE, THE FIRST thing he noticed was the noise. Hundreds of people, most of them wearing the robes of Mordum's priests, were gathered around a large pit that had been dug. Aramis guessed it must have been created recently, as the dirt was dark and fresh.

The crowd was chanting, but he couldn't make out the words. The ringing in his ears was hindering him from making out their words. He also had a pounding headache. He was standing upright, bound by thick ropes across his legs and chest. Aramis tested their strength. They didn't budge. He tried to summon his blade, but nothing happened. The connection he felt to the Mark was nonexistent. Glancing down, he saw why.

His tattoo had been cut and the skin was pinned back, keeping the two pieces from touching. *Disgusting,* he thought. The way his arms were tied, he couldn't reach to remove the small metal pins. He looked up. He was standing atop a raised platform in front of the pit, overlooking the crowd. It was like looking at a sea of blackness. There were hundreds, if not thousands, of the robed men. All of them followers of Mordum.

Aramis cursed them under his breath. He listened intently to their chanting. He could only hear it faintly above the ringing, but he could swear that the words were calling to him. He grew uncomfortably warm. Something was happening, but he didn't know what. The crowd continued their chant, and Aramis suspected they were saying the same words, over and over.

The sky filled with storm clouds. They came suddenly, with incredible speed. Solid black, roiling and churning like some sort of monster. The clouds devoured the tops of the castle's guard towers, crawling over them to consume them whole. The chill wind strengthened, whipping dust from the ground into eyes and mouths.

`677

A bolt of lightning flashed out from the clouds above, spearing the ground near the pit. Thunder exploded. The concussion knocked some of the priests to the ground. A small group of women screamed. The men who were still standing tried to calm them, but the women would have none of it. They fled in a mad panic.

"Forget them!" Adamar shouted from beside Aramis. He wondered if his brother had been there the whole time, or if he had just arrived.

The storm clouds raced across the sky, battling the sunlight, defeating it easily. The sun fell, overcome by darkness. Night was upon them, a night thick with swirling dust. Aramis could see nothing, not even his own feet. The next second all around him was illuminated by another devastating lightning bolt. Rain slashed sideways, coming at him all like arrows fired from a million bowstrings. Hail pounded on him like iron-tipped flails, cutting and bruising. Lightning walked among the crowd, casting its flaming spears. Thunder shook the ground and roared.

The rain fell harder, if that were possible. Aramis wondered how long the raging storm could last. It felt like a lifetime, like he had been born in the storm and would grow old and die in the storm. The rain and ice pelted him and felt like stinging nettles across his entire body. He could only lower his head to try and shelter his face, but even that seemed futile.

A lightning flash momentarily blinded him. The blast deafened him. The force of the thunderbolt lifted a man off his feet and slammed him back down. The bolt had struck so close, Aramis could hear the sizzle in the air and smell the phosphorous and sulfur. He could also smell burnt flesh. As his sight slowly restored, he looked in the direction of the man who'd been struck. The priest's flesh glowed red beneath a black crust, like a hunk of overcooked meat. Smoke rose from it; the wind whipped it away, along with flecks of charred flesh. The skin of the man's face had burned away, revealing a mouthful of hideously grinning teeth.

Adamar braved the wind and rain and leapt down from the platform, landing at the edge of the pit. He grabbed a sack from one of the cowering priests and climbed down into the pit. From Aramis's vantage point, he could barely make out what his brother was doing. Adamar reached into the sack and pulled out something white—bones. He lay them out, piecing them together until it looked like a skeletal man lay in the dirt. Then he pulled the wineskin out of the sack and poured the blood on the bones. He covered the skull with it and even kneeled to smear it, ensuring the entire skull was covered. Then he pulled out a small box and dumped out what Aramis assumed were the ashes.

The wind died. The rain softened to a steady downpour. The hail ceased altogether. Thunder rumbled a drumroll, which seemed to mark time with the pace of a strange figure of darkness steadily growing nearer with each illuminating flare. The storm receded, carrying its fury to the other side of the castle, to other parts of the world.

Soaking wet, Aramis shook the water and muck from his face. The wind was cold and crisp and chill, and he was shivering. The dark cloud filled the pit, obscuring Adamar within its clutches. Slowly, yet steadily, it flowed forth out of the pit, coming towards the platform, towards Aramis. An intense feeling of dread spread through him. He struggled against his bonds again, but they wouldn't give way.

The shadowy cloud pooled onto the platform at his feet, gradually shifting and turning until a vague outline of a man formed. The face was insubstantial and shifted amongst itself, never staying the same. Despite that, Aramis knew exactly what—who—stood before him.

"Mordum," he whispered.

The form pulsed in recognition of its name. Suddenly the pins in his arm came loose and clattered to the ground. His skin rolled back together, healing by the power of the mark. Heart thudding against his chest, Aramis stared into the face of darkness, the face of death. And then the shadow plunged into his mouth.

—

Adamar climbed out of the pit just as the shadowy cloud that was Mordum entered Aramis's body. He watched in envy while Aramis's body twitched and jerked as Mordum fought for control. Suddenly, a horn split the air. Adamar looked from tower to tower to see who was sounding the alarm. Spotting a guard waving a flag, he ordered one of the priests to go find out what was happening.

He turned his attention back to Aramis. His younger brother writhed and his eyes rolled into the back of his head. "He's putting up a stronger fight than I expected," he muttered to himself.

A tremor shook the ground, following quickly by another. The horn sounded again, this time from the other side of the courtyard. A whistling sound filled the air. Adamar looked in every direction, but he didn't see anything. A crashing sound echoed through the air.

"What is going on?" Adamar demanded angrily. The priests were standing around confusedly. They began to murmur among themselves. "I have to do everything myself, it seems." Adamar pushed through the crowd toward the first guard tower he'd spotted that had been sounding the alarm. As he got closer, it was evident something was wrong. Soldiers were running towards the main gate, hauling long timbers.

"My Lord," a breathless soldier hailed him. "Creatures," he gasped. He placed his hands on his knees and bent over, trying to restore his breath. Adamar waited impatiently while trying to get a view beyond the gate.

"Forgive me," the man finally said. "There are creatures attacking the gate. I've never seen the like before. The others are trying to fortify the damage from earlier." The soldier's eyes strayed towards Aramis and the pit.

"Creatures? What do they look like?" Adamar asked.

Metal clanged as the gate shuddered inward. Shouts and curses rose from the soldiers who were trying to brace the damaged gates. Adamar stalked to the crowd of soldiers, leaning left and right to try and see what creatures were attacking his castle. And then he caught sight of one of them, just barely. Its head was large and round and looked like a stone.

"Golems," a voice said. Adamar turned to see his remaining body guard standing beside him.

"What?" Adamar said, wondering where his guard had disappeared to. "I've never heard you speak before," he added.

"Golems," the templar said. "They are creatures formed of magic and earth. There are few who can summon them."

Adamar looked back at the gate. "How do you kill them?" he asked.

"You must kill the one who summoned them," the templar answered.

"What are you waiting for?" Adamar demanded. "Go deal with them!"

The templar wavered for a brief second before bowing and leaving. The hesitation was not lost on Adamar. *What,* he wondered, *could give a templar pause?* As far as he knew, nothing could stop Mordum's most powerful servants. Perhaps the templar was not used to fighting solo. The blasted Prophet of Edria has killed his other templar guard and Mordum had not answered his call for a replacement. He pushed his doubts from his mind.

"My Lord," the priest from the crowd jogged over to him. "There are creatures attacking the gate."

"So I've seen," Adamar said, his annoyance plain.

"To the west, a large army is approaching."

"How large?" Adamar asked.

"I think you'll want to see for yourself," the priest answered.

"Show me."

The priest led him across the courtyard to a curved stone stairway that led upwards to the battle ramparts. They climbed the flight of stairs quickly and Adamar saw a trio of soldiers pointing in the distance.

"Let me see," Adamar growled. He took the spyglass from one of the soldiers. *If that priest is exaggerating ...*

Lifting the device to his right eye, he gazed out across the plains and scanned the horizon. At first, he didn't see anything. Then he noticed a plume of dust. He followed its length until he found the source. A black mass encompassed his view. He tried adjusting the device, but he only made the image blurry.

"Someone fix this thing!" he shouted in frustration. The soldier he'd taken it from adjusted it and handed it back to him. This time, the image was clearer.

Cavalry. Hundreds, if not thousands, were riding straight toward him. His hopes soared as he thought they were more of Mordum's mercenaries, but his hope quickly turned to surprise when he saw the banner being carried at the front of the army.

The flag of Keswick.

Adamar clenched his jaw and threw the spyglass. It clanged as it struck the stone.

"Orders, my Lord?"

Adamar's thoughts went rampant. An army marching on him. Creatures at his doorstep. Mordum would soon fully possess his brother, if he hadn't already. He needed to hold them off.

"Ready the catapults. As soon as the army is within distance of the walls, rain hell on them."

He left the wall, taking the stairs two at a time. He ran towards the pit. Climbing onto the platform, he noticed Aramis's body had gone slack and pale. Turning his attention to the crowd of milling priests, he shouted, "To arms!"

The priests glanced askance at one another, obviously confused.

"An army approaches! We must hold them off until our dark lord has taken his vessel. Quickly!"

Adamar knew he might be pressing his luck. Although it was known that he was favored among Mordum's servants, his official rank was not very prestigious. The Prophet himself was likely among the crowd.

In a display that Adamar found truly beautiful, the horde of priests threw back their hoods and summoned their armor and blades. The hissing of mist overpowered any other sound, including the clanging of the gates. A sea of shiny blackness filled his vision and pride swelled within him. This would be *his* army soon.

"To the west!" Adamar shouted as loud as he could. The legion of priests streamed forth, heading to the gates.

He turned to Aramis. It didn't look like he was breathing. *Good,* he thought. *If Aramis is dead, then Mordum is in control.*

Everything was going in his favor. Aramis was dead, the priests were following his commands, and soon Mordum would walk in his midst. Mordum would bless him with the Mark and he would be the new Prophet. All his sacrifice, everything he had worked for, had led to this moment. He shook visibly with excitement.

The clash of steel and the shouts of battle erupted nearby. Adamar turned his attention to the raucous. A small band of men, perhaps thirty of them, were clashing with his soldiers less than a hundred feet away. Adamar looked to the gate, but the creatures had not breached it. In fact, the priests swarmed the gate, pushing it outward and attacking the stone golems.

How in Mordum's name did they get in here?

Drawing his own sword, he leapt off the platform and ran to join the fray. As he neared the battle, he recognized one of the men as Aramis's priest-friend. He'd heard the rumors of the man. Supposedly, he was a priest of Edria before she was killed. If that were true, then his armor and blade had left him. He would be an easy kill.

Adamar charged into the fight, bringing his sword in a downward arc toward the priest. He immediately regretted it as soon as he'd engaged the man. From afar, he appeared to wear normal armor. But as he stood before him now, he realized that the priest still had god blessed armor. He tried to retreat.

"Come now," Mel called after him. "You aren't very brave without your templar guards, are you? Come, let's dance."

Adamar sprinted away, fleeing the battle altogether. He could hear booted steps of pursuit. He ran towards the platform, desperately hoping Mordum had gained full control of Aramis's body. As he clambered on, he risked a glance over his shoulder and saw the priest had been intercepted by his soldiers.

His stomach dropped when he saw that Aramis's body was gone. The ropes lay at the base of the stone slab. He whirled around, bracing for battle. Yet Aramis was nowhere to be seen. Another horn, this one different than the last two, split the air. Adamar looked from the empty slab towards the gate where the priests were swarming out into the main city. Biting his lip in indecision, he left the platform and made his way back to the battle ramparts.

The soldiers were gone, but the spyglass lay where he left it. Snatching it up, he checked to see if it had broken. The only damage was a few scuff marks on the metal. The lens was still intact. He looked out at the advancing army. They were closing on the main city gates. Black armored priests were forming into ranks outside the city, preparing for close quarters battle.

Figuring out how to adjust the device, he turned it to the gates. Large piles of stone lay strewn about. He grinned triumphantly, knowing his templar had found those responsible for the creatures. The last of the priests filtered out of the gates, rushing toward their fellows outside the city. A thunderous boom filled the air and drew Adamar's attention. Flashes of light coming from the approaching army crackled to life, forking their way toward the ranks of Mordum's priests.

The magical lightning shattered upon an unseen barrier. Black flames erupted from the priests and spread across the distance, striking the cavalry. Both men and horses were consumed by the unholy fire. Screams of agony reached Adamar's ears.

He grimaced. He had seen battle before and had even killed. And despite his loyal devotion to the god of the dead, he found that he just couldn't stomach the sounds of the dying. Perhaps it was because they reminded him of his own impermanence. He knew then, in that very moment, that he was afraid to die.

Adamar shook his head to clear his mind. There would be time to think of such things, but it was not now. The enemy was almost to the formation of priests and then the battle would be on in full force.

He imagined what the priests might be feeling. Their hearts pounding, adrenaline coursing through their veins. They stood foot to foot, packed tightly together, with not much room to maneuver. The less space between them, the less of a chance a horseman had to get through. Seconds felt like eternity. And then the army washed up against the line priests. The noise and commotion was loud and rumbling. Adamar stood straight-backed, his chin high. He turned his gaze away from the clashing armies and up to the sky above them. It was dull and gray.

An explosion rocked the ground outside the city. Both sides were thrown into silence. Adamar used the spyglass to see what was happening. Some sort of magical blast had killed hundreds of his priests and soldiers. Their bodies lie smoldering on the field.

The smoke cleared to reveal two forms, both clothed in white robes. Their faces shined brilliantly and Adamar had to look away, lest he be blinded.

"Wizards," he growled under his breath.

"No," a voice beside him said. It startled Adamar and he turned to see Aramis beside him. His hand went to the pommel of his sword, but Aramis raised his hand and Adamar was paralyzed. He couldn't even move his eyes.

Aramis looked to him and Adamar knew that it was not his brother inside the body. Not anymore.

"They are not wizards," the undead voice said. "They are gods."

Had Adamar been in control of his body, he would have given his lord an incredulous look.

"It is time, though I am not ready," Aramis said. He lowered his hand and Adamar's paralysis faded. He fell to his knees.

"My Lord Mordum," he said in a trembling voice. "Grant me the blessing of your Mark. I beg you."

Aramis, or Mordum as he had become, looked down at Adamar. "I do not have the strength to spare," he answered. "Rise, and tell me what is happening now. These eyes are not like my own."

Adamar rose and looked out at the battle. The priests in the rear echelons were already streaming back through the city gates. Many had no idea where they were going, only that they wanted to be far away from the blood and the death.

"My—your," he quickly corrected himself, "priests are fleeing. They are retreating through the gates. Our enemy has routed us!"

"They need a leader," Mordum said calmly. He looked at Adamar and began to whisper words his mortal ears could not hear, then he pointed to where the priests were fleeing. Adamar's body rose into the air and flew over the castle walls towards the battle.

Adamar felt his stomach do strange things as the wind clawed at him. The clouds parted. A mote of sunlight fell from the heavens and touched him as he descended onto the battle field.

"To me!" he shouted. "Rally to me!"

He blazed as if dipped in flame, lit from above with the light. His shout brought the fleeing priests and soldiers to a halt. They looked to see where the call came from and saw Adamar outlined in flame, blazing like a beacon fire. Mordum's servants halted in their mad dash, looking up, dazzled.

"To me!" Adamar yelled again.

The soldiers hesitated, then one ran to him. Another followed and another, glad to have purpose and direction once again.

"Get into formation!" he ordered.

The soldiers and priests came running back, bringing their weapons to bear and lining back up. Adamar felt glorious. Mordum had used him to stop the retreat. All the men's eyes were on him now. *Now who is important?* He cried at them in his mind. *I am!*

"Charge!" he screamed.

His army charged forth, clashing into the ranks of their enemy. He stood still as they flowed around him, watching the death and destruction that ensued. The air begun to buzz. Adamar looked up to see a wave of arrows, hundreds of them, flying toward his position. His eyes widened in terror. He looked back to Mordum, issuing a silent prayer for protection. Yet his lord was nowhere to be seen.

The arrows rained down around him. The feathered shafts struck through visors of helmed soldiers or took them in the throat. More arrows flew, more bodies fell. The panic-stricken soldiers and priests faltered, halted, trying to discover the location of this new enemy. More arrows hummed through the air. Men screamed and fell. The dying were starting to pile up like hideous cordwood in the cut, forming a blood-soaked barricade.

Adamar cursed as the enemy crashed through his forces. He ripped one of the arrows from a fallen soldier and eyed the feathers. The colors were familiar. And etched into the wood was the symbol he least wanted to see: a phoenix bursting from a pile of ashes. The symbol of Talvaard.

The ground trembled beneath his feet. He spun around and spotted the source. One of the golems was coming straight for him. He turned to run, overcome with fear. And then something hit him in the left eye. His mind screamed that he needed to run, but his body screamed in agony and would not obey. His right eye barely recognized the feathered shaft that was lodged in the left before he had the sensation of falling. He crashed to the ground on his back, his head striking something hard. He told himself that should have hurt, yet he felt nothing.

The golem came into his blurred view. His eye was welling uncontrollably with tears. He tried to blink them away and only felt the right side of his face. *What's happening to me?!* his mind screamed. His heart was pounding furiously against his chest and his ears were ringing. He watched as the golem lifted its leg to step on him. He was powerless to move.

A wave of heat washed over him as a blinding streak of light struck the golem in the side of its head. The stone creature turned to face a new attacker and Adamar lay there, giving silent thanks to whoever had just saved his life. He knew he couldn't stay where he was, yet his body refused to cooperate with his commands. He didn't know how much time passed as he struggled to roll onto his side, but eventually he managed to do so.

He lay there, expended, watching the battle continue to unfold. It was hard to tell who was winning. The bodies of both sides littered his view. He tried to get up, but he was dizzy and couldn't keep his balance.

So, he crawled. It was arduous and tiring. His hands touched blood and dismembered limbs, yet he struggled on. He didn't know where he should go. Nowhere was safe. Mordum had abandoned him. Everything had fallen apart so quickly. Every so often, his arms faltered and he lowered himself to the ground. He had to turn his head to keep the arrow from lodging any further into his skull.

Though he wanted to give in many times, he continued onward.

14

THE COMBINED FORCES OF KESWICK and Talvaard pushed Mordum's forces into the city. With the gods Zevea and Tael leading the charge, the priests of Mordum fell to blade and magic alike. The army pushed its way into the main courtyard of the castle. Standing there, alone, was a man.

Zevea and Tael closed in, approaching cautiously. Though it was Aramis's body, they knew who really stood before them.

"So, we finally meet in the flesh," Zevea said.

"Why have you come here?" Mordum asked.

"You know why," Tael answered. "What you are doing is forbidden."

"Yet here you both are, in mortal bodies as I am."

"This is different," Zevea said. "We have left our celestial home to stop you."

"My power is greater than yours, and grows by the minute," Mordum laughed. "Kill my servants as you will. Even in death, they still serve me."

"We will crush you," Tael said. "We should have killed you when you were weakened after your first attempt to take this world for yourself."

"You couldn't kill me before, and you can't kill me now."

The gods eyed each other in silence. Tael was the first move. He charged Mordum, swinging a large battleax in an 'X' pattern. Mordum stood still until Tael was a few feet away, then dove down and rolled, coming up behind Tael and slashing him across the back with his onyx blade. Mordum immediately turned to meet Zevea's attack. She wielded a metal staff and struck at his head.

Mordum easily deflected her attempt and spun towards her, slashing a long gash down her arm. She cried out in pain, something foreign to her, and brought her staff around to block Mordum's second strike. Her wound was deep and she was bleeding profusely. The arm was almost useless.

Tael tackled Mordum and the two went crashing to the ground. They wrestled and rolled around, fighting furiously. Zevea wanted to strike Mordum with her staff, but the two were rolling around too much for her to risk hitting Tael.

A thunderous blast rattled the ground. Zevea struggled to see what was happening. Tael stood up, a smile upon his face. "We are vic—" bloody spittle flew from his mouth and he staggered before falling to his knees. A look of surprise spread across his face as his hand touched the mortal wound in his chest.

Zevea felt fear for the first time. She watched as Mordum rose and calmly walked to Tael, easily swinging his blade and removing Tael's head. Blood spurt and the head tumbled to the ground, followed by his headless body. Zevea screamed. First her sister, and now Tael. Mordum, she knew, would never be satisfied.

She tried to grip her staff in both hands, but her cut arm was numb. She backed up slowly as Mordum came towards her.

A flash of silver caught her attention and she saw Melchiades rushing Mordum. It was suicidal.

Mordum turned and met the priest with a flourish of his sword. Their blades clashed together and sparks flew.

"Leave Aramis's body, now!" Mel yelled at him.

Mordum laughed as he parried Mel's strikes. "This body is mine now. Aramis is gone."

"I don't believe you," Mel growled. He fought furiously, trying every maneuver he knew to get close to Mordum, but the god was too quick.

"Are you really going to kill Aramis?" Mordum taunted.

"You said he was gone," Mel cried.

"Perhaps he is, perhaps he isn't. I suppose you will never know."

Mel knew that Mordum was trying to confuse him. He believed Aramis was alive. Somewhere deep inside, he was sure, Mordum held his friend's soul prisoner. He tried to keep his mind focused on the battle, but he kept thinking to what Aramis had told him. Mordum could not be defeated by sheer force or a killing blow. There were specifics. And unfortunately, Aramis had only divulged some of the details. He was already tired. His muscles screamed at him, burning intensely. He couldn't keep up the fight. And this time, there would be no welcoming goddess to give him his life back.

Mordum rushed him, trying to end the fight quickly. Mel blocked the god's charge with his shoulder and his armor cracked from the blow. From his peripheral, he saw Zevea flinch as if in pain. Could she feel what was happening to his armor?

The courtyard began to fill with soldiers. Mel tried to keep his attention on Mordum, but he did notice Garrick. *Where did the man's loyalties truly lie?* he wondered.

His answer came quickly as Garrick joined the fray. His black armor and sword glinted faintly in the dull light of the sun. He attacked Mordum.

The god turned angrily towards Garrick and without a word or movement, Garrick cried out in agony and collapsed to the ground, clutching his chest.

"How dare you?" Mordum thundered. His voice echoed off the castle walls of the courtyard, deep and booming.

Mel saw an opening and charged Mordum, stabbing his blade into the god's side, between his ribs. Mordum turned and punched Mel in the side of his face, sending him reeling. He lost his grip on his sword and fell hard onto his back. Mordum towered over him, raising his own sword for the killing blow.

An arrow slammed into the side of Mordum's head, exploding with magical sparks. Both Mel and the god turned to see Lynessa, the Lady of Keswick. She stood a few feet away, holding a bow. She was surrounded by several priests in gleaming silver armor. Mel recognized them as Zevea's servants. Lynessa nocked another arrow and drew the string back, pointing it at Mordum.

"Release Aramis," she said.

Mordum laughed.

"Your army has been routed and you are outnumbered. God or not, I like my odds better than yours."

"Foolish mortals!" Mordum bellowed. "I am God of the Dead! I cannot die!"

The gray clouds above began to darken. The wind picked up. Lightning flickered in the growing darkness above them and thunder filled the air.

Mel knew that if they didn't kill Mordum now, he would come back again. He would continue to bring death and destruction upon the people. He looked to Zevea.

She was pale and weak. He could sense that she was dying, could feel it in his armor. It wouldn't be long before his tie to her power was severed and he would be without his armor and blade.

The dagger ... her voiced filled his mind, weak and barely a whisper.

Dagger?

The one I gave to Aramis. It is more than it seems ... it can kill him.

Mel looked at Aramis's body and saw it sheathed at his waist. How could a rusty old dagger kill a god?

Trust me, she bade him.

Mel looked to Lynessa and gave her a hand signal. He didn't know if she saw it or not, but there was nothing else to be done. He pushed himself onto his feet and reached for the dagger. Mordum began to turn and face him, but another of Lynessa's explosive arrows struck him in the chest. The concussive force threatened to push Mel backwards, but he dug his boots into the dirt for leverage and forced himself forward. He snatched the blade from Aramis's belt and jabbed the rusty dagger into Mordum's chest, his aim true.

The blade pierced his heart.

The hilt of the dagger became red-hot and burned Mel's hand. He cried out and let go of the blade in shock. His armor began to dissipate, but he couldn't take his eyes off Mordum. The dagger glowed with a blinding white light, piercing the darkness within Aramis's body. The blackness in his friend's eyes dimmed, slowly returning to their natural color.

Aramis's mouth opened in a silent scream and the black cloud that was Mordum rushed out, disintegrating into the air. Aramis's body collapsed lifelessly to the ground. The dagger's glow dimmed and then faded entirely.

Mel rushed to his fallen friend and pulled the dagger out. Aramis was pale and didn't appear to be breathing.

"No," he whispered over and over. "Please, no." Tears stung his eyes. Had he killed his friend by killing Mordum? He looked to Zevea. Her body lay not far, but she was faintly moving.

Come ... she called out to him.

Overcome with grief, he could barely comprehend the word. He forced himself to move and went to her. He wiped his tears. The life was quickly fading from her eyes. She opened her mouth to speak, but no words came out.

You ... can ... save him.

"How?" Mel cried. "Please, tell me how!"

Zevea closed her eyes. *Come near ...*

Mel lowered his head to her, inches from her face. She opened her mouth and breathed out a golden wisp of air. He gasped when he saw it, and the wisp flew into his mouth. He was filled with a tremendous power.

Breathe into ...

And then her presence was gone.

Mel stood there, not sure what she intended to say. Panic filled him. She said he could save Aramis, but he didn't know what she was going to say. He fell to his knees at Aramis's side, tears streaming down his face. He turned his friend's face to face him and stared into his lifeless eyes. Agony wrenched his heart. He began to sob uncontrollably. He placed his head on his friend's shoulder. He would have prayed, but he knew there were no gods left to hear him.

Lynessa knelt on the other side of Aramis and Mel saw that she too was crying.

Mel raised his head, looking at her. "Why?" he cried. The golden wisp flew out of his mouth. Lynessa's façade of strength broke and she shook her head.

"I—"

The wisp flew into her mouth. Her eyes widened in surprise. She had felt the power, Mel knew. She looked down at Aramis and shook her head again. Leaning down, she pressed her lips against Aramis's in a soft kiss. As she exhaled over him, the wisp slipped out of her mouth and into Aramis's.

Mel saw it and wondered what it could mean. Time passed and Mel dared not move lest he miss something. Lynessa eventually rose to her feet and walked away. Garrick knelt beside Mel and placed his hand on his shoulder.

"We should probably move his body," Garrick suggested quietly. "He paid the ultimate sacrifice. We should honor him for that."

Mel ignored him. Eventually Garrick left, too.

I should never have left him, Mel grieved in his mind. *I should have followed him. Even though Adamar tricked him, I should never have let him out of my sight.*

And then he thought he saw Aramis's chest rise. It was almost imperceptible, and Mel doubted whether he actually saw it. Then his chest rose and fell. Mel wiped his eyes, wanting to be sure of what he saw.

He wasn't seeing things! Aramis was breathing.

"He's alive!" Mel cried out. "He's breathing! Someone help me!"

Garrick and Lynessa rushed to help, followed by others. They lifted him gently and carried him inside the castle. Mel led them to Aramis's room and they laid him on the bed. Lynessa ordered everyone to leave except Garrick and Mel. The three of them took turns watching him while the other two dozed off.

Three days passed uneventfully.

"I'm afraid I must go," Garrick said on the third day, breaking the long silence. "I don't want to, but my duties cannot be ignored much longer."

Mel nodded. "I understand," he replied. "When he wakes, I will tell him you were here."

"Thank you," Garrick said.

"No," Mel shook his head. "Thank you. For honoring your word to him. And for risking your life. Standing up to Mordum like you did …"

Garrick shrugged. "I don't know how I did it," he said.

They stood quietly as they stared at Aramis's body, still except for his breathing.

"I will come check on him after I have things in order," Garrick said.

Mel nodded and Garrick left the room. Mel was surprised that Lynessa would not leave Aramis's side. Another day passed before there was a change in Aramis.

"Water," a voice woke Mel. He rose from the chair he was sleeping in and saw that Aramis had his eyes open.

"Water," Aramis rasped again.

"Thank the goddess!" Mel exclaimed. He rushed to pour a glass of water from a carafe the servants had left, almost spilling it in his excitement. Bringing the cup to Aramis, he helped hold it while Aramis struggled to lift his head up to take a drink.

Aramis fell back against the pillow. His eyes shifted back and forth across the room. "Where …"

"We're in the castle. This is your room," Mel answered. "How are you feeling?"

Aramis moved his head weakly to the side so that he could look at Mel. "I feel like death," he whispered. "Mordum?" he asked.

"Dead," Mel said solemnly. "And we nearly lost you as well."

"How?" Aramis rasped.

"We'll get to that when you are better. You should rest."

Aramis's eyes slowly closed and his breathing slowed. Mel watched worriedly, but soon realized Aramis had fallen asleep. He looked up as Lynessa rose from the chair she had been sleeping in.

"What's going on?" she asked.

"Aramis was awake," Mel answered with a smile. "He spoke a little, but I told him to rest."

"Oh, thank Zevea," she whispered.

"I couldn't say it any better," Mel said.

Aramis slept through the rest of the day, waking as dinner was being brought in by the servants. Having regained a small amount of strength, Aramis was able to sit up. The three of them ate together in silence until Aramis spoke.

"I feel like I've been trapped in a dream," he said. His voice was stronger.

"The last few days have felt like a nightmare," Lynessa said quietly.

"How long have I been out?"

"Almost four days if you count today," Mel answered. "It's good to see you awake. I was afraid …" he left the sentence unfinished.

"My body feels like it fell down a mountain," Aramis said, rubbing the muscles in his right arm. "What happened? All I remember is the storm, and then … it's all foggy after that."

Mel took a deep breath and related everything, pausing hesitantly when he got to the part where he stabbed Aramis in the chest.

"How am I alive?" Aramis asked.

"Zevea," Mel replied. "She did something. She gave you a breath of air, but it was … different. I can't explain it."

Aramis was surprised. The goddess had saved his life? All the anger he felt toward the gods hadn't left, but maybe he could forgive them in time.

"Where is she?" he asked. "I should probably thank her."

"She's dead," Mel said, the sadness in his eyes evident. "Mordum dealt her a mortal wound. He also killed Tael. Zevea helped you with her dying breath."

Aramis digested the words. "If the gods are dead," he said, "then we have no one to rely upon but ourselves. Just how life was before all of this."

"Well," Mel paused, "there are other gods, though I don't think they meddle in the affairs of men as much."

Mel glanced to Lynessa. "There's something else," he said. He looked back to Aramis. "I didn't get the chance to tell before, when you …" he trailed off.

"Lost my wits?" Aramis finished for him, smiling wanly.

"I would have said it a bit more pleasant, but yes. We found Lord Bavol."

Aramis raised his eyebrows. "Where is he? Is he all right?"

"No," Mel said. "He was dead. Murdered, by the looks of it. By Mordum's orders, no doubt. And you know we found Hannah."

Aramis closed his eyes and bowed his head. "I'm sure she must hate me."

"No," Mel answered. He motioned to one of the servants and then left the room in a rush.

"What of Adamar? Is he dead?"

"I'm afraid I don't know," Mel said. "We haven't found his body. He's just … gone."

A moment later, the servant returned with Hannah following closely behind her.

"Aramis!" she shouted. She ran to the bed and jumped onto it, wrapping her arms around Aramis. Weakened as he was, he could only smile as she tackled him to the bed.

"Careful, please, m'Lady!" Mel cried in exaggerated terror.

"It's fine," Aramis said. He returned Hannah's embrace and they stayed like that, holding each other for a long moment. Finally, Hannah released him and helped him sit back up.

"I'm so happy you are alive," she said. Her eyes welled with tears and one escaped, sliding down her cheek. Aramis reached up and wiped it away before kissing her.

"Me too," he said.

Lynessa cleared her throat. Everyone turned their attention to her. Her simmering anger was apparent. "Who is this *Hannah*?" she asked, glaring coldly at the her.

"She is my betrothed," Aramis answered, confused by Lynessa's reaction.

Lynessa stiffened. "Well … congratulations. I'm glad that you are back with the living," she said. "I must be going. My army and my city are waiting on me."

"Thank you," Aramis said to her. "I know you had your own problems in Keswick to take care of, even after the Warlock had been dealt with. Thank you for coming to my aide. I am indebted to you."

Lynessa curtsied, her anger still noticeable. Then she turned and left the room.

"A woman scorned," Mel said softly as he watched her go. He looked at Aramis, wondering if there was more between them than Aramis had let on.

—

Lynessa fumed as she strode across the courtyard. How could he choose another woman over her? She had welcomed him into her bed.

Fine.

If he didn't want her, she would find someone else. She ordered her army to begin moving out.

As she led her army across the plains of Oakhaven, she watched the vultures pick at the bodies that had fallen in battle. She led their pace and they marched slowly home. Ahead, something caught her attention on the road. As they neared the form, Lynessa realized it was a man crawling on all fours. His head turned toward them as they approached and she caught sight of the arrow lodged in his eye.

"Help him," she said, thinking he might be a wounded civilian. His clothes were dirty and tattered. "Let the healers help him and bring him back to me."

The soldiers did as she ordered and she welcomed him warmly, inviting him to come and live in Keswick. The man gladly accepted the offer.

—

Adamar heard the approaching army before he saw it. He wanted to move before they saw him, but he was too weak. His injuries had taken their toll and it was all he could do to crawl as slowly as he was. When he heard the lady order her men to help him, he smiled. He knew someone would take him in. Someone *always* took him in.

—

Jovanna could feel herself drifting along the currents of magic. Everything around her looked real, but it all felt different. Someone was there, just out of her sight. When she tried to see who it was, the shadow moved, always staying out of sight. After a while, she gave up.

Time was nonexistent.

Eventually, she began to feel weighted down again. Once, her eyes fluttered open and she glimpsed a stone chamber. She had grown accustomed to the darkness and wondered if death blinded everyone. Feeling finally came back to her, and she could feel her muscles. They ached and felt like fire when they twitched.

And then her eyes opened again, and this time they stayed open. Her gaze took in every detail of every stone above her. The small grooves and cracks, the cobwebs, everything.

She was different. And she was not alone.

"I wondered when you'd find your way back," a smooth voice said. It was a woman.

Jovanna turned her head. The woman was beautiful. Her skin was bronze and her eyes were a vibrant green. She had flowing long hair, so blonde it was almost silver. Her wrists and ankles were adorned with gold and silver bracelets. She wore a thin, sheer robe which did little to cover her nakedness.

"Who are you?" Jovanna croaked.

"My name is Vashah," the woman answered.

"Where—" Jovanna's voice cracked and her body shook with a coughing fit. Vashah brought a bowl filled with water and helped Jovanna drink some.

"You are in my home, atop Red Mountain," Vashah said. "You came very near to dying after killing that elf."

"Tairu," Jovanna said, the battle a blur and her memory fractured. "How did I get here?"

"King Garrick had his physicians rescue you off the battlefield before they marched to Oakhaven. There was nothing they could do for you. You were beyond the healing of any but the oldest of us."

"Us?" Jovanna asked, confused.

"Wizards," Vashah said. "You are a wizard. A true wizard. Not like those who play at it in Palindrom."

Jovanna remembered that place. Cignus had taken her in and taught her. He never understood her, though. Never understood that she was *different*.

"Why am I here?"

Vashah smiled. "I'm going to train you."

—

As the weeks passed, Aramis regained more of his strength and things slowly became more stable around the castle. Servants got back into their routines and the castle quickly became a swirl of politics and business as usual. Eventually, most of the people found it difficult to imagine life had been any different the past few months.

Most of the nobles loyal to Aramis's father had been killed, replaced with younger men whose character was akin to Adamar's. After the coronation—a small ceremony with only a few in attendance—Aramis's first act as king was to remove anyone Adamar had put in power. They were given the choice to leave the kingdom or be locked in the dungeon. Most of them had accepted the first option.

Aramis also issued a decree that all the towns and villages that had been burned and attacked by Adamar's men were to be immediately rebuilt, with everything to be funded by the royal treasury. As the word spread, the people who had fled their homes slowly returned. Crops were replanted, barns rebuilt, and livestock tracked down.

There was still so much to do, Aramis knew, but the first steps were the hardest. He and Hannah were married after the coronation, and since they didn't have the time to get away from their duties, Aramis promised Hannah a lavish honeymoon once things in the kingdom were back in order. How long it would take, he didn't know.

Mel, acting as the Chamberlain until Aramis could find someone to appoint, began a spiritual journey to find a new god to serve. Aramis thought he was a fool, but he kept that to himself.

Each day brought new troubles, but also things to be thankful for. The scars of Mordum's war would probably never be fully healed, but only time would tell.

Aramis looked forward to a bright and hopeful future.

THE END

ACKNOWLEDGEMENTS

I want to thank all of the Kickstarter backers who helped bring this omnibus edition to life.

Without you, the interior illustrations wouldn't have been possible, and they make this edition so much more epic.

ABOUT THE AUTHOR

Hey there!

I write fantasy and space opera, and you can find all my books in many different ebook stores. You can check out my website for more information about my books, my next projects, and events I'll be attending.

If you enjoyed this book, I'd love your feedback in the form of a review on Amazon or Goodreads.

Thanks for reading!

-Richard

Website: www.richardfierce.com

Facebook: www.facebook.com/dragonfirepress

TikTok: www.tiktok.com/TTPdSrPTBx